ANTHONY RETURNS HOME

Successful, joyous, he is back to rejoin his friends, to claim his inheritance. But Don Luis, the Marquis of Vincitata, is back, too, with a hatred of Anthony that is implacable. As Anthony's fortunes rise, Don Luis schemes against him. In France, he tries to engineer Anthony's death; in Spain, he plots his financial ruin; but it is in America that he aims his final vengeance against the illegitimate son of his unfaithful wife, the adventurer, the lover, the man called

ANTHONY ADVERSE

Read the first two parts of *Anthony Adverse*:
Part 1, The Roots of the Tree, 81-439-3 .... 2.50
Part 2, The Other Bronze Boy, 81-621-3 .... 2.50

Books In This Series
by Hervey Allen

Anthony Adverse Part One: The Roots of the Tree
Anthony Adverse Part Two: The Other Bronze Boy
Anthony Adverse Part Three: The Lonely Twin

Published by
WARNER BOOKS

ANTHONY ADVERSE

PART THREE

The Lonely Twin

Anthony Adverse

PART THREE
The Lonely Twin

by
Hervey Allen

**Decorations by
Allan McNab**

WARNER BOOKS

A Warner Communications Company

ANTHONY ADVERSE

WARNER BOOKS EDITION

Copyright 1933 by Hervey Allen
Copyright renewed © 1961 by Ann Andrews Allen

ISBN 0-446-81622-1

This Warner Books Edition is published by
arrangement with Holt, Rinehart and Winston

Cover art by Jim Dietz

Warner Books, Inc., 75 Rockefeller Plaza, New York, N.Y. 10019

W A Warner Communications Company

Printed in the United States of America

Not associated with Warner Press, Inc. of Anderson, Indiana

First Printing: March, 1978

10 9 8 7 6 5 4 3 2 1

"There is something in us that can be without us, and will be after us, though indeed it hath no history of what it was before us, and cannot tell how it entered into us."

—Sir Thomas Browne.

To
Edna Allen Rickmers

CONTENTS

PART THREE

The Lonely Twin

BOOK ONE

In Which a Worldly
Brother Is Acquired

Chapter One

Reverberations

DON LUIS leaned back in the coach, which had been comfortably repaired at Dijon only a month before, and inhaled the scent of the vineyards about Livorno with considerable satisfaction.

He was nearing the end of a year's journey from Madrid by way of Paris, and the certainty of resting his bones in a good bed that night lent an additional charm to the admirable vistas along the ancient highway between Pisa and Leghorn.

These, however, he was fully prepared to admire for themselves alone.

After an absence of nearly twenty-five years upon his estates in Spain, the Marquis da Vincitata was returning to visit Tuscany, the land of his predilection. And he was thinking, as he leaned back in the luxurious, albeit somewhat faded upholstery that still lined his old-fashioned coach, that a return to Italy must ever be to every civilized European a home-coming.

He had even composed an epigram about it.

At the particular moment when he swept with a clatter of sixteen hoofs through the hamlet of San Marco he was attempting to write the epigram upon a small slate which he kept handy for the purpose. It was not often possible to write when travelling, although the coach was now slung upon the best steel springs. But so level and straight was the Roman highway, which had lately been repaired by Bonaparte—so smooth was the stone pavement upon which the coach was now rapidly and invincibly rolling, that in this instance Don Luis had no difficulty whatever in writing upon the slate without breaking the delicate point of his stone pencil.

At this triumph of modern engineering he looked up with an amused and faintly-pleased expression about the eyes. The crow's-feet on the pouches under his heavy lids contracted a little ironically and he started to drum with his thick, powerful fingers on the surface of the slate which rested on his knee. The scent of the vineyards had caused him to remember something that interfered with his epigrammatic style. Finally, with an angry motion of his club-like thumb, he obliterated what he had just written upon the slate. He looked at the smudge and laughed, for he had not really intended to wipe out the epigram but to destroy only the uncomfortable memory which had just been forced upon him.

During the course of his frequent journeys—and upon diplomatic business he still travelled a great deal —the marquis had composed several thousand epigrams. He first set them down upon the slate and later transferred them to an elegant, morocco-bound notebook that reposed together with a pack of cards, the latest French novel, some goat cheese, and a bottle of white wine in a small locker on the side of the coach. This alcove had once, long ago, held a figure of the Madonna belonging to his girl-wife.

It was a bright memory of the dead woman, vividly but unconsciously forced upon him by the odour of grape blossoms, that had interfered with his writing. He looked annoyed. He brushed his hand over his eyes, and went on again.

The peculiarly sardonic and sententious style in which Don Luis composed his epigrams was a balm to his injured ego which had never ceased to suffer from the wound inflicted upon it by the unfaithful conduct of his wife. It was for that reason that there were thousands and not merely hundreds of epigrams now safely copied into the morocco notebook. Don Luis had thus taken his revenge on fate by secretly continuing to drip vitriol upon everybody and everything under the sun. His sarcasm was a kind of spiritual pus that he wiped away privately with page after page of the notebook.

Outwardly Don Luis had scarcely changed at all. He even looked a little better preserved. Indeed, there was something about the marquis that reminded some close observers of a living mummy. One almost crippling attack of the gout had brought a Spartan diet into his regimen. He lived principally upon sour wine, cheese, and goat milk. And he knew exactly how to physic himself after those banquets for which even a Spanish grandee and an old diplomat semi-occasionally had to unbutton.

For a man well up in his sixties the conde de Azuaga, as he was known in Spain, was really remarkable. But the most remarkable thing about him was that the world went on taking his spry, youthful vigour and unimpaired energy as a matter of course. It did not, except in a few cases of old men who enviously failed before him, remark his vigour at all.

In Estremadura, where Don Luis had spent a great deal of his time, the life was both healthy and hardy. Those who survived it in infancy usually lived to a vigorous old age. There were priests there who had been known to have had children at the age of ninety. And it was for that reason that the nobility in the neighborhood of Don Luis' estates frequently sent to Valencia, or other provinces, for family confessors whose ripe old age was less likely to break forth into ridiculous blossoms. In Estremadura there was,—yes, undoubt-

19

edly,—there was something in the air. Don Luis had breathed it in calmly, and preserved its fire.

After a decade of retirement in Estremadura the marquis had gradually begun to resume his position of natural influence and inevitable emolument at the then much disordered court of Spain. For this he was excellently fitted by both inheritance and long practice. At the supine court of Charles IV he possessed an enormous advantage over even the most selfish of timeservers; he was no longer troubled by any social conscience whatever. Over those who matched him in this respect he was still superior, for his own selfishness was complex and conservative while theirs was simple and immediately voracious. Those dull glimmerings of virtue, which even the most lupine of statesmen occasionally employ as beacons of direction in an otherwise purely opportunist piloting, did not in the midnight oceans of Don Luis' soul mark even a distant headland. He steered only by the fixed star of self-interest with a Machiavellian craft. It was in this sense that the conde de Azuaga was in a very real way a "prince" among men.

The Marquis da Vincitata and conde de Azuaga had in fact been endowed by an all-wise Providence, that accomplishes its mysterious ends with the deadly foil of evil as well as the sword of justice, with an awful and profound mind. That the colour of his soul was Stygian was only natural, for it is in the darkness of night that mental lightning without thunder makes its finest display when it strikes. The marquis' self-interest consisted in what he was interested in, and that can be described most laconically as a passionate desire to hold back the hands on the clock of time. With that end in view he had gradually thrown himself back into the ways and places of influence, body and soul.

Don Luis had within him a strong sense of the trend of the age; of the becoming of men and peoples in the stream of time. And as this, when combined with the practical ability to influence events, is undoubtedly a trait of genius, the advent of the conde in his gloomy coach at the Escurial just before the French Revolution broke out had marked a distinct epoch of pause in the history of his own peninsula. He proposed to preserve it as a perfect Christian Tibet, and for a time he succeeded.

He left no record of his strange and stilling influence. He wrote nothing, except the epigrams in his notebook. His method was the ancient, and often most effective one in human affairs, of a devious personal influence. He attached himself to the right men and left them at exactly the right time. He drove hither and yon in his gloomy coach, which for many years had remained slung upon the chains with which he had furnished it for his wife's martyrdom. A call paid by the suave, and inevitably correct, conde in this vehicle driven by a cat-like coachman was like receiving the ambassador of smouldering subterranean powers whose force is known but whose depth has never been plumbed. Virtue and sanctimony were forced to listen to his wisdom with respect, while the superficially sinful were left both envious and scared. A few ardent young spirits who opposed him had been questioned as to the basis of their curious opposition during the last ample days of the Holy Office. Thus, opposition to Don Luis was always dangerous; co-operation inevitably paid. Consequently, the ends he fostered throve, and the web, which the constantly widening circle of the peregrinations of the coach left upon the map of Spain, found an ever more and more powerful and alert spider sitting upon the faded rose-coloured upholstery at its shifting centre.

Don Luis was not "popular," of course. It had never occurred to any mob to shout, "Long live Don Luis," or to any assembly of notables to drink his health. It would have seemed preposterous, unnecessary. He somehow carried with him everywhere, and under every conceivable circumstance, the suggestion that he would inevitably outlive and prevail over those with whom he dealt. All this was largely due to an unquenchable desire for revenge upon life which now directed the movements of the marquis' soul. He would have liked to stop all other life than his own. And in that event he would have valued his own existence only because it would have enabled him to watch over a universal calm. The marquis was therefore known as a "conservative."

Indeed, there was only one positive desire left in his still active but negative nature. It was an harassing sensuality that still hoped for long-protracted and callous intercourse. It constituted, as it were, the secret, youthful vigour of his senility, and, when actively exerted, held a certain kind of mysterious and unexpected charm for older women. It was for this reason that the marquis as he made his rounds always kept at least one of his drooping eyelids half open, and he was no longer at all particular as to where he could slake a passion that was both dull and violent at the same time.

His reactionary hopes, however, had not prevented him from making those necessary outward concessions to change without which even a "conservative" cannot conserve. These were for the most part exhibited in his astute political manœuvres, his meticulous dress, and in the constant, almost affectionate, rehabilitation of the coach.

He liked to recall that he had won the coach from the Duc d'Orléans at a lucky run of cards in what he looked back upon as better days. For various reasons he had cherished it and rejuvenated it from time to time. The vehicle had almost become a part of him. In the course of time it received new tires, new wheels, new axle-trees and new shafts. It had been dragged over Spain, Portugal, and France by horses and mules that had died in its service and left the body of the coach behind them. Only that had remained the same. In its lines were expressed the luxurious amplitude and the heavy ruthlessness of the ancien régime. Its cat-like coachman had been promoted. He still rode upon the box in a coat-of-many-capes like a tom cat dressed in frills. But Sancho was now Don Luis' valet and general factotum, and the coach was driven by his son, a young man with grey hair, a round, ocelot-shaped head, and wide, greenish eyes. This personage, known as the "Kitten" in Madrid, flourished a whip and said nothing except to his horses or mules. These he occasionally addressed in a tempest of lewd squalls, while he drove with an uncanny skill that seemed to be reckless.

Towards the end of 1799 Don Luis had gone to Paris to try to arrange the little matter of transferring the southern part of Portugal to the prime minister of Spain. He and the First Consul Bonaparte had found that they understood each other. Pourparlers had rapidly changed into conversations during the course of which the character of the Prince of the Peace, the queen's favourite, and the general sorry mess of affairs at the court of Spain were amply discussed. These conversations were carried on with a masterful directness on the part of the first consul and a faultless, self-serving innuendo on the part of Don Luis that rapidly brought about an understanding between these two men as their admiration for each other increased. Napoleon saw in the marquis one whom it would be wise to favour in order to use; Don Luis beheld in Bonaparte a man whom it was imperative to serve well in order to profit amply. They got on.

"What sort of a man is the Prince of the Peace?" asked Bonaparte whirling about upon Don Luis, as he walked up and down looking out upon the gardens of the Luxembourg which he was just about to leave for the Tuileries.

"A man of large parts, citizen-general, necessary and assiduous in the service of Her Majesty both day and night."

Bonaparte smiled wanly.

"I have heard that he is also the friend of the king," he said. "Is there no one to whose interest it would be to enlighten His Catholic Majesty as to the state of his own domestic affairs?"

"Several, now in exile, have made the attempt," replied Don Luis. "But His Majesty's family party at the Escurial has been carefully arranged to insure the royal peace of mind. I might add that the unique relation the

23

Prince of the Peace holds to the king has thrown a new and romantic light upon the power and privileges of a viceroy."

Napoleon smiled again, this time not so wanly. He began rapidly to discuss the basis of a new treaty with Spain in which the payment of a larger annual subsidy to France was the most important item. It was at this interview that Don Luis first mentioned to Napoleon the possibility of the cession of Louisiana to France. He merely suggested it, as it were. It was difficult to transfer bullion from Mexico to Spain on account of the British fleet but a continent could be transferred at Paris, by a stroke of the pen. Napoleon shook his head. It was ready money he wanted. But he remembered the suggestion and turned it over in his planetary mind.

The upshot of several such conversations was surprising to several persons. The Prince of the Peace failed to get his Portuguese principality but was assured of French support at the court of Spain. For this he could grind his teeth—and be thankful—to both Don Luis and Bonaparte. The precise way in which the gratitude was to be shown was carefully provided for and understood beforehand.

The Duke and Duchess of Parma were also surprised. It was agreed that they should pack up and move their thrones to Florence, as Napoleon had new arrangements for Italy in view and was graciously willing to endow their Etrurian Majesties-to-be generously, at the expense of a helpless ally. Don Luis was commissioned to inform them tactfully of the little surprise in store for them, after arranging certain details beforehand through the Spanish ambassador at Paris.

The mission to prepare the authorities at Florence was one which for several reasons filled Don Luis with a peculiar satisfaction. He liked moving royalties, who had to pretend to be thankful to him, like figures in chess. He liked returning to Italy, where the Renaissance had been taken seriously, he said. There was a decidedly Roman pagan side to Don Luis. He had finally reduced his Christianity to nothing but ritual with

24

no moral implications. And a trip to Tuscany in particular coincided exactly with certain private business of his own in that region.

Thus, as usual, Don Luis was able to conduct his own and the public business as one. Before leaving Paris he had obtained certain letters from the first consul which insured the return of his confiscated estates in Tuscany. The dilapidated castle and small hill-town of Vincitata was nothing to Napoleon, who was therefore glad to return it to Don Luis upon whom he counted for further confidential advices when he should return to Spain.

In all of this Don Luis had been acting as the confidential agent of the Prince of the Peace. But he had seen fit to see eye to eye with the first consul, because perforce he must, and because as a matter of fact, it was in that way that he could make the best terms for Spain. At least he had obtained the promise of French support for the policies of Godoy, the queen's favourite, who was already anathema at home. Don Luis was also casting an eye into the future as every good diplomat should. A vague but stupendous outline of the plans of the young Corsican general with the Roman head had begun to dawn upon Don Luis. On one occasion the general in the coat with green facings had honoured the marquis with one of those metaphysical discourses on European affairs which so many people had made the mistake of not taking seriously. Don Luis did not indulge in that error. He had experienced a curious sensation while he listened to Napoleon, one of having participated in a similar interview somewhere else, very long ago. It had, he told himself, a kind of Trajanic ring about it. Just why, Don Luis could not be sure. But the experience of recall had been a powerful one. He dismissed that, but he retained in his head the vision of a great European empire with Paris as the new Rome. This suited the spiritual politics of Don Luis, and for the first time in many years there stirred within him an emotion akin to enthusiasm. For a minute or so the two men, who were conversing across a desk with the map of Italy laid out upon it, had been bound together in a profoundly deep and naturally flowing conversation as to the destinies of European civilization. It was above religion, national politics, and folk morals. For a minute or two what the Roman Empire had accomplished centuries before was reconstituted in a room over the portico of the Tuileries in Paris in 1800. Two free and ruthlessly candid intellects had dropped the petty conventions and prejudices of feudal provinces and looked upon Europe as a whole. Don Luis remembered afterward that Napoleon had lapsed into Italian in the excitement of finding himself understood, and he considered that to be the most majestic compliment which could have been offered him. Indeed, he looked back upon that interview as the crowning moment of his career. It had had about it the flavour of a meeting of Roman augurs, but of augurs who took themselves seriously and had eagles to unleash. Don Luis was able to add a few quotations and observations from some of the Sibylline books of the West. Then, as it were, the curtain had been withdrawn again. The sense of immediate communication in a mutual dream lapsed. Napoleon went on in French.

It was this that had caused Don Luis to smile ironically as he swept over the Roman highway, recently improved by Napoleon: It was only a small spur of the great system that had once linked Europe into one Latin whole. It was possible, however, that the whole system might now be repaved. He hoped so. It would give to life in the West a principle of direction in which every individual might participate with a sense not only of becoming, but of being with a sense of having been. At the present time society in Europe was composed of innumerable tangents from a curve that had dropped into a burst of shooting stars in the Renaissance and Reformation. Every person who was possessed of anything more than a purely conventional consciousness was now aware that he must steer by himself alone. Those remnants of the curve which still remained in Italy and Spain were hanging in limbo. It might be possible that a French segment would complete the old; no, a new and more magnificent Roman arch. Britain could go to hell her own way. What could be done with a people who had subordinated everything to a desire to trade? No, no, they were out of the arch forever. Barbarous! Don Luis reached for his slate again. The horses seemed to be galloping in hexameter.

It was at this point that the odour of grape blossoms had interrupted him. As an odour will, it recalled with extreme vividness certain scenes of his own secret life. The gears of his mind were suddenly shifted from impersonal politics to purely private considerations, as though a hand from without had been laid upon them. It was curious how those two seemingly disparate worlds were bound into one and made inseparable by the rapid and unceasing motion of the coach. As the vehicle rounded the curve at the southern end of the village of San Marco, Don Luis felt himself pressed back into the upholstery by the invisible hand that laid upon him the feeling of motion. He leaned against the momentum and stuck his head out of the window, bawling at Sancho not to go so fast. For some reason while the coach had swung him he felt angry. But the mood soon passed and, as he looked out over the landscape covered with vineyards in blossom, he was immediately presented gratis with a view of a somewhat similar countryside on a spring evening a quarter of a century before.

The coach he remembered was ascending a hill on a road through the midst of vineyards, approaching the Château of Besance. On the very seat where he was now riding sat his wife Maria. He remembered how the sunset had dazzled in her golden hair.

He turned, almost expecting to find her sitting beside him, and shivered a little at finding nothing there. The now faded rose of the old upholstery was merely touched into a sort of mockery of its ancient splendour by the approaching sunset. Here and there, over the back of the carriage, moved a few spots of shifting pentecostal fires.

The marquis felt suddenly as if he would like to get out of the coach. Where, after all,—where was it taking him? He felt for a minute that another hand than his own had really directed its motion. He had only collaborated with it. Perhaps he had not done so well in being sure he was always the master of its direction. A rare emotion crept upon him. He felt a little fearful of being all alone where only the lights and shadows of the outside world flickered over the inside of the old carriage —exactly as his thoughts flickered through his mind. He stuck his head out of the window again . . . "what, for instance, had become of Maria's child?" It might be a wise precaution to inform himself. The convent where he had left him was in the immediate neighbourhood— the "Convent of Jesus the Child." Don Luis smiled ironically again and decided to pay a visit to the mother superior. He could very easily concoct an excuse. Should he?

Just then they topped the rise of a small hill. In the valley beyond the marquis saw a large, rambling building with red roofs. An immense plane tree rose out of its midst about whose top a flock of pigeons was circling preparing to return for the night. It was this glimpse of the place which decided Don Luis to take advantage of its vicinity.

He called to Sancho and pointed. The man raised his eyes slightly and nodded. "So they *were* going to stop there again after all!" Sancho had wondered if they would. With the same grinding reverberations that the tires of the coach had aroused from the same stones twenty-five years before he caused the vehicle to pull up before the lane leading to the convent.

This time the marquis was somewhat longer in transacting his business at the convent than he had been on his previous visit. He had a long interview with the mother superior, whom he found to be an able and evidently painfully discreet woman. She was now directing the most exclusive convent-school for aristocratic young ladies in Tuscany. Mistaking Don Luis for a wise parent with a daughter to educate, she insisted

28

upon showing him over the entire establishment. Don Luis was forced to be politely patient, and to look at kitchens, laundry, and schoolrooms. He reflected as he went through the kitchens, as a revenge for being bored, that everything that woman used even for cooking had been invented and was made by man. He afterwards entered this in his morocco book. In the courtyard, however, he lingered with genuine admiration. Never, he thought, had he seen so antiquely somnolent, so pagan and classic a fountain. The statue of the bronze boy, who stood staring at the water with those peculiarly blind eyes that Phidias had perfected in Western sculpture, caused the cold springs of the marquis' internal aesthetic tears to melt discreetly. He even murmured a few words of admiration to Mother Marie José, who, thinking them to be an ironical compliment, tried to hurry him through what was now a long-deserted portion of the establishment; one of which she was thoroughly ashamed.

As a matter of fact, Don Luis, as a connoisseur, would have liked to own the statue. He inquired as to the missing twin. The mother superior did not even know what he meant. She looked at the statue of the lusty young boy somewhat askance. It was unnecessarily exuberant, she believed. Rather an unfortunate representation of the Christ Child for a girls' school, she thought. She could not discuss that, however. "Probably the twin was carried off and lost during the Renaissance," reflected Don Luis; "lonely enough in some modern garden even now, perhaps. Ah, well, he could never hope to find the twin." They went on into the refectory where upwards of thirty young ladies, dressed in elegant, but unbelievably prim costumes stayed with whalebone, sat bolt upright saying nothing. A sad-faced sister read to them of the blessed poverty of St. Francis, while they ate an iced sherbet.

"The niece of the unfortunate Duchess of Parma," said Mother Marie José indicating a gypsy-like girl near by . . . "The young Countess of Monteficuelli," she whispered.

29

That young gypsy managed to look discreetly down her nose at Don Luis. Don Luis allowed the lace from his sleeves to droop a little more elegantly, and bowed. He might have been acknowledging the presence of the Empress of Austria. The compliment was at once discreet, impeccable, and tremendous. To a young girl overwhelming. The breath of the world he brought in with him caused the envious bosoms of the other young ladies to stretch tight against their whalebones even in the Convent of Jesus the Child. Mademoiselle Monteficuelli blushed. Don Luis felt suddenly much younger again.

". . . And we have many other noble names represented here," the mother superior was saying. It was her principal argument. "Permit me to show you the rolls for some years past." She had often won her bid by laying her face cards upon the table.

It was exactly what Don Luis had hoped for but had been at a loss to bring about. Once having begun on the records, he pretended great interest; he kept going back. It was not difficult at first. Every teacher will talk about her school, for since that is all of life that she knows, she thinks that is all there is in life to know how to talk about. But finally Mother Marie José became anxious. There were certain entries in the 1770's which she was *not* anxious for any prospective patron to see. The curiosity of the stranger, however, was insatiable.

"What is this?" said Don Luis, scowling, and looking somewhat scandalized. "An orphan boy, Anthony, apprenticed to the English merchant John Bonnyfeather, what! what!" Here his face darkened like a thundercloud. There could be no doubt he *was* shocked now.

"Dios!" thought Don Luis. "Who would ever have thought *that?* To his own grandfather! Impossible! No, true! Yes, it *must* have been Maria's child. Here was the receipt by the old merchant for the little madonna and his own ten gold pieces. Even the black bag and the cloak. Hers!" He felt her cold hands in his own again as on that night in the mountains. A sudden chill went to his heart. Life was not so simple as he had

30

thought. He wished now he had left his wife's bastard in a basket in the mountains. Nature has a way with her. This unlooked-for eventuality actually gave him a headache as if he had received a blow between the eyes.

Mother Marie José felt much the same. She had always feared that entry would be misunderstood. She hastened to explain the presence of an orphan boy with the greatest detail. Don Luis now saw all the records. She forced them upon him. There could be no doubt about it. For a few moments he sat with an expression that almost reduced the protesting mother superior to tears. At last seeing the effect he was producing on the good woman, he rapidly recovered himself and reassured her.

"Believe me, I understand the matter *fully*," he said.

He determined to remove any unpleasant impression from her mind by an act of generosity. "After all the woman's worst failing is a little profitable snobbery," he thought. He would have to be careful, therefore, how he offered to confer a gift. The convent was no longer the home of charity. A way out of the difficulty came aptly to his mind.

"You have evidently mistaken my motives in visiting here, madame," he explained. "I myself am childless, but in former times my family were among the many noble patrons of this holy place. I have not been in Italy for many years, but, as I was travelling this way, I could not refrain out of a sentimental, yet I trust pious, prompting of the heart from paying you a visit. You will understand, therefore, that my curiosity about your records was a natural one, *ahem* . . . I might say an inherited one. Permit me to congratulate you upon your superbly judicious management; your highly distinguished clientele."

Mother Marie José blushed. The scar under her headdress burned with pride.

"It was my hope," continued Don Luis, "to confer some passing benefit upon you. Charity, of course, is now out of the question. Your excellent management! But I feel sure, or rather I make bold to hope, that

31

you will not refuse a mere memento of my regard. That old statue by the fountain now——" Don Luis could look embarrassed when he liked——"it is . . . well, it is scarcely what one would choose as an item of ecclesiastical decoration under your present circumstances. The ancients were of course naïve even in their piety. We have become more chaste. More may now be left safely even to the imagination of religious young ladies. Do you not agree with me?"

Mother Marie José lowered her head.

"Of course! Well, it was my hope that you would permit me to have an elegant, modern bambino in the best Florentine style installed, and the——*er*——somewhat outmoded, not to say dilapidated statue now in the courtyard removed. I should make only one condition. The gift must be anonymous. I am going on to Livorno tonight. I will send the workmen some time this week. Do not give them anything, the rascals. They will be well paid."

He looked at her keenly.

The mother superior was making self-satisfied and pious noises in her throat. Not only had she swallowed the bait, she now seemed to be chortling over the sinker.

As she parted from Don Luis at the door, she gave him her blessing with such a genuine warmth and humility for having misjudged him that he was forced to bend low to hide his natural emotions under the touching circumstances.

In the coach it was not necessary to conceal them. He sat there, as evening fell and he began to approach Livorno, with a look of mingled grimness, curiosity, and amusement.

In settling his connection with the Bonnyfeather estate and closing up the old building which he had rented to his erstwhile father-in-law, there might be more to settle than he had supposed. Well, he was ready for it. In a very short time he would know.

Just as darkness came he drove into the courtyard of the old Casa da Bonnyfeather and got out of the coach. The place seemed to be deserted. He felt annoyed. He had sent word of his arrival. But, no. There was a light coming through the chink of a shutter. Somebody, a female, was coming out.

"Good evening, my good woman," said Don Luis.

Faith Paleologus looked at him and smiled.

Chapter Two

Old Friends Grown Older

THE *Unicorn* had been battered about the Bight of Benin and generally bedevilled by gales and head winds for many weeks after leaving the Rio Pongo. Captain Bittern finally fetched a tremendous leg away across the Atlantic before he put-about and beat back for Gibraltar, gradually edging north. In early April he at last made port at the Rock, where with two topmasts and most of the rest of his top-hamper blown away, he had to refit and revictual.

Anthony was at a loss what to do with the ship. His own nationality was so vague that he was afraid of serious legal complications over her prizes when he finally came to settle his affairs in London with *Baring Brothers & Co.* It might be difficult to explain to an English court how a gentleman who had taken an oath of allegiance to the King of Spain, and had for long run an establishment under the Spanish flag, also owned an English ship that had been preying on French and Spanish commerce in the meantime.

He finally decided to get rid of the *Unicorn* by sending her under Captain Bittern to London and having the Barings sell her while they were still acting as Mr. Bonnyfeather's executors.

This plan suited Captain Bittern to a "t." He asked only for the padded chair as a keepsake. He received the entire cabin furniture, plate and all.

"Very handsome, very handsome, indeed, Mr. Adverse," he said, turning a little red in the face. He had asked for the chair only to save £2.3, he told himself. He could never admit his one romantic slip. Somehow the wind had been taken out of his sails with getting the chair, and so much else, gratis. He almost wished he had waited for the auction. He was sure the chair would have gone for,—well, just about £2.3. Now it would only make a good elder's seat at the chapel in Spitalfields. Certainly not at the cottage. Certainly *not!* —after what had occurred on that chair. He wound the chronometer—his now—thoughtfully. It was a nice chronometer—but it was too late now. It would always be too late. All the time left to him was bound now to be highly respectable. Well, he had seen a good deal in his time—in the time that was past.

While Captain Bittern refitted, Anthony began to find his way about Gibraltar. With a good-sized draft awaiting him from the Barings and a fat letter of credit on London, there was not much trouble in doing so.

It was amusing to see, as a sort of foretaste of what might come later, that he easily and rapidly became a person whose importance was taken for granted; whose antecedents were honourably involved in property. Already a door-opening rumour of his being a young man of great wealth had gone the rounds. The *Unicorn* was thought to be his "armed yacht" which he had contributed to the cause of king and country—and, if his patriotism had proved profitable, who was there to cavil at that? Before a week went by he was "commanded" to dine with the governor.

Indeed, he found he might linger on at Gibraltar indefinitely, passing the clear, spring days, that slipped over from Africa so early with a breath of summer in them,—days that set the flowers in the quarry gardens on the Rock to blooming madly,—seeing people, eating dinners, riding, being introduced by and to hopeful mothers, who tactfully withdrew leaving him "alone" in the moonlight—while they watched.

He might go to tea every afternoon in neat, bare, little military houses with green jalousies outside and pretty women within pouring Bohea out of china more sinolesque than the Chinese. Would he have Scotch marmalade or ginger out of neat, blue jars covered with rattan? To tea or not to tea—that was the question. People like the Udneys, and cool, tall girls like Florence were everywhere. And it was all very pleasant, very pleasant indeed to be back again in this world of his own kind; a world of uniforms, bonnets, long white gloves that wrinkled at the elbows; of white bread, yellow butter; skirts with white, mousy slippers twinkling under them, and always tea, jam, cards, whisky; the boom of artillery from the heights, the ships' bells below, and the shouts of the stevedores. Then there were Sundays when all the sailors marched to church. And the purple-blue of the middle, mother-sea made a moat around it all.

What with the ships of the fleet coming and going and a big wartime garrison on the mysterious Rock, there were endless dances, receptions, and affairs. Innumerable boats were always going and coming with dapper little "snotties" in charge, who sprang out on the quay and drew their ridiculous dirks while they landed in charge of a boat's crew of great bearded fellows in glazed hats with a yard of ribbon falling over their left eye; men who could pull, and pull all together.

Here was all the assurance of British official society, naval and military, with its well-ordered social classes, the stratified atmosphere in which it lived and breathed. But with the dullness of peace times worn off. For these were stirring times. Security was given a fillip by the constant hazard of war surrounding it. Respectability was hurried while lovers and husbands made love as men who might never come back again to women who would be left behind. Everywhere was that unarguable moral fervour about "us and ours" that it is the peculiar genius of the English to manufacture and to store up in vast, static quantities before, during, and after a national fight. Like the sparks from a cat's fur, most potent in bracing weather, it snaps at the least stroke the wrong way in war time. Then the lion is feeling his best with his mane full of great and petty lightnings.

At first Anthony was almost taken-in by this inherent righteousness and moral potentiality generated by the necessity to win. It was overpowering, especially in the wardrooms of the fleet, or at an officers' mess ashore; over the port with the candles lit and gold epaulettes drooping down the shoulders of scarlet tunics. Then it was especially convincing from its calm self-assurance and quiet understood boasting and humour; in its ignorance of what it was really opposed to.

It was especially convincing to Anthony, since it was carried on in what he felt to be—more than any other —his native tongue. Of course, he was assumed to be of them, and therefore with them and for them. What other side could there be than "ours"? And besides it was not possible for them to understand one whose fate had turned him into a mere European, a wanderer of the West which no longer had even the ghost of an imperial political body in which to contain its oversoul. The age for that had gone by, or had not yet come. By accident he had fallen into that vanished age. Its ideal had been reinforced in him in Africa, where he had unconsciously looked back upon Europe as one. Now suddenly, suddenly as if into a steaming hot bath, he had stumbled back into Europe at Gibraltar to find it divided against itself and vapouring and seething in a kind of prolonged explosion.

Even in a few days' time at this English outpost Anthony had found himself both attracted and repulsed in an infinitely complex way by his brothers of blood and tongue. They were a delightful people, but they seemed to have forgotten something which he remembered and

37

to be content not to look for something which he must find. If he had ever had any false spiritual pride he had left it in the valley with Brother François, yet he could not help but feel that he belonged to a larger unit than to any that all the stir of affairs and the social order at Gibraltar had now to do with. That society was self-sufficient. It was even too self-contained. It was insular, cut-off. He must look for a larger, perhaps a more empty country, he felt.

This was the essence he distilled from the total experience of plunging back into the world of the West at a British post. At Gibraltar the light of the days he was living in was concentrated into a narrow circle and made more intense by the broad sun-glass of the nation focused behind the fortress. Here England was projected in all its various colours in the living prisms of its garrison, men, women, and children. He thought of this one bright Sunday as he watched the garrison and the citizens of the English town being paraded, and parading to church, the Church of England.

He went in and listened to the service. He could do little more. Here were many of the forms he knew, strangely preserved but somehow having suffered a clammy sea-change. The many things which they were now about and still sought to embody were not the *one* thing which they were once devised to show. That supreme unity had somehow vanished. There was no doubt about it, only the god of England dwelt there. He was perhaps a captain, even an admiral in the British service. The Spirit of the World had gone. God was no longer Our Father, but the god of our fathers—and of "us"—our fathers' precious children. How had that happened? He did not know, but he felt it. Then he remembered something else like it otherwhere.

What was it Mrs. Jorham had felt uneasy about in the churches in Havana? Was that still another thing, too?

After the service he climbed with a party of officers up to the pinnacle of the Rock—that is forever England's—and looked out over Spain, and across the straits back and down into Africa. And he let his eyes wander freely over the blue sea and the arms of it betwixt and between. And again it all seemed equally good to him, part of the great indivisible world, of which, despite an already large dose of it, he knew he could never see and hear, taste and smell—and feel and think about enough. The range of cannon was surely not the criterion of the boundaries of it for those who were invisible spirits of another time; those who, even while the guns muttered, could slip between.

They descended the Rock again to Sunday evening tea and potted-ham, while a salute rang out in the harbour below. For Anthony it was a parting salute. He still might have gone on to London in the *Unicorn*. Next day he let her sail for "home" under Captain Bittern. He sent Juan "on leave" to Tarifa, his native town, near-by and regretfully sent Simba with him.

Taking the able little purser, Mr. Spencer, along with him, Anthony found passage for Malta in a naval supply ship. At Malta he hired a fast felucca and its crew to slip him into Livorno. They glided into the harbour one dark night only a few hours after Don Luis had dismounted from the coach in the court of the Casa da Bonnyfeather.

Anthony, Mr. Spencer, and a few chests and belongings, among which was the bundle taken from his room at Gallegos that had not yet been untied, were all quietly set ashore on the deserted quay of the Darsena.

Anthony was standing again at the same corner where he and Father Xavier had shared the orange between them over fifteen years ago. He was sure now that he had received the larger half. Along the familiar water front the dark water lapped in the starlight. But the Darsena was well-nigh deserted. Since the French and English had been quarrelling, commerce had languished, especially by larger craft.

It seemed curious not to be going home. Surely,

surely John Bonnyfeather would come down the old steps at the casa to greet him. The fire would be blazing under the portrait of King James and the misty room aglow. But he was gone and the casa was only a pile of stones now, one of a series of house fronts along the quays. Impossible! He could not resist going to see. It was only a few hundred paces away. He left Mr. Spencer sitting rather disconsolately on the piled luggage. Under the arches his heels echoed. This was the gate.

It was open, swinging a little in the night wind and creaking. There was not a light in the court. Overhead the stars burned like lights on a sable pall. The fountain was still. It had been turned off. A mysterious air of fear seemed to rest over the whole place. It was like looking at a tomb. What was that vast vague outline against the stars, a vehicle of some kind, a hearse?

He tiptoed in, reluctantly, aware of a kind of hostility that emanated from the great coach. Perhaps it was due to its strangeness, its great bulk, the dead windows agape in the night, the funereal droop of the trappings from the driver's seat. What was this catafalque doing here? In the vague starlight it took on for him the outlines of the hieroglyph of warning. It simply meant "beware." In the stables beyond a horse stamped three times hollowly. It seemed as if a curtain somewhere in the night was about to go up. He was vaguely aware of a stage lying behind it. All the stir and expectancy of a play was there, waiting. A cloud passed and the stars shone through. He turned away disappointed. For a minute it seemed as if he had been about to see through. The feeling of something grisly and oppressive returned. The Casa da Bonnyfeather was positively hostile. He had not expected that. He poked his head into the coach just to prove himself. It smelled of Malacca snuff. He tiptoed out. The gate creaked in the wind behind him. The arch boomed hollowly.

Mr. Spencer was still sitting on the luggage when he returned.

"Wait just a few minutes longer," Anthony said, "and I will get you help."

Anthony took the familiar short cut to the square of the Mayoralty and a few minutes later found himself knocking at the door of the old Casa da Franco. There was now nothing but a neat brass plate on the door with the legend "Herr Vincent Nolte, Banking and Foreign Exchange." But a light streamed out over the threshold as if there was someone living here and awake to welcome him. Nevertheless, he had to knock several times. He heard voices calling in German upstairs. Feeble steps approached and someone fumbled at the door chain. "Franko," the Swiss porter, stood there. "Why, he has grown old!" The man recognized him. "Mr. Adverse!" It was a glad cry, a welcome given unconsciously. The old fellow made quite a clamour over him. Someone looked over the banisters and giggled. A tall woman with corn-coloured hair and wide, blue eyes was coming down the stairs in a dressing gown and slippers. Anthony looked up at her rather startled. She was like a Valkyrie.

"Don't you know me?" she cried.

"Das kleine Fräulein," whispered old Franko.

So it was. It was his little Mädchen who used to sit knitting by the window.

"Du lieber!"

She came and kissed him laughingly on both cheeks.

She led him upstairs holding onto his arm, stopping to tell him the family gossip on every step. By the time they got to the landing with the brass rail about it and the statue of Frederick the Great in its niche, they were both in gales of laughter.

"His Majesty Vincent is still asleep," she called out.

"The devil I am," sang out Vincent, his voice now grown richer and deeper. He had only waited to dress. He came down holding out both his hands. "We've been expecting you for weeks!" They stood grasping each other by the elbows. "My God!" said Anthony.

The tears sprang into their eyes as they looked at each other. "Come up," said Vincent, "and see how you like the bedroom with the new chintz curtains. Anna

41

has been getting it ready for you every day for a month."

"I have not," she said. "It's *been* ready."

A faint reminiscence of beer and sauerkraut brought the room they were about to enter to Anthony's view before the door opened. And there it was; the long table and carved chairs, the pewter, the geraniums in the window and the bird cages with cloths over them. Franko was hurrying about lighting candles. One of the maids was setting a corner of the table evidently for a midnight supper. Old Frau Frank hurried in out of the kitchen whence savoury odours exuded. The lines on the side of her nose were much deeper. She peered more under her moony glasses. But the arms that came out of her short-sleeved wrapper were still rosy and strong. Her grey hair and cap belied her.

"Ach—ach!" Anyone would think Anthony had been her son.

"Do not kill the fatted calf, Frau Frank," he laughed.

"Nein, nein, shust a leetle snack. Kaffee und . . ." She disappeared into the kitchen again. The door banged on a clatter of dishes. A tray with Münchner and pretzels came. Excuses, more food would follow.

"Prosit."

Anthony, Vincent, and Anna.

They sat down and started to talk to one another all at the same time.

Anna was going to be married soon—"think of it, little Anna—ja wohl"—to a rich Düsseldorfer. A look of bland happiness overspread Anna's features suddenly making her look like a young mother with milk in her breasts. This approaching marriage was somehow the most important news. Anthony seemed to have come back just to hear about it. The girl described the home of her betrothed at Düsseldorf. Anthony sat watching and listening, all at once feeling a touch of melancholy. It was for this that his little Mädchen had been knitting and sewing even years ago; even when she didn't know it. How naturally and inevitably some women fulfilled themselves! And yet the quality of life was rich for

42

Anna. Yes, he knew that. There were tones in her voice, the way her hands moved, and her feet—to music—to *the* music. Not guitars in the moonlight. No, no, heavily-strung viols auf dem Grünewald, deep, unhurried, low-toned instruments invisible where the sunlight filtered through the oak branches and the Kobolds could be heard clinking briskly in their smithies under the huge, dark roots. Sweet forest, strong and ancient and blithe. Her bracelets clinked like hammers on elfgold. He sat dreaming about her, and the music welled up in his heart in a splendid chorus. A new experience. More than a tune, full-throated, manifold. She tossed her head in the lamplight. The suite ended at last with the sound of birds in the branches, and a flute somewhere away off in the cool, quiet glades. Dear Anna! He would give her something beautiful for her wedding, and there would be gifts for all her babies when they came. She looked at him, and seeing he understood the current of her life, suffused her eyes with his own. Vincent looked on in the current, too, and smiled. The flute ceased.

Frau Frank had come in with a pot of steaming coffee. She sat down wiping her hands on her apron while two tears ran down the runnels in her cheeks as she described Anna's trousseau. Schön, sehr schön. They began to eat pigs' feet and sausage. The wedding dress just basted together was shown him in a ribboned box. An immense cake powdered with nuts and cinnamon was brought in; more coffee, very black; more beer—wine. The world became softly rosy; the room delightfully bright and warm. Every shining pewter and silver thing duplicated it.

Vincent opened a new box of cigars with a small, gold knife on a chain. He rattled his seals. He was as much of a dandy as ever. But he dressed now with a careful solidity and a lambent good taste about him that just managed to be impressive and colourful without being crass. He dressed as if someone were just about to strike a beautifully polished brass gong—but had sounded a full rich tone on a harp instead. His was the latest French mode now. He felt the Continent was going that way—Bonaparte's. The English were in the offing for a while. He lived by Paris and not by London. While the armies and ships were deciding it between them—he lived on the Continent and made loans. He looked, and he was, prosperous.

Yes, he was going to Paris—had been waiting for Anthony to join him. They must talk it over, tomorrow. There was a great scheme under way amongst the bankers for floating the next French loan. Certainly he was in on it! And he had a proposition to make to Anthony. He had the very best connections now in Paris—the very best. There were *some* people he wanted Anthony to meet in Paris on his way to London. He took it for granted Anthony was going to London. But they could go as far as Paris together. "Think of it, my boy, Paris! —travelling together—old times again! Ach!"

"Herr Gott, Toni, I do luf you," he said suddenly overcome. "What a grand gentleman you have become. And now you are rich, too! Ooo—ooo—it is all coming true, everything we dreamed and more." He started to cry into the beer from sheer happiness and the tremendous, alcoholic sentimental implications of the divine past. Everything in which he himself had taken part was romantic to Vincent. Consequently the future was magnificent by implication, for some time in the future he would be looking back upon it as his past. The tears actually dropped into the foam on his dark beer. And yet Vincent Nolte was in all details of business the most practical of men. He was a sheerly German combination of moonlight playing across the hard marble of a banker's façade behind which the owner counted his marks with a nosegay of forget-me-nots on his counter. He kept his accounts of interest due in an iron safe with a knight painted on its oiled door, ate sausages— and cried or laughed over his beer. And in addition Vincent had spent most of his youth in Italy.

"Ach, Toni, I have great plans. You shall know them tomorrow."

They sat looking at each other very happy, pleased, agreeably surprised with the changes of time.

Anthony saw that from Vincent the last of the pink, rabbit-like impression was gone. His hair prematurely verged toward grey and stood up in a mane in which the ears were lost. His mouth had hardened. The eyes could be cold as they were blue. His high, white stock made him positively impressive with the expanse of splendid waistcoat beneath with a solid splurge of gold seals and a heavy chain across it. There was a round chin that might have been voluptuous if business had not hardened it sufficiently to make it look merely abundant and successful. He emanated an optimistic but convincing warmth. An able man on the make.

To Vincent there was still something decidedly mysterious and strongly reserved about Anthony. But the suggestion that this something might be vague and weak, in the final analysis not sure of itself and incapable of action, had vanished. As a banker Vincent had already acquired a considerable knowledge of people. Some men he knew intended to do what they promised but could by no means do it. The signatures to the well-meaning promises of incapable men were the hardest and most necessary things to watch against. He had, at the first, accumulated a number of small signatures like that. They had cost him dear. "Bad paper." Really one was safer in dealing with a rogue than with people who under other circumstances become other men. The world was too much for them. Anthony was not one of those.

One did not know exactly who or what he was—that was the aloofness of him—but one was quite sure that Anthony himself knew what and who he was now; that he was secure within himself and that "there was good security there." And Vincent felt instinctively as he looked at him that evening with all the keenness and illumination of a fresh view, while he was still a stranger, that Anthony had seen much more of the world than he himself had. Vincent was a little jealous of that, and yet, he was proud of it, too. One could not place Anthony exactly as belonging to this class or to that profession—or to just one nation. He was fair and blue-eyed, northern, but browned now; bitten deeply by some land of constant sun. How tall and strong he was. And yet when he had first come in Vincent had not noticed it. It was the way he moved and dressed that concealed it. Obviously one could not think of Anthony's clothes as being put on. They seemed a part of him. Vincent had never quite been able to achieve that. No, there were always clothes on Vincent Nolte. And he knew it. He saw them himself. Yes, "there is a difference between being a mere man of the world and a gentleman at home in the universe," Vincent remembered. He had not read much lately—the new French loan—but it had been said in a good German book.

But that smooth grey suit, almost silken in texture, the easy roll of the collar, and the neat flamboyance of the cravat—how did it all manage to sit so quietly upon Anthony from his varnished boots to the grey pearl pin at the throat? How the head rose up from the wide shoulders that supported it! Yet he had thought of him as being slim. He must have found a tailor at Gibraltar. The English were good at that. "It will be interesting to see what he does with all the money," thought Vincent. "I wonder if he knows how much he has? Tomorrow," he began. . . .

The door at the end of the room opened and old Uncle Otto shuffled in. He was in slippers and a dirty dressing gown. Anthony jumped up to greet him. It was a shock to find that the old man's mind was nearly gone. He remembered Anthony, but he did not know that he had been away or that he had come back. Only his general kindliness remained as a vague sort of friendship for all that moved. He responded to the warmth of the greeting. Here was an occasion, a general-warmth. He sensed that. He even brightened a little. He clutched Anthony by the arms looking up at him, trying to remember something. "Thou," he said. He smiled immensely pleased at understanding so much. His teeth were gone. Then for a minute a queer look of instinctive, childlike understanding came into his face. "Thou hast found the light," he cried. "Thou hast it! Warm," he said. He tried to lay his withered old head on Anthony's shoulder. They led him away. Frau Frank was greatly embarrassed. She treated him like a child. "Be polite," she said and almost shook him. Uncle Otto objected.

He sat in a chair and gesticulated and made noises. It was impossible not to look at him. "Go to church," said he suddenly. "It is there. I found it. My wife hung bedclothes over it, sheets. But it is there. It shines through. God has given it to his little boy again. And I am so small, so small."

"Uncle, uncle," said Anna. "Here is a footstool. Do sit up now."

"Ja, give it to me. I will pray on it," he cried. "Anna, my little one, thou knowest, too. Let me."

She held him up soothing him. Vincent shook his head.

"We have had a hard time with him," he said.

"Die deutsche, evangelisch-lutherische, protestan-tische Kirche," exploded Uncle Otto.

"Ah, the poor little papa," said Frau Frank, wiping her eyes. "Do you know he seems to hate me now. He says I am lost." She could not keep from weeping. "It is terrible. And I am the mother of his children. You would think he might remember that. But no. He sits brooding. You would think he saw something away off. It is nothing that he looks at. Eyes like the sky, wide. Ever since Buonaparte came that day and he was arrested and locked up he has withered. Now he is just a moon-baby."

Anthony tried to comfort her.

"Buonaparte?" shouted the old man. He shuddered and seemed to wilt. "Brigand," he muttered. He looked around apprehensively and collapsed into a sort of breathing heap.

Vincent was much annoyed at having the evening impinged upon this way. He bundled the old man back to his room. But Frau Frank, who went along with him, came back afterwards to listen and sit with her hands folded in her lap, watching the young folks. Anna insisted on hearing from Anthony where he had been. He began to tell her something about it. He had to go on, and the hours slipped away rapidly. Vincent and Anna sat spell-bound. Frau Frank finally tiptoed to bed unseen. They would not let him stop. At last the light began to come through the window. The birds in the cages began to stir.

"Good Lord," said Anthony, breaking away suddenly out of the midst of Africa, "it's morning, and that poor fellow Spencer is still sitting on my luggage at the quay!"

They roused Franko and sent him out with two boys, who returned in a few minutes with the boxes and the young Englishman. He drank some warm coffee and staggered off to bed with a pale, reproachful look. Anna giggled. They snuffed the candles and went to bed themselves.

Outside the dawn began to break in the square of the Mayoralty at Livorno. Anthony could see two tall poplar trees, one on each side of his window. "The best thing about Europe," he thought, "is the beds. No, it is friends! I am home." He slept till noon.

Chapter Three

What Banking Is About

VINCENT NOLTE was now doing most of the banking and financing for the port of Leghorn and the surrounding territory. He had been among the first to see that the struggle between England and France was going to be a long one, and to arrange his business accordingly. Regular trading had almost ceased, but there was considerable intermittent running of cargoes as the fortunes of war varied in and about the Mediterranean. Livorno had become the centre of this activity. Most of the travellers who came to Italy or crossed it still landed there. The profits on what cargoes did come into the port were enormous, and there was a large fleet of small craft, sloops and feluccas, that slipped from port to port, from Italy to France to Spain, and back again.

Vincent had promptly closed up the old merchant firm of *Otto Frank and Co.* about five years before and devoted himself to taking risks on cargoes. He made innumerable small loans to small shipowners at high rates.

He took care of letters of credit, and slipped bills of exchange through the blockade whether it was the British or the French who were in the offing. In a short time he had concentrated in his hands a surprising volume of business. People in Rome, Florence, Genoa, and Venice depended upon him. The ruling families and bankers of the whole northern part of the peninsula now corresponded with him to transact innumerable affairs, from delivering letters to buying French wines or English manufactures for them or selling their oil. "Nolte can do it" rapidly became a byword.

From this kind of petty business it had been only a natural step to making larger loans of all kinds for short terms and at high rates. In the high financing of the various petty states of Italy Vincent was soon heavily involved. Into his schemes he had drawn bankers at Paris. In short, he was now embarked upon the troubled but interesting sea of European finance during the Napoleonic wars.

The whole lower part of what had been the old Frank warehouse was now taken up by Vincent's clerks, and the ground floor of the dwelling on the piazza was given over to his private bank, its agents and secretaries.

On the morning after Anthony's arrival he had spent the time as usual in his bureau, but at noon he informed his chief clerk he would be "absent from the city" for a day or so, and went upstairs to Anthony's room where they had luncheon together. He brought with him sheaves of papers. Seated together, looking out on the wide piazza, Vincent began to discuss with Anthony the state of his own and his friend's affairs. For the first time Anthony now had the opportunity of reading John Bonnyfeather's will.

The old man's business acumen and foresight were abundantly plain. For some years, prior to 1796, he had been busy rapidly converting his assets into cash, both his ships and merchandise. He had deposited these sums with northern bankers at Hamburg, Rotterdam, and London. In doing all this he had sustained some inevitable losses. But at the time of his death toward the end of 1799, his whole estate, which amounted as nearly as Vincent could then figure it to about £93,000 sterling, was in liquid cash assets concentrated in the hands of *Baring Bros. & Co.,* of London, his executors.

The only items yet to be liquidated were the *Unicorn,* some merchandise which still remained in the vaults of the Casa da Bonnyfeather, and a lease on that building, which still had five years to run at rather a heavy rental. The fourteen prizes which the *Unicorn* had "accumulated" rather complicated matters, since nothing could be done with the funds which their sale had brought until the estate was finally settled. To do that "It will be absolutely essential for Mr. Adverse to hasten to London, after he settles his affairs at Leghorn, with as little delay as possible," wrote the Barings.

"Your affairs here," said Vincent, "consist in being identified and accepted as the legal heir under the will according to the forms of the local law. There will be little trouble over that, I feel sure, for I have retained your old friend Baldasseroni to look after the matter. But until you personally probate the will at Livorno the Barings write that they can do nothing in London but invest. You must arrive there with all papers in due form for proving your title as John Bonnyfeather's heir. Here is a list of the documents that will be necessary, sent on by their lawyers."

Anthony laughed to see that the Barings' solicitors were Messrs. *McSnivens, Williams, Hickey & McSnivens.* He now sent for Spencer and had him bring up the accounts and correspondence which the purser had brought with him from London. Most of this consisted of the accounts and disposition of the sums deposited from Havana for Anthony's share of the Gallegos trading. They amounted with interest to £16,834. Vincent whistled.

"You have lined your nest well, my boy," said he, not without a touch of envy. "I myself never know just where I stand as most of what I have is constantly being loaned out, and the best security is now liable to be swept out as the map changes. However, I guess I can take a risk on this."

He tossed the latest letter from the Barings across the table.

> . . . we are greatly relieved to learn by your last advices that you have heard from Mr. Adverse from Gibraltar and that he will soon be in Leghorn. It is also exceedingly satisfactory to learn that you know him personally and are familiar with his antecedents as he is, of course, a complete stranger to us. Kindly advise him to make all haste with his affairs in Italy and impress upon him the convenient necessity of his repairing to London without delay. It will greatly oblige us if you will explain to the gentleman our desire to close-out our connection with the Bonnyfeather interests, as we are primarily merchants and traders, and have consented to act as executors of this estate only at the instance of the senior member of the firm, Sir Thomas Baring, Bart. He for personal reasons of ancient friendship consented. Our situation, however, is somewhat anomalous. Your good offices, Mr. Nolte, will be greatly appreciated in making our position clear. You may advance Mr. Adverse any sum up to £1,000 on our security, should he desire it, at the usual commission.
>
> Latest advices from Paris indicate that a peace will probably be negotiated shortly, etc., etc., etc.

"Well, how much do you want?" asked Vincent, rattling his seals. "Shall we spend an hour or two haggling over the rate?" They both laughed.

"Wait for a while till I see," said Anthony. "I brought a little gold with me from Africa. Now what else is there to do here besides probate the will? The merchandise still at the casa, of course . . ."

"And the lease. I advise you to buy out of that for a lump sum. The property, as you know, belongs to the Marquis da Vincitata, who, by the way, is now in town.

He has made it convenient to come here to talk over with me certain details as to the forwarding and refunding of the Spanish subsidy to France, through Leghorn. You see the British watch the French ports like hawks, and sending bullion over the Pyrenees is a ticklish matter even when they can get it from Mexico. I have arranged a rather clever method of exchange through a neutral state." Vincent puffed himself a little and they both laughed. "Evidently the marquis wants to close out his own affairs here too and you will have to see him. He will want to sell you the old casa, but don't buy. Watch yourself, for he is brilliantly canny. Oh—there are also the legacies to some of the old servants, under the will. I see McNab comes off well. Well, now, I should say you could close-out all these matters in a week, get the will probated, and start with me for Paris, say, next Sunday?"

"Why Paris?"

"I will tell you. Believe me, you are not the only one who has been doing things since you left here. I have a proposition to make to you, Toni. Now *do* listen to me." He ran his hand through his hair in considerable excitement.

"You see, it is like this. The expenses of a general European war have surpassed the most spendthrift imaginations. The royal mistresses of the ancien régime with all their intrigues; our formal old dynastic wars were positively impecunious adventures in bankruptcy compared to what has been going on now more or less continuously for over a decade. People who based their calculations of government expenditure on the experiences of other times cannot even imagine the demands of the present. To cope with modern conditions it has taken men of a new cast of mind, men whose mental and financial speculations leap across old national boundaries to embrace the affairs of the whole world in a planetary economy. Naturally, there have been only a few people capable of this scope of thought and management among either bankers or politicians. Certain Jews, of course, who have always understood the world

53

to be one market, have profited. Then there is Pitt, and a few British merchants and bankers like the Barings who have understood. But above all others in his capacity to keep the wheels of finance moving under the brakes of war is G. J. Ouvrard, the great Parisian banker. That man is a genius.

"For some years now he has been finding the cash for both peaceful and war-time operations of the French government. I would also mention a certain Monsieur P. C. Labouchère connected with the important house of *Hope & Co.*, at Amsterdam. He is a son-in-law, by the way, of Sir Francis Baring. I want you to keep M. Labouchère in mind—and—and there is also in the south of Europe," said Vincent with mock humility, "my humble self. Ja wohl, there is also Herr Vincent Nolte!"

In his excitement at this pleasant thought he offered Anthony a pinch of snuff in his best professional manner employed after the consummation of a successful deal. He began to walk up and down feeling his watch chain, while the tones of his voice became heightened and more metallic.

Indeed, as he went on explaining the intricacies of the majestic scheme he was engaged upon, the new and the old Vincent Nolte—the happy-go-lucky youth who liked to bet and take a chance on everything uncertain, and the new, staid young banker with a wise, knowing gleam in the corner of his eyes—twinkled in and out and played hide-and-go-seek with each other between the sentences as they fell from his plump mouth.

At one instant he was the incorrigible, gambling boy sticking out his tongue and licking his lips over some spicy anecdote of golden profit reaped by your lucky great-ones, and at the next the persuasive, solid, financial adviser and investor playing hypnotically upon the open vowels and deep gutturals of sonorous words as if a variation on his theme had emerged suddenly from a nest of wood instruments. Vincent was talking now in German and now in Italian. And frequently when he broke into the latter, there would be a sudden

54

little bubbling run on a piccolo, a kind of plunging laughter. Then he would be brought up short, stopped suddenly by a feeling of boyish inferiority from the past as he looked at Anthony. He would be embarrassed, standing there laughing at himself, with his heavy watch seal in his smooth, rosy hand.

Anthony admired Vincent; was glad of his success and proud of his friendship—and yet, as he sat watching and listening, he could not help but wonder in the back of his head how it was that the affairs of a continent tended to drift into the smooth, rosy hands of men like Vincent. To what was that manual gravitation due? But another thing he saw at the same time quite plainly. It would not do to laugh *with* Vincent when he laughed at himself. He must permit him to bury the ridiculous contrast between his past and the so-important present which his own presence inadvertently evoked. "Yes," thought Anthony, "I must be careful how I recall old times to him. He is not sure of himself yet. The plaster of the professional manner is only beginning to set. It must not be jarred loose or the lathing will show through. I shall always, with Vincent—until a good many years have passed—always take the present enormously seriously." So he sat grave and silent, looking like a staid young merchant himself. On this basis the two young men continued to get along famously.

"And so," said Vincent all over again, but very much the banker now, and determined to remain so, "you see it is like this:

"What all the governments must have is bullion in immense quantities. And at the present time that is exactly what they haven't got. England must have it to pay her sailors and her subsidies to her allies to fight France: the French need it to pay their soldiers and buy colonial produce from neutrals while they fight England. At home both governments make their paper money go somehow. The Bank of England suspended specie payment five years ago, and French assignats also went clear out of business. Now it is francs. But try to

55

get metal for them—try it! Yet both the English and the French have to have hard money when it comes to making their settlements abroad. Only victory or peace will make their paper money generally valuable, and no one knows who will win. No, they have to have cash—gold, silver. And who has it? Why, that placid old milch cow, Spain."

He nodded at Anthony wisely.

"But the money is not *in* Spain. Oh, no—that is the joke. Bonaparte would have had it long ago if it had been there. The bullion—immense supplies of it—is locked up in Mexico. For years now the veins of Potosi have been bleeding into the Mexican treasury and the great pool of silver lies dammed up there. Spain has not been able to tap it, for the British fleet sails between. It was M. Ouvrard who was the first to get around the difficulty, and more or less by accident. Bonaparte had played a joke upon him.

"Ouvrard had advanced great sums to the French treasury and had through influence received the contracts to furnish both French and Spanish fleets with supplies. In payment for that he was given by Bonaparte six useless Spanish royal drafts on the Mexican treasury for the accumulated sum of four millions of piastres. Finally Ouvrard, who was nearly ruined by this, sent his brother of the firm of *Ouvrard De Chailles & Co.*, of Philadelphia, to Mexico. He reported that he had seen there the marked chests set apart as a separate deposit for the liquidation of the six royal drafts in Ouvrard's hands, and that besides that seventy-one millions of coined silver dollars were lying idle in the Mexican fiscus waiting to be shipped to Spain. It was in the next stroke that Ouvrard showed himself to be a financial genius.

"He knew that Pitt with his endless demands on the Bank of England had put the governors at their wits' end to furnish coin even for foreign subsidies, and he also knew that just at that time the East India Company was under the necessity of obtaining great sums of silver for Eastern trade. He, therefore, approached Pitt, through the neutral firm of *Hope & Co.*, at Amsterdam —you remember I told you that Labouchère there was the son-in-law of Sir Francis Baring—and he was consequently able, through the pressure of the Barings on the prime minister, to agitate the matter of permitting at least some of the Mexican hoard to be released.

"Pitt was at first obdurate and blustered a good deal about trading with the enemy. But as hoarding continued and the stringency increased, Pitt became more and more inclined to listen to the representations of Sir Francis Baring. At last the matter was arranged, and although England was at war with Spain, four British frigates were dispatched by secret arrangement to Vera Cruz with orders on the Mexican treasury, supplied by Ouvrard through *Hope & Co.*, at Amsterdam, for many millions of silver dollars. Just how much no one here knows. For these drafts on Mexico Ouvrard received drafts to a like amount on British merchants for colonial produce and merchandise, which was imported by way of Holland and the Hopes into France.

"It was said that the six chests marked for him were also brought over as 'tobacco.' I am not sure of that, but I do know that he sold the foreign merchandise all over Europe at enormous profit. The British, of course, received the silver dollars in England and some of them were restamped and put into circulation by the bank. The rest were poured into Europe and India. Those loosed in Europe soon gravitated, due to the exactions of Bonaparte, to France. Both the fiscal and commercial situations were relieved all round—and the war could go on."

"How did Ouvrard get his Spanish drafts for such large amounts?" asked Anthony.

"Oh, I thought I had made that plain," said Vincent. "Spain has by treaty been paying France an annual subsidy and Ouvrard took Spanish drafts on the Mexican treasury, which had been sent to France, in payment for his loans to Bonaparte. Bonaparte was glad to palm them off on him as they seemed uncollectable." Vincent laughed.

"Now bear with me," he continued, "and I will show you how *we* come in." He looked significantly at Anthony.

"The relief already experienced by this welcome supply of Mexican silver has been so considerable and profitable that the combination of Ouvrard, *Hope & Co.*, and the *Baring Bros.* contemplates further action along similar lines. They have now under way a plan to get the bulk of the Mexican bullion to the United States and to reship it, or the goods which it purchases, from that neutral territory to England and Europe, chiefly, of course, through the Barings at London or the Hopes at Amsterdam. I may received the southern consignments here at Leghorn, and, if even a few cargoes reach me, at the present price of colonial produce my fortune will be made. Ouvrard, of course, will continue to furnish the capital in the form of his drafts on Mexico, and the rest of the affair would be carried on by either English or American ships sailing from one neutral port to another. Ships consigned to the Barings or to *Hope & Co.*, or their correspondents, and insured by Lloyd's would run an excellent chance of being allowed to proceed even if searched by British cruisers. It is really a remarkable plan, don't you see? For those in the charmed circle the blockade is to be broken and both England and France will profit by the silver. That, of course, is a dead loss to Spain, but somebody must pay for war.

"Now here is what I want to interest you in, Toni, my boy. At several places in the United States it will be necessary for the Hopes, who are the go-between in this affair, to have confidential agents-resident for the purpose of receiving the Mexican bullion, shipping it, turning it into neutral goods, and investing it for the time being until it can be safely and profitably transmitted to Europe in the most advantageous way. These agents will set up business as regular merchant firms, correspondents of the Barings and the Hopes, and the bullion will be turned over to them ostensibly as their operating capital. Naturally, as great sums will be involved and the whole success of the operations will depend upon the discretion, honesty, and ability of the agents-resident in America, the posts would be filled with carefully selected and marked young men. I need not add that it will be profitable—but above all it would be interesting.

"Your old friend David Parish, by the way, has been asked to go. I have also been asked to take-over at New Orleans, which is in Spanish territory, but a convenient place for receiving the dollars. I cannot go, however. My operations here are already too large and important to think of giving them up. In short, I have other plans. But you, my dear fellow, would be ideal for the post. You are footloose, well-off. You can speak English, French and Spanish. You have already engaged in deals with Spanish colonial officials and you are now on your way to see Sir Francis Baring himself in London.

"You see it all seems to point to you as the ideal man for the New Orleans post, and I believe you would like it. You always used to say you wanted to see the world. Well, here is a marvellous chance to go on seeing it and to engage in its affairs honourably, and I have no doubt with great profit. Why not, why not? Don't just shake your head. Herr Gott! Do you know, I have written about you already to Ouvrard, and to Labouchère at Amsterdam. I want you to meet them, the French bankers particularly, and that is the reason that I especially want you to go with me to Paris. Now *do!* It is only tentative as yet. At least come along and talk it over with them. That can do you no harm. That will be seeing—meeting the world, Toni. And what else would you be doing anyway?"

"Ah, yes, that is true," thought Anthony, who was not over-persuaded. "What else shall I be doing?" At last he promised Vincent to think it over with more enthusiasm than he felt.

"So David Parish was still alive. Curious he should put it *that* way. And he might be seeing him again—see *him?* Tow many children did Florence have now?" he wondered, and sighed.

"Oh, it won't be as bad as that, *really*," said Vincent a little nettled.

"Dear Vincent," said Anthony, "I was thinking about something else. I appreciate all your thought of me. I—I was thinking of little Florence Udney." They both laughed together now. And this laughter was always a bond between them.

"Aha. I always suspected something there," said Vincent. "Well, Parish has not done so badly. Entertains Talleyrand at Hamburg, I hear. Mrs. Udney has been living with them. I'll bet she never plays 'Malbrouk' to Florence any more."

He whistled a snatch of the old tune that unexpectedly trickled like moonlight into Anthony's thoughts. Vincent smiled at his friend's expression. A clerk opened the door.

"His Excellency the Marquis da Vincitata is in the *case* asking to see Herr Nolte. We thought we had best tell you, sir," said the boy still looking a little pale about something.

"That's right," said Vincent. "Come on, Anthony. Let's go down. We both have business with him. Let's tackle this old fox together."

––––––––––––

Don Luis was sitting leaning forward on his gold-knobbed stick in the rather handsome room Vincent had fitted up for himself as his office. He managed to convey the impression to the two young men as they came in that they and not he were being received. Anthony was at first rather fascinated by the older man, whose manners were so suave, formal and polished as to carry even into the little *case* looking out into the square at Leghorn the atmosphere of the court of Spain. He treated Vincent with a consideration that was evidently flattering, though not without an ironical twinkle at times. And in his sardonic gravity Anthony was somewhat surprised to find himself included.

Vincent introduced Anthony by name, which conveyed nothing to Don Luis, and mentioned that Mr. Adverse was the young "Englishman" about whom— "you may remember, Your Excellency, we had some correspondence at Paris relative to his taking over the post as resident at New Orleans."

The marquis bowed a little more condescendingly than before.

"His Excellency, of course, is fully familiar with the Mexican matter I have just been explaining," added Vincent to Anthony, and then turned to Don Luis again. "I thought it might be well to invite Mr. Adverse to sit in with us on our discussion today before you and he take up the little matter of the Bonnyfeather lease. He is the heir, you know. I am anxious," smiled Vincent, "to enlist Mr. Adverse in the Mexican matter. You can rely on his . . ."

The marquis had started slightly. He turned half about in his chair to look at Anthony who was now sitting in the window with the afternoon sunlight streaming in from the square beyond. Anthony looked up. He was suddenly aware of a vital interest in the old man's stare. The old eyes licked over him from head to foot, half-veiled under their heavy lids. Anthony felt himself turning a little cold. There was an instant's silence, extremely tense and awkward for some reason.

"You have no objection I hope, sir," added Vincent quite anxiously.

Don Luis recovered himself.

"Certainly, certainly *not*," he muttered. "No, proceed!" he added with sudden fervour.

"One would think he was giving directions to his coachman," thought Vincent, angered at the tone.

A curious uneasiness had now gripped everybody in the little room. Vincent's caution was awakened by it. He wrote something on a card, and calling one of the clerks, sent him out hot-foot for the advocate Baldasseroni. "The old fox! One can't be too careful," he thought, and began to discuss with Don Luis some of the Spanish ramifications of the plan to import bullion from Mexico.

In this scheme Don Luis was strongly interested. He had recently had long interviews with Ouvrard at Paris and he began to recount at some length the turn that affairs had taken there.

". . . As for the arrangements for the cargoes and the minted money which are to be landed here at Leghorn, you must make your own terms with M. Ouvrard in Paris yourself. He and I have come to a very satisfactory understanding, I might add, as to the honorarium to myself and the Prince of the Peace. We shall deduct that at Madrid," smiled the marquis. "All that arrives here you can figure on as net for yourself in computing your own percentage. I trust a *fair* part of the original value finally gets to Paris, Herr Nolte. We leave that to your discretion. Remember there will be more than one cargo." He grinned a little wanly, and continued.

"It has also occurred to me that the matter of shipping produce from the Spanish West Indies direct could be arranged—possibly—by securing from the Spanish authorities themselves certain licenses to trade made out in blank, you know. I forgot to mention that to M. Ouvrard in Paris. Will you do me the honour of suggesting it to him when you see him as a proposition coming from me? Neither of us need suffer if M. Ouvrard cares to perfect such an arrangement. Assure him, please, that I can bring it about. Someone who speaks Spanish well should come on to Madrid sooner or later to negotiate the matter. In the meantime . . ."

For nearly half an hour Vincent and Don Luis continued to discuss the details of trade, finance, and politics involved in the combination of M. Ouvrard, the Hopes, the Barings, and Herr Nolte.

Anthony listened surprised at the ramifications of the scheme; at Vincent's grasp of details and quick suggestions, which evidently kept Don Luis on the qui vive.

As time went on, however, he began to become more and more aware of Don Luis, and in an unpleasant way. The man filled him with an unaccountable dis-ease and an unreasonable hostility. Here was someone who, without the slightest reasonable cause for doing so, he felt was an enemy; a being to beware of.

As he sat in the window listening to the discussion the feeling became stronger and stronger. It was absurd, he told himself. The old man had hardly said two words to him as yet; had only favoured him with a few side-long glances. Yet he was sure, was perfectly sure, there was a hostile appraisal in those eyes. He felt toward him very much as he had felt toward Mnombibi that night when he had seen him in the glass. But why? There was something a bit toad-like, something of the sardonic Punchinello countenance in the older man. But why should that make him loathe the very way he wore the buckles at his knees?

His spine crept a little coldly as he looked again. He was glad of the sunlight striking warmly through the window onto his own coat. Well, he would *not* look at him then. He would look away. Where was it he had felt that way recently; eerily repulsed—warned off? Ah, yes, in the courtyard at the casa the night before—and with Mnombibi.

Now that he came to think of it, now that he was looking away, he still seemed to be seeing Don Luis in a glass somewhere, somewhere—an ugly little fellow. The noise of the talk grew far away and buzzing—an ugly fellow, spider-like—"pshaw!"

He turned to the window and began to look over some bound magazines. Why did Vincent keep old things like that lying about? Some old consignment probably that had miscarried. The *European Magazine* —April—nine years ago! Good Lord! He turned it over and began to read with one part of his mind:

This extraordinary young man's taste for fame was so early displayed, that a female relation of his persists to say, that at the age of five years, when a relation of theirs had made him a present of a Delf bason with a lion upon it, he said, he had rather it had been an angel with a trumpet to blow his name about.

On quitting this female relation to go to London, he said, "I wish I knew Greek and Latin." "Why," replied she, "Tom, I think you know enough."

"Aye, but," said he, "if I knew Greek and Latin, I could do anything; but as it is, my name *will live two hundred years at least*."—Chatterton used to say, that . . .

A sound in his ears like a distant pistol shot made Anthony suddenly look up. The marquis had sprung back the lid of his patent snuff box. The conversation with Vincent was evidently over. Don Luis took a pinch and brushed some loose grains off his vest. He snapped the lid to again. A faint odour of Malacca snuff drifted through the room. Instantly the coach in the courtyard and the clouded, starry sky of the night before came into the part of Anthony's mind which was not reading.

Don Luis was speaking to him.

At the other side of his mind, as if in a glass pressed close to the corner of his eye, a vision of the coach with light flashing from its windows streamed off into starry space against a rack of wild-looking clouds . . . "the . . ." he turned the page

. . . *the* greatest oath by which a man could swear was, by the honour of his ancestors.

The type on page 286 of the old *European Magazine* slipped uphill into oblivion as he closed it quickly, suddenly aware that the conversation which he was about to begin with the marquis was a dangerous one and concerned him vitally. At the very first tones of Don Luis' voice he had been instinctively on his guard. He had almost flinched as he heard them.

It had been no small test of Don Luis' now nearly automatic finesse that in the conversation with Vincent he had never fumbled once, although a great many ideas had been kept going. His mind too, had, as it were, divided into two parts. That facet directed toward Vincent was compact of politics, finance, and calm caution; that turned toward Anthony was in a rage and a secret turmoil. For when Vincent had introduced Anthony as Mr. Bonnyfeather's heir it had instantly occurred to the marquis that this was also the apprentice from the convent—Maria's child. It would be just like fate to play a grim trick like that on him. He went hot and cold at the thought. "Just like the humour of Beelzebub!"

During the talk with the young banker Don Luis had occasionally stolen glances from under his heavy lids at the other young man who sat in the window where the sunlight fell across his hair. And it had given the marquis a sick feeling about the heart to notice that the ends of that young man's curls, where they were thin and the light came through them, twinkled with red and golden glints as he bent over his book there—"damn him." For an instant Don Luis saw the face of Maria sitting in the coach bathed in the light of sunset as they rode along; as they rode along and along toward the Château of Besance twenty-five years ago. O God, how he had loved her—and hated her! And here was the son of the young Irishman seized of his grandfather's estate by an act of God—or the devil, who knew which, —reading a book. Oh, splendour of the white Corpse of God! It was true.

At that instant Don Luis felt that the Controller of Fate hated him—and he returned that sensation cordially. He hated the world, and he determined, as he had never determined before, to throw himself against it. In a way which only a Latin European could understand he took the course of events as a personal insult. Fate had outwitted him. He would be even with it yet. He writhed a little in his chair. Then he steadied himself, took a pinch of snuff—and turned to Anthony who had just closed his magazine.

"I understand you are to be congratulated as a *very*

65

fortunate young man, señor," he began in a silken tone. "It is not every orphan who finds a benefactor and manages to inherit his estate. No doubt, if your parents were alive, they too would be charmed by your felicity." He smiled a little. Somehow he had managed to be insulting. The blood rushed to Anthony's face.

"I have been fortunate in some respects, sir. But I had no idea until shortly before the death of John Bonnyfeather that I was to be his heir. And I have no relatives I know of, no one to share with me in what you have been good enough to style my 'felicity.' "

"Of course, I did not intend to insinuate that you were a designing young person," resumed Don Luis. "My interest in you is, after all, a natural one. Perhaps you may recall that I had at one time the peculiar honour of being your benefactor's son-in-law?"

"And might have been his heir," thought Vincent pricking up his ears.

"I had never heard *that*," said Anthony obviously astonished.

"Do you mean to say," said Don Luis icily, getting out his pocket spectacles and looking Anthony over as if he were a curiosity, "that your—a—guardian never mentioned to you that the Marquis da Vincitata was his son-in-law?"

"Never," said Anthony, looking that nobleman over so calmly that Don Luis could scarcely sit still.

"The cool young liar," thought he.

"I heard your name mentioned once or twice casually as the owner of the premises upon which Mr. Bonnyfeather conducted his business. But nothing more."

"I will ruin you for that remark," thought Don Luis —and in the intense struggle of his inner feelings permitted himself an instinctive question which he would ordinarily have carefully suppressed. He seldom laid himself open to rebuff.

"Did the old Scotchman never mention his daughter to you at all?"

A thousand speculations were rushing through Anthony's head. He felt himself on the edge of a gulf into which if he could only look he might know his own mystery, but . . . "the greatest oath by which a man could swear . . ." and he seemed to hear the grave tones of the old man's voice in the courtyard that day exacting his promise. "Why was it? Why had Mr. Bonnyfeather made him promise? Who am I?" he thought. For an instant he looked with a peculiar speculation at Don Luis, with an expression of self-struggle that the marquis noted instantly as he leaned forward a little and gripped the arms of his chair.

"That is a point which it is a matter of honour with me never to discuss," said Anthony. "I am sure that Your Excellency will understand me if I put it *that* way."

"He knows," thought Don Luis. "I 'will understand,' eh—I *do!*"

The implacable look with which he favoured Anthony was not lost upon Vincent, either, who saw at the bottom of everything a financial trap. Doubtless Don Luis had in mind the possibility of contesting the will.

"I might add," said Vincent suavely in what was meant to be a soothing voice, "that the matter of probating the will has, of course, been carefully attended to."

" '*You* might add,' " repeated Don Luis witheringly, while preparing to go. "Well, adding is quite in your line, isn't it, Herr Nolte?" He turned swiftly.

"Good day, Don Antonio Adverso, perhaps we shall have the honour of meeting again." He bowed mockingly but with a grave face.

"Ah, who knows?" said Anthony in Spanish. The lines about Don Luis' mouth contracted a little. He took his stick and went out.

"Now what the devil?" said Vincent after he had left.

Anthony was striding up and down. "How those noblemen of the old school do despise us bankers! Well, I shall show him a thing or two." He called into the office to send up Signore Baldasseroni, the advocate.

"Now as soon as this lawyer fellow shows up go out and get the matter of proving the will attended to instantly, my dear fellow. I hope that you do not mind my having lied a little for you. The old one is evidently on your trail."

"Do you think so, too?"

"I am quite sure of it," said Vincent. "If ever I saw one man hate another——"

"My God, what have I *done?*" said Anthony with a half-humorous, half-serious quirk.

"What is the use of moral speculations?" asked Vincent. "The thing to do now is to register the will. Will that lawyer *never* get here?"

The door opened and a fat, little man with a limp, carrying his hat in one hand and mopping his brow with a flaming orange bandanna, entered quite out of breath.

"Why, Signore Adverse," he panted, "this *is* a pleasure, an unexpected pleasure. I haven't seen you for years. La la, how you've thickened up!"

He went limping about, very effusive, clapping his hand to his tail every now and then. "Of course, I remember you." He made a wry face. "You were there when that M. Toussaint put a bullet in my behind. A sad, a memorable occasion, very sad." He launched out into a description of his acute sufferings as a cripple, meanwhile laughing and hopping about like a wren. The whole atmosphere of the room cheered up. The sulphur reek which Don Luis seemed to have left behind him was blown away by the breeze that had puffed in through the door with gay Signore Baldasseroni.

Vincent soon cut him short and explained the situation. Signore Baldasseroni produced a huge watch and noted that the office of registry would close in twenty-two minutes. He and Anthony gathered their papers together hastily and tore out. Down the sunlit street they went and across the piazza to the Mayoralty, with the little advocate hopping along with his hand on his hip and chattering.

They registered the will. For an increased fee the

clerks kept the office open beyond the usual sacred closing hour. Every paper was stamped. Signore Baldasseroni produced the most grave and respectable witnesses, whom he seemed to keep on tap. "They will swear to anything," he whispered. "I hold them for a small monthly retainer. I trust, Mr. Adverse, you will see fit to repose your legal business at Livorno in my hands. My retainer is reasonable, my refreshers modest, my reputation unblemished. This I admit, signore, rests upon the questionable evidence of my own applause, but you may verify it if you will. Permit me to call one of my witnesses, *Beppo*."

Anthony laughed and clapped the little man on the back. "I feel quite safe in your hands," he said. "I shall instruct Herr Nolte to remember you from time to time on my account. What I want is someone who will keep an eye to my interests and not turn up as the counsel for the other side, witnesses and all. You know that *sometimes* happens here. But we, you know, have been through an affair of honour together and I am the star witness to your constancy during trials."

Tears sprang into the eyes of Signore Baldasseroni. "Ah, thou alone knowest to the full my bravery," he cried. "Toussaint and McNab they always laugh when we meet. If you would only tell the clerks here, signore, it would enhance my reputation."

"Some time when it will not embarrass your modesty as it would now, I shall do so," whispered Anthony.

They crossed the street together—friends for life—while the clerks looked over their gold coins and locked the big bronze door. In Vincent's *case* Anthony paid the spry little advocate a great many compliments and an astonishing retainer. They all had a bottle of wine together.

"You have done well," said Vincent after Baldasseroni had left. "You can depend on him now in the matter of the lease and everything else. And that is important. For Don Luis might otherwise persuade him to change clients. It is the curse of law practice here. Baldasseroni keeps a whole boarding-house full of witnesses, with costumes. He always wins my cases. Our old friend Signora Bovino, by the way, makes a wonderful witness in cases involving domestic disputes." Vincent grinned and put his feet over the arm of his chair. "Well, let's go up and see what the women are sewing on now. Anna's preparations are a triumph."

For the rest of the afternoon Anthony sat in the window under the bird cages while Anna, Frau Frank, and Vincent chattered; while the women and two sempstresses sat stitching at Anna's trousseau. There was something so bright and airy in the room, so domestic and home-like with the constant flashing of white thread and needles with gold thimbles on white fingers twinkling in and out through soft folds of delicate cloth, that the two young men from time to time looked at each other in mutual enjoyment of peace, happiness, and home.

"After all, this is what banking is about, isn't it?" laughed Anthony as Vincent passed him to light his pipe in the kitchen.

"Ja wohl!" said Vincent.

Anna smiled quietly over her embroidery and held it up to the light.

"See," said she, "it is a white dove with a red rose in its mouth. Now what colour must I make its eyes?"

On the perch just above her, where the warm rays of the afternoon poured through the open window and the curtains waved in the breeze, a canary began to blow golden bubbles of sound from its throat. It sang as if its heart would burst.

"Ach," said Anna, "Ach, mein Gott! I am so happy."

Anthony looked out into the empty piazza. In the breast of his coat the proven will of John Bonnyfeather, merchant, of sound mind and sound body, crackled drily. A lump came into his throat.

In a few days all this would be gone forever. For some reason or other, just why he could not remember now, he was going to London.

The canary sang again and again.

Chapter Four

Don Luis Reflects
By Candlelight

THE inn of the "Blue Frog" had for several generations been one of the best kept caravansaries of the Mediterranean littoral. Perhaps more than any other institution in Livorno—and it was an institution —it had realized the original dreams of the Medicean founders of the free port by attaining a complete cosmopolitanism.

Like all really great inns, it had not depended for support nor derived its atmosphere from a purely genteel clientele, which is so dully alike everywhere. It had catered to everybody, from travelling cardinals to sailors getting rid of their pay. And it had done so by sprawling out along the piazza into various pavilions where each kind of man could find others like himself gathered together eating and drinking, playing and talking according to his nationality and class. In that respect the "Blue Frog" was unique.

But its reputation depended upon, and had been

71

spread abroad chiefly by distinguished travellers; by prosperous ship captains and merchants who had tarried under its roof memorably. And the common item in their universal praise of the "Blue Frog" was always its abundant and tempting fare.

It was the boast of its proprietor, one Lanzonetti, that any guest at his inn could obtain there, not only the best in Italy, but that no matter from what remote portion of the globe the traveller hailed the inn kitchen could also supply him with his favourite, native dish. Lanzonetti had been able to do this by gradually assembling a bevy of remarkable cooks from sundry regions and by collecting from every traveller—who either condescended to take an interest in his "universal menu" or to order a strange dish—a recipe, which the innkeeper immediately proceeded to enter in a carefully cherished book, to experiment with and to improve upon.

A cellar of inspiring proportions and catholic selection contained everything from the rice wine of China to Canary vintages. It was especially rich in importations from England and Germany of brewed beverages of all kinds. In the next cave was a museum of choice sausages. Lanzonetti's main success as a host, however, had been due to two cardinal principles of cookery; he never permitted a woman to enter his kitchens, and he had a whole battalion of saucepans always bubbling over innumerable small fires.

In the late 1770's the "Blue Frog" had been at the height of its prosperity and glory. The art of eating and drinking had during that decade attained among the privileged classes in Europe a high crest of perfection from which it afterward for many confused decades declined. The traveller of the day was usually a landed, frequently a titled gentleman, with leisure and elegant discretion; possessed of taste as well as appetite. The nice craft of purveying to him might be rewarded by reputation as well as gold. Lanzonetti had won both. His recipes were much sought after and went out to all the world like tracts of a society for the propagation of the gastronomic gospel in foreign parts. As far away as "Strawberry Hill" Horace Walpole had learned how to coddle eggs in mulled wine.

Don Luis had stopped at Lanzonetti's at that, to him, regrettable period of his life when he had been making the arrangements for his marriage. On account of his present abstentious diet he remembered the place with more than the usual pleasure of an old epicure. It was only natural upon his return to Livorno even after a quarter of a century that he should again put up there. But alack and alas—the good "Blue Frog" had meanwhile suffered a sorrowful transformation.

To be sure, the main building of the inn still looked across the piazza at the establishment of Herr Nolte directly opposite, but it was no longer known as the "Blue Frog." It existed, or rather it languished, under the now fatal name of the Osteria dell'Inglese. A recent hasty attempt had obviously been made to obliterate the unlucky designation by painting out the last word of it with the device "Français." But the older letters were again showing through, and the now nearly ruined proprietor, a tall, thin Tuscan by the name of Fratello Rabazzonie, could not even afford a little new gold-leaf to repair what amounted to a serious political error on the part of his sign. Indeed, in his own spare body the proprietor seemed to personify the lean and sickly times he had fallen upon.

Upon the night of his arrival Don Luis had looked Rabazzonie over doubtfully. He did not believe in thin innkeepers, and there was dirt on the man's apron. Nevertheless, since it was late he risked taking the front chamber on the second floor overlooking the piazza. He was quite tired, and although the room smelled mouldy and the bed was a distinct disappointment, he slept tolerably well. The marquis had left the coach at the Casa da Bonnyfeather, after having refused to stay there despite the preparations and the rather pointed welcome of Faith. For it had suddenly occurred to Don Luis as he descended from the coach in the courtyard that the matter of terminating the old lease had not yet been negotiated and he *might* be laying himself open to a technical charge of trespass by staying in the house. The horses, however, he had risked leaving in the deserted stables under the care of the Kitten. He brought Sancho along to the inn.

Don Luis was awakened shortly after dawn the next morning by the arrival of luggage under the charge of some noisy porters at Herr Nolte's just across the square. Breakfast was poor, luncheon terrible, and the unexpected encounter with Anthony that afternoon unnerving. On the evening of his second night in Livorno Don Luis sat in his dingy chamber at the Osteria dell'Inglese confronted with what for a man in his condition was a "ferocious" supper. The blue veins on his forehead stood out even farther than usual as he rang violently and demanded the proprietor.

"Landlord," said he, when that individual had entered and sat down without permission,—"another evidence of degenerate times," thought Don Luis,— "landlord, this food and this room," he swept his arm around overturning a decanter, "*might* be considered hospitality by shipwrecked sailors with desperate appetites and sea-sore bodies, but by no one else. Do you call this supper? The oil is rancid, the wine sour"—he went on for two minutes—"the servants decrepit and the beds Procrustean."

"No one has ever complained of being bitten by anything but fleas before," said the surprised host. "I tell you, citizen . . ."

"Citizen?" roared Don Luis. "Citizen of what? Don't you know they don't talk that way any more—not even at Paris?" (Twenty years ago, he reflected, he would have caned the man for a similar ignorant impertinence.) "But what the devil *has* happened to this inn? One used to be received here as a Christian gentleman instead of like a relapsed heretic at a country branch of the Holy Office. The bed! Do you expect to charge patrons for the privilege of being put to the question? Holy Zacharias—and Bellerophon . . ."

In the course of a quarter of an hour the landlord,

who had at first sought to defend himself, was reduced to a few stealthy tears for his own misery and a lurid description of his misfortunes in order to stem the tide of steady abuse that flowed into his ears as if they had been manholes in a flooded street.

The man's misfortunes it so happened interested Don Luis, who now felt a little relieved at having successfully vented his spleen upon him. And he also saw in his story a certain confirmation of his own opinions as to the recent decline of civilization. Any inn, he felt, was a social barometer; this one in particular had been so for all Europe. And its glass was now low, *ergo*. Condescending to indulge himself in a bottle of fine, old Greek wine fetched by the landlord's suggestion from the last rack in the cellar, he finally put the tips of his stubby fingers together, leaned back, and listened to his host's recital with a philosophical air of "God help us all."

"It is the times, signore," said the man, coughing a little and spitting into his handkerchief,—"the terrible times that are responsible for your pitiable supper in what was once the abode of cooking. You remember it otherwise, you say. But consider, how can I help it? My wife, when I married her, was a woman well-off. It was her *all* that went to purchase this inn for me from the retiring owner, Lanzonetti. He agreed to help me supervise the business for a year. But he was a smooth one, that fellow, and he hated to see another going about in his place. He died only three months after I came— and would you believe it, sir,—but the jealous dog took his famous book of recipes into the grave with him. He had it buried in his coffin, clasped to his breast. It is with him now—in hell. My trade fell off—naturally! Distinguished Englishmen, for example, who ordered turtle soup and received frogs' legs instead, became violent. With my wife always in the kitchen, the old cooks soon left. To retrench my losses I gradually closed up one after the other the various extra pavilions along the square. The inn—he shrinks inward towards his great warm heart in the kitchen, year by year. In seventeen-

75

ninety nothing but the main house is left. The frog has lost his legs! I change his name and hire me all new servants who remember not the times before. Seventeen-ninety-four—most of the men go with the army. No one remains to serve here but old women. The English have stopped coming. Seventeen-ninety-six—the *great* General Bonaparte, he arrives. Ah!—*all* business ceases then. I am forced by decree to keep open. To live I must sell the fine, old wines to soldiers. I change the name again. But no good. All Frenchmen are in the army. No one travels. My wife goes off with an Austrian hussar to Vienna. Only two crones are left who stay on for bed and board. Eighteen-hundred-one—*the very distinguished gentleman from Spain* arrives and complains of his 'despicable' supper." He shrugged his cadaverous shoulders hollowly—"What would you, signore? What can I do?"

"There will be a peace shortly, I think," said Don Luis, sympathetic in spite of himself. "Your trade may pick up again."

"It will be too late," cried the innkeeper, letting his long hands fall loosely on his sharp knees. "I have the terrible sickness of the lungs. Long before peace comes I shall be hunting that swindler Lanzonetti with his book of recipes through hell."

"You will find him frying in his own grease in the most comfortable spot there," said Don Luis. "But tut-tut, man, it's not so bad as you think. (It's a great deal worse.) Cheer up. At lease you are rid of your wife."

"Sí?" said the man.

"Sí!" said Don Luis.

He had been moved by certain items in this tale of woe and now wished to offer a certain modicum of sympathy. He dismissed him with more kindness than the man expected after paying him on the spot and right nobly for the wine, which had been offered as a present. The innkeeper could not resist gold, however. Wishing Don Luis good night in a mournful voice, he left him alone with the cobwebbed bottle and one candle.

76

"At least the fellow had enough sense to understand the delicacy of a disguised gratuity," thought the marquis. "He might have been a democrat and *so* insulted. Well, good luck to him—in hell.

"Yes," thought Don Luis, "he and I have lived through some strange times the last two decades or so. It was a better world when we were born. Nowadays the wives of innkeepers—and others—go off—*ahem*— with hussars. 'Eighteen-hundred-one,' as that fellow says, June twenty-third my own dear wife's bastard so unexpectedly turns up." He clenched his hands.

" 'Anthony,' eh,—takes after his sainted mother. Has his father's reach. Leave him to Providence? Shall I? I suppose the sins of the fathers may still . . . I might try to help that idea along a little, circumspectly, of course. No more errors, no more going too much out of my way. Let opportunity serve." He sipped his wine slowly.

He did not mind so much finding that Anthony had inherited his grandfather's estate. He regarded that as merely a gratuitous insult, a quizzical prank of fate—a —a long deferred slap on the jowl after he had carefully and patiently wiped away the spittle of outrage from a too-trustful eye. Probably he might expect that in the nature of things. No, it was meeting again with the young gentleman at all that had upset him. He had done his best to prevent that. It had, in spite of him— occurred. And how much did the "young gentleman" know? Everything?

He gulped another glass of wine and wiped his lips, which were still red and a little too full like over-ripe cherries with a worm at the heart.

A number of frantic moths were circling rapidly about the big glass candle-shade on the table before him. To Don Luis they seemed to be making visible rings in the air as his eyes grew heavier and a little bleary. Behind them his mind was strangely active. Indignation and old Greek wine are peculiar stimulants. When he felt as he did tonight he often found relief in venting his thoughts on the morocco notebook. It was better than sheep over a stile at any rate.

Futile anger is the base counterfeiter of epigrams, he wrote. His hand trembled a little—and then: *Three things never elicit any enthusiasm: a pregnant bride, a reasonable religion, soup without seasoning.* "Perhaps I am drawing too much on my own past experience," he thought, "but the soup tonight was saltless. Why must everything be personal?" He dipped his pen again.

Men say they can discuss their affairs dispassionately in the terms of general propositions. But let a man make a remark about the enormous amount of quackery in medicine, for instance, and a woman will immediately wonder how much he owes his physician. In nine cases out of ten the woman is right. It is the tenth man, a genuine philosopher, however, whom she will set down as a fool. She understands the others. Why is it, then, that women seldom or never write poetry, which is the art of talking about one thing in the terms of another? There is a reason: In poetry women are talked about in the terms of something else. That appears to them to be a waste of time.

"Prolix," thought Don Luis. "I am tired, and ordinary in thought tonight. I *have* had better nights. Let me see." He fluttered the pages of the book backward scanning it listlessly . . .

"Education of the Young"
Boys should be kept in a monastery until they are old enough to be condemned to the galleys for life. Girls . . . "damn them!" He flipped a solid inch of pages and nearly broke the back of the book. The writing he was looking at now was firmer than usual. His hand had not trembled when he wrote this: *Once tangle the threads of two lives firmly together, and no matter how apparently remote and disparate their future courses may become, it is quite likely that it will require the good offices of the blind lady with the shears to cut the final tangle.*

Certainly the meeting this afternoon tended to confirm him there, he thought.

He dropped his quill and lay back pondering. He was in a state where, with his body too sleepy to write, his mind nevertheless galloped on; speculating; throwing off grand, shadowy visions; coining figures of speech and tags of phrases; watching itself and talking to itself about what was always going on in the old house just under the thatch.

"—which is now getting rather thin in spots under your wig," said a disgruntled voice with a note of suppressed terror in it.

"What is the use of thinking about *that?*" demanded another.

"In fact what is the use of thinking at all?" a whole crowd seemed to shout. A single-toned voice went on like the blood in the listener's ears:

"What you *think* is a candle there with the moths going around it—and around and around it—is really the planet Saturn."

"Yes, and wouldn't it just be a good idea to blow out Saturn and go to bed—be in a dark room, tired eyes."

"A dark room? Yes! With the Dutch countess whom you met travelling once, at Besançon—the dark room there, ah—here it would smooth out that inner palsy that you are still shaking with after being so angry this afternoon."

"*He* was there this afternoon."

"Well, we have not decided what to do about him yet. What—to do?"

"Let by—the countess was five years ago. And how are you now?"

"*Can* I still?"

"I?"

"Not a doubt—never!"

"Let's all get in the old coach then and drive around to the Casa da—Palazzo Gobo tomorrow where *she* is. Let's try."

"It's rather shameful at your age, though."

"Never think of it. No one need know. Who cares now if . . ."

"Get the lease arranged. Never mind *him*. Stay at your own house. She is still there. Do you remember you asked her when you were first seeing Maria what she was doing there—and she smiled just the same way? Why not? It will not be long now until no more beds—no beds at all—but one."

"Stop that. Think—what?"

"Why, how uncomfortable the bed here is. How the old house has tumbled down."

"Yes, it is like Europe. All the nice arts of living are being forgotten—and in a mad effort to make everybody comfortable and happy."

"But why *not* spread things out?"

"There never was enough to go round for everybody to have enough. No, it will all end in everybody, even those that have something now, having nothing—or getting things they don't want. What is life without land, rank, honour? Bonaparte, I tell you, has the right recipe for such philosophy—you stop it with soldiers. How to make them obey?—he knows."

"Aye, can't you see the inn 'shrinking,' as that fellow said? He didn't know why it was happening to him. Only a phrase, a name, 'Bad times, Bonaparte.' But it was that explosion in Paris that started to do away with the 'Blue Frog'—and other things—things I regret. Oh, what an ass was the sixteenth Louis! To let them come to Versailles. Even that day at the Tuileries the Swiss could still have stopped it. It was inevitable? Versailles had changed them into ceremonial kings. They couldn't act—only act. Versailles was a crest. Versailles was getting like something Hindu, Eastern, something completely conventional in art and life. It was a way, and something that could go on that way by itself. The West will never see anything like it again. Already they are forgetting what it was in itself. Bonaparte should have been—be king."

"I dedicate myself to making him so!"

"Don't be pompous."

"For unto us a child is born, unto us a son is given: and the government shall be upon his shoulders . . ."

"Rejoice, rejoice, the prince of war is born, eh?"

"Now you are being silly and impious."

"Not to myself. *I* know what I mean."

"Not to myself—umph!"

"None of this is meant for the book. No, no, don't rouse me—the me that writes. I know what I think. I pin my old hopes on this new man from the past. I talked with him in Paris. I remember. He is inevitable."

"It is all inevitable. The past is always inevitable. How could it have happened any other way than it did?"

"Is the future inevitable? Can't it happen any way?"

"No, it only seems to be open for anything. In reality it is already as inevitable as the past."

Here a wizened old man with very white hair and beard, who looked a good deal as Don Luis might at ninety, suddenly thrust up a wide, flat stone under which Don Luis *knew* he was always hiding. He stuck out his tongue and shouted, "You are a fatalist!" whereupon the stone fell down on him like a lid again. Some of the white hairs of his beard were caught under it. They kept on twitching in a horrible way, especially one pointed tuft.

Don Luis stirred uneasily in his chair. He had been expecting this to happen—he remembered now. The old party under the stone usually presaged trouble. He could orate the marquis into a nightmare when once aroused. Don Luis therefore hurriedly began an argument that he pretended was meant for himself alone. But out of respect for the head, which he knew was still listening under the flat stone, he addressed himself to himself in his suavest and most diplomatic manner.

"Let us, then, take an example," said he. "*Was* it inevitable that King Louis should stop the Swiss firing on the people that day at the Tuileries?"

The beard caught under the stone twitched violently. (Don Luis' face twitched in the candlelight.) He gasped. The old man was looking at him again.

"How can you ever know enough to argue *that?*" said the greybeard, and began raising the stone farther

81

back like a lid. Don Luis suddenly slumped lower down in his chair.

"Well," said Don Luis defiantly, "let us take something I *am* thoroughly familiar with, then,—something from my book, for instance."

"*Our* book," corrected the head, his white throat beating like that of a snake or a frog when breathing.

"*Ours,*" repeated Don Luis hastily, afraid the lizard body of the old man would appear, too. It was nevertheless some satisfaction to be corrected by someone who looked like himself.

"Ours—I will repeat the passage for you, *Once tangle the threads of two lives together, and no matter how remote and disparate the course . . .*

"I remember it," hissed the head testily, and threw the stone back with a bump. Don Luis felt a distinct ground-shock as if a distant powder magazine had exploded somewhere. It annoyed him. (He had just slipped off the chair onto the floor.) He shouted indignantly.

"I was merely going to apply the passage specifically to test the truth of it. I was merely going to ask myself how it is that after I, as a reasonable man, take all precautions to prevent it, this bastard turns up again. Don't you see that the truth of the passage *we* have written *and* the idea of inevitability, past and future, are bound up in that?"

"Certainly I see *that,*" said the old man emerging triumphantly now and snatching the argument out of Don Luis' mouth—"since you ask me—" he added softly.

Don Luis groaned. He *must* get this terrible old man out of his head. He tried to brush him away like a fly. It was almost impossible to move his hands. He just managed to touch his forehead—and knocked off his wig.

"*Certainly* I can see that," continued the old man not at all disturbed. "It is all perfectly simple. Any event will do in a case like this, either King Louis's Swiss or your own meeting with the young gentleman this afternoon. All events in history are equally mysterious. They simply happen. We, as it were, merely stumble across them. One thread crosses another. But let us take your meeting this afternoon. *Why* did it happen? But you admit it is futile to ask *why*. *How* then? Well, I am not so sure you could show me how it happened. Let me see:

"By following your separate threads of existence backward and forward across the pattern of events it might be barely possible to see how the encounter this afternoon happened. But only partially. You do not know all the facts. It is quite true that your lives were once looped together long before when the child was born. For a short time they even ran in parallel lines, which, I might point out to you, became visible in the ruts made by your coach between the mountain inn where Maria died and the hole in the convent wall through which you, sir, so trustfully thrust the black bag, and the stuff that was in it, back onto the loom of God.

"You thought the parallel lines might safely be allowed to diverge and become lost in the general pattern of Europe after that. You were willing to chance that they might come together at infinity. You could settle the account then, you thought. Perhaps you forgot how deep and how far the heavy wheels of your coach have cut those lines-parallel into the roads of the past.

"With a little larger view of the nature of things, at the time, Don Luis, you might even have allowed for the tendency of threads which have once been brought so closely together by the teeth of the weaver's shuttle to run across each other again at some other point in the pattern. After all it is by an infinite number of such crossings that the dots in the pattern are made, and it is an infinite number of those dots, where one individual thread crosses another in the warp and woof of events, out of which whole scenes in the tapestry of history are woven.

"That web, a tapestry, or pattern—whatever one may conveniently call it, when considering it as a cross-

83

section of a sliding future passing across a flat page,—
is constantly being created and interwoven out of the
stuff of human lives. It is now, at this instant, as it always has been before, made up of an incalculable number of separate threads marking the course of lives.
These have in themselves each a certain amount of free
will that resides in the essential tensile strength and the
calibre to which they have originally been spun; in the
colours of character in which they are dyed. And between the compulsion of the weaving shuttles and the
free will of the threads there is always a certain amount
of interplay in order that this piece of weaving with
living matter upon the loom of history may proceed.
For as every weaver knows, there must always be due
allowance for unexpected give and take. It is only where
the threads cross one another that they are firmly inter-
locked and loop-stitched together; tied up in a knot.

"But that living web must also proceed out of the
past by some living compulsion dictated by a tendency
in the general scheme of things akin to the particular
compulsion in an egg or seed to change only along certain peculiar lines into what is always becoming something else, but always within certain bounds; never the
maple into the oak tree. Thus as in the particular thing,
so in the great general Thing of history—the huge exud-
ing, creeping, weaving proceeding eternally and mysteriously goes on.

"This living web, which slides mysteriously out of
the past from beyond the vaguest, fabled memory of
things remembered, extends into the future complexly,
strangely; utterly transcending the mightiest powers of
even immediate anticipation. It grows, that is; it
changes. And on either side invisible binding filaments
of it extend beyond our human senses like the cords on
the side of a piece of weaver's work that are afterwards
cut off. These are what hold it on the frame of things
and they are not even known to us. So now you have
the loom backward and forward and from side to side.

"From above and underneath it is forever being
worked upon by the moving shuttles that go and come

and never pause, and by the wheels of direction that rack and shove the fabric on, always in one irrevocable direction. And now, you see, you have the loom from all sides.

"Thus any particular crossing of the threads, or knot in the fabric, any event, is merely a point at the centre of a sphere which has been tied or has come to pass because of forces working upon it from all sides at once. How then say that one thing is a cause and another an effect, when each is alternatively the other according to how we call it? Above all, on a flat page, how show conclusively how one knot in two threads got tied, much less project a general pattern?

"How, for instance, convince yourself, my dear sir, because you once carried a child in a coach from the hole in his mother's side to a hole in a convent wall that you must inevitably meet that child again when he has grown to be a man—and on a particular day in a certain banker's office, in Leghorn, Italy? Or, to put it the other way, how could you be sure when you abandoned him to God that you would or would not meet him again? In fact, how can you be sure you will not keep on meeting him again, or never see him at all? Is it fate, or is it chance, is it cause and effect? Well, that depends finally upon the nature of the Eternal Weaver and his method of procedure. By the way, what *do* you think of Him, Don Luis? For it is upon your conception of his nature that you will act and conceive all other men to be acting. Not upon what he is, but upon what you conceive him to be. That is where your interplay as a thread in the fabric comes in, isn't that true? Well, what *do* you think of Him after all?"

To this demand of the voice there was in the soul of Don Luis no answer at all, only the sound of chanting in a cathedral.

The little man upon his stone now became visible again. He laughed and jumped up and down upon it till Don Luis struggled in his sleep.

"So, you prefer to stick to your own particular little question and let the major premises alone. That makes

85

action easy, of course. Even if it ends in disaster. Those who trouble the gods have little time for men. Now *there* is something for Your Excellency's morocco book." The shrill laughter of the little man with the beard caused the man slumped down beside his chair to groan in his sleep.

"Go back to hell," he said aloud. The chill echoes of his mumble boomed through the mouldy chamber of the old inn.

The little man suddenly flipped the stone upside down and disappeared into the earth. On what had been the bottom of the stone Don Luis now began to see a dull phosphorescent glow that slowly took on, while he watched it as if hypnotized, the changing, shifting character of the web he had been dreaming of.

On the table the candle which was now nearly burnt out began to jump and flicker. The wick fell flat and burst momentarily into a broader flame. The moths began circling more rapidly about it.

On the now glowing map before him Don Luis began to follow among a thousand other visions the future track of the coach. It led straight toward an immense range of mountains whose snowy pinnacles glittered distantly in an unearthly moonlight. The coach drove on across the plain. He and someone else were in it. Suddenly the face of the housekeeper at the Casa da Bonnyfeather looked out of it much painted and bedizened and with a supercilious, satisfied expression of vulgar pride that caused him to laugh. A look at the range of sawtoothed mountains ahead served to silence him.

His dream now gathered up into an overpowering sensation of speed. There was a chasm just ahead. The speed became unbearable. Don Luis felt himself in the coach, falling. He braced himself for the crash. It came as a nervous shock that half opened his eyes. The coach had hurtled off into space and burst against the opposite wall of the gorge amid a shower of sparks and little lights that twinkled out from and all over the map on the stone before him. This had now suddenly grown gigantic as if he were looking at a whole hemisphere at once. Its shifting outlines were so huge and so writhing with life as to be terrifying beyond thought. On it the gigantic mountains into which the coach had recently fled were now only tiny, glittering lines like a clump of glow-worms seen by their own light. All about them rolled and tossed the twinkling camp fires of armies. The red glare of burning cities coloured the night. Here and there puffs of white powder smoke shot through with vivid red lightnings broke out. Into the midst of these Don Luis was suddenly plunged. The smoke reek was intolerable. Men were killing each other in the darkness on all sides. A tremendous salvo of artillery burst out just above him. He tried to scream but could not.

Clear over the face of the map, usurping it and taking its place, sprang out the Roman features of the little Corsican general to whom he had been talking in Paris across the desk only a short time before. It was like looking at a Caesar's head on an Augustan cameo ten miles high. The laurel wreath on the brows glowed intolerably as with the concentrated blue light of millions of diamonds. The mouth opened to speak. Another terrific crash of artillery which lit the head with lambent flames woke Don Luis from his sleep.

He had slumped down onto the floor and was leaning in an agonizing position against the slipping chair behind him. A thunder-storm accompanied by violent bursts of wind and sheet lightning was passing over Livorno. The rain spattered through the shutters. On the table the draught had thrown the wick onto the candle drippings. Inside the big glass shade the tablecloth had taken fire and was smoking and rapidly running holes with sparks.

Don Luis dashed the lees of the wine over it. Muttering a few sleep-drugged imprecations upon everything in general, he staggered stiffly to his bed, stepping on his wig as he did so.

He was awakened next morning by the glare from the piazza beyond striking through a broken lattice of the decrepit shutters directly into his eyes. It was still quite early.

87

He rose, dashed a little cold water on his face, and going to the window with the towel still in hand threw the offending shutter open and looked out.

As fair and clear a June day as ever dawned on Italy after a thunderstorm filled the square at Livorno with sparkling light. The sky overhead was a faultless blue bowl. Against the wall of Herr Nolte's establishment opposite, someone in dressing gown and slippers was seated leaning over a cane in the sunlight and drinking in the first warmth of the morning with all the hunched-placidity of a crouching and withered old man. Don Luis looked at him while wisps of the dream of the night before gradually cleared from his head. To see someone so much older than he freezing in the sunlight while he still felt as strong and vigorous as he did that morning, unconsciously filled him with sudden joy.

"It is going to be a good day," he said and flipped the towel. "There is one old fellow over there whose thread in the general pattern has nearly ravelled out. What an idea the web was. I wish I could catch it up in a sentence or two for the book. Por Dios! what tricks the brain plays on us when it is going to sleep. Does it? —or do you *see* your ideas then? I shall have to tell Bonaparte about Europe and his head." He laughed, and then turned a little pale. "Madre! I must be getting senile myself. I shall soon be relating my dreams. Can't you see them muttering, 'Here he comes!' Old? Not yet, by Lazarus! There are a good many surprises left in this old carcass."

He began to rub his arm vigorously with the towel. A number of gamins gathered below looked up and pointed in his direction. In the sardonic features of the figure moving in the square of the window above, one of them had suddenly seen a likeness to Punchinello. A burst of laughter followed to which Don Luis paid no attention.

Carts laden with vegetables and flowers, with their wheels muddy from country roads and the storm of the night before, began to call upon their customers and to cross and recross the piazza, leaving a pattern of wheel marks on the washed flagstones of the square. The interlaced designs rapidly grew more intricate. A flock of milch goats making its morning round left here and there the seal of a small cloven hoof.

A convoy of convalescent soldiers going home rolled rapidly across the square, the wounded riding on caissons, wagons, and nondescript vehicles requisitioned from the countryside. Some sat silent, holding bandaged arms clasped to them painfully, others smoked. A small group on one wagon broke into a snatch of song. A peculiarly brazen trumpet rang out the notes of "Column right." Don Luis started. He had been looking at the growing pattern on the flagstones fixedly for some minutes now. It was hopelessly intricate; beginning to fade in the sun. He turned, rang for Sancho, and gave him orders to prepare his breakfast himself. "The food here," said he, "gives me the vapours. Or perhaps, it was that Greek wine last night."

"Your Excellency should drink only what we have brought along," said Sancho picking up the wig and removing the burnt table-cloth without comment. He tied a large napkin around Don Luis as if he had been a child. "Foreign wines give you indigestion now. You must remember, sir."

Don Luis leaned back and looked up at his whiskered servant, laughing a little.

"The bottle last night was in memory of my honeymoon here—some time ago. You remember, Sancho?"

"No, señor," replied the man looking at him solemnly.

"Thou art a comfortable servant, Sancho," said Don Luis.

"What would you think if I asked someone to travel with me in the coach back to Madrid, Sancho?"

"A duenna for your nieces? One is greatly needed. Certainly—an excellent idea."

Only Don Luis smiled now. "Have the coach around at nine this morning. I have some legal business to transact—about that lease."

"Sí," said Sancho and blew out a small spirit-lamp under the breakfast bowl.

"And tell that señorita at the casa to prepare for me after all. I can't stand it here any longer. The beds at the casa are at least comfortable."

"Sí," whispered Sancho.

"Now then—" said Don Luis.

Sancho raised the bowl of chocolate to his master's lips and held it there. His master's gnarled hands, like the paws of a monumental lion, lay heavily on the table as he leaned forward. The chocolate was exactly the right temperature.

Don Luis sighed.

Chapter Five

The Coach and the Berlin

IN THE cobbled area behind what had once been the ample stables of the "Blue Frog," Anthony and Vincent suddenly emerged from the door of the old coach-house, tugging together at the long shaft of a four-wheeled carriage.

The vehicle followed reluctantly out of the gloomy arch as though indignant at being forced into the light of day again.

"Come forth, Lazarus," shouted Vincent, heaving mightily.

Answering, ghostly squeaks from the rusty axles caused Anthony to explode. Just then the front wheels came upon the incline, and to a sound like that of a cat running across an organ keyboard an old berlin galloped its two frantic steeds in shirt-sleeves into the alley below. They swung the pole just in time to avoid being crashed into the wall opposite. The old carriage, its windows hung with cobwebs, came to a halt with a despairing screech.

Even the dying Rabazzonie—who for once had made a fortunate deal and sold something for more than it was worth—laughed until he coughed violently. He looked at the scarlet spray on his handkerchief—and put the coach-house keys back in his pocket, still surprised at finding them jingling on something else metallic there.

Having brushed off the straw and dust amid a good deal of back-slapping and mutual banter, the new owners of the old berlin resumed coats and began to examine their purchase with rueful faces and an occasional chuckle.

"I warned you not to buy it in the dark," said Vincent.

"*You* warned *me!*" replied Anthony hotly. "Why, you were so anxious to get it yourself that you kept bidding against me in there. No wonder Rabazzonie wouldn't take it into the light, though."

"Toni, it was mad of you to give hard coin for it. Look at it!"

"Not so bad after all," sniffed Anthony. "Wait till I'm through with it."

Yet he was forced to grin with Vincent, too.

For the relic of antiquity which stood resurrected before them was like all dilapidated old carriages in having about it an air of insufferable complacency. "In me," it seemed to say, "you behold the *ne plus ultra* of something that has *so* unfortunately passed. In me you behold the fate of all particular styles. Some day your own wheels will stand still in time."

Meanwhile, the spiders and cockroaches abandoned it to run back into darkness, as if they too knew where the past had gone, while the carriage remained to stick out its tongue at the present.

The green paint clung to it in scales and its mouldy leather curtains hung limply like folded bats' wings. Its roof was sadly buckled and sway-backed. Two large, dusty lanterns glared like a stage-dragon's eyes, one on each side of the box whose moth-eaten hangings hung down in elf-lock fringes. Behind, a high, hooded seat cocked itself up like an extravagant pump-handle tail, while the shaft in front burrowed into the ground. Standing there in the bright sunlight of the silent alley, the old berlin resembled a cross between a griffin and a snipe that had been disturbed hibernating but had now comfortably gone to sleep again in the very act of digging up a worm.

Anthony and Vincent kept on joking about it despairingly with the full, flat irony of young men while they continued to scramble in and out of it as if trying to wake it up; slamming its chattering doors, examining its wheels and axles, poking its cushions from which the mice leaped. Then with as much gravity as if they were driving to Schönbrunn for an audience they sat down in it together and burst into peals of laughter at their own expense.

"At least the wheels are all right," insisted Anthony.

"Yes, but we just *can't* go to France in it," groaned Vincent. "They will arrest us for émigrés trying to return disguised as ghosts in the family coach."

"It was you who suggested it," replied Anthony, poking him in the ribs. " 'Member? You said that after the battle a year ago the Austrians requisitioned everything on wheels to retreat in and the French came and took everything that was left—or something logical like that —and that you can't sit a horse—and that this old berlin was a great idea—and that you were the only one that remembered its existence—and we should certainly be captured if we went by sea—and——"

Vincent groaned again. "That's right, rub it in."

"Of course," continued Anthony, now enjoying himself greatly, "it *will* look strange for that prosperous young banker, Herr Nolte, to drive into Paris in what looks like Richelieu's désobligeante exhumed." He bit off the end of one of his much prized Havana cigars philosophically and gave another to Vincent as a consolation.

Vincent sat back puffing it, gloomy enough. All that he had said about getting a carriage this side of the Alps was true. And he had set his heart on making the trip to Paris with Anthony not only in comfort but in privacy and luxury. The old berlin, which he knew had been accidentally overlooked by frantic quartermasters, was a last hope. The Tuscan posts were not only impossible, they were improbable. And a saddle did give him piles. No doubt Anthony thought that was funny. It wasn't.

Having now reached an impasse on the subject of the berlin, they continued to sit in it quietly for some minutes, smoking their cigars in the warmth of the brick alleyway which was pleasant enough at that hour in the morning. Vincent was trying to rearrange his plans for getting to Paris. He was greatly disappointed at finding the old carriage hopeless.

It was all very well, he thought, for Anthony to sit there blowing smoke out of the windows as if they were already on the way. But he, Vincent Nolte, had important international business to transact at Paris. He had an appointment to keep with M. Talleyrand, and several bankers. And, as usual, he was being left to make all the practical plans. Undoubtedly friend Anthony was still somewhat of a dreamer. From the expression on his face now you would think he was a boy again playing coach—looking out of the window that way! Well, that would never get them to Paris—never!

"As a practical man of affairs, Vincent, did you ever consider the philosophy of modern travel?" asked Anthony suddenly. Vincent stirred uneasily.

"No."

"Well, it goes something like this: None of us are content any longer to live in the present and to enjoy things just as they are. We are always thinking about the past or the future; trying to readjust what has already happened to us or making plans ahead. The present under those circumstances hardly ever exists for us. It is always, in our days at least, just a time-between. In other words, we never *are*, we are always just about to be.

"Travel is the one exception to this perpetual uneasiness of always becoming. It is only when we are travelling that we exist as we were meant to exist; in the present. Everything then becomes quite vivid and real. We have left the past behind us and the future must wait. There is nothing to be done about it. So just for a little, in transit, we give up our dear rôle of being our own tin fates and live. Suddenly it is now—for a while. And we are happy; surprised how pleasant it is to live, to be ourselves. I have noticed that a great many people can find each other and be friends when they are travelling, but let them once arrive and they lose themselves and each other again. They wonder, 'How could I have ever found *that* fellow interesting on the ship or in the coach?'

"Do you know, when I first set out to see the world I thought it existed only in the places I was going to. I was in danger of becoming a series of deferred destinations. Now I know that travel, that 'in-between' is the time when one lives. I am going to try to turn all destinations into part of one journey, the long journey from the beginning to the end, you know."

"What a philosopher you are getting to be, Toni," laughed Vincent. "And just like all the rest of them. Here you are philosophizing about travel, and all that, while sitting still in a funny, old-fashioned, useless coach that won't go. No, I haven't thought about 'travel.' But I notice that I shall have to make the practical plans for this journey. It's lucky you know one or two men of affairs, my boy. But I have a little business to transact at the bank this morning." He started to go.

"Now, *my son*," said Anthony making him sit down, and returning his paternal manner with interest. "You're quite mistaken. The trouble is you are just like all the rest of the bankers, you can't even apply philosophy at second-hand."

"Fo!" said Vincent.

"No? Well, I'm going to prove it to you! 'As a matter of fact'—as you always say in your letters—I have a little surprise in store for you this morning. I am going to show you what money *can* do. You know you laughed at my making a strict, eight o'clock appointment with Rabazzonie, who, you say, has more time than anybody in Livorno. He hasn't; he has very little time left in Livorno. Didn't you see the red spots on his handkerchief? I took no chances and bought the berlin last night—cheap. I just let you bid it up this morning in your excitement and gave him the difference. After all, what are a few measly scudi more or less to a rising young banker? Now wait a minute. That isn't all. The play really begins at nine o'clock. I have arranged for a little meeting here, a kind of post-mortem over our deceased friend the berlin. They ought to be here soon."

"Who are *they?*" demanded Vincent a little sulkily.

"Our old friend McNab for one. I put this little matter into his hands."

"Oh, you know how to pick your agents well enough," yawned Vincent, pretending to be greatly bored and stretching his feet out on the opposite seat resignedly. "McNab can make a Spanish dollar weigh an English pound. Toni, you're an old fox to make me give Rabazzonie twelve scudi extra. I'll charge it on your account as expenses. I certainly will."

"He needs it," replied Anthony. "Call it charity."

They both grinned now. Since Anthony had come back he and Vincent had been matching wits in several directions. This was a rather unexpected score. They were now about even. They sat waiting for McNab and his work-gang to appear, smoking contentedly.

"Almost nine, now," said Anthony, taking out Mr. Bonnyfeather's watch.

"What a turnip it is," remarked Vincent. "And all that spread of heavy seals on the chain. I don't envy you that part of your legacy. A little old-fashioned, eh?"

"Tut, tut," said Anthony.

A rat scuttled along the ancient brick pavement of the alley and stopped to look them over. It was very quiet in the old berlin with the leather flaps hanging down. Vincent jogged Anthony's elbow. Through a slit in the front they could see that someone had entered the end of the alley from the square. He was standing relieving himself against the brick wall. It was Don Luis. They laughed. He was so furtive and yet hearty about it.

"The old goat," whispered Vincent. "Look how he stamps around. It's still a positive pleasure to him. If you want to know what a man's like, watch him against a wall, when he isn't looking. There's philosophy for you."

But just then Don Luis looked up suddenly becoming the marquis again. He had smelled cigar smoke. Glancing down the alley, he saw the grotesque old berlin with wisps of smoke curling up from it. Its lamps positively stared at him. He had a good mind to rout out the boys who must be in it, apprentices smoking their masters' cigars. "And the best Habana at that. The young thieves!" He gripped his cane.

In the berlin Vincent and Anthony held their breaths.

"Pshaw!" said Don Luis, and strode out of the alley. He was busy that morning getting the antique statue from the convent safely shipped off to Spain. They heard the door of a coach slam and the heavy wheels rolling away.

"Would you have run if he'd come after us?" laughed Vincent.

"Yes," said Anthony. "Do you know, I hate that man, Vincent."

"Why?"

"It's unreasonable, I know, but I hate him just the same. He makes me feel desperately uncomfortable and insecure. I can't help it. Damn him! I want to fight him —if he only wasn't too old."

"It's just as well then you let Baldasseroni close that matter of the lease with him instead of having a personal interview—even if you didn't come off so well."

"Oh, well, let him keep the stuff in the cellar, and the old furniture! The last time I went to the Casa da Bonnyfeather, the evening I landed, I walked up to the old place and looked around. And there was that great coach of his standing like a hearse in the court. Do you know, I felt warned-off. The coach smelled of snuff,

97

and when I got the first sniff of it next day when I met the man in your *case . . .*"

"Oh, you're getting to be an old woman," said Vincent. "But here comes McNab. Now what is all this about? Here's the great Signore Terrini, too."

Not only were McNab and Terrini coming down the alley but half the master workmen in Livorno as well. There was Beppo Tulsi the blacksmith, Garnarlfie the cabinet-maker, and the little upholsterer with his apprentices. Their shoes clattered like a squad of soldiers. McNab spoke up rather proudly.

"It was na sae easy as you maun think, t' gather a' the great-hearts ye now see before ye togither for a tryst the morn, Mr. Anthony. They're a' sae bashfu' an' min at trustin' a body the noo. Sin' the French came every ass maun hae his hock in guid siller laid doon in his ain fist. Min' yoursel' or they'll be playin' nieve-nieve-nich-nack wie ye.

"Mon!" he cried, giving a start as his eyes for the first time took in the complete decrepitude of the berlin. "You'll no' be bamboozled into throwin' away guid, bright siller on yon negleckit, auld-warld trumbler, will ye? I wouldna ride a leaguer-lady o'er the plainstanes in it."

"Now, now, Sandy, hold your horses," laughed Anthony, "the money's not spent yet, and——"

"Na, na, but it's *aboot* to be," cried McNab, "and I'll hae na more to do wi' it." He continued to stay, however, out of curiosity.

"Terrini," said Anthony leaning out of the window and tapping that now shabby artist on the shoulder, "do you remember that sketch of me you did in Mr. Udney's library years ago, when I was a boy?" Terrini nodded uncomfortably. "Well, you have been using it ever since, haven't you, for the body and hands in the portrait of every merchant's brat you have daubed in Leghorn. I know how your best talents lie. Well, take the body of the old berlin and work it up into a fine modern portrait. Something fit to carry a prince of the blood travelling incognito through foreign dominions,

98

something that will convey—without attracting undue notice—a sense of wealth, stability, and the utmost modern good taste. That's all I want you to do with the old lady, Terrini."

Vincent lay back beating a little dust out of the seat before him with his cane, whistling softly.

"I give you carte blanche, Terrini, as to materials, wages, and your own designs."

"Mon!" exclaimed Sandy as a last protest.

"The only stipulation is that you submit all your accounts to McNab for approval after the work is done."

Sandy grinned. "There, there," he said to the artist whose face had fallen. "I won't be cutting your own profit more than half and the costs two-thirds, rely upon it."

They all had to laugh, for McNab knew them and they knew McNab. He had not lived in Leghorn for half a century without learning the fiscal peculiarities of his neighbours.

Leaving the smith looking about under the carriage and the rest gathered about Terrini in earnest consultation, Anthony, Vincent and McNab strolled over toward Vincent's *case* across the square.

"Well, are you satisfied, Vincent?" asked Anthony. "Sandy here will, I hope, be able to find us some horses somewhere." They were all talking in Italian now.

"Aye," said Sandy with a rueful shake of the head. "But I hate to see you leaving Livorno again, Master Anthony."

"I'd take you along if you knew where you wanted to go, Sandy."

"Thank you, sir," replied the Scot, his face becoming sad and perplexed, "but there's the rub. Since you've distributed the old master's legacy, Faith is the only one of all the old crew left at the casa that knows what she wants. It's curious, but none of us seemed to realize that the old life there was really over until Baldasseroni settled that lease for you and the old landlord took over the place again. It was too bad about the furniture. I've slept in that bed of mine for two and forty years."

99

"I'm sorry about that," said Anthony. "I should have thought of it."

"No, no, there's nothing to reproach yourself about, sir. The old master left us all enough to buy—mony a guid bed and a wee house to put them into." He broke into Scotch for a phrase or two, apparently a little excited about something. "But there'll be nobody to lie in them but ourselves and it *will* be a bit lonely—for me at least," he added significantly.

"You don't mean to say that Faith and Toussaint—" said Anthony.

"Aye," said Sandy.

"Was he happy?" asked Anthony.

"Like a boy with his first girl—for a while."

Anthony suddenly felt cold.

"Mon!" cried Sandy forcibly, "yon's a terrible woman. It must be inside the skull of her. Past middle-age and every new moon she's like a goat on the hills again. Did you ever see her eyes then, peerin' oot o' that great bonnet o' hers when she goes out? Do you know, Mr. Anthony?" They had come to a stop now. Vincent gave them a look and walked on. He was not in this, he saw.

"Yes, I know," said Anthony. McNab was still looking at him. His gaze became more searching.

"You don't mean to tell me that she bothered you when you were a boy, sir?" Anthony did not reply. He had grown silent again.

"Puir laddie!" exclaimed McNab. "Why didna ye come to me?"

"You know why," said Anthony looking at McNab. He had just guessed why himself.

"Aye," said the old man lowering his eyes. "We all paid there. And she's my ain cousin, too. But when she gave me the go-by and took up with Captain Bittern that time——"

"Oh, *did* she?" said Anthony. Suddenly they both laughed.

"By gad, she must have been sent into the world for educational purposes!" Anthony exclaimed. Somehow he suddenly felt relieved at what McNab had let slip. Since so many had shared in Faith she became a cosmic experience. He and McNab, and Toussaint, and Captain Bittern—and—and—were brothers. He linked his arm in McNab's and they went across the square. For the first time in their lives they were really talking to each other.

"Yes, sent into the world," replied McNab, "but not by God, by auld hornie. It's not her Scotch blood, of course."

Anthony grinned.

"Well, well," continued Sandy, "I suppose it's the mixture then. She's a kind of she mule, you know. Some mule mares are always in heat but Percheron, stallion or jackass makes no difference, they never gender. I suppose," speculated Sandy, "they want something they haven't got and keep trying for it. Yon woman's verra parseestant. It's the cradle and the grave with her." They had come to the steps of the office now and stopped.

"Will you come and have a talk; stay for dinner?" asked Anthony. "The Noltes, you know them from old times, they'd want you."

"No, no, thank you, sir. I'm moving to my new lodgings this afternoon. But I wish you'd send for Toussaint and talk with him, Mr. Anthony. You see the landlord, the marquis, is coming to stay at his own house. Toussaint and I have to get out but Faith is staying on, sir."

"What!"

"Yes, sir, there's no doubt of it. There's something up. Long before you came to the casa, in the old days, I think there was something between them. She was Maria Bonnyfeather's maid, and when the marquis came a-courting the old man's daughter, well, Faith was around, too. And——"

"I see," said Anthony. "Well, I shall send for Toussaint to come round for supper tonight. I wondered why I had been seeing so little of him. Good luck to you, Sandy, you know any time you . . . that is if you ever——"

"I know, sir, I know. And I'll keep in touch. It's the old blood that calls to us all. Good luck to *you*, Mr. Anthony—Adverse."

He shook hands and left Anthony standing on the steps pondering. The closed door again! He shook his head as if to clear it of cobwebs.

Anna called down the stairs to him. "Come up, Toni, I want you to meet somebody." They were all talking German and laughing up there excitedly.

"So her prince from Düsseldorf had come, had he?"

Why was it as he ascended the stairs he began to think of Angela? Something in Anna's voice, he supposed.

Pearls!

Why hadn't he thought of it before? That was exactly the wedding gift for—Anna.

In the courtyard of the Casa da Bonnyfeather, where the foul remains of stagnant water in the fountain were fast being licked up by the sun, leaving a film of green slime behind it, Toussaint Clairveaux was loading two small chests onto a cart. One contained his clothes and the other his library of second-hand books.

These, a few clothes, and the small legacy left him by Mr. Bonnyfeather were all that he had accumulated during about half a century of labour and existence. The legacy he had invested in a small cottage on the outskirts of Leghorn.

Faith stood on the steps watching the chests being carried out in the same mood that she had watched the departure of Mr. William McNab some hours before; that is, with considerable satisfaction. She had quietly completed her arrangements with Don Luis for remaining on as his housekeeper, and she was now seeing the last of the old régime depart with a complacency that bordered on enthusiasm.

The fact that for some time past she had allowed Toussaint, faute de mieux, an easy access to her bed made no difference to her feelings of relief at his departure. They had merely been left alone together with the establishment practically closed up, and it had amused and soothed her to allow Toussaint to think that his lifetime of devotion was being rewarded. McNab had merely laughed and let them alone.

Toussaint as usual had built up a romantic and blissful future on the basis of what he considered to be Faith's surrender to his long siege. "Her heart's citadel has at last capitulated," he assured McNab.

"Just temporarily starved-out," replied Sandy, and went his own way, waving off the demands of Toussaint for an apology as one would placate a child or a madman.

Toussaint on his part had bought the little cottage with vines about it some time before and furnished it charmingly. Since the great revolution had somehow failed, he and Faith would now live apart in a dream of happiness close to the heart of nature in the hills. He had even tried to read *Emile* to Faith. The embrace which followed after one paragraph he could never forget, never!

He now wiped the sweat from his forehead after lugging out the chest of books and arranged a sack on the seat.

"Tiens," said he. "All is ready, mademoiselle. Have you packed your bag? We can return for the trunks later." He stood waiting for her in a dramatic stance.

Twenty years before there had been something hawk-like and gallant about the little Frenchman, a kind of ardour which only the young intellectual fanatics who had brought on the revolution for the rights of man had possessed. It was their mode, the peculiar sign of their class and generation. It had not been funny then, because it was dangerous, genuine, and new. In his own mind Toussaint was still one of those, who, if you would only listen to him, could bring the golden-age out of a cocked hat. He extended his own, now frayed and worn-out, toward Faith, and stood waiting with his brown cloak at just the right droop from shoulder to

103

ankle although it was a hot day. The "consummation of his love" had given him all his old confidence. The hat was even arrogant.

"Come, mademoiselle," said he.

To Faith the little man standing in the courtyard had nothing hawk-like about him. He looked to her like an old bantam cock crowing defiantly upon a deserted dunghill. She smiled, and deliberately began to close the big double doors. She took out a great key from the ring on her belt.

"You may leave it in the keyhole," called Toussaint, climbing into the cart himself.

"*May* I!" she said and burst into a peal of mocking laughter.

He looked up startled—just in time to see the door close her in and him out, and to hear the lock shoot home.

The man on the cart burst into a roar of laughter. "Pretty neat that!" He hated the French anyway. They had taken his other horse.

Toussaint ran up the steps and beat at the big doors frantically. No answer. He poured through the keyhole the kind of eloquence that was out of date. That it came from his heart made no difference to the closed doors. Only the echoes in the courtyard replied to him. He heard them now. He heard his own voice. For the first time he recognized it for something frantic and ridiculous; something which even the stones hurled back. It struck him down. He lay on the steps and writhed while his ego withered. Then he lay still.

The man on the cart got down after a while, picked him up and dumped him like a sack into the back of the cart beside his chests. Toussaint, the works of Rousseau, and sundry out-of-date garments were drawn out into the country and deposited at the vine-covered cottage. The carter gave no change for the gold piece which the small man, with his head sunk on his breast, proffered mechanically while he sat on his library by the roadside. It was a hot day.

104

About twilight Toussaint got up and went into the silent, little house.

He sat there for some hours with his head in his hands. A full moon began to peer at him through the window. "Clair de lune," said he, and spat.

He went out now to one of the chests and opened it. From a compartment on one side of his books he took out one of a pair of duelling pistols. It had not been fired since his affair of honour with Signore Baldasseroni.

"I shall do even better this time," he said.

He removed the charge carefully and cocked the piece.

"Meldrun!" said Toussaint Clairveaux to the moonlight, and put a bullet through his brain.

About the same time at the Casa da Bonnyfeather Don Luis was climbing into the bed of his late father-in-law with almost pious grunts of satisfaction. Outside, the shadow of the coach stretched half-way across the court in the moonlight. The bed was undoubtedly a good one and the sheets smelt of lavender. Indeed, the marquis had every confidence in his new housekeeper.

He had even left the door of his room open.

For Anthony, the news of Toussaint's mad little tragedy served to give a dark poignance to rejoicings at the Casa da Nolte over the marriage of Anna to her Düsseldorfer and to the brightly concealed agony of Frau Frank at her only daughter's departure with her husband. Anthony said nothing about it until Anna had gone. But he could less than ever abide the thought of the strange new order at the Casa da Bonnyfeather. There was now something distinctly gruesome about it. With Anna away, the life of the Franks' house seemed to have vanished, too.

The whole past at Livorno lay heavily upon him. He wished to be rid of it forever now and to settle his affairs in England. With a growing impatience he awaited the revamping of the old berlin by Signore Terrini. Some days went by. Uncle Otto continued to sit in the sun and mumble. Then late one afternoon Terrini himself drove around in the rejuvenated berlin and even McNab had to admit that the "siller" had been well spent. The carriage was a little masterpiece, much too smart, indeed, for the sturdy but rather plebeian nags harnessed to it.

The ridiculous high seat behind was gone. The vehicle had been slung evenly on new "C" springs so that it no longer seemed to be always about to bury its nose in the earth. The wheels were lacquered jet-black with bronze lions' heads worked on the hubs. The remodelled body was decorated with oval panels and the glass of the windows and the door was set in the same graceful shape. The top was no longer sway-backed but hip-roofed. And the whole carriage was enclosed with the fine, grained leather, enamelled in blue, for which Leghorn was famous. Furthermore, the top was so contrived that the rear half of it would let down as a hood, otherwise kept in place by two polished metal rods. All the seams of the leather were held together by a bronze filigree that traced itself over the entire upper half of the carriage as a metal vine. The box was covered with grey felt ending in dark blue tassels, and there were two bronze side-lamps held in the beaks of eagles, which Terrini himself had designed and cast.

The little artist, who for a long time had found no work in Leghorn except the designing and decorating of coaches, had surpassed himself, and he was obviously proud of his chef-d'œuvre.

"Of course, signore, with cost no consideration!—" He waved his hands as if the berlin could take wing and might be shooed away.

And indeed he had managed to express in its lines a lightness and grace that were astonishing. The long sweeping curve of the back with the platform for the trunks had bronze handles for the footman to cling to. It gave the final effect of a piece of flying light-artillery with metal gleaming in the sun.

"There will be nothing like it in Paris, Toni, not even the aimables who drive out in their 'Anglo-cavalcados' to Chantilly can rival you," said Vincent, who was a little envious.

"That is what I thought," replied Anthony and smiled a little. "I told Terrini here to give me the latest mode, and he has done so."

"Yes, I have done so. The Greek mode is going out. It is the Roman effect I have striven for," gratulated Terrini. "Look at the bronze chains on the poles and the harness fittings, classic. You must get better horses in France."

"We shall. But we might as well begin now on the present team here and the postilion and try to smarten them up."

Next day little Beppo, the Florentine vetturino, who had been engaged as one familiar with the passes over the Alps, was lifted out of his large jack-boots and leather coat and provided instead with a smart livery of bottle-green and a half-moon cocked hat with a tricolour cockade. He was also induced to drive from the box, although he preferred to ride one of the horses. That, however, was too old-fashioned to be tolerated.

Beppo drew double wages, for they had decided to go light and not to take on a footman until the other side of the mountains. Consequently he was effervescent with his unbelievable good luck in a slack time. In a few days he could manage his team like a charioteer even from the box. He cracked his bronze-handled whip while he rolled through the now comparatively deserted streets of the town on practice drives in the early morning. The blinds would be opened a little and excited voices behind them would comment upon the dashing appearance of the little berlin as it whisked by. Some oil meal, a clipping, a tail docking, and the removal of what had at first appearance looked like mops over the horses' feet, vastly improved them. At least they looked as if they might show a clean pair of heels.

Vincent attended to the passports. He had official

107

friends. Otherwise there might have been difficulty for Anthony, who could not prove that he had been born. Described as a Tuscan gentleman on pleasure bent, he and Vincent set forth early one August morning in high spirits. There was an ample hamper of delicacies cooked by old Frau Frank, who kissed them both and saw them off with her blessing and tears.

As they trotted down the ancient street the last thing Anthony saw was the Swiss porter Franko bowing his affectionate thanks at the open door, and the already corpse-like face of Uncle Otto with his mouth open, asleep in the sun.

In the cool of the morning the horses whirled the little berlin on its slickly greased axles across the worn flagstones of the Mayoralty and flashed into the Strada Ferdinanda.

The team had just settled into a good spanking trot when a coach-and-four going at breakneck speed dashed out of a side alley and recklessly bore down on the berlin. The driver of the coach had evidently lost control of his horses and for some minutes the two vehicles galloped side by side, racing together down the Strada Ferdinanda toward the north gate. Poultry, and unfortunate fruit and flower vendors scattered before them like leaves in a gale.

Beppo had swerved only just in time. He was now doing all he could to rein in his own team, badly frightened, excited, and all for making a bolt of it. In this resolve they were much encouraged by the four splendid, coal-black horses racing beside them neck and neck. Ears laid back, eyes straining, and foam flying from their bits, the four galloped as one in their black collars, drawing after them easily and with a steady pull a huge, black coach piled high with luggage. It rolled along evenly upon its heavy iron tires that sang as they struck the paving like a dull bell.

There was something both ominous and thrilling in those iron tones. Anthony and Vincent had at first braced themselves for the crash that it seemed must inevitably follow. Then, as nothing happened, they sat back again tight-lipped, watching the familiar houses flash past and listening to the alarming, staccato tattoo of the galloping horses' hoofs. They were both thinking of the same thing. The arch of the Porta Pisa a short mile ahead was wide enough to admit only one vehicle at a time. Presently Anthony leaned back and laughed. Vincent looked at him as if he had just discovered he was riding with a madman.

The coach and the berlin, as though attracted by some invisible force, now gradually began to draw nearer to each other as they rushed down the middle of the broad avenue; dust rolling behind; spokes glimmering in a mist of speed.

The madness of the horses had spread its nervous contagion to both drivers, who were now exalted by excitement above all ordinary cares about life, limb, or happiness. They had now but one fatal end in view— to get to the narrow city gate first. Meanwhile, they began to abuse each other in the most provocative Spanish and Italian filth,—grandly pianissimo and fortissimo—and to pray profanely to the horses to burst their wheezing guts, but to get first to the gate. A mile of heartbreak had already made the sobbing nostrils of the poor beasts look like the bells of inflamed trumpets —then breed and skilful driving began to tell and the light berlin, which had a small lead, slowly but inevitably began to lose ground while the heavy coach gained.

A wail of all but feminine despair from Beppo, a tempest of chuckling squalls like the triumphant cries of a victorious tom cat from the box of the coach led the mere owners of the two racing carriages to suppose that they might now *possibly* be able to register an opinion with the drivers as to the immediate necessity of their deaths.

It was for that reason that both Anthony and Don Luis thrust their heads out of the precisely opposite windows of the coach and the berlin at the same moment—and found themselves looking searchingly into each other's faces. At the same instant the wheels of both carriages struck the smooth granite ramp that led to the narrow arch of the Porta Pisa.

"Good morning," called Anthony, leaning nearer. "We seem to be bound to meet."

Don Luis looked at Vincent, who was lying back in the berlin with a pale face; glanced at the black tunnel of the gate, where the guard was now beginning to run about frantically, and peered at Anthony again. In the three seconds which had thus passed the horses had taken as many strides nearer the inevitable crash.

The face of the young man only a few inches from the marquis was nevertheless quite calm and smiling. He seemed to be enjoying the situation. A reluctant gleam of approval widened the fixed smile on Don Luis' lips. The tires continued to sing brazenly. It was quite plain the coach could not gain enough in the short distance that remained to avoid collision.

"Well?" said Anthony.

"*You* pull up," shouted Don Luis. "I can't. My horses——" The rest was lost as the coach again forged ahead slightly.

"Beppo!" roared Anthony, "pull up."

The little Florentine, who was letting his horses rush toward the archway with the bits in their teeth, while he sat staring at death hypnotically, was suddenly awakened from his trance and stood up, jerking the heads of his team violently.

The coach passed the berlin in a flash.

It made straight for the archway. A sentry who was just running across the roadway with a chain suddenly thought better of it and darted back.

The whip licked out like a snake over the backs of the four coal-black horses. It burst like a series of pistol shots under the echoing vault of the arch through which the coach, now rocking frantically, disappeared with a sullen roar.

A tremendous running about of the military, in the same kind of flurry that follows the disappearance of a fox from a raided hen yard, marked its transit.

The tardy fury of the guard was now vented upon

the berlin which dashed up just in time to be halted by the chain. Vincent's well-meant and really profound thanks for the obstacle which had finally stoppped them was taken for sarcasm. Both he and Anthonny were arrested and rearrested as one sleepy officer after another was aroused to come down, rubbing his eyes and cursing at being awakened at dawn. The captain, who came down last, was chagrined at finding no one but the well-known banker Herr Nolte and his friend, both with passports in order, being detained apparently for nothing. He in turn cursed the guard and returned to bed. The runaway having been explained, drink money distributed, and the horses rested, the berlin was now permitted to proceed while a disappointed crowd dispersed.

The last familiar object which Anthony saw as they topped the first rise on the way to Pisa was the tree above the convent with the pigeons circling about it. "Contessina—where was she?" he wondered. He might stop—but it was only a passing thought. Vincent was in no mood for whims just now. Still pale, Vincent applied himself from time to time to a sumptuous array of silver flasks in a leather chest on the seat before him. His colour and eventually his high spirits began to return. Long before they reached Pisa his own remarkable calmness in the face of danger was thoroughly re-established in his own mind. As he looked at the place from a distance, not only the tower but the Baptistry seemed to be leaning.

They were approaching the walls and jumbled roofs of the town after sunset. It seemed fitting that they should drive through its grass-grown streets in the twilight. For Pisa appeared to Anthony to be a town glimmering upon the confines of sleep; the few cloaked citizens they passed, to be wandering somewhere in a detached dream.

Vincent had to be helped into the inn, *Grande Albergo Accademia*, a deserted, rambling place about whose doors a throng of whining beggars instantly gathered. They started up from holes and byways; they

111

came gliding out of the dusk, exhibiting their sores, withered arms, crippled babies and filthy rags in the rays of the dim lanterns of the berlin, till their numbers became alarming. Vincent's ill-timed, drunken generosity brought more. The innkeeper at last fell on them with Beppo's whip and cleared a passage to his own door, shouting a warning to Beppo to keep a sharp eye on the luggage.

Supper, such as it was, being over, and Vincent asleep on a table, Anthony took a short turn in the starlight of the old square where the tower leaned and the dimly striped front of the Duomo and Baptistry, from which the town seemed to have receded in order to leave them alone to their own peculiar beauty as things memorable and apart from the ordinary affairs of mankind, served only in some sort to compose his mind. He felt curiously disgruntled tonight.

The first day of the trip by which he had set such great store had been disappointing. He had listened to Vincent talking, trying to reinstate himself after the fright of the runaway. He had listened mile after mile. He hoped by tomorrow that Vincent would be able to live with himself without talking about it. He decided if necessary to give him a day to sleep it off. He had something to do at Pisa that he did not wish to be disturbed in.

Perhaps, though, it was Italy that was disappointing. He had never realized how poor and how barren Italy was. Could it be he would find all of Europe like that? Africa and the West Indies had given him new eyes.

These old lands where people had lived for untold ages seemed worked-out. Or was it the climate? The soil itself seemed tired. Plants and animals were scarce. Travellers always talked about "the luxuriance of Italy." Where was it? People existed here on a round of the comparatively few things they could grow, grapes, wheat, poultry, and some reluctantly slaughtered domestic animals. They were ingenious in making many combinations of a few things. But underneath was poverty, the poverty of nature. He remembered the genuine luxuriance, the abundance of the plantations at Gallegos. And there were no taxes there either. Here the cost of being oppressed and thwarted was frightful. The supper tonight!—sour wine and macaroni—the crowd of beggars at the inn door—ancient, festering misery. He had never in the worst slave gangs seen anything like that.

These beggars could, of course, feast their eyes every day on del Sarto's St. Agnes in the Duomo—where Angela had sat on the steps starving, and had found Debrülle.

"Why had John Bonnyfeather asked to be buried in Pisa?" he wondered.

A wave of homesickness for the hill at Gallegos, with the moon on his palm trees and *La Fortuna*'s lights twinkling in the river below, swept over him. Or—he would like to be going home to a good rum drink in Cibo's patio at Regla. And tobacco—Europe knew nothing about tobacco. What was snuff? A mere whiff. He lit one of his precious, black cigars and felt better. Havana—there was a town that knew what plenty meant! He sauntered back to the inn followed by a shadow that near the window, seeing he was a stranger, began to whine and hold out a hand. He turned about to curse it, man or woman. And then remembering Brother François, gave the hand a piastre he found in his pockets from old times.

Very tired, he slept soundly and cleanly on the rear seat of the berlin and was awakened by the loud crowing of the poultry in the stable yard. Vincent was not up yet. Except for a poisonous old woman who brewed him some coffee, there was no one about. He went into the square and looked about again. Surely this was another place, not the town of the night before.

On that magnificent early August morning Pisa was magical. Light with a red-purple tinge streamed from its stones. He thought he had never seen anything so fantastically beautiful as the Duomo and Baptistry alone there across the square. And the reason for the leaning tower was now self-evident. It gave the last, perfect, wizard touch. No, there was nothing like this anywhere. He took a deep breath of the cool morning air and plunged his head in the fountain where two young girls, one with her jar on her head, stood watching him with smouldering brown eyes. They went away laughing.

"Si può far' un píccolo gíro della città, signore," said a mild-voiced old man, peering up at him from under the wreck of an incredible felt hat. Anthony finished drying his face.

"No," he said, and then relented. There was something curiously prepossessing about the figure of the old man before him, who was dressed exclusively in patches and had only one stocking.

"The other went yesterday," explained the old gentleman, for such he was by his accent. "It was silk, and you know, signore, even the aged *must* eat occasionally. True, I have not yet been able to stain my other leg. But I scarcely hoped to find custom this morning. Heaven has sent you. Accept me as I am. For a soldo I will——"

"Done," cried Anthony. "Do you know the Campo Santo?"

The old man raised his head and smiled. "Si," he whispered. "It is where the rich are sometimes buried even yet."

They slowly walked across the square talking; old harlequin in patches proving by every careful intonation and nice usage—as genteel poverty having worn out its good clothes must do—that he was the product of better days. His face looked drawn and transparent and he tottered a little. They sat down on the cathedral steps for a moment.

"Perhaps you will breakfast with me?" said Anthony after an erudite little talk about the beauties of the Duomo died away faintly.

The old man could not deny his Adam's-apple a twinge of anticipation.

"A glass of wine now?"

"Thank you, signore, I shall accept your first invitation with pleasure, but only after we return from the Campo Santo. To tell the truth, I have not eaten—at least not this morning," he added hastily. "Let us go while it is still cool."

Anthony accepted this compromise with the old man's pride. He rose and walked less hastily.

"Perhaps," said he after a little, "a host might be permitted to offer his guest an arm."

It was gratefully accepted. And with age leaning thus on youth they entered the frescoed cloisters of the Campo Santo with its low green mounds, where long shadows and the bright glints of morning mingled together along the grass and under the peaceful arcades like memories of grief and joy resolved.

And Anthony knew at once why John Bonnyfeather had asked to be buried at Pisa. Here the past could never be disturbed. Here he was deeply lapped in it forever. He had retired into the still green walls.

"Don't bury me at Leghorn near to that fellow Smollett," he had once said, as usual veiling his gentle humour in a half-serious joke. "I do not like his vibrant, Protestant twang. It would disturb me. Give me consecrated and silent earth." Anthony remembered now.

He stopped the old man from telling him how the earth in the place had been brought from Mount Calvary.

"Yes, I know," he said. "'I am looking for a grave."

"If it is a new one I shall know where it is," said his companion. "There are not many who can afford to be buried here now," he added with a strange touch of pride.

"About a year ago," explained Anthony.

"Ah, the old merchant from Leghorn! Yes, he was the last. A very quiet funeral. It is over here, signore, close by the way out."

The grass had already covered the mound that they now stood looking down upon. In the crumbling remains of a low brick wall that crossed the place, probably the ancient foundations of some forgotten

115

tomb, was set a new white stone. The inscription was in Latin, not of the best:

Near Here Rests in Peace
A Caledonian of Noble Blood,
The Last of his Name,
A Faithful and Loyal Subject
of
James III
King of England, Ireland, Scotland
and France
——— : ———
He lost his titles but conserved his honour.
God prospered him and he remembered
In turn the poor and the fatherless.
Pray for him

In trying to carry out the last request on the stone, Anthony found himself at last addressing his verbal thoughts to John Bonnyfeather. He could not think of him as dead. He seemed merely to have withdrawn himself into this quiet place as if he had gone down the hall at home and shut the doors of his room behind him. In the back of Anthony's mind arose a half-conscious impulse to knock at the stone and enter. He would find Mr. Bonnyfeather seated at his desk writing with a plume pen, or with his slippers on reading a book. Something in Latin. It would be cool and quiet there. And he would ask a question.

What was the strange tie that bound him to John Bonnyfeather? Was it blood?—"noble blood?" "The last of his name"—said the stone. Perhaps his race still went on. That smiling girl's face in the miniature—who was she? Something deeper than he could understand, something essentially mysterious but real linked him with this dust asleep in the Campo Santo at Pisa. He was sure of it now. What was it that he had promised never to try to know? Faith knew. That sardonic old marquis knew—something. *He* had been John Bonnyfeather's son-in-law. Great God! Could that man be his

116

father . . . ? No, no, impossible! He knew his own body well enough to know he was not of that flesh. "To . . . the fatherless," said the speaking stone. Blessed comfort in that line of script.

It was curious, it was not grief he was feeling as he stood thus whirling a thousand things from the past through his mind, it was transcendental respect, an abysmal regret that he would never be able to make the old man know that his boy had grown up and come back again wise and feeling enough to understand and to be grateful. That was what he would have liked to try to whisper to him down through the short grass on his new grave; and to say: "Yes, I know *now* that honour is the best of all things and the hardest to keep, and that you were the most honourable of men. No dross could buy your sacred dreams and no vicissitudes purloin your self-respect,—and so I more than love you for it."

Then came grief. For he suddenly saw that such complete things can be said only to the dead when the caricature of the body has gone, leaving the portrait of the spirit clear and luminous; when we cannot even catch at their hands again to ask to be forgiven or to cry out that in all charity now—with the sorrow of life upon us and with the love of Christ, and of man, and of woman, and little children in our hearts—we too understand, forever, and too late.

A sigh from the old guide, whom he had utterly forgotten, roused Anthony. With a look of complete weariness and exhaustion the old gentleman had just sat down on one of the grass mounds to wipe a bead of sweat from his forehead.

"I am sure," said he after a little, fanning himself weakly with his faded hat while looking up and smiling, "that whoever is beneath this mound will not grudge me a moment's rest out of his easeful eternity. I *am* a little tired this morning." His mouth trembled faintly as he put on his hat again.

Anthony's heart troubled him that he had kept so pleasant an old man standing so long in the sun. There

117

was a touch of half-ghastly, old-world grace about him and his patches. It was, he thought, a little like talking to the ghost of John Bonnyfeather disguised as a respectable Lazarus. A little like him—out of the corner of one's eye—a sort of ragged-glimmering of lost, coffined gallantries.

"Come," said Anthony, "did you think I had forgotten my breakfast invitation?"

"By no means," replied the old gentleman, again frankly grateful for the support of a young arm. "But you must not suppose I was thinking *only* of that, signore. I was truly,"—and he looked up ingenuously —"I was truly thinking of you. I, you see, have my own dead here in the Campo Santo. And I so much desire to speak of them this morning," he hurried on, "that I thought, as I looked at you—I thought you would understand how the hunger of the heart is sometimes greater than that of the belly, and that you would let me tell you their names just so they might be on the lips of the living again, in the morning light. Will you?"

"Why, yes,—of course," said Anthony.

"Well, then," said the old man, "lean down . . ." He whispered two names.

"My little girls, you know." He straightened up proudly as if the syllables had renewed his strength. "Here they are—only a few steps—this way. And we can go out that gate there. Here they are!"

It was quite evident that the old man was looking beyond the carpet of tenderly cared-for flowers that covered two small mounds side by side—that—to judge by the light in his face—he saw angels sitting in the tomb. His parchment-like skin shone with a reflected glow.

They stood there quietly for a minute or two.

"Thank you," said the old gentleman, as they went on out the gate and across the square. "To me you are no longer a stranger here," he continued still holding on to Anthony's arm. "The dust of both our families mingles in Pisa, signore. For me that gives you the freedom of my city. If I still had my own house, you

118

should be my guest. It was that one over there." He pointed to what had once been a fine dwelling, now much dilapidated. "I come of an ancient family here, the Raspanti," he muttered. "And, I also am the last of my name."

For a moment before going into the inn they stood at the door and looked at the old house, where a collapsing balcony once beautifully carved staggered across a blind, shuttered front of flaking pink plaster. "None of us have ever been beggars, signore—may I ask your name?"

"Adverso," said Anthony. "But come, Signore Raspanti, it is only fortune that makes you my guest this morning. *My* good fortune," and he made the old man that stiff, old-fashioned bow that Father Xavier had taught him at the convent years before. He thought he had forgotten it.

The old man removed his hat with the true, antique flourish and put it under his left arm. He placed his right hand over his heart.

"You are very hospitable, a man of honest feeling, Signore Adverso," said he, and entered the inn with a sigh.

Vincent was already up and about with his high spirits renewed. Beppo was shaving him in a chair while he urged on the old woman who sat in the corner to hasten her plucking of several newly killed fowls. Vincent gave a shout as Anthony came in, and with the soap still on his face rose to meet Signore Raspanti with a gay formality. He shouted through the lather.

"Toni, we are going to begin our journey all over again today. That damned runaway shall not count as part of it. It was just bad luck."

"No, no," said Beppo. "They meant to drive us down. They flashed out on us from the alley on purpose like—*that*."

"Look out," roared Vincent, "you will cut my throat. Jesus!"

"But I am *right*, signore," insisted Beppo.

"Perhaps he is!" mused Anthony. "Here, landlord, a

119

glass of wine for Signore Raspanti, my guest,—and some biscuits. Until breakfast comes, you know," he said to the old man, who looked grateful.

"Nonsense," roared Vincent. "It was just the horses. Anyway we are going to start all over again from Pisa this morning on top of a worthy and a proper, soul-sustaining breakfast. Ah, we are good at breakfast, aren't we, Toni? Do you remember? Some Asti, land-lord. Look alive, man, get your spit going."

He sat up now looking fresh and pink after Beppo's scraping, rubbing his fat, full chin half comically and laughing from sheer inward good-nature just as he had when a boy. His spirits were catching to all.

A slight tinge of colour like rouge on a wax rose began to show even on the yellow parchment face of old Signore Raspanti. He sopped his biscuits in his wine and let them rest against his gums while he sucked without making a noise, noblesse oblige. He instinc-tively disliked disturbing noises. He hoped that the ticking of Signore Adverso's watch, for instance, which he had stolen from him in the cemetery, and which was now making an alarmingly vulgar noise in his own tat-tered waistcoat, would not disturb any ear but his own. One *must* think of others. He instinctively put his hand back over his heart in that gallant, old-fashioned way.

The landlord came in from the court dragging one of his half-naked brats by the hair, who whimpered as he was set to work at the spit.

"Four chickens! One apiece," bawled Vincent. "One for the guest and Beppo!" He waved toward Signore Raspanti, who rose and bowed, with his hand still on his heart in grateful but careful acknowledgment.

The landlord smiled. He began to lay the table for four. If the gentleman wished to eat with his servant, he had drunk enough wine that morning to have his ec-centricities catered to. Before Signore Raspanti, how-ever, he left only wooden spoons, and smiled again. Three law students from the university dropped in for coffee before lecture and sat looking on.

The old woman who had just split open the fourth

chicken broke into a lament. It was a laying-hen full of ripe eggs. Everybody laughed at her dismay and profane lamentations.

"Put them in the gravy, mother," said a fat priest from the Duomo who just then wandered in. He gave everybody his blessing, including the law students who laughed at him, too.

"The father watches the inn chimney, signore," said one of them to Vincent. "When he sees smoke he comes over to extend the blessing of the church to those who are able to make the spit turn." The priest grinned sheepishly but with great good-nature.

"Even the light haze of an omelette will bring me running now," he admitted. "Since the French burned my little farm I grow lean." He took in slack on the immense rope about his waist. "That will do, I think, Pieto," said he to the urchin at the spit. "Let me see." He rose and going over to the fire twisted a wing from one of the chickens without even stopping the wheel. "Yes, it is quite done. Just at the turn, signore," he cried, turning to Vincent. "I like mine not too dry. Do you?" Everybody laughed at his cool impudence.

It was impossible not to include everybody. Indeed, nearly everybody was just waiting to be included.

"Draw the tables together—here," said Anthony.

"Gentlemen, will you join us?" shouted Vincent to the three law students. They looked at one another as the younger generation will when bidden too heartily by their elders, even to a feast.

"Do," said Anthony, "join us in our little celebration. It will have the blessing of the church, I am sure." He winked at the young men. Hesitation vanished. There was a great scraping of chairs being dragged over the tiles.

"What are your favourite wines, my friends?" asked Anthony. A babble of local vintages drove the old woman to the cellars with her hands over her ears.

"Two bottles apiece," roared Vincent after her. The students now looked impressed.

"Father," said Anthony, grinning.

The priest gabbled something in Latin while the steam from the fowls curled up from the table under his nose. It was a laconic grace.

The meal began with a clash. In a corner by the spit the young urchin looked on gnawing dreamfully on a drumstick.

The discovery of the morning proved to be the students and the new wine to which they introduced the company. It was the first of the local harvest and only lately pressed.

"In a few days, sir, it will be acid and ordinary," said the oldest of the trio, a tall lad with flashing eyes, a restless air, and an immense mane of jet-black hair that he continually tossed back out of his eyes. "But just at this stage of working it is full of bubbles and creams as you drink it." His gay talk in a strong French accent ran off the surface of things very much as the bubbles effervesced from the wine. The priest stuck to Canary and smiled. He had a good reason. The new wine was light to the taste but proved heady. In a short time the table was seething with talk and beggars were gathering about the inn, attracted by the noise and rumour of plenty.

"Open the door and let in the sunlight," bawled Vincent.

"And the rabble, too?" inquired the innkeeper. "Father, can't *you* do something?" the man asked, seeing the crowd outside.

The priest went out and closed the door behind him. They heard his voice for some time but could not hear what he said. When he came back he left the door open and no one was there.

The innkeeper nodded his acknowledgment and admiration of the father's powers of speech.

There was a sudden lull of talk as the sunlight streamed over the table.

"Saints and angels! What time is it?" queried the youngest and palest student anxiously. "Remember,

122

you Jacopo, there is a lecture in the porch at nine."

"On the Code Justinian," mumbled the dark-headed boy into his mug. "Dry, oh dry!" He poured the remainder of the priest's wine into his own glass and drank to the company, giving the two "illustrious signori from Livorno" a neatly turned toast of thanks.

"Have you ever rolled in the dust of the civil law, signori? You would know then how I hate to leave this —and you," said he, putting down his glass. "But it must be almost nine, isn't it?"

Anthony fumbled for his watch.

The bell of the campanile began to tell the hour. Shouting to one another and calling their hasty farewells, the three students dashed out and raced down the street. They took the life of the party with them.

Silence fell on the little common-room of the inn. Anthony sat looking across the table at Signore Raspanti, who was apparently watching a spider on the opposite wall.

"You look ill, Toni," said Vincent. "Has the new wine been . . . ?"

Anthony waved him off and continued to stare at the old man.

"What time is it, Signore Raspanti?" he asked.

"The bell has just struck nine, I believe," answered the old gentleman with a little quaver. "Shall I go out and see?" he added, rising hopefully.

They were all looking at him now. The seconds ticked out by the stolen watch against the ribs of the old man measured his heart beats. His mouth fell open and he shook.

"Have you by any chance lost your watch, my friend?" said the priest to Anthony.

Anthony nodded. A rush of blood clouded his face.

"Give it to him, Raspanti," said the priest harshly.

The old man brought the watch with its dangling seals out of his breast and slowly pushed it across the table toward Anthony. Then he collapsed, weeping hopelessly with his head in the gravy plate.

123

"Pig!" shouted Beppo, jumping up and starting to shake him.

Vincent pulled him off. "Leave him to the police," he growled. "Go and get the horses harnessed and wait. We leave shortly."

"A word with you, signori," said the priest. He took them both over to a corner.

"Do not call the police, I beg you. Let me tell you something about this old man. He is a pitiable case. He married unhappily. His wife left him with two baby daughters. They both died on the same day, and as he had no means left but his house, he sold that to bury them both together in the Campo Santo. Otherwise it would have meant the common pit. He did not turn beggar as he might, but for years has acted as cicerone in Pisa. When travellers came here in the days before the war he made just enough to exist—and to get one of his daughters out of purgatory. Now only a few travellers come. He starves. Maria is in heaven and Euphemia in the fires. He says they both suffer at being parted, and it is his fault. Can you imagine that? It is only lately he has begun to take things. When a traveller comes now he gets what he can. The tick of your watch, you see, would have been heard in eternity."

"Hum!" said Vincent.

"Forgive him, signori, for the love of Christ." The fat priest's face worked painfully. "I am not his confessor, you know, or—" he put his hand over his mouth. "He goes to one of the canons at the cathedral. I saw the seals dangling from your waistcoat this morning, signore, when you went across the square with old Raspanti, and I thought—yes, when you came out of the Campo Santo with *no* seals dangling from your waistcoat, I thought—'Euphemia will soon be in paradise, provided I do not inform the canon. And if I inform the kindly looking young signore, Euphemia will not go to paradise and old Raspanti will go to jail.' I really came over here to see you both. The old man was hungry, too, no doubt of it. Well, you know what has happened. But I do not think the police are going to

124

help. Anyway, you have your watch back, and—Well, he will be hanged, you know."

They all looked again at the old man lying with his head in the plate of gravy. He did not move.

"How long have his children been dead?" asked Vincent.

"Over ten years," replied the priest reluctantly.

"Gott im Himmel! and all that time this canon what's-his-name has been sharing the poor old devil's tips. What do you make of that, Toni?" shouted Vincent. "The lousy swine."

The priest put his fat hands over his ears now. Anthony pulled them down again.

"How much?" said he, "to get Euphemia out of the canon's hands?"

"About twenty soldi will see her through—now, I think."

"You think? Perhaps I had best go to your metropolitan here."

"No, no, I am sure of it."

"You will tell him so before I leave?"

A reluctant nod gave assent.

Anthony went over to Raspanti and raised him up on his chair. He wiped the tears and giblets off his twitching old face. Then he took his watch and put it back into the old scarecrow's waistcoat. Then he threw his cloak around his shoulders.

"You make a mock of me, signore?" gasped the old man. "I did not *lie* to you in the cemetery. They *are* my children there."

"I love you," said Anthony and kissed his dirty, smeared face.

"Great God!" said Vincent in complete disgust.

"Now, father, you *tell him!*" insisted Anthony.

"Landlord, landlord," shouted Vincent, "the bill!"

"Come on, Vincent. He'll find us soon enough," cried Anthony, and rushed out still sick at heart.

"You're drunk," laughed Vincent as he stumbled down the corridor after him.

They climbed into the berlin just as the anxious landlord dashed out after them waving both his apron and the bill frantically. He was paid.

Anthony detained him, talking to him for some minutes in rapid Tuscan. Money changed hands. "Si, si, si, si, si. A place at my own table from now on. A bed. The Scotchman from Leghorn will see to it, you say. Have no fear . . . Yes, certainly it was the priest. The canon! that *is* a good one. The French hanged him a year ago. The wrong man, you say. No, they were right there, too. But here comes the one they missed."

The priest rushed out of the door, his face a fiery red. "Gone?" he shouted to the landlord. "You let them go when . . ." Then seeing the berlin he stopped short and tried to grin.

Some beggars began to close in about the coach whining.

"Here are your twenty-*five* soldi," said Anthony, pouring them into the priest's hands.

"Five extra for possible accidents in limbo," he growled.

"Signore, signore, stop, let me thank you," screamed old Raspanti, coming down the corridor. "My children are in paradise. I thought . . ."

"Get on, Beppo, drive off," Anthony shouted.

"Alms, alms, for the love of Christ, alms . . ."

The berlin dashed out of the beggars circling about the fat father, who held up his hands in terror.

"Would you rob the church, you swine? You black . . ."

They heard no more. Looking back, Vincent saw the old man with a smeared face, with Anthony's cloak flopping behind him, trying to run after the berlin while he waved his tattered hat wildly.

He looked at Anthony who said nothing.

"Did you give him Mr. Bonnyfeather's seals, too?" asked Vincent.

"No, I kept those," replied Anthony, taking them out of his pocket and looking at the old crest on the middle one.

126

"You weren't as drunk as I thought then," grumbled Vincent. "But that is the last time, my boy, that I buy *you* any new wine, anywhere."

Chapter Six

Over the Crest

IN THE marble porch of the Via Emilia Professor Monofuelli was droning away in Latin to about a dozen sleepy students upon the inexhaustible subject of the Civil Law.

During the recent French and Austrian struggles over Italy the University of Pisa had almost closed its doors. The restless times had drawn away many of its students, contracted its revenues, and even scattered the faculty. Professor Monofuelli had come over from Padua to lend a helping hand.

He felt, however, that he was not being fully appreciated. Five students had slept through his entire—and celebrated—lecture on the Pandects only the afternoon before. And it was not much better this morning.

To be sure it was both sultry and shady under the old, marble porch, open on one side to the empty and grass-grown street. The benches in the hall near by had gone to make Austrian soldiers warm only the winter before. But certainly it was hot enough now. The professor wiped his forehead with his handkerchief and brushed the snuff that fell out of it off his faded peach-coloured, velvet coat.

Perhaps he was just the least bit sleepy himself. He had given only an hour to the distinction between *fas* and *jus*, but without his usual enthusiasm. And three students had been late. They had missed *fas* entirely. Well, it was a distinction that those who merely expected to practise law could ignore. But historically—historically *fas* was important. It was all very well for Dontelli at Bologna to ignore *fas*, but there could be no doubt about it that *jus* had developed out of *fas*. He would give it to his students. He would repeat it for that fellow Aristide Pujol, one of the late ones. He had come in late with two others, at a quarter after nine at least. They had been drinking somewhere (he knew)—new wine! That was all very well, but then—then there was *fas*. He rapped on the desk and reversed the hour-glass. The red sand in it began to run the other way.

"Signore Pujol—*signore!*"

That young gentleman sat up.

"Aha! signore, attention! I am about to repeat something for you. It is not my custom to repeat myself."

"Only your lectures," thought Pujol.

"You are from beyond the Alps, my young friend, aren't you?"

"A Frenchman, Excellence," grumbled Pujol proudly.

"*Ahem*, all the more reason then that you should not waste your time in Italy in sleep. How many times does the distinction of *fas* appear on the twelve tables, my friend from Gaul?"

"Once, I think," grumbled Pujol.

"You think? Well, you are correct. Repeat the passage—the law itself."

The young fellow did so.

"Not so bad for a barbarian, I must admit, Pujol. But the accent, your Latin accent is terrific. It is worse than that of the barbarians from the schools in Britain. Now listen, that denunciation goes like this." The professor filled his lungs.

129

"Patronus, si clienti fraudem faysit, sacer esto."

But the professor was startled by the flat effect of his own voice. He was used to lecturing in a room with a dome in it at Padua. There he could tell the difference between the Latin of Ulpian and the Latin of Gaius by the sound in the dome. His own genuine accent came back to him. But here—here there was nothing; no return; no sonorous, encouraging effect. Only sleepy students gaping up at him. And that young Frenchman laughing at him, laughing! In his indignant disappointment he absent-mindedly reversed the hour-glass again. In a few seconds the sands ran out. A gust of applause swept the porch, the first he had received since arriving at Pisa. He cleared his throat for a philippic *contra* Aristide. It should be remembered and remembered, but——

At that moment the sound of rapidly approaching wheels turned every head away from him.

A smart, an extraordinarily handsome, little carriage was coming down the street. Just then the back hood was let down by an arm reaching around out of the window. It revealed two quite young but evidently very prosperous gentlemen sitting side by side on the rear seat. One was tall and spare with a peculiarly ardent expression, golden-brown hair, and a pair of eyes that looked searchingly out of a sun-browned face. It was a face so regular and yet so alive and mobile that you remembered it. The other young man was astonishingly blond, white and pink. And you felt that some day he would be fat and contented. Just now he was laughing, with his arm thrown back over the open hood, displaying inadvertently a handsome ring and a positively gorgeous expanse of waistcoat. Both young men were wearing high, English hats of remarkable mould under the wide brims of which their hair curled and flopped. The bronze, and blue leather upholstery of the carriage glittered; the horses approached at a spanking trot; the driver flourished his whip in a decidedly intoxicated manner.

There was something so gay about the whole equip-

130

age, such a debonair assurance seemed to accompany it, that Professor Monofuelli instinctively consigned it to hell in one erudite malediction while he rapped for order and a return to *fas*.

The sound of his well-worn gavel was the signal for the Frenchman Aristide Pujol to rise, throw his books down the steps, and rush out of the porch just as the little berlin was passing.

He ran along beside it for a few yards—"just like a beggar," exclaimed the professor later on in disgust—and then leaping on the step began to talk to Anthony, who leaned forward to catch what he was saying.

"You are going to Paris, aren't you, signore? I heard you say so this morning." His eyes shone with excitement.

"Yes, can we take a letter for you?"

"No, signore, but——"

"'But what?"

"Will you take *me*?"

"Why!—well, there is hardly room."

"I could go on the box, sir. I can drive. I will do anything you ask on the way. Serve you and the signore. Take me. I am rotting here at Pisa. I must go—*go!*"

"Go?" said Anthony.

The young fellow nodded, tears in his eyes.

"We can't delay for you, you know."

"No, no, just as I am, now."

"Well, Vincent?"

"Why not?" said Vincent.

"Climb up," said Anthony. "Stop a moment, Beppo."

By this time all the students in the porch had rushed out onto the steps and were craning their necks after the carriage. They broke out into a clamorous shout when Aristide climbed onto the box. But he did not look back. He went on. His former classmates returned to the lecture and threw themselves down on the hard stone benches rather desperately.

"Great things are doing in France, Excellence," said one of them as the little man began to rearrange his much-fluttered notes.

131

"So I have heard," said the professor opening his book again. He sighed audibly. "But, that our conversation may return to the point from which our Gaulish friend has just digressed—let us ourselves return to the law. As Cicero has so aptly said for us: 'Though all the world exclaim against me, I will say what I think: that simple little book of the Twelve Tables, if anyone look to the fountain and sources of laws, seems to me, assuredly, to surpass the libraries of all the philosophers . . .'"

The berlin trotted out of Pisa into the green, rolling country beyond and took the road for Florence at a more rapid pace. Beppo began to sing as the hills about his native place began to become familiar.

At Florence they stayed only long enough to rest the horses, to arrange for some travelling papers for Aristide, and get him a few clothes. He had left in his vest and shirt-sleeves.

Both Anthony and Vincent were glad they had given way to impulse and taken Aristide along. A merrier, a keener, and more willing helper they could scarcely have found. And he was painfully grateful. His constant, half-impudent but always good-natured comments from the box amused and sometimes convulsed them. He had also, Anthony soon discovered, the faculty of causing things to get done. "My mother was from Gascony," he said, "and my father from Auvergne. I therefore understand how gullible, how selfish, and how kindly in little things most men and women are. You make them laugh, and then—omelette." He could drive well, and he understood not only the civil law but horseflesh. "At Milan, signore, if possible, we should get other and more horses. These were not good enough even for Austrians to retreat on."

Soon they were heading north again and leaving Tuscany behind. The first certain notice of it was the change in the type of roadside shrine and the shorter horns of the cattle.

That Tuscan type of shrine, where every article used at the Crucifixion, from hammer and nails to spear and sponge, is displayed with terrible, literal exactitude, while the figure of Christ himself is omitted or made conventional as a mosaic in St. Sophia, began to give way to more naturalistic representations of the Passion. At these, no matter what their mode, Anthony tried not to look. For his own reasons the sight of any cross was a peculiarly painful reminder. Indeed, it is doubtful if any traveller for centuries had passed casual, wayside crosses with such a living knowledge of the reality of the scene they attempted to represent. Yet he could not ignore them. And they constantly gave rise to certain trains of thought which for his own mental health he desired for a while to let lie dormant.

He had come to the conclusion that he must for a year or two at least try to obscure in normal human companionship, at not too highly emotional a level, the incandescent light of the visions of his African experience, which still dazzled him, especially at night.

He had not opened the bundle from Gallegos with the madonna in it. That was to wait for a while, although it was along with him even now, travelling in the dark boot of the berlin, just as the knowledge and the harvest of all the memories in the bundle travelled in the closed box of his mind, waiting. When he looked at that little figure again he must be able to do so with a whole and healed soul; with tender but level eyes.

Yet reminders of Brother François were constantly leaping out upon him in Italy. They staggered him at times; almost forced him into hysterical, dramatic—and hence he was sure—eventually foolish action. He had kissed the genteel old thief at Pisa and given him his cloak in return for stealing his watch. And Vincent had said he was drunk on new wine. Well, he *had* been drunk, but not on new wine. "Wine of the vintage of A.D. thirty-three," he thought as he looked up to catch the shadow of a cross arm falling across the carriage.

133

Yes, that was the trouble. He must not be "drunk," not even upon old wine. Wine should be sustaining: "Give us this day our daily bread."

He was glad that Vincent understood. How much he needed a practical, happy, able friend like Vincent, who loved him and yet loved the world, too.

He had told him all. Vincent had wept, and yet he could laugh at you when you were "drunk"—and get you along over the particular roads of the world which you had to travel, towards Paris—or London, or whatever was the immediate rational goal. Yes, thank God for Vincent!—and let the horses trot now,—where was it they were going?—oh, yes, towards Milan, with that good-natured, keen, human, young Pujol on the box next to the ridiculous Beppo.

He gave himself up to being a traveller and nothing else.

He enjoyed the halts; the women about the town fountains; the inns, half stables, half human dwellings with something of the antique world left over that he had glimpsed and shared once with Angela. Certainly in the inns of Italy the fragments of it were scattered over her hills and along her still half-Roman by-ways. *Antiquia*—that was a good world, refreshing, real, and primitive. He enjoyed waking up mornings to its sounds; the loud peasant dialects, children playing, and the comfortable noises of cattle, lambs, doves, and chickens. In Africa he had missed the sparrows, he found.

But he was not to see much of Lombardy. As they emerged onto the level and often swampy plains a cool wind had come down from the snowy mountains to contend with the summer heat. The whole country was veiled in mist. Long rows of poplars loomed through it. It lifted only occasionally for bright, plangent gleams of level, green meadows and white towns. They heard the muffled bells of unseen chapels ringing through it. Or carts loomed up suddenly and were swallowed like wraiths, as they trotted on into denser fog and cooler weather.

And it was now that they first began to hear the voice of bugles and to meet frequently with French troops. An occasional column of them forced them to draw up and pull aside. Their trumpets shouted afar off, echoing.

"It is the voice of France," cried Pujol. "Soon, soon I shall be chez moi." He began to shout and sing.

They could see nothing of Milan as they approached it. It was late one evening and the moon over the city was only a bright, fleecy blur in a world of silver fog that veiled the houses and the cathedral spires from sight. Milan was nothing but glimpses of the legs of passers-by from the knees down in the light of blurred lanterns; moonlight along the bases of walls, and link boys making a red smudge drifting through the mist. But the inn near the Scala was a good one. No fog could veil that. They stayed for several days.

They sold the old team and bought four new horses. None too many to pull even the light berlin over the Simplon, which pass they had decided to take instead of the Great St. Bernard, followed by Napoleon only the year before, but since then cut to pieces by supply trains and artillery.

From being little better than a dangerous wagon track only sometimes passable, the Simplon, over which Bonaparte had chosen to maintain his communications with Italy in the future, had already been made practicable for troops and carriages in all but the worst winter weather. The French idea was to make the Simplon available for artillery and wagon trains at all times, and to that end they had already pierced tunnels and galleries on the Lombard side and were at work in great force on the Swiss slope grading and constructing avalanche shelters.

"If you can get the permission of the French commandant here to take the route, signore, I would do so," said the innkeeper. "By far the better you will find." Vincent had little difficulty in having their papers stamped "par la nouvelle route militaire."

Aristide had also proved himself such an able diplomat in negotiating the deal in horses that Vincent told him he had already earned his way to Paris and supplied him with suitable clothes. In fact, the whole party was now provided with rugs, gloves, and heavy coats that seemed incredible to Anthony after years in the tropics and in the present Turkish bath atmosphere of August in Milan.

It finally cleared up a little on the last day of their stay and they drove out on the Corso to try out the new horses with Aristide handling the reins. Beppo, with his troubles doubled, was now only too willing to ride behind, his new, braided coat-tails flapping in the wind quite à la mode.

On the Corso, despite a decided wispiness that still draped itself along that magnificent drive, the Milanese fashionables and nobility were already out, driving in the handsome turnouts for which the city had been famous for two centuries at least. The berlin was accompanied through the gate by a tumult of other carriages.

Indeed, driving on the Corso, rain or shine, peace or war, was the chief test of social position in Milan. One either drove and lived or did not drive and vaguely existed. Noble families impoverished by the troubled times, often reduced to an abject poverty indoors, nevertheless frequently managed to maintain, at the expense of appetite and clothes, a vehicle of some kind with two beasts to draw it. One would not do. One old marchesa who was known to be nearly starved, anaemic from nothing but cabbage soup and crusts, was much admired and pointed out when she drove daily in the still tolerable family coach with crest and running footmen. When one of her horses died the local assembly of nobles had provided her another by subscription. All this was current gossip even at the inn.

There was certainly something very Spanish about the Milanese, Anthony thought as they drove along the Corso with the sun glittering on the spokes of varnished wheels and the jewels of heavily veiled women. Spain was to be seen not only in this inevitable custom of the evening drive after the siesta but in Milanese manners and talk. The stately salutations, the simultaneous removal of hats by gentlemen, and the fluttering of black lace and painted ivory fans as the carriages passed and repassed reminded him of the Alameda de Paula at Havana. And the town was full of Spanish architecture.

He long remembered this drive with peculiar pleasure; the sun falling in trembling pencils and half-mystical gleams through the melting mist about the ghostly scarved poplars, with the dark prickly mass of the great cathedral dominating the town behind; the river of carriages streaming along to the sound of subdued feminine laughter and the sharp snap of fans; to the gleam of jewels in the sunset. What a splendid river it was, the most civilized he had ever seen.

And not a little of the pleasure came from being an acceptable, even a notable part of it. For the little berlin with its blue leather traced with bronze leaves, its four fine horses now in spick and span military harness with scarlet blinkers, caused many a head to crane on its neck.

Whether the young men who sat looking out over the lowered hood, smoking black Cuban cheroots,— which, they had accidentally discovered, created almost a furor wherever they went,—were found as acceptable as the berlin, they had not time enough in Milan to discover. But a number of eyes that examined them over the tops of fans seemed more friendly than critical. And the fans reminded Anthony of Dolores. In fact, for some reason or other, Milan, as he explained it to Vincent, made him homesick for Dolores.

"There is no use going through the world thinking of cities in the terms of women one has loved and lost," said Vincent, a little jealous as he was forced to listen for the second time to a tale of Dolores and dolour. "If you do, when you once get to Paris, you will never be able to admire another town."

"How do you know, Vincent?" said Anthony, who really had some doubts of Vincent as a cavalier.

"My boy," said Vincent, "when we do get to Paris I am going to take you around to a little house on the

Rue de Vielle du Temple. It was formerly the hôtel of an ancient and respectable, a noble family. But it now belongs to a certain young banker from Livorno. I want you to look it over and consider its—well, modern advantages. In fact, I have hopes you will like the place so much that you might decide to acquire another near by. Several kinds of business, mundane and even semi-domestic, can be transacted most satisfactorily in one of these refurnished, family hôtels. Since the Terror they are all the rage. You might send for Neleta—or Dolores—or——"

"Dolores is not the kind one sends for," interrupted Anthony considerably irritated, "and as for Neleta, I am done with all that kind of thing I told you."

"Tut, tut, mon vieux, you speak as if you were feeble and travelling from one source of hot restorative waters to another, and in vain. You will presently recollect yourself. Why, if you don't look out, you will be talking of marriage like an impotent young man or a debauched ancient. Remember you are not a *poor* bachelor."

"I *have* been thinking of marriage."

"But not of getting married, I hope," groaned Vincent. "That is quite another thing."

The argument, for it developed rapidly into that, continued until they had made the turn on the Corso several times and were returning for supper.

It was now late twilight, and the mist was beginning to settle again. Aristide lit the lamps. A number of belated carriages, as though seen through a curtain of thin, silver gauze behind which a procession of lights was taking place, likewise hurried rapidly home toward the city gates. The effect of a carnival in Brociliande was soon heightened by multitudes of fireflies and the rising of a harvest moon.

Aristide drove rapidly. They began to overtake one carriage after another and to pass them swiftly. Vincent and Anthony both leaned over the sides of the open hood, letting the cool evening rush into their faces while feasting their eyes on what was a truly marvellous scene. A glow of torches moved on the distant

138

battlements where the night guard was being posted, and wisps of mist caressed their cheeks from time to time with smooth, cool fingers. As they drove into and out of these fog pockets, suddenly the whole scene as if by art-magic would be cut off and then renewed before their eyes. They exclaimed to each other with astonishment and delight. It was like watching a feast of lights in elfland through a magician's milky crystal where the vision was now clear and now clouded by less tangible dreams.

Then, suddenly, as they flashed out of a streak of fog, a familiar shape loomed up before them. To Anthony it seemed in a curious way to be the centre of all those other dreams, driving through the mist. And although he had come across it suddenly and recognized it instantly, he felt that he had been looking at it for a long time before; that it had been waiting for him behind the curtain of mist; that it was inevitable that on this particular drive he should overtake the coach of Don Luis.

This time he would pass him or know the reason why.

He touched Vincent on the arm and felt immediately that he had electrified him with his own unreasonable excitement.

"Get on, Pujol, get on, *pass that coach*, and don't let it overtake you. Hold tight, Beppo," he cried.

The whip cracked. The startled horses leaped ahead, going at headlong speed while Aristide stood up.

Don Luis, also going at a fast clip, heard a carriage coming up behind him at such a pace that he turned to look back. He was in no mood to race on the Corso, but he hated to be passed. Like *that!*

For just as he leaned out the berlin flashed by. The coach lamp glared into the berlin; the lights of the berlin shone for a moment into the faintly rosy interior of the coach. Sitting upon the faded upholstery in the moonlight with her arm in Don Luis', Anthony saw Faith Paleologus dressed in the extremity of fashion with a necklace of emeralds smouldering about her neck. She gave a faint scream as she looked into the berlin and

139

Don Luis burst out with an oath. Both of them were as startled as Anthony. Then the berlin passed the coach.

They heard the coach picking up speed behind them, the whip snapping, and the lumbering of wheels. The two vehicles streamed down the Corso with the fireflies swirling behind them, regardless of protesting cries from other drivers.

But this time it was the berlin that flashed through the city gate and left Don Luis to the indignant welcome of the guard.

To have a lot of smoky lanterns poked into the coach and flashed over himself and his mistress until the whole carriage stank of tallow, of garlic and sour wine from the candid mouths of French conscripts caused him positively to flow with profanity. He considered the incident to be a deadly insult. He began to recollect who he was and "what" had caused it. He sent Sancho out to find where Anthony and Vincent were staying. From midnight on, a smug little man with grey whiskers watched the inn.

———————————

The berlin set out for the mountains about daybreak. It was followed a few hours later by the coach with four horses and two lead mules that ate out of the Kitten's hand like tame rabbits. As usual Don Luis had a plan, and, as usual, the plan was not entirely impractical.

Don Luis leaned back well pleased with it. Before they were over the mountains he hoped in several directions to have solved for all time his long standing and harassing domestic problems. It was still foggy and he occasionally poked his head from the window to make Sancho stop and listen for a carriage ahead. Behind him the wheel tracks of the coach and berlin stretched out in lengthening parallel lines.

Meanwhile the berlin, about ten miles ahead, had ascended out of the fog and was rocking along at a

140

steady trot with the jagged, snow-glittering pinnacles of the confused, cloud-haunted Alps ahead and the golden statue on the tip of the cathedral spire behind losing itself rapidly in the blue sky with an occasional parting flash. The plains of Lombardy far below were nothing but a smooth lake of mist, with poplars on hilltops sticking up as if fishermen had staked out their nets here and there in the placid sea. Just before nightfall the hearts of all the travellers in the berlin were at once rested and uplifted by the fantastically beautiful islands of Lake Maggiore springing from water turquoise in the sunset and in the midst of archangelic scenery.

"Nothing in the world is so unbelievable as Isola Bella by moonlight," said Vincent as they left it behind after supper to push on to Duomo d'Ossola at the foot of the pass. They arrived there with tired horses towards midnight. Aristide insisted that there must be ample rest for the animals before they began the ascent. "They will be able to start tomorrow evening," he said. "That will give us full daylight towards the summit. And the ascent par le clair de lune, messieurs," he said—for he had soon discovered with joy that he might just as well speak French as Italian to his friends and employers— "c'est merveilleux. I have seen it that way before, superbe, ravissant, incomparable, virginal." Having paid the Alps the greatest compliment possible in French, he went off to examine the shoes of his horses, whistling in the half-frosty air.

Already the breath of the mountains had brought back to Anthony a feeling of light, boyish vigour that he had forgotten since some cold winters in Livorno years before. He began to enter fully now into Vincent's high spirits and Pujol's gayety, even to surpass them. He was in fact entering upon the long, sustaining vigour of ripened manhood verging toward its crest.

He stood out in the roadway that night at Duomo d'Ossola under the stars and the now preternaturally clear moon just beginning to wane but with its black markings clear as an etched plate, and listened to the rush and whisper of the snow-fed Ticino that filled the

141

air with a continuous, low melody that came from no direction at all. The others had already gone indoors to find what cheer they might at that late hour. And as he stood there listening to the lonely voice of the mountains implicit in the snow water that forever fled away somewhere into the night, the mood of a great and yet a calm and serene exaltation fell upon him, lifting him out of himself and comforting him.

And it too had its own music that also came from nowhere.

Without effort, as if he were only a listener, began a magnificent concord of the abstractions of innumerable sounds. The voices of the great heights and ramping crevasses, of the snowy pinnacles glittering in moonlight uttered themselves through him, plucking from his heart-strings an inconceivably majestic and complicated harmony addressed to the stars and the black mountain sky beyond. The hymn died away at last with a soft, satisfactory, almost human melancholy, somehow exquisitely pleasurable as if the heights murmured regretfully now of their memories of past ages to the plains below.

It was a purely personal, an automatic, an incommunicable experience. It did not occur to him that some men attempted to set such things down. He knew nothing of staff and clef. "Music," he said, "go on." But the thing was not to be summoned. It occurred. All that he knew was that in that moment the meaning of the night enriched with all his past experiences of solitude, passion, grief, love, and joy had suddenly been transmuted for him and made understandable in the terms of sound.

There was no motif or prelude in this experience as there had been in that concord of wood sounds that he had heard as he looked at Anna that night, now ages past in Livorno, it seemed. His music tonight had been full, complete; devoid of weak longings and little regrets. It was the cry of his being at the full.

"Well, so let it be then for a while." He turned and followed the others into the inn.

"Tomorrow," he thought, just as he swung the door open, "we shall be going over the crest and on, down into France."

The osteria, or "hôtel" as it was now called, at Duomo d'Ossola was immemorial. Apparently the only change that had afflicted it since the elder Pliny had come that way gathering magical, Alpine plants was in the numbers and generations of its fleas. The hams and flitches of bacon hanging amid its rafters were contemporaneous with its ancient oaken beams, and as tough. But there was no doubt about their being well smoked. For the fireplace consisted of a great pile of stones large enough to roast a whole ox, over which a cave-like cupola of baked, red clay led upwards, presumably in the direction of several flues.

It was true that some smoke, on the principle that accidents will occasionally happen, escaped by this Gargantuan yet ridiculous chimney. But for the most part it lingered infernally and habitually about the shoulders and knuckles of hams, the leeks, the garlic, and the sooty bottles and crocks in basketry containers that perpetually threatened the guests who moved beneath them with a fatal rain of preserved plenty should the roof ever collapse—a contingency not so remote as the landlady was disposed to think.

At night the sole light in this hell's-kitchen was from a small flame lost in the huge fireplace. About this, as Anthony entered, Vincent, Pujol, and Beppo were seated on three-legged stools. They were impatiently waiting while several sleepy and well-smoked girls and an old woman with complexions like the hams were attempting, with all of the usual clamour, lament, and confusion of primitive females trying to perform a simple domestic action—to scramble some eggs. All that was lacking was the eggs. Beppo had kindled the fire.

A long consultation in mountain dialect, an argument, an outburst of fury on the part of the oldest woman, a loud slap in the face for the youngest granddaughter—finally began to produce results. The older women climbed into a loft leaving the girl who had

143

been slapped to do the honours. A hen under, or rather over, the delusion of raising a family was loudly disturbed in one corner by the slapped maiden and relieved of six of her prospective cares. These mixed with some herbs in a pan were put over the fire. But the hen proved to have been right after all.

It was Aristide who confirmed her. He had volunteered to take what he called les haruspices. He sputtered, holding his nose, and dumped the sacrifice out into the fire.

Frau Frank's hamper was now drawn upon and still proved itself triumphantly adequate. The girl, who had attempted the omelette, and who still sat wretchedly upon her stool, was invited to share in the cold sausage, bread and wine. She was soon not only comforted but by far the most amiable of the party. Rugs were spread upon some benches, Beppo flung himself upon the floor, and the party entered upon a gallant attempt to rest.

From his bench in a far corner Anthony watched the grotesque shadows leaping amid the rafters. The place was like a witches' brothel. In the centre on the stone "altar" by which the girl still sat with her unbraided elf-locks snaking about her face, the fire leaped fitfully, now flickering out into the darkness of the room with a smoky-yellow tongue and now licking the inflamed, sooty sides of its terra-cotta cavern when the draught veered up the chimney. From the benches where Vincent and Pujol were stretched out, and from the lean curs on the floor, arose occasional lightning movements denoting fleas stabbing home. Presently the daughter of the house got up and looked about her.

After considering the several benches deliberately, she walked quietly over to that upon which young Pujol was resting and began to climb in under his blankets.

A foot placed firmly on her stomach, and propelled forward by a vigorous straightening of the young man's knee, hurled her back toward the hearth, where she gracefully collapsed upon a stool and passed a few interesting moments trying to inhale. She then resumed her expression of rapt contemplation, finally arriving at the conclusion that apparently she had been repulsed.

Everyone in the room except the snoring Beppo was now watching her, secretly convulsed. After a while she got up again, rubbed her stomach, and obviously began to consider once more the now-rather nice question of —"with what man shall this young woman sleep?"

"Love is a wonderful thing, Toni," whispered Vincent. "Did you keep your boots on? You may need them."

"Monsieur is jealous," hissed Pujol.

"*You* interfered with nature, Aristide," muttered Anthony.

These mutterings and groans not sounding inviting, the girl decided that the united opinion of the bench was against her. She made no appeal. She walked over and quietly inserted herself under the horse-blanket on the floor with Beppo. A few sleepy grunts of surprise, ending in a dying fall, and sighs of settling satisfaction showed that a delicate situation had been gratefully accepted by Beppo.

Nevertheless, the benches proved to be by no means lonely couches. Each traveller soon shared them with cohorts of fleas. In a short while a spirit seemed to move all three at the same time toward the inn yard. Here they met amid oaths and laughter to engage in a mutual hunt by lantern light. Beppo was either immune or was solaced beyond mere flea bites.

The berlin they found soaked with dew. They dragged some straw from the stables and spreading their rugs upon it again attempted to rest. Looking up at the familiar northern stars, fresher and clearer against the black mountain sky than he had ever seen them before, in spite of the moon, Anthony finally counted himself to sleep by trying to number the infinite.

Perhaps it was unfortunate that he did so, for some time between midnight and morning Don Luis quietly passed through the village in the coach.

A few hours' rest farther down at Arona had apparently sufficed for Don Luis' horses. He had guessed that the berlin would stop over at Duomo d'Ossola, most travellers did so, and he made sure of it by sending Sancho to have a quiet look at the inn yard. There Sancho had not only seen the berlin empty, but its crew all laid out on straw in the moonlight like so many corpses. He reported as much to his master, who nodded contentedly and drove on. By daybreak the coach was miles ahead and making good time up the Val di Ticino toward the pass.

As he looked down onto the plains a little later, Don Luis was delighted to see a violent thunder-shower moving down the valley far below him and sweeping out toward Ossola with blowing arcs of rain. He could have asked nothing more than that the tracks of the coach should be erased. It had not occurred to him that they might be. He had had to chance that, and now— This time, at least, the gods seemed to be with him.

He remarked to the Paleologus, who was sitting beside him, that it was raining in the valley. It was the only general remark he had made to her since leaving Milan. She acquiesced to the weather—and his opinions about it. Otherwise their conversation was nil. Faith understood her position exactly. Her rôle was not that of a talkative companion.

At Milan, in a renaissance of almost youthful bravado during this unexpected Indian-summer honeymoon it had been the noble marquis' whim to flaunt Faith before the world on the Corso as his mistress. For that he had bought her some astonishing costumes and jewels. She had carried them well. She had carried it off with just the requisite amount of subdued impudence toward respectability and enough triumphant vulgarity to proclaim that she was his mistress and not a female relative.

In short, she had allowed herself with a cunning blatancy to be seen for exactly what she was, a handsome middle-aged harpy with something genuinely mysterious about her inherent in a look of suffering about her deep

146

eyes and wide brows as if her daemon had led her through fiery landscapes looking for a rare incandescent blossom that she had never found.

Such was the mistress with whom, at the age of sixty-eight, Don Luis found solace, comfort, and an unexpected release for fires that still smouldered warmly under the hard, cool lava of his own exterior; fires that were still capable of darting forth in a subterranean pit flashes of yellow flame as if a deposit of sulphur had suddenly sublimed after having nearly boiled away.

Over the meeting of two such volcanic natures there was bound to be a certain amount of stench released which might possibly arouse the hostility of nose-holding neighbours ploughing in greener and more domestically-fertile, in less scoriac fields. Perhaps, that is one reason why such women as Faith invariably reek of perfume. She had chosen for hers a combination of musk and sweet-poppy that was slowly but surely overcoming the odour of stale Malacca snuff with which the coach had long stunk.

For stenches, moral or otherwise, Don Luis now cared very little, however. Indeed, he rather enjoyed their piquancy. He had found what he wanted, and, without any undue commotion, he intended to enjoy it before he died. An event, by the way, which still seemed remote to him.

In Italy, where he was now known in a few official quarters only, it had pleased him to be perfectly open about his affair after leaving Livorno. Going through France, and upon his return to Spain, he intended to be a little more circumspect; to let his new star dawn slowly upon his more intimate friends and relatives rather than to have it burst suddenly out of a cloud which might throw some of its shadow on him.

Sancho's suggestion had therefore been followed out and Faith was now dressed with a taste and restraint that might indicate a duenna being brought from Italy for the instruction of certain young grandnieces in Madrid. She had accepted this temporarily less glamorous rôle with alacrity and understanding.

147

It still permitted her to make Don Luis thoroughly comfortable wherever they went in a hundred small ways that he had never known or had long forgotten. He realized, now, that with great means he had long been living a kind of Spartan camp-life under the rather stern care of Sancho. In short, he had much needed a woman to look after him. Now he had found one who, without disturbing his thoughts or threatening any legal or social complications whatsoever, comforted the man. In personal service Faith was solicitous by day and ingenious at night. And it so happened that she was the only person in the world who could sympathize over Don Luis' past without at the same time wounding the proud marquis' honour.

The Paleologus on her part knew all this. She wanted security. In finding it in Don Luis she felt her cup ran over and she did not intend to drop it or spill it lightly. This was her last chance, and she played for it consummately. As they drove over the Simplon they were supremely well-pleased with each other.

Don Luis did not intend to have his plans interfered with a second time, particularly by the son of the man who had wrecked them before. He intended to put a final stop to trouble from that quarter. The trivial incident of the race on the Corso at Milan had outraged him beyond all ordinary imagining. He planned to act this time so that, whether he succeeded or not, no blame could attach to him. But he was now a little superstitious about Maria's son. He might fail. Experience had taught him that. If so, he determined to be still in a position to bide his time.

It was with these thoughts in his mind that he continued to ascend the pass as rapidly as his four horses and two mules could be persuaded to drag the coach toward the clouds.

———————

The violent thunder-storm accompanied by pelting globs of hail had struck Duomo d'Ossola shortly after

148

dawn and driven in the tired sleepers in the courtyard. They found an even more elemental disturbance going on inside. The old grandmother had descended early to get breakfast for the party and had stumbled over Beppo and her granddaughter as one object. When Anthony and the others rushed in shaking the hailstones and rain off their hats and clothes, she was beating her granddaughter with a convenient piece of firewood till the girl's ribs resounded. She had also just finished-off Beppo who was dazedly looking on from a far corner by the single light of his one, as yet, unclosed eye. The girl was now screaming more with terror than with pain, for it looked as if her grandmother meant to kill her. The dogs barked and howled, and the imprecations of the old woman rushed out of her mouth like the sound of the hail against the tiles.

Seeing that the gentlemen were not for murder before breakfast, she finally left-off to sink down exhausted, weeping by the ashes of her hearth fire. The girl, feeling her bruises and sobbing, attempted to rearrange the tattered remnants of her bodice which had been nearly clawed off. In this she was gallantly assisted by Pujol, who felt a genuine remorse for having brought this trouble upon her by his repulse of the night before.

"I should have sacrificed myself. As a Frenchman I should have managed it sans scandale," he assured Anthony. "Now look!" He pointed to the girl, the old woman, and Beppo all in misery.

Beppo it was plain would be of little use going over the pass. Both his eyes were now closed. For him the old woman had nothing but curses. She spat at him like a lynx when he blundered near.

"Now it is the fourth generation. *His* brat! I shall soon be having travellers driven away from the roof by its squalls. May the evil-eye wither your womb like a dried tripe, harlot, little bitch," she screamed, seizing her club again. The girl shivered. "Pig, stunted boar," she screeched at Beppo, waving her stick.

"Why don't you keep him on here, mother?" suggested Vincent.

"I have kept too many men in my time," said the woman. "What they want is a fire, a bed, and something to eat. The less they have to move on their feet after a while, the better they like it. Soon they are flabby and nothing but a mouth. The breasts of my mercy for them are dry."

"But this fellow is a vetturino and you need one about an inn like this. We already owe him a hundred soldi and we will leave him as much more for the girl's dot. That is something, isn't it?"

The old woman still muttered but sat considering.

Beppo groaned.

"Make it two hundred, Vincent," added Anthony. "I will go half."

"Two hundred soldi," said Vincent reluctantly.

"That is something," admitted the old woman. "I need a horse, too . . ."

"Otherwise we shall just take him and drive on," said Vincent.

"Three hundred soldi, altogether?" asked the crone looking up.

"Sí," murmured Beppo, "my wages, too."

The old woman clucked with her gums. "Come here, girl," she said at last. "Get down the dog-grease and set your betrothed to work on your back. He might as well learn now how to salve a morning's beating so you can get breakfast."

The swollen-eyed Beppo without further comment began to rub the dog-grease into his future wife's back. Secretly he was well satisfied, but he did not intend to admit it. His had been, he thought, an excellent night's work. The woman in Florence could shift for herself now. Well, he wasn't married to her. What did she expect?

Pujol was delighted. There would be one less man to haul over the mountains. Vincent had been quick at getting off for less than it would have cost to keep the useless Beppo in France. Anthony felt he had assisted

150

at making peace. Breakfast such as it was passed off well enough.

Pujol was ready to start earlier with a lightened load. As soon as the roads ceased to be torrents he gave notice of harnessing up. The storm rumbled on into the plains behind. The old woman sat counting over her three hundred soldi by the rekindled fire.

No one would have recognized her as Lucia, the kindly, pleasant maid of Maria Bonnyfeather less than thirty years before. In that time she had had three husbands and thirteen children. The inn at Ossola she had bought with the last of Don Luis' gold pieces after much wandering about amid Swiss villages in the Italian cantons. She had no more idea who Anthony was than why the French had eaten her out of house and home the year before and given her only paper money. As she attempted to bite some of the more doubtful looking soldi she regretted her teeth. She put aside one soldo. It was to send to her first husband's cousin to put edelweiss on Maria's sunken grave. No soldo, no edelweiss; she knew the Swiss. Now that her little slut of a granddaughter had a man she would take these soldi and go back to Tuscany. She would like to be buried where the sun was warm. Holy mother, the snow in these mountains! It gave her bones the shivers. And that little fool would have given herself away just for the fun of it. But what was to be expected, with soldiers about the place the whole year before? She would leave the happy couple—her blessing. She wrapped a few yellow-grey locks about a peg of a comb that seemed to be fixed in her skull, scoured her sooty face off with the under-side of her second petticoat and went to the door to watch the berlin start.

———————————

"How do you suppose people ever come to be as horrible as these?" asked Anthony, looking about for the last time at Duomo d'Ossola and its inn.

"It's their own fault," grumbled Vincent comfortably.

"They don't have to be here. Just bad human nature, I suppose."

"Perhaps," replied Anthony, unaware that the reason he was sitting in the luxurious little berlin was because Don Luis had decided not to let him stay on the knees of the filthy old woman peering out of the door and trying to curtsy to him as well as her lumbago would permit. "But I suppose fate does have something to do with it."

"Not much, Toni. It's what a man does for himself that makes him what he is. What can you expect of these people though? Look at those two brats there, for instance."

Two half-naked boys were peering at the varnished doors of the berlin which reflected their delighted grimaces.

The view which included a number of lean, rooting sows was certainly not encouraging. From every crazy balcony with a tottering stairway rotting up to it, from every eccentric hovel along the street,—terrific scarecrows male and female, gaunt and starved faces, rheumy-eyed and goitred carlines and fearfully-peaked children could be glimpsed gathered to see the rich travellers leave. The bolder or more desperate beggars were also gathering.

"I am starving, signore. The soldiers have left nothing." . . . "Signore, I want something to eat. I tell you I am hungry, my belly grinds." . . . "I fought for the Austrians—and now look," said an old soldier revealing a seethed stump. "Dear and very charitable milords of England, I have a dislocated hip," drooled an old woman. And she had. "Dear and very charitable milords, rich and gracious signori, my hip has kept me in hell for twenty years. My hip, sweet and kindly signori, for the love of God and his saints, signori, my poor old hip. I can neither lie, stand, nor sit, signori. I am hungry and in great pain. It is true." Her palsied hand slid into the window, shaking, and gnarled as a griffin's paw—"My hip, milords of England, rich and high-born gentlemen of God, my poor old hip, my hip . . ."

152

"Get on, Pujol, you rascal," roared Vincent. "Never mind that little buckle."

The babble for alms grew threatening and clamorous. They were forced to throw out some small coins to get the horses through the mewing mob.

"God bless you," screamed old Lucia, secure in her soldi. The beggars scrambled and cursed. The berlin strained forward through the mud. Children ran up the street after it holding out their hands and screaming. One persistent little urchin who raced with them half a mile finally got a coin the size of his little toe nail.

"Farewell!" he shouted with his last breath, and collapsed by the roadside clutching the picaillon.

"That is the last of Italy," said Vincent. "Why, Toni, what's the matter? You look pale."

"It's the high air I guess," replied Anthony, and looked out of the window at the incredible mountains just ahead.

The last of the Italian hamlets was left behind as they started upward more noticeably. Soon they could look back at miles of little villages apparently asleep in the warm sunlight below. The sound of cow bells ceased. The roar of the snow rivers became louder. They climbed up a slanting plateau through an inferno of wind-tortured trees which were already shedding their leaves. Already it was noticeably colder. Remnants of the morning hail-storm glittered along the roads and in tree boles like fresh-broken glass. The wink from these beds of scattered diamonds answered the blink from the snow-fields above. The breath of the horses became faintly visible.

Now the way pitched upward violently. All roads travelled before seemed to have been level. They were dragged through a region of bare rocks, pebbles, and boulder-débris where the horses panted and struggled. The angry tumult of a river suddenly leapt myriad-voiced out of the earth. The road became a skidding track along the edge of a gorge filled with mad, rushing froth and uptossed arms of spray hundreds of feet below. They crossed the torrent on a new bridge over its raving water and struck into the living stone of the mountain between two walls of rock.

It was a mere cleft with the daylight leaking down greyly as if through a crack in a vault overhead. Even the gloom failed them as they headed for a cavern where their voices and the sound of the struggling hoofs were lost completely in the subterranean thunder of a cataract that hurled itself close by into an invisible cleft. Only the weight of the water could be felt making the earth shudder. The mist rose before the mouth of this newly-pierced tunnel in spectral veils. It coated the leather of the cushions and their clothes with pearls of moisture as they entered its darkness lit only by the foggy rays of the lanterns. Here the road took its upward way along a cliff with the river bellowing a sheer quarter of a mile below.

They spun out of this cave into full day to cross over another dizzy bridge. The road contorted up and up through the fierce barbaric gorge of Gondo overshadowed by black-fronted terraces and the smooth lowering foreheads of precipices that put their heads close together a thousand feet above as if plotting some overwhelming mischief while throwing cyclopean gloom and staggering shadows along perpendicular miles.

"You should have seen this by moonlight," shouted Aristide, while he breathed the horses. "That is a real test of driving. The pass is not what it used to be. The work of the French engineers has already made a great difference."

But Anthony was glad they had come by day after all. There was still plenty of opportunity for Aristide to prove his skill in tooling along the horses. And the grandeur of full light on the infinite view was beyond all expression and experience.

They were ascending the last rugged ravines of the pass, now overlooking planetary wastes of black rock; peering down valleys floored with clouds that opened suddenly to reveal further eagle-haunted wells of space full of clear, slippery air with toy villages in a lake of sunlight at the bottom. Yet they were still looking up at

154

Gargantuan heights over smooth, rosy snow-fields lying in the wrinkled patterns of hollows and crevasses. And from these half-frozen beds of moisture torrents slipped away to foam down the faces of cliffs. They leaped sheerly into nothing, hanging in tremendous sliding beards of water that smoked into pointed, swaying clouds of vapour still unsupported a mile below.

Here and there the arcs of more distant waterfalls glittered like the bow of promise, and directly above and beyond them, filling the whole moon-like landscape with a reduplicated bellowing roar, the main stream of the Gondo took at one leap the abyss out of which for many hours they had now been climbing.

It was frequently necessary to breathe the horses now. It was piercingly cold. They walked often beside the berlin both to ease the beasts and to keep warm. Their red mufflers floated out behind them in a keen, icy blast that howled and shuddered. The bronze vine against the blue leather of the carriage was now etched in white frost. Despite the great altitude and the difficulty of breathing which they stopped often to overcome, they were exhilarated, intoxicated by infinity below and around them and by the crisp, clean lightness of the frosty air. They shouted with pigmy voices and sang. The impalpable glaze of some infinitely thin but slightly opaque substance seemed to have been lifted from their eyes and brains, permitting sight and feeling to become utterly clear. A hitherto unnoticed weight was gone from their shoulders.

Towards the middle of the afternoon they emerged upon the smooth snow-field at the summit of the pass, scurrying with wreaths and wraiths of snow. Here the wheels sank into the drifts and the horses floundered.

The French were building a hospice a short distance beyond. Black figures gathered like numbed bees in the snow about the already frozen foundations.

"Winter has set in a month early up here," said a young corporal who approached them and examined their papers before one of several timbered huts whose chimneys smoked invitingly. "We will give you a lift

155

over the crest. The first shelter for the night is about five miles below. The engineers for the new road are staying there. You will find good company and wine. The first consul is impatient—'le canon quand passera-t-il le Simplon?' he keeps asking, they say. Now there is a man who makes things go. All marches when he but speaks."

They went into one of the shelters for some brandy and warmth while a team of oxen with old army blankets on them was being driven up and hooked to the pole of the berlin. Then they set out for the last haul through the drifts up to the crest marked by a rude, wooden cross.

Neither Vincent nor Anthony spoke as they trudged up the final slope in the track broken by the carriage. Already the western lights were beginning to redden. Over the plains of Lombardy the thunderstorm of the morning had grown into a vast, rolling cloud-pall washing against the domed fronts of the Apennines. It was a sea of ink clouded with silver. From it, at a seemingly infinite distance, the rays of the sun were dashed back onto the snows of the summits with infernal tinges of red that turned them violet. Here and there long pencils of light searched down into red, lighted patches of the valley floor streaked with silver rivers, infinitely, unutterably far, and sheerly below.

Towards the arc of the crest the titanic skyline of the Alpine ranges with snowy domes, with the sheer, wind-fretted needles of superior peaks, began to dawn upon them as they raised the view into Switzerland beyond.

They stood for some time on the ridge of one of the world's high gables, just where the track passed the rude cross of the ridge itself, and looked about them.

"That," said Vincent, "is France down there." He pointed westward as though towards the plains of another planet that appeared in a dim golden haze beyond a riot of peaks where the earth dipped away into nothing.

Anthony looked eagerly. He was seeing the world at

last. This was the top of the tree of life again. Below in the golden haze was the great courtyard.

It was their whim to ride over the crest. They went back a little and climbed into the berlin from which the oxen were now unyoked and standing with their breath blowing out beyond them like patient, fiery monsters stalled in the snow. The nostrils of the horses smoked too while their coats steamed faintly.

"You will find it not such bad going from here down," said the sous-officier. "The snow is less on the other side just now, and then—it *is* going down. Merci, merci bien, messieurs." He threw up his hand in farewell.

"Allons," shouted Pujol.

The horses plunged forward through the snow, seeming to know that relief was just ahead. The berlin came to the crest, slanted, and began to slide downward on the other side of the pass.

Chapter Seven

The Force of Gravity

TRAVELLERS who have been ascending a mountain in a carriage and have long felt the force of gravity pulling against them are invariably surprised and relieved when they finally top the crest and begin to roll down the other slope, aided instead of hindered. They now have the impression of being personally favoured by a new and friendly power after having overcome the unreasonable opposition of the old. That this impression is unconsciously taken for granted by them is only to say that it is the more profound. Then, to this fundamental feeling of release and relief is immediately added speed; speed, which confers an added illusion of freedom and power.

It was certainly so with the passengers of the berlin. Their sudden access of good spirits upon topping the pass lasted them half-way down the first descent. The night spent in the company of the French engineers near the crest did nothing to take the edge off their exhilaration; quite the contrary. But they were no longer so impressed by the tremendous height. It had become external. Their passage next morning through the new, arched ways under the glaciers, where icicles hung like dripping stalactites, became merely a novelty, an adventure in the realm of ice. The galleries of shelter for voiding avalanches were only a clever convenience whose pillars threw amusing effects of swiftly alternating light and shade into the berlin. The brakes seemed to be answering the nasal twang of the detachments of General Turreau's sapeurs doing their best to make the way smooth for cannon before winter came. With these ragged soldiers lately detached from the Army of the Rhine Pujol exchanged a hundred carnal remarks about their scarecrow appearance. Remarks which, as it proved later, were to be remembered against him. But nothing could now dampen the high spirits of the young Aristide, a Frenchman returning to France.

Below the regions of snow the road had been temporarily completed, and they no longer met any troops. They met with no one at all. Perhaps it was for that reason that they gradually became more silent as the day wore on and they began to realize the berlin as nothing but a small fly-like object crawling over precarious bridges, down the sheer faces of granite cliffs, and through the twilight of horrible ravines toward the gorge of the Saltine, which roared louder and ever more ominously below.

They could only hear the river. The gorge was covered by a stagnant, grey cloud that seemed to have taken refuge there from the wind which continually ravelled away one end of it, where it extended out into the clear area of the lower valley. As they descended into the cloud's upper mists the day gradually became darker, and in the gorge itself the white river whirled and swayed downward over its riven blocks and boulders to disappear in the twilight beyond as if it would lure those who followed the road along its banks to inevitable destruction.

The cloud, which had been a grey floor from above, was, seen from below, a dark, glimmering ceiling leaking and dripping a kind of pearly rain into the canyon. And this misty-drift was also flowing downward toward the mouth of the gorge, draping the bold escarpments and Gothic rock pinnacles with funereal scarves of strangely glowing mist. A more gloomy and purgatorial vista could scarcely be imagined. And it was all the more impressive and depressing to those in the berlin, who were suddenly plunged into it as though they had been flung into a limbo where darkness was hiding, because they knew that above and below them the snowy mountains and the green valleys were still bathed in cheerful light.

The adventure which overtook the berlin in the gloomy gorge of the Saltine always seemed to Anthony to have happened in a dream. That it came suddenly, was fatal, and occurred apparently for no reason at all, only enhanced its nightmare quality. There were even certain grotesqueries about it.

Anthony left the berlin to answer a call of nature. It was just where the new road made a sharp turn around a shoulder with another sheer face of rock some little distance ahead. He was forced to climb a small hillock for the sake of privacy, and as he sat in that semi-contemplative frame of mind peculiar to certain occasions he happened to notice that the old road had formerly swung inward behind the hillock just ahead of where the berlin was waiting. Presently he started to return to the carriage that way.

The short stretch of abandoned road had only one set of wheel ruts on it. They were made by broad, firm tires like those of an artillery caisson. A number of horses, at least four, he casually noted, perhaps more . . .

He happened to glance away from the river and up the old road. He saw the wheel tracks led straight into the face of a small rise in that direction. His curiosity was aroused. Since Africa a trail meant something to him—and here was a manifest impossibility.

Sheerly on the impulse of the moment he followed the old road for a few yards and came to a face of shaly rubble where, whatever-it-was, and six horses, had driven into the hill.

There could be no doubt about it. There was no room here to turn and the thing had not backed out. The hoof marks all led one way. They, and the broad, heavy wheel lines went directly up to a twenty-foot embankment—and continued into it. It looked as if something infernal had concluded just at this point to go home. In the Plutonian scenery of the dark gorge that conclusion did not seem so unreasonable. For a minute he stood nonplussed. He kicked some of the shale aside and saw that the wheel tracks did continue into it. A small slide followed the motion of his foot. It grew. A miniature avalanche of stone and earth followed. He leaped aside to avoid it.

Doubtless *that* was why the engineers had driven the new road into the solid cliff face around the turn just ahead of where the berlin was waiting. The old route was a short-cut, but through precarious ground.

He wondered if "whatever-it-was" had pulled through that slide of shale . . . if Faith and Don Luis were sitting inside the hill there, covered up, coach and all, with tons of rock. He had not thought of the coach since leaving Milan but he now knew that he was looking at its trail, a trail that led fearsomely into the heart of a hill.

Lord, how unreasonable his imagination was! It gave him the creeps to think of those two sitting in there in the darkness, forever—and yet he hoped they were. He hoped they were, with everything that was in him; walled-in; thoroughly checked for good and all. No more driving about. That coach, he knew it now, had been bound upon some vast mischief. "Let loose," was the phrase, "let loose." And now it was walled-in. Hurrah!

But was it?

Instantly he was made cautious by that thought. "It might have gone through." He laughed at himself. The problem became a practical one. "*Got* through," he meant. "Let's see——"

161

With considerable caution in order to avoid starting any more slides, he climbed from rock to rock over the mass of débris across the old road. The wheel marks continued on the other side of it. "Too bad!"—but they did go on——

For about a hundred yards along a kind of deep rut that went down just ahead through a "V"-shaped opening between rocks. That slide must have just missed them as they passed. He felt sure of it—had *just* missed them. Why had they turned in this way? Why?

He ran along the sunken road, crouching, and suddenly found himself looking out into an empty, misty space just ahead.

The old road now dipped down violently. The wheel marks here were deep, fresh! He climbed up behind a big boulder and looked down.

The coach-and-six—so he was right about that—the coach-and-six was standing on a good-sized mound about a hundred feet below him and only a giant's stone-throw away. All the horses and mules were harnessed. Someone wrapped in a cloak was dozing on the box. The horses' heads were hanging, but all pointing down toward the new road along the edge of the gorge. The thing was waiting there in the twilight, every line of it—waiting.

Anthony looked about him carefully. Someone must be on watch, he thought. He had no doubt now that little Beppo was right. Don Luis *had* dashed out on the berlin purposely at Livorno. They must have been waiting there in that alley. It was to have been an "accident." And now they were waiting here in a titanic alley, nature's own; and they had the berlin in a magnificent trap. He could see it all at a glance. The whole scheme lay below him laid out on a chessboard. "Coach to move and check berlin"—for good and all. He wiped his forehead. For the first time he understood fully what the hatred of Don Luis meant. That man and Faith were sitting down there in the infernal, cloudy twilight of the gorge, waiting.

A skein of mist detached itself from a sharp rock-

162

needle and lengthened out, slowly stretching downward. It drifted quietly through the dark, open windows of the coach. While it did so he stood spell-bound.

The mound on which the coach stood was the height of ground in a boulder-strewn amphitheatre several acres in area indenting one side of the gorge. The new road swung into it suddenly, coming downstream around a bald shoulder of granite. It then continued directly along the edge of the gorge. There was no wall along the edge yet. Not even a rail. It went off sheer. From the depth below small clouds and mist were rising. The river, by its distant roar, must be a quarter of a mile away—down.

Anthony smiled grimly. All that the coach had to do was to dash down from the mound onto the berlin when it came around the bend. The "angle of incidence," he told himself, had been nicely calculated. The vehicle on the inner track was bound to win. The berlin would certainly be forced into the gorge.

Just then he heard Vincent and Pujol calling him.

A whistle immediately came from the granite shoulder just above the road. "So that was where they were watching!" The man on the box of the coach came-to with a start and gathered up the reins. Even the horses were listening.

Anthony turned and dodged back along the old road, keeping low. He had been gone about ten minutes. He slithered down over the débris and came out upon the berlin. Pujol and Vincent were now bawling for him lustily. His expression was enough to silence them instantly.

"Have you seen a wolf?" began Vincent.

"Worse," said Anthony, and rapidly outlined the trap ahead. He drew the scheme of it in the road for Pujol, who looked at it calmly. Anthony hoped for a suggestion from Vincent. But the practical man of affairs had now nothing to say.

"You have pistols, monsieur?" asked Pujol.

Anthony nodded.

"We might go up and get that fellow on watch. M.

163

Vincent can guard the carriage here." Pujol smiled at Anthony.

"*I* am ready to go, too," said Vincent, getting out firmly but very pale.

"It won't do, Pujol. That fellow up there on the rock will see us coming and bring the others down on us. I had thought of that," replied Anthony.

Vincent got in the berlin again—rather hastily.

"I know!" said Pujol. His face beamed. "Look here!"

He dragged Anthony over and showed him a cotter-pin through the end of the shaft-pole. It had a ring in it. "There is a little catch underneath," said Pujol, "that holds it in. We can remove that and tie a spare rein through the ring. Pull it, and the horses go forward harness and all leaving the carriage behind. You pull the pin and put on the brakes. I will ride the lead horse. Do you see? It is the coach that will go over—in between. Right *through* us." Pujol waved his hands.

"Good for you, Aristide," said Anthony.

They set to work frantically. The little catch was pulled out; the rein fastened through the ring.

"What are you doing?" said Vincent. They paid no attention to him. Anthony was talking swiftly to Pujol.

"They only heard you calling," he said, climbing onto the box while Pujol prepared to mount the left lead horse. "They can't see us for about fifty yards yet; not till we get clear of this hill. Then it is about two hundred more around the turn, a very sharp one, mind. I suppose the signal for bringing the coach down on us will be a shot—to make us look the wrong way. *Don't look back.* I'll shout when I pull out the pin. Gallop on. Don't let the horses stumble when they jerk loose, mind that. Ready?"

"If you fellows . . ." said Vincent sticking his head out.

"Go," shouted Anthony.

Vincent was thrown against the back seat violently. The berlin tore down the road. "I might have left Vincent out of this," thought Anthony, "but—" He heard a pistol shot overhead. They began to take the curve.

"Much, much too fast, Pujol," muttered Anthony. He was pale enough himself now. The berlin began to slide toward the edge. The horses ahead swung around the curve. He checked the little carriage with the brakes. It swung; it almost pivoted. The right rear wheel glittered in space. For a fractional instant it spun free. There was a bump, and the berlin hurtled on.

Inside, Vincent swallowed his lights. A pistol which he had taken out dropped from his hand. The berlin was tearing along the edge of the gorge out of which the mist rose. Into this home of clouds Vincent vomited.

With one hand on the brakes and the other on the rein to the cotterpin, Anthony looked back and saw the coach coming down from the mound. The Kitten was driving standing up. He had not expected the berlin to come around the curve at a mad gallop, and he was lashing his horses. He expected to strike the berlin a glancing blow while moving on an inner circle, and then to sheer off and in. It looked easy—and it would have been. But now in order to catch the berlin at just the right point the coach must itself come headlong down the little hill. Much faster than Don Luis had intended.

It was doing that. The Kitten seemed to have gone mad.

The clatter of twenty-four hoofs, and the heavy wheels rushing over the stony ground to his left burst upon Anthony's ears above the roar of the cataract below on the right. He looked—shouted—and pulled the pin. He clamped down the brakes. He was nearly thrown off.

A space had instantly appeared between the berlin and its four horses that were now galloping frantically down the road ahead, dragging the thrashing pole and tangled traces after them.

Through the clear interval just ahead of where the berlin had come to a violent stop the huge, black coach and its six beasts rocketed off into the cloudy gorge.

It made an almost complete circle in empty air.

The Kitten had tried to swerve. He had pulled the

lead mules around violently. But the coach had gone on; swung its three teams like a whip lash, and snapped them off the road.

Those brief instants had seemed long. The Kitten was still standing up when he went down. The last thing Anthony saw was the two mules trying to gallop in. They fell scrambling. Their faces, their long, writhing lips, white teeth and eyes went over the brink. The worst thing was the faces of the two mules. They had understood. . . .

From the gorge not a sound came back. It was some seconds before Anthony realized that he was sitting listening intently, waiting for a crash that would never be heard.

At last he stood up on the top of the berlin and looked about him. It was only now that he fully realized what the stratagem had implied—death. He took it for granted that Don Luis and Faith were both down there in the gorge of the Saltine. He was not glad of it now, and yet he could not be sorry. It did not seem to him that he had done wrong.

Down the road Pujol put in an appearance coming back with the horses, which had galloped far before he could check them. He knew what Pujol would say, "Voilà, monsieur; allons-nous-en."—And they would go on. He started to climb down.

"Vincent . . ."

Just then he heard someone laughing.

It was Faith Paleòlogus.

She and Don Luis were standing up there on the mound looking down at the berlin. They were only a short distance away. Sancho was sitting at Don Luis' feet and rocking himself to and fro. His master had put his hand on his head. Echoed from the rock faces of the cloudy amphitheatre, the cool feminine laughter was reduplicated unbearably as if the gloomy, sardonic spirit of the gorge were holding its sides over this chef-d'œuvre of a jest.

And to Faith, there *was* something enormously humorous about the disappearance of the coach. Don

Luis' plans had been *so* well laid. The Kitten was *so* sure of himself—and suddenly gravity had taken charge, flicked the coach off the earth and left them all standing there with Pujol racing on down the road like a madman. The horseless berlin with Anthony standing up on it looked exquisitely helpless and silly. How surprised the Kitten must have been—that sure little fool-of-a-man. *Flick*—and he was gone, mules and all. She had had to' lean up against a rock to contain herself. She was sorry Don Luis had lost; and she was glad Anthony had won. So contradictory a rush of emotion demanded laughter or tears even from her. It was overwhelming. She must make a noise. She began to choke——

"My morocco notebook is gone," said Don Luis childishly, in a tone of voice that might have announced the fall of Rome.

Faith had instantly become a machine for laughter.

"Taisez-vous," growled Don Luis after a while. Her curious half-hysteria was a little catching even to him. "Sancho here has lost his son. They are a family which has served mine for generations."

"The last, señor," whispered Sancho. "Gone?"—he waved toward the river as though he could not believe it.

"I'll take the whip to you, madame," said Don Luis fiercely.

"Gone!" said Faith, and went off again.

It was true. There was no whip. The coach which carried it had gone—the coach had gone! He realized it now, fully.

"Fetch me a club, Sancho," roared Don Luis.

"There are nothing but rocks here. Little ones," whined Sancho. The tears that streamed down his face were for his son. He sobbed and picked up a handful of pebbles.

"Hell's-devils!" rapped out Don Luis—and burst out laughing, too. The coach had gone; he and Faith remained. In that laughter they were married.

"You didn't think I would be such a fool as to sit in

it, too?" he asked, taking her by the hand almost sympathetically.

"No, no," she replied. "I never thought that! I wasn't laughing at *you*."

"No, at the other thing," he said satisfied. "Well, it does interfere sometimes."

She nodded.

They watched Pujol fastening the pole onto the berlin again.

"Not so bad," admitted Don Luis grudgingly.

"*Very* good," said Faith.

He nodded.

Anthony picked his hat off the ground. He hesitated a moment before clapping it on again. Then he made a flourish toward the mound, and pointed toward the berlin with it.

"Do you want to go down in *that?*" said Don Luis, turning to Faith. "We might, you know."

"No," she said.

Don Luis took off his hat and bowed his refusal.

The young man below replied. He put on his hat and climbed into the berlin.

"That particular incident is closed," said Don Luis. "Now how the devil are we going to get down the mountain?"

In the distance the berlin trotted around the next rock shoulder, going down.

———————

Vincent was really in a bad way, Anthony discovered as soon as he climbed into the carriage. He simply could not forgive himself for having shown the white-feather. He insisted that he had. It was painful. Besides that he was really physically ill. They stopped frequently while he got out.

He felt better when they emerged into the sunlight of the valley below but Anthony could see that the shadow of the gorge still lay between them.

"I want to talk to you, tonight, Vincent," he said.

"Oh, do you still want to?" asked Vincent.

"Why, of course. Do you suppose I have no sympathy for any other way of feeling but my own? Now it won't do to have you suspecting me of despising you. Don't be ridiculous. Buck up."

It was better after that. They hurried on through several villages in the upper reaches of the valley. Anthony was determined to out-distance Don Luis completely now. Doubtless one of the army wagons would pick them up. A work detachment came down every evening. It would never do to find himself in the same inn with him. But, my word, it would be cold up there this evening. He wondered what they *would* do.

They came to the last part of the descent, a series of zigzag roads down a succession of terraces that towered above and slipped away into nothing below. And beyond that—soft, warm weather; a valley glittering gold and green with pastures and wheat-fields; the bronze, yellow, and copper-covered domes and spires of a Swiss town.

Here they put the tired, strained horses in a comfortable post stable, Pujol, tired as he was, saw them all rubbed down before he came in to join Anthony in the hospitality of a genuinely civilized little resort.

There was a party of Protestant merchants from Geneva who had driven over to spend the last of the summer. Anthony thought he had never seen such extremely decent people. They were more impeccable than the most respectable English and seemed to belong to no class. "Freemen," he thought. The place was spotless, supper delicious, everybody spoke French and there were no beggars. For the first time in his life he ate fresh, unsalted butter and saw thick cream. Vincent, poor devil, had gone to bed. "My, what he is missing!" he thought. There were some pretty good things in Europe after all—de la crême, par exemple,—and——

He went out whistling, and looked up at the Gargantuan barrier over which by some miracle he had come to this clean, fresh, civilized, warmly-human little hotel. His whistle died away. The contrast seemed a little ridiculous—but good. Perhaps he was revelling a little too much in it. Faith and Don Luis up there nearer the glaciers might be spared this sense of ant-like smallness tonight. They might be finding themselves in a place more fitting to their souls than their bodies. There was something tremendous about them, he felt. "Equals of mine, of a different kind. My opposites, but equals. We have met, and passed. What next? No, I am not flattering myself. There is no one to hear. And I know myself now. I too might have gone down standing up. I am grateful. Do *You* hear? *I* am grateful."

And he ran his eye up the vaulting terraces only a few miles away. He threw back his head to look up the smooth, snowy slopes. He bent his neck back to see the huge, glittering peaks and pinnacles up there glistening amid the glittering stars. Such things as these also were in Europe.

Somewhere along a mountain road half-way up the barrier, like a spark crawling imperceptibly down a wall of sheer darkness, descended a tiny, winking light.

He watched it for some moments, thinking. Then he turned out of the chill, clear night to go in. A light was also shining in Vincent's window. He was waiting for him then.

Anthony meant to have a good talk with his friend tonight. To unburden his heart. He meant to tell him how he had set out over the mountains with a certain ideal in his heart, an ideal that had been reinforced by that experience at Pisa. How he meant to try to grow in the grace that had been Brother François's until he could return good for evil—and how he had carried out that resolution by causing the death of a man and six helpless beasts. And his friend had thought that he would despise him because he, Vincent, was not capable of great physical courage. Why was it that Vincent had always looked up to him; had in most things been Anthony's follower even when they were boys? It was true. Now, if their friendship was to endure, Vincent must know how and where Anthony had failed—and failed time after time. He would tell him that. He

170

would tell him how he had failed in Africa. Vincent was not the only one who faltered and grew ill on high and dizzy roads—not by a long shot!

He opened the door of the room and saw that his friend had been waiting for him anxiously. The room was bright with candles. Vincent looked up from the bed, where he lay still rather pale, to give him a delighted and relieved smile.

"I heard you whistling in the garden and I thought you might have forgotten," he said.

"No, no!" He felt a little awkward and was at a loss how to begin.

An old charwoman in a spotless, frilled cap and glistening wooden shoes came in and made the fire. She gave them both a cheery good night. It was easier now. They seemed at home when she had gone.

And so they talked well into the night. They talked about everything with all the windows and doors of their spirits open. They passed in and out and saw each other's dwelling houses with no locked rooms.

"—And I think," said Vincent, "that under certain kinds of trials I too could be courageous. In fact, I know I could. And I am sorry that I was annoyed over the berlin, because you were smarter than I was about it and made a lovely, swift thing when I could see nothing but old bones. Do you know that I have been taking it out on you all the way from Livorno in a hundred little ways? I felt it necessary to be superior— Mein Gott! I was—jealous!"

"Why, do you know I must have been insufferable about the berlin myself, Vincent. And the funny part about it is I meant all the time to give it to you. I was going to wait till Paris. You remember I laughed when you said, 'There is something in the latest mode,' that day at Livorno when Terrini brought it around. Well, I thought then of your calling on M. Ouvrard in it; how surprised you would be when you knew it was yours. Then I began to like it *so* well. Oh, well, you see how it was. But there—the berlin belongs now to Herr Vincent Nolte."

"Ach, mein lieber Freund," said Vincent, his eyes shining. "Es ist für ewig."

"Ja wohl," said Anthony and laughed happily as he went out.

"Toni," Vincent called after him in a stage-whisper as he went down the hall to his own room, "I did forget to tell you something." The plump German face of Herr Nolte peering through the half-opened door looked very red under the flannel night-cap. But it was very serious.

"What?"

"I was thinking of getting married myself." The door closed almost violently.

And so the Alps were crossed.

Chapter Eight

The Plains of France

OUT of Switzerland, through a canton where all
the women wore round fur caps even in September, as if the country were garrisoned by shakoed
regiments of females, they trotted down to Vevey along
the metallically smooth reaches of Lake Leman. Then,
leaving the miniature villages of chalets clustered behind them at the feet of mountains, they pushed on to
Fribourg.

St. Peter, standing there in the public square with a
key so large—"that the lock which it fits has to be
opened by gunpowder," said Vincent, did not detain
them long.

The disconcertingly rickety bridges over mountain
torrents, the steep downward slope of the snow-thatched
roof of the world were now left behind.

Toward Bâle the road meandered playfully and without much reason from one village to another. The
women here, even the little girls, wore broad white
stomachers with small aprons, fan-shaped hats prinked

out of white gauze. The old men stood smoking large white pipes before very small inns. Every house had its thatch descending in low overhanging eaves over pointed windows set with round panes like bottle-ends, and each seemed to be the cottage in the wood to which the ogre lured children with candy. Only the ogres were gone while the fair-haired children remained. "Plainly, this is the toyland of my German nursery books," mused Vincent. "The forest has been cut away and left the villages exposed. Any person can see that." And he was much pleased by the fancy.

Everything pleased them mightily now. They moved in an amber haze of enjoyment somewhat heightened by a conscientious sampling of the various brews and vintages of the several neighbourhoods through which they successively passed.

"I think the horses are thirsty again, Aristide," Anthony would say.

"Oui, monsieur, ils souffrent. Ils s'en mordront les pouces."

So they would all get out, to let the horses drink, until the surfeited beasts dipping their soft noses in sparkling pails would only wrinkle their lips a little in the water and stamp with surprise at so much damp solicitude.

As they went down the valley both the brews and vintages grew better. "Wine rises to its peak in Burgundy and beer foams to its crest in Bavaria," quoted Vincent. "The spirits of the right and left bank thus rival each other in a balance of excellence. Along this route one can enjoy both sides at the same time." But for all that Anthony noticed that Vincent stuck to beer rather closely and he to wine. And this was now the most serious difference between them.

"Toyland" seemed by a natural transition to extend itself into an elfin country that they passed through by night going on into the early morning hours. It was the tumbled landscape of the Jura Mountains, or rather hills, for they seemed nothing more than that after what lay behind. But they were musical with waterfalls under the late remnant of the moon, pines and crags faëry with September mists. And so on to the famous hostelry of the "Three Kings" at Bâle, where the Rhine ran green and clear under its windows; as yet unmuddied by the long expected autumn rains.

At Mulhouse they were both moved to get on faster. Leaving their own horses behind them to be brought up by easy stages, they hired post and galloped down through Colmar to Strasbourg with fresh relays every few miles. Aristide sat in the berlin now enjoying himself beyond measure.

If he was not the soul he was at least the wit of the party, and he knew how to argue them past the columns of French troops along the Rhine roads till even the wagoners let them go by with a grin. Here began a second foretaste of that song of bugles that grew into a swelling chorus as they continued down into France until the very spirit of the land seemed to be giving tongue and to be loosing its silver élan, and bright, brazen "Ça ira" into the golden atmosphere. If the church bells had been the subdued hymn of Italy, the bugle, when the church bells were now silenced as often as not, was the voice of sovereign France. Only in the walled cities the old iron clangour from the steeples still went on. But it was answered now by the trumpets of recruits drilling for the armies of the first consul that shouted back from the fields and from the walls and citadels over the roll of revolutionary drums.

Strasbourg, however, seemed quiet enough. There was something undisturbable about it, Anthony thought, with its towering cathedral spire and the crooked streets full of peak-roofed houses.

Before one of these the berlin stopped.

It was the house of one of Vincent's new relatives by the marriage of Anna, a relation for which there was no word in any European language to express at once the remoteness of its degree and the heartiness of its recognition. Just as the cross on the Simplon had marked the height-of-land of their journey, the hospitable house of the glover Herr Johann Bucer at Strasbourg marked the

175

summit of wassail, good-humour, and gusto of the trip.

Life in Livorno had not altered the fundamental Teutonic tastes of Vincent. Amid a host of new, blue-eyed, burgher "cousins" and straw-haired river-maidens from the Ill and Breusch, he advanced to the complacent sound of city rebecs in the chambers of the Aubette where, despite the Revolution, the gavotte and minuet still survived. He drove to the Temple Neuf on Sunday with the berlin packed full as a case of sausages with juvenile Lutheran relations. He went to sleep with the rest of the Bucers, Von Stürmecks, Brants, and Toulers while the pastor passed the sand twice through his hour-glass in Alsatian Deutsch. He sat at the place of honour, at a succession of boards too firm to groan under the hams, Würste, fat geese, pâtés de foie gras, and Hochheimer which they had been built to bear up under, while he and Anthony ate, danced, dozed, smoked, and talked themselves into the heart of the family to the vast delight and relief of Anna at Düsseldorf, who received in due course of post an account of these rejoicings in the refined hand of a female cousin.

> ... And there had been *a good deal* of talk, too, my dear Anna, for no one could have been more gallant than our cousin and his friend, and some modest hopes and speculations on the part of certain prospective Hausfrauen whose cheeks are too firm to tremble but not too red to blush in spite of all the cooking. I hope you will be coming here next spring for your first lying-in which I hear is ...

Anna's eyes overflowed with mixed feelings as she put on the pearls which Anthony had given her, for dinner that night. Ach, if he would only marry into the Von Stürmecks it would be schön, sehr schön. Everything with Anna was schön.

But Anthony had no intention of doing that. It was evident that Vincent had, however. And it became necessary for his friend to remind him that the berlin was at least expected to carry them to Paris and was not meant solely for the delectations of Fräulein Katharina Geiler, charming and incapable of walking as she might be.

"For my part I have now seen the collection of watches made by Uncle André, the collection of ritters' swords assembled by Uncle Franz, and tomorrow I am to *hear* the collection of musical spheres and scaled glasses in the camera of des alten Onkel Fritz. Vincent, I just can't listen to it. Not to another glass, or sigh over the sorrows of Werther while the taps drip in the cellar. My capacity has been reached. And you know I have stood by you loyally, too."

Vincent admitted it with gratitude; admitted even his now somewhat vague engagements with M. Ouvrard and other bankers—in Paris. After a formal call upon the Fräulein and her mother and a supper at Herr Bucer's that promised to ruin their digestions permanently, they found Aristide with some difficulty in a house on the Bröglieplatz and prevailed upon him to harness up their own horses which had also been eating their heads off. And so westward now till the peaked roofs, the star-like citadel of Vauban, and the high spire of Strasbourg vanished from view as they left the valley of the Rhine behind and headed across the pleasant land of France.

If he had been alone Anthony would have continued on down the Rhine and crossed the channel from Holland, but he wanted to complete the trip with Vincent and to meet some of the bankers in Paris, particularly Ouvrard, which Vincent was so anxious to have him do.

Vincent had by no means permitted the subject of the Spanish-Mexican silver he had discussed with him at Leghorn to drop out of sight; in fact, they had discussed it frequently as they drove along. It now began

177

to appeal to Anthony as "something to do" for reasons of which Vincent had no idea.

It was doubtful, Anthony felt, if he could bring himself to settle down in Europe anywhere. He would not feel any violent national enthusiasms. If anything, by sympathy he was inclined to feel himself English, but the sojourn at Gibraltar had done something to jar that. The idea of going to America where he might put his roots down in new soil appealed to him. If he remained in Europe he would have to give allegiance to some sovereign or society for which in reality he would probably never feel more than an assumed loyalty. That this was in many ways unfortunate, he acknowledged. But that due to his upbringing and later experiences in Cuba and Africa it was also true, there was no use denying. How become a Spaniard, a Frenchman, or an Englishman overnight? No, it would be like his oath to the King of Spain in Havana, taken but not registered. But once in America he might become part of a growing community, not the master of it as at Gallegos, which was a personally cultivated mushroom, but part of a living, growing organization in which he might find a wide scope for his ideals, his abilities, and his natural desires. Then too, the adventure of the thing appealed to him. "New Orleans," "Louisiana,"—the names called. He would still see the world and he was already aware of something that most Europeans, even intelligent and travelled ones that he had met, did not seem to have an inkling of—that Europe was not the world, Europe was only a small, at present he could see, a very disturbed and disturbing part of it. "Yes," he thought——

"The subjects which men think about and to which they attach the significant verbs of action should always maintain some connection with objects—out of which after all the subjects develop. The trouble with the verb *to be* is that it is intransitive. And there has been a lot of intransitive thinking done in Europe in the past. I suppose devoting your life just to being yourself, and you nearly always follow someone else's pattern, is

178

rather selfish. If a great many people should all start out just 'to be themselves,' following no set pattern, things would get pretty rotten and static. The French seem to have gotten tired of that plan and broken it up. They are probably trying to find a new one. That may be what all the excitement is about. A little hysterical to judge by the bugles and drums. I wonder what that man Bonaparte thinks? What are his subject and his object? Evidently he is a kind of human verb between them. I tried being just that at Gallegos—to do, to do, to do—it is not enough. Besides my object was wrong there. It nearly ruined the subject," he chuckled. "What else was there I learned?

"When I was a child Father Xavier said in effect, 'Be (a certain kind of man) in order to please God—the church will tell you what pleases God. You can become in that pattern by doing what you are told to do. Take the wafer and seal the bargain.'

"John Bonnyfeather said, 'Be honourable (my code) and devote your life to transferring goods from one place to another. You can live on the tolls *like* a gentleman.'

"Cibo said, 'You can't become anything but a healthy, pleasure-loving human animal—act in such a way as to be wise within those limits. Happiness will follow.'

"I said to myself, 'Do in order to keep on doing. Life is action—' and in four years I nearly went mad. I can see now I much mistook Cibo.

"Brother François said, 'Lose all sense of your own being in doing good to others—in that way you will be reborn in God. In Christ is the pattern which the church preserves. Imitate Him.'

"And now where am I? Physically, somewhere between Strasbourg and Nancy going west. Politically, nowhere. Financially, lucky. Spiritually, waiting in a limbo to make contact again with the world. For that is the first step in carrying out my own vision of the plan. I must in some way put down roots in a place, associate myself in primary human ways, somewhere, somehow, and soon. And the first step is to know and to find

179

people. And why not men of great affairs as well as little ones? My wealth and my training make it possible. I have cemented my boyhood friendship on this trip with Vincent, who loves me. Why not let that be the entering point and this Spanish-Mexican business the wedge to follow after? It will provide a thousand vital associations. I might drive it in deep—to a wife. I might drive it *home*. And besides what else—I can't become a mere spending dilettante. Well, I shall talk with these bankers at Paris, and with Sir Francis Baring in London, and M. Labouchère at Amsterdam on the way back from England—if I come back. I might live there, of course. Poor Florence!—Yes, I shall at least find out, and then——"

"We ought to get to Metz sometime tomorrow," said Vincent sleepily. "Make up your mind, my boy, I'm going to sleep for the first stages of this journey to Paris. I can't help it. Strasbourg has worn me out. And I really must, I really *must* you know, be able to think when I come to talk to Ouvrard—and Talleyrand!" Vincent whistled and sat up uneasily. "Yes, you were right, we delayed too long. You should have made me leave before. For that Katharina now I really do not give a damn. What did you think of her?"

"Sehr schön," replied Anthony non-committally.

Vincent nodded after a while and sank back to sleep as well as the road would permit. At least the cushions were soft and the springs strong. A smile gradually gained over his anxious expression. "You are right, Toni, sehr schön. It was worth it. We shall see these fellows in Paris just the same. I wonder if, after what has happened, I should still deliver Don Luis' message to Ouvrard—those blank permits for Spanish produce from the colonies, you remember."

"Yes, I don't think the marquis is one to let his hates interfere with his income," replied Anthony. "Besides his little plan was directed against me."

"*I* was in the carriage, too, don't forget," muttered Vincent.

"That was merely accidental from Don Luis' standpoint, I suppose."

"I think you are right—again," said Vincent after a while, and dozed off along a good stretch of road.

"Why was it so many people took his advice or depended upon him when it came to acting?" Anthony wondered. Here was Vincent. Their association had been and continued to be almost boyish. Yet Vincent, he knew, was an astute and able man. Important men had entrusted him with important affairs; believed in and counted upon him. Yet he was turning to Anthony for advice and the signal to act just as he had always done. Of course, Vincent's professional manner was different. The natural and domestic lining of his professional front was exposed to Anthony—and yet? And there was Pujol out on the box, ambitious and keen. He had left Pisa to get into the main current. Young Aristide was no fool. He said he did not intend to forget what he knew about the law—and he knew a great deal. He couldn't stand hearing it talked about any more. He wanted to practise it in Paris. And somehow, somehow, Anthony knew it, Aristide had picked him as the means to put himself upon his way. He would expect Anthony to help him—and he would. Perhaps that was it, he not only would—he did. The quality of one's personality was a curious thing. It reached out and drew others along with it. It had drawn an ex-slaver, a German-Italian banker, and a law student all into the little berlin and the horses were drawing all of them together to Paris.

The swift drumming of hoofs fell like music on his ears. "Go"—the command still seemed authentic. Its fulfilment contented him. He looked out with satisfaction upon the shifting landscape; lost himself in it.

They rolled into Nancy about midnight, after considerable trouble at the gate, and slept like logs. Pujol had made a fast trip.

From now on they settled down to travelling in earnest. The autumn of the year 1801 was dry and crisp. The rains delayed interminably. The roads smoked with dust under the horses' feet while they overtook the lumbering diligences that looked like travelling houses; while the important military posts rushed by them. An occasional detachment of Moreau's ragged cavalry ambled along with a disgruntled air, recalled from the Rhine. They were discontented. Their victories had not been won under the eye of the first consul. Their battles did not count. It was whispered their general was in disgrace. To Aristide's quips they replied with curses.

At Varennes an old sergeant descended from his horse and kicked Aristide all around the stable yard. The sport was like to become popular. Other troopers prepared to join in. Anthony and Vincent were forced to interfere and provide enough pourboire to last the troopers to the Marne in order to get Pujol off. From an upper window a hard-bitten major looked on approvingly in a uniform which still affected a Jacobin slovenliness. Vincent thought of protesting to him.

"I would not do so, monsieur," whispered a neat-looking young corporal. "They say the major was with Carrier at Nantes, one of the old terrorist enthusiasts. Ma foi!" The young fellow started violently and froze to attention. The major was roaring at him.

"Sartain, cochon, what are you saying to those aristocrats, you rascal?"

"Rien, mon major!"

"Throw them out," roared the officer, evidently full of wine.

"We will go," shouted Vincent. "I shall complain of this at the Tuileries, monsieur le major."

The major's face clouded. "Les Tuileries!" and then, "This is Varennes, citizens. You remember—Varennes?"

"We are going," Vincent assured him.

"Oui? A l'enfer," muttered the major and went back

182

to his bottle. The older soldiers looked at them sullenly and jibed at the berlin.

Pujol said nothing now. His bottom throbbed as they drove hastily out of Varennes, and there were indignant tears in his eyes. "I will get that major some time," he said. "Wait!"

"Nice customer, that," said Anthony.

Vincent was purple with rage. "Wait!" he also said. He looked out over the wide waste of the Argonne where the clouds were drifting serenely along the wooded ranges. He was thinking how times were changed since the Prussians had been driven back here —and bankers were not without their influence again. "We and the serene, indifferent landscape remain," he thought. "The farms and trees push over the graves while interest goes on. Idealism is very expensive and the voice of the people dies away into the chest of the first consul—which is now empty and needs Mexican dollars, I understand."

"What are you grinning at, you old miser?" asked Anthony.

"Did it ever strike you what a wonderful thing geometrical progression is in peace times?" replied Vincent. "I mean applied to government consols, you know."

Anthony shook his head. Vincent had his moods too, sometimes. They galloped through Les Islettes and slept at Sainte-Menehould.

———————

The vineyards and small hill farms began to change into the wide wheat-fields and the towered granges of level farms as they pushed on towards Paris. Here and there a gaunt fire-scarred skeleton of a château rose amid fire-blasted park trees.

"Not many aristocrats have seen fit to return yet," muttered Pujol. "I hope my father will be able to keep his new lands in Auvergne. We don't want the émigrés back. What an ass that major was. Vive Bonaparte! He

183

knows the solid people who are behind him. No mobs and no seigneurs. Just let us keep the land."

They stopped at Mourmelon to let the horses rest, and looked out over the broad plateau on the other side of the river.

They crossed the rolling Champagne slowly. The beasts were tired now and they could get no relays. All the horses had been taken for the artillery or were being kept for the military couriers. It was lucky they had their own. At Rheims they had to fight to keep both teams. Vincent had to produce all his credentials. As it was they were regretfully allowed to proceed.

"A great requisition and impressment is under way," explained an old officer in what had once been a royal regiment of the line, one of the maison du roi. "Times *have* changed I can tell you. Now everybody must serve under the Revolutionary law. The newest arrangements for enforcing it have just been perfected in Paris and they are trying them out first in the valley of the Marne under the eye of the first consul. He is driving about from one arrondissement to another, I hear. Watch you don't meet him—with four horses. War with England, they say."

"I thought it was to be peace," said Anthony. "The negotiations are under way I was told."

The captain leaned into the window of the berlin confidentially, where it stood before the prefecture on the square at Rheims. He shrugged his shoulders till his epaulettes flapped. "Peace? Yes, for a little perhaps. But what is it, la paix? Only a little time to let the old world wheeze and breathe easy after a good blood-letting. In a few years its veins are swelled out dangerously again. In the forehead they begin to throb. And then—it has another stroke. It calls loudly for the basin and knife to save it. Le roi, le peuple, le Premier Consul, what is the difference who the surgeon is it calls upon? The operation is the same. I have in my time seen them all operating. The people are the worst. They like guts all over the place covered with symbolic olive branches and doves. Beautiful!—les fêtes de la paix, little white doves with red feet and those cheesecloth arches, quelle magnificence! I have trained my horse to rumble behind when he passes under them. He is an old war horse and understands. And what after all are all those young men doing in this classe which Bonaparte is calling to the colours—to preserve peace, of course—ah—one must hasten to add that. Why, I will tell you, trying to keep the girls quiet and placid and endeavouring to drink up each harvest as it occurs.

"Venus, le vin, it is not sufficient. Men must live even if only for a few weeks. War is vivid, a thing of flame and thunder. It takes one out of the house under the stars. It exchanges the bubbling of babies for the mewing of eagles and the cough of cannon. What is the difference if one dies? One dies anyhow. I am sorry, of course, for those who lose their superior colons for Schömberg-Lippe—quel dommage! But for France— what are a few bones, a leg? if France asks it? Is it not then a leg of honour, a limb beyond compliment, a foot shrivelled in the divine fire? Voilà!" He roared suddenly caught in the flames himself.

A tremendous fanfare of trumpets came beating back from the façade of the cathedral at Rheims. The square vibrated with it. A squadron of glittering, spick-and-span cuirassiers trotted across the place, its musicians ahead on grey horses. People drinking under the little awnings about the place rose, and turning white in the face, screamed. The scarfed staff at the prefecture ran to the doors and windows and shouted. The regiment had come to aid in numbering the people. The patient Jewish-looking saints and the long angels carved on the front of the church, where Jeanne d'Arc had crowned her rascal sovereign, looked out as they had for eleven centuries, and trembled. The bells above burst out, the gargoyles grinned. "Vive Bonaparte, vive Napoléon," roared the streets of Rheims, "vive la France."

Pujol sat and gaped. Something had happened to France while he had been toying with *fas* and *jus* at Pisa. The old captain rushed away.

"Get on," cried Anthony. The berlin started. "That captain was drunk," he said.

"They are all drunk here," replied Vincent. "Don't let it catch you."

"It's got Aristide, listen to him shouting up there. Vive everything." They were galloping recklessly through the main street.

"Don't kill the horses, Pujol,"—Anthony looked out of the window grinning. Pujol suddenly looked ashamed. "Vive la loi," he muttered—"I live by that." They went more slowly and carefully now. Rheims with its roaring steeple was left behind.

They descended upon the Marne at Dormans just above Château-Thierry. They asked the way of the curé, "Tout droit." The first consul was just across the river at Crezansay yesterday, mustering. "Look out," he said, eyeing the horses. They laughed and went bowling along, the river on their left.

"We are lucky to see the Marne valley so beautiful and sunny this time of year," said Vincent. "Did you ever see anything so golden and peaceful? The spirit of the harvest seems to be resting here just now. Usually by October it is soggy and full of driving rain. One might imagine that little valley of the Verdon across there to be undisturbable with its overhanging forest-clad heights looking down on the spires of old villages. Look how the meadows and the stubble of the wheatfields reflect the light. It is as clear and white as the wine they grow hereabouts. That deserves a better reputation than it has, by the way. It's a little like the Rhine along here, but chalky soil, you know." He leaned out, gazing across the river with a genuine enthusiasm for the landscape rare for him.

"Would you like to live in France, Vincent?"

"It depends upon how rich I get, and how safe property is going to be here. Yes, sometimes I have thought of it—Paris? I have been living there for about half my time the last two years, you know. But I was thinking of the country rather; a place to settle down in. And right along here is one of my favourite spots.

It reminds me of Germany, a miniature Rhine. I would like to be able to take that old castle of Martel there on the hill and rebuild it."

"And bring Katharina from Strasbourg for its princess," hinted Anthony.

"Ja," said Vincent.

"Living in France because it reminds you of Germany is a very curious German reason to live in France, isn't it?" teased Anthony. "And of course it *must* be a castle on a river."

"Ach," replied Vincent a little irritated. "You mistake me. It is because it is so beautiful just here. Everyone has favourite spots. Call it my castle in Spain then. A castle in Spain might suit you better, nicht wahr?"

"It might," admitted Anthony, "provided——"

"Dolores," grunted Vincent. "But *do* look at my view now. Around the curve here we begin to see Château-Thierry. Am I not right?"

And Anthony had to admit he was. There was an unexpected, delicate charm about Château-Thierry dreaming in the sunlight, set in the midst of flat, emerald meadows along a steel-blue river with enormous, bold, green hills behind it. They came upon it around the curve suddenly and there it was lightly poised by the river-bank like a white bird about to take flight; the arches of its white bridge leaping easily; its inexpressibly graceful belfry soaring against a background of verdure; the flying buttresses of St. Crépin's church rising in splendid uplifting curves; the golden clock tower and copper spires glittering above ivory houses— lacelike, wonderful, a village that had become a little city and kept the charm of both.

"La Fontaine had his house somewhere hereabouts," mused Anthony. "I remember Toussaint talking about it. He came here once to see the poet's library. Great rows of books all bound in sumptuous leather by the Sun King, he said. Poor Toussaint! I wish he were here now. This place reminds me of some of his dreams."

"I can't imagine shooting myself. Can you, Toni?"

"No—not exactly. Not now anyhow."

187

They turned into the main street and found themselves unexpectedly in the midst of old acquaintances. It was the troop of cavalry that had treated them so roughly at Varennes. As they drove past the prefecture someone gave a shout. A couple of troopers ran out and seized the heads of the horses. Their old friend the major was standing on the steps smiling significantly.

"Bonjour, messieurs les aristocrates," said he. "So you haven't got to the Tuileries yet—not even with *four* horses?"

They were forced to alight.

Major Luçay—for they were soon only too familiar with his name—was, they also discovered, in charge of the requisitions and enrolment of recruits in the arrondissement. The local civil officers were evidently afraid of him. He and his sullen veterans of Hohenlinden had been temporarily detached on their way home to perform what they considered to be local police duty and were cursing their mal chance in meeting the general who had given them orders. The induction of recruits and the requisitions had been merciless. It was noticed that Luçay was especially severe on young men from the better class families. He would listen to no pleas for exemption however reasonable. The atmosphere at headquarters was turgid.

Without even waiting to inquire who the travellers in the berlin were, the two best horses were led off. "We take them in any event," coolly remarked the major, and then proceeded to examine their papers and passports with an eye microscopically critical.

He was evidently disappointed to find Vincent and Anthony were foreigners, and their papers in order. With Pujol it did not go so well. His certification by the French commandant at Florence as a French student permitted to return home caused Luçay to smile under his dirty, red moustache.

"He is simply a vagrant of military age," he said. "Enrol him, sergeant." And Pujol was enrolled. "Since he knows horses, put him down for a cavalry dépôt." That was all the reply made to their continued protests.

188

Poor Aristide was in tears. "I am ruined, M. Toni, I shall lose precious years. I am a student of law. I go to practise in Paris, monsieur le major," he shouted at Luçay desperately.

"The law is that you be enrolled," said the major. "It is finished. Take him away."

"M. Toni," cried Aristide aghast as he was led out, "M. Toni!"

"I shall see you through, Aristide," said Anthony.

"Wait!" said Vincent.

"No doubt, Herr Nolte," said the major leaning forward and looking Vincent in the eye, "no doubt you will have me cashiered for this."

"Well, since you suggest it, major," replied Vincent, "I shall."

Luçay digested this with difficulty, and it was made no easier for him by the scarcely repressed cheers of the civil staff. The mayor, a scared, thin little man, wrapped almost to extinction in the folds of a tricolour sash, followed the two foreigners through the door. He would have liked to kiss Vincent on both cheeks for his temerity.

"I am helpless, monsieur, I want you to know that," he cried, standing on the steps. "I apologize that this outrage has overtaken you in my arrondissement. This major is a Jacobin—one out of the Terror who still persists."

"We know about him," said Vincent. "I shall go to my friends in the right places at Paris."

"Bon! But I wished to tell you that the first consul is even now at Nogent, only an hour's drive down the river. If monsieur *has* influence?"

"Come on," said Anthony. "Let's see him. I'll drive. Merci, monsieur le maire."

They climbed up on Aristide's box together and started. "That way, that way," cried the mayor, pointing. Just then the major came to the door. Vincent looked back at him and took off his hat. The man looked uncomfortable.

"I'm proud of you, Vincent," said Anthony.

The two gentlemen on the box of their own berlin drove leisurely out of the town of Château-Thierry. The least appearance of nervousness or flight would, they felt, bring the redoubtable Major Luçay after them. As it was from the steps of the prefecture he watched them go, regretfully they thought.

Once across the bridge over the Marne and around the first short curve in the valley, Anthony touched-up the horses to a good fast pace. The remaining team missed its leaders and was inclined to shy at every opportunty.

"We shall certainly have to pick up another driver between here and Meaux," said Vincent nervously. "Anyway it would never do to drive into Paris on the box ourselves."

"We won't have to do that," replied Anthony firmly. "Who that you know is likely to be with Bonaparte at headquarters?"

"Are you really going there now, Toni? It might be better to go on to Paris. I know Fouché there. He and Ouvrard understand one another. I thought . . ."

"Now look here, Vincent, let's see this thing through now. You want your horses and driver back. Are you really going to let that rat of a cavalryman make you forget who you are? Of course not. We are going to the first consul himself if necessary. And we are going to get Aristide released, too. Make no doubt of it. He is going to drive us to Paris, and once there I want him started on the way to be an avocat, and by your influence."

"If you really believe I can do it, I will," said Vincent. "Coming to think of it, I do know de Bourrienne."

"Who's he?"

"Bonaparte's secretary. And he goes with him everywhere."

"There you are," said Anthony. "And here we are, too. That must be Nogent ahead there down the valley."

He began to fan along the horses and Vincent's indignation at the same time.

Chapter Nine

The Little Man At
Great Headquarters

FOR some hours on the afternoon of October the fourth, 1801, the hamlet of Nogent l'Artaud on the left bank of the Marne a few miles above Paris had temporarily become the nervous-centre of Europe and the focus of its most intense energy.

Napoleon had been moving about through the villages of the lower Marne valley watching certain provisions of his new law for the enrolment of recruits being put into operation there. He was carefully taking note of the temper of the population under the workings of an altered system of conscription, and watching its faults and merits before applying it universally. He had driven down from Epernay that morning, intending to return to Paris by way of Meaux next day. He had settled suddenly and unexpectedly upon Nogent as temporary headquarters, as it was his custom to do, by stopping his carriage in full career, getting out, taking over the principal house for himself and quartering his staff on the village. It seemed unlikely that he would choose such a place as Nogent, and that was precisely why he had done so. For it was in small places where no one expected him that he could best see for himself what was really going on.

France had been at peace with the rest of Europe for almost a year. On the very day that Napoleon stopped at Nogent he was expecting to hear at any moment that the preliminaries of a peace had also been signed with England. The news would be semaphored down from the Channel to Paris in a few minutes and a courier would soon find him on the Marne. At last reports the parleys at London had reached their final and critical stage.

These negotiations, and a thousand other things, were in his mind while he talked to the thunder-stricken officials of the little town, looked at the military rolls for the arrondissement, complimented the lieutenant in charge of the muster for his zeal, entered ten houses in fifteen minutes to see that entries on the rolls were men and not mere names, asked for the tax returns and re-marked some lax, local favoritism in regard to personal property returns, noted that a bridge at Nogent would relieve congestion at Château-Thierry in case of military operations in the Marne valley, that the heights just above provided excellent artillery emplacements to command that town,—and then walked back to headquarters with his tired young adjutant, wondering meanwhile whether Cambacérès or brother Joseph Bonaparte would be the first to bring him the final details of the English news.

"Probably Joseph. He will rush to point out how valuable his advice has been, while the amiable Second Consul Cambacérès will certainly get lost on the way and stop somewhere to dine. Still his dinners do have more influence than speeches. I wish my family would drop the democratic rôle now. Joseph and Lucien— how tiresome they are with their everlasting talk about 'public opinion, public opinion.' I am public opinion now. People believe what they are told to believe, and I

193

intend to tell them. Only one's family, of course, will never believe that.

" 'It is not going to last,' mother says. Pauline tells me mother keeps putting louis d'or into that coffer-clock with the sphinx on it that Kléber sent her from Cairo. Kléber, he hated me. Now he is gone. Well, one should not have empty cisterns in a garden in Egypt where Arabs with knives can hide. Mother will soon be hiding gold napoleons with *my* head on them. She *might* believe it then. Perhaps? But what does last? Institutions —a dynasty? Mon Dieu, if Josephine would only conceive! 'Climb into the bed of your royal master, little Creole.' Is it not soft enough? I will embroider it with imperial bees. Be the queen of the hive. Princes—I must have princes for the house of Bonaparte! Give me two years' peace with England—and then." He looked grimly at the eagles on the stands of colours before the door of the humble house he had chosen to honour with his presence. As long as it should be a house no one who ever passed its threshold could be able to forget that his shadow had once brushed it in passing. Already that shadow lay across the world.

Within, his secretary had cleared out the front room and set up the bronze-clamped camp furniture that now accompanied him everywhere he went. In the room down the hall his narrow, military bed with a soft mattress and a hard pillow was laid out. His valet had drawn the blinds.

"In half an hour, Bourrienne," said he. "There are today's letters to dispatch and last morning's post; the sack from Italy first. Sort it! No more widows' petitions! I want the Piedmont reports, too."

De Bourrienne replied patiently and sighed as his master and former schoolmate went down the hall. He missed his comfortable rooms and the smooth routine at the Tuileries. These country inspections were the devil. Napoleon lay down and composed himself for sleep.

Outside the guard was posted. A sergeant went through the house. He found a boy hiding in a cupboard. "I wanted to see General Bonaparte, only to see him," he kept bawling.

The man shook him. "Taisez-vous. The general sleeps. Little swine! Well, look then, idiot." He kept a firm grip on the boy's collar.

Looking into what was ordinarily his father's bedroom, young Pierre Mortier saw a man in a green uniform with white facings lying stretched out on a cot. He was lying on his back with his hands folded on his breast. The eyes were closed. The pale olive face was like a wax death-mask; like the profile on a coin. The slightly damp locks clustered about his brows and over one ivory ear. The nostrils were faintly transparent. The only sign of life about him was a faint wrinkling of his thin lips when he breathed, and the crease in one boot which also occasionally wrinkled uneasily as if the left foot twitched. Young Pierre did not know that England had hold of that leg. But he never forgot the room.

Usually it was as confused as his bibulous father who slept there. Now it was another room, preternaturally neat. It had been swept clean and everything familiar in it removed. Only the sunlight kept coming through the same crack in the blind just over the figure of the sleeper. On the peg where his father's dusty hat usually hung was a small-sword with its hilt in gold wrought in eagles set with diamond eyes. On this the sunlight lit and spattered.

It played in little metallic shivers over the walls. It lighted the face of the sleeping general on the bronze-knotted cot; gilded the uniform of young Beauharnais, the adjutant, who sat on watch with folded arms over against the wall. Suddenly the beam brightened, the hilt gleamed, intense the glory streamed. It lay silent across the faded carpet of the room of the father of Pierre Mortier, aged ten.

"The lightning—it sleeps," said the child breathlessly. "Dans la chambre de mon père!"

Bonaparte opened his eyes and looked at the boy out of his sleep.

Pierre saw the brown pupils widen, light like amber and darken again. The waxy lids closed.

"Voilà, Joséphine, c'est lui," muttered the sleeper inaudibly. On his brain the sunlit image of a boy's face transfigured with wonder and pride burned out slowly into nothing. He breathed once heavily and slept on.

The adjutant and the sergeant smiled at each other. Young Eugène de Beauharnais put his finger on his lips and motioned for them to go. He stuffed his handkerchief in the broken shutter. The grip on Pierre's collar tightened and he was marched off down the hall to the back door, but not in an unkindly way.

"Here," said the sergeant gruffly. "Here is a sou for some little cakes. Remember you saw General Bonaparte. *Thou,* thou little cabbage. Think of it! Now be off and keep quiet, or—" The sentry who passed just then with walrus mustachios and a gold tassel on his busby touched his musket fiercely and grinned. The boy dashed off happily. They were not so terrible after all. He had a sou and had seen the general.

"Il est colossal, colossal," he boasted as he shared the cakes with some other urchins up the street. But he said nothing about the sunlight. He was going to go back to his father's room to examine that later on. Something wonderful had come into that room, something that had certainly never been there before. Just then he and the other boys started to shout and run after a berlin, with two gentlemen on the box, that drove rapidly into Nogent with the autumn dust rolling up behind it in golden clouds.

It drew up before the house of Pierre's father where the new silk flags with the eagles stood by the door. The sergeant ran out. The boys stopped to watch curiously. One of the gentlemen was evidently very angry about something.

"General Bonaparte is sleeping and cannot be disturbed," said the sergeant firmly, twirling his moustache and looking the angry German gentleman up and down. One of the horses gave a loud whinny.

"Hein!" said the sergeant.

"It would seem that he may be disturbed unless you detail one of your men to take the berlin to the stables over there," said Anthony. "We have lost our driver. Here is something for the fellow who will look after the horses." He gave the sergeant a heavy coin and climbed down. The man's expression changed.

"If you have a real reason, messieurs . . ."

"We are not merely selling eggs, I assure you," said Vincent nodding towards several peasant women with baskets lined up across the street, waiting for the head-quarters commissary to appear. "It is a matter of genuine importance. Is M. de Bourrienne here or in Paris?"

"Ici, monsieur. You know him? Here, Frampton, take care of these gentlemen. They have business with the general." The sergeant pocketed the coin. "For God's sake get that mare's nose in a bag before she whinnies again," he said to the orderly. "If the general has been wakened—" he pulled his beard anxiously. "What name shall I give to the adjutant?"

"Tell M. de Bourrienne that M. Nolte, the banker, and a friend wish to see him immediately. Important!"

The sergeant went.

In a minute or so de Bourrienne himself came to the door. He looked none too pleased.

"Ah, good day to you, Herr Nolte." He bowed in a perfunctory way at his introduction to Anthony.

"General Bonaparte is asleep now," he said. "And if you have come up from Paris to worry him about the rate on the funding of that next advance on rentes I advise you to return to Paris before he wakes. He gave Ouvrard himself a bad half hour over that only Monday last. Surely you must know it. He will certainly recollect you, and——"

Vincent interrupted him.

"It is something entirely personal, a military matter, not financial at all. And I have no doubt, monsieur, you can yourself aid us, if you only will, without annoying General Bonaparte. In short, we have been outraged and I come to you for redress."

"Tiens," said the secretary looking much relieved.

"That is different. Come in. Orderly, chairs. Will you excuse me for a while, messieurs? You see I am vitally engaged for the moment. The first consul wakes"—he drew out his watch—"in fifteen minutes." He sighed a little and wiped his brow. Vincent and Anthony sat watching the scene before them with great interest.

In an adjoining room some staff orderlies were rapidly setting up field-desks and chairs and arranging pens and stationery. They were so precise about it that it was evidently a matter of long-standing and perfected routine. An adjutant looked in and checked every pen, ink-pot, sand-box and quire of paper. He rearranged the large chair in a better light. Two civilian clerks entered and sat down on camp stools. They sat waiting, alert, uneasy. On a large table in the main room, where Anthony and Vincent were sitting, three assistants were sorting dispatches under the watchful eye of de Bourrienne. Orderlies brought in large leather bags. The secretary broke the seals. The contents were dumped out and rapidly sorted.

"Milan and Piedmont," said de Bourrienne. "Let the others alone." His eyes and his hands flew over the contents of the spilled bags. A small pile of documents rapidly accumulated in a little green basket. The rest were seized upon by the clerks who began to endorse upon them and throw them into other leather bags hung before them.

On the small pile in the basket before him de Bourrienne began to operate. He put the letters from the Bonaparte family into a small box marked with a "B." There were several of them. Those from Lucien Bonaparte, then at Madrid, he put with the Spanish dispatches. He looked through the rest of the documents with marvellous rapidity and wrote out a description upon each. He arranged them in a certain order and put them back in the green basket.

Two couriers, who had just found the whereabouts of the first consul's headquarters, dashed up. Their dispatches were also brought in. De Bourrienne put his hand to his head and smiled at Vincent. Just then

198

Beauharnais came down the hall and looked in. "All ready?" he asked, and returned.

A minute later they heard the sound of a crisp, rapid step and the sharp click of a scabbard against a boot. Everyone in the room rose and felt as if they were runners in a race waiting for the word "go."

A short man with a head a little too large for his body entered the room. He stopped, looked. Energy radiated from him like heat from the sun. Everybody present was positively electrified by it; swept out of their own orbit into his. The force came from the head, from the eyes, and under the brows. To be suddenly faced with it in the ordinary course of life was equivalent to opening a cupboard to take down your hat and finding a cobra looking at you with its hood spread. The next move would be with the terrible head. And you knew, you felt eternally certain, that the head knew what that move would be. All action except that which it initiated was paralysed; what it once began must be followed out.

"At ease," said a high, clear voice. Someone else seemed to have spoken. The work went on; seemed only to have begun. The dispatches seemed to be sorting themselves. Bonaparte held out his hand blindly. De Bourrienne put the green basket into it. "Et, monsieur le banquier-là?" he said, looking keenly at Vincent. He did not appear to see Anthony. Nevertheless, both of them rose again and bowed. De Bourrienne murmured something they could not hear.

"Eh bien!" replied Bonaparte, and slipped into the room where the two civil clerks sat waiting. They dipped their pens. He began instantly to dictate letters.

From where he sat against the wall Anthony could see diagonally into the room opposite where Napoleon was working. He could even hear part of what he was saying and catch glimpses of him as he passed walking up and down. An intense quiet and absorption had gripped the house. All noises now came from outside except the scratching of pens, the flop of papers into bags, an occasional low-spoken direction from de Bour-rienne.

Outside the sentries paced alertly, very erect, conscious that the general was awake again. Horses stamped at pickets between the trees down the village street. Orderlies came and departed. Now and then a dusty courier dashed up with a clatter. Others left and the sound of their hoofs died away in the distance toward Paris. The long afternoon sunlight began to verge toward the close of day. The high, clear voice in the other room went on. Bonaparte also paced back and forth there like a sentry. He was dictating to the two clerks alternately.

They sat at opposite ends of the room. He passed between them, leaving a terse paragraph with each as he turned. He was dictating a letter to the newly appointed superintendent at the Ecole Militaire, prescribing certain changes in the courses of mathematics for artillery officers: ". . . those who show themselves incapable of feeling and tracing the abstractions of geometry from the models of cones and cylinders in cages which have just been supplied should be slated for the infantry. It is essential that every artillery officer in the French armies should from now on be capable of seeing the parabolas in various trajectories as physical facts. His mathematics and physics must coalesce . . ." and then his sword would gleam as he passed the door again, and Anthony heard him say to the other clerk: ". . . it is too early yet to assume openly that the newly acquired districts in Piedmont are French soil. They should still be treated merely as garrisoned districts and the local laws respected in so far as it may be convenient. In a year or so from now these districts may be incorporated in a department. In that event this matter should then be referred to . . ." and so it went on.

His head sank a little forward on his chest. His arms went behind him as he walked. Presently he went over to the green basket and began to read its contents letter by letter, but at the same time from some other portion of his mind he kept both the clerks busy. He threw the letters on the floor as he read them. He read, talked and walked on; ordering, reorganizing, building bridges, establishing schools, directing the kind of cloth to be used in women's dresses, urging on the codification of the law, repairing prisons, and confirming court-martials, arranging for the exchange of the officers captured by the British in Egypt, altering the procedure of the new tribunals to try brigands and the form of the oath to be taken by returning émigrés, refusing Mme. de Staël permission to return to Paris, dictating the movements of the returning columns of troops from the Rhine. New clerks stepped in and took the places of those worn out. The voice continued rapidly, smoothly, tersely, inevitably, bringing order out of chaos, hope and energy out of despair, changing the history of the world.

Trying in vain to keep up with him, the indefatigable de Bourrienne and the secretariat about the table toiled on and said nothing. They were engulfed. Napoleon had slept for half an hour previously. He went to sleep instantly and he woke as if he had just been re-immersed in the source of energy. He awoke with a mind as clear as spring water but as incisive as acid. But it was deep and wide as well as limpid. In it an entire epoch as it was on any particular day was poised just upon the verge of becoming something else; was held in suspension; every part of it generally and particularly from armies to individual corporals, from cities to houses and roads seen clearly, understood and in process of being manipulated by a will that had not yet become merely the habit of ego, by a body not yet the host for cancer. For the next four years the first consul and emperor continued to wear out relays of ministers and staffs of generals without a sign of fatigue. He first charged France with his energy and then exhausted it. Nothing on earth had been seen like it since the days of Julius Caesar.

The scene before them was so charged with the vital atmosphere of time in the making that Anthony and Vincent felt themselves to be participating in it directly

201

and waited for de Bourrienne without remarking that he was keeping them doing so. In Anthony's mind the constant appearance and reappearance of Napoleon pacing across the space of the half-open door of the opposite room became synchronized until Bonaparte appeared to be nothing but the pendulum and governing instrument of the machine in motion all about him. Although the impression was only a half-conscious one at the time, it was nevertheless the deepest and the most lasting that Anthony carried away with him. It was with a start of surprise that they saw de Bourrienne break off and begin to cross the room toward them with the evident intention of hearing Vincent's complaint. The secretary drew up a chair and sat on the arm of it swinging one leg over the other.

"Believe me, messieurs, I am delighted to have the excuse for an interruption. For five days and two nights now in half a dozen villages"—he wiped his face with his handkerchief—"this has gone on. But I hope you have not had a serious misfortune." He looked at Vincent, who rapidly related his troubles with considerable eloquence and heat.

"Most exasperating and a piece of unwarranted, petty spite," said de Bourrienne. "But it will be somewhat difficult for me to do anything about it directly. I can issue no military orders, you know. I am only the general's secretary. But I tell you what I will do. I can send in a memorandum about this occurrence among the papers that go in to be signed in a few minutes. In that case he may ask to see you personally, Herr Nolte, and he is not very fond of you bankers as you know. Do you care to risk it?"

Vincent nodded. "Decidedly," he said.

"Very well then." Taking a pad on his knee, de Bourrienne wrote rapidly. "Will that cover the facts?" He read the note.

"Quite. Only the major's name is Luçay, not Lacey," said Vincent.

"Thanks for that correction. Names that go in there

202

must be right. Luçay? Luçay?—where have I heard that name before?"

"With Carrier at Nantes, they say."

"That may help you." He scribbled something more on the memorandum. "Confidentially, we are weeding out the 'friends of the people,' you know. Well, wait. It will not be long. I wish you luck."

He went back to his work but then looked up suddenly and said, "Do me the honour of remaining for dinner this evening, messieurs. Pardon my preoccupation. I should have asked you before. It will not be much to boast of, a military mess. But there may be amusing talk."

They accepted with delight.

"Your papers go in shortly now," said de Bourrienne, and went on again.

"Will Bonaparte be at our table, do you suppose, Vincent?" asked Anthony.

"Hardly, de Bourrienne and his civil assistants probably mess alone on these inspection tours. He is much liked, you know. Very friendly. You may be surprised to hear that he has dined with me at my hôtel twice. Ah, wait till you see that place, Toni! But there go our papers."

The voice in the room had ceased. De Bourrienne had immediately sent in the bundle of papers to be signed. He knew better than to lose an instant. Napoleon sat at his desk now. His pen flew in that indecipherable scrawl which was already his signature. He stopped. He was reading a brief memorandum in the clear hand of his secretary.

"General: The notorious Jacobin Luçay is at Château-Thierry. 'Major.' Army of the Rhine . . . fomenting discontent . . . merciless requisitions . . . M. Nolte and friend robbed of horses and driver . . . requests immediate return. Proceeding to Paris on business of rentes with Ouvrard and M. Talleyrand."

"Luçay? Luçay? Ah—that red-moustached scoundrel of the Noyades, who tried to interfere with my emplacements at Toulon. What is he doing at Château-

Thierry? That *is* curious. He used to be in the artillery."

He scrawled an order and gave it to an orderly. He gathered up the signed papers and came out. He stopped to say something to de Bourrienne when his eyes fell again on Vincent and Anthony. He came over to them and they both rose. He was looking at Vincent.

"Well, monsieur le banquier, I have sent for your man and beasts. Also for the person who detained them. When he arrives we shall see. You *are* M. Nolte, aren't you?"

Vincent bowed.

"Ah, yes, I thought I remembered you and M. Ouvrard together one day about the Mexican bullion and treasury drafts. So! You see I seldom forget. That was a year ago, wasn't it?" He seemed to take great satisfaction in this.

"Your remarkable memory for names and faces is famous, mon général," said Vincent. Napoleon looked pleased.

"It is inconvenient to some people. Well, have you succeeded in getting any more Mexican dollars? No? About to—bien! I must talk to you after dinner about it. Bourrienne—" He looked at his secretary. "Good, you have already been asked. My Bourrienne often anticipates me. A rare quality. He does not abuse it." He glared at them suddenly. "I have found, M. Nolte, that you bankers frequently do. You are a sad lot, you buzzards that follow my eagles. Do you suppose I do not know what a fine thing your friend Ouvrard has made out of his army contracts? And now it is supplies for the Spanish fleet. Mon Dieu! I am going to dust some of the crumbs off him. Tell him so." Bonaparte folded his hands behind his back and looked up at Vincent and Anthony who towered above him like a couple of ostriches over a bantam eagle. He suddenly became aware that the room must be secretly amused by this, and hopped up on the table where he sat cross-legged with his sword over his knees. He felt his short stature keenly at times. It was one of the things that forever drove him to lengthen his shadow.

"I should regret being made the messenger of ill-will between two of the ablest spirits of the age," replied Vincent.

"I am not sure I can accept your compliment on the basis of that comparison, M. Nolte," said Bonaparte, taking up an ivory ruler and beginning to tap one boot sharply. "It implies at once too much and too little. What do you think?"

"Both General Bonaparte and M. Ouvrard are masters in their own fields. That your own genius embraces and includes that of M. Ouvrard he would be the first to admit. It is for that reason I feel your message might carry a too devastating criticism. M. Ouvrard, as well as M. Bourrienne here, has faithfully anticipated your desires upon occasions. I am sure he looks forward to being able to continue doing so." Vincent smiled engagingly.

Napoleon was not displeased. He distinguished instantly between respect and servility. "Well, we meet upon common ground at least, M. Nolte," he said. "No, you do not give way. It would seem that your interest in your friends is not entirely expressed by percentage. That does you credit. Let us admit then, I do not know M. Ouvrard in the same way that you do. Quel dommage! *Like* my good Bourrienne, you say, M. Ouvrard anticipates my desires. I reply—not without his *own* 'anticipations,' and I understand they are always negotiable. Come, you must admit there is a difference in their motives."

By now the entire room was listening with ill-concealed curiosity. Napoleon's love of baiting bankers was notorious and well appreciated. He was now merely relaxing himself after a strenuous day's work, and it was all the more amusing to him that with a certain mischievous maliciousness he had been able to entangle in an invidious and damaging comparison the name of the greatest financier in France and that of his sensitive secretary who was present. Hearing his own name mentioned several times, de Bourrienne could not help but follow the argument, and he was now only pretending to write with his face burning. Napoleon looked at him and chuckled inwardly.

The little man seated on the table bending the ivory ruler across his knee was intensely pleased in his own curious way. He never laughed heartily. He seldom smiled. His sense of wit and humour was caustic and brazen. Even his lighter moments such as the present one resembled a rapidly spreading patch of verdigris on polished bronze. He had now succeeded in making everyone in the room thoroughly uncomfortable. He had placed one Herr Nolte, banquier, in the uncomfortable dilemma of denying an influential friend or of traducing M. de Bourrienne in his own presence. Meanwhile, he, Napoleon Bonaparte, remained the centre of all this uncomfortable attention and was perfectly at ease. He now smiled and bent the ruler on his knee till it appeared ready to snap.

"Come, M. Nolte, what have you got to reply to that?"

"The motives of both gentlemen in serving, Your Excellency, must be correct," replied Vincent, who was tired of being sport at another's game and wished to have done with it.

"Oh, you merely evade me? I shall ask your very tall friend here, then? Or is he too a banquier? Do not be embarrassed, my Bourrienne," he cried, turning half-way about. "What is there to blush about? Je suis sûr que ce généreux monsieur la vous fera la grande justice!"—he let one end of his ruler flip pointing straight at Anthony and looked at him. "Well, monsieur?"

"M. de Bourrienne, I am sure, mon général, does not feel any embarrassment at having his motives for serving you discussed openly. It is only your great confidence in him which so affects him."

"Present this gentleman to me, Bourrienne. Upon my word he deserves it of you," said Napoleon.

There was a general relief at this end to so uncomfortable a verbal skirmish. De Bourrienne and Vincent now withdrew a little and talked in low tones. The clerks, at a nod from the secretary, departed, leaving only the orderlies on a bench in the corner. It was only a short time till the mess would be served and work was suspended.

"This is the only hour when the general permits himself a little leisure," whispered de Bourrienne to Vincent. "I can tell you it is a boon to his staff. But I am afraid your friend is in for a good quizzing, by the signs. The general's method is to squeeze the last drop of information out of anyone who looks interesting and then leave him like a dry sponge. But you have doubtless experienced being cross-questioned by him yourself. Let's go over and sit down a while. I am still waiting for a courier. I hope your horses do come tonight. With the staff quartered in the village, there will not be even a garret room." They sat down, Vincent congratulating himself that he was not in Anthony's shoes.

For Bonaparte was now standing immediately opposite Anthony looking up at him quizzically, his legs apart and clasping the ruler behind his back. It was so much like a big boy being called up by a little schoolmaster that de Bourrienne and Vincent were both forced to stifle a smile that neither wished the other to see.

"Disembarrass me of your height, monsieur," said Bonaparte pointing to a chair. He sat down himself with his boots stretched out before him, looking at the toes. "I have seen you before, I think," he continued without lifting his eyes. "You are very tall. Are you an Englishman?" He looked up now.

"From Livorno," replied Anthony.

"Yes! You were standing there once in a window looking down at me. Beside you was a man with the face of a fanatic."

"That is so, mon général," said Anthony, obviously amazed.

"Fanatical faces in upper windows within easy pistol shot of my carriage are always impressive to me, monsieur. Like M. Fouché, I have the habit of spotting and remembering them."

"I am not a fanatic, mon général. And neither Your Excellency nor your minister of police has any cause to remember me," said Anthony, making no effort to cover his anger.

"You mistake me, M. Adverse. I did not say *you* had the face of a fanatic. What has become of the man who did?"

"He shot himself—recently."

"Bien, such fellows are bound to shoot somebody. In this case both wisdom and determination seem to have pulled the trigger together. So you are from Livorno?"

"Si."

"Did the clothes you are wearing now originate there, too?" asked the little soldier quietly and in Italian. He continued to study the toes of his boot.

"No."

"Where?"

"In Gibraltar. Nevertheless, General Bonaparte, I am *not* an Englishman," insisted Anthony in undoubted "Livornese."

They continued for some time in Italian. Bonaparte was soon satisfied on that point. It was not a conversation but a series of interminable questions from the little general in whom Anthony now recognized the typical insatiable curiosity of an Italian islander displayed on a cosmic scale. Certainly the grilling was as severe a one as he ever underwent. Now that Napoleon's Anglophobia was laid aside, there was no longer apparent any point or direction in his curiosity. It simply spread out over the map. It demanded to know what was going on everywhere Anthony had been—and how. There was obviously no malice in it, Anthony recognized. He soon saw that Bonaparte felt he was conferring an honour in using him as a human textbook, manifestly to be thrown aside when the information should be exhausted or prove dull. Indeed, he now found some amusement himself in what took on the form of a game of knowledge, and on that basis, a ghost of a smile passed between them. Nor could he help but appreciate the keenness of the questions as he felt the quality of his personality as well as endless facts being brought out by his replies. Perhaps that was what Bonaparte was after. He was always interested in and looking for men. Or perhaps he was only curious as usual, or amused. Anthony could never be sure. All that he knew was that the quiet, incisive questioning went on till he felt wrung dry.

Napoleon was insatiable about conditions at Gibraltar, but not more so than about Havana. The predicament of the Spanish governors-general of Cuba amused him. "Go on," he said, "tell me—" and he propounded a string of questions. "I thought so," he replied. "And so you found yourself in Africa. On the Rio Pongo? Where is that?" "For ten minutes one would have thought he intended establishing his capital there," said Anthony to Vincent afterward. "I found that I knew more about Africa than I thought. It is a curious thing, Vincent, to have another man's will reach out and force you to remember things you did not know you knew."

"Eh bien," said the insatiable little man finally, after at last permitting Anthony to talk himself for some time about trade in Africa. "Good—I see you are a man of affairs and business. Neither of us is entirely the fool of circumstance then. That is much. Yes, it is something to achieve anything; to make a thought become tangible. With most men it dies in 'I think' or 'I say.' How difficult to combine *I think* and *I do*. Thought in action—that is to be like God." He tapped his boot with the ruler, seeming rather to have spoken to himself. Then he leaned forward almost violently.

"That is why I do not like bankers," he exploded in Anthony's face. "And in another hundred years if I do not stop them they will own Europe—the world. Financiers cannot act. They never *do* anything. They are passive, they spin webs and every wind, blow peace blow war, brings them flies. They are not the fit repositories for power. What is the use of a power that forever keeps still? A powerful oyster, hard outside and jelly within. An oyster cannot act, move—GO!"

209

He leapt to his feet and swung about with the same motion. He stood listening with his back turned, while the last word he had uttered still rang in Anthony's ears with the force of gunpowder.

Anthony sat looking up at him. He felt as if he had been given a ride on the outer ring of Saturn and flung off into space.

Napoleon was listening to the sound of a horse at full gallop coming down the Paris road.

"From London, Bourrienne," he said. "Yes, I am sure." He folded his arms and waited.

And it was thus that Anthony always remembered him, standing there, alive, the bronze forehead touched by a pencil of sunlight. The motes in it seemed to be streaming out of him into the room.

———————————

"You will excuse me, I am sure," said de Bourrienne, glancing at them significantly. "Here, Jancey," he called down the corridor. "Look after the general's friends." A grey-haired clerk in staid, black clothes led them through the house and out onto the lawn behind it. The Paris road ran along one side of the space and on the other the turf slipped down easily to the river. Under a number of horse-chestnut trees, towers of molten gold in the late October afternoon, the orderlies and mess attendants were laying several long tables with white cloths.

A fat young officer hurried over to meet them.

"Your names and ranks, messieurs, if you please," said he. "I am the adjutant of the mess and must seat you. Have you servants? I could use them."

"Unfortunately, no," laughed Anthony.

"Detained for the cavalry by a major at Château-Thierry," grumbled Vincent.

"Oui? That is too bad." He reeled a little. "But it is gay here, isn't it?" he cried. "I have had them set the tables under the trees. A remarkable autumn to be able to do that. Warm and dry. But—nom d'un chien!—

210

what should we care about the weather? One of the carriages of M. Cambacérès has just arrived here, a little too far ahead of him. It was loaded with good burgundy. What could a good mess officer do?" He steadied himself. "Come, confirm me in my opinion—about the weather." He led them to a small rear room of the house piled with baskets of wine.

"You see I *am* a mess officer. I like it. I would rather be that than a general of division." With his tongue in his cheek, he poured out of one of the second consul's cherished bottles, a dark purple wine that filled the little room with an inspiring bouquet. "*Um-m-m,* yes, it is gay here," he insisted, looking out the window at the scene beyond. "An incomparable lawn, little birds singing their hearts out in the sunlight"—he gulped the glass—"oh, how ravishing the country is; nom du petit Jésus! for nearly a week now I have not seen a woman without sabots, but courage, tomorrow we shall be in Paris. I contain myself therefore, and—I contain a good deal. Just now I contain four bottles of the excellent wine provided by M. Cambacérès, the second consul of the Republic.

"Encore? Oui! I insist. I am, I tell you, the mess officer. The wine of the second consul. Le gros, le beau, the innocent and sensible M. Cambacérès who understands what government is about. To the second consul —and your good health. The first consul, he drives about inspecting, winning battles. Making people do things. All are uncomfortable wherever he passes—everywhere. Suddenly this afternoon at the third bottle I see it. I, the mess officer, have my vision enlarged to proportions *co-co-co*lossal. I see,—what do I see? In the front of this house the first consul of the Republic conducting what he thinks is the government. Is it? What is behind it? Why, this!" he cried, running up and down now, keeping his hands on the table. "This!" he kicked, and one of his boots came off. *"This!"* and this time he finally kicked open the door which he had been aiming at. "Voilà," he shouted. "Voilà la vraie France qui persiste toujours." Caldrons of soup, long loaves, piles of roasted fowls, and salads greeted their eyes and a general reek of savoury steam and odours drifted out to them from the little kitchen where all was a scene of confusion, the several headquarters chefs stumbling over one another in their haste in a kitchen meant for a small civil family. The little officer leaned in and laughed.

"Is it that progress advances itself in here, mes enfants?" said he to the cooks.

He stood for a while in the entrance with one boot in his hand, hopping about like a fat duck. The cooks roared at him and shut the door. He had been drunk ever since M. Cambacérès' carriage of wine had arrived.

"Come, messieurs, come. I still want to show you my view of things. My view of politics. Messieurs, I insist upon it. No, it will not be necessary for you to take one boot off. Not at all. One merely returns to the lawn. One *throws* one's boot and follows it." It went smashing through the window. "Voilà! Maintenant!" He led them outdoors, and placing his feet wide apart, suddenly ducked his head down and looked through his legs at the men setting the mess tables under the trees.

"That is what the government is really about. All governments." He was holding onto his own fat legs now, patting them with satisfaction, while he continued to gaze upside down and purple in the face at the scene behind him.

"Take my view of it, but for an instant. It is revealing. I *insist*. From here the yellow leaves on the ground under the white tables . . . *beautiful* . . . someone has been tossing gold about there. I will roar if you do not look—my way."

There was no getting out of it. Either they had to take the mess officer's view of things or he would undoubtedly "roar." And then—they would be found there. It would be ridiculous—and they would be able to explain it only by laughing; by laughing as they were now.

So they bent down and looked. Three of them in a

line. Their hats dropped to the grass and their hair hung into them. The mess officer made appreciative noises.

And it was in that position that Aristide found them, coming suddenly around the corner with the chief clerk of M. de Bourrienne in his sober black suit.

"Voilà!" said the old man. "But what is it that it is?"

They rose scarlet-faced. "Here is your servant, messieurs," said the grey-haired clerk sadly, backing off a little with his eyes large and round.

Aristide sat down on the step and began to hold his ribs while they shook him. The old clerk looked on scandalized.

"I shall report this. I shall report you, M. Latour, you the adjutant of the general's mess, to M. de Bourrienne. You have seduced the guests of the first consul."

"Pas du tout, pas du tout," insisted Latour. "Come, Jancey, you sad old Huguenot. Take my view of things." He started for the old man, who fled.

Latour, Vincent, Anthony, and Aristide remained beating one another on the back.

"Encore une autre," cried Latour, staggering a little. He led the way back to the little room beside the kitchen.

In another room at the front of the house Napoleon and de Bourrienne were reading the London dispatches which the courier had just brought. The news was incredibly good. The preliminaries of peace had been signed, and the British ministry had agreed to concessions which had been advanced only as diplomatic demands. France was to regain her lost colonies.

"This is the greatest victory of all, mon Bourrienne," said Napoleon. "The empire which the Bourbons lost I shall regain—these colonies from England, and Louisiana from Spain—all in a year. It is incredible. Dealing with this ministry is not like dealing with Pitt. Let them keep Malta. I will quarrel with them over that later. Give me a five years' peace to raise armies—and then—" He

213

began to stride up and down the room, his feet winged with triumph. Nothing could stand before him now. He felt exalted above all that had gone before. The lowly steps that descended into the past—incredible that he should have ever had to traverse them. A vast imperial staircase led into the future. At the top, still distant, exalted, stood a figure of himself crowned with laurel. Up and down the stairs crawled a host of ants that had once been men. He wiped his feet on the carpet and laughed.

"The major Luçay reports himself," announced an orderly.

Bonaparte looked at the man but did not see him. He was planning the next step on the staircase. "These fools on the Tribunate shall be silenced. One law—and one will to enforce that law. A broom for the ants in opposition. Cambacérès must force on the code. Le code Napoléon." A fat, lazy fellow the second consul. Pliable—but slow. They were all so slow. Some would not move at all. For the immovables—a hypodermic injection of lead. He smiled, more arrogantly than a few hours before. . . . This peace with England—who would have thought it possible on such terms? They must be in a bad way across the Channel. The continental system was ruining them. No more imports from England. People would have to do without tea—and sugar. Surely patriotism should be able to do without tea. Besides, those who had their feet on imperial stairways were not likely to trip over teapots. No, no, Austria was the next hazardous step. Next time he would crush her. . . . He clenched his fist and looked out the window.

Brother Joseph, a little fatter than he used to be, had just driven up and was climbing out of his chaise. A bourgeois Italian. It reminded Napoleon of Ajaccio. The biggest merchant in the town—eating an orange under an awning—or the most prosperous country gentleman near by. My God—he wanted to put a crown on that head. If he could only get the family to live up to him. Joseph couldn't even be taught to look

214

stiff-necked under a fashionable hat. He looked a little uncomfortable now—from the neck up. An umbrella, eh! And it was the driest autumn in years. He wasn't going to give it to young Beauharnais—was he? Le parapluie du frère de l'empereur se présente à l'adjutant du staff. He could see it in the *Moniteur* for a few years ahead. That kind of thing could undo the crossing of the Alps. Bon Dieu! He *was* giving it to Beauharnais! Josephine was right. This kind of thing must be stopped. He rushed out.

"Joseph!"

"Napoleon, mon frère, congratulations. Didn't I tell you if you would write to M. Fox it would turn the trick? And now he is coming to see you, you the friend of liberty. Now we can all settle down in France safely." He kissed Napoleon on both cheeks. Beauharnais stood by at attention holding the umbrella over his arm.

The greatest man since Julius Caesar stood at the door of the little house in Nogent perspiring. He had just been defeated. In the presence of his invincible elder brother a curious lethargy came over him—always. Joseph had only to appear and Napoleon was little brother again.

"Come in," he said. "I am glad to see you. Give your hat to Beauharnais, too." There was some comfort in making Josephine's relatives realize who the Bonapartes were anyway.

"Damn them," said Beauharnais as he hung Joseph's dusty hat and umbrella on a peg in the little hall. He shoved the hat sidewise and went out to drink with Latour. He found the party in the little room was very merry.

Napoleon, Joseph, and Bourrienne did not even notice Luçay although he had stood up as they passed through.

He sat down again fuming as the door closed behind them. The aristocrats were coming back. But who was this little Corsican general to keep a patriot waiting? "Luçay, friend of the people of France," Marat had

215

called him that once. He remembered it. He sat cursing the work of time.

The mess bugles shattered his bloody reverie. Bonaparte came through the door.

"Oui, il faut manger," Joseph was saying with an air of great wisdom.

"Good evening, citizen-general," said Luçay rising in his dishevelled uniform and scraggly moustache like an apparition of the past before Napoleon. The old official title, now tacitly disregarded by all who were wise enough to do so, grated dreadfully on Napoleon's ears. "Citizen-general—" and he had probably just signed a peace with England. Who was this fool? His eyes took in the sans-culotte major hastily.

"Luçay—M. Nolte's horses," whispered Bourrienne.

"What are you doing at Château-Thierry, Luçay?"

"I and my veterans were ordered there to round up recruits by one of the aristocrats on your staff, citizen-general. Otherwise we should now be being paid off in Paris, I suppose. That is *if* the citizen-general is really going to pay the Army of the Rhine." He smiled slowly.

"And so you enforce the law by taking a pair of good horses from a fat German banker, *citizen-major*."

"Yes, for the Republic, citizen-general."

"No, for the republican Luçay. For his farm to which he returns like Cincinnatus to plough after the wars— on land also furnished by the aristocrats. Is it not so, *citizen-major?*" They stood looking at each other. Luçay's eyes were glaring.

"Well," said Napoleon at last, "you may keep the land. *I* have guaranteed that."

"Tyrant, to think I have lived to serve you!"

"Do not let that trouble you, *citizen*," said Napoleon. "Give me your sword. Take it, Joseph."

On the way through the hall Joseph Bonaparte hung the sword of the friend of the people on the same peg with his own hat and umbrella. Napoleon smiled. He felt a sudden appetite for supper as a burst of talk floated in from the lawn. The staff, both military and civil, were already waiting for him about the tables. They all stood silent as he took his place.

"Begin," said he, and sat down abruptly.

Anthony and Vincent were sitting at de Bourrienne's table. The meal began dully enough. After the time they had spent drinking with Latour and Beauharnais in the little room, sitting out in the twilight with the rather silent company assembled under the trees seemed flat by contrast. Napoleon and Joseph Bonaparte were some little distance away at another table and confined their remarks to each other. De Bourrienne was tired and said little. Most of the others at the table were under-secretaries and clerks. The sound of faint conversation, an occasional laugh, the sunset jargon of birds and the voice of the evening wind through the branches above gave a certain low-toned solemnity to the occasion. A row of heads along the street wall, where the population of Nogent had gathered to watch the first consul eat, began to drift away.

All this was changed, however, before the second course was laid.

A great coach accompanied by a small escort of cavalry came rumbling up the Paris road. A trumpet burst out. Everyone started laughing. A cheer went up from the street.

"Voilà," said Latour, stooping down as he hurried past toward the gate. "The real government has arrived. Now you will see."

The coach came in and drove ruthlessly across the lawn. It stopped not far from where they were sitting. In it sat a man of great amplitude in all his proportions. A wide, cocked hat nodding with red, white, and blue plumes perched a little awry on his forehead. The plumes nodded and curved over his large, beaming face like flames. The coach shook and leaned as he got down out of the door with some difficulty, disclosing as he did so lacquered half-boots with gold tassels, a wide expanse of white breeches, smooth and tight as a sail in a gale. Then his tremendous tricolour sash appeared and above it a blue coat embroidered with golden laurel leaves that climbed up into the points of a monstrous high collar—as he finally disentangled his broad shoulders from the coach and stood upright. He was not fat. He was well proportioned. He was simply vast. And he stood there in the sunset with his plumes waving above him like a Gargantuan specimen of the Gallic cock about to crow. The crowd along the wall cheered. Some of them thought that Bonaparte had just arrived.

"Cambacérès, the second consul—" said one of the clerks in reply to Anthony's glance of inquiry.

"It may be an amusing evening after all," de Bourrienne confided to Vincent.

Everybody, even Napoleon, was already looking pleased. Cambacérès hurried across the lawn to Bonaparte's table where room was hastily made for him and a young man who accompanied him. Two chairs were brought. But only one of them, that for Cambacérès himself, was set at the first consul's table. They saw Cambacérès presenting his young friend to Napoleon, who was apparently none too pleased to see him, for he called out to Latour and coolly directed him to seat the newcomer at another table.

The rejected guest was brought across to de Bourrienne who received him with some embarrassment but kindly enough. A place was found for him next to Vincent and directly across from Anthony.

"Permit me to introduce myself, monsieur," said he, his voice trembling slightly. "I am M. de Staël. I trust none of your clerks, M. de Bourrienne, will be troubled by my presence." He added this bitterly. The colour raged into his cheeks again. Napoleon's affront had evidently been a bitter one. De Bourrienne hastened to introduce Vincent and Anthony and to engage young de Staël in conversation. He responded gratefully and with evident relief, but a cloud passed over his face from time to time as he glanced at the consular table.

Anthony thought he had never seen so completely

civilized-looking a person as the youth who now sat opposite him. Young de Staël's easy gestures, and the gentle tones of his voice, his exquisite costume, and his animated but powerful expression all conveyed a peculiarly memorable effect. His features were not regular or handsome according to any usual standard. He was simply and quietly distinguished, charming and satisfactory without exerting himself. Of all those at the headquarters mess that evening, not excluding Bonaparte himself, de Staël was the only person whom Anthony truly envied. Indeed, he already felt indignant with Napoleon for having rebuffed him; in sympathy with his cause—whatever it might be.

Vincent, de Bourrienne, and de Staël were soon engaged in talk. Jancey, the grey-haired clerk, next to whom Anthony was seated, had little to say. He still looked upon Anthony with disgust and made no bones about it. His expression resembled that of Mrs. Jorham when she was looking at the cathedral in Havana, Anthony thought; sour and not a little suspicious. Nevertheless, although he was forced to sit silent, he was soon aware of a subtle change in the whole atmosphere of the occasion.

It emanated from Cambacérès. At the first consul's table a great deal of laughter and loud talk was now going on. Cambacérès had come to congratulate Napoleon on the peace and to bring him the details of the negotiations. The news of the occasion spread from table to table and magnified by rumour was soon all over the place, among the guards, and out in the village.

Napoleon sat in the centre of all this flattered into good humour by the incense offered him by his good-humoured colleague; content to sit, as he liked best to do, the apparently indifferent cause that radiated success. Even in the garden of the simple house of the horse-leech at Nogent, where he had chosen to quarter himself, he was the centre of glory. And it was the second consul's intention to heighten that effect. It was not mere flattery that led Cambacérès to do this. True, it might pay. But the future arch-chancellor of the empire took a peculiar pleasure in being a sort of horn of plenty for the government; in extolling the first consul by distributing good cheer in the form of diplomatic dinners, official feasts to functionaries, and popular carousals. It was all there was left under the Constitution for the second consul to do. It suited his nature, and he did it well. There was an unexpressed understanding between himself and the first consul about it. Tonight if the first consul of the Republic was bestowing peace, Cambacérès as his colleague had come up from Paris to see that plenty should accompany it.

Four apparently empty post-chaises that had followed him now began to be unloaded. They contained innumerable packages prepared by Beauvilliers, the Parisian restaurateur. Cambacérès sent for Latour and amid much raillery forced him to discover the whereabouts of the wine which had arrived "dangerously early." Bottles of the excellent vintage which Vincent and Anthony had already sampled were now distributed to all. The simple fare already prepared by Latour's cooks for the headquarters was sent to the guards, who at some little distance away gathered about the camp fires along the river and began to sing and cheer. Cressets were lit. The scene became brilliant.

The scarlet-and-blue uniforms of the mess attendants moved about in the red glare of torches. They were bringing dishes from the deceptively empty-looking post-chaises to the long staff tables under the horse-chestnut trees. The yellow leaves drifted down and lay upon the white cloths about which the gilded and booted staff of the first consul of the French Republic jangled spurs, flashed epaulettes, and held up glasses of the excellent burgundy of the popular M. Cambacérès like so many rows of rubies in the torchlight.

"To the health of the first consul." Napoleon had replied with "Glory and prosperity to France." It was his only active part in the proceedings of the evening which was now obviously handed over to Cambacérès. Napoleon even sat a little apart under the largest tree with his chin on his hand, looking on. In his simple uniform and plain sword over his knees he stood out with startling contrast to the all but weird variety of the brilliant uniforms of his staff. The expression on his face did not change at all. Only his eyes moved.

He did not laugh over the English Goose, "cooked for the occasion," which was produced as the grand finale from the now genuinely empty chaises, nor applaud a really apt reply to Cambacérès made by brother Joseph. He merely sent for his cloak as it grew cool.

Anthony sat watching him from the "civil table" of M. de Bourrienne, where the secretaries sat, which was somewhat withdrawn from the others amid the shadows. All there felt themselves to be spectators and had now for some time said nothing to one another. De Bourrienne had accepted a cigar that glowed in the gathering darkness. Along the wall most of the town was gathered to watch the first consul eating, as only a generation before it had once gathered in the same place to see the king of France and Navarre dine hastily under the same trees on his way to Rheims. Hearing the news of the peace, the little mayor of Nogent came to offer his congratulations. He was received by Bonaparte and sent to one of the tables, where he and his sashed assistant fared well. Undoubtedly peace was a good thing and the first consul the saviour of France, if one took a mess officer's view of the situation.

"Didn't I tell you?" whispered Latour as he passed Anthony once. "M. Cambacérès knows what it is all about." He tripped happily on. This was the only "after dinner conversation" that came Anthony's way that evening. Vincent, de Staël, and de Bourrienne were now silent. Jancey had turned his glass down and gone in to write. The whole affair was suddenly terminated unexpectedly. Cambacérès held a surprise, however, to the last. He had brought some fireworks from Paris.

A burst of rockets soared over the river to the delight of all those watching along the wall, and as a finale a large "N" framed in burning laurel contrived to float for some time in the air and reflect itself in the water. This brought an acclamation from the soldiers encamped along the Marne and from everybody else—except young de Staël—and the ex-major Luçay, who with the citizens of Nogent had been watching the rejoicings from the street. He now turned away, his heart full of dark imaginings, to ride off with a burning "N" in his brain.

Napoleon had been visibly pleased by the "N." He now left his chair to go in, and the groups around the tables scattered.

"Come in," said de Bourrienne. "There will probably be a brief conversation this evening in the house. And the first consul, M. Adverse, wants you to talk with M. Cambacérès about Africa. Please recollect to do so. Cambacérès, you see, is responsible for the African Company which has just been renewed."

"I shall consider myself included as the second consul's guest," said young de Staël.

"As you will, monsieur," replied de Bourrienne, and they went in.

Anthony found himself left alone with de Staël as they crossed the lawn towards the door of the now brilliantly lighted, little house.

"You and Herr Nolte have had a rather strenuous crossing of the Alps, I hear," he said. "He has been telling me about it. Would you recommend the Simplon route?"

The others had hastened to separate themselves from de Staël in so marked a way that he could not but notice it.

"In another year the new road will be . . ." began Anthony.

"Do not let me embarrass you, M. Adverse," said the young man suddenly. "It will perhaps be better if you do not permit Bonaparte to see us together." He stopped by the threshold looking proudly miserable. The others had already entered.

"I do not know what differences you and General Bonaparte may have, monsieur," said Anthony, "but I shall be glad of your company now or upon any other occasion."

De Staël looked at him gratefully.

"I have come to request General Bonaparte to grant my mother permission to return to Paris. I am afraid it is useless. She is a woman whom he hates. But I shall persist," he said simply.

Anthony had never heard of Mme. de Staël, but he wished her son's mission might be successful and said so. They walked down the little hall and entered together the front room of the house from which a hum of voices proceeded.

The dispatch tables had been pushed back against the wall. Napoleon sat in a chair by the fireplace with his boots resting on the empty grate and his cloak still wrapped about him. He looked sallow and cold beside the ruddy Cambacérès standing with his plumes almost brushing the ceiling.

Bourrienne, Vincent, Beauharnais, and a number of staff officers were seated about talking in low tones. The gathering had about it the feeling of being only temporary; about to break up and go to bed. Everyone except Cambacérès looked tired. From the look of headquarters that evening anyone might have supposed a dull, minor campaign to have been finished and the staff to be returning home. A lackey in plain livery who passed about some coffee and rum was the only mark of state.

"These inspection tours are not without their compensation," Anthony heard de Bourrienne remarking to Vincent as he came in. "It is a relief from the formalities of the Tuileries"—but his attention was instantly transferred to the two consuls.

"*But,*" Cambacérès was protesting to Bonaparte, "if you expect me to give state dinners and to entertain for the government, you must permit me to import civilized delicacies. One must have sugar, and it does not grow in France. Where do you suppose the nougat came from tonight? It's no scandal. Smuggling is now universal. I must have those fellows released. The prefect at Boulogne must be instructed. Every ambassador has this privilege . . ."

"Manage it then," said Napoleon. "In your case I acquiesce, but reluctantly. British trade must be struck down. I am afraid you as my colleague set a sorry example. But there is a gentleman I want you to talk to." He motioned toward Anthony. "He can really tell you something about the African project. I have questioned him myself. Does the company advance?" Cambacérès shook his head. "Like the codification of the law, I suppose. You must get on, mon Cambacérès, get on," he cried impatiently. "Monsieur, you—" he said pointing to Anthony. "Present him, Bourrienne, present him. Come here, M. de Staël, I wish to speak with you now."

The weary de Bourrienne presented Anthony to Cambacérès. But it was impossible for them to start a conversation just then. The room had suddenly grown quiet. Everybody was listening to the high, clear tones of the first consul. He had now turned about in his chair and was leaning back addressing young de Staël, who stood before him with a natural ease and quiet carriage that seemed in some sort to have recommended him. For Napoleon's voice was less harsh than at first.

"—far from annoying me, monsieur, your frankness has pleased me. I like to see a son plead the cause of his mother. You are young; if you had my experience you would judge of things better. I shall even explain myself. Nevertheless. I do not wish to rouse in you any false hopes. It is impossible that I should permit Mme. de Staël to return to Paris. I do not want women about who make themselves men, any more than I want men who render themselves effeminate. What use is unusual intellectual attainment in women? What has it always been? Vagabondism of the imagination. To what does it lead?—nothing. It is but the metaphysics of sentiment. I do not say your mother is deliberately a mischievous woman; I say she has that effect. She has a mind; she has too much, perhaps. But it is a mind insubordinate and without curb. She was brought up in the chaos of a crumbling order and a revolution. She amalgamates all that disorder and she might become dangerous. If she were repatriated she would make proselytes. I as head of the state must see to that. It would be weak of me to permit it. The greatest curse of nations is the weakness of will in the great-magistrate. The next is for him to be funny. The last and most fatal is for him to be serious and to permit others to make him seem funny. That is governmental suicide, madness. Sarcasm is the seed of anarchy. Hence, I shall not let your good mother return to Paris to become the standard of the Faubourg Saint-Germain. She would make little jokes. She would attach no importance to them, but *I do*. My government, M. de Staël, is not a joke; I take all matters seriously. I wish this to be known, and you can tell it to the world."

"But my mother wishes to see only a list of acquaintances and old friends which she will submit to the minister of police," interposed de Staël.

"Fouché, bah! He can arrest pickpockets and assassins but not ideas. No, no, my young friend, the trouble with you intellectuals is that you do not yourself understand the importance of ideas. They are like new mechanical inventions. Some are clever; most should be suppressed. Their social implications are dangerous. Their cleverness and convenience are generally seductive and illusory. Your mother lays ideas as a hen-ostrich lays eggs. She has no responsibility. I am to be left to deal with whatever hybrid hatches out—while she makes jokes in the Faubourg Saint-Germain. You underrate me, you even despise me as a man of action. Yet the philosophy of action, I say, is the greatest idea in the world. It is natural that you, the grandson of Necker, should not understand me. I am that idea, action; in me it is personified and exists in the flesh." He leaned forward now much excited and with imperial gestures.

"You have not read the last work of my grandfather," protested the young man, greatly perturbed; "in that he does you full justice. Perhaps it is the reports of his book . . ."

"I have read it from beginning to end—in two hours. Yes, he renders me pretty justice. He calls me 'the necessary man'! And according to him the first thing to do was to cut the throat of this necessary man. Why?—because he interfered with the ideas of M. Necker. Your grandfather was an idealist, a fool, an old nuisance. He was one of those theorists who judged the world by book and chart, who thinks man is an 'economic animal.' Economists are blockheads who make financial plasters to stop the running sores of the body politic. They do not even know that a nation may have a sick soul. Bankruptcy is an effect—a sign of dissolving organs. The money provided by the great M. Necker ran off like pus from the cankerous sores of France. Yes, I was necessary—indispensable, to repair all the fooleries of your grandfather; to efface the injury he has done to France. It was he who caused the Revolution.

"Now I wish you to remember this, M. de Staël. I do not address you alone but all those to whom you will return. You are still young and sensitive enough to feel when a man is sincere—even a great man. I speak for your own good as well. Remember, authority comes from God. Respect it. The reign of terror is at an end. I wish for subordination. The chaos of ideas is over. I am applying to them the solvent of action. It is only when ideas are embodied in force that they attain energy, work. Listen. When I was your age, monsieur, I thought of rivalling the fame of Newton. It was the world of details which then attracted me, the action of force on atoms. Newton has very little to say about that. It is important. I could not follow out my thought. The profession of arms was forced upon me by circumstances, but I made certain analogies from the world of nature, the rôle of chance, of what happens when one thing collides with another. And I did not forget that they *were* analogies and that there is also the world of men. You have a good head. I suggest that you follow out my train of thought—there is the institute. *There* is a career for you. But no, you will go on making epigrams in the salons. I foresee it. At the age of sixty—a book of amusing little recollections and bon mots, par M. Auguste de Staël—Bah, monsieur, that is death. That is what your mother, whose cause you plead without understanding her, will do to you. Let her go to Vienna, she will learn German there—encore un autre talent pour la femme. How old are you now, sir?"

"Eighteen," said de Staël, with tears in his eyes.

"And only the son of your mother," Bonaparte smiled quietly at him. "Awake, M. Auguste de Staël, or it will be too late." He rose dramatically.

"Does your mother need funds?" he asked as an afterthought.

"She does not ask for them, mon général."

"Then she shall not receive them," said Bonaparte.

A trumpeter outside began to sound tattoo.

The first consul got up to leave. "Bourrienne, we return to Paris tomorrow. Joseph, I wish to see you. M. Nolte, you and M. Ouvrard I shall expect shortly on the Mexican business . . . I am glad to return your horses. You will not be troubled further. It was an excellent thought of yours tonight, mon Cambacérès. We are all in your debt." He returned the salutations of the company and disappeared with Joseph Bonaparte down the hall. All now looked at Cambacérès.

"Bon soir, mes amis, I know you are tired," he said. "My poor boy, I am sorry to have brought you from Paris for such a wigging," he continued, taking young de Staël by the arm. "I should have known better. Auguste, you have met this gentleman?—M. Adverse?"

"I shall not soon forget his courtesy," replied de Staël and took leave of Anthony with great warmth.

"Bon," exclaimed Cambacérès obviously pleased. "You will come and talk to me in Paris about Africa then."

"I should not presume to advise you, monsieur," replied Anthony.

"Nonsense, of course not." He lowered his voice. "We understand the enthusiasm of Bonaparte. I shall be glad to see you. Doubtless you can tell me much."

Anthony thanked him and joined Vincent who was taking leave of de Bourrienne with many expressions of gratitude. The little secretary saw them to the door and they hurried out to find Aristide.

"I'll bet you he will be with Latour," laughed Vincent—and he was. They insisted that he should come with them. After three "last" glasses with the adjutant of the mess they accomplished their cruel desire.

"How did you manage to get in there, Aristide?" asked Anthony.

"By flattery, monsieur. Must we go now? Burgundy like that is scarce. We have been lucky, I think."

"There is no place to sleep in the village."

"We might stay up all night—in there."

"Get the horses, Pujol," said Anthony. "We must be in Paris tomorrow. You will end in the army yet, you rascal."

"Ah, I am truly grateful for that," he cried. "Wait for me at the gate. In two minutes!"

Their last glimpse of headquarters was a curious one. As the berlin drove off down the Paris road they saw M. Cambacérès, the second consul of the French Republic, leaning over the wall in conversation with an old peasant woman with a basket. A sentry near by stood at present arms.

"He was pinching the breast of a duck," shouted Aristide from the box as they rattled out of Nogent. "I saw him."

"Your driver is zigzag, Vincent," said Anthony. "A little less noise, Aristide," he called, looking out the window. "You will bring down the patrols."

"But it is true, M. Antoine," said Aristide, bending down very confidentially, and dangerously, "they tell me that the second consul buys *all* his own poultry."

They both leaned back in the berlin and laughed. "My God, what a day!" cried Vincent. "Do you know, up until this moment it has all seemed to be perfectly inevitable. But we might not have gone to headquarters at all."

"But we did, and it was worth while, wasn't it?" said Anthony, and smiled to himself in the dark.

"Decidedly," agreed Vincent.

"Get up, all my four horses," cried Aristide triumphantly from the box. They sped on through the night and found beds at a late hour in the little village of Rebais.

———————

But it was not to be their last glimpse on that trip of Bonaparte. On the road between Esbly and Lagny he overtook them, descending upon Paris.

It was a long section of new highway lined with young poplars lately planted. They heard the bugles coming up behind them. An outrider with a trumpet appeared suddenly on the crest of a hill and galloped past at a furious rate with his horse in a lather of foam. He motioned the berlin to one side violently. They drew up. Nor did they have to wait long.

Four splendid Arab horses with grey coats and white feet suddenly flashed into view and came down the hill with their hoofs in perfect time. Their bodies grew out of the perspective inspiringly and leapt past with a tension against the beautiful, light carriage like that of tireless, steel springs unwinding in oil. Napoleon was reading a book. De Bourrienne sat facing him. They came out of the perspective and they dwindled into it. The drumming of hoofs thundered; diminished rapidly. The four horses leaned all together as they took a distant curve. The varnished back of the carriage, with the cocked hat above it, flashed in the sun once—vanished. The trumpet ahead had already died away incredibly into the distance. It floated back now as if echoed from the distant past. The carriage had seemed to be going faster than time.

There was something inexplicably impressive about the vision which had just passed. For to all who sat in the berlin it was not the mere sight itself that lingered in memory. It was the curious, complex feeling of the meaning of it. A meaning for which there was no word, and which seemed to be embodied only in the man with the cocked hat who sat reading in the carriage and yet was going so fast that he was overtaking events.

"It is not the same as when we saw him in Leghorn, is it?" said Vincent.

"No," replied Anthony. "Somehow that was just an amateur, a preliminary affair."

The other carriages and escort were evidently miles behind. They did not wait for them.

They whipped up and followed in the wheel tracks of Bonaparte.

It was late in the afternoon when they finally displayed their papers at the old gate of Picpus and found themselves at last rolling through the narrow and crooked streets of the Faubourg Saint-Antoine.

It had been necessary to hire a driver at the gate, for even Pujol admitted his inability to cope with the apparently crazy ruthlessness of Parisian traffic.

Anthony was thoroughly confused by his first glimpse of the whirl and maze of a great city. All sense of direction was lost in him. The short streets twisted and turned and ran into one another in a seemingly hopeless maze. Most of the roofs were peaked and the fronts of the houses leaned back, which served to give some light to the narrow streets. There were no overhanging balconies as in southern towns. A wilderness of chimneys and dingy swinging signs, the latter fast falling into decay in favour of the new street numbers painted on every door, was the principal mark of the changing era. Now and again a glimpse could be caught over the roofs of the frowning battlements and turrets of some medieval building.

"The Temple," said Vincent. "They are tearing its tower down. The Bastille has gone, you know. This is the Rue des Francs Bourgeois and we are driving into the Marais. It is still as it always was. Look, that is the Hôtel de Sévigné. I feel at home in this part of Paris. It is not fashionable certainly, but rents are cheap. These cochers always pretend not to understand.

"No, no," he shouted, "*not* by Saint-Merri, *not* Rue Saint-Martin. You tell him, Toni. He knows I'm a

German." The little cocher in a glazed cocked hat and a coat of many capes grinned at Anthony as he repeated for Vincent, "Au coin des Blancs-Manteaux et des Archives."

He swerved suddenly to the right, drove through a labyrinth of dark alleys where sullen-looking workmen hurrying home shouted after the neat carriage. He managed to splash the horses and the body of the berlin in a vile smelling pool and then drew up suddenly before an old tavern with a soldier standing by a cannon for a sign.

"L'Homme Armé," said he contemptuously getting down.

"You pay him, Aristide," said Vincent, "and remember he splashed the horses for you. We shall leave them here. Now then, do you see that little turret on the house at the corner just ahead? Well, that is the Hôtel de Baule. You walk up there and turn to the left on the Rue de Vieille du Temple. I live at number forty-seven. When you have seen to the horses and locked the berlin in the shed, give the key to the innkeeper. He knows me. Come around then. I shall tell the concierge to expect you and the luggage. But mind you, I don't want to find all the bronze stripped off the berlin."

"I have been to Paris before, monsieur," said Pujol, and turned to settle with the cocher.

A crowd of gamins gathered. Aristide turned on the cocher with a torrent of invective.

"You have abandoned me to a Gascoigne," shouted the surprised cocher after Vincent and Anthony. He actually looked shocked. They looked back from the corner of the Rue de Vieille du Temple. The berlin was going into the inn yard.

"Wait a minute, Vincent. There is something I want to bring along myself," said Anthony. He ran back to the little inn.

Aristide and the cocher, who was now laughing, were preparing to sluice down the horses in the stable yard together. They were friends for life, it seemed.

"I forgot something, Aristide," explained Anthony. Out of the boot he extracted the bundle he had not opened since Gallegos and swinging it over his arm went to rejoin Vincent.

"Now, Toni, I am going to show you something," said Vincent again, and led the way down the narrow, old street. He stopped before a seventeenth century house with a wide gate boarded across. Its beautiful spandrils projected above the tops of the planks with dimly gilded spearpoints of wrought iron.

"It is quite safe to take down these boards now," said Vincent while they waited, "but I want the privacy they give. Before you leave for London you will be in love with the old place. A snug retreat for a young banker. We shall call on Ouvrard tomorrow, mon vieux. Toni, I want you to consider that Mexican business!" He rang again impatiently.

"I am going to," said Anthony.

"Splendid," cried Vincent. "But what have you in that bundle wrapped up in a woman's shawl?"

"My luck," said Anthony.

"Paul," shouted Vincent, beginning to hammer on the door. "Are you dead?" A little square in the boards opened and an old man who still wore his hair in a queue looked out.

"Nom d'un nom, c'est vous, M. Nolte! Quelle impossibilité!" He swung the gate back. A small courtyard full of Renaissance carvings disclosed itself. A little stairs led up with a sweep like those of a graceful woman's skirts to a raised green garden with a sundial. On the wall directly before them was a bas-relief of Romulus, Remus and the obliging wolf. Someone was hastily opening shutters upstairs.

A flustered-looking, flaxen-haired little bonne suddenly plumped out of the passageway beside them and began to curtsy with a dust pan in one hand.

"Where is Mlle. Hélène?" demanded Vincent.

"Alas," said the girl in Alsatian patois, "she has gone for a visit with her brother, the hussar."

Vincent coloured to the eyes.

232

"Never mind," said Anthony.

"But he *is* her brother, by the cross I swear it. You shall see," insisted the maid.

"Set covers for four then tonight," chuckled Vincent. "Tell them, Paul."

"Yes, yes. He really is her brother, monsieur, and a nice fellow. All has been quite in order since you left. Très comme il faut!"

"Well, well, so he *is* then. Send for our baggage to *L'homme Armé* and for the young man there prepare a room. The guest chamber for M. Adverse, here. He remains until he goes to London. And, Paul, the gate is always to be opened for M. Adverse night or day whether I am here or not. My brother! He really *is*, you know.

"Aren't you, Toni?" said Vincent, taking him by the arm with considerable emotion.

"Oui, oui, monsieur," said everybody all at once and laughed.

The little bonne sped before them up the stairs opening doors. They began to ascend spiral steps in an old tower. They turned down a hall with beautifully carved doors. Just ahead one was half-open that gave a glimpse of a polished floor with white reflections. Somewhere a small clock chimed seven times.

END OF BOOK ONE

BOOK TWO

In Which Prosperity
Enforces Loneliness

Chapter Ten

A Metallic Standard
Is Resumed

BEFORE he left Paris for London Anthony was so thoroughly engaged in the great scheme to pry open the rusty flood gate of the Mexican treasury and turn its stagnant pool of bullion into the thirsty channels of European finance that he had all but forgotten his determination to order life from within rather than to have it overwhelmed from without, a determination which he had brought with him and cherished out of Africa.

It was true that the inanimate form of that ideal still lay vague and dormant in the twilight depths of his being, but it was like the neglected image of his little madonna that he had brought back with him from Gallegos wrapped up in Neleta's shawl along with other memorabilia of the past—and toilet articles. It was seldom remembered, and never brought out for contemplation. It simply reposed, probably safely enough, in a closed cupboard at numéro 47, Rue de

Vieille du Temple, where he and Vincent Nolte for several months in the late autumn and early winter of 1801 conducted life in a gilded-bachelor style of existence that made them at once enviable, convenient, and valuable to a widening circle of influential friends.

Through the wrought-iron gates at numéro 47 came and went, not a constant stream, but a lively trickle of numerous petty bankers and a few great financiers. There were also merchants and agents of all kinds; politicians, and certain government officials and personages.

"The House of the Wolf," as numéro 47 had long been called from the Roman plaque on the wall, had in fact entered upon a new era and busy days. Those who now met there acted, talked, and thought in ways that were new and all their own.

To be sure, Vincent Nolte did not gather friends about him to hold them and arrange them like so many iron-filings in the lines of the force he radiated. But he did have a certain influence. He was one of many magnetized, though not highly magnetic personalities, possessed of a certain modicum of attraction and force that kept the various motes in the current of the times in motion. His local segment of influence was Leghorn and Southern Europe. But in Paris he fitted into the general sphere of European finance, and on the whole acceptably and ably. This was recognized by several and sundry, and the post of Paul, his concierge, was by no means a sinecure.

Paul, indeed, was an ideal concierge for the House of the Wolf—or for that matter, for any other house. He had seen the de Vaudreuils, its original owners, depart as ruined émigrés and he had remained loyally at his post while royalists, republicans, terrorists, directors, and consuls passed. It was he who had boarded up the gates in the secret hope that their beautiful griffins might sometime display themselves again, for he believed in the permanency of fabulous things. Certainly not even the griffins themselves could have been more fabulous than the styles of human character and

238

costume which had passed through his portals during the incredible decade. In the course of ten furious years Paul had been forced to become either an amused observer of mankind or a cynic. He chose the former.

"Eighteen-hundred-one, Year Nine, as the newspapers must still say, encore une autre mode. Hein, let us answer the little bell and see what it is like then," he would mutter, shrugging his shoulders. He had long ago learned not to be surprised by anything, and never under any circumstances to laugh aloud. "That is why," he said to Vincent, when the latter had retained him, "I am an ideal concierge."

On the whole, Paul felt, the world was once more becoming more credible. Those who now rang his bell were suave rather than grotesque and madly enthusiastic.

For in Paris in 1801 one was no longer a cultured-natural longing exquisitely for the refined simplicities of a pastoral Utopia or a carefully-unkempt ruffian provided with convenient anarchical rages and a pike to help usher certain philosophic ideas into the world and those who opposed them out of it. One was no longer even a trousered Grecian devoted to naked simplicities and frantic fornication. Outwardly one was a somewhat puzzled kind of Roman, hesitating whether to admire more the busts of Brutus and other republican regicides that the first consul had installed as a precautionary measure in the Tuileries along with himself, or, the now carnivorous-looking eagles on flags and standards that were undoubtedly beginning to preen themselves imperially and to look one way only as if prematurely afflicted with a touch of neck-stiffening, heraldic pip.

Inwardly, of course, much of all this was still unreal and confusing. One knew, if one had any flair for permanence, that it would pass; that one would secretly remain what one always had been—a good medieval European with perhaps just a saving-dash of the classic sciences and enough Semitic mystery and habitual morality to make life supportable. If one were

239

none of these things, if one were perchance madly oneself, or merely some hard-working French artisan or peasant, one was not one. One was not even a minus quantity. One did not count.

But the ones who frequently, and in some cases habitually, now passed through the boarded gates of the House of the Wolf were again among those who counted. Counting, indeed, was their all-absorbing interest. Nor did they reckon any longer by ancestors and family. Their houses were counting houses and their great names illustrious by firms. But none of them intended to count just one. One in their society, which was, if anything, Carthaginian rather than Roman— one was not anyone until one had become at least one-hundred-thousand something else; francs, guilders, pounds, dollars, or whatnot.

Nothing, perhaps, could have made this notable change in the ways of counting more apparent than a comparison of the little door-books kept by Paul, the first literate concierge of the House of the Wolf, and those of Paul the second, his son and proud successor. Under Paul the first the entries had been, even as late as 8th Janvier, 1785,

Ce Soir

La Princesse de la Tour d'Auvergne
M. le Duc d'Ayen, Madame la Duchesse de ditto
Le Curé de Saint-Eustache
Comte de Ségur, Madame la Comtesse de ditto
M. de Miromandre de Saint-Marie, Madame ditto
Docteur Franklin, philosophe, et sa dame (sans titre)

Under Paul the second the prestige of the House of the Wolf continued to be made manifest, at least to Paul himself, by such entries as these: 3rd Fructidor, An IX,

Ce Soir

Collot, de la mint
Barbé-Marbois, du fisc

G. J. Ouvrard, banquier
Herr Nootnagel, de Schwartz & Roques, Hambourg
Perregaux, banquier
Fulcheron, ditto
Cinot, de Cinot, Charlemagne & Cie.
deux autres—

and after each one of these entries was a faint estimate in pencil of the number of francs which Paul thought, or had heard, these guests of the house to be worth. The "deux autres" were merely Talma, the actor, and Nicolas Isouard, a young musician, both tolerated because M. Ouvrard patronized them and brought them along. But of course they didn't count. How could they?—they had nothing to drop through their fingers.

There were others that Paul merely jotted in his book; various bank messengers, brokers, and runners for commercial houses who had business with Vincent. These received no names. Only their business was noted. But no matter how the various comers-and-goers at numéro 47 were now entered in Paul's book their interest if not their business was always the same.

Most of them were to be described by the then rather new word "financier"; that is, the handling of the symbols of value, the game of it, and only incidentally the gain of it was their chief interest in life. In their various business schemes all social, political, religious, and racial differences were tacitly disregarded between them in order that commercial and banking operations might prevail and go on.

For the simultaneous disappearance in France of so many of the kind of people who had once lent distinction to the door-books of Paul's father, and the weakening of their hold on society everywhere else, had opened a new era for the kind of gentlemen who counted and figured in ledgers and on door-books in the year 1801.

Quite distinctly the possessors and manipulators of capital were coming into their heyday. The Revolution which had ideally devoted itself to the "rights of man"

241

had in reality cleared the way for the unrestricted power of the capitalist. The feudal aristocracy had vanished, and with it the social stigma upon "usury" and trade. There were now only two ways of really counting: either by bayonets or by money. The ballot box by which the new order had hoped to be able to ascertain the voice of God, also by counting, was already discerned by some astute men to be a human oracle that could be either bought or coerced.

Here and there international plutocrats, who were eventually to absorb the powers of autocrats, aristocrats, and democrats, had begun to appear. There were even a few isolated individuals who had already evolved the machinery by which the state was to be manipulated. But there were only a few of them, for as yet the theory of financial control was scarcely understood.

But it was already a social feeling, an attitude capable of being shared with others, accompanied by a genuine sense of growing importance even among the lesser lights and small-fry engaged in banking and mercantile operations.

They felt themselves able to say to one another with truth, "We are the coming men." Their class feeling was that of sharing an increase of power which was being daily conferred upon them by fate. That is one of the most potent feelings that unite men and force them to act together. They felt it strongly; they felt a growing air of triumph and mastery when they met together even informally. It shone in their faces and confirmed them in their manners. It overflowed in their correspondence—and in that era commercial correspondence first began to overflow the world.

Merchants and bankers everywhere in Europe and America, as if by mutual agreement, now abandoned the old separatist formulas by which they had so long operated. The mercantile and colonial era was already over; national restrictions were beginning to waver so far as they were concerned. In an age of constant warfare they began to collaborate, unconsciously for the most part and always "patriotically"—but nevertheless effectively and consistently to overreach, undermine, and checkmate the arbitrary regulations of hostile governments in restraint of trade.

Hitherto money alone had not been thought quite enough to entitle one to great consideration. In the end riches might procure but they did not immediately confer power and prestige. Certain human graces, certain inherited manners that included a not entirely material code of honour, above all, well-understood and definite responsibilities to both church and state had for ages been demanded and expected from those who possessed property. But now all was changed. The financiers in reality had no superiors in power, not even titular ones. They were accountable only to themselves and their peers. In that sense, but in that sense alone, they had become aristocrats.

Bonaparte understood this. He felt some element of aristocracy to be inevitable and even attempted to re-create it. But he desired an aristocracy accountable to the state. "Aristocracy always exists," he insisted. "Destroy it in the nobility, it removes itself immediately to the rich and powerful houses of the middle class. Destroy it in these, it survives and takes refuge with the leaders of the workshops and people." Napoleon's hostility to financiers, his outbursts of rage and his sarcasms directed against such men as Ouvrard, were due to his comprehension of the fact that the financiers were not interested in anything but finance; that the unrestricted power of money in their hands tended to become a kind of ritualistic game, a thing-in-itself without any regard to its function as a political and social fact, just as the monarchy had become a ritual without meaning at Versailles only a generation before. In the European empire Napoleon hoped to create, the financiers were merely to play a necessary part. To the unrestrained power of plutocrats the little man at the Tuileries was consistently hostile.

"What is a merchant?" he once demanded of a crowd of Hamburg bankers and traders. "I will tell you:

243

A merchant is a man who will sell his country for a small-écu." This was hyperbole in miniature. Nevertheless, truth was present. M. Ouvrard, for instance, and the other guests of the House of the Wolf did not intend to sell their country for a small-écu. No, no! The accusation was unjust; they sweated under it. They were men of larger interests. They would not sell their country for anything less than several milliards of grand-écus. But they knew that they could do it. And some of them, those with the greatest financial acumen, had already set out not only to sell their own country but all the others in the world "into the bargain."

The smaller-fry still acted on more traditional principles. The thrill of power also attended them, but it was not their sole motive. Vincent, for instance, loved to be domestically important, to be able to provide the means for and to engage in a kind of medieval merchant-class life such as that still carried on at Strasbourg. That life was gross perhaps, but at least it was ample and generous. It still supposed that the profits of trade were to be spent in a whole-souled way for human relations and family life. It could still value a friend for himself and not solely for his influence. Vincent's struggle was carried on between a desire to retain some of these "Hanseatic values" and the fascination for purely abstract financial power which the period of war-time finance opened up to him. Was he to remain a merchant living in a whole-souled way or to become a manipulator of government securities and loans devoting himself to the game? He was not generally conscious of the situation. It became visible to him only as the necessity for decisions arose upon various separate occasions.

To Anthony the game of finance was never in itself overpoweringly fascinating. By training and experience he understood its methods of procedure and it was only natural that he should enter into it rather than take up politics, or go into the army, or merely amuse himself going about spending. A man without a country speaking several languages, he found himself peculiarly

244

adapted to take part in international schemes. He could even lose himself in them to a certain "successful" extent as a mere actor in a rôle which fate seemed to have thrust upon him, because there was no other to play. Like a great many young men, then and since, he felt forced to go on doing something "real" even if his ideals remained locked up. He was not the only one whose madonna was in a bundle in the cupboard.

Yet with Anthony there remained in a peculiarly vivid manner the memory of another rôle, of another way of acting which implied a choice of his own instead of a mere assignment by fate. It would turn the world from a place in which to write letters and speak lines and play financial and other games into a reality, and yet into a mystical city where one could be a whole man and act like one.

Anthony still hoped to work through one rôle into the other. In a curious way, which only his own personality could envisage and contain, he entered upon this attempt by taking part in one of the greatest international financial intrigues of the time. It was a great plot. Through it he hoped to take his place in the world, and then . . .

In the meantime the mode of existence at the House of the Wolf offered every facility for becoming involved in the financial currents of the time.

The two young men felt themselves to be quite in the main stream of events. For a while this was a highly satisfactory sensation. If Anthony had his reservations he was not inclined just then to state them even to himself. He felt drawn by the tide and swam in it, although not so heartily perhaps as Vincent who swam with it and felt glorified. Neither was fully aware where the tide was taking them. They felt themselves to be going—and that was enough for the time being. Certainly it was better than stagnating, which seemed to be the only alternative.

They arranged life accordingly and the House of the Wolf by consequence became entirely masculine. "Love" even in its more ephemeral and lighter manifestations seemed out of place in what had become essentially an abode of finance. Masculine associations were bound to predominate there. The only human affection which could flourish in such an atmosphere was friendship. Perhaps it was even more to their credit than they knew that they were able to cherish so well the bond between them. The strains put upon it served only to bind them tighter. Not until years later did they understand that in this loyal association lay the principal element of their success. It enabled them both to act with a confidence which neither could have experienced without the assurance imparted by a completely trusting partner. In the warmth of this understanding and loyalty the natural petty jealousies upon which young men's partnerships so often founder were transmuted into so many friendly rivalries. They became merely the urging of the spur toward a success to be mutually shared. And because of this friendship between them they seemed for a while to be living in halcyon days.

The final "divorce" of Vincent from la belle Hélène, who had for some time previous to Anthony's arrival shared Vincent's loneliness, was indicative of a new era. The parting of Vincent and Hélène was not painful. It was amusing. It was even characteristic of belles Hélènes everywhere.

She had never returned from her visit with her "brother, the hussar." She had simply continued on in his fraternal care. He, however, had called one afternoon, politely, suggesting that, *as he was the best fencer in his regiment,* his "sister" was entitled to compensation for having been suddenly surprised out of her boudoir. "Her chagrin, monsieur, was of a terrible completeness at not being asked to return. Her modesty has been shattered by your suspicions. Elle souffre."

"I shall be liberal," said Vincent—and he was, "but there is no reason, monsieur le frère de mademoiselle, why mine should be the only private house in Paris where liberté, égalité, and fraternité are still practised

246

with a complete sans-culotte abandon. That legend reads well only on *public* buildings now. I hope you agree?"

"Are you also a good shot with the pistol?" inquired Anthony apparently from mere curiosity and over his newspaper.

"The profound sentiments of monsieur le banquier are acceptable, I am sure," said the military gentleman, departing hastily with some francs.

"I don't want to interfere with your domestic arrangements, Vincent, even temporary ones," continued Anthony, feeling in honour bound to lay at least one posy on the cenotaph of the vanished mademoiselle. "I can make myself comfortable chez *L'Homme Armé,* you know."

"Ach—that you should think so!" cried Vincent. "What was that little bud-of-love to me? It is a relief that she has departed. It is terrible for two people to try to read the same newspaper from one knee. I know *now* I was tired of it. Anyway, Paris is a young man's paradise. There are two Eves here under every forbidden tree. Besides, you know, I left my heart with that great rosy-one at Strasbourg. Du lieber, it is for *her* that I suffer now!" And he looked so comical and so sincerely and sentimentally miserable at the same time that they both enjoyed it immensely.

Anthony was wise enough, nevertheless, to take the hint, if it was one, about the newspaper. He had both *Le Moniteur* and *La Liberté* brought up every morning. And this feeling of each to his own newspaper and an open exchange of views afterwards became the spirit of the house and pervaded the entire establishment, affecting to some extent all those who came there.

The shutters on the rez-de-chaussée looking out on the little court and the green garden with the sundial were now thrown open, and they breakfasted in what had once been the drawing-room of the ancient hôtel, eagerly discussing the news, planning a thousand projects and the day's adventure—for all serious business

247

was still that to both of them when they were together —with a flow of understanding and a facility for sound invention and prevision that astonished them both; which, indeed, occurs only when two minds are thoroughly at one and working profoundly at ease together. A shared responsibility made decisions doubly easy. And, as is so often the case when two friends collaborate for the sole purpose of collaborating, the practical results of their work were accompanied by astonishing good luck. For a month or so during the late autumn of 1801 in Paris this was true with Anthony and Vincent to an unusual degree. All that they undertook prospered. The more off-hand they seemed to be about it the better it went.

They began by calling on Ouvrard, a vigorous and florid man who received them, as he did everyone who would engage with him in his schemes, eagerly. No one at that time, not even he himself, knew how rich he was. It was only his schemes that were complex and subtle. He himself was in his address and manner simple, direct, and kindly enough. On that particular day he and Vincent discussed eagerly a speculation in government stocks in which they were both vitally interested. It was only toward the last of the interview that apparently as a side issue the Spanish-Mexican scheme came up.

Ouvrard showed immediate interest, however, when he learned that Anthony was shortly to visit the Barings in London, and why.

"It was my thought," said Vincent, "that here is an opportunity to urge upon that important firm, and possibly to present to Sir Francis Baring himself, the full details of the scheme at the instance of a gentleman of independent fortune who is already favourably known to them as a client; one whom they cannot suspect of any political motive. That, as I understand it, has been what has so far delayed our progress. We

248

advance slowly by correspondence. Letters are cold."

"It is very difficult to be candid and explicit in this matter and entrust it to the posts," said Ouvrard. "I can see your point. Well, would you be willing to convey certain proposals to Sir Francis Baring in person, M. Adverse?"

"Provided I was fully acquainted with the contents, M. Ouvrard. I should at least want to know the nature of the risks I might be taking."

"Practically none, I assure you."

"I think it is also important," added Vincent, "that if M. Adverse is eventually to take over the agency at New Orleans he should be fully acquainted with the whole plan, for it is at New Orleans that the initial supplies of bullion, the whole capital for the enterprise, will first be received into neutral territory. In a sense, if the thing goes over, all operations will begin from there."

"Ah, pardon me," cried Ouvrard. "I had not identified your friend here with the person you had written me about for the post at New Orleans. The name slipped me." He turned to Anthony with much greater interest. "I recollect you now. You have had considerable experience with Spanish colonials, haven't you? I thought the suggestion of your going to New Orleans excellent. But how will the Barings feel about it?"

"I cannot be sure," replied Anthony, "but it has occurred to me that since my entire fortune is now, and I trust will remain long, in their hands, they could not find anyone who would be better bonded from their standpoint for handling the large sums which would have to pass through my hands at New Orleans."

"An excellent point," agreed Ouvrard. "Well thought of. It seems in a way to slate you for the post. For to tell the truth, you touch upon the crux of the matter there. It has been impossible so far to agree upon the method of investing the capital in the United States, once it has been released; that is, we disgreed about *who* was to do the investing there. As there will be in the aggregate millions of dollars released from Mexico by my drafts over a period of time, its deposit and temporary investment in America before its eventual transfer to Europe, whether in the form of merchandise or specie, is a vast problem."

"I should not care to be involved in that," said Anthony. "I should prefer to have my duties at New Orleans, provided I go there, confined solely to the receipt and transfer of the specie. I should then deliver it to whatever agents in the United States may have been designated."

"The profits for the agent will largely be in the 'temporary investments' he may make, I should think," smiled Ouvrard.

"I should prefer merely a reasonable percentage for handling."

A card was brought at which Ouvrard looked. He got up and put his fat hand on Anthony's arm.

"*And* expenses, M. Adverse, do not forget expenses." He smiled. "But the details must be settled later. You must excuse me now. It is the secretary, de Bourrienne," he whispered to Vincent, "the new advance on the rentes, I suppose. Now when shall I see you next? Supper tomorrow chez vous? Non! I dine with M. Talleyrand. The next day? Bon! Wednesday evening, then."

He followed them to the door. "*What* a charming equipage you have, Nolte," said he as he glanced out of the window. "Where can I have it copied?"

"A present to me from M. Adverse."

"Ah," sighed Ouvrard his brown eyes watering, "the latest London mode."

"Let me send it around to fetch you Wednesday," said Vincent. Ouvrard looked childishly pleased.

They bowed to de Bourrienne as they passed him going out.

"You have not met any more patriots who like horses, I hope," said he laughing. "Did I tell you that fellow, what's-his-name, was dismissed?"

"No, but we rather suspect M. Ouvrard here," said

Anthony. "He has taken a fancy to the berlin, too."

Ouvrard roared and clapped him on the back. The door closed. It opened again. "If I were you I would take up those consols, Nolte. Mais oui!"

"Well, I said I would have that major cashiered," said Vincent with tremendous satisfaction as they drove home after the interview, "and I *did*." Anthony said nothing.

"Ouvrard is a genius but the most vulgar one in the world. Did you notice how he said 'Talleyrand'? But anyone who has anything to lose can take dinner with Talleyrand. Gott! that old fox, he can smell the cheese in the beak of any corbeau a mile away—and make him drop it. I should tell you, mon vieux, that Ouvrard is said to be partial to young men. I think you can go to New Orleans if you want to."

"Damn," said Anthony. "But why do they always take me for an Englishman—the latest London mode, you know. Pshaw!"

"Because you look and act like one, Toni," said Vincent with a shrug.

"But I don't *talk* like one."

"When you are not speaking English, no. But what's the difference? Well, I am going to take Ouvrard's tip and invest in this last issue of the government stock. You had better come in with me, too. It will go up, you know. Let's go to the Bourse now."

Anthony was surprised at the amount Vincent put into French consols. So was Vincent when he got home. "But government securities are bound to go up with peace coming on," he insisted. Yet he looked anxious and read his newspapers Tuesday morning avidly.

The consols had gone down a little.

The dinner with Ouvrard Wednesday evening, however, was a cheering affair. After several hours' talk over the wine he finally spread his hands out on the table, leaning down on his fingers as if he had cards under them, and said, "Attention, messieurs," like a little drum-major.

"I am about to make you a proposition.

251

"You must be aware, M. Adverse, that in talking with you this evening I have, to be frank, been acquainting myself with you along several lines. The business is an important one and I wished to be satisfied first about a number of matters. Suffice it to say I am. Also, Nolte, I am inclined to think that your suggestion of leaving all the details of the handling of the capital in America to the Barings, if they will undertake it, is the only solution. The matter sums up this way then: I supply the drafts on Mexico; the Barings undertake to get the specie or its equivalent in goods to Europe, making as much as they are entitled to in the process. I will see to the disposal here of whatever comes through their agents." He rubbed his hands. "In that way I can at last recoup myself.

"Messieurs, at the present time I have at my *case* bills on the Mexican treasury for seven millions of dollars. Think of it! They are sight-drafts made over by the Spanish royal treasurer to France as part of Spain's annual subsidy by treaty. The first consul has given them to me to pay me for feeding and clothing his soldiers. He has laughed and thought to ruin me. 'The silver is there,' he said. 'Go and get it.' Well, now we shall do as he suggests. This is my plan.

"You, M. Adverse, will take with you to London my Mexican drafts to the extent of one million dollars. You will suggest to Sir Francis Baring that this is only a first earnest of my desire to further this enterprise and that the money when realized is to be used as working capital for the firms or agents which he may see fit to set up in America. You will also tell him, that as soon as he has his arrangements perfected in America and in Holland, for I imagine that is where most of the goods will be finally received for European distribution, I shall supply him with further drafts for as large amounts as he can handle at one time, and without question. And I am prepared at this time to guarantee that within the next two years I can furnish him drafts to the extent of thirty-five millions of Mexican dollars if he can arrange his forwarding operations on a large enough scale. Urge him to do so. One affair of three millions has already been pulled off. Why stop? I *must* realize on this Mexican paper or it will ruin me. And what is it to the Barings if I make my own arrangements with our government officials here to admit goods on the side?"

"There is also the British blockade," said Vincent.

"That is their affair," cried Ouvrard. "This is a matter of international finance; each side will have to fool its own government. All sides will profit. It is a good thing. A tremendous amount of idle capital will be put to work. And peace will shortly be signed anyway. We must catch fish while the tide serves. I am afraid the peace which is still negotiating will not last long. When do you start for London?"

"In a few days."

"Bien, you will want certain credentials to pass you over the Channel. See Talleyrand, also Fouché. I shall, as it were, smooth the path." He stroked the table-cloth gently. "When you are ready call at my *case* for the drafts. You must not let anyone see them or permit even a rumour that you have them to leak out, for if Bonaparte learns of this he will immediately smell a mouse.

"And now then, good night. It is a great mission you go upon. You will not suffer by it, be sure. Be careful how and what you write above all things. The best letters are those that are never written."

He swung his luxurious cloak, lined with Russian furs, about him, gathered up his purple gloves, his huge beaver hat, and the stick with a carnelian handle and left with a rich suavity of manner that his walk denied. He ground his boots into the floor as if they were sabots.

They went downstairs and saw him into the berlin which he had now offered to buy.

"You still think it advisable to hold onto this last government issue?" asked Vincent, leaning into the carriage. Ouvrard looked at him calmly. He gave an almost imperceptible nod.

253

"Talleyrand has borrowed money to take it up," he said, and raised his eyebrows.

The berlin started down the narrow street, its candles burning dimly. Behind its oval window the large, white face and huge hat of the banker looked out like a florid picture set in too-refined a frame.

"I wonder if he was lying?" muttered Vincent.

The next forty-eight hours were some of the most troubled ones that Anthony had ever spent. For two days he thought Vincent was going mad.

From somewhere came a rumour that the peace negotiations were being broken off. A young German banker who had also bought the last government issue heavily ran in to tell them about it next morning about ten o'clock. He was green and shaking. He consumed half a decanter of brandy. Vincent could take nothing. His pink complexion was now a dull, smooth white. They drove headlong to the Bourse. The square was a pandemonium of coming and departing carriages with the gamins employed as messengers rushing about. The police had already resigned and were standing in the slow drizzle with their long capes wrapped about them, taking what shelter they could and merely looking on.

"That is a bad sign," said Vincent gloomily. "Fouché has been known to act promptly when there is no truth in depressing rumours."

It was impossible to force their way into the old buildings from which a constant yelling, as if a thousand poisoned dogs were all dying there, proceeded.

They finally worked across the square and took shelter from the rain in a small shop, where a number of other investors were sitting around. Chairs were being let-out there for a franc an hour. In them those who were being ruined sat as long as they could keep from rushing out to sell. Others immediately took their places. Quotations were brought in every few minutes by boys, who yelled out what was written on the small wooden blocks they carried showing the stock, the hour, and the price. In the shop these were passed about dismally from hand to hand and then stuck in a wooden frame, each stock on its own line.

As the day wore on it was curious to note that the successive waves of men who came to sit in the chairs were more and more handsomely dressed. All the small spectators had been sold out. Only those who thought they could still afford to hold on, or who held such large blocks of consols that they could not sell now without being ruined, would still pay a franc for a chair.

Limonades and sour wines were no longer brought in. Nothing was ordered but the best cognac and coffee for the gentlemen in ruffled stocks, deep, brown coats with many-capes, silk waistcoats, and elegant boots, who nervously compared notes in acceptable accents and exchanged snuff as the market continued to fall.

Vincent said nothing and sat perfectly still. A downward swoop of ten points at one fell blow after a brief rally about two o'clock seemed to have left him frozen.

"Is it so bad?" said Anthony. "Hadn't you better get away from it for a while?"

"I must stay," croaked Vincent hoarsely. "It is *all*. And Anna's, too. I borrowed." He put his hand on his friend's arm and drew him down to whisper, "I know how a man could shoot himself now. I'm not going to." He smiled through clenched teeth.

"Don't think I would let you be washed out, mon vieux," said Anthony.

"I shall see this through myself, Toni. God bless you," said he, and continued to sit.

A young man dressed in silk and broadcloth, with his dapper boots resting on a chair for which he had paid an extra franc, began after a while to talk to Anthony. He had a dark, Jewish cast of features and wore large rings.

"Are you hit very badly?" he said.

"If it stays down, yes," said Anthony, not caring to explain that his only interest was his friend.

"That is exactly the way I feel," said his new acquaintance. "I don't believe in the rumour of the ne-

255

gotiations with England being off. And I'll tell you what it is, I believe Ouvrard and old Reynard Talleyrand between them are responsible for starting war rumours. When things go to where they want them, then they will buy in. I tell you I have been expecting it. Yesterday this issue started to go up, and I learned then that it was Talleyrand's agent who was buying in large quantities. He stopped at eighty-seven. Then Ouvrard went to see Talleyrand. I'll bet what happened was this: Said the old fox to the fat pig, 'Why not put it down, buy it in cheap, and then put it back again?' Joseph Gallatin, the Swiss banker, was at Talleyrand's last night too, and this morning when the Bourse opened *he* got rid of a large block of governments. That started things. 'No peace with England. Old Gallatin must know,' said everybody, 'He was at Talleyrand's only last night!' And now look! Even the peasants are beginning to come in with one or two bonds. I tell you, if there was anything to it, if the market was in any real danger, Fouché would have closed the Bourse at noon."

They went over and looked through the shop windows, where a stuffed baboon stood displaying on both arms gentlemen's canes and knick-knacks, which were the usual stock in trade of the place whose chairs were now at a premium. The rain had turned to snow. The steps of the Bourse and the square were packed with a sea of backs, hats, and hunched shoulders watching the black boards upon which a clerk leaning out of a window wrote hieroglyphics from time to time. A groan went up from the mob.

"Five off, at a clip!" said the young Hebrew to whom the hieroglyphics seemed to be familiar.

Vincent came over and joined them, shaking. "I believe Ouvrard *was* lying the other night," he said. "They are down to thirty-four, and I bought at—Mein Gott!" He moaned. A gamin with a set of discouraging blocks rushed in. An old aristocrat who looked as if he might have been a courtier at Versailles in his youth dropped a snuff-box on the floor and wilted as if he

256

were going to have heart failure. Anthony picked up the box for him. It had a portrait of Marie-Antoinette on it. The old man extended it with a trembling hand but with the grand manner.

"It is a curse, monsieur, for having bought republican securities. 'Securities!'—it must be M. Voltaire there in the window who called them that."

He rose, took his cane and lunged at the baboon which collapsed into a corner of the show-case, grinning diabolically at all those in the room.

"I am going to sell, *sell!*" shrieked a staid-looking man apparently addressing the monkey. He rushed out. Two others began to shuffle their feet uneasily.

"Ouvrard has just jettisoned two thousand shares," yelled someone, sticking his head in the door. "Do you hear, Henri? Oh, he is gone!"

As if at a signal everyone in the place but Vincent, Anthony, the old aristocrat and the young Hebrew rushed out. They rolled over each other getting down the steps. A handsome, middle-aged banker picked himself up out of the gutter after his colleagues had stamped him flat, and wrung the mire out of his beard. The young Jew broke into an ecstasy of laughter, looking up at the face of the baboon. Vincent began to move toward the door, shaking. Anthony laid hold of him.

"Wait, Vincent," said Anthony. "I don't think he was lying. I feel sure of it."

"I *sell,*" said Vincent. "Enough to get home on!" Anthony looked appealingly at the young Jew who was regarding the little drama before him quizzically.

"Stay and get rich, monsieur," said the Hebrew with sudden sympathy, his smile vanishing. "Why not?"

Vincent hesitated; collapsed in a vacant chair. Anthony gave him a drink from a glass of brandy someone had abandoned.

The old man in the corner snickered behind his hand.

Suddenly a roar went up from the mob. A carriage escorted by police was trying to make its way to the Bourse. It lodged half-way across the square. Someone, they could not see who, got up in it and shouted something.

"It's a messenger from the Tuileries," said the young Jew going out on the steps. "I can see his scarf."

The mob about the carriage began to swirl. In five minutes everyone in as many blocks knew that the rumour of renewed war with England had been officially denied.

A boy dashed up and thrust a note into the hand of the young man on the steps. He walked in smiling triumphantly.

"Ouvrard is beginning to buy," he said. "Now you will see. That lot he threw on the market was only to save his face."

"Up we go," he shouted, snatching a block from a passing gamin.

The confusion outside was now indescribable. A great crowd of hatless men rushed out of the Bourse and down the steps, waving their hands frantically. The mob outside broke up into eddying groups buying and selling. The old man in the corner got up and going over to the window put the stuffed monkey back into place almost affectionately. He then went over to the young Jew and extended him his snuff-box.

"For the first time in the history of my family to one of your race, monsieur. *Do me the honour*. I have been watching your face during the last hour and it is the most beautiful one I have ever seen. It has been worth forty-five thousand francs to me."

He bowed and went out.

Vincent joined in the laugh. He seemed to have been healed by a miracle. They waited till the Bourse closed, shook hands with the young Jew, who declined to be driven home by them, and wound their way through the groups in the streets who were still eagerly buying and selling while shaking the snow off coat collars. Everyone understood what had happened now. Everyone was trying to recoup himself. Consols soared.

"I shall sell tomorrow morning before the big ones

begin to cash in and the crest falls off," said Vincent. And he did.

He came home enormously complacent.

"How much did you make?" asked Anthony grinning.

"Toni, I shall never tell you," said Vincent. "I have learned my lesson. I shall never risk my reason again. I am ashamed."

Anthony laughed at him. "So our friend the Israelite proved a *profit* after all," he said after a little.

"Yes," cried Vincent leaping up. "But it was you who kept me in that chair. You! And now I am rich. Du lieber Gott, I am rich!"

"If I were you," said Anthony, "I would turn those paper francs you have made your profit in, into coin of some kind and make a cache of it in England. I begin to see now how wise was old John Bonnyfeather in several ways."

"I'll think it over," replied Vincent. "But first I will recoup Anna, and I am going to transfer her investments to *Hope and Co.,* at Amsterdam. How *could* I ever have borrowed from her? Think of it!"

"Yes," said Anthony, "when I was sitting by you in one of those damned hired chairs that day I saw Anna sitting in her window at Düsseldorf, under her canaries. There must be flowers in that window, too. I guess she will be big with her baby by now. You remember that day at Livorno when we both agreed what banking was about?"

"Ja," said Vincent, and sat silent for a while. Neither of them ever referred to the matter again.

An urgent letter from the Barings, this time addressed to Anthony, served to hasten his departure from Paris. Old Sir Francis Baring himself had written briefly, enclosing his few lines like something alive encased in the documents which surrounded them.

My dear Sir:
    Only a lifelong esteem and boyhood friendship for your benefactor persuaded me to undertake

259

the administration of his affairs. It is that alone which now prompts me to tender you my advice.

Delay no longer. I am in receipt of your letter of recent date and I shall be pleased to see you personally when you arrive here. But no matter how alluring the prospects of future gain may appear to be in the Spanish-Mexican scheme, to which you allude so enthusiastically, your further tarrying in Paris at this time is like to endanger what you have already inherited. Between a comfortable certainty and a gilded possibility no reasonable man should ever hesitate. Suffer me at least to remind you of that. I assume that you are reasonable.

The accompanying letters will inform you of my particular reasons for writing you this. As you have not been brought up in England, you may not perhaps fully appreciate the evils of falling into the hands of those who at a staggering charge turn the hearty, human curses of their clients into feeble legal-prayers to the Court of Chancery.

The enclosed advice from Messers McSnivens, Williams, Hickey, and McSnivens is therefore, be advised, sufficiently alarming. I trust we shall be able to stave the matter off until you arrive.

Your humble obd't servant,
Francis Baring, Bart.

"Well, that settles it. Doesn't it? If Ouvrard isn't ready to have me go yet I shall leave anyway. Go!"

"Let's drive round and see him now," said Vincent seeing that Anthony was so determined. For some days they had not heard from the banker.

The rest of the day was a busy one. They found Ouvrard at the Tuileries with some difficulty but as it proved later fortunately with Talleyrand.

"Come in, come in," said Ouvrard, after the servant whom they both bribed and threatened to announce them at the ministry of foreign affairs had finally done so, "I have just been going over our scheme as it now stands with the bishop upstairs," he whispered, grinning. "He can see no reason why with peace coming on we should not begin operations promptly." He filled his chest for a long talk but Anthony took his opportunity.

"That is exactly what we all feel, M. Ouvrard, and as I am leaving tonight for London I have come to you for the drafts you spoke of desiring me to carry to Sir Francis Baring."

"Tut, tut," said Ouvrard, still puffed up like a fat peacock with the wind he had inhaled for a long period. "Tut, tut, I don't want you to leave right away." The plump hand had come out and rested on his arm as if it would detain him.

"I am sorry, monsieur, that I am unable to make my own convenience entirely yours," replied Anthony; "perhaps in any event you will aid me with having my passports properly endorsed. I understand that despite the suspension of hostilities there are still difficulties."

"Tiens!" exclaimed Ouvrard, stepping back. "It is someone like you that we need to put action into this affair. I myself, I talk. Yet much is accomplished by talk, you will observe, much is done by words . . ."

"The passports are the first step now, aren't they?"

Vincent looked shocked that so important a man should be interrupted in the midst of his words.

"You are right," said Ouvrard. "Come up and we will see Talleyrand now."

They found the former bishop of Autun looking out the window with his back towards them when they entered. Anthony caught a glimpse of his face in the full light as he looked out across the Tuileries gardens and before he seemed to be aware that they had been announced. He did not turn instantly. He seemed to complete his thought, whatever it was, and then turned. Anthony felt it to be a curious thing that the expression on the face of the minister of foreign affairs had not altered in the slightest as he came forward a few steps with a slight limp to acknowledge their presence. He seemed to accept them simply as facts with the self-

261

same completely quiet smile, a very slight one, with which he had been looking out at the grass and trees a few seconds before.

There was something vaguely familiar to Anthony in that smile, something just a little sinister in the shell-like curve of the lips which the smile overcame but did not cancel. Theirs was a moulded self-possession. The eyes, rather small but steady and keen, confirmed the self-possession of the mouth without adding anything to whatever faint warmth the smile might have been useful enough to convey.

And yet the man was not cold. He was animated, alive, no doubt of it. But imperturbable. By always compelling all who approached him forever temporarily to suspend their judgment as to his motives he perpetually kept their attention—and then he would vanish, usually with a portion of Europe in his portfolio.

"Permit me, citizen-minister," Ouvrard was saying —"mes amis, Herr Nolte, whom you will remember, and M. Adverse."

The citizen-minister bowed, limped once and sat down, at the same time indicating that there were other chairs with a courtesy that seemed to make standing up only a little less futile than sitting down. For a moment they hesitated.

"In America, where I lived for some time," said Talleyrand impersonally, "they have a marvelous contrivance called a rocking chair. I have long thought of furnishing the suite of the minister for foreign affairs here with them. They give one the impression of always being just about to attain equilibrium without ever permitting anybody to do so. Do be seated, gentlemen."

They did so while he continued, "I hear you are to be congratulated in holding on to your government stock through the recent flurry, Herr Nolte. There were only a few who were wise enough to do that. They say a certain young Frankfort Jew also made a great fortune."

"I did not make a great fortune, monsieur," began Vincent.

"He became only moderately rich," put in Ouvrard laughing.

"Well, what more do you want me to do for you, gentlemen? I do not suppose, of course, that you came here to express your gratitude. The rumour about the negotiations being broken off was absurd. M. Ouvrard will confirm me, I am sure."

"Ridiculous," said the banker. "The first consul could not have chosen a more fitting person than his brother Joseph to negotiate the treaty. Look how well he did at Campo Formio. I trust you will say so, M. Adverse, in the proper quarters when you arrive in London."

"I shall be delighted to do so provided the citizen-minister can see fit to smooth my way across the Channel."

Talleyrand opened a cahier before him and began to finger its leaves. "Your purpose in going to—London —monsieur?"

"Is to transact some private affairs with *Baring Bros. and Co.*—and—" he looked at Ouvrard, who smiled encouragingly, "to convey to Sir Francis Baring several Spanish compliments from M. Ouvrard."

Talleyrand smiled. "Your formula is apt enough, M. Adverse. I also hear you have the habit of making friends. M. Auguste de Staël expressed himself warmly about you yesterday at Cambacérès'. I admire Mme. de Staël enormously. I am under great obligations to her."

"It was nothing, I merely acted on impulse, I assure you."

"I have no doubt of it," replied Talleyrand. "When do you leave for London?"

"Tonight, if possible."

"And you are living now at?"

"Forty-seven, Rue de Vieille du Temple—wih Herr Nolte."

"The House of the Wolf," said Talleyrand amused. "Now when I was at Saint-Sulpice I remember . . ."

he smiled and waved his hand—"and you are gay there?"

"Very," said Anthony and was echoed by Vincent.

"That is well. You sustain a certain tradition. I will tell you that much." He looked at them both with a reminiscent satisfaction. "The twins of the wolf, eh! But come, that is my affair.

"What I was going to say to you, M. Adverse, is, that since you are going to London, I wish you to deliver certain letters for me personally. They will be sent around to you with the rest of your papers this afternoon. Now when you deliver these letters merely say this; that I am *personally* sincerely desirous of a lasting peace between England and France. Convey that impression from me as a *personal* expression of my opinion to those to whom the letters will be addressed. Ah,—two things more—assure Sir Francis Baring that no difficulties will be thrown in M. Ouvrard's way by me—quite the contrary. The first consul's attitude on British goods you understand is unalterable. But colonial produce, that, of course, is a different thing.

"And now, monsieur, this is really important. From a certain shop in Bond Street—I will write the name on this slip—I wish you to have sent to me twelve dozen pairs of ladies' gloves, grey with pearl buttons, and this size." He put the piece of paper about his own hand, marked it, and handed it to Anthony. "Mme. Grand will wear no others," he said to Ouvrard.

"In spite of your doubts as to gratitude we are all grateful, citizen-minister," said Vincent as they rose.

"De fait," cried Ouvrard.

"La gratitude n'existe pas," said Talleyrand. "But do not neglect to get the gloves at least, M. Adverse. I shall reimburse you for them," his eyes lit up a little.

He did them the honour of limping to the door before bowing them out.

"Who is Mme. Grand?" demanded Anthony, going down the stairway.

"Sh," said Ouvrard. "La bishop—ess. And now let

me drive round to the *case* with you. Ah, the little berlin! I wish you would do something for me in London, M. Adverse," said he, lying back and taking up most of the room on the rear seat. "Have your dealer reproduce the little vehicle for me, but upholstered in red morocco. An improvement, I think."

"I shall see what I can do with my dealer," replied Anthony. The man looked pleased.

At the bank Ouvrard delivered to Anthony ten drafts on the Mexican treasury, each for one hundred thousand silver dollars.

"They are sight-drafts," said Ouvrard, "signed, you will notice, by Godoy, the Spanish prime minister, and by the royal treasurer of Spain. Anyone who presents them is entitled to receive the specie."

"There is nothing to prevent me from cashing them for myself then?" said Anthony.

"Nothing but yourself," replied Ouvrard, sealing the package. "Well, it would not be *quite* as simple as that. One does not call with a wagon for a million silver dollars, you know, and just drive off. When the time comes certain letters of identification and confirmation will be provided for me by M. Talleyrand to the Mexican government. But you know the procedure in such cases. Do not lose them, though," he said, raising his finger half humorously. "It would ruin Herr Nolte."

Anthony looked from Ouvrard to Vincent.

"Why," laughed the banker, "didn't you know Nolte has gone bond for you?"

He delayed them for another hour going over endless details.

"My God, Vincent, why didn't you tell me you were going bond for me?" said Anthony fingering the package with the drafts gingerly as they drove back to the House of the Wolf. "Suppose something *does* happen to me!" he exclaimed again as they got out of the berlin.

Vincent did not reply but in the courtyard he stopped and putting a hand on Anthony's shoulder pointed with

265

the other to the plaque of the twins sharing the milk of the wolf. "From now on, as always before already," he said in German, "between us it is still going to be like that?"

"Yes," said Anthony, "and a fine picture of two young bankers sucking the guts out of the state . . ."

"Ach, go on with you," said Vincent. "It's a good sign, a lucky one, Gemini—this is a gay house. Even Talleyrand said so. I wonder what he . . ."

"A government messenger has been waiting for you for an hour, monsieur," said old Paul just then appearing from within breathlessly. "I have been watching him while he waited. That was why Jean opened the gate."

They rushed upstairs like two boys. Anthony signed for the packet from the Tuileries and scarcely waited till the messenger was gone to break its seal.

"Look," he cried, "an order for government posts as far as Havre. The prefect there is to 'expedite my waftage,'—what a curious expression."

"Give me the first post billet," said Vincent, "and I will send Paul out with it now to the government stables. How will it do to have them call for you about nine? A last dinner here, you know. And your luggage will take time."

"That reminds me of something, Vincent. I want you to take care of this bundle for me." He brought it from his room.

"A woman's shawl, eh," said Vincent grinning.

"No, no, that is not it at all. There is something in it which—oh, do not ask me to explain. Keep it safely here till I return. I leave it with you—in the House of the Wolf," he added solemnly.

"Very well, Romulus, Remus hears you," smiled Vincent, and then looked solemn enough as he took the bundle and locked it up.

At the hour of nine exactly a light post-chaise with two horses and a government postilion drew up at numéro 47. A sergeant of gendarmes emerged from it.

"May I see your papers, monsieur?" He examined

266

them carefully while two leather trunks and a valise were being strapped on.

Vincent stood holding a lantern lugubriously over the signs of departure.

"I wish you would do something for me when you get to London," he laughed, imitating Ouvrard, and leaning into the carriage at the last. "Have your dealer line this with red-morocco-and-pink-and-green satin— and bird-lime—" he flashed his lantern over the battered interior of the old post-chaise ruefully. "And keep yourself warm, Toni, mein Gott, England is not Africa! Wait, wait a minute, you have forgotten something." He stormed back into the house.

For a minute the grim, grotesque shadow of the postilion and his horses, the post-chaise and its vacant windows stood waiting, leaning forward a little, projected on a blank wall across the narrow street by the lantern Vincent had left on the curb. The ancient bell at Saint-Merri near by tolled a quarter. The sergeant looked impatient. A little snow was beginning to fall.

"All in the house wish to thank you for your extreme generosity, monsieur," said old Paul. Anthony shook the old man by the hand. A horse stamped. The gate flew open and Vincent rushed into the street and began to stuff something through the window of the carriage.

"For winter," he cried, "to keep you warm, Herr Gott, to keep you warm."

"Allez," snorted the sergeant.

Anthony wrung Vincent's hand as old Paul dragged him back, and the post-chaise clattered up the crazy old street. It turned left and rattled along the cobbles of the Rue Saint-Antoine. It turned right, and passing the dark front of old Saint-Merri, headed north along the Rue Saint-Martin, a straight Roman road.

The post-chaise was not going any faster, however, than had the chariots along that same road seventeen centuries before. Nor was it, perhaps, going quite so safely.

"Monsieur goes armed?" asked the sergeant.

"Yes."

"Bon! It is well. I go as far as the Porte Saint-Denis with you. I do not leave the city. You will receive your first galloping relay and an armed guard at the gate. It is better since the first consul has sent around his tribunals. But the post of the Republic is not the post of the days of the kings. Few travel, everything has fallen off. In my boyhood for a few écus one could send a package or even a money order on a banker from any city in France to another. They say if Bonaparte is made king things will go better. Perhaps? He makes good roads for soldiers. But one can no longer send money and letters safely. The Revolution has made men less honest than they were when God was in heaven, the king on his throne, and the devil in hell."

"Are you a legitimist, sergeant?"

"No, monsieur, but in these days I would simply advise you to go armed. Such moral sentiments as still exist do not help deliver the mails. I know that. I myself have secured you a carriage with sturdy wheels. That Committee of Safety was so busy removing heads that they had no time to put on wheels. You had best buy your grease too or the pigs will answer when you drive past. They sell it at the barriers. And now I leave you, citizen—bonne chance." He would not be paid. "My opinions cost me a great deal," he said and went into the guard-room laughing.

Anthony felt for his precious papers. They were still there.

At the Porte Saint-Denis before the barrier a fire was leaping like a wild beast in an iron cage. The horses were changed rapidly. Four, instead of three, were now attached. A glowing brick was taken from the fire and put in an iron box. This on a bed of sand was put in to heat the carriage. It was now beginning to snow still harder. A north wind rumbled against the old battlements, the red fire leaped fiercely in the black night. Would they never get through comparing his papers? The sergeant on guard came out with them at last. "All right," he muttered. The armed guard climbed up on the seat behind. "If the citizen would be kind enough to provide cognac?" said the sergeant. "I can get it at the gate canteen for him. It will be cold for those outside." "Three flasks," said Anthony. A rumble of approval and the slapping of the guard's hands on the roof followed. The brandy came. All took a swig. The barrier was suddenly opened letting the wind sweep in bitterly. The postilion broke into a torrent of abuse, and leaning low along the back of the beast he was riding, lashed his teams forward into the storm.

It was the first great winter storm Anthony had ever seen. A gale of a distinctly arctic character was sweeping down from the Pas du Nord accompanied by flurries of fine snow. The roads were frozen as hard and as smooth as iron. The horses which knew every foot of their own familiar stage with a stable at either end galloped steadily by the light of a waning November moon. The guard on the open seat behind crouched low behind the trunk on the roof and beat his arms about him to keep his hands from freezing. Occasionally the horn blared and a dog barked. Then the devouring sound of the hoofs and wheels continued.

Inside the heat of the brick gradually died away. The windows steamed over by the breath of the solitary traveller in the post-chaise became more opaque as they froze until he sat insulated in a little world of frosty moonshine. He wrapped about him the heavy bearskin rug that Vincent had stuffed through the window at last. He drew his feet up on the seat under him and sank back gratefully into its comforting folds. The world outside seemed to have fallen away. He could not sleep, but as the swinging and rocking, the long forward slide of the carriage continued and the cold became more bitter and penetrating, his process of retreating into the rug continued and he withdrew farther and farther into himself.

He heard them change horses at Villiers la belle Gonesse but after that no more.

Sitting half-awake and numb in the amazing cold,

269

he now retained only what seemed to be the fundamental residue of realization. He was being taken somewhere swiftly and he felt now that he was travelling absolutely alone. Within him was an utter stillness and calm. If he could only retain that. Was it possible? He wondered.

Chapter Eleven

Your Humble Obedient
Servant

London, 28 December, 1801

DEAR VINCENT,
I arrived here on Weds., the 27th inst., coming up by coach from Plymouth through as bitter a snap of winter as anyone remembers having seen. The trip across the Channel was like to be my last.

You know we both wondered why my departure was arranged by way of Amiens. It was plain enough when I got there. The conference to make the treaty of peace is getting under way there and there is considerable coming and going of envoys, secretaries, and personages by way of Havre de Grace. Otherwhere the blockade is still strict. I received every courtesy as a "messenger." At the prefecture I ran into M. Joseph Bonaparte who was just coming out from seeing the prefect. He remembered me although not my name. I think he thought I was you, but he soon caught himself up very pretty. He told me how Luçay was dismissed. We really did not have so much to do with that as we thought.

It did me no harm, I think, to be seen talking with the first consul's brother. The prefect gave me an order for a special dispatch lugger at Havre when I should arrive there, which I did two days later.

I shared the ridiculously crowded little cabin with a young English diplomat by the name of Spencer, with de Lanark, another messenger of Talleyrand's, who looked at me somewhat askance because I would tell him nothing, and young Lord Francis Russell, son of the Duke of Bedford, who was accompanied by his tutor, the Reverend Hinwick Orlebar. The last two were returning from a tour of the lower Germanys and had been blown into Havre by the gale which scattered the blockade it is said from the Scheldt to Finistère. By some influence here the Englishmen were permitted to depart and were glad even of the crowded cabin. As I was in a merry mood at getting off in such style I had the innkeeper send down a large hamper of wines and eatables, which proved in the event a mighty comfort to us all in extremity.

Young Russell was especially desirous of spending Christmas with his family in Bedfordshire and he and I combined with the persuasive metal to prevail on the skipper to put to sea, rather against his own better judgment I think, and the protests of the tutor, a clerical gentleman with small stomach for gambolling with Neptune. There was a lull in the gale the morning of the 19th inst. We put forth, got half-way over, and had raised the cliffs when a brawling norther cold as the hinges of doom swept us down channel like so much fluff. The seas were mountainous and all we could do was drive straight away. The crew, four sea-rats in red knitted-caps, and their pock-marked captain were all but worn out. The water-butt went by the board, and no fire could be lit. My basket with two fat geese, some pastries, and several bottles of wine served to keep us alive. The cold was unexpressible. Your bear rug saved the life of the clerical person, if that is

272

anything to you. He sat wrapped in it eating goose's drumsticks occasionally and praying continually. The other gentlemen, Spencer and de Lanark, rolled about puking on the cabin floor. Their plight was truly miserable, especially so since young Russell, who still had the merciless humour of a boy that can see but not yet feel the miseries of his fellows, plagued them unmercifully by offering them bits of goose liver with emetic results. The sight of his tutor praying in a bear skin sent him into gales of mirth. As I was afraid some in the cabin might gather enough strength to do him bodily harm, I took the young bear up on deck, where, despite the spray and the cold, we managed to be gay and shared our wine with the crew, who were grateful.

Taking it altogether, the experience in the Channel is one of the worst I have ever had. On the third day we got a glimpse of the coast that the skipper recognized as a bit of Cornwall, and as the wind blessedly relented and veered, we were enabled to beat back up the coast into Plymouth late on the afternoon of the 23rd.

I went to the "Swan," as nothing could have induced me to take the night coach for London which all the others did, except Mr. Spencer who came down with a bad attack of pleurisy. I went out and got him a leech who bled him. He seemed very weak, poor fellow. Young Russell and his tutor hired post and were both pressing I should come along. In this I am flattered to believe they were sincere enough but the invitations of sons and tutors do not necessarily imply the welcome of fathers, especially if they be great ones, so I saw them off in a flurry of snow with a merry toot of the horn and young Francis waving his hat and shouting back "Merry Christmas."

A sinking sensation of being left alone followed (Christmas is made much of here). I went back to the "Swan" and a good sea-coal fire and excellent dinner in my own room, where, for the first time in a week, I was both full and warm—and thankful to God

273

for still being able to do so. The lugger is shipping a new mast, I hear.

I strolled about the town next day. This is the cleanest country I have ever been in. It is strange to hear English spoken everywhere and by everybody. My talk is a little curious, I fancy, but passes well enough. They take me for Scotch if for anything. I shall devote considerable attention to polishing the roughness off my tongue and write you in nothing else. This is the language in which I find I do most of my thinking. Little else was spoken, you may remember, behind doors at the old Casa da B (what a polyglot world Livorno was). I also took occasion to provide myself with innumerable warm clothes. I shall gradually become hardened to the northern winter, I suppose, and it will do me good, but at present I do suffer greatly. Almost as good as your bear skin are my Havana cigars for comfort. My stock is running low and I grow alarmed. They smoke the Virginia leaf in pipes here. Only the best is tolerable.

The pleasantest thing that has yet happened to me in England overtook me in Plymouth. I found Mr. Udney in the public room just as I was about to leave for London. He gave a rumble and a shout when he saw me and would not hear of my going up. All my things were carried back upstairs again by his order. Saving your own welcome, I have never had a man so glad to see me. I was quite overcome, and I believe he was, too, for he did swear dreadfully. Had just driven down from his place near Totnes in Devon to transact some business in Plymouth. Really an excuse to get away from a lonely old house, I take it. Mrs. Udney is in Amsterdam on a visit to Florence, the Parishes having recently removed there from Rotterdam since David has now joined interests with *Hope and Co.* in Amsterdam. If I return that way I shall see them. Mr. U. much cut-up over Florence's having no son or "any other children," as he puts it. He claims it must be David's fault, who I gather is rather a cold fish. The old man is a breeder of horses and I shall not set down

274

his speculations about dear David which were not only frank but downright technical. He was greatly interested to learn that I was going up to London to claim my inheritance. It seems he knew of it through the registering of the will all along. When I told him *I* hadn't, he cursed J.B. for a sentimental old Jacobite. He is quite sure I was no relation to J.B. and told me how he and Father Xavier arranged to have me apprenticed. All quite accidental, which in a way relieves my mind. After all, when you come right down to it, a great many people do not know their parents any better than I do, even if they do know their names. What do you know about your own father, for instance? (I don't expect you to reply.) The upshot of it was we had Christmas dinner together, and a right merry one, and I got off for London next day leaving the old gentleman, whose hair is quite white now, standing with a very red face in the door of the "Swan," thumping his stick and swearing and insisting that I must come down to Devon for a visit, which I think I shall do, if conditions permit.

I got here the 27th, awful weather as above mentioned, and am staying at the Adelphi. This morning I called at *Baring Bros. & Co.* to notify them of my arrival and was most courteously received by Mr. John Baring. If not glad, they were certainly relieved at seeing me, as also to discover, I think, that I was not a Sicilian or a Red Indian. I have an appointment for tomorrow, when I may be able to mention that I have an important matter to convey from M. O. to Sir Francis. I requested Mr. John Baring to convey my profound appreciation, gratitude and respect to his father, at which he looked genuinely pleased. I think the slaving business gave them the idea I was a rough and ready customer. I was—but I am not.

You shall hear from me directly as to further developments. This letter is sent by way of Helgoland and Amsterdam by a special messenger maintained between the Barings here and Messers *Hope & Co.* there. The blockade is unrelaxed. I have not yet bought M. T.'s gloves for him. If you want to know what London is like breathe heavily on your shaving glass and then try to look in it. That is as much as I have seen of it so far, so I will not give you any "reflections." This rather in haste as the Barings' messenger calls for it shortly and sails tonight. With luck you should have this in two weeks. There is some talk of re-establishing the Calais packet and mails. I think of the House of the Wolf fondly—heaven fend for you and good luck follow.

Your humble obd't servant.

A. A.

P. S. Send by way of Messers Hope at Amsterdam when you answer and address me care of *Sir Francis Baring, Bart & Co.*, Bishopsgate Street, London. They operate abroad as *Baring Bros. & Co.*

To Herr Vincent Nolte, at the House of the Wolf, 47, Rue de Vieille du Temple, Paris.

London, 9th January, 1802

Dear Vinc,

Almost a month has gone by since I wrote you and I suppose that by this date you must have my first letter. A great deal has happened in that interval which I shall attempt to relate rather in the order of its occurrence than that of its relative importance.

First, my own affairs financial are satisfactorily in order; secondly, the great Spanish-Mexican business, if not launched, is at least set up on the ways and lacks only about £100,000 to knock the blocks from under it and start it moving. That is a large "only" I admit—but to the events themselves:

My own humble affairs were settled with greater dispatch than at first seemed likely.

On the 29th of last month I called according to appointment at the counting house of the Barings in

Bishopsgate Street and was received by Mr. Charles Wall, who oversees most of the routine correspondence of the firm. I was taken to the second floor office, a splendid, panelled room furnished with teak furniture and various Indian rarities assembled by Sir Francis, who for many years has been a director of the Honourable East India Company. He now, I find, seldom appears in the city and has turned over the practical conduct of his affairs to his older sons Thomas and Alexander.

In this ample but arctic room I found assembled about an immense teak table in which the candles, for there was a rayless fog outside, reflected themselves funereally, Mr. Thomas Baring, John Hickey, Esq., of the firm of McSnivens, Williams, Hickey, and McSnivens, barristers; a gentleman by the name of Flood from the Bank of England, and several accountants and clerks with various piles of papers. Mr. Thomas Baring seated me beside himself and Mr. Hickey, of whom more later, accepted one of my precious Habana segars after smelling of it like a posy as if it had been an unexpectedly large refresher, which indeed it was. We then, together with Mr. Wall, who took notes, settled down to business.

The first matter taken up was the sum due me from my remittances to the Barings from Africa. These I found to my great satisfaction had been turned into ready money deposited in the Bank of England, and despite the heavy discount on the acceptances of the original foreign bills of exchange, amount with accumulated interest from the Bank to 17,034 pounds sterling, ten shillings, and four ½ pence. The transfer of this goodly sum from the account of the Barings to myself was effected with due formalities by Mr. Flood. I then paid Mr. Thomas Baring 2½ % net for his firm's handling of the transaction and gave and received receipts. All this was properly witnessed, stamped, recorded by notaries and I know not what else. The whole transaction was overlooked by the genial Mr. Hickey, who with an apparently casual manner combined the eye of a hawk, and at one point shook the precise little Mr. Flood into an ague by pointing out that by the omission of a comma in the transfer the whole sum was made liable to be claimed by the crown. Mr. Flood protested his good intentions. "Pooh, pooh," said Mr. Hickey, "don't dribble self-serving testimony, Mr. Flood, punctuate. Nearly all the tragedies in the lives of my clients come from little *commac* effects. I have a notion to live luxuriously on the fees arising from this one for the rest of my life by not putting a *period* to it. What will you compound with me for?" Mr. Flood's hand shook as he inserted the comma and Mr. Baring laughed. Hickey is an Irishman, or his father was, and he is said to have made the original pun before the woolsack about litigants being the lambs that furnished the fleece to stuff it with. I tell you all this because I thought you would like to know how the Barings conduct business, since you transact a good deal with them yourself.

The firm is purely a family affair. Sir Francis is responsible for and still directs its policies. As an old member of Parliament and one of the most powerful of the Whigs he has great political influence. Thomas looks after the London house with Wall who is his brother-in-law. Alexander is now in Amsterdam with the Hopes, and, as you know, M. Labouchère of that firm married a Miss Baring. The Barings and Hopes act as one apparently, the latter looking after continental affairs. They are to all intents and purposes a family unit. There is also a Mr. Henry Baring, who I understand is very brilliant but addicted to high play. He and David Parish are very close. They are brothers in whist.

As soon as Flood left, after requesting me to call around and identify myself with certain officials at the bank, we went into the matter of the Bonnyfeather estate. I produced my copy of the will probated at Leghorn and other papers, which Hickey found in order and expressed his satisfaction over. He would, he said, in a short while if all went well, be able to put me in possession of the estate, which had been invested by the Barings in ways too numerous to mention here. I asked Hickey what he meant by "if all went well," and he replied that a very ridiculous but none the less serious situation threatened the inheritance. Without going into the legal phraseology and technicalities of it, for which I naturally take my attorney's word, let me explain—because it is—or rather, thank God, it *was* funny.

You will recall old Captain Bittern of the *Unicorn,* no doubt. Well, when I left Gibraltar I gave him the cabin silver and furnishings, among them a chair which he particularly affected for some reason; a chronometer, etc. This was just a small token of appreciation for years of faithful service, and he was not a man upon whom one could press banknotes. "Independence" is his watchword.

When he returned home he quite properly removed these effects to his own lodgings. The ship was then sold at auction by the Barings. The young cub of an attorney in charge of the proceedings dug up an old ship's inventory, and finding that Bittern had removed the cabin furniture, etc., he had the good old skipper taken up for larceny and the goods seized. This was bad enough, the Lord knows, but worse followed.

Captain Bittern had presented the chair to a chapel at Spitalfields, the shrine of an obscure and fanatical Protestant sect known as the "Muggletonians." Furthermore, that chair had been consecrated as the seat of the prophetess, an ancient and fiery old party by the name of Johanna Heathecote. When the bailiffs arrived to claim "her chair," as near as Hickey and I can find out, a riot of no inconsiderable proportions unrolled itself.

Spitalfields is a hungry weaving neighbourhood with a lot of people thrown out of employment by the war. Before the rolling around in the chapel was over the friends of the saints had assembled outside, attracted by what seemed to be more than just the ordinary scuf-flings of schism.

When the bailiffs, battered and bleeding, emerged with the chair, the crowd, recognizing in them the enemies of mankind, made common cause with the saints and forced the poor fellows to take refuge in a stone stable near by, where some rascals set fire to the straw. The mob, for it had rapidly grown to those proportions, then turned its attention to the bakeshops in the neighbourhood and was proceeding to I know not what further mischiefs when a detachment of the guards and a number of special constables fell upon them, arrested a number of poor souls, put out the fire and rescued the bailiffs who were all but smothered but still had the chair.

Thus the throne of Great Britain triumphed over the chair of the Pythoness of Spitalfields, the latter being sold next day at auction to a Jew for something under £4. God save the King.

I give you Hickey's account of the affair more or less. Several murky fellows found with bakers' loaves under their arms, who are no doubt honest workmen when there is any work, were locked up by the authorities along with the fighting prophetess and the Muggletonian saints and elders. Of course, nobody at the Barings' knew anything about this until it had all happened and the saints were keeping the rest of the prisoners at the Old Bailey awake by singing nasal hymns.

This all happened about three months ago. All of those taken up have now been discharged except two louts with bad records who it seems did set fire to the stables. Hickey did his best to smooth matters over, —enjoyed it in a way, I gather—says that old Johanna Heathcote almost ruined her chances by preaching to the judge and insisting that his lordship was damned now and for all eternity for meddling with God's people. An excited young attorney objected that her evidence was irrelevant and immaterial and his lord-ship was so pleased that he chuckled the saints out of the dock. It must really have been rather grand, I gather, but it nearly cost me my inheritance.

God's people and Captain Bittern were outraged. They might have proceeded against the Barings in several ways. I don't understand the exact situation. Suffice it to say, that if they *had* entered suit for the return of that chair the ownership of the *Unicorn* would have had to be adjudicated. As the ship and her dozen prizes were part of the Bonnyfeather estate, and as some of the prizes were made after Mr. Bonnyfeather's death, the status of the whole estate would undoubtedly have been involved. The Barings were only executors, and for an alien heir who had not yet appeared to make good his claim. The whole thing hung on nobody's questioning who owned the property before I established my rights under the will. If a suit was started many a poor barrister would scent big pickings, Hickey says, and the whole thing would have galloped into Chancery. I might then have spent all I made in Africa (and the rest of my life in London) trying to get something for my children, if I ever have any. When I tell you, Vinc, that the whole estate with the sums realized for the *Unicorn* and her prizes comes to £137,000 odd you can imagine that I looked across that table at the Barings with considerable interest while Mr. Hickey explained. It wasn't so funny then.

Mr. Thomas Baring had been the first to realize the grave state of affairs when a deputation from the Spitalfields conventicle headed by Captain Bittern called upon him. They wanted their consecrated chair given back. Luckily they had retained no counsel and Mr. Baring sent for his, Hickey, whom they listened to as he had aided in getting them released. I am vastly indebted to that man. He suggested to them that they should be legally represented. Luckily for me the poor souls actually asked Hickey to recommend them counsel. He had counted on that. They even wanted him to act. He explained why he could not, without making them feel he was "on the other side," and secured a young cousin of his who consented to advise them.

It was arranged to refurnish the Muggletonian chapel at Spitalfields, to contribute to their charitable fund and to settle the Heathecote woman in rather snug lodgings for life. Thank God she is old, as all this comes out of my pocket. I am afraid Hickey is a sad old fox as he went for six consecutive Sundays to service à la Muggleton at Spitalfields. I believe he would have been converted to keep them out of court. The red carpet and cushions for the benches certainly helped, and the chosen people were at last got off the subject of the chair—all but Captain Bittern. He insisted on the identical chair and threatened to undo all the good work by bringing suit. Hickey had the good sense not to offer him money and of course started a frantic search for the chair. He had, he thought, traced it a day or two before I arrived and he went to reassure Captain Bittern. The old fellow was sullen, however, and would say little. When Hickey told him I was in England he brightened up, however, and admitted he would see me. This was the situation on the morning of my first interview with the Barings.

So we went out to try to get the chair worth £137,000.

It is past midnight now and I shall put off till tomorrow the account of what happened. I had a good dinner tonight at Wattiers and—my eyes are heavy. You shall hear, too, of the Mexican affair in due course. It marches.

22nd January

(I meant to finish this ten days ago but have moved my lodgings since. Will tell you about that later, but have missed this week's messenger to Amsterdam. No mails yet. Anyway, I shouldn't care to trust what I have to tell you to the French posts.)

Out of a conceit for convenience I shall entitle what I am writing you tonight—

Your Humble Obedient Servant and Captain Bittern's Chair

As soon as we left the Barings we took coach and hurried over to Threadneedle Street, where I identified myself and my signature with certain of the bank's officials as Mr. Flood had suggested, and from whence I departed with a goodly sum in banknotes but could get no gold. I also settled with Mr. Hickey for a well-deserved but nevertheless startling fee. I must confess to you that when I drew this money which was partly the proceeds from selling my fellow men I had a superstitious qualm that perhaps Captain Bittern's chair was to be the instrument of my being scourged by Providence. If so, it seemed curious that I alone should be singled out.

We now took coach again and called at various places, with which I am not familiar, where Mr. Hickey expedited in so far as he could the acceptance and recognition of myself as the lawful heir under the will. The fees were again in each instance—large. We then proceeded in the general direction of a place called Hammersmith where we arrived about two o'clock in the afternoon, and had a most vile luncheon of heavy lumps of soggy dough and boiled mutton with small beer. We then set out through various highways and byways—wiping away the beads of perspiration caused by the difficulties of digestion—in search of the house of the Jew who was thought to have bought the chair at the auction and to reside in this vicinity.

I must for the moment, however, return to the subject of the luncheon. The English speak of being "fortified" by such food—and the idiom is a just one. For two hours that afternoon I felt as if one of the citadels of Vauban in a characteristic star-fish outline had been built of solid masonry in my bowels. The assaults of digestion were successful only after a prolonged rumbling of nature's artillery.

I should also have mentioned that the carriage we were riding in was the property of Mr. Hickey and was provided with a wheel-and-notch contrivance registering distance on a dial, the like of which I had

283

never seen before. It is certainly ingenious although not very necessary. There was also in the carriage with us a nigger servant who had been left with Mr. Hickey by his cousin William that is now in Bengal. Although he was wrapped in a suit of quilts, the poor black devil's teeth chattered with the cold. He is much persecuted by the other servants when left at home alone and prefers to accompany his master and freeze rather than remain alone at the house. I tried some Arabic on him but he only continued to click his teeth. A large beefy Yorkshire man drove us. In this style we got as far as Starch Green, inquiring for a hypothetical Hebrew. At last we learned from an estate-agent that a German by the name of Mayer had taken a house in the neighbourhood of Shepherd's Bush and that we must return that way by Goldhawk Road. As this nomenclature sounded promising we did so.

By now it was half past four, foggy and beginning to get dark. As we drew up before a gloomy, dilapidated mansion of pretension to former affluence my heart sank.

Mr. Hickey remarked that the place must have been built by someone on the outside of the South Sea Bubble just before it burst—and, indeed, it had that sullen look of having been surprised at birth by the sudden withdrawal of the silver spoon from its too-expectant mouth by the false fairy Finance. Hickey looked at it and laughed.

I could obtain entrance only to the rear garden and that with some difficulty along a porch of collapsing pillars. Eventually I found myself in the rear close, where much to my surprise I found a very neat and semi-Corinthian doyecote devoted to what appeared to be the scientific raising of carrier pigeons.

There was no one about, not even a dog, but as I stood there in the yard there suddenly came out of the foggy sunset a whirr of wings and a pigeon like a bolt from somewhere else. It alighted and entered daintily by a small door in the cote. I was somewhat startled at the same instant to hear from somewhere in the house the distant tinkle of a small bell. How the device was arranged I do not know, but I am sure the bird and the bell were no coincidence.

I was just about to knock when the back door opened and a young woman, obviously a Jewess, came out. After some little difficulty she secured the bird which had just arrived. She did not observe me, for I stood back under the shadow of an old wagon shed, but I saw her remove something from the tail-feathers of the pigeon and return to the house. "From father at Frankfort," I heard a man's voice exclaim in German. "He should start them earlier in winter. The night confuses the birds sometimes." Just then the door closed.

Certain now that someone was within, I went round to the front door and beckoning to Hickey to join me —knocked loudly. The same young woman who had secured the pigeon opened the door.

"Is Herr Mayer at home?" I asked in German.

"Ja," she said, noting the carriage over our shoulders. "He has just returned from Manchester," and ushered us in.

"Rachel, you should not say I am just from Manchester. Let no one be unnecessarily informed," I heard the same man's voice admonish the girl in the back of the house.

"*Ssh,* they speak German," she replied.

"What!" cried he. "Are they here already, impossible!"—and then raising his voice—"I shall be with you directly, Jacob, I am only in my gown now."

We both looked at each other and laughed. We also looked about us with considerable curiosity.

The house had evidently been furnished from a number of auctions. Every piece in it was second-hand. But the interior had been made as spotless as the outside was dilapidated, and I am bound to say that a great deal of nice taste and discrimination must have been evinced by the person attending the sales. For all of the furnishings, rugs, carpets, clocks, sofas, desks, and secretaries; everything from the andirons to some warm oil landscapes on the walls must have been bought-in with as careful thought as no doubt it was bid for. And most of the pieces, if one did not look too closely, matched. But there was a strange air about it all. No one could have possibly mistaken it for an Englishman's house. Here and there was an oriental or bizarre bit, something of unknown use, which gave the effect of suddenly coming across in a book written in a European language a page printed in Hebrew. I shall say no more, save that drawn up before an unlit fire was the chair of Captain Bittern, reupholstered, and I am bound to admit, a handsome, ample piece.

I had scarcely had time to gather these impressions when we heard steps coming down the hall and Herr Mayer entered. He was considerably startled to find that we were not "Jacob"—and so was I—startled I mean —for the gentleman before me was none other than the young Hebrew who had sat next to us in a hired chair through the flurry in rentes in Paris.

He gave a whistle of surprise, and then begging my pardon bade us both welcome with grave courtesy.

"I am charmed to see you," said he in German. "Our last meeting was such a profitable occasion that I cannot help but remember you pleasantly, although I do not know your name."

I told him.

"I hope that does not belie my remarks about your luck," he replied.

"I hope not," I said, and sat down firmly in Captain Bittern's chair.

Herr Mayer looked at me and raised his eyebrows. "Then—?" said he.

"I am in peculiar difficulties, Herr Mayer," I said as frankly as I could, "and, through a strange train of circumstances, you may be able to relieve my anxiety without any risk to yourself."

"I . shall be happy to lend you any reasonable amount, even a very large one on such excellent security as the Barings represent. Their word is as good as their bond. It was unnecessary for them to send their attorney along with you," said he glancing knowingly at Hickey. "To what extent am I asked to oblige you? Money is tight you know . . ."

As all this was in German Hickey was none the wiser.

"You mistake me," said I, "although naturally enough. I have not come to borrow. I have come to buy. And I have brought Mr. Hickey along just to assure you that I am completely . . ."

"I have no doubt of it," said he smiling.

"—sane," I continued, "and that I would be more than considerably obliged if you would consent to part with the very comfortable chair in which I am just now sitting."

"To *what?*" he asked amazed. We looked at each other. I saw an expression of pain and amazement flash from his eyes. He appeared extremely hurt as only a proud and sensitive Jew can be.

"I buy second-hand furniture," he said at last, "but I do not sell it, Mr. Adverse. You are unfortunately mistaken as to the nature of my business"—he was indignant now—"I am afraid I cannot part with the chair. As you say, it is a very comfortable one." An expression of scorn and contempt caused his eyelids to droop.

"Now you have mistaken me," I cried. "I certainly did not suppose what you think, nor have I come into your house out of curiosity. It seemed better to be quite frank about the reason for my coming here than to try by some subterfuge to purchase the chair and to fail, perhaps, by puzzling you and arousing your suspicions. I have simply come for the chair and nothing else."

"Why do you want it?" he asked, looking mollified by what I had said. "I am equally frank, you see, about my own curiosity."

"I am afraid I cannot tell you. My reasons are purely private. All that I can say is that the chair has nothing valuable whatever concealed in it, that your retaining it will vastly embarrass me, and that you will gain nothing by keeping it except a possible perverse satisfaction in doing so. That, I hope, you are incapable of feeling."

"Upon my word," said he, "I begin to see great merit in the lines of that chair." He smiled a little.

"Come," I said, "you have something that I greatly desire. That is valuable to me. I admit that. But that value exists only for me. You cannot realize on it from anyone else for the value does not exist for them. And I do not intend to make this chair valuable for you. In short I do not intend to permit you to realize on my predicament. I can simply go away, and I shall do so. I shall then regard your not giving me the chair in my extremity as a judgment of God. I shall go away without it."

At that he looked at me queerly, Vincent. I realized that now for the first time he believed that I was making an appeal to him man to man and not just trying to drive a good bargain.

"Surely," he said, "you did not expect me to make you a gift of the chair."

"Under the circumstances," I replied. "I felt that I was dealing with a man who might be generous enough to do so. I thought perhaps you would not permit the mere accident of your ownership of this article to ruin me."

"How much will you give me for the chair?" he asked after hesitating a moment.

"Not a penny, beyond the cost to you at the sale and your repairs. I thought, Herr Mayer, that you did not sell second-hand furniture."

"I don't," he said, "and so I am not going to sell this chair."

At least a half-minute's silence ensued. I saw him studying me intently. I decided to play my last card.

"May I take the chair with me now then, or shall I send around for it tomorrow?"

"So you *did* believe I might give it to you, after all!" he exclaimed. "You are the first Gentile I ever met who did not imagine that because I am a Jew I am also Shylock. That play I am sure has cost Christendom

288

infinite millions. Everyone who approaches us thinks he is an Antonio and acts accordingly. I thought you had brought Portia with you," said he grinning at Hickey. "How much do you think your client has given me for the nice chair he is sitting in, Mr. Hickey?" he asked in English.

"God knows," groaned Hickey. "I do not understand German." He looked at me apprehensively.

"Mr. Mayer has just made me a gift of it," I said.

"What! what!" grumbled the lawyer. "Why! I thought he was a Jew."

"I am," said Mayer with a fiery pride.

"Jesus Christ!" bumbled Mr. Hickey.

"Me too," put in Mayer. And at that it was impossible for any of us to restrain ourselves.

"Bring a light, Rachel," he called. The girl came in and lit the candles. We had been so intent on the chair that it was only now that we realized we had been sitting in almost total gloom. Mayer looked at a very large and handsome Swiss watch with enormous seals attached. Outside we could hear Hickey's Bengali coughing dismally in the coach.

"It is now nearly six o'clock," said Mayer, "and I wish you would both do me the honour of remaining for supper. We shall have to stretch it a little," he smiled. "I and my sister live alone here very simply, as you see. We have only come to live in England recently. I shall hope some time to have the pleasure of entertaining you both more magnificently. Who knows?"

He was so inexpressibly sincere and simple in his desire to have us remain that I accepted. Hickey, however, would not do so. "I must return tonight," he insisted. "How will you get home, Adverse?" he asked somewhat brusquely. "This is Hammersmith, you know."

"I shall be happy to send Mr. Adverse home in my own phaeton later on, Mr. Hickey," replied Mayer. "You will not wait and return with him?" he asked a little wistfully. I am glad to say Hickey responded nobly.

"Believe me, it is not prejudice which keeps me from dining with you, Mr. Mayer. I really do have to return at once. Permit me to say that through your accommodation of Mr. Adverse I consider you have also put me under a great obligation to you. I can assure you he does not exaggerate the importance of——"

"The chair," laughed Mayer.

"Exactly," said Hickey.

"Perhaps you had best take it with you in the coach, Mr. Hickey. My carriage is small and it will look strange driving through the city late at night with a large chair slung behind."

So Hickey drove off with the chair.

"It is too late to reach Bittern tonight," he said just before leaving. "Let us hope he has not made any move this afternoon. We must catch him first thing in the morning. I shall call for you at Bishopsgate Street."

My evening with Mayer proved intensely interesting. A great weight was off my mind. I felt boundlessly grateful to him. I was particularly touched by his sending the chair home by Hickey as if to remove all doubt of his intentions. He himself did not refer to it again. I thought the least I could do, however, was to satisfy his curiosity, which I did. He was vastly amused, and did not for an instant show any trace of regret, even when he learned how great an apparent opportunity to profit at my expense had lain in his hands. I am sure he realized that I meant what I said about not intending to bargain for the chair. But by telling him how great was my obligation I was also enabled to convey to him some sense of my gratitude. Our conversation flowed with a rare ease, nor was our compatibility due to wine. He was soon unfolding to me the state of his own affairs as I had already done with mine. As a genuine confidence had been established between us by the chair, the usual diffidences seemed to have been broken down as if by an acquaintanceship of long standing.

You would scarcely guess, Vinc, from my description of the style this Hebrew lives in that he and his family are already a power in European finance. His father, who lives at Frankfort, is a great collector of coins and medals and has just been made financial agent for the elector of Hesse-Cassel. He is also negotiating a loan of ten million thalers for the King of Denmark, in which I believe Ouvrard is interested. There are four brothers, Anselm, Solomon, Nathan, and Jacob. Anselm has great influence in northern Germany and is heavily interested in Prussian and Bavarian loans, Solomon has a branch of the house at Vienna also doing well, and Nathan, who is my friend here, was sent over to England about a year ago to arrange for the shipping of English manufactures. He has his own house at Manchester. The house here at Shepherd's Bush near London is only a temporary affair, rather a secret one I gather. Eventually he intends coming to London when he has established himself well enough to set up properly.

I call your notice at some length to this remarkable family as in my opinion you will soon have to reckon with them. They do business for some reason under the name of "Rothschild." Nathan will not tell me why.

Their system is a most interesting and vital one. From what I can gather they have a strict family compact by which the house is eventually to cover Europe. Each brother is to become a financial power in the particular capital in which he has been sent to reside. The children of the various brothers are to marry their cousins and the strictest loyalty is to be maintained, each aiding the other and all each other. The head of the house is to remain at Frankfort. They have already gone far toward building up this system. Jacob, who is still a boy, is eventually to take over at Paris. In the meantime Nathan is establishing the English branch and goes over to Paris frequently, which was the reason we saw him there that day.

These brothers already maintain a network of agents in influential places to gather news both financial and political and a complete system of pigeon posts from one capital city to another. By this scheme they are enabled constantly to anticipate the market everywhere both in buying and selling operations, but especially in government loans and stocks. They have also a number of fast sailing-craft in their hire.

The house at Hammersmith is, I take it, the pigeon post establishment for England. Seeing the pigeon arrive that day I first called on Mayer opened my eyes and I have since seen hampers of pigeons arrive, doubtless those to be dispatched from here. He has never said anything about this himself and gives out that he is a fancier which passes well enough. His sister keeps the house at Hammersmith without even a servant for reasons of secrecy, I suppose. That is typical. Nothing out of the family.

I have come to know Nathan rather well, however. Have seen him a number of times since our first meeting and the growing intimacy is evidently welcome to us both. He began operations here on very small capital but has increased it remarkably. The seeming rashness and boldness of his operations repulses some people, who do not know, of course, that he is trading on advance information. They think him merely lucky so far. I hope to succeed in interesting him in the Mexican scheme, but of that in its place. And now to bring my own affairs to their conclusion, as well as this long section of my letter which is really a sort of running diary for your benefit——

Hickey and I drove out early next morning to Captain Bittern's cottage at Chelsea where he is living with his niece, a widow with two little girls. Yes, we took the chair. Hickey did not alight from the coach, however.

I went in alone to see the captain, who I believe likes me, although no one would ever suspect it who does not know him. He seemed to regard me as a kind of providence, because I suppose I inherit, for him at least, the prestige of the head of the house which he served for nearly forty years. In relating his experiences in prison he broke down. I can only say it was for me a terrible experience. He has become a sort of minor prophet of his sect and was rabid about the chair. When he brought the subject up I simply said I had brought it with me of course; that I regretted his sufferings enormously and wished not only to restore the property that had been taken from him so unjustly but also to testify further my esteem for the works of the Lord at the Spitalfields Chapel and to provide for the proper education of his two grandnieces, who, as he kept saying, are "nice little girls— little girls"—and indeed they are.

To my great relief he acquiesced in this and actually smiled when the chair was brought in. He is to have the satisfaction of returning it to the chapel himself. At any rate all hostile threats of actions at law completely subsided and Mrs. Quaire as I went out followed me down the little door-yard and whispered that she would see that "uncle didn't make no more fuss," with tears in her eyes. So I left Captain Bittern sitting at ease in the chair. Counting Hickey's "honorarium" for what he calls "purely diplomatic services," that chair cost me well-nigh £700. Yet because it introduced me to Mayer I think it was worth it. I am greatly impressed by that man.

The light is beginning to steal through the windows of my new lodgings, yet my pen is still sliding on. There are no birds in London except sparrows, as yet, and I miss them. Lord, how dreary is the fog and snow! I long for the sun—where is it? I *must* stop now. The Barings effected the transfer of the Bonnyfeather estate to me two days ago and I have now nothing to fear except the well-known slings and arrows (do you know them in German?), and my own unknown capacity in the presence of a great sum of money. I need your advice. Tomorrow, by the gods, you shall have the Mexican business set down, and then the whole book can go off to you by the next messenger. I am lonely, or I would not write you so much. But to have

293

a single confidant anywhere is balm to the soul. And so I talk to you with my pen.

God bless me it's seven o'clock a.m., unless Protestant steeples all lie.

———————

27th January, 1802

So much for good resolutions about finishing my letter "tomorrow." I have missed the messenger again. Mr. Henry Hope returns to Amsterdam day after tomorrow, however, and has himself kindly offered to carry this across and see it forwarded to you at Paris.

I will give you a résumé here of the present status of the Mexican business rather than a narrative of how it has developed, with such comments on the personalities I have been dealing with as I trust will prove helpful both to you and M. Ouvrard.

As soon as the crisis in my own affairs was allayed I intimated to Mr. Thomas Baring that I should appreciate the opportunity of thanking Sir Francis in person. Anxious not to seem to be taking advantage of a personal interview, I also hinted that I had a confidential matter from Ouvrard to deliver to the head of the firm. I can tell you Thomas pricked up his ears, and an interview with Sir Francis, who was visiting Mr. Henry Hope at Richmond, where the latter is building a new house, was promptly arranged. The conjunction of the heads of both houses seemed auspicious.

I had just purchased a fine little turnout and provided myself in every particular with the proper clothes, sparing no expense and taking Hickey's advice. He is by way of being a conservative dandy and understands good form, the best tailors, dealers, and shops. I derive, I confess, an immense satisfaction in seeing a certain orphan arrayed impeccably. My armour! At any rate I drove to Richmond in that style of perfection which stops just short of foppery. My reception there by Sir Francis Baring and later by Mr.

Henry Hope, to whom the former presented me, will always remain one of the warmest recollections of this frigid isle.

We retired to the library, where there was actually a fire. Sir Francis was, if I do not flatter myself, almost affectionate in his manner. He was obviously gratified by my expressions of gratitude, in which, however, he cut me short to reminisce of his schoolmates John Bonnyfeather and your father Johann Nolte. He inquired eagerly about you, and repeated several times his sense of satisfaction that the "sons" of his schoolmates, for so he phrased it, should be doing so well in the world. "The best things in this world," he said, "flow from noble friendships. It is an immense satisfaction to me to find you young men continuing ours into the second generation. I hope you will both marry and have children." He was quite insistent on that point and also inquired about your operations in Paris. I was thus enabled to introduce naturally enough my bringing over of Ouvrard's treasury drafts.

Please tell M. Ouvrard that Sir Francis was greatly impressed by this evidence of his, Ouvrard's, confidence and serious desire to forward the scheme. He discussed the whole matter from his own standpoint most candidly and later called in Mr. Henry Hope to join us. In short we spent the whole morning on it. I stayed to luncheon and we resumed in the afternoon.

I shall not give you those conversations in detail till I return. The upshot of the matter is, after several such consultations, in which Mr. Thomas Baring and Mr. Wall have also been called in, about as follows:

Both the Barings and Hopes are convinced that Ouvrard means business. The initial drafts for a million dollars they consider ample to set up the machinery in America. They will, however, demand complete control of these operations without any interference as to the temporary investment of the funds in the United States and elsewhere; also the designation of the personnel of the firms to be set up in America and the merchants to be utilized there as correspondents in forwarding the neutral goods into which the capital will be turned.

The entire relation between the Barings in London, the Hopes in Amsterdam, and Ouvrard at Paris is to remain without exception confidential. All correspondence with England is to be avoided and M. Ouvrard himself is to come to Amsterdam to guarantee the Hopes of his ability to continue to provide drafts on the Mexican treasury to the extent he mentioned. Also they would prefer that he should, once the agents are established in America, place in their hands at Amsterdam further drafts to the extent of seven millions if possible, and five at least. The last I think will be a condition of their beginning operations, the drafts to be cashed by their agent.

If the above arrangements are agreed and adhered to by M. Ouvrard, both Sir Francis and Mr. Henry Hope pledge their good names to exert themselves to the utmost to replace in Ouvrard's hands, as soon as commercial operations will permit, the equivalent in value of his drafts either in specie or in goods. Their own method of profit and its extent must be left in their hands, and should losses occur they must be borne by M. Ouvrard out of the capital provided. Also there are to be no written agreements and the whole transaction is to rest, as it must and should, on the mutual confidence of all parties in one another's integrity.

Under no condition is the source of the capital involved to be revealed by anyone. It is also suggested that in this stage of the affair the necessary preliminary correspondence should be carried on between you and me; you to negotiate with Ouvrard, and I with the Barings and Hopes, thus leaving no direct trace.

Let me know as to M. Ouvrard's attitude toward these proposals without delay—for the Barings are extremely anxious if the thing goes forward to take advantage of the peace now being made at Amiens, the duration of which they do not anticipate will be long. Therefore, haste.

I enclose Sir F. B.'s personal receipt for the Mexican

drafts which he made for me in duplicate and one of which I retain. I am also arranging to have Montgomery and Ticknor build a coach for Ouvrard which will cost in French money about 14,000 francs. Does he desire it? It will be a magnificent one. I enclose the drawings which cost me £6, 8s, and I should like to be reimbursed whether O. takes the coach or not. Kindly convey my respects to him, and tell him so.

Now one thing more. Before the drafts for one million now in Sir F. B.'s hands can be cashed, an estimated expense of establishing agents in America of £100,000 will be involved. That must be forthcoming. Mr. Henry Hope at first insisted that Ouvrard should provide it all. I have, however, represented to him that the initial good faith of all parties should be made manifest in this, and he and Sir Francis have arranged between them to guarantee £50,000 of it. I suggest that Ouvrard should be asked by you to contribute £20,000, and that you, I, and Nathan Mayer take up the remaining £30,000 equally between us. (Take Mayer's participation in this on my word, if you will, and say nothing about it.) We understand each other. Sir Francis is satisfied I should go to New Orleans. That seems fated. Get me some maps and books about Louisiana.

All hail to the House of the Wolf. I shall continue to write whether I hear from you or not. Things are looking up here with the peace coming on. I have bought considerable English stocks on Mayer's advice.

> Your humble obedient Servant,
>
> A. A.

P.S. This should reach Amsterdam by February 2nd at longest—kindness of Mr. Henry Hope.

Dear Toni:

Your letter from London of December 28th last reached me somewhat sooner than you had opined, being brought down from Hamburg by P. T. Lestapsis, who has come here on business for Messers Hope. He is staying at the House of the Wolf.

I thank God you arrived safely and have had a cordial reception at the Barings. I shall await further advices as to the progress of your own affair and of the Mexican project, on tiptoe. Pray proceed as rapidly as possible in the latter. There can be no doubt Ouvrard is anxious to finish that. I shall tell you why.

He came storming in here two nights ago having had a terrible interview with the first consul in which the latter forced him to loan to the state most of his gains to date on government contracts, taking gov't bills on next year's revenue as security. Bonaparte is angry over the recent flurry on the Bourse, no doubt suspecting the cause, and has commanded Ouvrard to retire for a while to Castle Raincey—O.'s magnificent estate.

O. is therefore in a perilous position with most of his liquid assets in the hands of the government and is wildly desirous of cashing in on the Mexican drafts which the first consul cynically contrives to pay him for supplies furnished to Spain. My own idea is that Bonaparte intends to force O. to cash these drafts and knows that with his many associations he will in some manner be able to do so, in which case Bonaparte will be able to hold O. accountable for trading with the enemy and at the same time have the Mexican silver put into circulation here. I would explain this to the Barings and Hopes. To protect himself O. is anxious to put things into their hands—*and will make any terms not absolutely ruinous*. Anything is better than nothing. Now no more business till I hear from you further as to developments in London.

The news here is that the treaty making at Amiens proceeds favourably to France, your friend Joseph

Bonaparte and Talleyrand doing well for themselves. Rumour has it that the peace with the supine British ministry of Mr. Addington will be used by Bonaparte, who is soon to be known only as "Napoleon" by the way, as a breathing space in which to prepare for the invasion of England. There is no let-up here in military activity. "Napoleon" is more popular than Bonaparte. Rentes soar.

Here is some personal news for you—*important*. Don Luis is in Paris. He is arranging the matter of selling blank permits from the Spanish crown to trade with its colonies. These are to be put in the hands of Ouvrard for certain loans and concessions. O. has already approached me about fitting out ships at Leghorn to trade with Cuba. This may have important personal developments for you. Ouvrard also says, "If M. Adverse can successfully arrange matters in London with the Barings and Hopes *I shall accompany him on his way to New Orleans as far as Madrid* in order to perfect arrangements there by means of these permits for the shipment of specie from Mexico to Louisiana." So be ready. You and Don Luis may be doing business together yet! I met him at Raincey and he bowed most courteously without even the change of a wrinkle over our last meeting. Faith was at the Comédie with him the other night, looking handsome. Neither of them seemed to have suffered by their experience. I wonder how they got down off the mountain. They go to Madrid shortly I have ascertained.

Now one thing more. *Angela is here.* I saw her at the Opéra Comique in *Jeannet et Colin* in the leading rôle. She is no less a person than Mlle. Georges, who created such a furor at Vienna and Milan as the cantatrice in the operas at the Teatro della Scala. They say that at Milan a year or so ago the first consul was very partial to her and that he had scenes there about her with Josephine. He is also said to be calling upon her here, secretly; that she is his mistress! What there is in these rumors, of course, no one knows. Probably it is idle talk. No doubt simply because he applauds and admires her at the opera along with the rest of the world tongues wag. The only thing I can say for certain is that he is always present when she is on the bill and Josephine is usually absent. C'est ça.

Now I'll tell you what I have done. I have sent her an exquisite but not very large pearl necklace made-up by Fossin with that little rigmarole of names you used to keep muttering and laughing about enclosed. I am not sure I got them *all* right, but nearly so. I simply put the address of the House of the Wolf on it. Now tell me I have not done wrong. The pearls went yesterday and I have heard nothing yet. This it seems to me, Toni, is a real romance and I could not refrain from getting you into it just to see what happens. You can pay me for the pearls, mon vieux, a pretty sum, if you are angry. Yes, the lady is beautiful—and Herr Gott, her voice! Do not suspect me or be jealous even before breakfast.

Fräulein Geiler and her mother arrive tomorrow, "pour une petite visite." I shall hire a double coach, the berlin will never do, and we shall see the town. I am on fire. Thank God, Hélène has gone. Her "brother" has been arrested for killing a Russian prince in a duel over the cards. Six aces turned up in one pack which each claimed the other had furnished. "Cinq et un" they call it here. The prince was sent back to St. Petersburg pickled in brandy. I hope they will not guillotine poor La Force for plunging a Russian into paradise.

Your talk with Mr. Udney sounds interesting and throws a curious light on the past. P. T. Lestapsis tells me Parish is cold steel, able, terribly lucky at cards, and regards his domestic establishment as merely one means of advancing his one interest in life; to wit, D. Parish. Be careful there. David is on the inside with the Hopes and has made a great deal of money for both himself and M. Talleyrand, whom he entertained beautifully. Mrs. Udney I have no doubt revels in all this. As to Florence—who knows? I shall be amused to hear when you get to Amsterdam. I am sorry for the old man. If you go to see him be your usual silent self.

I shall await your next with mixed anxiety and expectation. I regard you as lucky and Ouvrard concurs.

"Certain people," he says, "have the habit of being fortunate in their collision with events. This has little to do with their ability or character. It is a product of personality plus a fated life rhythm. Their cogs fit into events when others find no slots. Hence, they turn with the wheels of the times and help turn them. My success in life is largely due to my being able to pick such people out by instinct."

I thought that might cheer you. I believe it, too. But that is not why I believe *in* you—you know—through everything. You return to this house when you return to Paris, remember that.

Your humble obedient servant,

Vincent Nolte.

P. S.   Your mysterious bundle is safe.

N. B.   I contemplate a long engagement.

London, 10th February, 1802

Dear Vinc,

No word from you yet, which is to be expected. This is purely personal. I jot things down from time to time and will send them on in a bundle after hearing from you.

Mr. Udney has written. I am to come down to see him in the spring if I am still here. Deep snow here now, a horrible form of the element that gets down your boots. My new apartments are in Farringdon Street close by the bookseller Routledge. I live alone with a valet and houseman. A woman comes in to cook and clean. I thought of taking up with a Covent Garden actress, one Mrs. Arnold, a young widow. My tropical lassitude has notably vanished. But the widow has a baby daughter and Hickey suggested other complications, so I shall remain in the paths of virtue. Hickey and I go about town a good deal. This is at my expense but he is quite frank about that and desires me to understand that he is not using me or selling his acquaintance as he can live as well as he wants to on his own income. And in this I believe him sincere for he has never failed to advise me correctly. He says as long as my Havana cigars last he will stick to me through thick and thin. I have also visited some clubs wtih Henry Baring and lost and won considerable amounts. This I ceased to do at the request of Sir Francis who is alarmed that anyone connected with the firm should be seen at the tables as constantly as is Henry. The young gentleman promptly dropped me when he found my estate was not to be the means of an evening's amusement. He goes to Amsterdam shortly.

I have called at M. Talleyrand's "glove shop." He enclosed in his package an English bank note with directions to purchase the gloves for Madame G. with that particular note. It must have been marked, for when I received the gloves I found there was something in each pair. It proved to be a large sum of money in bank notes and the following communication.

Monsieur: the letters you have been asked to deliver to certain persons have nothing in them but an authenticating signature. You will act accordingly.

I was at first greatly puzzled by this until it occurred to me that M. T. desired me to deliver only his *personal message.* Thus the letters with his signature would serve to authenticate me as coming from him and without any possible complications if they were stolen or lost or not delivered. The "glove shop" is, of course, French agent headquarters here. I shall avoid it in future meticulously as I do not wish to become involved in something I have no interest in furthering. It might totally ruin me. I returned the "gloves" by my man with an oral message to the "proprietor," saying I would deliver certain letters out of personal esteem for M. T. but that I must positively *not* be counted on in the future. My man George returned with the reply,

"Monsieur is wise." I related the whole circumstance to Sir Francis, who congratulated me on my good sense and arranged to have me see Messers Pitt, Fox, and the Prime Minister Addington.

Vincent, please call on M. Talleyrand, convey him my profound respects, and tell him I have "delivered the letters." That I found Mr. Pitt in a flowered dressing gown drinking port in the afternoon and that he said, after listening to my message, "Tell Talleyrand that even a sick hound knows the difference between an aniseed bag and the trail of an old fox trying to get the weather gauge by sneaking up wind. I greatly regret that due to the late hour the figure is a mixed one." For another three hours we discussed only port and the orations of Cicero. I had to be carried out and I assured him with tears in my eyes I was not a French agent. "By Gad, I never thought so," said he. "None of them they send to me can drink above four decanters. Tell that to Talleyrand, too. He employs nothing but white wine merchants to peddle his lies. Your Latin is better than your English, young man. It has been an afternoon. *Vale*."

Mr. Fox, whom I found at a pub, said, "The noble spirit of freedom, which is professed in France and practised in England, will light the mutual path to peace which both nations should tread. Tell M. Talleyrand that I am myself coming to France shortly and that I should be surprised but rejoiced to discover in him an ardent colleague."

Mr. Addington asked me what I wanted, after fingering the letter gingerly. When I replied, "Nothing,"—he laughed, and after some consideration said that he hoped M. Talleyrand would continue to enjoy good health. He asked me what I did in England and I was, I think, able to satisfy him on that score. He acted like a dull confused man. I was surprised to find him so.

Explain to M. T. why I cannot take his "gloves." I do not intend to be worn out and thrown away. The peace they say here will be ready soon. Now no more for a little.

Dear Vinc:

Your letter of the 10th instant arrived here today, brought on by Mr. John Williams Hope from Amsterdam. By this time you must have my second and I shall anxiously await your reply to my specific questions as to Ouvrard's guarantees.

In the meantime, the information you gave me as to O.'s situation I have passed on to the Barings and Hopes, and on the strength of it they are this week making full plans for the setting-up of the agents and correspondents in America. The heads of both firms are now in London and their conferences, which I have frequently been asked to attend, go on apace. Sir Francis is particularly impressed with the possibilities opened up by Ouvrard's being able to furnish blank permits to trade with Spanish possessions. He feels that they can be combined with our present plans to enormous advantage.

Angela! I dare not set down what passes through my mind and heart as I write that name. You did right nobly to send the pearls. Tell me swiftly what is her reply and where she lives. I do not believe the stories about her, but they trouble me. I find I care much. It will be hard to wait for your letters. I would like to hurry back to Paris. But it would be running away from the battle here. Good luck to your own sweet and ample Fräulein and you. Write—*send by special messenger*. All these expenses I will take up promptly when I return. Do not save money now. Its best use is to stop anxiety.

Vinc, please send by one of your feluccas out of Leghorn for my man Juan and my great dog Simba who are both near Algeciras in Spain. I wish them to meet me in Paris when I return. Juan would be invaluable about the House of the Wolf and Simba could be the night watch for Paul. I suggest you get skipper Manchori in his swift little *Stella Maris* to call in direct at Tarifa for them and land Juan at Marseilles. I enclose a letter to Juan. Also, on second thought, a good fat draft on Amsterdam to sweeten my accounts with you, pearls and all.

Instead of keeping this letter for further jottings I send it off tonight with a bundle of London newspapers via Helgoland. Only diplomatic mails as yet to France.

Get me Juan. It comes across me I shall need him.

Your humble obedient Servant,
A. A.

Paris, 3rd March, 1802

Dear Toni:

This in vast haste. All your letters, including that of February 19th last, had arrived by three days ago, some grossly delayed, also the newspapers which have been eagerly read and are already called for by borrowing friends.

I devoted a night to studying your correspondence in order to be able to act carefully, and snatching some sleep early in the morning, called the berlin after breakfast and started out to see Ouvrard at Raincey. We spent the day over the Baring-Hope proposals. Now then to speed all things to a conclusion:

Ouvrard accepts the conditions as laid down by Sir Francis Baring and desires both the Barings and Hopes to hasten perfecting the American forwarding arrangements without delay. He says should any doubt arise in their minds about any *particular* to proceed on the assumption that he has *already* approved it. He must realize on the immense sums locked up in these Mexican drafts and all means which lead to that end are proper means.

Let me add that you cannot overestimate the necessity for dispatch. Ouvrard is in a precarious way and if he fails it will precipitate a panic of major proportions on the continent. I myself have loaned him 500,000 francs.

As soon as the agents are ready to proceed to America Ouvrard will repair to Amsterdam and place in the hands of the Hopes any amount of drafts on the Mexican treasury which they may be able to handle. "Bonaparte is choking me to death with them," he says.

Now then—I enclose you a draft on the Bank of England for £30,000, mine and Ouvrard's share of the advance working capital which you and Mayer are to bring up to the agreed £50,000; the Barings and Hopes to contribute the balance of the total of £100,-000. Also a letter from Ouvrard to Sir Francis Baring in confirmation of your negotiations, which is to be the only correspondence, and which he requests shall be destroyed.

Now, mon vieux, a thousand congratulations on your able handling of this matter which has roused Ouvrard to an embarrassing style of encomium. Insist upon the post at New Orleans. The first pickings will be there, and millions of specie will pass through your hands. You are to return with Ouvrard from Amsterdam to Paris and he takes it for granted you will go on with him to Madrid. No details now, but prepare yourself. I know you can be as persuasive in Spanish as you are in English. As for your own inheritance being placed in your hands—thank God for it, and don't give away any more chairs. I read your account of that with all the thrill of a Gothic romance.

I have heard from Angela. I devote my next letter to her. Also I have sent for Juan by post to Leghorn today. Johann Frank, my cousin, carries on there well. The *Stella Maris* shall go.

Send me no more drafts, you ridiculous fellow, or I will charge you a ruinous discount storage on your precious bundle, and board and lodging for Juan and the hound Simba when they arrive. We are both rich, my boy! You remember too well the philosophy of McNab in estimating your friends.

Anna has a young Düsseldorfer, einen Knaben.
Ever your humble obedient servant,

Vincent Nolte

I have not seen Talleyrand yet. This must go *now*
by P. T. Lestapsis. Angela must even wait.

London, 13th March 1802

Dear Vinc:

Your letter with Ouvrard's confirmation and the
draft arrived here yesterday by Lestapsis—I love the
man's moniker—who arrived ory-eyed from lack of
sleep bringing it.

I immediately hunted up Mayer, procured his £10,-
000. Drew an order for my own and driving around to
Bishopsgate Street took up Mr. Thomas Baring, whence
we all proceeded to Richmond where we found Sir
Francis and the two Hopes at "East Sheen" and went
into conference.

The great scheme is under way. Inform O. that it
is being pressed night and day.

The Hopes return to Amsterdam shortly to perfect
final arrangements there and will wish O. to come to
them there in May.

This without further comment but vast relief. Doubt
not both our shares in this matter are appreciated
here. Lestapsis, the somewhat battered Mercury, goes
back with this and is waiting below as I write. Consider that without further advice all goes well.

Yr. H. O. S.

A. A.

For God's sake tell me about Angela, you devil.

Paris, 15th March 1802

Dear Toni:

I know you will curse me for my delay about Angela.
Business, my boy, before romance. I have seen Talley-

rand and he actually laughed heartily at your message, "Tell monsieur he has a gay spirit and has done well." Now Angela——

I have not seen her. She lives at Meudon. Debrülle, now old, toothless, and fatherly, called. He asked for you and would say little to me. He said he had written to you once in desperate circumstances years ago and heard nothing. I assured him you could not have received his letter in Africa. He seemed pleased to hear that you would be in Paris shortly and said that "Mademoiselle" thanked you for the pearls and would communicate when you arrived. I asked him if he needed funds. He said *not from me*, and departed.

I am sorry I cannot tell you more. Evidently I am not expected to call on Mademoiselle, and I shall not. It is rather curious. That is all.

Your friend,

V. N.

P.S. Instruct the builders to proceed with Ouvrard's coach, a draft will follow.

N.B. Take out your £6.8 for the plans.

———————

London, 30th March 1802

Dear Vinc:

Peace was proclaimed here today. Mayer knew it the morning of the 28th. A little bird told him before breakfast, which he took with me at Farringdon Street. We drove around to the Exchange and I put all I could muster into government stocks. A rumour as to a hitch in the negotiations at Amiens had sent government stocks down the evening before. They soared this afternoon after the heralds with silver trumpets went about. Very picturesque, to me a golden sound. I sold out this evening and made a cool £13,000 odd. Mayer's takings are enormous. He immediately came and borrowed £10,000 from me which I gave him on his own note without security at current interest. Our association is a curious one. He is very silent; so am

I. I know, for instance, he is not now recouping himself for the lost opportunity of the chair. He knows that I know it. His winnings on Change make no change whatever in him. That puzzles most Englishmen, I think. Nine-tenths of them pay no attention to any person who does not possess property. Poor men with ideas here are merely ridiculous. A Jew who is rich and does not care fills them with secret awe. The expression "A man of sterling character" exhausts all compliment here. There must be now, or there must once have been, Englishmen who were "beings" instead of "havings," but I do not meet them. My misfortune, perhaps, but a sore one. If I lived in England I should simply become property.

One of the most curious things about this country is everyone's horror of expressing any emotion. All the upper classes seem to have stolen their faces out of a wax works. The complexions are impeccable and the expressions moulded. I am frequently suspected and despised, I find, because my expression sometimes changes.

Mayer says that only the complexions of the English are due to the climate. The fixed expressions are due to the necessity of all respectable persons, i.e., all people with property, maintaining an emotional status quo as the custodians of things. They cling like clams to the rocks of property and they look like them, closed, shell-fast. Pry them open, and a faint muscular withdrawal takes place as the bivalve slowly shifts uneasily and gets a grip on itself in order to close tighter. Occasionally an impious foreigner, usually a Frenchman, inserts an uncomfortable fact or even an idea into one of these clams that has been taken off its guard while breathing. The shell then closes, and after a due period of expressionless effort at digestion, the idea is exuded in the form of a smooth pearl of wisdom in English literature. Respectable writings here are now confined solely to scientific and economic treatises. Everything else is purely romantic. Poets, novelists and musicians, it is thought, appeal merely to the emotions. Emotions are not real when no one has any fervent feelings except a fixed fervour about property. I argued with Mayer about this, and he is, of course, not being entirely serious.

Yet there is much truth in his way of putting it. Only the lower classes here, he points out, can still laugh, dance, sing, swear, drink and fornicate without being embarrassed about it. They have no property. But that will not last long, he says. "You ought to live for a while like I do in Manchester. They are tiring out the whole population on the weaving machines there. Those people no longer laugh. They drink to be able to forget. If the English win out against Bonaparte half the world is going to get to look like Manchester, because the English themselves must keep running away from it in order to live, and they have nothing but ideas out of Manchester to take along with them. The Greeks took Athens, the Romans took Rome, we take Jerusalem, and the English will take Manchester along wherever they go."

"Why do you come to live here?" I asked him.

"I will tell you why," said he. "On the continent the old quarrel between Athens and Rome on one side and Jerusalem, no, let us say Carthage on the other, is still instinctively understood. It is known, for instance, in France, Italy, and Spain that Jews are still oriental; that they dislike Greek symmetry and perspective and despise Roman order and logic. They are, in short, hereditary enemies of the classical state which insists on conceiving of itself as something eternal and divine no matter what its form. The Jews believe something else is eternal and divine and have no state. Their philosophy is not political. It is racial and individual. Their only organization is the synagogue and the family or firm. They therefore exist in, but apart from, Western society and are suspects. Now in Latin countries this is clearly recognized and precautions are taken by the Gentiles accordingly. There it is still an idea against an idea. But in England the state is merely a 'commonwealth,' a means of controlling interests, for there are no ideas of state above property. Anything, even religion, can be compromised, bought, and sold. It is the greatest auction of the ages. I find myself at home in Tyre and Sidon, London and Manchester, with Jerusalem destroyed; and I find myself still a stranger in Paris, with Rome—not destroyed. I am devoting my life here to removing those memories of Rome which still make it uncomfortable in England for Hebrews. It is like this: In Paris M. d'Ayen offered me a pinch of snuff for helping him keep forty-five thousand francs and his pride. In England I shall some day be elected to Parliament, out of respect for my property, and sell snuff to the local d'Ayens so that it will cost them dear every time they sneeze in my face. But they will not do so. Snuff is going out. It makes the English change their expression, and no man of property can afford to be seen doing that."

After that he borrowed £10,000 from me and sent me a snuff-box with Bonaparte's head on it. "I have no use for this one here," he said.

I think this snuff-box with the first consul's head, for which Mayer has no use; throws some light on why he borrowed the ten thousand as soon as I made it. He is investing heavily in the "commonwealth." From what I can gather a great portion of the family takings on the continent are also being concentrated in his hands and put into English rentes. He believes, I know, that in the coming struggle, in which this peace is only to be a brief breathing space, the English will win. I feel that my money he borrowed is as safely invested as it can be. Also I have arranged with the Barings to keep the bulk of it invested here, in which the example of Mayer encourages me. After all *England is an island* and the conflagrations of Europe are stopped by the Channel. That is the most important historical and geographical fact in the world.

10th April, 1802

This is a jotted letter again, you see. Your news of Angela, and Debrülle's strange visit fill me with both anticipations and forebodings. Of course, I never got his (or her) letter, which? I shall write you no more about Angela, because the subject tends to fill my mind. I loved her and I think I still do, though God knows what she may be like now. Still the past holds. I send you a brief note enclosed to be sent to her. Read it so that you will understand my attitude. It is possible Debrülle is merely after money from me, but I doubt it. Now no more about that till further developments.

Spring came here with a bound. The season is strangely advanced. I go down to Brighton frequently, where the crown prince has repaired very early this year. He is building an outrageous Aladdin's palace there called the "Pavilion," at a disgraceful cost. The bubble domes of it already begin to rise. I have a room on James Street near the sea and yesterday saw H.R.H. in a striped chariot, that seemed to have been dragged through the rainbow, driving along under my windows with a whole boatload of trollops—titled ones I suppose. He is a handsome dog but looked flushed and sleepy. These Hanoverians get no shouts from me. All the dukes, sons of the mad king, are wastrels, too.

There are over seventy coaches a day now they say to and from Brighton. The roads are wonderful and the way they change horses a marvel. I drive my own curricle and keep two horses on the route. Rather expensive. I have nothing else to do and find casual company at Brighton. I have found a pretty face at Cuckfield in the Weald of Sussex on the way down—or up—the most charming village I have ever seen. Hickey took me to White's where I dropped £56. At Brook's with Henry Baring I won £28 about two months ago. I shall call it even and let the clubs alone. There has been so much lucky chance in my life that I do not wish to tempt Fortune at her own game.

Brighton, 24th April

Have installed the pretty face from Cuckfield in my rooms at James Street here. We drive about a good deal. Dolly is a simple and true little soul, a cobbler's daughter. Parents dead. We orphans have joined forces. "Divided we stand, united we fall." This is a quiet, uncomplicated affair. We are just like a boy and a girl who are in no danger of being caught. The time passes without our knowing it. I stay out of London much now. I am merely waiting for the heads of the two houses to perfect matters here when I go with Mr. Henry Hope back to Amsterdam. A letter from Udney. I am to go to see him at "Spichwich" in Devon near Widdecombe-on-the-Moor. *We* go by way of Bath. Good-bye.

A. A.

P.S.   Ouvrard's coach is a-building. I shall ship it to Amsterdam and drive down to Paris in it with him, since that is *his* plan. Madrid has some attractions, you know. I do not fear Don Luis any more with his coach gone.

———————

London, 28th May 1802

Dear Vinc:

This is my last letter from England as I leave for Holland before the next French mail.

I returned to Farringdon Street yesterday morning after as ethereal a journey as any fallen angel can enjoy in this sphere. I drove with Dolly in the curricle as far as Bath, which I much desired to see. The trip down the New Forest with "the darling buds of May" breaking forth into a green haze and the birds coming in from the south along with the sun, the stopping off at little inns overnight with the noise of streams coming through the windows and my dear little Hebe in a dream of pleasure in my arms—is beyond the powers of expression to describe. And yet I am sure I can convey it to you, you sentimental old German compound of Rhinegold and moonlight. Only this was English moonlight in the month of May, and the magnificent road leading to Bath clicking under our wheels by day, a pair of fine little mares in neighing fettle to the curricle and the shining mail coaches sweeping by with the sound of their horns dying away and overtaking us as if a universal hunt were up and away. The guards *did* blow the horns at us, as might be expected when one does not remove one's arm from a girl's shoulders even for the Royal Mail. And I have no doubt we both shone under the hood with the same colour as Dolly's curls against my shoulder; with the kind of light that only lovers give off (or sunlight on willows) for we were really mightily happy.

Strangely enough I was all the more happy because this experience was made poignant by a conviction I cannot shake off that this is the last really youthful, love-in-springtime full of May buds and golden sunlight I shall have. It is true I grow older, but in England this spring I seem to have grown younger. The trip to Bath was like some of those morning drives with Angela about Livorno as a boy. Indeed, I think I have to some extent thought of Dolly as Angela.

We had a most glorious week in Bath, very gay, bathing in the morning and taking the triple glasses in the pump-room, riding about in chairs, and scaling the romantic cliffs that look down upon the town. Everyone goes to evening services in the Abbey after dinner, then the pump-room again, and then rushes out to the gaming tables and ballrooms and routs. This is the only town in England where I have continually heard happy music. I spared nothing for Dolly's gowns and she was in seven heavens at once. Her voice is so pleasant the bad grammar doesn't need to be noticed. Sussex talk. We stayed at a house in Great Poultney Street, number 36, where was a gentleman M.P., a Mr. Wilbur Farce, who finding I had been in Africa kept me up three nights running asking questions about the slave trade, till I excused myself for a more congenial occupation.

I left Dolly with a Mrs. Razzini, wife to a former

musician, highly respectable, and with an Italian under-standing. Dolly cried only a little (as the house is in Gay Street) and promised to wait for me—well provided, I might add.

I drove down to Exeter and thence over to Totnes, where Mr. Udney met me at the "George" and we had a *rouse* and a *bouse,* which is two names for the same thing. "Spichwich" is not far from Princeton and Widdecombe. It is a pleasant house at the top of a combe filled with ancient, mossy beeches and looks out over the moor from a space of lawn and terrace. Mr. U. alluded to Florence scarcely at all. Mrs. U. still at Amsterdam with the Parishes. The house very quiet, and I am glad of it, as I needed a rest and felt inclined to drowse with Mr. U. and the dogs before the empty fireplace. Much good ale, local hunting talk, riding over the moors that are haunted by something that speaks in the winds from over the heather; something sad and infinitely remote and of the far past and yet whispering always in one's ears. I am sure of it. You know I can hear voices. Mr. U. was like a father. I think we both agreed to play our respective parts. I enjoy finding "parents" here and there as well as other forms of casual affection. The greatest event at "Spichwich" was having the two churchwardens from Widdecombe, Messers Peter and Sylvester Mann, in to dine at which much broad Devon with brewed beverages to wash it down. I stayed on eight days and Mr. U. said, "Goodbye, my boy, I shan't see you again in this world damme!" and rode off with a very red face up a lane blowing his nose like a horn.

I returned to Bath to take Dolly back to Sussex and found her already engaged to marry one A. Taylor, the son of a baker, who peddles hot buns to the chairs and has made a good thing of it. I own this *was* a surprise, but soon saw its advantages and took Mrs. Razzini's advice to leave them both my blessing and depart. Dolly will have a decent dot. The widow, of course, must have helped them. *The banns were up*

315

when I returned. This is best for the girl, too. I drove back to London, lonely again, but relieved of the anticipations of certain tearful farewells.

But farewell now to London and England. I leave with Mr. Henry Hope by Harwich. My man is packing me now. I find your letters about various matters awaiting me and have read them carefully. But no answer to business matters now. All is well for the Mexican project. It will be launched from Amsterdam, from whence in a few days' time I shall be able to send you the final particulars, probably before I myself arrive at Paris. Ouvrard's coach (set up in neat cases) has gone on to Holland. I hope I shall find Juan and Simba at numéro 47 when I return. I long to see you again. My letters have only shaved the surface of events here. Thanks, my dear fellow, for your affectionate and unfailing thought of me—for the welcome that I know awaits me at the House of the Wolf and that lends such genial warmth to the offing. No trouble about passports now. From the Low Countries next D.V.

Your h.o'b.s.

A. A.

---

t'Huys ten Bosch,
Wood of Haarlem,
9th June, 1802

Dear Vinc:

I arrived at Amsterdam five days ago but have delayed writing in order to be able to give you more important news. Discussions have been going on here ever since we arrived toward perfecting final arrangements to set up the apparatus in N. America for forwarding the Mexican bullion. M. Ouvrard's not arriving until yesterday caused me considerable anxiety, as I could see that P. C. Labouchère, the active head of *Messers Hope & Co.,* at Amsterdam, was not inclined to move in the matter until he was assured that the further drafts on Mexico were forthcoming. O.'s arrival, however, settled all that. Not only did he bring the drafts but ten blank licenses to trade with Spanish colonies, which require only the names and destinations of the ships to be filled in and carry permits for cargoes both ways. There is now no drawing back and I give you below a schedule of the projected organization.

America

David Parish (of Parish & Cie, Antwerp) to be Resident Agent-in-Chief of all funding, forwarding, insuring, and investing in North America—to reside at Philadelphia, Pennsylvania, in the United States.

A. P. Lestapsis (of the Amsterdam counting house of Messers Hope & Co.) to be at Vera Cruz, Mexico, but under the Spanish name of "José Gabriel de Villanova," supposed to be acting for the House of Plante of Santander, confidential agents there for the Spanish crown. Lestapsis will cash the drafts at Mexico, forward the specie and look after all cargoes arriving under the licenses.

Anthony Adverse, General Receiving Agent (accountable to both M. Ouvrard and Messers Hope & Co.) resident at New Orleans, Louisiana, to receive all specie shipped by Lestapsis from Vera Cruz and to transmit it to Parish at Philadelphia.

Carlo Cibo, agent at Havana, Cuba (my suggestion).

Commercial agents at the ports of Boston, New York, Baltimore, and Charleston in the Carolinas to be designated by Parish upon his arrival in America.

Great Britain

Baring Bros. & Co., London. They, or the firms designated by them, to receive all specie or cargoes shipped to the British Isles and exchanged thence to Europe.

317

Messers Hope & Co., Amsterdam, to receive, and to assign to and designate all correspondents for cargoes shipped to the continent.

———————————

The Hopes have arranged through Mayer to have the "Rothschilds" at Frankfort look after the disposal of goods in the interior of northern Europe. Ouvrard will himself look after French and Spanish assignments, and you, of course, *it is understood* will be allotted the cargoes for Leghorn as correspondent for Italy.

Parish and Lestapsis sail shortly for America where they will, with the present capital subscribed, make all arrangements for setting up what will undoubtedly become, once the specie starts to flow, one of the major, if not the largest commercial operation of modern times. It is now expected that with the signing of the peace only comparatively small amounts of the bullion brought from Mexico to the United States will be shipped as specie to Europe. Not much in coined silver at any rate will be shipped at any one time, owing to the risk and the enormous insurance. It will be beyond count more profitable first to invest the capital in the United States and transfer it in neutral goods, cargo by cargo, taking advantage of the most favourable prices for colonial produce in the British Isles and Europe, by shipping it to the correspondents of the Hopes and Barings who offer the most favourable terms. They, of course, do not intend to cover or receive all *if any* of these cargoes themselves. They will simply designate the firms to do so. Thus neither the House of Hope nor Baring need appear on ships' papers at all. In case war breaks out again the whole transaction will be between neutral firms in America and neutral firms in Europe. Only the profits will accrue to the Hopes and Barings since their correspondents will, of course, handle such cargoes for the usual commercial agent's fee. But those profits will be immense, for with the English blockade and the French attempt to shut out all English goods, colonial produce is now at a premium all over Europe and the expectation is *to double the value of the original capital received in America by the time it reaches here.* Nor is that all, cargoes from the Spanish colonies will themselves first be sold in the United States at great profit.

David Parish will, therefore, have on his hands a commercial business, both the buying and selling of goods of all kinds in the United States. He will also have the rapid investing of colossal sums of money to look after (at least seven millions in the next two years), to say nothing of the amount of credit which the mere possession of the original capital in cold specie will generate. No one can calculate that, especially in a new country with a raw banking system. And all this, in order to facilitate its transfer to Europe at every opportunity, must be kept in liquid assets.

The meeting yesterday afternoon, in the cabin of one of Messers Hopes' ships, for the greater privacy, was a momentous one. Present: Messers John and Alexander Baring, Messers Henry and John Williams Hope, P. C. Labouchère, M. Ouvrard, David Parish, and your humble obedient servant. On account of the signing of the peace it seemed possible at the last moment Ouvrard might withdraw and attempt to cash his bills direct. I persuaded him, walking up and down the deck beforehand, not to do so. I represented that the peace would probably be of short duration, as most people think, and that *in any event* it was to his interest to have these vast sums concentrated in the hands of honest and neutral people like the Barings and Hopes, where the first consul could not lay his hands on them. This last argument went home, and we then proceeded to the cabin where the final arrangements were made.

Ouvrard particularly cautioned Parish of his responsibility for not creating either furors or panics in the United States owing to the sudden influx and withdrawals of huge sums in bullion; above all not to invest in lands in a new country where the temptation would be great. Parish, I think, did not much like being advised even by so able a man.

David has been chosen for the American post because of his brilliant management of certain colonial deals for the Hopes, successful owing to a consummate intrigue with Talleyrand whom he entertained, as you mentioned, so brilliantly some time ago. He is also great friends with Alexander Baring who married a Philadelphia heiress, Anne, daughter of a Mr. William Bingham, banker of that city, the richest man in the United States, it is said. Hence Parish's path in Philadelphia is smoothed. My own feeling about Parish is that he will organize brilliantly and administer—not so well. This will not affect me at New Orleans, however.

My work there will be confined to arranging the means of carrying the specie safely from Vera Cruz to Louisiana and to shipping it north. I am to receive 2% on all sums *received,* deducting my share in silver dollars, and charging all expenses to Ouvrard. It would be enormously risky to ship direct from Vera Cruz to Philadelphia, owing to British cruisers, pirates, loss by sea on a long voyage, and the staggering insurance. The run from Vera Cruz to New Orleans is a short one and the facilities for dribbling the specie north to Parish in small amounts on swift, little ships from Louisiana, without attracting notice or running the chance of losing several chests in a single disaster dictate the choice of New Orleans. Equally important is the fact that both the Hopes and Ouvrard desire to have me as a neutral receiving agent accountable to them both, thus preventing all argument as to the amounts of capital actually shipped and received from Mexico. Parish is not more than content. And so I go to New Orleans—but not instantly.

It will take Parish and Lestapsis some months at

least to proceed to the United States, organize their affairs there, and acquire agents. In the meanwhile, I am to go to Louisiana by way of Madrid with Ouvrard. By the time I arrive in New Orleans Lestapsis should be in Mexico, Parish ready in Philadelphia, and we shall begin operations. I look forward to *finally establishing myself for life* in a new country with profound satisfaction, and, I confess it, with enormous curiosity as to the outcome. Quién sabe?

The rest of my letter will be a short account of some of my more casual doings here.

After the meeting we all came out to this place, t'Huys ten Borch, Mr. Henry Hope's magnificent (I use the word carefully) country estate near Amsterdam in the Wood of Haarlem. It is quite literally a palace. The Hopes first made an enormous fortune by putting the empire of Russia into European finance, hence a striking presentation portrait of the Empress Catherine II hangs in the grand salon. There is also an extraordinary gallery of old masters, and a park and garden in the Dutch style beyond compare.

Mr. Henry Hope was sensible of my having influenced Ouvrard to continue in the enterprise, and after dinner one night called me out on a balcony overlooking a world of tulip beds and expressed himself unreservedly for that and my other diplomacies. I take pleasure in being praised by a man like him. We talked for an hour while Ouvrard held the others within about the pianoforte, his fat hands and great rings flashing over the keys in a masterful way—he is passionately addicted to music. Before we returned to the room the old man was telling me with tears in his eyes that he was being disgraced by his niece here, who is carrying on with a Dutch officer of dragoons, one Captain Dupff. I was both touched and surprised by this confidence and tell you it so that you may see in what personal estimation I am held by the head of this great house.

I spent the next morning with Ouvrard having his

coach, shipped here in sections, set up. He is childishly pleased with it. I shall almost be afraid to ride to Paris in it as it looks like the one the prince came around in to carry off Cinderella after the glass slipper fitted. There is a portrait of Fortune and her wheel on the ceiling, cornucopias spilling largess from each corner, red morocco upholstery, silver gilt hardware, mirrors! For *God's sake* come out to Raincey in the berlin and pick me up there.

I also dined with Labouchère, the Hopes' partner, with whom a rather curious incident. He insisted upon my meeting his "young sister," and on the way out to his place explained to me what an excellent match she would make and that "a young man with great interests to conserve" could do worse than to ally himself with Messers Hope & Co., Labouchère et al. I admitted the premises but nothing more.

On arriving at the gentleman's house I was introduced to his sister, who, although twenty-five in body, was I am sure not over ten years old in mind. She looked at me over an endless Dutch dinner with the blue, uncomprehending stare of a Dutch doll. Her proceedings were at last so ludicrous that Labouchère himself was forced to smile, and I departed early, leaving him smoking a pipe gloomily and shaking his head. I have said nothing and he appreciates *that*. "Py Gott it ees no gee-hoke," he said to me only yesterday. "Fifty thousand florins joost go to hell van she tie." He looked at me still a little hopefully I think. "Eef you *haf* friends," said he. So here you are, Vinc—florins and a silent wife, commercial affiliations, and a respectable brother-in-law. Come and grow fat—and tulip bulbs.

The big event was yesterday with a dinner at the Parishes'. Four of us, a very formal affair, with David at one end of the table with his eye on Florence at the other. Mrs. Udney, who did all the talking, just across from me. Mrs. Udney seemed labouring under some repressed excitement. She took such a pride in the style in which her daughter was being kept that it caused me to catch from Florence the only smile that I received.

Florence is a beautiful woman, pale, rather suppressed, and devoted to doing everything for David in the best possible form. He himself was most hospitable, talked entertainingly after supper, and made me welcome without a trace of doubt, for which I admire him. I said nothing about my long visit to Mr. Udney because I suddenly understood while talking to Mrs. Udney that *he* will never say anything about it to *her*. We ended with a rubber or two at whist in which David carried off the honours, apparently without effort. And so I kissed hands good night and promised to pay my respects before leaving.

I am glad Philadelphia is a long way from New Orleans.

The only feeling touch I had that evening was when I told Mrs. Udney I regarded my visit to their house at Livorno as the foundation of all my good fortune and wished to send her a small token of gratitude. She looked both pleased and touched and said she and Mr. Udney took a pride in me and would like me to write them from America. I sent her a beautifully jewelled watch with her monogram. And so *vale* to a house without children—and that indescribable air of futile perfection in a barren woman's housekeeping at the Parishes'.

I forgot to say that the sea treated me elegantly this time when we came over—a swift sloop from Harwich to Helgoland, the great smuggling centre, where we picked up Nicholas, the English consul at Hamburg, a strange person with a squint, who keeps walking over everybody's toes and perpetually apologizing. Hence known as " 'Scuse-me Nick." The voyage to Vlissingen was picturesque but uneventful. From there hither by coach. I am well. The Dutch dine one as if the trolls were making the ogres merry—Gargantuan and endless and frequent are the meals. I long for France again. We shall have some months in Paris, I take it. Ouvrard will be leaving here shortly and I shall be seeing you, and I hope Juan and Simba too, soon after you will be looking on this.

  With merry anticipations and profound gratitude,
    Your humble obedient servant,
        Anthony Adverse.

Chapter Twelve

Gloria Mundi

OUVRARD remained day after day in Amsterdam negotiating a loan to tide him over his embarrassments. His own financing was so intimately bound up with the French government's that it was impossible to extricate himself without also supplying the needs of the French treasury at the same time. It was characteristic of him that he undertook to do this indirectly; that the discussion, which went on for nearly three weeks at t'Huys ten Bosch, laid the basis for an immense loan to Spain to enable her to meet her obligations to France.

So far had the control of Europe already fallen into the hands of financiers that as yet neither the French nor the Spanish governments were informed of the many good things in store for them. Ouvrard simply made his arrangements to have the money available. After he had completed certain transactions with those in power at Paris and Madrid the loan was to be "offered."

Anthony was both impatient and fascinated by these proceedings. He was anxious to get to Paris, and every day spent in Amsterdam cut down his prospective stay there, for he knew it was Ouvrard's intention to hasten on from Paris to Madrid as soon as he could. Yet linger he must, for since he was to accompany Ouvrard to Madrid it was essential for him to be familiar with all the implications of the bankers' schemes.

"I rely upon your knowledge of Spanish, of course," Ouvrard said to him, "but you will not find yourself, when we get to Spain, a mere interpreter by any means. There will be, I foresee, many occasions when it will be much better for me to appear by proxy than in person. And from your handling of the Mexican affair in England I am convinced that you can do equally well in Spain."

There was, therefore, no way out but to listen carefully to the conversations about Mr. Hope's great table at t'Huys ten Bosch in the eevning and to visit various financial personages in Amsterdam with Ouvrard in the forenoon. This Anthony found was interesting enough; the amazing web of European finance began to become more generally visible to him as they called on the sundry Dutch spiders engaged in spinning it. In this intricate tangle he soon discovered that the Mexican affair was only one supporting strand.

Also it was impossible not to admire Ouvrard more and more as his resourcefulness, his wide, clear knowledge of men and contemporary affairs, and the strange persuasiveness of his personality exhibited themselves in infinite variety. While they drove about from one establishment to another he explained, speculated profoundly about the future, or reminisced about his startling rise through all the changes of the Revolution from his clever beginning as a young paper-merchant at Nantes.

So far as Anthony could discover the man seemed to have no personal life whatever. His whole existence appeared to be a series of brief but vivid contacts with merchants and financiers. Each one of those interviews actually was, or had in it the elements of becoming, a minor or a major crisis, as the case might be, due to the fact that the ownership of property always tended to shift whenever Ouvrard appeared. Thus the man moved in a perpetual state of importance amid the tense atmosphere of an excitement which he alone appeared to be able to control. His was the reputation of a legendary alchemist and a Midas combined. For it was whispered and believed that wherever he appeared he might turn to gold whatever he touched; and that he might also, in an equally mysterious way, transmute the best of bullion into lead. All this was accomplished by the magic manipulation of paper. Even the bankers he dealt with believed that. And there was some truth in it, for Ouvrard, who was the first great modern financier, had discovered that a gold coin was merely the concrete focal point for an enormous aura of credit. He was always careful to keep at least a faintly auriferous tinge in even the pinkest glows of credit which he evoked. So he remained a not altogether fictitious Midas. Both the empire and the restoration were enabled to exist largely because of him.

There was only one person before whom his prestidigitations were performed under a completely understanding and always watchful eye; one who always demanded the rabbit, and who did not care whether it came out of a sleeve or a hat so long as it could be used for soup. At the very name of Napoleon Bonaparte the fat tail of the famous financier resembled that of a plucked goose; one upon which not even the pin feathers remained, for he had been plucked bare several times.

"What have you been doing, Ouvrard, since I have been away?" the first consul had asked upon his return from his last Austrian campaign. "So you thought to control me by supplying my wife at Malmaison with paper francs." He tore up Josephine's notes and stood with an amused expression staring up into Ouvrard's astounded and blanching face. "Voilà, you are repaid. In the future, monsieur le banquier, you will remember that if I am not the fountain of credit I control its conduits." He took a turn up and down the room and laughed. "I am going to punish and educate you by forcing you to undergo a spiritual experience." Whereupon he had sent Ouvrard to four months' solitary confinement.

Of this, his only subjective experience, Ouvrard was never tired of talking. He returned to it while he and Anthony drove about Amsterdam or while he chatted in the room of t'Huys ten Bosch again and again.

He told how, to escape from his despair at finding himself alone, he had scattered a box of pins on the floor of his cell and picked them up one by one counting them each time to be sure that none were lost. Of this experience in prison he always spoke in the present tense while all the rest of his verbs invariably dealt either with the future or with the past.

"It is the hunt for the always one missing pin that keeps me sane," he said, half closing his eyes. "There are a thousand and one of them. One has been missing for a week. I find it at last in a crack in the stones of the floor. There is not, I am sure, a happier man in France now than I. I am successful once more." He opened his eyes as if to be sure he was not still in the cell, which was the only room that had ever genuinely contained him, and exclaimed, "What is the difference what one is busy at so long as the mind is completely occupied?"

"But suppose you cannot find the missing pin?" hazarded Anthony.

"Oh, I keep on looking for it. I am sure it is there and it's bound to turn up," laughed the banker. "I wait till I guess right as to its whereabouts or I keep on recounting them to be sure my mistake is not in numbers. I might have found them all, of course. It is best to be sure before looking again. But what is the difference? The day passes and pretty soon it is night anyway."

"Don't you get to counting in your sleep?"

"No, no, you mustn't do *that,*" insisted Ouvrard seriously alarmed as if he were giving advice to a fellow prisoner. "That's dangerous. You take exercise by chinning yourself on the window bars of your cell till you're tired-out and can sleep."

"Didn't you worry about the cracks some, too?"

"Well, I *do,* you know, a little. But then I find the pin. And you will have to admit there is a point to that. And furthermore let me tell you I borrowed the pins to begin with from the turnkey's wife who trusted me because I was in jail, young fellow."

He held up a warning finger and laughed as he climbed out of the coach before the doors of *Vandevar & Van Group* to arrange some details of his loan.

"In that crack," said he as they drove off again, "I found fifty thousand pins."

M. Ouvrard was in need of a great many pins, and he was not through looking for them in all the various cracks in Amsterdam until the end of July. Consequently it was the beginning of August when after a five-day drive down from the Low Countries he and Anthony finally arrived at Raincey. Vincent came out to meet them.

Nothing would do but that they must stay the night, for the great banker felt in a peculiarly affable frame of mind after returning from a trip in which he had not only rehabilitated his affairs but had laid immensely promising lines for the future. Château Raincey was his pride. Here only, in its superabundant luxury, he felt that his success became invisible. Could he have had the title of baron his cup would have run over. So they rode about the park that afternoon, where every vista of the ancient coverts had been formalized and an army of marble statues and unnecessary fountains introduced. All of the latter were squirting.

Surrounded by new Calypsos, Bellerophons, Venuses, Tritons, and Andromedas the deer moved about uncomfortably under the colossal oaks, annoyed by exotic shrubs and intrusive fenced plantations which supplied an excuse for an army of gardeners at a loss what to do. The statues looked smooth and smug and the whole domain gave the impression of trying to be formal without having arrived at a satisfactory reason for being so.

Ouvrard, of course, admired most his greenhouses and the endlessly trained wall-trees which supplied fruits out of season for his table. They were taken through a mile of glass houses and finally brought around to the model village where agriculture was being encouraged by the proceeds from rentes; where every picturesqueness was both old and new.

And then there was the house, miles of it. An old château at the front, it staggered behind into a "Roman bath" supplied with hundreds of windows and chimney-pots. Here one enormous room led on into another, streaked with afternoon sunlight as they toiled through it; silent except for the ticking of endless ormolu clocks; filled with vast, lion-clawed sofas, chaises-longues, and tête-à-têtes where no one sat talking to nobody about nothing amid classical braziers, Chinese jars, chairs apparently waiting for Cleopatra, and the hanged ghosts of swathed chandeliers waiting, waiting for some event so important that it could never occur on a mere planet like the earth.

"You see I live on a large scale but very simply," said Ouvrard, waving his chubby hands at two be-frogged lackeys to open the leaves of a cavernous portal for them at the end of a hall paved with mosaic. "These are my own little quarters where we can all be quite cozily comfortable." And the man was right, for he lived in what had once been the châtelaine's quarters in the old château, where the rooms were small, the ceiling low, and the furniture old, comfortable, and domestic.

In these quarters Ouvrard seemed to be an entirely different person; a simple and amiable man. Here he became amazingly personal again in all his anecdotes; grew plaintive about his painful corns and advised both his young guests as to the best place to get boots in Paris—and other really vital matters—while he sat paring apples and stroking his fat cat. He showed Anthony the famous box with the thousand and one pins still in it, and was desirous that he should count them. But supper intervened and splendour was resumed once more.

The three ate at one end of a series of long tables where a hundred guests might have sat down. Candles blazed upon silver pyramids that rose toward the ceiling and wax tapers glistened in the pendent masses of crystal that drooped toward the floor. A great sideboard ascended by a series of steps provided the high altar from which dishes, in an endless stream of opulent courses, were brought by sleek, middle-aged acolytes loaded down with looped aiguilettes. The wine flowed fragrantly out of the extremely distant past.

Although this dining-room was monstrous, it was too overpowering to be funny. Even the most sophisticated and cynical were secretly impressed and bowled over by it. For it was in fact the crystal cavern or cathedral of the deity of endless possessions, the nave and altar of immaterial finance transmuted into things. It expressed all that perfectly in its outlines and bodily services with the chief manipulator and possessor sitting at the head of the great table in the glare of a thousand candles and long mirrors. Lush dinners here, when anybody came, were the climactic experiences of Ouvrard's abstractly-conjuring soul.

Yet as he sat there that evening, no amount of wine could evoke in Anthony the feeling that he was sitting again at the table of the sun. He was somewhere in a subterranean cavern being served by jinn. Perhaps, if the cup were rubbed the wrong way, the whole table might vanish and leave them sitting in the dark.

They talked that evening of the decree of the senate and plebiscite which had made Bonaparte first consul for life.

"From now on 'Napoleon,' " murmured Ouvrard, "in the style of other kings. Well, well, we bankers will at last know how to proceed now. It is delicious to feel that for a while at least the world is not just going to dissolve again." He looked about the huge room, dark at the other end, with some satisfaction. "I remember," said he, "when Napoleon needed cloth for his ragged uniform coat. I arranged that for him through Mme. Tallien. And—I suppose—I shall keep on doing so till the end. Let us drink to the new era."

They did so silently, and were then led off to the picture gallery where a succession of classical scenes by David and other moderns of the same school depicted the Homeric adventures of statuary in paint. At the end of the gallery was a portrait of Ouvrard by one of David's pupils. They stood before it trying to imitate the self-respect and reverence of Ouvrard for himself as he called for a light and looked up at it. Upon a dock, apparently at ancient Ostia, Ouvrard in the toga of a Roman senator stood superintending the unloading of a preciously-freighted ship.

"If there are secret stairs behind this picture," thought Anthony, "I wonder where they lead to?" But there was no time for exploration, for once having penetrated to the inmost shrine of Château Raincey it was now time for bed.

"I shall not see you young fellows tomorrow morning when you depart," said Ouvrard. "I need some hours of rest, and shall sleep late. But hold yourself in readiness to leave for Madrid at any time, M. Adverse. And if I were you, I would take what time you will have here in Paris for preparing your affairs and your outfit for New Orleans. There are many fine things one can purchase in Paris which I understand are not on sale in Louisiana," he smiled. "But if you do as well in Louisiana as I expect there will not be many things you cannot purchase in Paris when you return from New Orleans."

Three lackeys with flambeaus led them off through dark corridors to widely separated rooms. Vincent and Anthony had scarcely had time to say anything to each other.

As he composed himself for sleep that night, for the first time since his landing at Gibraltar over a year before, a devastating doubt and a feeling of the futility of the course he was pursuing overtook Anthony. Perhaps it was the somehow exhausting tour of the park and château of Raincey that had done it. Was he devoting himself with Ouvrard to picking up a great many pins? Into what new crack in the cell of existence had he himself rolled? This afternoon especially he had been enormously bored. And when one is bored one is either being sinned against by others or sinning against oneself. So far the elation of returning to civilization had borne him along with it. He had crossed the Alps on the very wings of it, he saw. Tonight it suddenly seemed to have ebbed. Tonight at Château Raincey, as he hid himself in an immense and ornate bed in a vast chamber, where the only sound was a clock ticking dismally, the antithesis of that mood from which music occasionally welled up within him lay dull and heavy upon his soul. Upon the beach of time where he was walking suddenly the waves had ceased to say anything that he cared to hear.

A sudden impulse to abandon it all, to cut loose from the strings that bound him to property brought him up out of the bed again and took him to the window, where into a kind of dull, opaque moonlight he looked out into the night and beheld the statues standing about in the cemetery-like park.

The immense window stretched from floor to ceiling. It would be perfectly easy to step out of it—into what?

He slipped into a dressing gown, and leaving a candle beside his door to mark his room in the huge corridor, he walked downstairs toward a distant noise of human voices at the other end of the house in the servants' wing. Presently a light and the sound of dishes being stacked amid whistling and laughter stopped him before a closed door. He hesitated a moment and then pushed it in. It was the scullery. Four or five servants, men and maids, were finishing washing up the plates from the feast of two hours before. Silence suddenly ensued when they saw him.

"What is there monsieur desires?" said a young man coming forward respectfully. "Is the bell pull broken?"

Anthony shook his head.

"I wish to sit with you here a while and talk. Will you let me? I am very lonely in the big room."

Some of the girls laughed. The man drew up chairs to a small table and sat down with Anthony. For some time they were a little embarrassed. Then the young servant began to speak of the farm where he lived. He was interested in that. He was about to be married, and he was interested in that. They talked for over an hour. The others finished their work and went, one of the servants placing a cold fowl and a pitcher of milk before them.

At midnight Anthony returned to his room. The candle by his door had almost burnt out. He blew it out before the window and watched the faint ghost of smoke trail into nothing in the moonlight. Then he climbed into the huge bed and slept soundly. "Life is nothing but moods from somewhere else," he thought. Something of the peace of Jacques Claire, the chief scullion, remained with him.

He had forgotten to draw the curtains. A few hours later a magnificent August morning poured intensely through the shining eastern windows of Château Raincey and awakened him as with an embrace from the angel of light.

The new day brought a mood he never forgot. It was an exalted one, the mood of trumpets and bugles. As he looked out on the park that morning he saw two stags bounding and fighting amid the trees where the early, level fingers of the sun streamed through the aisles of the ancient oak forest. Even the statues looked alive and rosy now.

He dressed hastily without calling the valet and ran downstairs to find Vincent had done the same and was already at breakfast. They beat each other on the back

334

as if they were meeting for the first time. Indeed, yesterday they had not met at all. They both talked at the same time until they laughed at each other.

"Thank God, Ouvrard's not up," whispered Vincent. "Let's not take any chances." He gave orders for the berlin to be brought around without delay. "I have an idea this is going to be one of our rare days," he laughed as they heard the wheels grating in the drive.

"I have trunks from England," said Anthony.

"Have the butler send them on later by cart, then. Let us go swiftly and freely this morning."

That was easily arranged. No one at Raincey had any cause to complain of their tips. Something like a uniformed guard of honour of about twenty servants managed to get two or three hand bags to the berlin, with the maids bowing in a bank of short petticoats and bodices behind. The news that Jacques Claire had received a comfortable gift for his fiancée just after breakfast had electrified the usually tomb-like château.

"It was to be understood now why monsieur's coachman had embraced him, that tall young man who only looked like an Englishman, and besides, monsieur's coachman was a fellow of great élan and pride, unespagnol. Ah, the esprit of their meeting on the steps was beautiful. Monsieur had been so surprised, even overwhelmed—and no wonder. For the great dog had darted out from under the berlin like a lion and sprung upon him. Was it not drôle to see him seize monsieur's hand in his great fangs and mouth it?" Those who could not say "oh" and "ah" many times had lumps in their throats because of the sounds which the dog made. Such sorrowful and happy cries. And is it not well known that such animals are sagacious?

In fact Anthony had been nearly pulled apart by Juan and Simba as he came down the steps. The berlin had driven off with the dog leaping along beneath it giving tongue so that the stags on the other side of the wrought-iron pickets scrambled to their feet while M. Ouvrard stumbled out of his bed and peered through the curtains, to see what the devil all the confounded clamour was about. The sound of it died away joyfully down the Paris road.

It was three hours' rapid posting from Raincey to Paris along the fine, new river road that flowed like a satin ribbon along the bank of the Seine. Vincent was happy with the success of his surprise.

"Juan has done very well with the horses," he said. "In fact he can do almost anything from laying a new floor to pressing my clothes. It is almost like having Aristide on the box again. By the way, I have Aristide well started on his career as a clerk for Cambacérès. He writes dossiers for the new law commission. Simba I admit is something of a problem, perhaps you can manage him." He looked out happily at the smoke of Paris rising like a thin haze some miles away over the low hills. "Ah, it is good, Toni, to have you back again. Did you know Katharina has accepted me? Ja wohl!" They whooped together, causing Simba to bark again under the berlin. "I will tell you one thing more and then no more of anything either business or life but let us just live in today which is so bright and golden. One would almost think the Seine was the Rhine here today, nicht wahr? Well, Anna's little Düsseldorfer died. I thought you would want to know—even today. Don't cry," said he, wiping his own eyes. "It is all over now." A few minutes later they were both smiling again. "One must drive on, you know," cried Vincent, waving his arms.

They stopped to change horses where a canal boat was waiting sleepily in a stretch of locks where water-lilies grew. A child brought them a small bunch of these, roots and all, for a sou. They laid them dripping on the floor and drove on with their fragrance filling the berlin.

"Here we are driving on through the harvest again like old times," said Anthony after a while.

"Ja," smiled Vincent, "it looks as if peace had come to France at last. The first consul is a great man."

It was not until nearly half an hour later that they began to hear a distant song of trumpets, fifes, and drums. On Montmartre the cannon began to boom.

"I had forgotten," said Vincent. "Napoleon is holding a great review today in the Champ de Mars. It is to celebrate his election for life, I suppose. There will be a presentation of eagles and standards and the swearing in of recruits.—Juan," he cried, "try to get us in, in time for the march past. Drive to the Spanish ambassador's first and we will try to pick up Señor Montijo there."

Their pace quickened. The distant trumpets, the clashing of church bells and the boom of cannon brought a wave of the far-off excitement of the city rolling over the fields.

It was like approaching an African village, thought Anthony. Only there was no hysteria in this excitement of sound. It seemed to be controlled, regulated; to flow from a deeper and more lasting impulse than had the fusillades and tom-tom beating that greeted him upon approaching Futa-Jaloon. That was mere savage child-play compared to the mighty thunder rolling out over the peaceful harvest from Paris in this August forenoon while the peasants toiled in the fields.

As they drove through the city streets deafening peals of bells broke out over their heads from the steeples, while from every side the bands of the regiments in garrison sang marching troops to their rendezvous.

All Paris was streaming toward the Champ de Mars. Cavalry wheeled at the end of street vistas, and artillery rumbled. Citizens walked, rode, and ran. The guns on Mont Valérien and at the Invalides marked the minutes alternately. Here and there above the heads of the multitudes flags passed, swept along by a river of bright troopers that flowed like streams of blood or grey and blue and silver through the more drably-clad Parisiens. At the Pont-Neuf they waited while a whole brigade of artillery trundled past, trotting swiftly, relentless, all at the same pace, with little gamins riding on the axles and caissons, beside the cannons, waving their hats and shouting. It was tremendous and yet it was gay. It was Paris, the new Paris which had suddenly found itself and was rising stronger and cleaner and more magnificent out of the ashes, the blood, and the grime of the old. The endless front of the Tuileries from one pavilion to another was draped with colours and standards. It shone. Today the new-born phoenix who lived there was going to soar.

They hurried quickly through some tortuous by-streets and picked up Señor Montijo at the Spanish embassy. He could provide them with a permit for the ambassador's carriage-stand, which was why Vincent had remembered him. And with the dapper young undersecretary, glad enough to be able to chatter Spanish unreservedly, they soon found themselves admitted to the "cour des ambassadeurs" and pressing forward to the ropes with the families of the legations seated amid flapping foreign ensigns behind. A little crowding among the hangers-on, and they were looking out across the wide-level sweep of the Champ de Mars.

Perhaps it was not an accident that the stand for the ambassadors of foreign powers, and for what remained of the legislative bodies of France, had been placed directly opposite the reviewing tribunal before which the armies of the victorious Republic were to pass under the eye of the first consul. Certainly it was not an accident that his tribune reposed on the exact spot occupied by the Altar of the Nation only a few years before. The fierce heat engendered by internal and external wars had fused the two objects. To the vast majority of the spectators Napoleon and France, the Altar of the Nation and the tribune were now one and the same thing. A political poet and a dramatic military genius who understood the use of symbols had chosen this day of his elevation to the consulship for life to make them actually and visibly so.

Napoleon had been brought forth on a bit of tapestry covered by the legendary deeds of the heroes of Homer just after his mother had hurried home from mass. He liked to remember that. The birth of the first consul, who consciously intended to grow into the emperor, was now to recapitulate the original event. But it was France which was now laid out upon a classically decorated background about to be safely delivered of a demigod. He moved with great precision. The presentation of standards was to take place at high noon and to be followed by a great banquet and civic feast tendered by the municipality of Paris.

At 10.30 exactly the sudden cessation of cannon, church bells, and all military music announced that Napoleon was hearing mass at Notre-Dame. This impressive silence, in which the whole city seemed to participate as in a prelude of worship, lasted for nearly half an hour during which time nothing was to be heard except the earth-shaking tread of troops marching down from the Barrière de l'Etoile and massing along the embankments of the Seine. At 10.45 a sudden peal of bells proclaimed that mass was over and the first consul was leaving the cathedral.

At 11.00 the guns at the Invalides boomed the warning of his approach. A few minutes later his coach drawn by the six white horses presented by the Emperor of Austria after Campo Formio emerged from the gate of the Ecole Militaire and moved slowly down the Champ de Mars. At the same instant from the opposite end of the field a battalion of the guards began to advance to meet it. No commands were heard. In the huge vacant area of the fields of manœuvre there was nothing but the glittering carriage with the six superlative white horses; the advancing oblong of the guards. These two things must inevitably meet in the centre of the field opposite the tribunal.

Napoleon sat erect in the carriage. He no longer had colleagues. He was enormously alone. So great was the spell of that lonely figure in the transverse cocked hat and the green coat with white facings that the fascinated multitude looked at him, looked at the carriage advancing toward the guards, and the guards advancing toward the carriage, in electric silence. Its number was sandy. Everybody in Paris who was not blind or paralysed, an ancient or an infant was there. The people swarmed both barriers of the long fields from the Military School to the river; they climbed trees; they ascended backward in waves onto the adjacent housetops. No one uttered a sound. The carriage and the troops met. The guards wheeled with that magic of mathematical motion in life which only soldiers possess, advanced obliquely to each side of the tribune, counter-marched, halted, and came to present arms with fixed bayonets. On each side of the tribune there now extended a living wall of steel.

The man in the carriage got out with his hat on. He walked alone across the ample space that separated him from the tribune, the focus of countless eyes. He began to ascend the stairs through a forest of eagles. They tipped the flags, still tightly wrapped about their standards. These, when he descended the stairs a few minutes later, he would present rapidly to the troops. On each side of the stairs a colossal bronze tripod smoked. At the top of the stairs was a crude chair, and the sky.

A horse neighed and a woman screamed. The multitude broke out into a brassy roar. The sound grew in volume, died down, rose in ever ascending waves of delirious enthusiasm and lifted Napoleon to the top of the steps. He turned, stood there with his hat extended in his hand for five minutes and sat down. The regular acclamations from the troops on the river banks still proclaimed his name.

Something of a surprise now developed. A procession of young girls dressed in white and green, the youngest of whom bore a laurel crown on a satin cushion, approached the tribune. At this unexpected intrusion of the feminine into what had promised to be a purely military occasion the crowd shouted again. Napoleon came down the steps and held up his hand. A childish voice was heard reciting a brief ode in which "Paris" conferred the wreath of victory on her hero. Napoleon lifted the child in his arms while she placed it on his head, amid appreciative roars from the mob and soldiers.

Apparently by a happy thought of the moment he beckoned to the children to seat themselves amid the flags thus charming untold legions of Parisiens into pandemonium. The human noise eventually subsided. He reascended the tribune and lifted one hand.

From the lower end of the Champ de Mars a thousand trumpets smote the summer morning flat with one stunning fanfare of clear, brazen sound.

The bugle is the essential voice of France. Other nations employ the instrument to give military signals, but they merely blow upon hoarse war-horns by comparison. Through bugles the French soldier releases his sublimest emotion in a wordless song. In it are mingled the tones of the Roman buccina, the far-calling of the mighty horn of Roland, the shouts and shrieks of Joan of Arc. The song is irresistible. The trumpets are torches. From the mouth of French bugles flames the fiery, golden soul of France.

A front of trumpeters a quarter of a mile wide and four files deep started to march up the Field of Mars. Before them twinkled the batons of the drum-majors, behind them thundered twelve files of drums, snare, tenor, and bass. It was the massed field-music of the veteran armies of Italy and the Rhine. The trumpets ceased and the drums began; the drums stopped, a thousand scarlet tassels tossed, there was a brazen flash, and the trumpets spoke again. So to alternate thunder and lightning the long lines advanced like rigid rulers, scarlet and blue, scarlet and blue, legs passing; every elbow of every drummer thrown upward at the same time, rolling sound before them.

As the lines swept steadily forward the spectators began to go mad. The flanks of the marching lines aroused on either side along the barriers as they passed whirlpools among the people; dashed a spray of hats into the air. All those who were still seated rose as one man. It became necessary to shout, or stifle with excitement. Those who remained silent did so at the cost of tears. Here and there women began to faint and to be trampled upon. The drums and bugles passed on. Before the tribune the long lines wheeled, advanced, countermarched, and at one signal —stopped..

In the midst of this sudden, stupefying silence every eye turned once more to the little man in the curule chair. But he no longer seemed little. He stood now at the top of twenty-four steps exalted against the sky; above the eagles with laurel on his head. To the multitude, exhausted, but still beside themselves with emotion, still looking up at him, he had become a god.

In the blinding August noon a hot whirlwind swept down the field and vanished.

"It is the ghost of the Republic," croaked a voice in Anthony's ear. He turned astounded to see a venerable, clerical-looking man with a fine, wide forehead standing just behind him. He was clasping a green umbrella close to one side of his chest and muttering to himself. He had been weeping, too.

Just then the drums began again.

They were now tapping a cavalry trot. The god had not remained doing nothing long enough to become ridiculous. At precisely the expected moment the manifestation of his powers began.

All the landscape from the Barrière de l'Etoile to the Pont-d'Iena, from that bridge to the Tuileries, began to move upon the Champ de Mars in a sliding avalanche of men. The trumpets gave tongue, ceased.

A column of cavalry poured across the bridge, emerged on the level parade of the field like a bright sword thrusting itself into a brown body, and trotted along the west barrier. A bugle screamed. The leading squadron wheeled on a right pivot, drew sabres and charges. As each squadron reached the same mark it executed the same manœuvre.

The irresistible might of the god on the tribune was now visibly apparent. In a moment, by a majestic magic, the Champ de Mars was a square mass of armed centaurs, the earth shuddering as if with subterranean thunder, the sun playing with dazzling lightnings along the descending lines. So overpowering was the solid reality, the threat of weight in this mass of cavalry, that the spectators at the end of the field directly before it milled about in panic and tried to scatter. But at a point some hundred yards ahead of them the line drew off by the centre into column, rushed at an even more furious gallop through the central arch of the Ecole Militaire; hurtled headlong down the Avenue Saxe.

From the stand of the ambassadors, where Anthony and Vincent were looking directly across the middle of the field toward the tribune, the effect was a curious and memorable one. The horses seemed to be galloping furiously upon a treadmill. As each line passed it was immediately followed by another precisely the same. The motion thus compensated became static. The square of charging cavalry, renewed by its feeding column at the rear and drawn off in a similar flume of men at the front, continued to move at tremendous speed and yet to occupy precisely the same space of ground by the force of a calculated discipline in space and numbers. At the exact centre there was always an officer rising in his stirrups to salute the first consul. This continued for the space of nearly half an hour while the dust rolled until the field smoked; while the hoofs thundered.

It was some moments before the multitude became fully aware of this curious vision of irresistible force in furious motion maintained in status quo. All the recklessness, the threat, the enthusiasm, and the élan of the Revolution were still contained in the terrific square of charging figures upon which a perfection of order had now been conferred. All, without thinking, beheld this. They saw it—and the man who had brought it about was standing upon the tribune before which the colossal tripods smoked.

It was suddenly borne in upon Anthony that the silence of a few minutes before while the first consul had been attending mass was a mere salute to the past, the brief acknowledgment of a faded sacred memory. *Now,* in this overpowering and thundering present, he was participating with the French nation and all Paris in the living worship of Mars whose emanation stood opposite upon his altar, crowned with victorious laurel, playing with pure force.

The thunder muttered into a new and more continuous rumble. The lines of cavalry had suddenly changed into artillery. The square of men sitting upon horses melted without losing outline or substance into lines of men sitting with folded arms upon caissons with golden cannons flashing behind. A noise as of ten thousand chariots quivered in the air. The crowd broke into an ecstasy of cries echoed and re-echoed by the signalling bugles. Where had been the haunches of galloping horses were now lines of glimmering wheels with the smoke of battle drifting through the spokes. The cannons passed and the endless lines of infantry, blue, grey and scarlet, furnished and twinkling to the last accoutrement, strode after them, saluted the first consul, and passed. Their meaning was perfectly expressed by the sound of the enormous march music to which they advanced.

There were not many present who understood the full significance of these advancing lines. By far the majority of the spectators were now overpowered and satiated. They were merely waiting for the final scene of the occasion to go home. The Prussian ambassador, however, leaned forward a little. The lines did not move as precisely as did those of the guards of his master at Potsdam. They were, he saw, not composed of human automatons moving rigidly but of individual and enthusiastic men. Yet they were lines, lines that rippled with life and with the resiliency of beautifully tempered steel. The old general of Frederick looked up to the man on the tribune and at once admired and cursed him for the perfect sword he had forged. He knew that the world could be altered by it. He determined to make his speech to follow at the Hôtel de Ville even more flattering than that which his secretary had prepared. "Those who do not temper their metal must temper their words," he muttered gloomily—and looked at Napoleon again with reluctant admiration.

The first consul was now descending the steps distributing eagles to the various standard bearers who had been chosen to receive them. The newly recruited regiments which were to receive their colours were massed before him and their colour guards had come forward. On each step as he descended he plucked a furled flag from its socket and leaning forward with an imperial gesture placed it in the hands of a soldier with appropriate and inspiring words. As each soldier received his flag he unfurled it.

Thus, as the brilliant standards unfurled behind him, he moved to the bottom of the tribune. There, on the last step, he presented swords of honour to a couple of chosen veterans in a brief and fiery speech that all the recruits heard. Then he turned, pointed to the flags, and lifted his voice so that all the waiting regiments heard.

"Soldiers, these eagles and these flags are the honour of the nation which I deliver for safe-keeping into your hands. I shall send them in her defence where glory leads and victory follows. Swear that it shall be so, swear to defend them with your lives."

He raised his own hand.

A tremendous roar followed, the authentic sound of the military tumult by which conquerors are acknowledged. Paris had heard nothing like it since Julian had been hailed as Augustus and raised on the shields of his veterans at the Roman palace just across the river from Notre-Dame fifteen centuries before.

The review was over.

Napoleon mounted his charger and at the head of a brilliant staff rode off to the Hôtel de Ville. The multitude swarmed over the Champ de Mars in every direction. Coaches, citizens, and soldiers struggled with one another across the thronged bridges going home. The golden dome of the Invalides swam glowing

345

warmly in the azure mist of Paris on a hot afternoon. From the Jardin des Plantes balloons rising by virtue of hot-air floated over the devoted city and the gaping crowds. The device was still a novelty. They were magical. The distant strains of military music where the troops returned to barracks followed by groups of marching and capering gamins slept drunkenly on the molten August air. Trees drooped, and nursemaids with the next generation of conscripts in perambulators turned reluctantly home.

The huge crowd had pretty well scattered by the time they were able to get the berlin out of the enclosure roped-off for the diplomats. A fierce dispute over the precedence of departure between the Austrian and Portuguese ambassadors delayed everybody else. The American envoy, Mr. Livingston, aroused considerable laughter by at last walking out and hiring a fiacre in which he and a fellow citizen quietly drove off, leaving the monarchists involved in metaphysical questions. The British left next by force of several red-faced grooms and the good management of horses, and the Dutch followed behind. The upholders of the Houses of Braganza and Hapsburg were about to come to blows when the police removed the barrier and everybody drove off in all directions at once.

"The young man with Mr. Livingston," said Vincent, "is an inventor who is trying to sell to Napoleon a boat that is to go by steam. A fine Yankee notion that no one here takes seriously. He has tried to interest me and Ouvrard. He also has torpedoes on the brain. An amusing talker though—" but further conversation was checked when Juan drove up with the berlin. Simba, who had been shut inside it during the review, had torn off most of the upholstery with his teeth.

"I *had* to lock him in," said Juan. "When the music started he went wild. In his country, Señor Nolte, such

346

sounds on drums and horns mean the beginning of a lion hunt or a war. Of course, it is different here, but how was I to tell a dumb beast that?"

"Well, we shall just have to have it all done over again," said Vincent, climbing in gloomily and showing Señor Montijo to a seat from which the stuffing bulged. Anthony was some time in quieting the big hound which still whined and trembled and appeared in an ugly mood.

"You can't start so much excitement and not have something happen, at least with an animal," remarked Anthony to Vincent, who was a good deal put out over the appearance of the berlin. "I'll make it right, you know. It's too bad." Simba growled in reply and they had to laugh.

They dropped Montijo at the embassy and continued on across the old turning bridge by the Tuileries.

"Look!" said Vincent at a carriage that forged by them. Anthony had just time to catch a glimpse before the rather smart phaeton ahead turned a corner. A grey-haired man in a beaver and a young woman in a bonnet with curled plumes upon it were its passengers. Both were handsomely dressed. He could not see the woman's face. She sat with her grey-gloved hands lying in her lap almost resignedly. Anthony looked at Vincent inquiringly.

"Angela and Debrülle," said Vincent. "Shall we try to follow them?"

"No," he answered after a moment. "She might not want us to."

Vincent nodded. "Debrülle left a note for you some days ago when he learned you would soon be home. I have said nothing about it so far."

"Good, let us not think of it now," replied Anthony. "I shall want to see her, but just now I want to do nothing but go home to the House of the Wolf. Here we are in the faubourg now."

Vincent was pleased and showed it. They turned the corner by *L'Homme Armé* and drew up at "47" with a warm welcome from old Paul. Simba bounded out and darted up the circular steps before them barking. Once upstairs they began to rush about like a couple of boys home for a holiday. The trunks had come in from Raincey and Vincent was soon exclaiming with tears in his eyes over his gifts from England. Generous himself, it was a curious quirk in his make-up that always made him astonished and delighted when anybody gave him something. Anthony had taken full advantage of this.

"I am looking at the little plaque of the wolf and the twins with greater ease of heart than I have known since I left here," said Anthony, strolling over to the window and looking out with quiet satisfaction in his eyes.

"Ja!" said Vincent. He put away his gifts and had the water-lilies they had obtained that morning brought up and arranged in a bowl.

"For Anna, you know," he sighed. "Ach—that little Düsseldorfer. For two years she has been making things for him already," he muttered, rearranging the flowers that were now wilted. "With these roots though they will even bloom again perhaps. Sehr schöne Blumen."

"They *are* lovely," said Anthony. "Let us keep them here on this table while I stay. They are better than words. And we shall both know what they mean— *who* they are."

The flowers remained, expanding slowly in the water, reviving and slowly filling the room with a subtle fresh fragrance.

"And for only a sou!" said Vincent, smiling and brushing a fly off his forehead with his cuff.

A pile of mail Anthony disregarded, and they spent the rest of the afternoon talking in the deep chairs, coats off, a big meerschaum pipe and many Havana cigars accompanying their talk of all that had transpired, until it began to grow dusk. Simba stretched out on a rug beside Anthony and slept, the hair occasionally lifting along his spine while he growled in dreams at the sound of the distant drums still rolling here and there far away over the city roofs.

"It is complete now," thought Anthony, "even the wolf is here. If this afternoon could only last forever! Why not? Why did he always have to go? And this time it would be forever."

"Vincent, you will have to come to see us at New Orleans some time. You must."

"Ja," said Vincent taking the "us" for granted, "if Katharina will go so far. Himmel, you will not be here when I am married! Ah, who knows?" His eyes grew large and blue looking into the future, a little frightened.

"What do you see?" laughed Anthony.

"Nothing," replied his friend, "nothing. Do you remember that Bovino woman said I was to die poor and that you . . ."

"Oh, nonsense, Vinc. I have met some real witches since then. How you do remember things! I had forgotten that. It's getting dark. Let's go out to dinner tonight. Paris will be en fête after the review. Call a fiacre and let's dress."

"Ach, my new English clothes," exclaimed Vincent. "We'll go!"

Simba followed Anthony down the hall, nudging him. Juan was in the room laying out his things. Juan gabbled in Spanish unmercifully while Anthony was being shaved. Shouts of delight from Vincent's room over his own splendid appearance when arrayed in what came out of the London bandboxes announced his satisfaction with perfection. Juan, who considered his master's property to be his own, had calmly opened the bundle from Gallegos and extracted from it the set of razors Cibo had given to Anthony in Havana. These he had put in excellent shape and he was now running one of them rapidly over Anthony's chin.

"Does it go as smoothly as it used to at Gallegos?" asked Juan. Lying back in a big chair with his eyes closed, Anthony waved his hand in satisfaction.

"It is much better than when one is alone and compelled to do everything for oneself, isn't it, señor?"

"Much, *much* better, Juan," said Anthony so emphatically that Juan almost cut him.

"Sí," replied Juan, stropping the blade and looking down at his master whose eyes remained closed. "But you are not alone any more. Simba and I, we have come to stay with you. Wherever you go we follow."

"Even to the other world? I go to Louisiana, you know, Juan."

"Sí, señor, even to the other world," said Juan eagerly. "I am a little tired of this one," he added in a far-away voice. "That swallow I sent back to my town from the *Wampano-ag*—you remember, señor? Well, he must have fallen into the water or gone to the wrong chimney. When I got back home from Gallegos I find my girl is married to a fisherman and has two fat boys. She milks goats and fries the sardine for another."

"The world is full of girls, Juan."

"Sí, but is there comfort in numbers, señor? One should also consider that."

A few minutes later Anthony and Vincent were rattling over the cobbles of the old faubourg to supper at Frascati's. The gardens were brilliantly illuminated and there was to be a display of fireworks later in honour of the review. They picked up a young banker by the name of Joly from Antwerp. He had in tow a Count von Haxenthausen of the Royal Danish Life-Guards who aroused some amusement by comparing everything he saw in bad French with something else in Copenhagen, and there was also his friend, a Major Holstein of the Queen's Jäger from the Island of Amager, who said nothing at all but grunted with appreciation of the supper. They managed to leave the Danes watching large "N's" in fireworks coming out of a fountain surrounded by fiery pinwheels, and started walking through the salons furnished to the last extremity of gilding in the new Roman style.

It was the thing to do, to stroll at Frascati's, where everybody agreed that English politics were perfidious and men's clothes from London perfection. The women had been forbidden by the first consul to dress in English cloth. They managed to look quite acceptably Roman, some were still even quite Greek, in sandals, high waists and puffed sleeves half-way to the elbows in the silk of Lyons. The most striking thing about Frascati's, however, was its brilliant lighting. A thousand pounds of wax candles a night were consumed in the lines of chandeliers, inverted pyramids of crystal that ran the entire length of the salons. Lackeys in oiled canvas coats with a movable ladder went about snuffing them. The salon was the place to be seen; to stand by a pedestal and be admired.

They saw Garat the singer with a book of music in his hand talking to the dancer Frémis. The place was full of people from the embassies. Lord Whiteworth, the newly arrived English ambassador, hurried through to a private garden party with his own wife, which caused considerable surprise. Murat, the Governor of Paris, passed through after dinner with a brilliant suite.

"That is Mme. Récamier, the banker's wife, over there," said Vincent. "She comes here every Wednesday night to be seen and to play cards. It is said that he insists upon it as there are stories she is unhappy with him. There is the Prince of Nassau, the fat little fellow in the brown pelisse, coming up to talk with her. Most of those uncomfortable looking people are émigrés who have returned since April. You can tell them by the old-fashioned bow. Come over here and meet these Italians. Look, that is Miot de Melita with your friend Joseph Bonaparte. Come over; I know him. We should not lose this opportunity. Melita is an ardent Bonapartist and would turn all of Italy over to Napoleon—remember that."

They found themselves received casually but cordially enough. The consul's brother questioned Anthony eagerly as to conditions in England. Most of the talk turned on the recent suppressions and changes that had gone on in the Tribunate since it had offered opposition to the formation of the Legion of Honour, which Joseph maintained was a democratic institution.

"It is something that is likely to last," said he and then looked suddenly embarrassed.

"The only formidable opposition left," said Melita to Vincent, "is not from orators but from a certain general, Moreau," he whispered. "Have you heard the bon mot? Il n'y a que deux partis en France maintenant, les moreaux et les immoraux. Ah, I am afraid we are all among les immoraux here," he laughed. "Come and see me, Herr Nolte, about that municipal loan for Milan—tomorrow. Good!" They bade one another good evening and passed on.

"That *was* a stroke of luck," said Vincent. "Well, it pays to be seen here, you see. Look, there goes Mme. Grand, the lady for whom you got the gloves. Napoleon wants Talleyrand to marry her. There is certainly a good deal of the lady. Well, it is time to leave when the older dames begin to arrive. You would scarcely think there had ever been a revolution here, would you? Now I'll show you the other side of the medal."

They hired a fiacre and went to a dingy little place with a few candles in bottles, the Hôtel de Saint-Pierre in the littered alley of Saint-Pierre-de-Montmartre, near the Messageries. Here the girls still wore the red caps of liberty and nothing else, if one insisted. They did not, however. An hour of sweaty atmosphere and a bad imitation of the carmagnole purchased by a drunken Russian nobleman who had heard of "Liberty," and wanted to see her dance, sent them home sleepy and laughing.

"Poor Toussaint," said Anthony. "What would he have thought of Liberty in red drawers?"

"And even those were insecure," said Vincent.

Anthony began to spout pages of *Emile* as they bumped over the Paris cobblestones already replaced here and there by the smooth pavement of the new boulevards being laid by Napoleon. They laughed at the sound of the prose of Rousseau. They looked out at the horses ravished from Venice, the old Roman team sedately pacing against the sky on the new triumphal arch in the Place du Carrousel. They loomed high against the stars as if they had always been there and would remain permanently. They enjoyed an excellent little midnight supper looking out on the court at numéro 47 flooded by placid moonlight, where the shadow of Simba passed like a lion. And it was all vastly satisfactory, from the horses at the Carrousel to the shaded candles on the little table by the window over langouste en casserole, and other small platters, which consoled them for the disappointment of Montmartre and the despicable little Hôtel de Saint-Pierre.

Anthony did not feel at all like stepping out of the window tonight. The mood of the enthusiastically contented world of Paris and the new era was on him. He felt tonight that he had entered into it at last.

Before he went to bed he took the madonna out of the bundle that Juan had untied. Neleta, he saw, had smashed the mother-of-pearl inlay at the Virgin's feet when she had kicked it onto the floor at Gallegos. The shrine was also badly chipped. Probably travelling had done that. But the statue itself was unharmed.

Tomorrow he would take it to a jeweller and have it repaired. He left it standing on the bureau in the moonlight and went to sleep like a child.

And then tomorrow there was Angela.

Chapter Thirteen

The Swan-Song of Romance

"WATER-LILIES are fragrant," thought Anthony, as he sat alone in the big room next morning going over his accumulated mail. One bud he noticed in particular that had hung drooping on its stem only the day before had now revived and was beginning to open. The flesh-like pink-and-white of its petals was beginning to show. He renewed the water in the bowl, covering the roots completely, and turned to his letters again.

Most of them were current bills or tradesmen's announcements, remittances and statements from London. There was an ill-spelled note from Dolly at Bath, stumbling over a few sentences of awkward thanks—she was evidently quite happy—and, "He thinks I had better not write you any more." Again he was glad it could end this way. He lit his cigar with the note and watched the childish writing crisp into nothing.

Women, he reflected, on a purely banking basis were costing him a great deal. There was the prophetess at

Spitalfields—not *his* fault—comfortable for life, Captain Bittern's nieces, Cheecha, Neleta drawing something nice every quarter in Havana, if the receipts that came back with her mark were to be believed, and Dolly at Bath in a nice new cottage with her bunbaker. He reckoned up these payments as interest on capital and reflected that they would have represented at least the results of some years' labour in earlier times on the part of John Bonnyfeather—deceased. And now there were Angela's pearls. All that he could say was that it all seemed unavoidable. But in the future . . .

He sat fingering a note with a large monogram seal on it addressed in bold, precise German script. At last he opened it.

> Dear Mr. Adverse: I shall do myself the honour of calling Weds. morning next. Prepare yourself for a little journey to the suburbs by request, but under certain conditions which I shall be under the necessity of explaining to you. The precautions I think you will agree, when you understand, are sensible ones. All under this roof look forward to your visit with the profound expectation of long deferred hope. Do me the credit of reading nothing ominous or mercenary in these lines. From one who has been an ever constant friend and supporter.
>
> "PAPA" VON BRÜLLE

The note was dated Saint-Germain-en-Laye, Monday—and it was Wednesday morning now. He rose in considerable excitement and perplexity. Vincent had gone out to see Melita. "Damn that Milanese loan"—he would have liked to talk this over. It was decidedly strange. And Debrülle might be expected at any moment. *"Von Brülle,"* eh! Well, such things counted in this mad world. He called Juan and had himself arrayed in his best dove-coloured morning suit. During the struggle with the new boots "Herr von Brülle" was announced. Anthony descended to the big room again,

355

where the green window draperies waved lazily in the morning breeze and sunlight.

Debrülle was genuinely glad to see him—there could be no doubt about that. He came forward with great warmth but with the dignity of a man well past middle-age who still carried himself well.

Age had done a great deal for him. His erstwhile somewhat stagy heartiness had softened into a dramatic charm. His lion-like mane was still impressive but less luxuriant and streaked with grey-silver. A carefully trained moustache and a vandyke turning white contrived to be at once distinguished and benign. The deep tones of his voice were fatherly and reassuring. He was, Anthony observed, dressed with a perfection of taste and detail which only an actor could attain without merely seeming to be playing a part. He moved a little too impressively—and yet his gestures were sincere. Only a hint of something ever-present and yet unaccountable, the half-mysterious glamour of a hidden weakness and trouble that seemed to emanate palely from the starched frill of his shirt-front and his high-silk cravat might convey to a careful observer that alcohol and Debrülle were inseparable, long-suffering, and secret friends.

"Well, monsieur," said Debrülle in excellent and sonorous French, "your long-expected return from London is likely to bring pleasure to more people than you might think. A great deal of liquid has gone under the bridge since I saw you last," he sighed. "Let me see, it is now at least seven years ago, isn't it, since our little breakfast together at Livorno? And time has wings and shakes many things out of them. Some unexpected ones perhaps." He looked at Anthony benignly and smiled. Yet there was just a trace of amusement there, Anthony thought. It made him a little uncomfortable.

"And Angela?" Anthony asked. His voice shook quite unexpectedly. He could have kicked himself.

"Ah, I see that you still—care for her," smiled Debrülle. "It is only actors who can assume tones from

356

the heart. And you are not a very good actor, are you,"—he hesitated a little—"my son?"

"No," said Anthony. "I have never been *that*. Ah, I did not mean to convey any slur on your profession," he added hastily. "Do not mistake me, mon père."

They both laughed heartily.

"I should never have thought so," said Debrülle gayly. "In fact I have reason to believe that you have been more partial to us than you suspect. No, we began by being good friends under circumstances that might have caused trouble between unfeeling people. But we were never that. We *understood* each other somewhat unusually well, you will recollect. And I wish to tell you that I have kept a certain promise that I made to you that morning at Livorno. *Thus* was it made," he cried dramatically, raising his right hand. "Yes," he continued, recovering himself, "I *am* an actor, and you are not. So I must tell you that this is one of the great moments of my career. I have long looked forward to it. I wish to tell you that not only did I look after your little shepherdess, par le bon Dieu, monsieur, I made a great woman out of her." He dropped his cane and with great agitation stooped to pick it up.

"I want you to remember, my son, for I have a right in a way to call you that—I want you to remember when you go to visit her this morning at her charming little house at Saint-Germain, that she is not Cinderella sitting in the ashes in that kitchen at Livorno. The ashes from which she rose—ah, truly now to have the slipper tried on by princes. No, it will not be Cinderella that you will see or your little shepherdess, but Mlle. Georges, who is now the idol of Paris, the—" he checked himself and waved his hands emphatically.

"I—I have a right to say this to you. Angela may even tell you why; she is grateful. When I was a very young man I suffered greatly. I was betrayed, cheated out of life. Sorrow made me sentimental, I suppose. I have always been merciful to the young ever since. That is why I was merciful to you. In all things Angela has had her way. In everything but in the training of the voice and in acting. There only I have been her tyrant. But I, Debrülle, the poor singer, have taught her all she knows. I have sung for her myself when we starved, and held out the hat. Now the princes arrive—she triumphs. Pardon, might I have a little something to drink, monsieur?"

He took the fiery cognac gratefully. Anthony remained quiet.

"I am grateful, too," he said at last as the man sat looking at him curiously and drinking. "I owe you the greatest happiness I have ever known."

"Yes?" said Debrülle, "I am glad to hear that. And now *you* have come back. It is she who has insisted upon seeing you again. No, I have not opposed it. She has always had what she wants." He looked a little miserable. "What I am asking now is that you should not simply regard this second meeting as a beautiful romance, not even if she regards it that way. I would ask you to consider her situation truly; perhaps, even to remember others. No, I do not wish to intrude. Who knows what is in a woman's heart? For years I swear I have been only a father to her; old Papa Debrülle,"—he mumbled the phrase over several times half ironically, half tenderly—"but I have loved her, loved her—and I think I know now what that is. It is something a little hard to bear to the end sometimes. If you wouldn't mind it would help, I think, to have the decanter filled again. Ah—yes. Herr Nolte's cognac is excellent. I noticed that when I came here before." His hand shook a little as he poured out.

"I . . ." began Anthony.

"Do not promise anything," said Debrülle. "Promises only complicate life. And I am afraid when you arrive at Saint-Germain you might misjudge my motives."

"Then we do go this morning?"

"Why, yes, of course. What did you think? And yet after all it will not be so simple as *she* thinks," exclaimed the old actor, looking paler and worried, "and for a good reason. Mlle. Georges is now of great in-

358

terest to the government. Ah, of *great* interest," he insisted, getting up suddenly, clapping his hat crosswise on his head, his hands behind his back and walking up and down with an important frown and a subtle bit of mimicry that brought the little man at headquarters at Nogent instantly to life.

"Ah, you should see him in the garden," cried Debrülle, carried away by his own art, "walking with mademoiselle, plucking flowers. Thus. And becoming romantically pensive on a marble bench. A sword is always in the way." The shifting of Debrülle's walking stick caused Anthony to choke.

"You might have the Comédie at your feet with that act, Debrülle."

"And the police on my neck," laughed the old actor, pleased nevertheless at finding his divinest bit appreciated. "No, no, my dear boy, it will never be known. But can you imagine him when he forgets himself? No, it is incredible. He himself cannot believe it. He runs away from the memory immediately afterwards."

What Debrülle had actually seen and how much he was imaginatively acting it was hard to say.

Anthony sat feeling as if he had been plunged into a comic nightmare, something that was at once absurd and dangerous, laughable and terrible. So this was what was happening to Angela. And it was true! His emotions were too complicated for him even to try to name them.

"But the trouble is now that the house is watched," continued Debrülle. "Whether it is the first consul or Josephine that is having it done I don't know. Perhaps both of them—or Fouché?" He shrugged his shoulders. "It makes no difference. In any event it will be ruin to both of you if you are seen going there. Have no doubt of it. You can see that Angela is really anxious to see you to take this risk. I have thought of a way. It is so simple that I believe it will work. It will depend on your doing exactly what I tell you."

"What am I to do, disguise myself as a blanchis-seuse?" laughed Anthony.

"No, no," smiled Debrülle. "That is merely one of the forty-seven disguises listed generally as suspect under 'B' in the primer for gendarmes. There is also the nun with boots on who calls for alms. I once knew the list by heart from 'Allemand commercial avec bijouterie de Bingen' to 'Zingari avec les perruches sages.' It is curious that there should be only forty-seven ways of being just plausible enough to attract the notice of gendarmes. It is an odd number, undoubtedly. Now there are none listed under 'Q.' So I am inventing a safe one. 'Querulous old papa returning home alone.' This brandy is wonderful. What chance has Fouché himself against Debrülle thus inspired? Well, M. Antoine, this is the plan . . ."

A few hours later Anthony found himself seated on the floor of Debrülle's double cabriolet approaching Saint-Germain-en-Laye. There had been no difficulty. Apparently they were not even being followed. Debrülle tipped heavily at the toll gates so that no one looked into the coach. About a mile short of the village a farmer trotted out of a lane and took along behind them. "That is a new scheme," said Debrülle. "Let me explain our situation.

"Until the last opera season was over we lived at Meudon. Up until that time a certain person had not visited mademoiselle in Paris. She had merely received considerable evidences of his regard, continued from a former and more intimate acquaintance at Milan of three years past. Some weeks ago we were told to give out that mademoiselle would retire to the country for a complete rest and would remain there in absolute seclusion for the summer. This was not a proposal but a command. On our arrival at Saint-Germain very early one morning we were conducted to a little villa exquisitely furnished and beautifully appointed in every way. It is just at the end of the great lime-tree entrance of Lenôtre with a garden that has a private entrance from the Forêt des Lôges. There our first consul has

360

recently established in the old convent a school for the children of his Legion of Honour. Mme. Campan, a former femme de chambre of Marie-Antoinette, also maintains a school for young children at Saint-Germain. Hortense and Emilie de Beauharnais, Josephine's daughters, were educated there. Now both Napoleon and Josephine take a great interest in Mme. Campan's school and she advises him on all his educational schemes. There is therefore every excuse for him to come frequently to Saint-Germain. He often brings Josephine with him for long conferences with Mme. Campan and then makes inspections at Lôges.

"Now, Mlle. Georges' little villa is strategically situated just half-way between the new school in the forest of Lôges and Mme. Campan's in the village of Saint-Germain.

"Occasional and unsuspected opportunities for a little relaxation between inspections and conferences are now possible with Mlle. Georges. He comes by the gate that leads into the forest. For instance, Mme. Campan's pupils recently gave Racine's *Esther*. Pressing reasons of state unfortunately required the first consul to depart early during the performance while Josephine graciously remained. No doubt they met happily next morning. I was invited to see *Esther!*

"We at the little villa are very quietly watched to prevent anyone disturbing us—and for other reasons. I have long been supposed to be mademoiselle's papa and I can therefore go out. But when I do, I am always followed. Bonaparte himself thinks I am 'papa' and that Angela is a young widow. He found us thus in Milan. You see, my boy, I am playing a most difficult part, whether in a comedy or a tragedy I do not know yet. The gods have not yet written the last act. I wonder how you will collaborate with them. I have done the best I can." He looked out at the landscape with a tired and troubled expression. "I should like when this is over to return to Düsseldorf."

"Dusseldorf?" cried Anthony, looking up at him from the floor.

"Yes, I was born there," said Debrülle. "I love that town. But we are entering Saint-Germain now. Keep low." He himself shrank back farther in the carriage.

"Now," he continued in a low voice, "as we turn up the drive I shall open the carriage door a little just before we arrive at the house. When I say 'go' it will be almost opposite a flight of steps that goes down into the garden directly off the road. You must jump down them and below the level of the bank before the carriage passes on. You will find a little gate immediately before you. Here is the key. Go in without delay and see whom you will find there.

"You will not be seen," Debrülle reassured him. "The watch is kept from the road that looks down the drive. Once you are below the bank level you are safe. They will see no one get out of the carriage except myself. When it drives on I shall simply be standing on the steps with this bundle under my arm. See what I have brought her—" he cried—"but, no, we are too close now. Wait till we are at home. We shall not be disturbed at all, unless he comes. Then— in that case I would ask you both to remember poor papa who has always brought home the bundles and would like to die quietly in Düsseldorf. If necessary, hide. S'il vous plaît, monsieur." He moved down and shook Anthony by the hand.

They drove on a little and turned in. Anthony gathered himself for a spring. To the right of the road a grassy bank sloped precipitously.

"Allez-y!" said Debrülle.

Anthony jumped, tripped, and rolled down the slope, cursing and laughing, to rise dusting off leaves and grass. Before him was a small lyre-shaped gate in a high wall. He ran forward stooping, unlocked it hastily, and stepped through into the silence and green shade of the walled garden beyond.

The place was much larger than he had expected.

362

The wall enclosed at least a half-acre of tangled, neglected shrubbery and ancient oak trees. He could
scarcely see where the paths had been. They must have
been neglected for twenty years. A squirrel with its
cheeks full of acorns made him an elaborate and
ironical bow and departed. A gust of anger swept
over him. His knees and elbows smarted. The sense
of anticlimax at this lonely reception was unbearable.
There was no one in the garden at all.

He pushed on through what had become a thicket,
where only a few cultivated shrubs still lingered, putting
forth unnoted blossoms. Presently he stumbled upon
what had once been the main walk of the place, densely
shaded by venerable oaks. He sat down on a neglected
stone bench and began to pick the burrs from his
clothes. At one end of the walk he could see a door
half overgrown with ivy, and at the other sunlight
reflected from a pool with leaves floating in it.

He was not going to go up and knock at the door
as if he were begging to be let in. He would sit here
till somebody came to find him. Debrülle was a dramatic old ass—telling him to jump that way—into a
weedy wilderness full of squirrels. Well, he would sit
on this bench if necessary for an hour or two. And if
nothing happened he would go away. He had come
to find Angela, not Mlle. Georges. Let her wait. Let
Angela come to meet him at least half-way. At any
rate it was cool here. He had burst through the briars
overheated, almost panting. He was not really as anxious as all that, he told himself.

People did use this walk. There was a fresh print
of a small foot in the moss near by, a child's apparently. Certainly not Pan's—although it was so quiet
and so near the forest here.

He settled himself to cool off and wait. A long
while passed. A bird came, alighted on the arm of the
bench and looked at him. He did not move. The feeling
of summer-in-the-woods came over him. Angela would
come out presently—and they would go and sail leaf
boats in the pool together, "Maea, my delightful one,

little earth-mother." He began to mutter over the names of the lost children who had once stood by the fountain at the casa. There was comfort in the old spell. He closed his eyes to shut out the world. Nothing but the green oak shade, the very colour of the strong, quiet dream that lay deepest within him, remained. He sat there as though he were sitting alone at the bottom of a cool, deep well where the light struck down greenly, or as if he were playing under the tree at the convent again lying on his back and looking up through the leaves. It was something to be at home again. He sat drawing strength from it. On a few minutes of this he could exist for years to come.

The mood passed. Perhaps it was what he had been brought here for? Probably the best thing he could do now would be to go away. He and Angela had shared that mood together once. It was too much to expect to find it twice. Why should they? He opened his eyes. Things took shape slowly again out of the dim light. "What are tears for?" he wondered. "They always spoil the form of things. How damnably silly of me." And yet—these were not tears of self-pity. He was amazed as he realized that they were just drops of pure happiness that had overflowed from the superabundant waters of natural contentment which he had once more discovered within. Good water that! Life intoxicating in a world without end . . . clear now.

Standing before him leaning over the rim of a hoop he saw a boy of seven or eight years regarding him with a fascinated curiosity. They looked at each other with similar eyes for some time.

"What are you crying for?" whispered the child at last. "Aren't you glad to see me?" he added a little louder.

"Yes," said Anthony, surprised into a purely instinctive utterance.

The boy smiled. "Mamma said you would be," he ventured. A sudden embarrassment overcame him that leapt into excitement. "Can you roll a hoop?" he cried. "Can you? Look. I can."

He set off down the long walk striking the speeding circle, running, leaping. Anthony rose, looking after him. No one except himself had ever run just exactly like that. A pressure of triumph and emotion surged up into his temples. "Alive, alive!" The boy was living. He ran. The circle glittered before him. Suddenly the man standing by the bench bared his arm and put his mouth on it.

"Firm, living flesh, you are going on."

The waters *had* overflowed into the world.

"Angela, Angela!" he shouted. "Angela, where are you?"

He started for the door of the house. But the child, who had run to the far end of the walk, was returning now faster than ever.

"Wait," he shrieked, "wait! I want you to see *me*."

He found himself overtaken and surrounded as if by a crowd of little boys. He *had* to stop.

"Look," the youngster kept calling—"look how I can make it go!" and he began to drive his hoop, with which he was certainly most nimble, in skilful narrowing circles about the man who stood in the path. Suddenly he stopped it, and striking an exact imitation of the attitude of the large man before him stood looking up into his face. "Aren't you going to play with me?" he asked.

He took the hoop and they began to run down the path with it together—faster—faster.

"Look out, mother," shouted the child. "Don't! You'll stop it."

Anthony stopped and looked up covered with confusion. A soft, mellow laugh rang in his ears. She was standing in the path just ahead of him with the child clinging to her skirts and demanding his hoop indignantly.

"So I am in the way, am I?" she said a little wistfully, at the same time clutching her young and looking at Anthony half defiantly. The boy caught her mood and stamped his foot. "Go away, man," said he. "Let my mother alone!"

At that she laughed again and came forward and kissed him, while for a moment they forgot the child entirely. It was the same with them as before he had begun to exist.

Papa Debrülle let them in the door with a strange mixture of pride, satisfaction, and disappointment. The sight of them with the boy between them coming up the steps together caused him to gulp his Adam's apple ludicrously and dash the tears from his eyes. Hovering over them, he was overpowered by pride, a happy and sentimental old German.

"Ach!" he cried, blowing his nose loudly, "it is old Papa Debrülle who has always foreseen this. And now at last—the day—it comes. But you, Angela, you with whom I have laboured to make you great in expression, you and Anthony say nothing. You stand there each holding the boy by one hand. And it is the great dramatic moment of your life that passes! Have you not a single gesture?"

He sat down on the steps disconsolately and took the boy on his knees.

"You at least, little Tony, will not forget old Papa Brülla, will you?" And the child solemnly promised he would not, which moved them all greatly.

Debrülle in fact had not meant to watch. He had pictured himself as stepping aside. It was to be his crowning and perfect sacrifice. But when the time came he could not live up to his own plot. He had been forced as by a superior power to peep through the door at the scene in the garden, which he had planned. And not a gesture, not a single attitude, nothing of the training he had bestowed on Angela had rewarded his hungry eyes that fed upon the emotions of others. Debrülle, indeed, lived entirely vicariously. It was the secret of his constant interest, his love and sacrifice for others. And now those for whom he had slaved had refused to act. Yet hope ever springs anew.

"It is little Tony," he cried at last in more misery than he meant to show, "that I will make a great actor."

Somewhat comforted by at least having become the centre of things, they at last persuaded him with pathetic protestations of gratitude to come into the house. He sat at the head of the table and said grace. Angela and Anthony looked at each other. The child had shut his eyes tight sitting in a high chair. For a moment they gave themselves over to the illusion of domestic simplicity and peace.

Angela smiled inwardly. "What would Bonaparte think if he could know he had furnished the villa of Mlle. Georges at Saint-Germain for this?" She longed to be able to tell him, "that preposterous, sudden, little man." Yet—"let no one here be harmed by him. Let *me* win against the king of the world," she prayed in her simple heart, "since my lover has come back too late. Let me win alone."

Overcome, she took Anthony's hand and pressed it close to her just to be sure that Angela Guessippi was not living in a dream. It was her fear that his return would persuade her to try to do so.

If he had not believed by other testimony than his eyes Anthony would not have known at first that Angela was Angela. To be sure, he did finally rediscover in her, hidden somewhere, in certain tones of her voice and in what is permanent in the cast of anyone's features, his sweetheart of the pagan mornings about Livorno and the slim shepherdess who had sat beside him at the "wedding breakfast" at Signora Bovino's. But that was only Angela, the girl out of whom had grown and burgeoned Angela the woman. The woman had been unpredictable from her slim and modest beginnings. She came to meet him in the present, a Juno of splendid proportions with a golden voice, imperturbable, and yet majestically magnetic. She came as an incredible and an overwhelming surprise. Her self-contained vitality, the large but symmetrical and gracefully-moving bulk of her swept his sweeter but more fragile and younger memories of her irrevocably aside.

Anthony had not changed so much to Angela. She saw in him what she had both hoped and expected, her youthful lover grown into a virile and yet elusively charming man. Angela had become. Anthony was still becoming.

She was now in her first full flower. She knew what she wanted, and she intended to have her ambition, for which she had toiled conscientiously and unremittingly from childhood on with Debrülle, fulfilled. The child meant much to her but her great moments at the opera, and they were great ones, meant more. It might have been different. Under other circumstances she might have cared more for Anthony and the child she had borne him than for the place she had won in the world by her talents and work. But she was now just about to realize her ambition to the full and she saw no adequate reason for turning aside to try to colour the bold and unconventional, but nevertheless courageous and noble lines which she and Debrülle had sketched into their picture of life with the soft pastels of lost dreams.

Except for the lines of the plays and librettos which Debrülle had taught her, except for the notes of her songs, which she followed more easily than the printed words beneath them, Angela was still illiterate. But she had a prodigious memory and a calm, clear mind.

Seven years behind the footlights of northern Italy, Vienna, the lower Rhinelands, and Paris; the constant necessity of imagining herself into innumerable rôles had rapidly conferred upon her a sophistication that was both apparent and real. She understood other people and she understood herself. And all this was made apparent by the way she moved and by the sound of her voice.

She had learned, what so few woman ever learn: how to get up and sit down. She knew where to stand and where not to stand in a room. In short, she occupied space as if she had inherited an ancestral right to do so instead of having had an awkward, a boring, or even an animated nervous task thrust upon her by a puzzling plebeian necessity. In that, at least, she was still pagan.

Nothing is more difficult than to recall to life the peculiarly personal charm of a great actress or singer. Memories, letters, diaries, portraits—even the burning testimony of poets is in vain. Mrs. Siddons, Rachel, Jenny Lind—like the lamp that Hero lit, like the bells of Babylon, only a legend of their alluring glow and molten music now remains. But how different to have seen and heard. Only that way and in no other did men know *who*, and not merely what they were.

Who was Angela? Debrülle knew; Anthony. But all that anyone can know now is that Angela was Mlle. Georges; that all Paris on certain evenings waited for her impatiently, sat rapt in silence while she sang or walked and talked, and roared afterward with tremendous applause. Even that human meteor Napoleon felt an attraction which had produced at least a temporary eccentricity in his orbit. No one could do more than that to him. And if that seems inexplicable, as indeed it was to Josephine, then there is only one other explanation possible. And that is that Mlle. Georges was Angela.

To sit with her in the little music-room of the villa that had been so exquisitely decorated in Pompeian style while she sang and practised with Debrülle accompanying her, his grey, lion-like head nodding or shaking itself in approval or disapproval while the clear notes ran the gamuts of music and the emotions at the same time—that was actually to experience her charm.

She dressed in a white, high-waisted gown with plain gold bands on her bare arms, with open-work sandals caught with silver, the saffron edging of her thin cambric dress-stuff outlining its classic folds. To look from Angela to the portrayal of some Roman matron or an ample yet air-born goddess in the frescoes was to find a resemblance that seemed more than accidental. In that Angela was fortunate. Both the style and the dress of her features realized the conscious ideal of beauty of the time. She was not unaware of this and had made the most of it.

Debrülle worked her hard and yet in that both he and Angela found a zest and a pleasure. The room with the harp in one corner and the grey pianoforte with the mother-of-pearl inlay and the candelabra on each side with trim wax candles was the centre of the house. As for Anthony, he could have sat there listening and watching indefinitely.

"Ah, your tones are richer since he has come," said Debrülle. "Now, once more, that cradle song of Tantiani's. It is one of your best encores. It seems to quiet them. There is nothing, you know, like dismissing an audience in tears. Lean a little lower as you rock the cradle, Angela, and softer, softer as you leave the little one going to sleep. You must count ten steps to the door; one for each bar—and the last—smooth —ah, one hardly hears it. It is far, far away when the curtain goes down. Now then——"

And his strong hands would run over the keys smoothly, and standing there in the afternoon shadows of the music-room with the pianoforte chiming its quaint bell-like chords in quiet harmony the voice of Angela would liquidly begin.

She sang to him. In the weeks that he came and went at Saint-Germain she filled his heart with gracious music. In the evenings, after the boy had been put to bed, she would sit down by the harp and they would lose themselves together in the other world of sound. He sat silent. The words of her songs, when there were words, meant nothing. Yet at these times they found each other so deeply that to return to the device of sentences and converse casually seemed by comparison to be only touching finger tips in a grey mist.

At these times Debrülle also came and went in the same way that he had sustained his constant part in both their lives, but especially in that of Angela. In the later summer evenings when a cool wind was already beginning to fill the house and garden from the forest beyond as though with a premonitory chill, he would come into the music-room and lighting the candles on the pianoforte stretch out on its lyre-shaped, ivory rack some well-chosen sheet of music. This, as if by premonition, he always suited exactly to their mood. Then a duet of harp and pianoforte would begin, accompanying the voices of the man and the woman, who in all but bodily heredity had become father and daughter. Then Debrülle would be gone to keep watch on the terrace to see that all was clear when Anthony left the house and went home.

But it was not necessary to return every time to Paris. Anthony had taken lodgings about a mile down the lime terrace from the villa in a quiet little place that overlooked the town and the Seine. Saint-Germain was as always full of summer visitors, especially before and after the fête of Saint-Lôge, which was the crest of the season. His presence could be no cause for remark unless he chose to make it so.

And of course he did not. He and Debrülle between them took infinite precautions. They were able to manage his comings and goings through the forest gate behind, which at certain hours they discovered was not under observation. Indeed, the watch on the house was rather a desultory one, confined rather to shadowing Debrülle and Angela when they drove out and to occasional questioning of the servants. These were loyal to Angela. The two women who served her in the house and a nursemaid for the child were attached to her and had long been with her about the theatre. Nevertheless, their interest as well as their sympathy was enlisted. As the summer wore on Debrülle became convinced that the surveillance they were subjected to was not one of jealousy but for the protection of Napoleon himself from having his visits noted. He came seldom. When he did so it was not without warning, usually when they had notice of his being in the neighbourhood of Saint-Germain.

Thus for nearly six weeks through August and September Anthony was able to divide his time about equally between Saint-Germain-en-Laye and Paris. He was happy beyond all expectation.

Ouvrard was delayed and delayed. He was negotiating an enormous deal in wheat which was to be exported to Spain where the dearth was extreme. This had the secret approval of Napoleon who was gradually extending his net about the Spanish royal family. It was vital, however, to keep the price of bread reasonable in Paris, for it was known the harvest was a good one. Of this Napoleon had particularly warned Ouvrard. But in spite of his precautions his wholesale buying of grain became known. Speculators rushed in. The price of wheat in a year of plenty soared; approached famine prices. Unrest began to be evident in Paris about the bakeshops. The garrison found its cavalry suddenly increased.

Napoleon sent for Ouvrard and forced him to work out a new system of loans both to feed Paris and to supply the Spanish wheat. The genius displayed by Ouvrard in doing this moved Napoleon to reluctant admiration. In private he even admitted this to Ouvrard but he intended nevertheless to use him for the scapegoat. He was quite frank about it.

"You do not need to mind," said he. "You will soon be off to Spain, where you can appear just in time to save the government there by stopping the famine. That will put them finally in our hands. They blame the bad harvests in Spain on Godoy. Save him and use him. But here in Paris I intend to be the only saviour of the people. Let the price of bread go up two more sous. One sou this week and one the next. But no more. Do you understand? Then I shall step in. Already they are beginning to call upon me. But mind you if I have to bring in the artillery you will never get to Spain. You were inept, Ouvrard, in letting your wheat operations become known. I warned you. I shall simply use this as another occasion to demonstrate that France cannot do without me. But do not present me with any further opportuniites, my friend, or I shall have to ask you to retire to Caen. I shall take occasion to whip you in public soon. Do not forget to wince properly. Now make your arrangements to relieve the market here instantly. Let us be exact, let us say that on September thirtieth the price of bread falls four sous. I shall supply the edict and arrest recalcitrant bakers—you will supply the wheat. You can make up the loss in Spain. Do we understand each other?"

"As always," said Ouvrard. "But I would like you to remember," he added, "that no matter at what cost I have always seen that the troop rations are ample and honestly provided."

"I led them to victory when they were hungry, monsieur le banquier," said Napoleon, tapping his snuffbox. "You are like all merchants, Ouvrard. You are incapable of understanding me because you cannot understand my motives. Do you think men die for rations? Ouvrard, you are a great mathematical hog. If you ever threaten me again I shall give you a hypodermic injection of lead. Look, you stand there fascinated. Do you know why? You are afraid? No—you are hearing the truth. It convicts you to yourself." He waved him out.

With such speculations in the air the House of the Wolf was not without its interesting evenings. It was Vincent who was to convey the French wheat to Spain. Anthony spent about half his time in Paris and the rest at Saint-Germain-en-Laye. Yet, despite the intricate financial web that went on slowly weaving itself with wheat, Mexican silver, Madrid, and New Orleans in the offing, for him it was a peculiarly calm and serene autumn. Until Ouvrard should leave for Spain Anthony was merely standing-by waiting.

Paris, he discovered, was an excellent place for a wealthy young man to tarry in. He provided himself extensively, not only for New Orleans, but for the permanent life in America from firearms to a well-selected library. He read all the books he could about Louisiana, and he interviewed several people who had lived there at various times. In some sort his future there began to become vaguely visible. He pored over many old, confused maps. On the advice of a young Yankee who had floated down the Mississippi on a flat-boat and been arrested by the Spaniards for his pains, he took up pistol practice at Fantan's gallery, where a number of old duellists examined the finer principles of the art.

He and Vincent went about together endlessly. They were even invited once to the Hôtel Salm. They danced at a ball at the Tuileries. They dined—and then Anthony would go out to Saint-Germain again.

He spent long mornings there playing with the boy in the garden. They became complete friends. He brought the child endless gifts till Angela put a stop to it. They sailed boats in the fountain and they played bear in the thickets and leaves. They told each other long stories and conducted campaigns with armies of lead soldiers. And all the time Anthony filled his eyes with the sturdiness of the youngster who was a combination of his own body and the brown health and quiet serenity of Angela. All the time he kept filling his eyes and heart with the surprise and wonder of his living son.

He would take the boy to New Orleans with him. He began to dream of their life there with this child growing to manhood in the new country. He began to speak to Angela about it.

It was the child who forced them at last after weeks had gone by to come to some conclusion about their own relations. These—with a curious instinct on both their parts to let the delightful well-enough of the present alone—they had avoided coming to any conclusion about.

They had not renewed their intimacy on a passionate basis. With both of them that seemed already to have been fulfilled. They remembered it; it coloured all their association that summer, but as something which had been completed, which did not have to be repeated. There would have been something fumbling, something blundering and unnecessary about returning to physical beginnings. They had begun there, fulfilled themselves, and gone on. The days in the garden together with the child, the evenings in the music-room, a deep and quiet companionship which they experienced together as a kind of bright and tranquil happiness for hours at a time did not seem to point them inevitably to bed.

And yet they were in love with each other. They cared for each other more than anybody else. And they were happier together than when apart. Perhaps the crux of the affair was a certain sense of fatality that lay deeper than all else, an instinctive understanding and acceptance of the fact that do what they might, each had a separate life to live. And no matter how they met, they met ultimately to pass on and live apart.

Yet it was this feeling that also lent a poignancy to their hours. If it was not the same as passion, it brought with it a similar degree in intensity of emotion; a yearning and pity, a desire to love and comfort each other beyond the easy warmth of the flesh.

So fragile was all this, and yet so real and complex, that both of them shrank from laying rude hands upon the walls of dreams to tear them apart. They were content by a mutual understanding to live for weeks, snatching what hours they could together, in the present only; thankful for it, tacitly disregarding both the past and the future. To begin to plan anything was to begin to plan the end. And then suddenly one day they found themselves engaged, as they knew they inevitably would be, in doing just that.

They were sitting together watching the boy sail his boats in the pool at the end of the sunken garden during the afternoon hours which seemed to pass without beginning or end. An occasional low rumble of wheels from the high road beyond the wall and the distant notes of Debrülle composing a song at the pianoforte drifted through the thicket. He had been ardently telling her about his plans for New Orleans, hoping she might say something that would show she felt she might have a part in them, building carefully, erecting his air castles in the other world with open doors. But she had said nothing and he fell silent.

The boy by the pool had curled up and gone to sleep while he talked. It was for him more than for her that Anthony had been pleading, Angela thought. It had frightened her and *he* felt it. He faltered how to begin again. They both looked at the child each seeing the other in his face, and for an instant the awareness of the unity of feeling which had bound them so completely that night at Livorno brushed them with its wings again. She crept into his arms.

He kissed her. And an agony of regret for all they had lost in each other welled up in both of them unbearably so that all that had been their happiness and peace and pleasure in each other was quite suddenly and unexpectedly transmuted into pain, into an exquisite and impossible yearning for themselves to be as they had once been. Angela, who had thought that it would be so, lay still in his arms. As he bent over her it was suddenly revealed to him what the sorrow of embracing the beloved dead was like.

Instantly he was all defiance, determined to overcome the unreasonable and inevitable, driven to reasserting his own will and reconstructing life.

"This time you will come with me, Angela. What is the difference what either of us has done? We have found each other again. And this time there is the child—out of our dream."

She crept close to him, alive again.

"That much of it came true," she cried. "Do you care?"

"Care!" he exclaimed. "Am I not trying to tell you to? Why won't you come with me and bring the child? I will go anywhere, do anything for you. I can now, you know. Where shall it be—Italy, Germany, France? England!" He suddenly flamed up at the thought. "Marry me. I will give you and the boy a home there. You do not know how we could live in England. Away from this little man of battles that troubles your peace. All the best of the past is in England, the future safe, free. We could have our dream there again and watch the boy grow up, right, a

gentleman. Or will you come with me to America—
anywhere? Only it must be *our* life. Not music only.
Not precious moments snatched from something else.
Why not? We should be happy. What more is there we
can find anywhere than each other? Marry me this time.
Didn't I beg you before when I was poor and a boy
and knew nothing—only that I had found you and that
that was all? Why do you always go away from me,
Angela? Why? Something died in me that morning at
Livorno. You killed it. Yes, I know now I started to
die then."

"But you lived once with me, too," she whispered. He
did not answer her but did not let her go either.

"You cannot get more," she cried. "We were used
as we were meant to be. There is no reward except in
remembering what we were to each other. Forgive me.
I know now that I should have married you then. But
how could I know it then? What could you have done?
How could you have married me that morning, Anthony? There was too much against it. We did not
know enough to act in spite of everything, to live and
let the world die. I was a woman and I turned to
Debrülle who was a man. Time had not made you a
man yet. But what was I to do? I could not help that.
I did the best I could and I am grateful to Debrülle."

"I will take him along with us," said Anthony. "We
will not leave him alone."

For a moment she lay looking up at him. Her hand
went up to his hair. "Oh, my lover, my only lover," she
murmured. "You are very good to me."

"And so you will come with me then, Angela, Angela
Maea," he cried.

An indescribable sense of hope and relief, of life
become a livable certainty, overwhelmed him. He got
up in triumph and went over to lift up the sleeping boy
to put him in her arms. Then—then they would all be
together at last and they would get up and go into the
house and tell Debrülle. And hereafter it would all
be well. Why, he felt like a boy again, confident of
eternal happiness. He could have thanked his own little

virgin with a childish prayer. He must, he felt, thank something. She should stand by the hearth with the child in her arms. He picked up his little son and caught him to him, pressing his smooth face to his own. What had died in him was alive still in the child. Thank God, thank God for that. He turned toward her and came over the grass slowly, carrying the boy so he would not awake. He felt the relaxed childish form settle against his shoulder, the weight of himself and Angela and the boy. "Anthony" he was called! All this he was carrying at one time, knowing by sensation, by weight and warmth and by the sight of the unconscious, sleeping face that so moved his hope and pity—above all his pity—what it was to be the father of that child.

Angela had meanwhile been leaning back against the trunk of one of the old forest oaks that still lived on in the garden like the giant survivals of a sturdier time. She sat in a pile of dead leaves amid the roots. Through the thickets and garden tangles that were no longer formal came the notes of Debrülle's song for which he had now constructed his accompaniment.

It was a simple melody, his own words in German, sentimental and vague in meaning. Yet when joined to his music it meant something; something that was new and strong then in the world, the swan-song of romance. The music and the vague little lyric of Debrülle's, when the two were combined and the words and notes became one, was compact of a curious sorrow for itself that was already sweeping all northern Europe. It rose out of a conviction that the world was growing old, that the best of love, and high living, and advenure could be found only in the past. At best only a few moments of life at the full could be tasted in these days. One was no longer young enough, even when one was very young, really to live them, to be of them. Ecstasy was vanishing. Reality was old and hopeless or new and ugly. "We have parted," thought the thinker in the blind chamber, "the light is growing dim. Let us sit here and be sorrowful and do the best we can in the daytime. Psyche has left us. We are only bodies again. Oh! how beautiful she was. Make us a song, write us a book, give us riches that we may lure her back and be at one with her again. Oh 'magic casements opening on the foam of perilous seas' . . ." That perfectly forlorn view had yet to be provided. But already the generations had begun to move toward that kind of window, the last out of which the departing sunset glow of the living day was still visible. "Soon we shall be sitting in complete darkness," whispered the feeling of time, "look, even look backwards while you can."

Soon it was to be forgotten what those who crowded to the window were weeping about. The foam on the magic seas turned to madness, to froth. Tears were to become so terrible that they became funny. Men could no longer bear them.

But in Debrülle's time they were just beginning to wet the eyelids a little. Out of his own life and his own generation he had made a song about them. It was to be a new encore for Angela when the next season began. After the mock-classical play was over she would come out and sing this song. That was what the audience was waiting for; for this strange new yearning and sadness that brought them up standing, trembling and weeping, while the first consul sat in his box with Josephine under the wax candles, bored. What were they all weeping about? He would give them another Roman empire for which to die; order, glory, and stability again. Let emotions be saved for patriotism. Come back to the Tuileries, Josephine. Mlle. Georges was, of course, charming and after all he was a man. Yes, he understood the emotion of the people when she sang to them. He understood better than they did. He would possess the cause of it, Mlle. Georges herself.

She had been his prisoner all summer at Saint-Germain. He had not come often. He did not stay long when he did come. He came like a flame blazing, was quenched instantly and was gone. And then Anthony had come again. What was she to do? Debrülle had made her a new song with which to speak to the people.

What it was she said to them she did not know. The sadness of what Debrülle had lost himself he had re-created in her. The sorrow of her own loss of Anthony, her personal feeling in Debrülle's tune and words, she made them all one. The woman as always conveyed herself personally. But the world heard its time-feeling speak. She did not know that or care. She sang to it everywhere and it laughed and wept. Those were great moments. Something uttered itself through her. Something that Debrülle knew about and put into his little songs. She felt herself being used then completely. She was the voice of it, possessed. Anthony could never possess and use her again fully. The child had been their song. She had fulfilled herself there.

How could she tell him?

He was coming over to her now bringing the child. They were to live together again. He was demanding real life of her. He was strong and could live. Life was still the same as song to him. How could she face that again? The strength and the belief to do so had died in her. It had been transferred to the boy.

"Let Anthony keep him in his arms," she thought. "They can sing life together. Nothing is left me but music. It is too late."

She pressed her head against the rough bark of the tree closing her eyes and listening to the completed portions of Debrülle's song which he was trying over and over. His baritone in the distance and the rich chords of his accompaniment blent smoothly and came warmly through the leaves.

"Oh, there's never a dove in last year's nest,
    Or a swan to come back to me."

He stopped, fumbling musically for a better harmony for the next line.

"Debrülle, I will stay with thee," she whispered, and looked up to see Anthony standing there with the child, waiting.

She shook her head at him.

"What has happened?" he said, clasping the boy close. He woke and cried out, demanding to be set down. Anthony let him go. But he stayed beside his father holding onto his coat. She stood looking at the two men before her for a while. Then she put her hands behind her head and hummed the stave of Debrülle's song.

"Oh," said he miserably. "Is that the answer?"

"Yes," she whispered.

"And that means 'no,' " he said.

Neither of them moved for a minute. They were both white with emotion. He looked down at the boy who was dragging at his coattails.

"Keep him," she cried. She came forward and clutched at his breast a moment. He could not answer her embrace.

"We will tear you apart between us, won't we?" said she laughing distractedly, and kissed him. Then she burst into tears and fled into the house leaving them alone together.

He spent the bright agony of the rest of that afternoon in the garden with little Anthony. The pool with the dead leaves on it, the oak tree where she had sat, the green where for a moment with happiness found he had taken the child up from the grass to carry him back to his mother were engraved on his memory permanently. It was etched without colour by the sharp acid of the emotions he had undergone there as if his brain had been bled white.

All his comfort remained in the child. His sorrow was not for himself now, it was not the dizzy sickness of his first parting with Angela at Livorno. It transferred itself into calmness and resignation, into an overwhelming access of pity and determination as he looked at the child. As he played with him gently there, as if he were playing with some emanation of himself again in the convent garden, he determined to do well by him and not to use him unmercifully as a comfort for himself.

He sat down by the pool and began to help him sail

his boats again, losing himself with the boy on the miniature dream-ships that the wind blew back and forth. There was one water-lily growing there that they caught upon. In all the world which had gone pale white for him that afternoon it seemed to be the only thing that still retained its delicate warm flesh colour. Then he saw the boy's face close beside it puffing his cheeks out at a small sail. How the boat flew! The perfume of the flower came reminding him of the bowl on the table in Vincent's room.

He began to think of Anna in the empty house at Düsseldorf, of the pearls he had given her that had once made him think of Angela. And there was Anthony with his cool cheek in the water looking at the water-lily with wide-open eyes.

"Water-lilies are fragrant," he said.

"I love a big, cool flower like that," said the little boy. And then dashed cold water on his father in pure male embarrassment.

"Come on, my son," said Anthony. "I understand. I will send you home to one. Would you like that?"

The boy looked puzzled but the man was evidently in earnest.

"If I can take my ships along, too," he said.

"Bless you, all of them," cried his father. "And I shall give you more."

The child gathered up his little fleet contentedly and they went into the house together.

The music-room was going full blast. Debrülle was playing over his new song with tremendous enthusiasm. The pedals on the pianoforte thumped and squeaked. As if she would shatter the ordinary air and make an impossible but more ecstatic and passionate atmosphere in which to palpitate perpetually, Angela was hurling herself through the brief chords of passion and the weak longing and yearning of Debrülle's swan-song. The house, silent and subdued, with all the life in it halted in order to provide an intimate audience for the woman's loud, melodious cry for more feeling than existence could possibly sustain—waited—waited with the serene patience of inanimation, the sunlight basking upon its terraces, the wind tossing playfully in the tops of the ancient oaks in the garden. And with them on a bench in the shadowed hallway also waited the man and the child.

Anthony took the boy in his arms, and this time he offered no resistance. He sat contentedly enough upon his father's knee as if he had gladly taken refuge there from the furious and clanging bursts of sound for which everything else had been temporarily thrust aside—but was still waiting with sure prescience to resume. To all that, song and silent waiting, Debrülle had composed a perfect accompaniment. The pianoforte seemed to spill over with music, trying to interrupt life, trying to create something apart from it, yearning futilely over its inadequacy to exist, emotion without a cause or an end even in thought.

"Mother is singing again," said little Anthony.

At the sound of the child's voice someone in the music-room got up and closed the door. Whoever it was that did it managed to convey a hint of impatience at a universe that interrupted a song.

The man and the boy looked at each other and understood what each was thinking. They and the house and the things about them suddenly seemed to have ceased to be listening to the song in the closed room.

Anthony determined to take his son with him to Paris that night.

He went upstairs to the nursery with him to see about getting his things together. The nurse made no opposition, although she informed her mistress. With the swift understanding of a woman, and without any questions, she began to beg Anthony to be taken along. She seemed to regard the boy's departure as a fait accompli. A will in fixed determination can indeed make itself felt to be such.

It was now about six o'clock in the evening and the little boy sat quietly eating his last supper in his mother's house.

Behind the closed doors of the music-room Angela and Debrülle, with the scratched score of the new song scattered on the floor, sat in an excited, and on Debrülle's part, a reproachful and tearful debate. He did not wish to give up the child.

"You do not understand me," insisted Angela again and again. "You blame me and yet it was you who took me away from him and made me Mlle. Georges. You, Debrülle!"

"You . . ." he cried, rising up and tossing his grey mane back with his hand in a tragic gesture that was for once both dramatic and real. "You . . ." a conflict of emotion overcame him. But no one, not even he himself, ever knew what he was going to say.

"Listen!" she cried. "Ah, now—you see, you hear?"

Down the walk from the wicket that led into the garden from the forest came the crisp, swift tread of a pair of military boots and the click of a sword.

Debrülle fled.

Angela turned to meet the conqueror alone.

Chapter Fourteen

Panem Et Circenses

NAPOLEON had little or no curiosity about the
domestic establishment of Mlle. Georges. At
Milan some years before, when he had been
attracted by Angela in the first bloom of her success
and womanhood, he had become acquainted with the
fact that Debrülle existed and that there was a child
in the actress's house. Debrülle had long been accepted
about the theatre as Angela's father and mentor. He
was always addressed by Angela, and everyone else,
as "Papa." He looked and he played the part. As for
the boy—Angela was an actress and her great lover
had neither the curiosity nor the inclination to be
jealous of her past. She was a young widow, they said.
Possibly—why not? At least there were no present
difficulties; which was admirable. Also she had herself
proved discreet about their relations. It was Josephine
who had deliberately hunted up this obscure affair in
Milan herself. He had carefully ascertained that. He
had never forgiven her for it. Neither Angela nor

Debrülle had ever asked for anything. Naturally he saw that they were comfortable. The villa at Saint-Germain was even luxurious. He thought so as he strode into the little music-room and found Mlle. Georges standing there with her music strewn over the floor. But he intended to reward her, to be greatly generous as he could afford to be now. And he had thought of a way to be princely to Angela and to be even with Josephine for her unnecessary trouble. It would attract just enough attention thoroughly to annoy and rebuke her without really compromising himself. Paris would merely be amused. No one could prove anything. Editors, if necessary, could be prosecuted. But best of all Josephine had that very morning unwittingly suggested it to him herself.

It was the thought of it that gave him a more than usually self-satisfied smile as he strode up the path that afternoon. His coming was quite a surprise at that hour. He had just ridden over from Saint-Loque. He was delighted to find the evidences of the genuine consternation and pretty surprise which his arrival must naturally have produced in her strewn about the floor of the music-room.

"Mademoiselle!" said he, pausing a moment on the threshold to look about, "do not, I beg you, permit me to interrupt so lovely a thing as a new song. Let me be the first to hear it." He assisted her gallantly in retrieving Debrülle's composition and rearranged it for her on the little ivory rack. He stood by the pianoforte with his hand on his sword waiting for her to begin. She began her own accompaniment gayly. She began to sing. She got as far as

> "Yet creatures of wing that fly and sing
> Must fly if they would go free"

when the words choked her. Even an actress could go no further in her own tragedy. "Poor Angela, poor helpless me," she thought. She struck a discord and broke down weeping for herself.

Much touched by this display of great and genuine emotion, by the cries and tears which his arrival had evoked, he led her to a couch with eagles on it and sat down. Every eagle had an "N" in its mouth. He observed them with satisfaction. "Napoleon—Napoleon —Napoleon." The universe from armies to couches shrieked it back at him. He could hear and see nothing else. Doubtless, Mlle. Georges had been lonely without him. He had not visited her for a long time. Poor woman! He began to comfort her.

After it was over he would tell her about the surprise. The diamonds must certainly be magnificent ones or Josephine would not have asked for them.

———————

Debrülle had fled directly to the nursery both to be out of the way and to warn Anthony. He found him sitting having a bowl of bread and milk with the boy. Anthony refused to be moved by Debrülle or the fact that Napoleon was in the house. A certain hardness of mood in regard to Angela and her affairs left him cold. "As a matter of fact," he said to Debrülle, "the nursery is the last place where the great little man will come, and if he does he will find us all eating bread and milk. Have a bowl, my dear Debrülle. Marianne, a bowl of pap for the little papa."

The nurse, who was "ravished" by excitement, amusement, and the danger of the situation, as only a Frenchwoman could be and contain herself, departed wide-eyed for the kitchen, where she enlarged on the sang-froid of monsieur eating milk with the innocent while cet homme de l'enfer conduisait encore une autre victoire en bas.

"There is no more milk," said the cook showing signs of hysteria.

Anthony and Debrülle sat silent. They heard the pianoforte begin and Angela break off in the middle of her song.

"My words and music!" exclaimed Debrülle, "to think that he has heard them."

Anthony felt his mouth harden with contempt. Little Tony demanded his cabinet before going to bed. Anthony found it for him. The silence continued downstairs. Both the child and Debrülle sat looking grave for different reasons. Overcome by the situation, Anthony leaned back and laughed. He felt greatly relieved by that.

"How romantic it all is, my dear Debrülle!" he cried.

"It is life," whispered the older man dejectedly looking about him. "My God, how terrible that is!" He wiped his brow, which had broken out into a cold sweat at the sound of Anthony's laughter. "He hardly ever stays more than an hour," he added deprecatingly.

"Good night, little papa," said the boy, coming over to Debrülle. "I am going to bed now. Go away. I want to sleep. Where is mamma?"

Debrülle covered him up and kissed him.

"When do I go to town? You promised, you know, big man," said the boy, sitting up again.

"Tonight," replied Anthony, soothing him. "Go to sleep now and when you wake up I will take you along."

The boy looked at him with delight and wonder.

"I will go to sleep quick then," he said and shut his eyes determinedly.

Debrülle took Anthony by the arm and led him out of the room. He was weeping. They went down a long dark hall at the top of the house. There was a deep window at the end of it. They sat down there and looked out into the garden. It was twilight now. The house was still quiet downstairs.

"I think I shall go down," said Anthony, "and . . ."

"Don't be crazy," whispered Debrülle. "That would only ruin us all. None of us could avoid this, you know. It was fate. Do you think she could help it? Think!"

"No," said Anthony after a while, looking out into the garden, "I suppose not." He had suddenly seen

Angela in a new light. Perhaps it was for the good of the boy after all that she had given him up. Perhaps as Debrülle said, "she could not help herself." Debrülle's grasp on his arm relaxed. He heard him sigh with relief. Silence engulfed them and it grew darker in the long hall. He could no longer see Debrülle's face.

"When we left you," his voice began after a while whispering out of nothing, "we went on to Naples. It was there that Angela found that she was with child. I was doing well then. The company finally got to Vienna and the boy was born there. We knew he was yours. We called him Anthony. It was Angela who would not let me write. Ah, we were both proud. I had done well by her. She was also succeeding and working hard. Mon Dieu, how I worked her. It was a happy family. Mine, I called it. Can you blame me?"

"Then very hard times came with the wars. The theatres at Vienna closed. We starved, everything for the baby. It was then that I wrote you and I heard nothing except, long afterwards, that you had gone to Cuba. I sang in the streets for them and held out the hat. I never let her do that. Angela would never let me write to old Bonnyfeather."

"Thank you for that," said Anthony. "Your letters never came."

"I knew," said Debrülle. "At last we heard the theatres were open again in Milan and we followed the armies there. We both sang our way to Milan with the child. I knew Lotti at the Scala. It was there that Angela emerged. A lucky chance at a fine part and she triumphed. It went on night after night. She became great. It was at Milan that Bonaparte saw her. He came to our house. What could we do? You must know how it would be. At last we came to Paris. It was not because of him. No, it was not that. She came here to shine brightly and she has done so. It was only this summer we came into his grasp again. She suffers him, I tell you. She has done the best she can. The boy has had every care. I myself have begun his education. And now, you will take him from us?

"Yes," said Anthony, "he goes with me."

"Ah," said Debrülle—"he goes!" He said it with so much relief that for an instant Anthony was furious with him. Then he understood what he meant.

From the gravel path below came the rapidly diminishing tread of boots. They were almost—almost running. The muffled beat of hoofs from the bridle path that led from the little gate directly into the forest was heard and was gone. It was already quite dark. Apparently he had been completely alone. They had not even caught a glimpse of him. The stars were beginning to come out over the black mass of the forest.

In the darkness Anthony reached out and sought the old actor's hand. "I understand you both, now," he whispered. "You are a hero, Debrülle. I will do everything for the boy, not only because he is mine but for you and Angela. Believe me, I will not think of myself but of him. I have a plan. At Düsseldorf . . ."

"At Düsseldorf!" exclaimed Debrülle. "I have friends, relations there. I could be near him. Angela could sometimes come. It is home. But you were saying, yes, at Düsseldorf you were saying?"

"I can tell you later," said Anthony. "What can I do for you, my dear friend?"

Debrülle choked.

"Ach, mein Gott," said he in German, "you can get me a drink. It is wine that I want." He got up and stumbled down the hall.

"I will go down now," he said, pausing at the head of the stairs. "Wait. I will tell you if she wants to see you again." His feet dragged down into the darkness and silence below. Anthony heard him striking a light somewhere, the clink of glass, and the man coughing over a decanter.

"What an end to it all," he thought. "Debrülle's only refuge is a chemical reaction. Something to give the lie to fate." He sat waiting. "Well, it has been fate. What else could the man do? How otherwise could he escape

390

from the responsibility for four lives that he had romantically assumed?"

"Angela," called Debrülle.

"Here, mon père."

Her voice came up to him rich even in the note of
despair that he recognized, thrilling him as always. He
heard them whispering, a door closed . . .

—but whatever they decided he meant to take the
boy with him to Paris that night.

Presently Debrülle called him. "Come down now,"
he said.

He found the door from the music-room open, a
fan of lamplight lying across the hall. Angela was
sitting alone on the couch. A part of her dress which
had been torn was wrapped about her. She was very
pale and trembling. But he had never seen her so
magnificent before. Her dark eyes shone wide and
strangely. She looked up at him with a courageous
tenderness and a feminine patience and endurance
that overwhelmed him.

He loved her now. Loved her completely with no
romance or mists of dreaming, but clearly and wholly
in the grinning face of fact. She let him take her in his
arms.

"I needed your comfort just once in a time like this,"
she said. "It is cruel of me, but I wanted you to see
me now, I wanted you to understand. Do you see why
we could never live together again?"

And he knew that what she said was true. He tried
only to give her what comfort he could by holding
her close to him. For a few moments their hearts
beat together.

"Now take him and go," she said. "Do not ask me
to say good-bye to him, too. Tomorrow morning I shall
just say, 'He is gone,' but he is not dead for he is with
you." She kissed him for the last time.

"How can you, Angela?" he cried.

"Just as you can, Anthony," she said, rising and
standing triumphantly before him. He saw her supreme

now in her greatest part. "We can both finish our song."

"Yes," he said, "I know. Yes, we can do that. And so I will go again."

She caught her breath.

"No, no, do not touch me, do not touch me again. I couldn't bear that. It is enough."

"You are right," he said. "But, my God, I won't see you again. It is over." He turned to look back. She was standing there firmly, yet her hands involuntarily reached out toward him.

"Come and hear how bravely I shall finish this song which has been scattered tonight," she said and dropped her arms. "At the first night, the opening of the season, you know. I can sing it if I know you are there, Anthony."

"I will come, Angela."

"Good," she cried, with a miraculous gayety. "It is like you to promise that. Why, we are not going to be stopped, are we? The performance as billed is going on." She waved a sheet of notes at him. "I think, though, while I am picking up this scattered music from the floor you had better go. No, don't try to help me." They looked at each other and smiled. She stooped and started to pick up her score again. She rearranged it and put it back on the pianoforte. The wind had scattered it badly when Napoleon had gone out— the winds of the world.

Mlle. Georges went over to a mirror and looked at herself critically. Her dress was torn, she noticed.

"That sudden, little man. He had done that—mon Dieu!" She laughed.

And then she listened to her own laughter as critically as she was looking at herself in the glass.

"Debrülle was wrong," she said. "*This* is my great moment and I am perfectly cast for a tragic part."

"Come down here, mon père," she cried, for she could no longer bear being left alone. "I want to show you something. This moment is yours, too."

The audience she had summoned arrived with a bottle in its hand.

"Look," she cried, pointing to the glass, and she went through her gesture and laughter again and again. He sat watching the reflection, fascinated. She could repeat it indefinitely now.

"You taught me that, without you I could never have done it. I wanted you to see it now that it is completed."

"It is perfect," cried Debrülle. "Magnificent! My God, Angela, but you are a great woman."

She went through the gesture and laughed again.

Debrülle emptied the bottle, watching her till he nodded.

Four hours later, at half past three in the morning, Anthony got home to the House of the Wolf with his son asleep in his arms.

The last few weeks in Paris assumed a character which Anthony could never have imagined. The House of the Wolf was turned at one stroke from a bachelor's establishment run on strictly male lines to a domestic "child-garden" swarming with women.

Marianne, the nurse, and the wife of old Paul established young Tony in a nursery the day after his arrival. The two maids who came in by the day were always hovering near. Juan and Simba followed him about with a similar expression in their eyes. Anna came from Düsseldorf answering in person the letters which Anthony and Vincent had written. Katharina Geiler and her mother arrived shortly afterward, having heard the news from Anna on her way through Strasbourg. At the end of the month Frau Frank arrived, having made a record trip via Marseilles. She was positively jealous to find even Anna there before her and immediately assumed control of the house. Nothing could be done about it. Uncle Otto had been buried only a few weeks before, and the active old woman who had felt her life ended in the empty house at Livorno suddenly found it renewed and flowing vitally at Paris. She seemed to grow young again. Debrülle kept coming in from Saint-Germain and spent hours in the house. He regarded all the plans made for the boy as his own.

Anthony and Vincent, of course, had had no idea what a call upon maternity with a romantic plea in it would evoke. Life in its fullness had simply and un-avoidably descended upon them from all points of the compass at once. They undertook to cope with it as well as they could in a sort of mutual defence, which was of course only partly successful. That is to say that nothing turned out any longer as they had ex-pected.

Anthony would have been horrified at bringing all this down upon Vincent if he had not discovered from the very first that Vincent liked it. Vincent's surprise at finding that Anthony had a son seven years old—"at three o'clock in the morning and the father doing well," as he put it—was only matched by his pride and delight. He kept thumping Anthony on the back until his shoulder was sore. And Vincent was now "Uncle Vincent." When the women arrived he became, so far as the household was concerned, paterfamilias, and he liked it. He had written a few days later to Fräulein Geiler suggesting that they be married at Christmas. "Ja, you watch and see," said he to An-thony. "You are not the only one that can have boys. Wait,"—and when Katharina and her mother arrived to purchase the trousseau he went strolling about with a knowing air. The empty wing of the house across the court was now fitted up for the women. It was Juan who called it the harem. And in a curious way little Tony, who played with Simba in the court and liked him better than anyone, even his new papa, was the cause and centre of it all.

He was a quiet and self-contained little fellow, brown like Angela but with his father's eyes and hair. He had been used to constant changes of abode and living everywhere. Mother, he knew, had gone away some-where. She had often done that before. He saw De-brülle often. Everybody at this place made much of him. His new papa took him about Paris in a carriage and the tall cool lady, Mamma Anna, as he soon learned to call her, put him to bed at night. Already he liked her better than Marianne. Next to going to sleep with his head resting on Simba he liked going to sleep in her lap. All this he took for granted. How long was it going to last? he wondered. Nothing had ever lasted very long before, he remembered. They always went on to some place else. But he could not bear to think of leaving Simba. At the very thought of that he would get up and shout.

Anthony found himself in an abysmal difficulty about what to do with the boy. He wanted to take him with him to America. Yet everybody was against that.

"Yes," said Vincent, "when you have established yourself there and have a home. But to drag him with you to Madrid and then half-way across the world to New Orleans before you know what your life will be like there. Suppose he gets ill on the ship." He shrugged his shoulders. "Nice for you," he said.

He talked it over with Anna. Perhaps he had sent for her too hurriedly, he sometimes thought. He knew she would come. And she had. She said little, but it was plain she longed to keep the child.

"Let me have him if only for a few years. I will do well by him; love him like the baby I lost. When he is big and strong I will send him to you." But even now she wept at the very thought. It was Anna who said the least. She did not, like the rest, oppose him. But her every attitude seemed to plead with him. "Let me take this child home and to my heart." And, in a way, Anthony loved Anna. They were at peace together —water-lilies—it was to her that he instinctively and perhaps too impulsively turned.

As for Debrülle, he could see nothing but Düsseldorf, and education was his theme. There was truth in it. He also could not bear to lose the child. He too would retire to Düsseldorf shortly, he said.

Poor Anthony—they were all against him. "Delay —wait—after a while. When you are settled—when he is older—consider him instead of yourself." And it was that argument that finally turned him, for he had promised Angela to think of the boy first.

Anthony did not have enough experience with women in the full domestic round to know that not one of them who advised him so well and so earnestly upon this vital occasion could imagine his own joy and consequently his affection and yearning over the child. Like most people they were disposed to take paternity lightly. "Love" is supposed to have feminine connotations in human affairs. There is really no word to express the emotions and attitudes of fatherhood. The relation of women towards children is so physically necessary; so obvious and overpowering in its double necessity that the father can be easily lost. It is not until social chaos begins to ensue that the loss begins to be felt. Long before that, however, myriads of individuals deprived of the male element in everything but their bare conception begin to drift through life the victims of unchecked emotion. Historically the increasing dominance of woman is marked by emotionalism and revolution, romanticism, feminism triumphant, hysteria. The end is either a return to a balance, a reaction where the man reasserts his authority in the family, or anarchy. The paternal state, which tries to be Our-fathers-which-art-on-earth, is always accompanied by the loss of the subtle qualities of fatherhood in individual men. When patriotism becomes matriotism, nature and force reassert themselves in human affairs. Sympathy has been mistaken for the truth.

All the women, young and old, who united to persuade Anthony not to take his son with him did so for the reason that in each case they wanted to keep the baby. As his own feelings in regard to the matter had no name, he was at a loss how to persuade either himself or them that his desire to keep his son was right. Indeed, this was hardly discussed. There was a great deal of head-shaking and tongue-wagging over Angela. The boy had lost his mother. That he had found his father was scarcely important. What was needed, all agreed, was a woman to take Angela's place. And there was Anna, whose baby had just been buried.

So Anthony laid Isaac on the altar. It was agreed that little Tony was to go to Anna at Düsseldorf. For a while, of course, only for a while.

Surrounded by the approving faces of all at the House of the Wolf, he felt supported and fairly happy in his decision. Along with the boy his feelings persisted in reasserting themselves. Once as they rode through the Paris streets on some errand or other with the boy leaning against him and talking gayly of the magic sights beyond, the thought of parting with him became unbearable. "This is part of your being," said his voices, "and you are leaving it behind?"

"Yes," he answered himself determinedly. And something in him hearing its sentence pronounced died. At a toy shop he overwhelmed little Tony with too many gifts. He asked to go back to Simba.

"My God," thought Anthony. "They will ask to have Simba stay with him, too." He began to make much of the dog, which loved him blindly. When he stroked his head he growled and closed his eyes.

A message from Ouvrard made Anthony realize that at length the end of his days in Paris was at hand. They would be leaving Paris for Madrid about the end of September. Ouvrard himself began to come around in the evenings. Vincent had kept evenings sacred to the continuing of his affairs. In spite of his engagement, the boy, and the women in the household, banking, as he explained, had to go on. It did so now in the evenings in the sense that Vincent meant of keeping up his acquaintance among men of affairs in Paris. Paul was busy at the gate every night. Among the many who arrived and departed, Ouvrard sat usually till after midnight, looking tired. He had taken lately to drinking a good deal. His enormous speculations in wheat worried him. The price of bread was going up in Paris and interviews with Napoleon, which had now become frequent and harassing, put him under a strain that was visible in his face and motions.

At length one evening he came in looking much relieved and related what had happened that day at the Tuileries. An incipient bread riot had precipitated the interview in which the final arrangements for a little drama had been laid.

"All is now ready," said Ouvrard. "I am to be released at last. I have satisfied him that I can supply the wheat to the Paris bakers. On the first of October the price is to come down to normal when the shops open in the morning. But I am to appear at the Comédie, a comedy indeed," he grunted, "the evening before. It is the opening night of Mlle. Georges in *The Templars*. Bonaparte and Josephine and all Paris that counts will be there. After the play there is to be a 'riot,' a carefully staged one, outside the theatre. Thus the good shepherd of the people will learn with amazement that they are hungry. He will turn to me on the steps before everybody and give me a tremendous wigging. I will drive off in disgrace—to Spain. He will then announce that the price of bread is to come down and plenty restored. Next morning the edicts will be up all over Paris and the bakeshops open, full of good brown loaves. All I have to be is the villain. Hein, that is not so good, I am going be miles from Paris by morning. You can never tell how a little joke like this might end for the goat. And you, my boy," said he to Anthony, "must be prepared to leave with me in the coach. How will you like that? By God, I'll need somebody."

"I will leave from the theatre with you that evening," said Anthony. "I shall be at the play, too. I shall be waiting for you outside."

"Good," cried Ouvrard, looking much pleased. "There will be two villains then. Well, you still have a day or two to send your things on ahead. We shall travel light and fast ourselves."

Anthony nodded and looked worried.

"Don't let it trouble you," said Ouvrard. "The hostile mob will be hired, you know. It will not go too far— I hope."

But that was not what had worried Anthony. He had

398

just realized that he had forgotten his promise to Angela to hear her sing Debrülle's song. Now he would be there.

The next two days he dashed about doing last things frantically.

On his final day in Paris at about three o'clock in the afternoon Anthony found himself strolling down the Rue de Rivoli at a more leisurely pace than he had employed for some time past. A thin, bright autumn mist lent to the vistas and distances of the superb city of the West a nostalgic aspect which sorted well with his own mood within. Paris, which is so prone to colourful mists, especially in the autumnal season, seemed to be moving before him now, but at a distance; bright, gay, and absorbed as ever in its own vital interests, yet mysteriously tinged as if with a faint, transcendental purple like the memory of the funereal scarves of the remote past. They had vanished, but they had left behind them in the atmosphere through which the cheerful pageant of the present moved so gracefully and swiftly a trace and a tinge of mystery and sorrow as if the haunting presence of mutability were not altogether, not quite invisible.

He had just finished his last errand. At the House of the Wolf he knew Juan had everything ready for him to depart. That evening when the boy went to bed he would kiss him good night. He would not tell him he was leaving. Of course, there was to be no scene. It would just be "going to bed." And then, afterwards, he would go to the theatre to meet Ouvrard. Angela would sing her last song—the last for him—and they would drive away into Spain. He looked about him. God, how he loved it all, Europe, France, the civilized world into which he had been born, but where it was so hard, impossible almost to find a soul-satisfying part. What was it all about; why was he always hurried on through it at great speed toward an invisible and mysterious

399

goal? Why was it that from the lips of everyone from Brother François to Angela, always under different circumstances, but still as if with the repetition of a ritual, fell the fatal word "go"? What was the meaning of it, what was the sense of it? Out of what general underlying consciousness and necessity in everybody did this command and injunction inevitably arise? No one had ever said "stay," "tarry," except Neleta—and she was not really a European at all. Tonight once again he would "go." Go to Madrid and beyond that?—suddenly the vast and senseless abyss of the ocean rolled before him—he stopped, leaning up against the bars of a shop window—beyond Madrid he would fall through that abyss into the unknown, the new and other world.

"What is it all about?" he wondered. He would be utterly alone again. He stood there stopped, hesitating, even dizzy for an instant, groping for an inner necessity to keep on going. He closed his eyes to shut out the irrational moving world, demanding some answer. He must have stood some minutes apparently looking into the shop window. Nothing came to him but a faint image of the little madonna he had loved so much as a child. He had not seen her thus for a long time. This time he did not impatiently destroy her. Her return in some inexplicable way brought him a dim comfort. He was aware that she represented to him a source of inward strength upon which it was possible to draw. It was as though someone in a parching land, where he had long been wandering, had suddenly given him a sparkling drink of cool water. "So—that did not go, then? No, he could take that along."

"Would monsieur kindly step aside?" said someone. The world flooded back. An elderly gentleman with an elegantly trimmed beard and a gold-topped cane was standing beside him asking to be allowed to look into the shop window.

"Certainly, certainly"—he apologized for his reverie. The old man smiled.

"They are wonderful diamonds," he said. "I don't blame you."

On the 30th of September, 1802, the window of Fossin Frères, the smartest jewellers in Paris, was attracting a good deal of passing attention. There were only three things exhibited there but they were all well-worth remarking. There was an exquisite ebony case lined with black velvet in which reposed a necklace of giant blue diamonds sparkling like cold crystals of pure ice in a winter sun. Beneath them was a small placard inscribed by a master penman with inimitable flourishes:

Much Admired
by the illustrious, the Citizeness,
Josephine Beauharnais Bonaparte,
Consort of the First Consul

———

250,000 francs

The old gentleman whistled, and continued to feast his eyes upon the stones.

They and the case in which they reposed were set upon a kind of extemporized monumental hillock of black velvet drapery the front of which was a large, black stone polished until its surface was a perfectly reflecting mirror. It was placed so as to catch the street scene before the window in full, even to a small and melancholy image of the sun that seemed to flood the mirror from within its remarkably dream-like perspective with the light of another planet.

Miroir des Artistes

said a card at the foot of this melancholy and yet magic glass—and behind it, behind everything in the window, diamonds and all, forming a delightfully romantic background and set in a thin gold frame, was a landscape, which could only have been painted from a scene reflected in the glass. For it was not of this earth, it was a pastoral vista through the horned-gate of dreams.

"They say," said the old gentleman, "that Josephine

401

has been making life uncomfortable for Bonaparte because he will not buy her these diamonds. Her privy purse is as always exhausted and he has refused to advance her the sum. At any rate she has been here to see them three times. I know that, the younger Fossin told me. Well," he shrugged his shoulders, "it *is* a large sum. But they are glorious . . ." He continued to expatiate on them but his voice had become only a drone in Anthony's ears. He had lost himself in the reflection of the street scene before him.

When he first glanced into the black glass purely by chance and just as he was about to turn away, he had had a startling experience.

He felt as though not the scene itself, but the real scene as he saw it bathed in the colour of his own imagination was exposed in the window. Not only was the semblance of things as he saw them reproduced but the mood and philosophy of them, too. There it was with all the unity of reality, and yet set apart in the stone just as the world must be reproduced in every individual, as it was in himself, with both the images and his feelings about them contained in one another.

He watched pondering. It was another moment of wordless understanding like that of the vision of light. The small sun within the stone—for the scene did not at all appear to be on the surface; the illusion of three dimensions and a perfect perspective was even accentuated—illuminated the scene as if it were the very source of light. Far up the avenue a small carriage moved away into the darkness within; another drove rapidly out of it, passed by, and was gone. The faces and gestures of passers-by came and went in a perpetually perfect little pageant; went into the dark past at the back of the mirror, where they dwindled slowly as if into a failing melancholic memory, or came from and vanished suddenly beyond the boundaries of the picture and were gone.

There was something both amusing and irrevocable about this. You could not possibly tell whence they came and whither they went. They existed in the "now" of the mirror—and then no more. He did not connect anything that went on outside the boundaries with the activities in the mirror. It was all mysterious there, unreasonable, a perpetual coming and going apparently without order and cause. It was like his own days in the world; lovely, full of colour and feeling, dark and melancholy in the depths and yet a brilliant dream going on; going on without any cause. His own face remained the only fixture, as long as he was there to watch. Only as long as he remained there could he be in the picture at all.

How it had changed since he had first looked on it that day with Father Xavier on the water front at Livorno, without seeing his own face. Then it had all been outside, very clearly outside, beyond, and so clear and bright. How eager to identify himself with it he had been. How good the orange that the priest had stood sharing with him had tasted—and now— Why, one could be a polytheist in a world like this where everything was its own mysterious reason moving in a general atmosphere of illuminated melancholy. What if the colours *had* become more mysteriously perfect and romantic. They were only illusions. He could not help seeing the block and the scientifically polished stone in which they were all contained.

He must remember, in order to cast off the lost feeling that the picture transmitted, to look up, to recall that beyond its borders was . . .

A young man with a portfolio the same as that carried by M. Talleyrand's diplomatic messengers suddenly emerged from a cabriolet that had driven up to the curb hastily, and dashed into the shop. Anthony turned to go, his reverie for the time completely forgotten. He would never have given the carriage another thought, but just then a hand came into the shop window from behind the curtains and removed the diamonds in their case. Two or three loiterers gathered almost instantly looking at the now useless card. A gendarme was sitting in the carriage. The young man with the portfolio emerged as hastily as he had entered, gave those before the window a keen glance, and drove off.

"To the Tuileries," said a frowzily dressed woman who had been watching. "The price of bread goes up more every day. Certainly, but the Creole must have her diamonds. Two hundred and fifty thousand francs." A murmur of agreement arose. Quite a little crowd had now collected about the empty window. The woman spat on her hands and picking up her heavy basket walked off. Anthony lingered for a little out of curiosity. When he left a good-sized crowd was elbowing up to the window to read the card and to look at the place where the diamonds had been. He wondered if Josephine would wear them that night to the play. Before evening most of Paris was wondering with him —and going to find out that night at the Théâtre Français.

Anthony said "Good night" to his little son in the nursery at numéro 47 and turned away quietly. He had a devastating premonition that it was a final farewell, one which he could not shake off.

At the last minute he had a wild impulse to pick the boy up in his arms and walk out with him.

"Oh," said Anna, who caught a glimpse of his face. "Why, my dear, we hardly thought of you at all! Be sure, though, it is for the best."

She kissed him.

With Anna there to pity him he turned and walked out. She thought he was not quite as grateful as he should be and tucked in the child overcome with tenderness for him.

They had a brilliant supper. Everyone dressed gala for the great opening evening. Ouvrard came for them early. There were to be two parties in the best boxes that evening. Juan climbed onto the carriage as it had been arranged he was to take the place on the trip of Ouvrard's footman. Simba trotted under the body of the great coach engulfed in its shadow. Vincent and Katharina Geiler and her mother had kept them waiting and they arrived at the theatre late. The first act had already begun. There were some indignant murmurs as the lackeys lighted them to their boxes. "Ouvrard!" The whisper ran over the place. Talma, who was in the leading rôle as Ignaz de Molay, was indignant at the distraction and came forward spouting the lines

"Why interrupt my meditations when
I had withdrawn from money-grubbing men . . ."

to the vast delight of the whole audience and Napoleon, who could not have managed it better himself. Not having heard the lines, Ouvrard bowed to the applause which seemed to be directed toward him and the parquet shrieked with laughter. He wiped his forehead and sat down.

Renouard's *Les Templiers* was a melodrama in which the melody had already begun to encroach on the drama. Talma's "Grand Master" was a good, fat, ranting part. Lafond and Mlle. Georges were King and Queen. The latter was especially lyrical and was of course in love with the "Grand Master," while the King as the villain of the piece kept insisting in bass that the Templars must be suppressed. At the end of five thundering acts he was given his own way. Angela parted with her doomed lover in a duet which was encored twice. The curtain fell but the audience still sat waiting for the great event of the evening. Mlle. Georges was to appear as herself in a solo which had been written especially for the occasion.

Anthony had sat watching the curtain go up and down and looking out over the first-night audience. Certainly it was the most brilliant in the world. Coiffures and white shoulders, jewels, uniforms; the endless decorations of the diplomatic corps and the presence of innumerable generals with their staffs male and female blazed in colourful glory under the new patent chandeliers. These alone that evening had seemed to be real. For Anthony the play had passed without illusion. It seemed to be taking place like a meaningless scene in the glass in the shop window that afternoon. At the end, as had been prearranged with Ouvrard, he got up and left the box to be near the doors. The banker soon followed him rather nervous now over his own part in the little drama from real life that was shortly to take place on the steps; anxious above all to be sure of making his get-away. There had only been time to give Vincent a hand-clasp as Anthony left the box where Anna, the Geilers, old Frau Frank, and several guests were sitting. He went out and made sure that Ouvrard's big coach was waiting at the bottom of the steps. Usually the first consul's was the first called, of course. But the superintendent of gendarmes gave him a knowing glance and a wink. He was evidently in charge of the scene. An unusually large crowd of rather ragged persons had already gathered to watch the first consul depart. The usual groups of police stood about the portico and on the steps. Having assured himself that the way for Ouvrard's coach was open, Anthony returned and stood waiting at the back of the theatre.

Napoleon usually left the play before the end of the last act. But tonight he had lingered and kept Josephine. Everybody sat looking at them. It was Mlle. Georges for whom he was keeping Josephine waiting, said the knowing ones. "Now we shall see."

Suddenly Debrülle, looking enormously distinguished in a faultless black suit and with his iron-grey hair waving back, appeared in the orchestra and took charge of it. It was to be his triumph, too. Josephine sat fanning herself languidly. Debrülle raised his arms. Napoleon and the entire audience with him leaned forward. The soft prelude to the song began and the curtain rose.

Angela was standing dressed just as he had seen her a hundred times at Saint-Germain. But around her neck and flashing down over her breast rippled the diamonds

Anthony had been looking at in the window only a few hours before. He knew them instantly by the peculiar spread and the set of the necklace. But he would have known them anyhow. He looked at Josephine. She was just resuming again with her fan which had paused slightly.

The harp rippled and somewhere in the run of notes Angela's began.

With the door into the street already open behind him, Anthony stood at the opposite end of the theatre looking down a little at the stage. And as she raised her head to begin singing she looked directly up at him and he knew she had seen him. He stood waiting with his hat in his hand. As she had promised she sang her song bravely, overwhelmingly. She swept the whole theatre along with her into a mood of impossibly delightful sorrow for something unknown but lost, a mellow and golden yearning, a veritable swan-song.

Oh, there's never a dove in last year's nest,
Or a swan that comes back to me.
And my swallow that flew to the darkling west
Was lured by a magic sea.

Yet creatures of wing that fly and sing
Must fly if they would go free,
So my heart will follow the questing swallow—
Though he fall in the sunset sea.

That was all. It was over.

He raised his hand, holding up his hat to her as the applause broke out; jammed it on his head, and walked down the steps.

A wave of anger and hot resentment swept over him. Why couldn't she have come and lived with him? They were still clamouring about her song in there. Her triumph—and Debrülle's—suddenly seemed to him worthless; silly, sentimental. They all, Angela and the hundreds who were applauding her so madly, wanted emotion without being bothered by connecting it to anything in life. Great emotion and no cause for it! He had been sold-out, he felt. Even the boy had been snatched from him. He hated Anna, too. Nothing was left for him now but to begin life over again. There was that vast ornate coach he had had built for Ouvrard in London waiting for him at the bottom of the steps.

Well, he would go down and get into it. It was as convenient as any other vehicle in which to be carried away from all this.

He stood on the steps and lighted a cigar. The good, strong tobacco steadied him and he did not hate everything about him so intensely any more. He only calmly loathed it. He decided *not* to hit the gendarme who was standing near, after all.

Ouvrard, however, could take care of himself. He was in no mood to be baited by Bonaparte along with Ouvrard. There was no use in getting himself shot tonight—for a few diamonds. Anna had the boy——

He got into the coach and found Simba on the seat. "I closed him in," said Juan. "Underneath he growled at the crowd."

"Good old boy," said Anthony. The hound rumbled and the hair along his neck bristled. The audience was beginning to come out now. Ouvrard appeared on the steps.

A roar broke out from the crowd watching from the far side of the street.

"Bread! We starve. To hell with profiteers."

The police scarcely appeared to be able to restrain them from rushing up the steps. Ouvrard stopped and hesitated.

"Down with the bankers," screamed a shrill-voiced group of women.

"Bread, bread. We want loaves," chanted a deep undercurrent of male voices.

Napoleon and Josephine appeared. Pandemonium broke loose, in which cheers for the first consul, threats against Ouvrard, and demands for bread struggled to predominate. In the coach Anthony sat restraining the growling hound with difficulty.

408

By this time those who had emerged from the theatre, realizing that the anger of the mob was concentrated against Ouvrard, whose name was constantly being uttered menacingly, had withdrawn from him and surged back under the porticoes. He now stood half-way down the steps and alone. He had not meant to become thus entirely isolated. Things had just worked out that way.

Napoleon folded his arms and looked down at him frowning from the upper step.

A tremendous roar of approval went up from the street.

"Vive Bonaparte, à bas les banquiers."

The fashionably dressed crowd from the theatre stood silent and awed. They had not expected to emerge into a street full of the terror. They shivered. Here was the terrible people loose again. Only the little man on the upper step could save them. They waited. Napoleon raised his hand. The street grew quiet.

A group of women fishmongers waving petitions was permitted to come up and present them. Josephine clung palely to his arm.

"What! Bread is now ten sous!" he exclaimed indignantly.

"And no bread," screamed one of the women. "We starve in a year of plenty."

"Horrible," said the first consul. "The speculators have conspired against us. It is true what you say, my friends," he cried, tapping the petition which he had not read. "I shall see to it."

One of the women who had not long before sat knitting by the guillotine could not neglect her opportunity even if she had been hired.

"It is you fellows in epaulettes and the bankers who grow fat now while the people grind their teeth on nothing, citizen," she stormed, putting her hands on her hips. Unfortunately she was of an enormous bulk herself.

Napoleon grinned craftily. He was still quite thin.

"Which of us is the fatter?" he asked slyly.

They loved him for it.

He took her paper and went half-way down the steps toward Ouvrard reading it. Then he stopped.

"Citizens," he cried. "I have heard your complaints. They are just ones. I thank you. You have but to cry and I hear. Tomorrow the bakeshops will all be open. There will be bread. The price of the loaf is fixed at two sous. I make it so. I will punish those who interfere, those who speculate with the peace of our domestic lives."

He turned and stretched forth a hand to Josephine who came down the steps regally to stand beside him.

A stupendous roar of approval and enthusiasm leapt toward the stars. Again he raised his hand. Even to him it had become real now.

"And I shall begin to punish now," he cried. He turned to Ouvrard. "It is you and your confrères, monsieur le banquier, who have caused this silly dearth in Paris. Did I not warn you?"—Ouvrard bowed his head —"but you would not listen to me. I banish you to Spain. There is a famine there. Do not return until I send for you. It is just. Go"—and he pointed to the coach waiting.

In the midst of silence Ouvrard descended like a broken man and climbed in. Then the mad crowd, delirious with enthusiasm and approval, broke loose again.

They had started instantly but they could scarcely get through. The gendarmes were not pretending now. They were having a genuinely difficult time of it. Simba began to bay. At this unexpected note of fierce defiance from within the carriage a rain of filth began to descend upon it. Anything would do. As it turned a corner and broke away down an empty street a stone smashed through the rear window and struck Ouvrard on the head. He groaned, and wept from mortification. Small gilded pieces from a shattered horn of plenty in one corner descended upon his hair. They raced for the barriers while Anthony held onto Simba.

Behind them the silver trumpets of the first consul's

escort let loose. He was leaving the theatre now. "Vive Napoléon! Vive le Consul Premier!"—and on that night, for the first time, here and there arose a voice calling "Vive l'Empereur!" Napoleon smiled.

In her dressing-room Angela put the diamonds back into the case and bent over them. Her tears fell onto the black velvet where they sparkled like small, loose stones. She wished now she had not given him up. Josephine had not cared, after all. What a triumph!

Rolling southward that evening beyond the barriers, Anthony looked at Ouvrard stanching the cut in his head with a handkerchief dipped in cologne. Simba was quiet now.

He lay back and looked up at the figure of Fortune and her wheel in the ceiling. It was very dim in the reflected moonlight. Only the mirrors in the luxurious coach flashed as it rolled cumbersomely toward the Pyrenees. Some of the spokes seemed to have fallen out of Fortune's wheel.

"Jésus!" said Ouvrard, and shifted the handkerchief.

Chapter Fifteen

Shoes and Stockings

THE management of the Fonda of San Esteban at Bayonne devoted itself not only to the entertainment of travellers about to enter Spain but also to alarming them thoroughly over what they were going to encounter there. One would have thought that its suave, garlic-fed proprietor, Jean Pellicier, received a government subsidy from Paris for persuading his guests not to leave France. If he did not actually turn them back by his tales of robbery and bitter hardship to be encountered beyond the Pyrenees, he at least succeeded in detaining a great many, particularly the well-heeled ones, for several days longer than they might otherwise have lingered.

Much to Anthony's annoyance Pellicier was thus able by his undoubted gift for lurid narrative to delay the departure of M. Ouvrard and his little party from day to day. The great banker was in no mood to encounter further afflictions just then, particularly physical ones.

His chagrin over the last scenes at Paris, the stone which had bounded off his skull, the sounds and sights of popular contempt and hatred which had so signally marked his departure had completely unnerved him.

Loud indignation—even assumed indignation—had been a totally new experience to a man who had always been used to quiet triumph or at worst to private disgrace. It had seemed easy enough to agree to assume the rôle of scapegoat. Ouvrard had by no means anticipated the emotional effect which had followed: he now felt and acted as though he were really guilty, as if he had actually had the sins of others laid upon him.

As he lay back in the coach on his way down from Paris, with his bandaged head still throbbing from the bump on it, the vision of Napoleon descending the steps of the theatre so menacingly appeared between the flashes of light that troubled his eyes when the coach jolted into a rut. The clear denunciations of the first consul rang more and more accusingly in his ears. Then he would hear the answering roar of the mob, and with a perceptible nervous jerk he would re-experience in imagination the smashing impact of the stone.

There could be no doubt that the man was suffering. One glance at his face was sufficient to attest it. Anthony remembered how old Uncle Otto's ego had wilted after his encounter with Napoleon and he suspected that something similar but on a more important scale had happened to Ouvrard. In that surmise he was only partly right. The explanation lay deeper, for the events at Paris had jarred a deeply hidden but delicately poised balance in the banker's nervous system.

There were in his life certain primary emotional experiences which it was essential for him to conceal from others in order not to have to admit them to himself. While he had never been threatened with public scandal (he had even been meticulously discreet in obtaining his somewhat curious necessities), the finer and more sensitive side of his nature was greatly troubled over his vagaries and had often impelled him to imagine what it would be like to be exposed to contempt.

In reality Ouvrard's secrets were not so shameful. Had they been known he would have been laughed at and pitied rather than despised. But he had long ago convinced himself that he differed deeply from his fellow men; that his sins as well as his successes were great. His desire for financial power was therefore to justify himself in the eyes of others. Even his sometimes overwhelming generosity was a kind of blackmail paid to fate to induce her to remain discreet and kind; or to thank her for having always remained so. In his attempting to act the scapegoat for Napoleon at Paris a curious thing had happened; the prearranged farce had suddenly become an unexpected tragedy.

For the first time in his life Ouvrard had been exposed to popular contempt and he had wilted under it. That night on the steps of the theatre his feeling of guilt, which he had so long concealed even from himself with an almost complete hypocrisy, had suddenly triumphantly asserted itself. It substituted what he knew he actually had done for the imaginary transgressions against which the mob had roared. The effect was instantaneous and automatic. Reason was no aid against this mental self-conviction. It had seemed right to him that he should be pelted with stones. He had even enjoyed the confusion as a kind of penance; as a substitute for what might have been worse. He had driven out of Paris like a sensitive and quivering criminal, a temporarily broken man.

Like so many others of his type, Ouvrard had never given a thought to the nervous results of his own morals. To find himself suddenly altered by a subtlety within him astonished him. He was afraid. All his overpowering optimism and genial self-confidence had suddenly vanished.

The trip through the sombre regions of the landes from Bordeaux, with the autumnal fogs from the ocean drifting through the drooping pines, with the contorted

414

branches of cork trees mirrored in dismal, leaden ponds, had only served to accentuate a mysterious melancholy which he could not shake off. As they neared the frontier towards the end of a depressing October afternoon, the unearthly blue of the Pyrenees fading into vague, titanic outlines against a pale sky— at sight of which Juan had burst into joyful shouts —contrived to depress him even further. He thought of the unknown difficulties and dangers in the mysterious and "hostile" regions beyond them.

Only the firm, huddled mass of the roofs of Bayonne with its squat, canary-coloured church tower served to reassure him.

For to Ouvrard all the landscape of the misty country about him seemed to partake of his own inexplicable morbidity; to be haunted by vague but unpleasant and threatening titans. He sensed them moving secretly along the almost invisible wraiths of the ever more mystical mountains marching down into Spain.

But upon Anthony, who had already for some time given over the hopeless task of trying to cheer up his unexpectedly gloomy companion, the effect of approaching the Spanish marches was quite the opposite.

He already knew enough of Spain and Spaniards to hope that in the country beyond the Pyrenees he might be able to find certain mystical aspects of existence still conserved in space as they had once, in days past, been present in time. At least the monuments and evidences of such beliefs would still be visible, he thought, not only in buildings and fashions but in customs and speech and attitudes; perhaps in the minds and spirits of the people themselves.

Everyone who had been to Spain assured him that Spain was "behind the times." It was for that reason more than any other that he desired to go there.

"Few moderns," he thought, "can resist the exquisite compliment they pay themselves in patronizing the past. It permits them to assume that they themselves are superior and yet sensitive enough to feel and understand the merits of their own age above all others;

it permits them to assume tacitly that as time passes men grow better; that they increasingly triumph as the heirs of the ages as if nothing were ever lost in the process of inheriting."

And everybody in France and England had seemed so sure that the days they were living in were ineffably superior; that it was a great age, reasonable, liberal, cultivated, humanitarian, comfortable. "Yet it is curious," he thought, as he sat looking out of the coach window at the country about Bayonne, "that no one seems to miss something that I expected to find in Europe, but which is no longer there.

"No, it has curiously vanished, only a few vestiges of it remain. But I have heard that in Spain much modern detail and many small comforts have been sacrificed and even suppressed to retain eternal relations in time. I have heard that people still live there as though their own days were contained in a great brooding stillness.

"And perhaps, too, I myself have not learned yet to get the most out of travelling about the world and living in the present, living in the now only, as I tried once to explain it to Vincent. It may be that now is only complete when it is time felt in something that is not time.

"I can feel now-in-eternity in wild countries and on the ocean, for eternity remains in the landscape and the sea. That was the best of Africa. In America I may find it again. I do not find it these days among men in France and England. Yet I was born into it. It was in my courtyard at the convent. For a while as a child I awoke and I lived in an eternal now. I am looking for what I have lost.

"Now it is said that Spain is like a monastery where the lost faculty of living in an eternal present has been miraculously preserved. Well, we shall see!"

He looked at Ouvrard asleep against the cushions. His face was twitching. How could he possibly have told Ouvrard what he had been thinking? Ouvrard was going to bring about great changes in Spain. He was the advance emissary of Napoleon. Anthony looked away, and out across the Basque country and the darkening western ocean toward the mountains again. The Pyrenees, he knew, cut Spain off from the rest of Europe as a tremendous physical barrier, a wall against change, a grim, difficult reality. But at the distance of a few leagues they did not look to be merely mountains. They seemed to be vast curtains hanging down out of heaven as if they would preserve inviolate the secret of what lay behind them.

Ouvrard had looked upon them with foreboding in his present state of mind. But to Anthony, as the great coach rolled on through the greying twilight of the Basque country toward Bayonne, the thought of the strange far-country stretching before him made his heart leap up with the anticipation of penetrating beyond. Surely the land that lay there in the midst of smouldering amethyst could not be in the same world from which rose the squat, uncompromising church tower of Bayonne only a few level miles away.

And suddenly he recaptured the feeling of adventure, the hope that lay in the lure of the unknown. Even the necessity of helping Ouvrard out of the coach before the matter-of-fact hotel in the town and of seeing him safely to bed, for by now the banker had come to the conclusion that he really was a sick man, could not destroy it.

That night he and Juan went out after supper and loitered along the quays where fisher boats with dim lanterns burning under their half-decked cabins cast shadows into the mist drifting in over the landes from the Bay of Biscay as if here were a whole fleet of which Charon was the admiral.

"Yes, they are waiting to ferry souls into the west," laughed Anthony to himself, and told Juan the legend. Juan looked rather serious about it. The husky tones of Basques speaking their mysterious language occasionally rose with an astonishing effect out of these dark hulls. Spars, ghostly, half-furled sails and spidery rigging, the earthless smell of loot from the great waters

417

seemed to call to both of them to step aboard, hoist sail, and be gone.

"There must be a country somewhere where the woman who loved you did not always go away, where sons were not always torn from their fathers' arms. Was there? Was there no place on earth where even a glimmer of eternity penetrated the present?"

He returned to the inn, pondering.

Charon's fleet proved to be by far the best of Bayonne. In a week Anthony and Juan were both tired to death of this limbo between two worlds where French and Spanish were spoken indifferently as if they were one language. They were bored by the flat narrow streets and uncompromising canary-colored cathedral; by fish, rags, and stinks. All the life and colour of the place seemed to be concentrated about the Spanish diligences which they were forced to watch depart for Madrid daily while Ouvrard sulked and hesitated.

The banker's condition, Anthony was already aware, might change the whole tenor of the trip to Spain. He had become curiously timid and helpless. Even the smallest decisions were now too difficult for him to make. All the details of arrangements were left to Anthony and Juan. Anthony had expected to take a certain amount of responsibility during the trip, but he had not expected to have to make up the banker's mind for him. If things went on like this he would not only be "interpreting" but actually initiating and conducting the negotiations at Madrid.

To persuade Ouvrard to leave he had the drivers of the diligences brought up to reassure the banker. He gave out his presence under an assumed name to avoid rumours of tempting pickings going on before. He began with great care, and after careful inquiry, to hire an escort at Irún just over the frontier.

But despite the constant assurances of the jaunty mayorals who drove the diligences that the camino real between Irún and Madrid was the best and safest of roads, Ouvrard was not to be easily moved. In their leather gaiters, brown embroidered jackets, and peaked hats covered with velvet pompons he saw only the garb of such prosperous bandits as he had been warned he might expect to find. The suggestion that he should leave his comfortable, cherished coach at Bayonne and confide himself to their care in a diligence appeared little short of mad to him. He was taking a considerable sum along with him, and the first works in the noble tongue of Don Quixote that he learned to mispronounce lay embedded in the proverb, which his host assured him all travelers to Spain should get by heart, "La ocasión hace el ladrón."

So while Simba strained at his chain and barked at the departing diligences in the courtyard, Ouvrard sat in the common room listening to rumours and buying warm, woollen sashes to wrap about his middle, green phials of insecticide, sheets, soft pillows, blunderbusses for the guards, biscuits, mattresses and stew pots. In short, he strove to buy security for everything in a country where he was assured nothing was to be had, not even security.

He pored over a guide-book written by Pellicier which the innkeeper sold to his guests for ten francs. Page eleven daunted him:

"I would like to have something. I am tired."
"Have a chair," replies the Spanish innkeeper.
"Good, but it is nourishment I want."
"Well, what have you brought?"
"Nothing."
"What—nothing! Why, how can I cook it then? You are in Spain. The butcher's is there; the banker's yonder. Go and buy what you can. If there is any coal perhaps my wife will feel like cooking."

"Think of it," cried Ouvrard. "And we go *there!*" He purchased the carcass of a sheep, sausages, and some pickled fish of which he was very fond. There

419

was no room for a cask of wine. "But chocolate," he said, "makes me bilious." He groaned. Already his room looked like a ship chandler's store.

Seeing how things were, Anthony at last resorted to stratagem and suggested that Napoleon might change his mind and send for Ouvrard to return to Paris.

The next morning early they were on the way to Madrid.

They crossed the Bidassoa with the Spanish guards sleeping on the grass at the far side of the bridge. One of them rose and grunted over their passports until money changed hands. And then in the streets of Irún, lined with oriental-looking houses and overhanging balconies, they were suddenly plunged at one stride into Spain.

Here they left the horses behind them. Ten mules were harnessed to the coach. They were shaven. They were thin. They looked indecent. Every detail of their skeletons, their muscles, and their veins like the model of a river system stood out. It was as if ten rats with pointed ears and hairless tails had been furnished forth by an evil and sardonic magician. And each one of these mules was vicious in his own little way. Only the Spanish could understand them.

The escort was also picked up here. It consisted of six miqueletes, or guards, mounted on mules and armed with muskets. A professional mayoral drove the coach. A zagal, or footman, sat by him who was to do nothing but put on the brakes. Two grim ruffians known as trabucos armed with brass-mouthed blunderbusses sat on the top and smoked cheroots. All of these gentry wore rope sandals; sported breeches trimmed with buttons of filigreed coins. They shone in chestnut jackets with broad blue cuffs, scarlet sashes; choked in flamboyant cravats that thrust their heads up into peaked hats waving with ribbons and silk tassels. Only the knights of the road could afford such finery. They were a proud and distinct class.

"Vaya usted con Dios," shouted postmaster Ramón, from his little coach office at the Posada de las Diligencias near the gate at Irún, as, with all luggage strapped on outside and piled knee-deep within, the coach prepared to·start. A small crowd had gathered attracted particularly by the carcass of the large sheep which hung down over the rear of the vehicle staring backward with glassy eyes through links of sausages.

Ramón along with others was somewhat amused by the nervousness and solicitude of Ouvrard, who, now about to take the final plunge into the unknown, kept looking out of the window at the preparations, fidgeting, and rolling his eyes homeward over the landscape toward Bayonne as if he were leaving the earth instead of his own country. He could see the horses being led back over the bridge into France. "Where they belong," said the mayoral, walking along his teams of rearing, biting mules. "Mon Dieu!" whispered the banker huskily. To him the whole scene looked like the preparations for a journey to the moon. It was in truth grotesque enough.

The great London coach glistening in the bright, dry sunshine appeared to have been captured by a crew of bronzed bandits that had swarmed upon it out of the caverns of a bad romantic dream. It seemed to Ouvrard that he was the victim being abducted in some picaresque incident enacted out of the *Arabian Nights*. He sat back trying to live through the nightmare. To Anthony the spirit of adventure had suddenly embodied itself costumed and with an appropriate background. He sat puffing a cigar, the bouquet of which set the beggars to whining. He refused to have his enjoyment curtailed by Ouvrard. Juan, seated on the top of the coach, was touching his guitar and premeditating a song for home-coming. It was all familiar to him. To the escort and guards the occasion was nothing but itself—the usual, and after all, the best way of getting from Irún to Madrid.

And it soon proved to be the most rapid, too. Contrary to all foreign opinions, travelling in Spain, so long as one did not leave the great royal highways that had been constructed during the reign of Charles III,

421

was swifter and smoother than in any other country of Europe. There was not in all France a road that could compare with the camino real that led from Irún to the capital.

They were off—violently.

The ten liver-coloured devils hitched to the coach rushed up and down the alarming descents and inclines that mark the steep rolling country between Irún and Orayzún as if they were so many incarnations of the speed demon. The narrow road could be traced for miles ahead running like a taut, stretched tape until it lost itself among blue mountains. It zigzagged the hillsides and leapt deep, dry torrents upon bridges that seemed to be pierced rather than supported by slim, pointed arches. Always situated at the bottom of slopes these bridges were negotiated at a frantic gallop with brakes-off just as the level stretch of the approach was reached. The thin stone boomed like a drum under the heavy wheels and the cavalcade. Passing the lumbering oxcarts in the narrow highway was accomplished by volleys of whip cracks and miracles of skidding that left Ouvrard puffing. From the roof above, cheroot stumps tossed away by the zagals and mayoral fell fuming and sparking into the body of the coach. They burned holes in the upholstery and rugs of the helpless passengers and added the last diabolic touch. At a brief stop to breathe the mules and tighten the harness Anthony emerged and begged those seated aloft in the name of Spanish gentlemen to desist. A raising of hats and profound apologies followed. There were even bows, but after a few miles the rain of fusees was resumed.

Progress, however, was now slower as the mountains were approached.

They were passing through a country a little reminiscent of Switzerland. The houses were of wood and resembled chalets, but with their beams painted a deep blood-red. In the distance amid patches of green oaks and pines these villages looked like little flocks

422

of brown chickens gathered about the old hen of a church.

At Orayzún the relay was changed. It was like a battle of drunken centaurs. Amid biting and kicking mules, tangle of ropes and harness, squalls and brazen braying, the torsos of men suddenly reared up triumphantly above the dust and confusion as they passed the coach windows dragging the new relay into place by their noses, mounting them and beating back the menace of white teeth and rolling eyes with their heavy felt hats. All was ready when the escort, which had lagged behind, rode into town and the battle began all over again.

Standing oblivious to the clouds of yellow dust that rose about the coach as if it were the prize of conflict, morose figures in immense ragged cloaks and hats pulled down over their eyes watched the proceedings without further comment than a glitter of brown eyes above their muffled mouths and sharp noses. They looked like bedraggled brown hawks, whether caballeros or beggars it was impossible to say. In them were concentrated the poverty and pride, the indifference and the suspicion, the fatalistic spectatorship of the male population of Spain. It was impossible to tell what they were thinking. Perhaps they were not thinking at all. They remained standing, impassive. There was something Arab-like about them. They were the first touch of eternity in time that Anthony had found in Spain, and he continued to see them everywhere as long as he remained in the peninsula.

They were whirled indecently out of Orayzún and at nightfall dined at Astigarraga where even to Ouvrard his own fears of starving became ridiculous.

Beds, curtains, and towels were dazzling white, the inn painfully clean. Great mountain girls, set-up like dragoons and with thick chestnut braids falling to their waists, brought supper: meat soup powdered saffron colour with paprika, loose, white bread with a soft, golden crust. The puchero followed. Brought in separate dishes, it was finally combined into one on the diner's plate. Chicken, mutton, slices of roast beef, bacon and ham, spiced sausages stuffed with chorizo and pimento formed the foundation of this solid edifice which was then topped with a verdura of vegetables, greens, and the ever-present garbanzo or chick-pea—and over this was poured a highly spiced sauce. Juan showed them how to mix it.

They had just laid down their comb-like forks and narrow pointed spoons and prepared to retire when—the other courses appeared. Chicken fried in oil, haddock fried in oil; and then roast lamb, asparagus, and salad. By this time Ouvrard was laughing, for the door still continued to open bringing other girls with other trays. For dessert macaroons and almonds smoking from the roasting pan, then goat's-milk cheese, queso de Burgos, justly celebrated, and at last a little tray with a bowl of glowing coals for lighting cigarettes; finally Malaga, sherry and brandy.

"Juan," cried Ouvrard, "cut up the dead sheep on the coach and give it away."

"I will keep it for Simba," replied Juan. "In Spain it is not thought necessary to feed a dog. A sheep will last him to Madrid." Gorged to repletion, Simba slept on the top of the coach, his nostrils twitching at the cigarro smoke the rest of the way to Burgos.

They were awakened at two o'clock at night to set out again. The country became wilder and hillier, the inns more primitive, the villages "pueblos." In the province of Alava at the foot of the mountains of Salinas amid an uproar beyond description a "procession" of oxen was added to the five teams of mules. With goads, whips, and the help of men on the wheels, men moving up and down the long line of animals that disappeared around curves far ahead of the coach, they accomplished the ascent.

It was now day and cold; the Pyrenees behind them could be seen lying like great piles of draped velvet caught up into sharp ridges as if the gods had abandoned the planet just here and let their rich draperies fall behind them along an endless floor. Before them the silver filigree of snows on the black forehead of the Sierra Nevadas tumbled along a cold emerald sky. Azure and lilac shadows tinted their precipices below the long rolling snow barrier of their continuous crests. They were not like the Alps, tumbled, inchoate, and incomprehensible. These Spanish mountains were remote, regular barriers that seemed to have been raised with a purpose. In the dry clear air, but at a tremendous distance, they seemed to be walling-in a grim country inhabited by giants who might sit upon them, resting in Cyclopean blue-shadowed seats with their thin, white hair in the clouds and their mighty feet set like sphinxes on the red plains below.

At a distance, looking over the plateaus and escarpments, the tangled veins of dusty watercourses, the interior of Spain, treeless and without verdure, looked as if it could nurse such a race.

The moisture-healed slopes of Biscay were now far behind them. They were moving toward the plateaus of León. Something African had already crept into the landscape despite patches of beautiful cultivation, as if the Sahara from over the rim of the world had cast a stony mirage of itself upon these parts and barrenness were creeping north. They had first encountered it at Vittoria which they had entered by torchlight, the crescent horns of the oxen going on before them through the deserted and shadowy streets until the parador viejo was reached. Here there was much trouble with the authorities over baggage, hard mattresses at the posada, and nothing but a bitter jicara de chocolate when they left in the dark just before dawn.

As they pushed forward next day through Miranda the prophetic hints of barrenness they had already encountered began to be fully realized. The path to its full realization was a fitting one, the rocky pass of Pancorbo, which is the entrance to old Castile and León. Here they climbed through long, rocky narrow valleys like gloomy corridors and passed between the two granite monoliths that lean toward each other like an arch left unfinished by a race of giants. It is the gateway to old Spain.

All that was usual and familiar was now left behind over the heights of Pancorbo. Briviesca at the foot of the pass seemed to be a city in another world. Inns and stables were now one and inseparable. The road led on through a succession of evil villages grey as dusty lava. Pradanos, Castil de Peones, Quintana Dueñas, Quintanapalla—these were the towns of a country of bearded old women, withered, moled and wizened; witches who gathered about the fires at night to ladle guisado out of their giant pots to scare foreign travellers; hags who looked as if they might ride off on their thick brooms.

All the women went barefoot here, and for some reason Ouvrard kept complaining about this. He was plaintive about it. While they stirred the stew with long ladles he would complain of their lack of shoes.

Nothing was said in these wretched ventas that were usually placed just outside the walls of towns to avoid paying gate-taxes. They were the worst inns they met on the route. In the red firelight under the beams, muleteers and caballeros, children, and the great greyhounds of the country all alike sat silent awaiting the distribution of bread, salt, and meat.

"This is not like the south, not Seville, señor. See those fellows wrap themselves in their cloaks after supper, pull their hats down closer and take six puffs from a cigar. There is not even a song. The nostrils of the girls are like black caverns with snuff. It is so dry here even their stomachs must be puckered. I would be afraid to sleep under the same cloak with them. I have not even been asked. Shall I get out my guitar?"

"No," said Anthony, "this is no place for music, Juan."

Only once did they hear music. It was far away and late at night, a low, sinister singing accompanied by an eternal rattle as of hard dried peas shaken in a box in three-time. An eternal dry rasping that returned upon itself to a slow stamping of feet.

Tiime here in these huge, dry valleys was like time

426

at Futa-Jaloon. It did not seem to pass. Day and night might shift the colours of the landscape but time seemed to remain the same. The coach went on through it. It hastened but it seemed never to arrive anywhere. As they turned west toward Burgos, by the last hovel in the pueblo of Quintanapalla, Anthony saw a figure that remained with him in memory as the spirit of the place. It was that of a youth leaning against a pumice-coloured wall.

From the waist down his cloak had rotted away. But his straight legs, firm and brown as those of an Arab, braced him solidly against the wall. There, with his arms folded, and the remains of his upper garment thrown across his lean shoulders in magnificent tattered folds, he stood proudly; triumphantly existing; looking down across the sun-baked plains of León with black-diamond eyes. When the time came he would beget a son to take his place by the wall. With inexpressible contempt and immobility he watched the coach go by. Not even a silver onza cast at his feet could wring from his thin, incurious lips the customary "Vaya usted con Dios."

At Burgos once more they lingered.

Godoy must have received notice of their approach through the French embassy at Madrid, for the authorities were positively obsequious and the party found themselves lodged and entertained by the alcalde but with more ceremony than comfort. A letter from the Prince of the Peace was waiting for Ouvrard and was delivered resting on a brocaded pillow. It bade him welcome to Spain with a hundred abject and stately phrases. But the cunning favourite of the queen, who now ruled Spain with all the authority of both his royal mistress and her husband, rather than as a mere prime minister, was careful not to commit himself to anything in advance. He offered to send an armed escort of honour but at the same time he advised the banker to keep his arrival strictly private at Madrid for fear of arousing premature opposition to his schemes.

Pondering this, Ouvrard moved himself incognito to El Parador del Dorado, the best fonda in the city, and gave himself up to the luxury of physical comfort and mental misery, showering gratificacioncitas upon the mozos and muchachas until Juan interfered through sheer disgust.

"All these things, dos almohadas limpias con sus fundas, and such trifles I can obtain for you with a smile, a cigar, or a proverb, señor. Have you never heard the saying 'the generous pay more for a grape than the careful do for a bunch'? They will think you are mad if you go on showering double-duros about."

"I *am* going insane," said the banker. "Send for M. Adverse when you go, for I am afraid to be left alone."

When Anthony came into the room Ouvrard complained to him that ever since Paris he had felt himself "dividing within."

"Do not laugh at me," he begged. "I assure you it is so. I can explain it to you in no other way. I am at the present time not one but two men. That is, I know I could become either one of two persons. I cannot make up my mind yet which I want to be. I might remain, let us say, myself, the man you know, G. J. Ouvrard financier—or I might become, oh, *that fellow who is so interested in shoes!*" His eyes gleamed and he sat up. "Yes, I shall have to do something for him. Ever since Paris he has been becoming me. All these new scenes make it easier for him to be. Mon Dieu, do something for Ouvrard! He is being pulled apart."

So Burgos was a somewhat curious interim for Anthony.

The first "cure" that occurred to him for Ouvrard was wine. With this Ouvrard was inclined to agree. He would not see a priest or a leech nor would he try tobacco. For some days he stupefied himself and lay quiet under the influence of mountain Malaga fortified by brandy. It was necessary for someone to be on watch during his return to consciousness when his misery was extreme. Anthony and Juan took turns. In his leisure intervals Anthony managed to see a good deal of Burgos. It was the first Spanish town he had really had time to examine.

And he could have done no better. Here he found at least the relics and legends of what he had been looking for. Burgos the palladium of Spain, the home and tomb of the Cid, Burgos the shrine of Mary. He remembered it forever—the domineering castle and the mighty cathedral rising on the hill out of the clustering roofs of a rough half-circle of houses, the montañas behind him, the old walls and the green plantations along the sparkling river of Arlanzón at its feet.

While the great banker lay deep in the fumes of wine trying to decide in a troubled sleep who he might be, Anthony found who he himself had been or might have been in ages past. He explored this precious enclave in time where the living age of Europe was still preserved, and still to some extent dreamed alive and even walked in its streets. He explored it from the plaza with its naïve bronze fountain of Flora to the Gate of Santa María, where the image of the Virgin rose above the battlements along the river front, reminding all who entered that this was her town.

Indeed, in every conceivable place in Burgos, and in every attitude and episode of her story and legend, the goddess Mary was to be found. Here she was still a living reality. He thought of her and dreamed of her again as he walked the pleasantly planted little paths in the river valley toward the Isla and the nunnery of Santa María la Real, where Ferdinand and Isabella have left the story of the Conception carved over the gate.

In one of the cloisters open to strangers near the hospital for pilgrims he sat for hours surrounded by silence and the round-headed arches, and found before he left he could pray again.

He asked for help and guidance in bringing up his son. He sat hoping in a wordless petition for the return of his child. At least he recovered peace again.

As he threaded his way back to the fonda through the narrow streets, which the small river El Pico cleans and freshens by being led dashing along them in a stone watercourse, the swirling waters bore away with them the tumult of feeling and perplexity that had come with him from Paris. He was aware of the feeling of being at one with himself once more. Out of a renewed integrity of being he felt able to act. He was sure this was not due to any subtle change in his body; on the contrary, this feeling of health that brought with it a capability for happiness in all the incidents of life seemed to proceed from a conviction of wellness and peace within. It was an outgoing instead of an income.

"Yet how strange and unexpected are the accidents of life. How they vary between man and man," he thought. "While I find peace, Ouvrard lies there at war with himself, fighting for his very entity for some dim cause unknown. Perhaps I can help him now. How, I do not know"—and he returned to the fonda to find Ouvrard awake, anxious to talk with him. For hour after hour the man with a twitching face poured forth to him in a brilliant exposition his entire plan for the shipping of immense quantities of wheat to Spain with all its political and financial ramifications. He was high-strung, brilliant as though lit by a consuming fire from within, entirely the banker again.

"If I can only stay this way," he sighed. "What was the matter with me?"

"Do not remember," said Anthony and hastily expressed his admiration for Ouvrard's brilliant scheme, which had about it the elements of inspiration in its daring and originality. "And it was so lucidly and compactly explained," he insisted. He was being quite ingenuous, too. For it had startled him to come in and find a man whom he had left only a few hours before in a confused stupor, suddenly speaking with the clear accents of genius. His genuine astonishment and admiration showed in his face.

It was amazing how Ouvrard responded to that.

"So, then, you do find me myself again," he whispered. "Yes, I can see that you do. You do not know how much that means to me." A look of childish gratitude suffused his features.

"You will not leave me?" he said. "I am this way sometimes. Twice before! You will stay even if I become that other fellow for a while? Will you? There is no one to care, you see. No one!" He looked pathetically pale and anxious again.

"I will stay," Anthony promised. "I will see you through this time, my friend. And you are going to be well soon. I know it. You must rest and forget everything."

"Mon Dieu, I can go to sleep then," whispered Ouvrard, and sank back with the look of fear and perplexity fading from his face.

Nothing could have been more curious than those days spent at Burgos. There were other talks with the banker, who was slowly coming back to himself.

Thus between excursions into the town, replete with a thousand emotional and intellectual adventures, sounded the voice of Ouvrard discussing with nervous avidity the great deal in wheat; the means of obtaining influence in Madrid; shaping as he lay back in his alcove with a bloated, nervous countenance pale against the pillows the scheme that for the next five years dictated the economic and political history of Spain—while occasionally, only occasionally now, and far less frequently than at first, he would have to babble something about shoes.

"Keep the barefoot girls out of the room, Juan," said Anthony, "or we shall be here the rest of our lives" —and then he would go out to walk up to the Calle Alta along the wall of the castle, where in the old parish of St. Martin were ancient houses that fascinated him; La Casa del Cordón of the Velascos, where the Constable of León had lived, with the rope carved over the door, and the Casa de Mirando with a patio snatched out of a poet's dream. Or he would loiter through the Plaza Mayor with its new shops ranging

431

under noble arcades, where proud, penniless loafers in threadbare capas lingered wistfully and the children sold bright yellow flowers and incense.

Everywhere, in walls and at corners, on houses and in little churches, were the shrines of Mary, usually with a woman standing before them praying. The town breathed of this female worship. Apparently it existed because of it. And all these little shrines were only reminders and approaches to the great one, the cathedral in the centre of the town.

Its twin towers crowned with delicate spires of open stonework seemed to be fluttering with lace. Its clustering, filigreed pinnacles rose triumphantly and lavishly above the sombre roofs of the quiet city like a burst of rich music out of silence, suggesting the wealth and enduring sensitivity, the miraculous passion of the spirit aspiring to write its eternal thought of beauty above the flat and drear arrangements of physical life. There were three portals, and above the middle one with her motto worked into its magic balustrade, veritable memories of the Virgin's Conception, Assumption, and Coronation dreamed alive in the pliant stone.

Then he would pass through the portal into the interior.

What manner of men were those who had wrought this? Out of what rich daily experiences shot through with wisdom and vivid emotion had this flamboyant and yet austere testimony to the communion of the soul of man with the Eternal overflowed? What was the secret of the life-giving quality of that story that had inspired and contained it? Why was it being forgotten? Had the spirit of man tired in its attempt to commune with God?

Here in this cathedral at Burgos was the record of an incredible spiritual energy. Something not at all preoccupied with building things of use to enhance the ease of physical existence. It was beyond that. It was the expression of the attitudes and experiences of pure being that had builded here. How could the age out of which this had risen be called "poverty-stricken"? Those who had built and carved and painted here had been more than happy. They had left the record of their ecstasy in a divine orgasm of stone.

The very skeleton of the place leaped and vaulted upward. The lines of it suggested an energy terrible because illimitable in its proportions; a force greater than the body of any plant or animal could express. The most majestic avenues of palms with their interlacing fronds in the sunny sky overhead were only natural in their stresses and strains compared with these cathedral vaults and groined arches and buttresses that had caught the underlying mathematics of boundless space and expressed the terrible abstraction of The Thinker whose thought is the universe. That was the necessary element of terror and mystery in which the shrines of Mary and the altars of her Son, in which the stations of the cross were all contained. "That is why," he thought, "it is not comfortable to live in a Gothic building. The curves of it frighten one, they express the *super* natural; thought which transcends the necessities of matter and the world of the senses." No, those who had built here had not gone to nature for their forms as had the builders of pagan temples who made stone groves. When these men wrought, the spirit of man had already gone beyond that. Burgos had congealed out of abstract thought that was still the wholesome servant of emotion.

It had been necessary to cover the unbearable implications of its soaring arches with a wealth of natural forms; to fill its interior, floors, walls, and ceiling with a wealth of works of art that imitated the prodigality of nature. To dwell upon the labour expended, the patience, the excess of energy lavished upon them caused thought to stagger and lie down.

In its illimitable profusion Burgos was like the natural world itself. Even the dead gods were here. In a half abandoned favissa or storeroom, once the old sacristy, lay the damaged images and the abandoned figures of saints used in processions, with the time-darkened portraits of a hundred bishops of Burgos glaring at them from the walls.

Anthony was in a mood for all this. After his loss of Angela and the boy he lost himself eagerly in the emotions and thoughts of art and architecture, in experiences which were safe from any intrusion by man. Burgos for him was like healing music.

Especially, he loved to linger along the choir stalls in which the ancient wood with its yellow high-lights and mellow shadows seemed to be less a medium for handicraft than the dreamful substance of thought itself that the carver had suddenly arrested in motion. And what dreams were there, fantastic, prodigal in invention and as ruthless in imagination as those of God; another world swarming with foliage whose delicate tendrils sprouted into hands or legs. Here amid the fretted and contorted branches of a fabulous, submarine forest dolphins spouted wide-flaring sea-fans from dilate nostrils, sirens rode upon undulating dragons, while overhead claw-winged chimeras like the souls of misers emigrating to paradise flew above charming little islets situated upon the confines of sleep and sanity where cupids tried on capricious masks, gladiators wrestled, bears played upon harps while peasants harvested the fruits of elysian champaigns, wanton girls teased a monster to the point of ecstasy, and little boys squirted into shell-carved fountains with infantile, Rabelaisian glee. And yet—step back but a few paces—and all this became grave, solemn, part of the architectural unity of the whole building, a fitting frame for the pallid, austere faces of the canons themselves.

There was a stairway here, one mass of twisting monsters that ascended like a flame to a mysterious door that any man might be afraid to enter. And there was also the retable above the high altar adorned with cascades of silver and crystal suns, where from the fruitful breast of a recumbent Abraham spouted and soared upward the genealogical tree of Jesus Christ. Above it the Virgin sat throned in the clouds lit by

434

a glory as of far-off morning, while through the marble leaves and blossoms below her glinted the gold and silver of the moon and stars.

Down the enormous nave of the cathedral this inconceivable tree seemed to bear the fruit of glory at its radiant top and to shout Hosannah! It was impossible to turn one's back upon it. Even the long figures of the dead with stony hounds and bat-winged griffins at their feet, sleeping behind gratings and withdrawn amid the gloomy side chapels, seemed to hear it.

Afterward—after he had left Burgos—and only the dreamful symbols of it remained, it seemed impossible to Anthony that he had spent only a few days there. Concentrated into that experience were the merged messages of innumerable lifetimes hurled at him in the sublimated language of art. Chiefly he bore away with him an enormously enriched and nobler realization of the meaning of his dreams of the Madonna. He had added nothing to his personal philosophy about her. But in looking upon her life-endowing dream as it had also existed in the hearts of others and was depicted at Burgos on every side he had extended and clarified her emotional meaning in his own soul. In her, he felt, was the image of the way in which the Eternal Spirit was conceived by man.

On a door-post that was for the most part passed by unnoticed was a small image of her, exquisite but daring in its conception. She was not meek and contrite. She stood there with her head thrown back, breathing in with an expression in which sensuous pleasure had been transmuted into spiritual ecstasy an invisible influence from the flame-wrapped symbol of love. It was humanity in the transports of conceiving God.

And Anthony turned away from this, to remember it forever, but thinking at the time how he had wasted and debased himself and sought life only in the body —and found it denied to him. "Next time . . ." but perhaps this realization had come to him too late.

The premonition troubled him—and there were other things . . .

He was afraid, as Ouvrard continued to recover rather slowly, that a plethora of seeing and sights at Burgos might stifle his appreciation. There was, he was aware, a ridiculous side to it, as there always is to everything. He had only, for instance, to permit himself to be shown the renowned figure of Christ made of a stuffed human hide, painted, and crowned with real brambles to have taken once more to reading and snickering with Voltaire. But he did not wish to take the one step from the sublime. It was too easy. The threshold of the ridiculous is always a slippery one. He preferred to conserve what he had experienced in order to ponder upon it afterward like the memory of divine music uninterrupted by a fatuous and comical noise.

Yet he might have failed. High moods are not long in passing. But he was saved from loss of untarnished treasure by being plunged from the divine, not into the entirely ridiculous, merely into the human. For it was while he was standing one afternoon before the retable that on the other side of the high altar he discovered and overheard talking in common-sense English the Honourable William Eden and the honest and always whimsical Mr. Richard Ford.

His attention was first attracted to them by the sound of a prolonged chuckling wheeze. That he afterwards discovered was Mr. Ford's version of laughter.

———————

"So," said the cultivated voice of the Honourable Mr. Eden, "you still solemnly maintain that trout fishing is a more dangerous sport than bullfighting."

"Not solemnly," replied Mr. Ford, "there is nothing funnier than being right."

It was at this point that Anthony had overheard the wheeze.

"But, my dear Dick," rejoined his companion, interrupting his survey of the genealogy of Christ through a pair of German-silver pince-nez—which he folded up and put back in his pocket authoritatively, "I do not see upon what grounds you can possibly make such a silly assertion."

"As usual, you are looking at the matter from your own standpoint only," insisted the other; "suppose you consider it just for a moment from the standpoint of the trouts."

"Ow-ah," said William, making the English noise for surprise, "but first count your fish, count your fish before you catch them," he added hurriedly and looked at Mr. Ford in triumph as if he had found exactly the right proverb to quote him off the map.

"Egg, Billy, eggs! You are thinking of eggs. I say!" wheezed the amiable Mr. Ford.

Mr. Eden turned very red in the face.

"By God, so I was," he muttered. "So I was."

They joined each other in a hearty laugh. It was quite evident, however, as they walked away that Mr. Eden was rallying for another attack. He was making noises in his throat and merely trying to readjust his fish and eggs.

It was impossible for Anthony to restrain himself. So far as he was concerned the cathedral had vanished. He wished above all things to learn the outcome of this argument. "Why, after all—why *was* trout fishing more dangerous than bullfighting?" In hurrying to overtake the pair disappearing through the door ahead he nearly trod on the toes of an old canon who looked up with the expression of a Torquemada as he brushed past.

But he had missed most of the reply of Mr. Eden when he drew near them at last. He could just hear him saying a little indignantly:

"I am perfectly willing to take the standpoint of either the trout *or* the bull in the matter, but I still can't see how that alters the argument. Men, and for that matter horses—*men*, I say, are frequently killed in the bullfight. Did you ever hear of anyone's ever being pulled in and devoured by a trout?"

"Such fishes, when hooked, invariably escape," countered Mr. Ford. "But you will admit that if fishermen are to be believed the brooks must be full of them."

Mr. Eden snorted.

"You have reminded me of a danger in fishing which I had overlooked, Willum," cried Mr. Ford. "You have proved my argument. No, no! No, sir," he continued without permitting his companion, who was now waving his walking-stick incoherently, to reply, "believe me, you much overrate bullfighting. It is only a favourite subject for foreign authors who visit Spain to enlarge upon. As a matter of fact it is less dangerous than the most sedentary occupation I know of in England."

"How can you—?" Mr. Eden managed to say.

"Why, as the Scotch clergyman once said to God, I can prove it to thee by statistics. There are more aldermen killed every year in London by turtles than matadors in the whole kingdom of Spain by bulls. Now isn't that a fact?"

They both stopped short in their tracks to laugh again. Mr. Ford because he had just thought of the argument, and Mr. Eden because he had been vanquished in so jolly a way. And they halted so unexpectedly that Anthony almost blundered into them.

"By George," said Mr. Ford scowling suddenly, "*we're* being followed! Well, sir?"

"I couldn't help overhearing what you were saying in the cathedral just now, and I admit following you just to see how the argument turned out," said Anthony in English, turning red as a beet. "I hope I haven't . . ."

"Certainly not," said Mr. Eden.

"Quite," said Mr. Ford.

"By George!" exclaimed Mr. Ford, seizing Anthony by the waistcoat. For a moment he thought Mr. Ford must have serious intentions—"if it isn't made by

Rowland!" At the same time he exhibited the tag of the same London tailor on the top of his own vest. " 'Straordinary, precisely the same . . . Well, good taste and curiosity meet them. It is time we introduce ourselves—by George!"

They did so.

They discovered they were all staying at the same fonda.

"Dies mirabilis!" exclaimed Ford. "We only arrived there this morning—by diligence."

"You must pay no attention to him, Mr. Adverse," said Eden as they walked up the street to the fonda. "He is full of inconsequential facts. How would you suppose we arrived—in a sheet let down from heaven?"

Mr. Ford snorted but Mr. Eden went on.

"Dick is taking notes for a guide-book to Spain. Everything goes in it from *Abades* to *Zzonso*—"

"It is sadly needed. Every intelligent traveller feels the lack," Mr. Ford wedged in.

"—And when it is finished, two volumes of it," continued Mr. Eden, who was not to be put off, "it will be . . ."

"An excellent guide-book to Spain," thundered Mr. Ford, "full of that admirable redundancy of impertinent information with which every good guide-book should reek."

"Not at all," continued the even tones of his companion. "It will be like everything else you have to say. It will only prove your own theses. In this case it will merely show how superior everything in England is to everything in Spain."

Mr. Ford stopped and appeared to be threatened with apoplexy.

"Now take the argument that you just overheard, sir," continued Eden, taking Ford along by the arm. "All that were merely to persuade me to put off seeing the bullfight at Madrid in order to go trout fishing with Dick here in the mountains."

"Do you fish, Adverse?" exclaimed Ford hopefully. Anthony could see it was a crucial question.

"Indeed I do," he cried enthusiastically. "I love gaffin' sharks—"

"Sharks?" bellowed Mr. Ford. "Sharks! No, no, trout, salmon; trout, salmon!"

Mr. Eden leaned up against the wall of the fonda of El Dorado where they were now arrived and laughed immoderately.

"Another fact for your book, Dick," he shouted. "The snow-fed brooks *of the Sierras are not frequented by sharks*—make a note of it."

"Go to the devil, Willy Eden," grinned Ford as they entered the inn together.

Anthony stopped by the door astonished. In one corner of the room by a window Ouvrard was quietly eating a hearty luncheon.

He looked like a man who had just received overwhelming good news after a prolonged and exhausting anxiety. Anthony was at first afraid that he would resent the presence of strangers. But Ouvrard proved pathetically desirous of companionship and from the first got on with the newcomers uncommonly well. He exerted himself to be likable with all of his old charm to which was now added a certain dignity, as though he had passed through a great sorrow from which a sympathetic wisdom had been acquired. Most of his vulgar assurance and fat vanities had vanished. He no longer appeared to strut even when he sat down. What he lacked now was a certain faith in himself which still made it difficult for him to make decisions.

The irrepressible Mr. Ford by dint of unceasing badgering of Mr. Eden at last obtained his desire, and it was decided that the whole party should pause on their way to Madrid for a fishing expedition. They had now tacitly joined forces. Ford and Eden were delighted to have found a fellow countryman in Spain, for so they considered Anthony, and Ouvrard's apparent gayety under misfortune had recommended him to them as well as his boundless generosity. For his own reasons Anthony had hopes that with good luck a little fishing might serve to restore Ouvrard's self-confidence. So it was decided to send the great coach on to Madrid with Juan, Simba, and the luggage and to pursue the rest of their way by diligence. Most of the escort, which was consuming the banker's substance in gorgeous idleness at Burgos, now found themselves suddenly dismissed. They departed grumbling, and not without threats.

With Ford, Eden, and himself all well-armed and tolerably good shots, Anthony felt safe enough for any ordinary contingency. Indeed, he took very little stock in rumours of the perils of the road.

The departure was still somewhat delayed by the banker who had been bled too profusely by the leech he had at last employed. He finally, however, recovered from his weakness and they set out. Mr. Eden and Mr. Ford were provided with professional paraphernalia for fishing that they both carried with them as a matter of course. There were creels, reels, rods, and boxes of artificial bait by which Mr. Eden especially set exaggerated store.

———————————

The ancient diligence provided by the Compañia Catalines was of a seventeenth century vintage. It resembled an omnibus and was pierced along its preposterous length by doors and windows of contorted shapes as if its architect had had the Alhambra vaguely in mind. In the days of Isabella the Catholic, Mr. Ford thought that it had been painted in chrome and vermilion. Its behind, which was fatter than its before, was entered by a collapsible ladder that seldom failed to collapse. It was slung from spindle-spoked, concave wheels of gigantic circumference by cords of espartograss. The long benches of its interior, provided with red satin cushions adorned with chenille trimmings, did not in the end prevent bruising the bottoms of passengers, for this cabaña on wheels whizzed through space in a delirium of motion imparted to it by the united effort of ten vicious mules.

441

"And in this," said Mr. Eden, as he collapsed resignedly on the stern ladder, "we are going to fish for trout."

A peasant woman of superb and plastic proportions, under the impression that this was the public diligence departing for Madrid, was sitting in one corner of it when they entered. And it proved impossible to convey to her in any known dialect that she was in error.

"Try some of your damned arguments on her, Dick," said Mr. Eden at length beside himself with her obstinacy.

While the rest of them sat convulsed, Mr. Ford, who was an erudite gentleman, lavished Catalonian, Castilian and Aragonese upon her. Not even her expression changed. Her sloe eyes like those of a basilisk looked at him with contempt. He was at last reduced to gasps, a little bastard Basque, and maledictions in Latin.

"Nothing will move her but a derrick and a papal bull," he cried.

In the meanwhile the coach departed with Juan and Simba at the top. The great dog set up a dismal howling as he saw Anthony lean out of the window of the diligence to wave to Juan. They exchanged a gay farewell. The ribbons of the guitar fluttered from Juan's neck as the coach turned the corner. The baying of Simba diminished in the distance. For a moment a sinister feeling clutched Anthony. He turned to find the woman still sitting.

As a last resort the mayoral in an astrakhan jacket and sheepskin trousers was called in to remonstrate with her. But he might have been as Russian as he looked for all the effect his words had. At last she crossed herself. They all sighed. But she merely removed from her bodice a breast like a bean sack and applied its gathered nipple to the mouth of a small, pink pig.

"She is a wet nurse, señores. Doubtless she is employed at Madrid by a noble family and does not wish to go dry," said the mayoral, shifting his sheepskin trousers.

"Doubtless," said Mr. Eden, listening to soapy noises.

The woman returned the pig to a small basket.

"Do you realize, Willy, that this maternal succubus is going with us to Madrid?" shrieked Mr. Ford.

"Quite," replied Mr. Eden imperturbably.

"Vaya usted con Dios," roared Richard Ford at the mayoral. The man bowed.

They started.

Mr. Eden was forced to lend assistance to M. Ouvrard, who had been hooked in the deepest vein of his biological French humour. He took the banker's head on his knees.

Between paroxysms of laughter Anthony sat in the corner remembering at the same time with a sense of indescribable loss the fluttering ribbons of Juan. Mr. Ford and Mr. Eden began to get out little cards with artificial flies and feathered hooks upon them.

Anthony looked at them. How serious they were about it. To him life had lately become too ludicrous even to bear thinking about. Soon they would be fishing. Nom d'un petit nom! Think of that!

It seemed fitting that just about this point Mr. Ford should point out the town of Vibar and remark that the Cid had been born there.

"What did it matter? Suppose he hadn't been born," mused Anthony, just then unwilling even to think that.

Mr. Ford proved to be correct about other things. The headwaters of the river Urbel were found to be swarming with fish. The decayed town of La Pinza where they alighted was situated on a trout stream.

The lazy trout on the higher reaches of the stream could actually be seen basking in pools, big fellows. Once they caught the glint of salmon leaping a falls. But none of these fish would bite. No matter how carefully they cast and whipped the pools there was not a single strike. They changed flies; they rotated flies. They let their bait drift downstream; they drew it slowly up. Nothing, not a nibble.

443

It was irritating to return to La Pinza and find the pig being nursed.

"Caramba!" said Mr. Ford.

"Perhaps it is because zey are English flies and very ar*tifici*al," suggested Ouvrard towards the end of a second fishless day.

"Not at all," asserted Mr. Eden. "It is due to the phlegmatic temperament of Spanish trout."

"Try ze vurrum," suggested Ouvrard.

Mr. Ford looked horrified—and there were no worms.

"I vill show you zen how as a leetle garçon I take feesh in ze Vosges montaine." He began to take down one of his stockings.

They all gathered about the banker, whose preparations were mysterious.

He unravelled some brown yarn from one of his woollen stockings. He prepared a line with a small, clear pebble tied on just above the hook. He then broke off a short length of yarn and threaded it carefully on the hook with an end floating free.

"Ha," said the great financier, "ze vurrum ar*tifici*al. Now you see!"

They tiptoed over to a near-by pool, where lying on his belly Ouvrard lowered his contrivance directly before the face of a large gasping trout sunning itself under a great root with its head upstream.

The tame animal swallowed hook and all. Ouvrard jerked it out onto the bank. His triumph was extreme. He went about repeating the performance. He caught salmon as well as trout. He rose rubbing his hands. He was a successful man again. Respected, envied.

They filled their creels and returned to the village to be received as only successful sportsmen can be. The fish were delicious and the dinner hilarious. Even the wet nurse appeared to enjoy it. They lingered for days in these high, clear valleys amid the towers of ruined castles and dashing waterfalls. Anthony enjoyed himself hugely. Ouvrard was shouting like a boy. Half

444

of one stocking was ravelled away. Ford and Eden were deep in the bliss of endless argument.

When they decided to leave at last, the woman took her place in the corner of the diligence, without comment. She rode with them to Madrid. She alighted at the Puerta de Hierro and gave the mayoral fifteen reales ten maravedís. She disappeared around the corner into the sunrise with her pig in the basket.

The diligence moved on through the streets of Madrid now slightly acrid with wood-smoke. It was December and the washerwomen in the dry rut of the Manzanares were forced to break the ice on the few remaining pools. They left the diligence in the Calle de la Montera. Mr. Ford and Mr. Eden parted from Mr. Adverse and M. Ouvrard with mutual admiration and regret. They also went their several ways; Anthony and Ouvrard to the Fontana de Oro where they refreshed themselves on agraz mixed with manzanilla wine.

Neither Juan nor the coach had been heard of. "Mañana," said Anthony to Ouvrard who looked worried. "Mañana. Remember we are in Spain." Yet Juan should certainly have arrived by this time. "What," he wondered, "could have become of him?"

At three o'clock in the morning he was awakened by the deep baying of Simba.

Chapter Sixteen

The Prince of the Peace
Beyond the Pyrenees

THE baying of Simba did not awaken Anthony immediately. Yet even in his sleep—for the sound started him dreaming—he knew that something was terribly the matter. At one time he thought he heard Juan calling him, too—far-off. But he forgot that when he awoke. Only a strong impression of the eery and sinister had been added to the bell-tolling voice of the great hound that echoed through the caverns of his nightmare. He struggled up in bed. It was real.

Simba was in the courtyard below.

The scene in the patio while he stood by the window, instinctively drawing on his clothes, was so vivid as to tinge with its wild, emotional colouring his entire sojourn in Madrid. The great court of the posada of the Fontana de Oro was awash with red torchlight and fleering shadows. And in this atmosphere of funereal-macabre all hell was let loose.

446

At first he could make out nothing but glare, smoke, and pandemonium. Then—

Simba was baying at the open gate. He was being kept-off by a crowd of half-dressed mozos and link-boys with clubs, sputtering flambeaus and a raving pack of curs at their heels. Under the black arches of the stables, amid skeletons of coaches, more torches were making red rings and ovals in the darkness as they were whirled into flame while grooms armed with pitchforks and shovels rushed out.

Just then Simba charged.

The scared waiters and yard attendants scattered before him. A pistol went off, followed by a shrill howl of agony from one of the coach dogs. Simba tossed another over his shoulder, a big, black-spotted fellow with its throat torn out. Just around the corner from the window a door banged. Before it the fierce clamour as of a wolf-pack in at the kill, followed by worrying sounds, began. The curs scattered. One of them was being eaten alive. Then there was another shot.

All this had taken about ten seconds. With his trousers on backward, and the exaltation of battle in his heart, Anthony rushed out. At the bottom of the stairs which he descended headlong in the darkness, and at the end of a long corridor, several whey-faced waiters in shirts and drawers were standing in the dim rays of a smoky lamp peering out into the darkness through a grating. A man nursing a sprained wrist and groaning sat on the floor with a pistol still smoking beside him on the tiles.

"Body of Jesus!" cried another as the sound of sniffing and claws traversed the threshold, "it's the devil himself." Several crossed themselves. They clutched at Anthony's arm as he approached to unbar the door.

"Santiago, señor, there is a great mad dog out there! Would you let him in at us? Caramba, crazy English-man, what can your little stick do? For four days now he has terrorized the whole quarter and stood-off the

447

guards at the Puerta de Hierro. No one can hit him even with a bullet."

"My dog!" said Anthony. "Open the door."

At the sound of his voice an indescribably fierce and pathetic whining came flowing in over the sill.

"You see—he knows me."

He whistled. The hound began to throw himself against the door till it quivered. His voice filled the entire inn.

Anthony picked up the empty pistol from the floor and pointed it at the group of scared but obstinate servants. They broke away from him, racing up the passage. He pulled the door open and stood behind it. Luckily it opened inward or he would have been devoured by frantic love. It was fully five minutes before he could venture out and throw his arms about Simba. When he did so the dog put a grizzly head over his shoulder and moaned with affection and relief. He twitched and trembled all over.

In his room upstairs—no one had offered to stop him—he examined the dog carefully. One of his ears had been shot or half bitten off. It was hard to tell which. A great peeling scar as if from a knife wound raked half-way over his shoulders and along his back. It looked as though a gigantic cat had clawed him. And he was starved and stone-bruised and filthy.

Anthony talked to him in Arabic. "What is it, Simba, what happened?" he cried as he sat on the floor with angry tears in his eyes trying to bathe the wounds. The hound whimpered.

But his powerful tail continued to flog the floor in a mad tattoo of joy at having found his master, while at the same time he rested his muzzle on Anthony's knee and in his own language poured forth a story of outrage and tragedy. There could be no doubt of the emotional meaning. That was clear. Only the incidents were lacking.

"I won't leave you again, my friend," cried Anthony. "That's a promise. Give me your paw."

He swore, washing out the deep cut on Simba's

back. It was evidently some days old and badly caked. The noise in the patio outside had subsided. Simba rumbled on in his chest.

Ouvrard came in in gown and pantoufles. He was much perturbed.

"Hein, when I was a little boy I used to wish animals could talk—and now this one does. Mon Dieu, if he only had words! How did he ever find us here?"

"Picked up my trail in the streets, I suppose. We walked here from the Calle de la Montera, you remember. Pure chance. He may have been wandering about the streets hunting for me. He would do that."

"Juan must have arrived in Madrid then. Where do you suppose he is?"

"Juan?" said Anthony.

They looked at each other significantly. At Juan's name Simba had begun to bark.

They spent the next day inquiring for Juan and the coach but no one had heard of it or seen it. On the following morning they went to the authorities but they had no better luck there. Simba was well known. Sí! everybody knew Simba. He had appeared suddenly from nowhere and had terrorized the streets. The señor would do well to purchase a stout chain and to look carefully to the staple. It was fortunate that only beggars had been bitten. Gold would heal them. The alcalde bowed them out.

"Mais, c'est impossible," complained Ouvrard. "That a coach, ten mules and a man should vanish. I will wait till I can bring pressure to bear in high quarters. It will not be long. I shall soon have their bread here at my mercy." He ground his teeth. "We shall see then, par le bon Dieu! We shall see."

In some respects Ouvrard proved to be an able prophet but it was many and many a long day before they heard of the coach. And Juan——

"Poor Juan!" thought Anthony. He had not given up looking for him yet. But his heart was filled with foreboding at Simba's crying at the name of "Juan."

And so—the great deal in wheat got under way,

unluckily enough, while Anthony did his own hair with the ghost of Juan leaning over his shoulder; while Simba slept in the bleak winter sun in the patio, keeping his secret, growling and licking his wounds.

———————

They did not stay long at the Fontana de Oro. Richard Ford called one morning to see how they were getting on and casually confirmed them in their opinion that it was the worst hostelry in Europe. "Not only are the beds populous but the muchachos play guitars in the patio while you are being eaten. That is carrying cannibalism too far." Messrs. Ford and Eden departed for Toledo behind the usual number of mules, and they saw them in this world no more.

They took the hint of the departed, however, and moved to the Casa de los Baños, kept by one David Purkiss on the Calle Caballero de Gracia near the Puerta de Hierro. It was much frequented by government couriers, who came there to remove the mud of Mercia, Aragon, and Valencia from their anatomies. But as M. Ouvrard never bathed, having once caught a cold at Arles in doing so—he merely wiped his face and sometimes his neck in the morning with a powerful gillyflower cologne—the adobe in the baths was to him immaterial.

These moves on the part of Ouvrard were not unimportant. His rise to influence and the course of his negotiations with the crown ministers during the government's speculations and peculations in wheat could have been marked by them. The humble taking-off place was the establishment of Señor Purkiss. From thence M. Ouvrard rose and eventually soared into more congenial, luxuriant, official, and exalted surroundings, all in the course of about six months. His way-stations towards the golden sunshine of royal favour after taking-off from the Casa de los Baños were in rapid succession La Fonda de Genies in the Calle de Peregrinos, the French embassy, the Palace of La

Buena Vista in the Calle de Alcalá, belonging to the Prince of the Peace, and the apartments of Philip V at San Ildefonso.

Anthony did not follow the banker. He remained with Señor Purkiss and kept comfortable vigils in a suite of rooms with a large fireplace. He hired one Pedro Manuelos, a polite and silent edition of Sancho Panza with some sartorial technique, to look after him. In the absence of Juan it was a consolation to be shaved without conversation. His complete loneliness began to pall upon him. He missed Vincent. He thought despairingly of Angela. He read a deal of Spanish literature good and bad. He fondled Simba, of whom, as his one remaining friend and fireside companion, he became unduly fond. So much for blustering evenings spent indoors.

The world outside was a different matter. He was busy there, a cog in a great intrigue, and he was still fascinated by it. He took immense pains with his Spanish, trying to banish from it not only the mannerisms of a foreigner but all traces of the colonial accent he had acquired in Cuba. His pleasure in high Castilian became an all but sensual thing. In the language, he felt, resided all that was living of the genuine magnificence and the true greatness of Spain.

A large part of his time was taken up in going about with Ouvrard whose Spanish was at first infantile. He got on rapidly but in the beginning of his negotiations he was dependent on Anthony. As Ouvrard did not wish to disclose fully the nature of his mission nor the policies of Bonaparte toward Spain, which he was initiating, he took some care for a while to whom he revealed his presence in Madrid .He desired to make his first approaches without arousing unnecessary opposition.

There was a streak of genuine diplomacy in the banker. He took due note of Spanish pride, punctilio, and prejudice. He wished to work through them rather than against them. Avarice, flattery, and persuasion were always his face cards in a pack where fear was a carefully played ace of clubs. It would have been well perhaps if Napoleon had not finally insisted upon making clubs trumps in Spain. Ouvrard did not think it was necessary to take all the tricks in order to win. "No," said he, "Godoy is the knave, which in this game takes the king and queen." He began therefore by sending Anthony to the Prince of the Peace to make known his arrival at Madrid.

"You might sound him out a little and learn all you can. Keep your eyes about you. Get him to talk. Here are a few leading questions—and a letter from Bonaparte. You will obtain audience as a confidential messenger from the Tuileries. The initial impression you make will count for much. I would arrive in an ordinary cab. We want no attention now. Meanwhile I shall myself go quietly to the embassy and arrange for some credits. All my gold and luggage was in the coach, you know. No papers, thank God! It is ridiculous, but I haven't even a change of linen left. Must we start the conquest of Spain in dirty shirts then? Bonne chance, mon garçon. I see your ruffles are still fresh."

They each took an antediluvian hackney. "Mine makes a noise like a pig whining," thought Anthony.

Coaches, however, were not the only things giving vent to hungry sounds. The bad harvests had filled the streets of Madrid with beggars. As the government was bankrupt, and the king did not take even enough interest in the queen to prevent his being a cuckold, there was no hope that he would suddenly become a father to his people.

There was only one fountain of bounty left in the country, one turgid source of honour that remained. It was the man who slept with the Queen of Spain, the Caliph of Ali Babas since the world began, a noble beggar on horseback who had stretched forth his unashamed hands to fate murmuring, "Por el amor de Dios," and received the golden fleece and the usufruct of the Indies. Whatever was left he alone might still give away. If the beggars licked their lips when he passed it was from envy as well as hunger.

452

It was upon this remarkable individual that with not a little well-concealed curiosity and natural contempt Anthony was about to call. His introduction, delivered in the name of Ouvrard, was a brief note in the lightning-like script of the little man in the Tuileries.

Thus Mercury jolted on in his squeaky chariot down the Calle de Alcalá with the paper thunderbolt of Jove in his pocket.

——————————

Don Manuel de Godoy Alvarez de Faría Ríos Sanchez y Zarzoa, Prince of the Peace, Duke of Alcudia, Count of Evora Monte, Grandee of the First Class in Spain, Commander of the Knights of Malta, Knight of the Golden Fleece, Grand Cross of the Order of Charles III, President of the Council of Castile, Generalissimo of the Spanish Armies, Colonel of the Household Troops, High Admiral of Spain, etc. etc.,— sat in an upper room of the palace of La Buena Vista and looked out through the high windows at the dank light of a Madrid morning in April. The room was cold, but Don Manuel was notoriously a warm-blooded man.

Nevertheless, he gave a slight shiver. He was listening to the wheezing drone of a blind man hawking handbills just under his windows on the Calle de Alcalá. God alone knew what they were saying about him now. And that fellow with the saw-like voice was especially persistent. He went to the window. Yes, it was the same man led by that half-starved, black bitch like a hound come from hell to guide blind Rumour about the streets. He sighed, picked up a pen, threw it down again and subsided into his chair by his desk. He would sign the papers—mañana.

It was a gorgeous desk, almost effeminate with its small medallions of heathen goddesses and its miniatures of court ladies set in wreaths and scroll work. It had been sent by Louis XV to Philip V on the latter's birthday. Now it belonged to Don Manuel. Under the desk was a handsome pair of legs—also the property of Don Manuel. They were well shaped, a little gross and too vigorous. Yet they went perfectly with the desk; that is, they were of the same era; obviously idle, sensual, over-decorated, and effeminate, because no longer meant merely to support a man. They were for something more than that, as their costume showed: shoes with high, red heels, plump calves in puce-coloured stockings, a diamond garter with a cameo miniature of the Queen of Spain on it, and above that a Dionysian development thrust rearward into a soft green silk cushion and clothed smoothly in canary-coloured knee-breeches. A complicated arrangement on his breasts of looped ribbons and cordons of the various orders to which he belonged, or that now belonged to him—it was hard to tell which—had only one disadvantage. They made it difficult for Don Manuel himself to see the blazing diamond star pinned over his left nipple. But the sweep of his shoulders clad in rich, blue watered-silk and hung with gracefully drooping epaulettes with tassels of spun gold was manly. Above their straight line rose a flamboyant countenance with red, sensual lips, a flat aquiline nose, and a high Gothic forehead so narrow as to convey the impression that there was not much in it. That impression, however, was instantly relieved by a wealth of dark-brown ringlets that swept luxuriantly away from it in long romantic waves upon which the white ribbon that confined them slept like the sail of a becalmed treasure galleon seen from afar.

Such was the grandee of the first class in Spain who was now annoyed by the wheezing of the blind beggar selling handbills in the street below.

There were no newspapers left in Madrid. With a diligence that might otherwise have been commendable Don Manuel had seen to that. But there were still handbills. Despite the greatest care, they continued to appear from time to time. And they were always hawked by the blind. News in Spain was invariably sold by blind men. It was a Castilian trick. Even in Madrid it was impossible to convict a blind man no matter how complacent the alcalde might be before whom he was haled for selling libellous printed matter. "I have not seen the great infamy attributed to the King's Minister," they would swear by the heart of Jesus. And the joke was always appreciated. "Go then, and God go with you, innocent one. You have broken no law."

It was true. Even "Yo—El Rey" could do nothing about it.

Godoy had often thought of complaining to Don Carlos about the lax state of the press law. But invariably the king would ask to see the handbills. And that was distinctly *not* to be thought of.

It was becoming painfully apparent to Don Manuel that there were some things that even El Rey could not do. Fixing the price of bread, for instance, or paying the troops out of an empty treasury. It was not Don Manuel's fault that the harvests had been bad for two years. Yet people blamed him for it. How unreasonable —in fact, "Caramba!" And to have the people hungry and the soldiers penniless at the same time was a foul conjunction for a royal favourite.

"Hunger has no punctilio."

He could remember copying that for old Dr. Guzman, his tutor, only a few years ago. It was just after he had first . . . first fully convinced Her Majesty that he was a man of large parts—and natural understanding—fully equal to lightening the most burdensome duties of the king. Her Majesty had been most gracious. In preparation for his becoming the choricero not only should he be able to play the guitar, she would also have him taught to read and write. It would be convenient. So he had learned to sign his name, beautifully. And he was fond of quoting all the proverbs he had copied for Dr. Guzman.

"*After lightning there is thunder.*"—"*Another Tuesday will follow Monday.*"

When he presided over the Council such profound saws gave him a certain air of wisdom.

It was only Don Luis da Vincitata who dared to laugh. Dios, how he hated that man! He would never forgive him for having given him the title of "Your Peculiar Magnificence." Don Luis had moved it in full council and it had been passed with acclaim. To think that for a year he had been charmed by it—"Your Peculiar Magnificence." It was not until Don Diego, his secretary, had whispered into his ear that . . . shocking. it was quite shocking.

But he saw the point. He was not one to dismiss a secretary for frankness. He did not wish to be flattered. The great should have the truth told them. Yet; it must have taken a good deal of courage to tell a man of his peculiar magnificence what Don Luis had said.

Still, he had not let them laugh at him for long. He had married the infanta, Doña Tuda, and that had made him a nephew of the king, a "serene highness." It was Don Luis who had suggested that Doña Tuda should be made "lady-in-waiting." She had not had to wait long.

He started. He had never thought of it before. Could Don Luis have been making fun of him with his wife's title, too?

He was very suspicious of that old man now. Don Luis had tricked him nicely enough on the transfer of that province in America to France. *Lou—Lou*—what was its name? Oh, yes, Louisiana! Monstrous! He had never meant to part with it. He had been cajoled out of it. Don Luis had assured him when the secret treaty was made that it was only "put in pawn," his very words, only a security for the payment of the French indemnity. And then—Bonaparte had sold it to the Yankees for fifteen millions of dollars. He licked his lips. That money would have been welcome in Spain. And now they were blaming him for that, too.

Perhaps it would be a good thing to get rid of Don Luis da Vincitata? Somehow or other he always seemed to play into the hands of Bonaparte in the end. It seemed to him now, as he sat thinking over the past, that ever since he had been at court it was Don Luis who had really directed the course of events. Yet he was only a councillor, a mere confidential agent of the crown.

Yet since he owed his introduction to court to Don Luis he had naturally been willing to take his advice— to be grateful.

He remembered how Don Luis had driven down to Badajaz in that great gloomy coach of his one July morning in '84, he was only seventeen then, and found him swimming and strumming a guitar by the banks of a stream.

"Put your shirt on," Don Luis had said. "I am going to take you to court and make a royal body-guard out of you. You play the guitar well, don't you, my boy? Take it along—to accompany your other instrument. You may be able to play some notable duets. Her Majesty is much given to stringed instruments."

And so this old friend of the family had driven off with him just as he had taken his older brother to Madrid before him. "But I am much disappointed in your brother," Don Luis had told him. "He forgets his friends. Now I think you will go further. You are much more of a man." And Don Luis had been right. He was always right. That was the trouble with him. But he ought not to keep him waiting this way. He was no longer a boy with a guitar. He was the Prince of the Peace and, as Don Luis must know (damn him!), the father of the queen's youngest son. Don Luis knew a good deal, didn't he?

He reached forward on the desk and began to play with the sander. It was a silver figure of a peasant sowing. When you pressed the spring the peasant swung his arm and sanded your letter nicely. He amused himself and scattered sand all over the top of the desk. In the anteroom he could hear Don Diego skylarking with the pages. When he was a boy he had loved to be tickled, too. *But now it was different.* Few people had any idea what the Prince of the Peace had to put

457

up with. Her Majesty was still *so* playful—and then there was Doña Tuda—the infanta. As his wife of course she had her moments. There were two of them to look after and he was thirty-five now. He was coming to appreciate how a man might devote himself to experimenting with nothing but water-clocks, as the king did.

He never got any credit for his good ideas, and lately they were blaming him for everything. Few people suffered as much for Spain night by night as he did. Did they think he could be a father to the royal family and a father to the people, too?

He walked over to the window and stepped out on the balcony. Would Don Luis never arrive? It was eleven o'clock now. Well, there he was getting out of that new coach of his. The latest London make. It had been a joy to ride in it yesterday. Marvellous springs. Don Luis' remarks about the wheel of Fortune painted on the ceiling had gone a little too far though. After all, who was he to dig the Prince of Peace in the ribs —and grin?

"Bread, and the beggar on horseback," cried the blind man, waving his handbill. "A new ballad, señores. For a maravedí, read. Famine, and a warming pan for the queen's bed. Read, señores. For a maravedí. Bread and the beggar on . . ."

Don Manuel closed the window behind him angrily and stepped back into the room.

"Good morning, Manuel," said Don Luis. "How is it with you—by the Grace of God?"

Don Manuel resented that. He resented all that the intimacy implied and the tone in which it was conveyed. But there was such a sturdy and vigorous air about the hale old man who stood before him, whose outline seemed to occupy a square in space rather than an oblong; above all there was such a complete unity and calm self-assurance conveyed by the massive mahogany features and the grizzled temples of the old lion, that Don Manuel quailed. Instinctively he started to whine a little.

"Do you hear what they are saying about me out there?" he asked plaintively.

"Well, can you blame them? They are very hungry and there is nothing like the lack of a few meals to make poets write. Under your beneficent administration we are like to have a renaissance of satire. The acid muse never sings clearly with pie in her mouth. She needs mouldy crusts to thrive on."

Don Manuel felt the edge rather than the point of these remarks.

"The dearth *is* extreme," he admitted. "And I have not been able to do anything about it. It now amounts to famine—"

"Pooh!" said Don Luis "Spain has been hungry ever since we drove out the Moors."

"—and the soldiers near the city are unpaid," continued the Prince of the Peace with a note of genuine concern for the military. "Even the household cavalry is six months in arrears. I have a remonstrance here." He lifted a scroll of paper that rustled ominously.

"Eh!" said Don Luis. "You should have let me know before this. I will do what I can. But it will take at least a month to drive swine in from Estremadura." They both remained silent for a few minutes.

"Can't you do something with the new French ambassador?" asked Don Manuel.

"You mean toward withholding the payment due on the subsidy?" Don Luis looked doubtful. "I might," he said at last.

"It would save us," cried Don Manuel. "We could import wheat and pay the garrison for the winter."

"And then what?" asked Don Luis.

"There may be a better harvest next year—and the Mexican flota will soon be in, shiploads of silver bars, seventy million dollars by the viceroy's account."

"I have a little bad news for Your Serene Highness," replied Don Luis. "An advice has just come through by way of Paris that the British have annihilated the Mexican treasure fleet."

459

"What? Why, we are not even at war with them!" shouted Don Manuel.

"We are now," said Don Luis. "When a nation captures and sinks your ships at sea, then it *is* at war with you. Need I enlarge on that?"

"But what excuse have they? It is national piracy!"

"They consider the cession of Louisiana to France a hostile act," replied Don Luis. "Now that it has been sold to the Yankees the Mississippi is forever closed to England and Bonaparte has received fifteen million dollars. It will enable him to go on with his English war again."

"That is *your* fault," bellowed Don Manuel. "You assured me that the province would eventually be returned. It was only to be held as security. You brought M. Lucien Bonaparte here to confirm that while he was still ambassador. You have permitted Napoleon to embroil us with England. We are ruined." For some minutes Don Manuel in an unusual but sincere access of passionate anger and alarmed patriotism, not unmixed with personal forebodings, bellowed on.

"Calm yourself," said Don Luis after he had listened as long as he cared to. "If you go on this way your voice will be ruined for accompanying the guitar. That would compromise your position with the queen even more than you say I have." He grinned a little. Don Manuel sat panting.

"As usual you are only partly right," Don Luis continued a little languidly. "That has always been your weakness as a statesman from the time you first went to bed with the queen. It is true that I desire to see France and Spain aligned against England and I worked for it. But I also hoped to build up a great Latin empire in America, and, as we were weak in Louisiana, I thought to preserve it by transferring it for a while to the more powerful protection of France. That was arranged for in the secret treaty after my discussions in Paris with Napoleon. Both Lucien Bonaparte and I were sincere—I believe the first consul was, too. M.

Lucien writes me that he opposed the sale of the province to the Yankees to the very last, even to the verge of the bath."

"To the what?" croaked Don Manuel.

"To the *bath*, I said. The final papers were signed by Napoleon in the bathtub."

"Did he offer any excuse?"

" 'I need the money.' "

"Oh!" said Don Manuel inanely. "Does he bathe often?"

"No. We shall be able to keep Mexico, I think."

Don Manuel grunted. "At any rate we are done for here," he said despondently. "They are already rioting in Barcelona. They call themselves anti-clericals."

"Take advantage of that," cried Don Luis. "Organize a similar party here. You can sack a few monasteries, seize the loot, and then garrote the ring-leaders. There are enough silver crucifixes and pyxes in some of these monasteries to pay the army for a year."

"Or—I might seize the funds for the hospitals and give them government securities instead," cried Don Manuel looking brighter.

"You have your moments," Manuel," admitted Don Luis.

"But then what? That is only a temporary expedient at best."

"I have a plan for you," said the older man seizing his opening. "I want you to send me to Mexico to look after the safe forwarding of treasure there. You can give me special letters of instruction to the viceroy."

"But the British," objected Don Manuel.

Don Luis raised his hand. He began to explain to the Prince of the Peace the plan of M. Ouvrard to forward Mexican bullion to Europe. It took him a long time to explain it to Don Manuel.

"Well, I suppose so," the favourite finally admitted suspiciously, remembering Louisiana. "It seems the only way out." Then he looked more cheerful. A way to rid himself of Don Luis had suddenly occurred to him. "Shall I have the necessary credentials to Mexico made out and signed by the king?"

"Yes. And there is one thing more," said Don Luis.

"There always is," muttered Don Manuel. He looked up inquiringly, however.

"Before I leave I want my wife made lady-in-waiting to Her Majesty."

Don Manuel raised his brows in surprise.

"Yes," said Don Luis, "I have allied myself with the descendant of an imperial house, a lady with a noble past, a Paleologus. A quiet wedding in the country."

"I congratulate you," said Don Manuel. "I shall speak to Her Majesty about making a place for her among her camaristas tonight."

"Do so," said Don Luis. "It always pains me when I have to go over your head to ask the king for a minor favour. His Majesty is always willing to gossip, though."

Don Manuel winced.

"And this fellow Ouvrard?"

"I advise you to listen to him. He is the mouth of Bonaparte."

They bowed to each other more coldly than usual as Don Luis withdrew.

On the mantelpiece in the gorgeously furnished anteroom where Anthony had been kicking his heels for half an hour an ormolu clock began to strike noon. The two pages stopped skylarking and stood by the portières ready to bow stiffly as the latch on the cabinet door clicked.

"Now, monsieur, if you will give me your letter for His Highness," said Don Diego, extending his hand.

Don Luis emerged. He and Anthony stood looking at each other. The pages unbent and looked up at Don Luis in surprise. His hand remained behind him on the door-knob.

The clock suddenly became audible clicking away in its glass case.

While the clock ticked for twenty seconds or more both Don Luis and Anthony were thinking at a speed which no timepiece could record.

Don Luis was not merely made uncomfortable by being confronted by Anthony again. It was true that at the mere sight of him a lifetime of emotion never failed to shake even his iron-clad equanimity. But there was now something more than that. He had thought Anthony was dead. It was like being confronted by a determined ghost. For a moment his hand did not leave the door-knob.

So Sancho had lied then. Or the ruffians he had hired to waylay the coach had sold-out. It was only the servants that had been murdered. The details could be ascertained later. The result was clear. Anthony was standing there, and Ouvrard must be in Madrid, too. Probably both of them had escaped. He had failed again.

His hand did not leave the door-knob yet.

There was fate in this. A sudden resolution formed itself in his mind. He had tried three times now and lost. All that was connected with Maria was unlucky for him. Had been so from the first.

The game was about even so far. Why not call it off, forever? Tempt fate no further. Wisdom consists in not paying too high for anything. He would not be surrendering. He would merely be calling a draw.

The door-knob clicked.

Meanwhile an extraneous fact had forced itself upon him, just as in times of great pain the sufferer will notice the presence of a fly on his hand. The face of one of the pages looking up at him was that of a sardonic young imp. "I wish I had a son like that," said the old man's mind. "He is like me."

"Of what blood are you, my boy?" saïd he breaking the tension that all felt.

"Pedro to serve God and Your Honour and of the family Sidonia, Your Apostolic Reverence," said the boy who traced in Don Luis a certain humorous resemblance to the papal nuncio who had called only the day before.

Don Luis was delighted with this impudent tact.

"Here is something to get you into trouble," he said, and spun him a gold piece that never touched ground.

"After all, Maria's son was like her. A good type, too. The extreme opposite of his own. But a mould that he had once admired. Fate evidently needed both of them in the world. Goth and Latin." The dark man turned to the fair one.

"Welcome to Madrid, Don Antonio. It is somewhat of a surprise to find you here."

Anthony was vastly astonished. He had seen Ouvrard's coach at the door with Sancho dozing on top of it as he came in. A hundred speculations as to what Don Luis would do when he confronted him had run through his head as he sat waiting. But he had not expected this move. There was absolutely no hostility in it. Intensely on the alert, he suddenly felt disarmed. It was not only the words of Don Luis' greeting. The fire and brimstone were absent. As usual he said what he thought.

"Nothing could surprise me more than to be welcomed by Your Excellency. I should have thought it impossible."

The older man looked at him quite frankly. "You are mistaken, Antonio," he said. "I would like to talk to thee for a moment alone."

If anything could have astonished him more than the use of his first name familiarly it was the note of appeal in the old man's voice. He looked at him keenly for a moment.

"I can see no objection," he said.

Don Luis looked relieved. "Don Diego, if you and the young gentlemen will do us the favour of withdrawing for a moment?"

464

Don Luis motioned toward a long table and they sat down on opposite sides of it.

"I trust you will not misunderstand my motives in what I am about to say, Don Antonio," began Don Luis showing signs of conflicting emotions—which he gained the better of as he went on; "nor that you will expect me to explain. It would be impossible for me to do so. Nevertheless, I hope we may arrive at an understanding." He paused ponderously.

"I have never desired to trouble you, Don Luis. Recollect, you have been the aggressor. Before we discuss anything I therefore feel entitled to make clear to you how I feel. Since I am certain that there is nothing petty in your nature, it has been forced upon me that your motives for wishing to be rid of me must be profound ones. That they inhere in the past is so obvious as to be inescapable. Perhaps you suspect me of either possessing knowledge which I do not have or of a determination to investigate. In either case you would be mistaken. I do not wish to pry into the motives for your hostility. *Why* I do not is my own affair, and, to set your mind at rest, known to me alone. But I must also say this: if you persist, sir, in harassing me I shall feel forced out of pure self-defence to investigate what otherwise I should feel in honour bound not even to speculate upon. I shall say no more."

"Believe me, you put your case even more strongly than you suppose," said Don Luis. "I can now fully credit what at first I am bound to say seemed to be impossible; that is, that you had neither a knowledge of nor a desire to pry into certain matters of the past. But recent events in my domestic affairs have already confirmed me in that opinion. I allude, sir, to my nuptials with the lady who had your youth in charge. She is a better friend of yours than you may be disposed to credit."

Anthony could not conceal a look of astonishment.

"I am seventy," said Don Luis, "but I am still young enough to desire happiness. As we get older loneliness does not become more attractive. My pride in my wife is that of Pluto for Proserpine." A menace seemed to have crept into his tone. "You may shortly have the honour of meeting her at court."

"Is the old man getting garrulous," wondered Anthony, "or does he wish to seal my mouth about Faith? All this is only just as impossible as—life." Don Luis was looking at him but there was now no hostility in his glare. On the contrary . . . !

"I wish you both peace," Anthony said quietly. "What is it you desire of me?"

"Just that," replied Don Luis, "peace. From now on let us agree not to annoy each other in any way. Let the account be closed; paid in full. I admit that I opened that account with you. But you also admit you are not in a position to judge of my motives for doing so; that you do not even desire to know why. I leave it to you to close it, if you will, for both of us and with honour."

"Where is my servant?" asked Anthony.

"Where is *my* servant?" replied Don Luis. "As for the coach . . ."

"It is before the door waiting for you now," exclaimed Anthony. "Let us waive that in our account. It is M. Ouvrard's. You can settle it with him. But my man?"

"*Upon my word I know nothing about him,*" insisted the marquis.

They looked at each other for a moment steadily.

"For my own reasons then," said Anthony, "and not for yours, I accept."

They rose simultaneously and bowed. Anthony with a little stiffness that he was at no pains to conceal; Don Luis with a stately courtesy and grandeur which implied that in the young man before him he at last acknowledged fate as an equal. Anthony could not know why, but he felt the great resignation and equality of that gesture to be the genuine sign-language of the old man's heart.

466

A minute later he stood by the window watching Don Luis drive off. The hair that rose into points on each side of Sancho's cocked hat was now a peculiar grizzled grey; his smooth mouth sinister. "Beware. He is always driving . . . with the great vigour of evil" . . . where had he? . . . he remembered now. Brother François. In the cabin of the *Ariostatica* that night . . . a feverish vision. It must have been that. Why should it occur to him now? What connection? Unfathomable. He could not trace it down into the dark depths of intuition.

What mysterious vendetta had he and Don Luis been engaged in? Their hostility was psychic, instinctive. He had felt that from the first. Its roots went down into the darkness beyond reason or memory whence bitter juices are drawn. And where was Juan? He choked. Had he been right in meeting the old man half-way, after all? Now that he and Faith had joined forces, perhaps something was completed. Loose ends had met. The dark ring could be left hanging in space. He saw it, like a spinning noose in a cloud. Why? What? He longed to know, bitterly.

How curious! It was as hard to give up this hate as it would have been to deny a love. "John Bonnyfeather —if you can hear me—I have kept my promise in splendid difficulty." A sound from the land of the living recalled him. He turned to find that the secretary had returned to the room. He seemed more respectful than he had been before, almost obsequious. He must have delivered the letter from the Tuileries then.

"His Highness is waiting for you impatiently, señor. This way if you please."

He had not entirely shaken off the mood of his reverie as he stepped into the room. Out of the corner of his eye he caught the grin on the face of that imp-like page as he announced him.

"Don Antonio Ada—*vairs*," shrilled the urchin as if a bowstring had twanged.

Don Manuel Godoy, Prince of the Peace, stood against the light before the high window. He shimmered

467

in silks and diamonds. His soul glittered with success. There was nothing dim or chaste or virtuous about him. He was like Ganymede in the strong arms of Jove, rosy—and only a little troubled. Proud that he had been snatched up to dwell upon Olympus, he had the easy expression of one who might still discern clouds but only by looking down upon them.

And instantly—without having any volition in the matter—even as he stepped through the door, Anthony knew that he had been sped like an arrow to strike this glorious creature down.

Against so inhuman an institution he recoiled with horror and denial. He felt a great pity for the man before him. Sympathy begets sympathy. Don Manuel responded nobly. And in this seemingly auspicious atmosphere of fellow-feeling they met.

"You come to provide us with the staff of life, I am told," said Godoy graciously, letting Bonaparte's open letter flutter to the floor. "Need I say that in that case you are welcome to this hungry Madrid and to Spain? When will M. Ouvrard do us the honour of calling himself? I am impatient to see him. Let us waste no time on polite preliminaries. People starve."

"I am prepared to lay the general scheme before you now," replied Anthony. "M. Ouvrard will discuss it in detail if you are favourably impressed with the plan."

"Let no one disturb us, Don Diego," said Don Manuel. "You may close the door. I shall be closeted with this gentleman for some time."

Thus the great deal in wheat, Mexican silver, the Spanish royal family, and the peninsula of Spain got under way.

The grim archer, if he had any lips, might have laughed. Certainly he would have grinned as he watched the first arrow he had loosed flash to its mark.

———————

Don Luis had not lied to Anthony when he said

he did not know anything about Juan. He had left Sancho in Paris some months before to keep track of Ouvrard. He frequently employed Sancho in private espionage and had found his old servant both clever and faithful. Sancho never appeared himself in these affairs of his master, which were so closely connected with government intrigues that it was hard to tell just where the public business ended and began. He was only the agent. He supplied the means and directed others whom he took into his hire or bribed.

In Paris he had been harboured at the Spanish embassy as a butler, and it was not long before he was receiving a stipend from M. Talleyrand for supplying enough tidbits of gossip to gain him some credence at the ministry of foreign affairs. In this way he had been able to mislead the French on one or two minor matters and at the same time to devote himself to ferreting out the business of M. Ouvrard while under excellent cover.

Knowing what he already did know of Ouvrard's affairs, Don Luis was enabled to piece out the information which Sancho forwarded him into a clear picture which frequently permitted him to act or to give advice that seemed to have about it the quality of a mysterious prevision.

He was particularly anxious to know exactly when Ouvrard set out for Madrid in order to warn the Prince of the Peace, over whom he must retain his influence in order to advise him how to act. Sancho had therefore been instructed to follow Ouvrard as soon as he set out and to keep a close tab on him as he travelled through Spain.

Don Louis' policy was a complicated one. He was convinced that the only hope for Spain was to entangle it firmly in the Napoleonic net. His patriotism was genuine, but of a far-seeing, almost metaphysical variety.

He saw his country in the not-too-remote future as the thriving province of a great Latin empire with its people secure in a code of well-administered law; with the arts reviving and commerce flourishing in the midst of a federated European peace. The bright and rising star of the new and fortunate Caesar at Paris was to bring this about. Thus in a curious way characteristic of his time Don Luis was able to reconcile an intense conservatism and an all but radical idealism. Spain was to progress but by going backward. The Middle Ages were to be swept aside and *Hispania* was to rise out of order political and ecclesiastical; out of flourishing cities, bursting oil presses and flowing aqueducts. Individuals and institutions which stood in the way of this were to be swept aside. Even religion to Don Luis was political. Indeed, it might be said that Don Luis' religion was politics.

As time went on, and it seemed more and more probable that old as he was he might actually live to see his dreams and hopes realized, Don Luis had changed from a purely static reactionary to one who desired to accelerate the trend of events. His growing enthusiasm re-endowed his hale, old body with an all but youthful energy. He enjoyed an iron-clad health. The solution of his domestic difficulties and the companionship and comfort which he found in his new wife, who was not only looking after her husband but engaged as well in pious works, seemed to have turned the clock back for Don Luis even as he would have liked to turn it back for Spain.

Some marvelled that one who had sat on the council of the old king should still retain his influence upon the reigning monarch. Only a few realized that Don Luis dominated him. Yet it was so. He was the conscience of the dull Charles IV. He held the whip-hand over Godoy by his knowledge of that guilty secret of which he alone could have convinced the king. The queen was afraid of him. His influence had provided Crown Prince Ferdinand with the tutor who afterwards persuaded him to play into Napoleon's hands. The old man held no official position except his place on the Council of Castile. There most of the government business went on before his eyes. He said little. He looked down his nose while the ministers squabbled. Floridablanca, Count Aranda, and Urguijo had all had their day and joined one another in impotent retirement. Don Luis da Vincitata, Conde de Azuaga, at the age of seventy remained to advise the king whose advice to take and Don Manuel Godoy, the queen's favourite, what advice to give to the king.

The first faint rift in this admirable arrangement, admirable at least for Don Luis, coincided with the journey of Ouvrard to Spain and was due to the fact that he was accompanied by Anthony.

Sancho had not expected that. It was a complete surprise to him. He saw in Anthony not only an enemy of his master, the bastard son of the wife who had betrayed her husband, but also the destroyer of his own offspring, the late lamented "Kitten." The hard-bitten old tom cat's hair rose at the sight of Anthony riding towards Madrid in the luxuriant coach of Ouvrard, while his own son and his master's long-cherished vehicle kept each other dizzy company in some whirlpool at the bottom of an Alpine gorge.

At a discreet distance behind he had trailed Anthony from Paris. The delay at Bayonne had served to wear out what little patience and restraint he may have had. He sat brooding for days in a dark hole nourishing his implacability. The second delay at Burgos had done the trick.

Sancho there persuaded himself that he would be doing both his master and himself an excellent turn by knocking the passengers of the coach on the head before they reached Madrid to make further trouble. He felt that his arrival with so fine an empty vehicle to take the place of the one he knew Don Luis still grieved for might go far towards explaining the mysterious disappearance of its former owner. As for Anthony, he expected his own reward there, and no questions at all from Don Luis, perhaps even a pat on the head.

So he departed from Burgos a day before the coach, knowing that it would soon follow, to arrange a royal

471

welcome for it with some cloaked gentlemen of leisure not averse to being paid in advance to plunder. They lay in wait not far from a convenient spot where the camino real entered a defile in the desolate hills north of Madrid. Sancho himself, out of a delicate hesitation to involve his master, remained at a convenient hamlet near by.

All did not go as smoothly as might have been expected. It was true that the coach was handed over to Sancho about dawn one morning without his asking any questions and with no one but the mules as witnesses of what had taken place. But a great deal had evidently taken place. The noble caballeros who had engaged in the adventure of the night before seemed to have been overtaken by a pack of wolves. One of their gallant company was missing, and the rest could only be described as "all chewed up." Only the large sum in gold which they had found in Ouvrard's strong box could begin to console them for the united loss of an ear, a kneecap, several fingers, and various convenient if not essential muscles amongst them. Sancho's failure to mention the presence of Simba was commented upon with a wealth of simile that exhausted the animal kingdom and the calendar of the saints.

"Go, and the devil go with you," they said, and slunk home still grey in the face.

Alone in the box, save for Juan's guitar which had been overlooked and was still strapped to the iron railing, Sancho drove down the road toward Madrid in the greying darkness. It was no help as the light grew brighter to see that the guitar and its ribbons were splashed with blood. He wiped this off with his headkerchief and throwing it on the road drove on at a headlong pace.

But he was still some miles out of the city when the dog overtook him. He came out of the darkness behind and followed silently for some miles. Then he began to give tongue.

The little cat-man on the box shivered. He lost his hat. The dog picked it up and trotted along beside him looking up at him. He was evidently judging the distance for a leap. Sancho lost his head. He lashed at Simba with the whip. The hound dropped the hat and began with a devilish cunning to stampede the mules.

He took an unholy joy in it. He nipped them when they lagged. The sound of his furious baying, the rumble of the black coach, dim in rolling clouds of dust, roused successive hamlets that morning and died away down the road toward the city. The rumour spread that Satan had been caught out after cock-crow and was fleeing back to hell carrying a shrieking soul along with him.

Be that as it may, at half past six in the morning ten foundered mules staggered through the Puerta de Hierro with an hysterical little coachman on the box who begged for an armed escort to take him to his master.

Nor did this appear such a joke to the guard a few minutes later when a lion-like apparition with a voice like a cathedral bell stripped the leather breeches off a horrified sergeant and rushed past the paralysed sentries with nothing but a bayonet scratch to show for it. Sancho got his escort but they rode in the coach. The reign of terror in the streets had already started.

"You fool," bellowed Don Luis beside himself with rage when he at last understood Sancho's story. "And you bring ten mules and a bloody coach into my courtyard so the crime will come home to me! Christ deliver me from thee. Get out of my sight."

But a few days' cogitation and a talk with Faith put another aspect on the matter. Don Luis decided the best way to do was to brazen it out. He would treat the coach as his own, and drive about in it. No questions as to whose it was would then arise. He was considerably amazed to discover that Faith had tears in her eyes. "For the boy she had nursed," she said. Well, it was a natural explanation. He called Sancho and punished him by making him drive about while the dog was still loose in the streets. Nothing happened. The regiment on guard was changed, and the incident forgotten.

Don Luis was not superstitious, far from it. But under the circumstances it was only natural that he should have felt his heart flutter for the first time in his life as he came out of the door that morning and met Anthony. He was getting to be an old man.

That was one reason he had decided to compromise with fate in the form of Anthony.

But there was still the coach and M. Ouvrard. Don Luis now felt badly in need of a magnificent lie. Something that would out-Spanish a French banker.

At last a splendid idea occurred to him. He chuckled over it. He felt relieved at having the vendetta of a lifetime settled at last, and arrived home in high spirits. He called Sancho an amateur murderer, and cackled with Faith over the dinner table about her going to court. There was only one fly in the ointment.

Since M. Ouvrard was still in the flesh, perhaps he himself would not find it necessary to go to Mexico. The Frenchman could be trusted to see that the bullion was actually shipped. Everything depended on that. Well, let Don Manuel make out his credentials to the viceroy at Mexico. He could simply stick them in his pocket and stay in Madrid. At his age that would probably be the wisest thing to do. He drank his Canary a little thoughtfully, however.

———

Anthony had no idea that he would remain seven months in Madrid. Yet until the last few weeks before his departure for New Orleans the time passed rapidly enough. At first there was a large number of people to be interviewed with Ouvrard who, as soon as his plan had been officially accepted, set up shop.

The banker's scheme was vast but in its main outlines a simple one. The Spanish government was bankrupt, due to the failure of the treasure fleet to arrive from the colonies and an archaic system of farming the domestic revenues. And there was also a condition of famine with all of the usual attendant unrest.

Ouvrard offered a loan, which he had arranged for at Amsterdam the year before, sufficient to tide the government over its immediate crisis. He offered to ship into Spain, from the huge reserves that Napoleon had permitted him to accumulate in France, wheat in abundance and at a reasonable price. All that he asked for security was a blanket assignment in the form of sight drafts dated six months in advance on the royal treasury for the principal and interest due him. He had only two modest stipulations to make: that he was to be permitted to have an adequate supervisory control over the collection and disbursement of government revenue as long as the crown was indebted to him, and that all loans for a period of some years should be negotiated through him alone.

All this seemed too good to be true—and in the end it was. But to the Prince of the Peace and the harassed crown ministers in the early winter of 1802, G. J. Ouvrard, and his obliging assistant Señor Adverso, seemed to have stepped out of the diligence in Madrid like gods from the machine.

Within a month after their arrival the treasury found itself bursting with cash. Wheat was flowing in from Marseilles by the shipload and the price of bread lower than it had ever been. Surprised garrisons guzzling their back pay and wolfing their rations had nothing to grumble about but new shoes. His Majesty was enabled to slaughter three hundred seventy deer with the help of two field pieces and seven hundred horsemen. Her Majesty and her ladies appeared again in new gowns and real jewels. The voice of Don Manuel Godoy's guitar was once more golden—for it was through the Prince of the Peace that Ouvrard made most of his "arrangements." To make happiness happier, when the first loan showed signs of exhaustion it was given a new lease of life by another advance.

Who now so popular as M. Ouvrard? He was received at court and by the nobility. He was blessed in the streets by the populace and followed about. And all those connected with him shared in his popularity. He was always a very busy man and so was his secretary. They set up shop for a while at the French embassy. And then, in order to salve national sensitivity and suspicion, Ouvrard moved to the ground floor of the Palace of the Prince of the Peace.

The staff of this modest little bureau, called the "Office for the Consolidation of Foreign Loans," in reality controlled the government and destinies of Spain.

Ouvrard seldom appeared there. He left the direction of its affairs to Anthony who had for his assistants several discreet French and Spanish clerks whose mouths were closed by magnificent salaries always paid. Most of the work consisted in reorganizing the machinery for collecting and disbursing taxes by gradually appointing foreigners to various key posts; Frenchmen whenever possible, or those known to be reliable and favourable to Ouvrard's policy. Careful accounts in double entry were kept with a rough trial balance struck at the end of each day. For the first time in history it was possible to say just how much Spain, and M. Ouvrard, were worth. There was a constantly growing volume of correspondence between Ouvrard and Paris; with bankers in Holland; with French grain dealers and merchants all over the world; with the Spanish authorities at home and in the colonies.

Every effort was now made to ship all the bullion and colonial produce possible through the British blockade by the employment of neutrals. In particular every pressure was put on the Barings in London and the Hopes at Amsterdam to hasten the organization of the mercantile machinery being organized in America by Parish. The whole success of the scheme in Spain was dependent upon the success of Parish in the United States. If the funds lying dormant in Mexico could not be transferred to Europe either in the form of bullion or negotiable goods to establish credits, Ouvrard was done, the bubble would burst.

476

He had about two years to go. Then the loans which had been made by the bankers in Holland to the Spanish government would be called. With this money he had started the boom in Spain, financed the government, and purchased French wheat. All that must be repaid out of Mexican silver, since the domestic revenues of Spain were not sufficient to meet this charge and the demands of the French treasury for the stipulated subsidy at the same time.

It was a great gamble with the American ramifications becoming more and more important as time went on.

Ouvrard, however, was not satisfied with merely making a great profit on wheat and government contracts; with his commissions on loans; with having the operations of the Spanish treasury concentrated in his hands as a monopoly. He went on expanding and obtained licenses in unlimited numbers for trade with the Spanish colonies. These permits he peddled about Europe to various merchants, stipulating in each case for a percentage of the profit for himself and the Spanish government. These operations combined in 1805 in the firm of *His Catholic Majesty Chas. IV, G. J. Ouvrard, and Company*. The banker finally moved to the Escurial and directed his affairs from the palace of the kings of Spain.

Then Napoleon sent for him to Paris. He disgraced him and mulcted him. M. Ouvrard's trading operations and the emperor's European system had come into hopeless conflict. But Napoleon retained the grasp on the Spanish treasury and fiscal administration which Ouvrard had built up. It was the entering wedge. The entire royal family and Godoy were next taken over and imprisoned in France. Then followed the French columns, the occupation of the country, and King Joseph Bonaparte at Madrid.

But all that was in the future. Success and inflation were now in the air. Ouvrard was in his element. Life was so interesting and real for the banker, he had again become the financier so successfully, that the

477

other fellow under his hat who was so interested in shoes could only roll his eyes occasionally. He grew fatter and dressed more gorgeously. He kept driving about from Madrid to San Ildefonso when the king was there; from San Ildefonso to the Escurial, where the queen for the most part stayed; from the French embassy to the palace of Buena Vista, where Godoy held court on an equally royal and more prodigal scale. There were innumerable people of position to be seen and interviewed in order to secure their influence.

"It is true," said Ouvrard, "that we shall consolidate our position in Spain"—and without warning he would pick up Anthony at the Bureau of Consolidation and drive anywhere.

Thus amid accounts, letters, interviews, calls, court functions, and long secret conferences at the French embassy, where Beurnonville, the new French ambassador, Don Luis, Ouvrard, and sometimes Godoy, and Cabarrus, the agent for the Spanish treasury, frequently met—Anthony's winter in Madrid was a hectic one.

Afterwards he could recall very little of the intricate negotiations, the conflict of personalities and interests, the infinitely complex web which Ouvrard spun until he was enclosed in it himself along with the flies he lured. And he doubted whether anyone else could follow it, or understand it, or remember it for long.

To take his own mind off it for a few hours in order to enjoy life was to feel all of its gossamers slipping out of his brain and to look back upon the whole scheme as a dusty cobweb hanging in some dark garret of the mind.

Those who got anything out of the negotiations, he observed, kept their minds fixed on a few primitive factors—and withdrew in safety with several chests of a positive material-something, a profitable concession, or a definite bribe. He pondered this and began to turn over the routine at the bureau to the clerks and to the chief agent sent on from Paris, one Maurice

Dreyfus, who was deep in the confidence of M. Beur-nonville and interested in nothing but finance.

Anthony did not intend to permit Ouvrard to prevent his going to America. He kept that thoroughly in mind. He was not going to be a fly in the web left buzzing over papers. Still he made the most out of going about with Ouvrard into high and curious places while he waited impatiently for news from Parish that he had perfected his arrangements and that it was time to take up work at New Orleans.

Once relieved of the technical nonsense of accounts and secret correspondence at the bureau, of the immense flubdubbery of finance and merchandising-politics attempting to deal with life on the basis of the mathematics of things, Anthony's senses began to become vivid again, since he began to give play to his emotions once more. The streets of Madrid no longer looked white and unreal to him when he went out.

He began to feel the life in them. He experienced it in its own terms of feeling. His brain was no longer bled white as it had been when he emerged from the Bureau of Consolidation after having maintained a fixed state of mind from morning till night.

"No wonder, those who live that way eventually become interested—well, in shoes, let us say. One cannot always be nothing but your esteemed correspondent, or the causer of additions in books, without having an immense wealth of feeling left over to lavish upon something." He laughed as spring began to return, as the dry winter winds that swept the streets of the capital began to grow mild and a little humid, when the smell of wood smoke began to be replaced by that of early flowers hawked through the streets and piled in great bunches about the approaches to the Puerta del Sol. Who could pass them by, or their girl vendors in short skirts and brilliant bodices, looking back over their shoulder—a high comb, a short, impudent puff of a cigarette, a gleaming smile? Not Anthony. One must at least buy an early rose. "There are tides in the affairs of man as well as in those of finance," thought Anthony and purchased a few early roses. One could rise even from the ashes of dead fires, he discovered, surrounded by pleasant little flames that warmed but did not burn.

"So!" said Ouvrard, "you are *not* going to stay here in Spain as my agent and conduct the bureau for me? After all this you are going to New Orleans? And so you make the most of it here, eh? Ah, I can see that."

He tried to look disappointed and angry but he only succeeded in looking envious. He even had to laugh when he was punched in the ribs in a familiar way. He liked to be with Anthony. In his company it seemed to the older man that it was really worth while being rich, that life was worth trying to buy.

The Manzanares had its brief flood and poured roaring under the great bridge. The days grew warmer, hot. M. Dreyfus at the Bureau of Consolidation settled his square-rimmed spectacles on his more than Roman nose and complained of the antiquated formula which M. Adverse had used for figuring interest on national debts.

Anthony and M. Ouvrard drove out through gales of spring flowers to the court at San Ildefonso.

Out of a welter of recollections of Spain and Madrid a few memories always remained clearly with Anthony. There were of course innumerable bullfights. To be precise, seventeen in all. For the return of prosperity brought with it a consequent lavish outlay on the part of the authorities, and the populace craved not only bread but bulls. From a state of thrilled-fascination his progress to satiety at these spectacles was a rapid one.

The slaughter that season was unusually comprehensive. Maddened animals, wreathed in smoke and a necklace of firecracker banderillas exploding in the flesh of their necks, charged and galloped, bellowed and died tamely or magnificently, while los aficionados went through a succession of splendid frenzies. But whether the bull expired with a buen estoque or by the media luna, the end was always the same.

Ouvrard sickened a little on these occasions. The spectacle of worn-out and blinded horses treading in their own bowels or dragging their glistening, liver-coloured guts behind them for yards was always to him overpowering. He complained of the stench. Yet it was necessary to go if one was to be thought of as "the friend of Spain." The seething colour and frenzy of the multitude in the great ring remained with Anthony. He took to watching the faces about him as being even more enthralling than the spectacle in the arena. His composite memory of them was that of the expression of Spain.

He came to the conclusion that it was difficult, if not impossible, for a foreigner to understand what the bullfight was about. That it satisfied a deep craving of the Spanish nervous system there could be no doubt. Mere enjoyment of suffering as an explanation; the usual complaints of cruelty indulged in by aliens were, he was sure, superficial and beside the mark. They were too easy. For there was some deep expression of the meaning of life in this ritualistic spectacle. It was drama, a tragedy in which the heroism, danger, and chance were real even if the setting was artificial. It was the nearest approach to reality that a theatre could make. It seemed to him to be an expression of the triumph of the spirit of the people over the land, over the climate, over the aridity and barrenness of the landscape and the rigid social and class conventions in which the Spanish nature dwelt.

Spain was ancient. It impressed him as being antique. The hand of the past lay heavily upon it. There was a certain overpowering monotony in its landscapes and sunlight. Its life moved slowly and languidly with a dolce far niente. It was true that a curious hint of northern Africa, like the promise of a far distant and yet inevitable doom, was reflected from its skies, as though they remirrored the brazen Saharan lights into the north with a prophetic glance. And such things are what colour a people's soul as they live out their planetary destiny. One could not imagine too much, however. There was also diversity, there was brilliance, a flaunting of colour in buildings and costume, a hint of passion and intensity in the swish of skirts, in the swagger of caballeros, in the little boys playing el toro, always playing el toro, violently. But all these passionate things were seen by contrast. They had about them the aspect of a protest against something grim and Baal-like, something implacable in the land itself that even in the cities was never far withdrawn. And then——

Suddenly, out of all this welled up in a reassertion of unexhausted and undaunted energy the seething and frenzied spectacle of the bullfight.

In the bullring the Spanish people became united. All classes and distinctions fused into one passionate entity. On the sullen forehead of the bull was laid all that was Baal-like and implacable. He stood there staring at Spaniards, black, horned, bovine, the obstinate and ferocious emanation of the land. And the Spanish people in the persons of their gaudy and brave matadors, the beribboned cavaleres of Spain, played with him; ever holding him in fear and admiration, but having their revenge and torturing him amid the flapping of cloaks, the glitter of swords and the galloping of horses. And then they finished him off, they triumphed over that old bellowing el toro with punctilio and ritual. The short sword of Spain went down between his horns and into his heart.

Yes, one could scarcely doubt this feeling. El toro was a sacrificial victim, he was dragged off in triumph. And when he was driven down from the hills in droves, before he went into the arena, those who could not even afford tickets for the ring to see him die waited with knobbed sticks along the streets to whack him as he went past in clouds of dust.

It was religion, this merry hatred of bulls. It welled up from something deep in the feelings of Spain. Spaniards who felt it did not need to understand it or to have it explained. It was in their blood.

In the patio below his window at the Casa de los Baños Anthony watched the gamins playing el toro. One afternoon the game became unusually boisterous and realistic. A number of lounging, adult figures wrapped in capas condescended to stop and watch so well-acted a mock spectacle. The boy who was being baited made an excellent bull. The sport became fast and furious. At a given instant the children's imaginations fused and the game became real. Hysterical urchins closed in from all sides and began to kill the "bull." The clamour was shrill and fearful. Simba rose on his chain and bayed at the other end of the court.

By the time he reached the patio Anthony found that some of the men standing about had already interfered. And apparently none too soon. Young señor Toro stood bleeding and battered, his clothes in fragments; swollen and trembling with the lust of battle and excitement. He had a deep gash in his scalp and the blood trickled into his eyes. But he was not surprised nor frightened. He stood there bullet-headed and proud with the men who had dragged him from sacrifice laughing at him.

"So they were going to kill thee, little bullkin," said one.

"Sí, señor," replied the lad, draping the remnant of his rags about him grandly. "I was the bull." And he limped out as if it were the most natural thing in the world that he should be butchered.

Whoever the god that lived in Spain before Christ and Mohammed came, he had almost received a human sacrifice that day.

Anthony decided that this game of el toro was a Spanish religion he could not participate in to the full. And he was glad of that. Still one did not go to the bullfight just to be sorry for the horses, like Arabella Hookham Frere, the sister of the British envoy. Decidedly there was more to it than that.

In April the entire court moved to Madrid to celebrate the Infanta Maria Isabel's first communion. Afterward there was a great state dinner at the palace. Anthony had reasons for always remembering it, although it was an accident that he went and sat where he did.

Beurnonville and Ouvrard had indulged themselves beyond measure at the opening the night before of a new French pâtisserie in the Carrera de S. Jerónimo where the tarts were full of invention, genius, and apricot jam. On the way home they had stopped to drink bottled beer and lemon juice, much admired in Madrid.

The ambassador of France and the envoy of Mammon were soon laid prostrate in adjacent beds at the French embassy. A sudden use was found for large Sèvres vases that had hitherto merely adorned the hall. A state banquet was now unthinkable. So they were represented respectively by the chargé d'affaires, de Calincourt, and Anthony, both scandalously gay at the misfortune of their superiors and their own good luck.

"Let us arrive in the state coach," said young de Calincourt. And they did so, with the precedence of the ambassador, while the Flemish company of the Garde de Corps in their facings of yellow-and-silver on duty in the courtyard came to "present" to the arms of France.

"The madrileños call those soldiers chocolateros," remarked the young Frenchman in rather too loud a voice as they emerged between a wall of lackeys.

Don Tomás de Iraqui, colonel of the regiment of Pavia, immediately came forward twirling his blue-black moustache and scowling. "Permit me, my dear colonel, to congratulate you on the martial appearance of your men," added the young chargé d'affaires hastily. The colonel broke into a blue-black smile under his brass helmet as they passed on.

"Phew!" said de Calincourt, "a close call. That fellow is the devil with pistols."

They crossed the court in the red glare of torches escorted by liveried link-boys. Behind them the heavy coaches of the ambassadors continued to arrive to a continual clash of arms. The rumble of wheels, the voices of men and the low laughter of women were lost in the vague echoes of the vast court. Before them the great palace glowed from one wing to the other with soft, yellow lights and the glitter of crystal chandeliers behind lace curtains in the still unfinished square windows. Above the glazed balcony and between the arches heavy statues of the Iberian Roman emperors looked down from dark niches, while overhead on the balustrade of the flat roof a company of the kings of Spain advanced with stony faces glittering in the moonlight. It was the quality of this façade to make one pause to look up and then hurry past it into the portals.

They ascended the famous state staircase between the marble lions. Lackeys in the livery of Castile, like so many coloured statues, held flaming flambeaus on every fourth step with halberdiers between them who struck the butts of their halberds in salutation on the stone.

As it was half past six, and the guests were arriving rapidly, a continual thumping swept past them upward through the whirling flames of the flambeaus to where the bewigged statue of Charles III grinned at them with his baboon-like face at the top. Here they were met by the Duque del Parque, commander of the Royal Guard, glittering in a gold-inlay cuirass and a helmet bursting into a gigantic white plumed crest. He inquired their names and rank and passed them on to the ushers.

" 'All this will end in a clap of thunder,' says the first consul," whispered the irrepressible de Calincourt as they were led through an endless range of enormous state apartments with ceilings a riot of Tiepolo's tepid frescoes; with velvet, glasses, tapestry, gold-tasselled

485

furniture, and lace. Hundreds of grim portraits glared at them and seemed to march with them down walls lined by stiff guards in jackboots and scarlet-and-blue.

"Here is nothing amusing, all is truly royal," the Frenchman continued as they walked suddenly out of comparative gloom into the glare of the Salón de los Embajadores with two empty and lonely thrones under a canopy at the far end.

The number of guests invited was upwards of three hundred; dignitaries, the diplomatic corps, nobility, and distinguished persons. They assembled rapidly but they seemed to make no impression on the vast room. There was not a single note of gayety or happiness. Conversation went on here and there in low tones if not in whispers. Underneath the oppressive ceiling, where the majesty of Spain, the virtues of dead kings, and the costumes of the provinces flaunted heavily, sublimes rasgos de sublimes ingenios, the company sat weighed down, lost amidst colossal pier glasses and gigantic marble tables; pale under mountainous portières of crimson and purple velvets.

"Apollo himself would be a mere glow-worm here," acknowledged de Calincourt, impressed at last.

It was no small test of the amazing virility and physical brilliance of Don Manuel Godoy that he appeared to shine and glitter even in these overpowering surroundings. His arrival, indeed, served to inject positive signs of life into what had promised to be a decidedly leaden occasion. Despite the almost frantic efforts of several Bourbon sovereigns, who had imported from France the traditions of gayety, the Spanish court had never ceased to retain a certain funereal air. Godoy could by some personal magic dispel this.

Into the dark, straight tunnel of the lives of the royal family, which had as its most gorgeous vista the candles of requiem mass in the mortuary chapel at the Escurial, Godoy came like a ray of sunshine dancing with all the colours of the rainbow along their cavern path. This sunny quality of his nature and a certain dog-like fidelity, a warm, human tenderness and affection had endeared him to both king and queen. They could both afford to overlook his amatory irregularities, they felt, at the price of retaining through life, in the case of the king an unswerving personal friend, and on the part of the queen a lover, who, if he sometimes wandered, always returned. It was a curious and a complicated relationship but it stood the test of tragic circumstances and the long lapse of time.

It was this man, who at the height of his success and favour now entered the room where the subdued guests of the court were apathetically waiting for the sovereigns to appear. Contrary to all etiquette, he was leading the youngest son of the queen, the Infante Don Francisco de Paula, by the hand. A veritable rush now took place in his direction, for no matter how much he was envied and hated he was also fawned upon by all those who had anything to obtain by his favour. And nearly everyone from ambassadors to country grandees had something to obtain.

Some crowded about the little prince, by far the most jovial of the royal family, and listened to his childish wit and gayety, which had already endeared him to the court. This they knew would recommend them to Godoy even more than direct flattery, for he was passionately attached to the brown-eyed little prince whose father he was said to be. In the meanwhile Godoy conversed gayly with all who approached him, from time to time making an anxious survey of the apartment as if he were looking for someone who was expected but had not yet arrived.

Young Don Francisco, skipping across the room through the wilderness of gigantic chairs and tables, jauntily commanded the musicians to strike up. This they hesitated to do before the sovereigns had appeared, but they were also embarrassed to refuse "His Highness," who, just tall enough to peer over the top of a balustrade, menaced the first-violin with his royal wrath. They compromised, and a much subdued pianissimo of wood instruments began to breathe through the vast apartment the "Woodland Moments" of Bec-cherini.

The atmosphere immediately cleared. A great many people were soon on their feet moving about. The giant chairs seemed to disgorge the company from their maws. The sound of light chatter, an occasional laugh with an undertone of reserved masculine voices, and ringing sallies in the high, clear voice of young Don Francisco marked the turning point of the evening.

While Don Juan Antonio Melón, the king's cham-berlain, moved about distributing the cards of prece-dence with names of the ladies that gentlemen were to take in to dinner and the precise order of the proces-sion and seats at table written upon them, the empty thrones at the far end of the room seemed to have withdrawn even farther into solitude and aloof disdain.

Anthony found himself pledged for the evening to the dowager Countess of Montarco, a raw-boned widow, whom he thought Don Juan took a certain malicious punctilio in pointing out seated under a Gargantuan purple curtain on a green chair. This com-bination not even her liberal rouge, diamonds, rice powder, and the stiff brocaded dress and whalebones of the previous reign could entirely overcome.

"Jésus!" whispered de Calincourt, who had drawn Mlle. Zinoviev, the ravishing young daughter of the Russian ambassador, and was looking over Anthony's shoulder at his companion's fate, "my hearty commis-eration. But she is very pious, they say."

An hysterical yodel on a flute, representing an Italian composer's idea of a nightingale luring his mate by moonlight, made the moment none the easier to bear. It looked like a terrible evening. This was the court of Spain and etiquette had spoken. Yet Anthony could not bring himself to bow before the old harpy under the portière. He looked about him in despair.

There were plenty of young and beautiful women in the room. That one, for instance, talking to John Hook-ham Frere. Her back was so perfect in that long white gown and her golden hair in a little Grecian knot was reflected so delightfully in the pier glass that one did not even need to wait to see her face hidden just then by the ample shoulders of Albion's statesman. She tapped Frere on the shoulder with a fan and he moved away laughing. Anthony drew in his breath—and held it.

It was Dolores who had been in eclipse.

The lights in the room seemed to eddy . . . he saw clearly again.

Since his arrival in Madrid he had scarcely thought of Dolores. He had not even inquired. After Angela the world had seemed denuded of possible mates. Rose girls—they sold flowers for the buttonhole—no more. And now—now he was about to conduct the horse-faced relict of Don Quixote in to dinner. Intolerable.

"Never! Something *must* be done about it."

A lackey approached him. "Señor, His Highness has been trying to get your attention for some time."

He looked up startled. Godoy was undoubtedly looking his way anxiously and nodding. Anthony crossed the room rapidly to where he was standing somewhat apart from the crowd talking to Don Luis. A Milanese suit of mail with its visor down on a stand just behind them gaped open-mouthed over their heads.

"Where is M. Ouvrard, Don Antonio?" inquired Godoy anxiously. "Several matters have arisen which I hope to discuss with him tonight."

Anthony explained the banker's condition so vividly as to cause even Don Luis to smile.

"Most unfortunate," said Godoy, "but you can probably tell me! Have the pay chests for the dock-yards at Cadiz left yet?"

"His Highness as Grand Admiral of Spain is naturally solicitous for the payment of our loyal mariners," said Don Luis with a grimace. "His zeal does him great credit," he remarked as he bowed and withdrew. An angry flush rose in Godoy's cheeks.

"They leave Wednesday. Do you wish them delayed?"

"Ah, you anticipate me, Don Antonio. It would be

most kind of you to request M. Ouvrard to do so. Another, a more pressing need for the money has arisen here at Madrid. The queen—" he stopped for a moment—"Her Majesty has decided to refurnish her equipages—new horses. *Devil take that old man!*" His resentment against Don Luis suddenly flamed out. "To tell you the truth he is most exasperating. Er—no, you will not say anything, I know. You have been most discreet since you have been here. I observe you do not even ask for anything. Others are not so. I have done much for Don Luis." He drew Anthony into a window-niche and continued rapidly.

"I want you to do something for me, Señor Adverse, a personal favour. You will not regret it! Some time ago Don Luis had me obtain for him special letters to the viceroy in Mexico, commissioning him to expedite the silver shipments from there. Tonight he coolly informs me that *he* has decided it is unnecessary for him to go." Godoy grew livid as he said this and paused.

"I am sure we should not want his interference at Mexico," replied Anthony instantly on his guard. "We have already our own agent at Vera Cruz, you may recall."

"True, I realize that. Our arrangements have altered since the commission was granted. But, I shall be frank with you. *I* wish to have Don Luis go to Mexico."

Anthony started. "It might ruin us," he began.

Godoy laid his hand on his arm. "Don't you see the old man has built his own trap? If M. Ouvrard will only suggest to His Majesty that the services of Don Luis will be *required* in Mexico—"

"But—" objected Anthony.

"Why, then," continued Godoy, "I will simply have the instructions to the viceroy in regard to his mission slightly altered. He can be sent into the northern provinces of New Spain to expedite the flow of silver from the mines. Oh, I shall do his rank and ability full justice! He shall go as governor of the most distant desert province in the north. Of course, I forget its name. Santa Fé, isn't it?"

"I am sure I can't enlighten Your Highness," replied Anthony pondering.

"Well, there are maps, fortunately," sighed Godoy, "large ones with very small towns on them. Now you will speak to M. Ouvrard about both these matters, won't you?"

"I shall speak to him tomorrow," said Anthony, "It is most necessary he should know."

"Bueno!" exclaimed the Prince of the Peace. "Recollect we are dealing with a dangerous old man."

"I am well aware of that," said Anthony with conviction; "but there is a little matter in which I wish Your Highness would aid *me* tonight."

"So?" said Godoy.

"I have been placed at table with the lovely countess yonder—" cried Anthony, pointing out the old woman across the room.

"Ah, she should have a parrot perched upon her shoulder," grunted Godoy.

"—and I wish," he continued, "above all things to sit next to that lady over there."

The sleek, black eyebrows of the Prince of the Peace, which lay across his brows like two smooth, fat leeches, crinkled slightly and then lay still again as if they had resettled to their congenial task.

"Doña Dolores de Almanara, eh! Well, your taste does you credit, señor. But I warn you. Her husband is a rich old Mexican hidalgo whose jealousy is as deep and dark as his mines. And the lady is rumoured to be cold."

"I had the honour of her acquaintance some years ago in Cuba. The rumour is not well founded."

Godoy laughed. "I will do what I can for you," he said. "Let me see. Go and fetch the roll of precedence for me from the chamberlain," he said to a servant to whom he beckoned. "Peste!" he cried a few minutes later. "Don Melón is bringing it himself."

"I merely wished to remind myself of some of the names from the Russian embassy, Don Juan," roared Godoy, running his eye down the lists.

491

"Most difficult," squawked the old man who was quite deaf and thought everyone else was, too. He pulled Godoy down to him confidentially. "Barbarous!" he cackled into his ear, "but all spelled correctly, every one correctly." He went off tapping the paper with a knowing air.

Godoy and the Russian ambassador exchanged a wink. He then turned to Anthony.

"It is impossible to change the rolls, señor. Once the order of precedence is settled only a revolution can alter it. But the gentleman who is to sit with Doña Dolores is standing over there." He pointed out a tall, cadaverous young man. "He is the Count Lancaster of Portugal. There is royal blood in his veins, so ancient that even the English have forgotten it. His tastes are expensive and his barren estates covered by thin sheep. He might be willing to exchange cards. Well, I shall do all I can for you. I will introduce you myself." He sent for the man.

"Everything at the court of Spain can be bought except the crown jewels," murmured Godoy as the count approached, "and they are at present in pawn. It would be most embarrassing if Their Majesties should have to conduct the next audience in dull pastes. I trust you will endeavor to delay those pay chests, Don Antonio."

"I shall speak to M. Ouvrard," repeated Anthony.

"This gentleman has a gallant request to make of you," said Godoy to the count as he presented him to Anthony, "which I shall esteem it a favour to have you consider." With a brief inclination he left them alone. . . .

"Your proposal is to say the least unusual," said the Portuguese, his dark face showing no signs of relaxing in hauteur. "The privileges of birth are valuable, especially if one does not happen to possess them," he added condescendingly.

"And even if one does they may be valuable," countered Anthony.

The man shrugged his shoulders.

"I am prepared, señor, to bet a thousand dollars on the turn of our dinner cards that you think they are worth no less."

"I *have* gambled," confessed the count smiling, "but always for high stakes. May I ask you to point out the lady whom you wish to bet I will sit with?"

With great misgivings Anthony pointed her out.

"Corpo de Bacco," cried the count. "It is the angel of constipation herself!"

"Two thousand!" murmured Anthony, prepared to bid his entire fortune by millenary units. "Paid to-morrow in new-minted coins."

A gleam as if from bright reflecting metal appeared upon the countly forehead. "Señor," said he, "your princely offer does adequate homage to my rank."

They laughed and exchanged their seating cards.

With a feeling akin to the anticipation of a crisis Anthony left the empty suit of armour gaping by the wall and went to find Dolores.

She saw him coming toward her half-way across the room. Her eyes widened and her hands for an instant fell into her lap and lay there. Then, with that familiar gesture that he remembered so well, she reached up as if to arrange flowers in her hair. It was the ivory comb that he had sent her from Africa which she was wearing. She settled it a little more firmly. And then, moving her fan slowly, waited calmly enough.

And so he knew that she had not forgotten him.

———————————

Whether Dolores' husband was of as jealous a nature as Godoy had indicated, Anthony never discovered. He had only time to present himself with the usual compliments and to watch the white-haired Don Guillermo limping off to find his own table-companion as hastily as his old legs would let him. Then the doors at the far end of the room were suddenly thrown open and a master of ceremonies carrying a

493

black wand announced, "His Majesty, the King of Spain." A white wand next announced the queen from the opposite doorway, and the entire company rose to their feet and crowded forward to be able to see and make their bow when the sovereigns should appear.

First there came walking backward out of the king's corridor the Duque de Bejar, an emaciated grandee with spidery legs. He was clad in bright yellow silk and held aloft with a trembling arm a heavy, silver candelabrum whose candles guttered in the draught. He heeled outward and hindward as if making geometrical leeway, covering a remarkable stretch at each backward step.

Immediately afterward there appeared in the arch against the glow of flambeaus behind him a tall, thin man with fine silver hair and a curved nose that projected over his chin. He had remarkable, childishly-blue eyes that matched the colour of his faded coat pulled down from one shoulder by the weight of the mighty gold and diamond star flashing on his left breast. A tight, white vest laced with gold, crossed by a blue ribbon and buttoned with emeralds, seemed indispensable to prevent his chest, which had already slipped, from collapsing about his knees toward which it pendulously tended. He wore leather hunting breeches splashed with deer blood, which he was said never to have changed except for his coronation and marriage, white hose gartered with scarlet ribbons, and Cordovan shoes with red heels and gilt buckles. The most remarkable thing about him was his circular profile and the bland futility of his florid countenance frozen between affability and surprise. Charles IV of Spain walked eagerly. All in the room bowed low and the ladies swept him curtsies, to which he replied by a slight inclination from what had once been his waist.

The king took his place standing before the empty thrones and was followed across the floor by a detachment of halberdiers clad in yellow-and-scarlet silk who trod noiselessly and whose steel weapons glinted with

494

bloody lights. They seemed a fitting prelude for the sinister figure which followed them.

Gloomy, pale with ennui, and with his hands blotched by futile chemical experiments, Ferdinand, Prince of the Asturias, followed his sire apathetically, dressed in dull green and indifference, haunted by his grinning tutor the Canon Escoiquiz and by Matias his valet and the slinking Moreno, an assistant barber, who had been given court rank and followed him like a cat. He bowed to the court unseeingly and stared at it with a fixed snapping-turtle expression to which his curled side-whiskers, his low beetling brow, his parrot-like nose and Austrian jaw protruding far beyond his upper lip combined in a startling effect of senseless ferocity. All the vices of the Bourbons and the wrong obstinacy of the Hapsburgs were stamped upon his features and lay dormant in his soul. He had the flushed cheeks of a tyrant when excited. He looked like Caracalla come back to trouble the world in knee-breeches and a mulberry-coloured stock.

The Prince of the Peace, the ministers Cabellos, Cabarrus, and Don Gaspar Melchior Jovellanos; the knights of the Golden Fleece, and the Order of Christ, having ranged themselves about the sovereign in an open circle glittering with orders—the queen at a given signal advanced.

To Anthony, unused to the bizarre whims of royalty, the guard of Her Majesty provided a shock.

She was announced by a pack of Spaniels whose long, shaggy, brown bodies with almost invisible feet dragged their lengths slowly out of the door before her and undulated over the green carpet like so many silky caterpillars crawling across a leaf. A dozen or more of these pop-eyed harbingers, which all seemed to be suffering from Graves's disease, always preceded her.

Queen Maria Luisa, slightly double-chinned with a fine dark down on her upper lip, dressed in the new Greek style but with diamond pendants in her tall wig, paused in the doorway with superb bare arms clasped

495

with pearl bracelets locked with rubies, her ivory shoulders shining under the candles, and curtsied to her spouse.

A gasp of flattering but sincere admiration arose from the court. The eyes of Godoy sparkled. The queen was leading by the hand the Infanta Maria Isabel still in her communion costume of Mirandella lace so ancient that a golden-ivory glow tinted her wintry veils crowned with lilies and sparkling with frosty diamonds. Alone among the royal family she was wholly beautiful, arch, gracious, with exuberant colouring, a princess with a certain poetry in her glance, and a deer-like walk. At sight of her, in whose honour they had assembled, the ancient Catholic loyalty of Spain burst into a discreet enthusiasm of welcome and the rapid clicking and breezy opening of painted fans.

"The rest of the royal children are being put to sleep, I suppose," whispered Dolores, which were the first words he had heard from her. She was smiling a little sadly. "I envy the queen her beautiful daughter."

"Yes, but not I when I am looking at you—señora," he said, putting her gloved hand over his arm.

"Don't," she said. "We are only going in to dinner, you know. You must promise me not to forget that. Do you hear me?"

"Yes," he replied, "I think so." And to himself, "Do I hear you? Am I really standing here with your arm, Dolores, on mine? 'What will I do in Europe?' "—he remembered asking himself that at Gallegos long ago. The thought of a naked orphan scuttling through a big iron gate at Livorno flitted before his eyes. And now —how that boy enjoyed dreaming he was in the palace of the King of Spain. In a moment it would all vanish. . . .

She looked up at him laughing, understanding his mood, and pressed his arm. "They will be going in in a moment now," she said. "I am glad . . ."

His Majesty, who always argued with his chief musician Olivieri, at last had done. The brassy "Royal March" of Jarnowick boomed out. Marshalled in perfect precedence, the procession set out led by the royal family and the halberdiers.

To Anthony, who now looked down at Dolores, with flushed cheeks and a mounting excitement and delight, the evening had already taken on that aspect of a gloriously-coloured opium dream, mad with light and splendour, which it never lost. He accepted it and doubted it at the same time as one of the supreme surprises of life that seemed too vivid to be true.

They moved through a succession of colossal corridors with groups of guards and domestics standing about lost in the perspective; with the gleam of steel and the intense scarlet of the robes of the papal nuncio Casoni burning on ahead of them; with the music growing fainter behind.

Past an endless succession of cabinet treasures and objects swept from the wealth of Europe and the Indies the glittering serpent of the procession dragged its length slowly.

"C"-shaped tables with the guests seated on the inner side surrounded the banquet hall facing the long, straight board of royalty and the ambassadors at the far end. Mersquitz, the queen's confessor, said grace assisted by two acolytes and an almoner. From the royal chapel farther down the corridor the scent of stale incense mingled with the fading sweetness of the pastoral lilies with which the tables were trimmed.

Into these unexpectedly complete and perfect hours which had been vouchsafed him, Anthony merged himself, forgetful of the past and future, wholly content to be sitting next to Dolores and listening to her voice. And she also. Yet the intense and quiet joy of the man and woman who were meant for each other, who revelled alone together in an island of mutual consciousness amid the other feasters, was all the more poignant for their awareness of what was passing in the river of time.

All the dying order of the Old World surrounded them in its deathly complete and uniformed ranks. Constellations of heavenly-named honours winked from the breasts of the exalted gentlemen to the crescents and jewelled comets caught in the cumulus clouds of ladies' hair.

Liveried servants were pouring vintages of the early years of the eighteenth century; years long vanished. The last cask would soon be broached, the last toast flung. Versailles the beautiful and perfect epitome of all this was dark and silent. The world had swept around it and gone on. "All this will end in a thunder-clap." Only the calm before the storm surrounded the palace of the King of Spain, where the great company feasted while the mellow, saffron lights glowed from its windows like the dwindling radiance of a pharos that is being left behind. Without giving a thought to it, every feaster felt that he was rapidly floating away from it down the river of time. That feeling gave the zest and spirit of the occasion. It lent it its *carpe diem* and its hectic glitter; the "high" taste to meats that had been kept too long; its hysteria of loyalty for the feeble crown.

In the midst of this it was surprising for Anthony and Dolores to find without an effort an island of refuge in each other, a still and quiet section of eternity in time. Yet within it they lived more vividly than those without. It was quiet and still there only because it was nearer the whirling centre of things. No wonder that for a few moments they played, and played successfully, that they had always been together and would never part. "If it were only so," was the overtone in both their minds.

So it mattered very little what they said to each other.

Anthony found himself telling her of his wanderings and his hopes. He even spoke to her of Angela and the child he had left behind. And in a few words she understood.

"Do not doubt," she said, "go on. You have done well. I fail greatly, too." He long drew comfort from that.

They did not allude much to Cuba. All but the fact

of their meeting there now seemed childish—the moonlight and the garden. They knew they had grown now into man and woman moving in strong sunlight and deep shadows; moving on into the afternoon of life with night ahead.

Her marriage had served to link enormous haciendas in Mexico. There were no children. Don Guillermo was old. A faint flush stole into her cheeks. After tonight Anthony must never try to see her again. Pastures must be kept welded to silver mines. Her life was lived for the peons on those estates. Much could be done for them and she was devoted to that. They would return to Mexico soon. She travelled great distances there, rode hundreds of leagues on horseback. Beyond El Paso del Norte was a great wind-swept country she loved.

They had a great house in the capital, a serene city, where Popocatepetl and the "Sleeping Woman" dreamed under blankets of snow in the soft sunsets and dawns. Names, places, a whole life and world he had never heard of flashed into hazy being mixed with strange glows and exotic colours while she spoke. Her husband was rich and powerful. His wife could be very useful to many. God had bound her to him. Yes— she was content.

A blast on a silver trumpet brought their world to an end. They plunged back into time. The company rose. The last toasts were drunk standing amid a wild enthusiasm of drawn swords. Castile and Aragon hailed their king.

"Viva el Rey . . . viva . . . viva . . . viva."

He saw her elderly husband come and lead her off. They bowed politely, distantly.

"Farewell, ma doña."

"Adiós, Don Antonio." She smiled over her shoulder.

Royalty left by a private passage and the guests streamed out to lose themselves in the vast, deserted apartments beyond.

He stood for a moment looking at the chair where she had sat.

"Has the señor lost anything?" said an officious lackey coming up.

"Sí."

The man began to look under the table. Anthony laughed and walked out. Under his feet he felt faint earthquake shocks. The organ in the chapel was rumbling. The king insisted upon requiem mass every night after midnight before he slept. Don Carlos himself frequently impersonated the corpse. The stones of the palace were trembling.

In the courtyard he met Don Luis. The old man was waiting for him excited about something.

Don Luis wished to make sure that Ouvrard would *not* suggest to the king the advisability of his going to Mexico. He would make good the matter of the coach with M. Ouvrard. It was not his fault that he had it. It was equally embarrassing to return it or to explain. Would Anthony smooth the way to an interview with Ouvrard? If so, Don Luis would be glad to tell Anthony certain matters of great interest concerning the past. That would explain everything. Don Luis wiped his brow.

"I shall speak to M. Ouvrard in any event," said Anthony.

"*But not until you have seen me first*, Don Antonio!" cried Don Luis. "It is something that concerns you vitally. You must hear it now. Come to me at the hour of the siesta, tomorrow. There will be none to disturb us then."

"Very well, I shall do so," said Anthony, after a little pause.

At that Don Luis took him by the arm and led him across the court.

"Your promise brings a great calm to me," he said. "Old ghosts must be laid. I wish to be haunted no longer. I am old. I shall soon be joining them." He laughed languidly.

"Let us begin now," he added. *"Señor, I wish you to meet my wife."*

Anthony turned, startled. They were standing by the coach under the arches. From the window a white hand was extended to him.

"All that was a long time ago," said the voice of Faith Paleologus out of the darkness. She spoke in English with her old Scotch accent.

"Eh?" said Don Luis.

Her hand moved searching blindly. Anthony bent over it and kissed it.

The great coach drove off into the night leaving him alone under the stars.

———————

But the meeting between Anthony and Don Luis, in which Anthony was to have learned "certain matters of great interest concerning the past," never took place. The accounts of the good and evil of a lifetime cannot be balanced by explanations, and the books closed. The balance is carried forward into other lives; into actions and reactions until equilibrium results. Only time can liquidate in full. Don Luis' offer had been made too late.

Madrid can be lonely, sultry and hot at the hour of the siesta. Its vistas, especially in those quarters occupied by the houses of the wealthy and powerful, are frequently silent and deserted. The inhabitants are only slumbering. Yet, except for the rumble of a distant carriage or the sleepy whine of a beggar in some comfortable alcove, the streets are as dead as those at Pompeii. The feet which traversed them only a few hours before seem to have vanished and to be no more.

On the afternoon following the state dinner Anthony stood before the gate of the Casa de Azuaga ready to keep his appointment with Don Luis. He peered through the grille into the patio. There was no one in sight.

The house was a little sinister. One of the oldest in

501

Madrid, it had been constructed at a time when defence could not entirely be overlooked even in domestic architecture. There were heavy, iron gratings, a frowning, blind façade, and a decidedly narrow gateway calculated rather to prevent than to welcome ingress. In fact, the old building vaguely reminded one of Don Luis himself. Although the patio had been planted with trees and a formal garden laid out in it, only a dim glimpse of greenery could be caught from the street through the grim shadow of a tunnelled arch.

Anthony knocked. An echo answered. He tried again. There was still no sign. He became impatient, for he had an appointment with Ouvrard later and he had no doubt but that Don Luis would take his own time. At last he reached in, unlatched the gate with some difficulty, and walked into the patio.

After long thought the night before, he had arrived at the conclusion that he was no longer called upon to refuse to hear what Don Luis might have to say. He had kept his promise to John Bonnyfeather. The mystery of his birth, whatever it was, now concerned him and Don Luis alone. Don Luis would soon be dead, in the natural order of events, and he alone would be left to know—whatever there was to know. He could not even be sure that Don Luis could reveal the mystery of his origin. But he thought so. For a hundred reasons he felt sure of it. If Faith knew—he could not help that. So far as he was concerned he would continue to keep the secret safe from the world, if there was anything dishonourable in it. And—he seemed to see Faith's hand coming out of the darkness and to hear her saying, "All that was a long time ago."

There was nobody in the court. He started across the central path of the garden toward the door. Perhaps Don Luis himself was waiting for him there. A hedge momentarily cut off the view of the house. The path led to a central oval.

There was a new arbour here that had recently been planted about a formal fountain. A statue stood above a pool. He looked at it casually—and could scarcely prevent a loud cry of surprise. It must be the Other Bronze Boy, the missing twin. At least it must have been cast from the selfsame mould. This was not a mere resemblance.

And then—as he examined it more carefully—it was borne in upon him with irresistible conviction that it was actually his old companion of the convent pool, the Bronze Boy! If he knew anything in the world, he knew *him*. He knew his own brother!

There was the dimple in the left-cheek, the mark of a stone he had once thrown at the Bronze Boy—a thousand years ago, it seemed now. It was the only thing Father Xavier had ever whipped him for. For a moment he felt himself wriggling on the knees of the priest again and shouting with pain. One did not forget things like that. Sacrilege!

If Don Luis had committed a personal assault upon him he could not have been more outraged than he was now. Indeed, that would have been only physical. But to have ravished this statue away from the fountain and the tree—that was to commit a spiritual nuisance in the holy place of his soul, to dissolve its bonds of permanence with the past. The refuge to which he had returned in dreams and reverie had been invaded and spoiled beyond repair.

It seemed horrible to him that the Bronze Boy was in the possession of the Old Man. He did not care how it had got here. The fact, with all its overpowering emotional significance, its mysterious and sinister overtones, was more than he could bear.

He understood by the nervous shock with which he had blundered upon that part of himself held prisoner here what the nature of the influence of Don Luis and of Faith had been upon him. He apprehended it figuratively; with a mental nausea; with a blind fear of fate, and of the power over him which it implied.

No, he would never see Don Luis now. He could not even bear to think of it. There was something here which impelled him to flight; to go on forever thrusting off that influence; denying it, balking it. If the Bronze Boy was a prisoner, Anthony at least could still walk out of this garden free. He had better do so while he could.

"Go?"

Yes! go now. Go to the new world beyond the ocean, torn loose like the Bronze Boy from the roots of the past—perhaps even from the roots of the great tree. Be it so. What did it matter who his parents had been; their names? They were dead to him. He had come out of darkness. But in the courtyard he had been born into the light. And the light remained in him. It was part of him. He could take that along—forever.

He stooped down and washed his hands in the fountain. He held them up like a cup before the statue and let the stream run out through his fingers like the years that had gone. And then he held them up to the light, cool, empty, and clean.

"Farewell forever, old playmate," he said, looking up for the last time into the antique-youth of the bronze face with its blind eyes watching the water with that mysterious archaic smile.

He felt as though that stare followed him as he walked out. Then he discovered as he neared the gate that after all he had not been alone.

Sancho lay asleep on a bench by the wall. His back had been turned that way as he came in. At least he felt sure Sancho must have been there then. Sancho evidently took his siesta seriously. His sleep was audible; a kind of faint purr. On the ground beside him was Juan's guitar.

It was the same one Juan had bought that day with Cibo in Havana. The one with the Indian's face carved below the bridge. He picked it up very quietly and holding his hand across the strings walked out with it. It would be missed.

Don Luis, at least, would know he had made his call.

Half an hour later, like a troubadour in a cab, he

arrived at the embassy to keep his appointment with Ouvrard.

Anthony was determined to leave now without further delay. Even Ouvrard had to agree that it was foolish to wait any longer for letters from Parish. If the Mexican scheme was ever to go forward, it was time to be preparing for the reception of the bullion at New Orleans.

They spent the balance of the afternoon winding up several matters. Ouvrard talked a great deal. He was still recovering from the dire effects of beer and lemon juice and lay abed looking out wistfully over the covers as though he would like to plead with Anthony to remain, but did not know just what inducements to offer him or exactly how to go about it. Anthony had always been a puzzle to the banker. There were several awkward pauses now in their talk. It seemed as if Ouvrard was always on the verge of a sentimental appeal which he just managed to avoid. At any moment— Anthony winced.

"I have sent a draft in your favour to Herr Nolte. The size of it may surprise you—pleasantly," said Ouvrard at last, glad to find himself talking business. "At any rate it will obviate any foolish arguments on the value of your services for many months past. Knowing you as I do, I was bound to anticipate that. Now no protests. It is too late. You underrate the importance of money, Anthony. I am sure you do. I tell you you cannot have too much of it."

"Let us not argue that now, monsieur," replied Anthony. "I suppose it all depends upon what you think you can buy."

Ouvrard shifted his hands uneasily and changed the subject. "As for Don Luis and the coach—my boy, *leave that to me*. I think Godoy's suggestion of bundling Don Luis off to Mexico rather a good one. Don't you?"

Anthony said nothing. He sat looking grim.

"Ah, yes, poor Juan," cried Ouvrard. He reached out for the guitar and examined it. "Undoubtedly his."

505

He shook his head and began fumbling with the strings. "Poor Juan!"

"I shall speak to the king," said Ouvrard, picking out a little tune with his thumb. The guitar jangled as he put it down.

"Wild, wild is the child," its ghosts of music seemed to say.

The vision of the barrier beach at Gallegos suddenly obsessed Anthony. He rose and stole out of the room for a moment.

He had meant to go back. But once in the hall—where the Sèvres vases had all been replaced—he decided not to do so. He simply went down and got into the carriage.

"To the Prince of the Peace—and be smart about it," he said to the driver. He would get what letters he needed to the authorities at New Orleans and his passport from Godoy—now.

"Hey," cried Ouvrard looking out of the window, suddenly aware of what was up. "What am I going to do with this guitar?"

"Keep it. It belongs in Spain."

A look of pained surprise sat on the face of the banker.

"Just throw me down my hat that I left on the table. It's all I want," cried Anthony.

Ouvrard's pale face disappeared from the window.

The carriage drove off.

"Hein," said the banker, looking out again, "that clever young fool has gone! And without . . ."

He sat on the edge of the bed holding the empty hat in his hand. His eyelashes were suddenly wet. He gave the hat a kick.

"If he had only left me his shoes!—those beautiful boots he had on the first time I saw him—why, the history of Spain might be different."

Suddenly he cringed. He was alone now, absolutely alone again. He gave a great French gesture of resignation, climbed back into bed, and pulled up the clothes.

A few days later Anthony and Simba sailed from Lisbon in the good ship *Lothair*, Captain Edgecombe, bound for New Orleans.

END OF BOOK TWO

BOOK THREE

In Which the Tree Is Cut Down

Chapter Seventeen

By the River of Babylon

"**L**AND HO!"
Out of the blue bowl of the Gulf—a distant
black line like the rim of the cup brimming
over. The tone of daylight shifts. The free rhythm of
the ripples alters. The sun no longer splinters dazzling
upon a glaze of pure blue. Over a vague waste of tan-
coloured miles, where the water still retains an implacable urge southward, the Mississippi languidly
pumps the yellow blood of a fat continent into the
slowly contracting and expanding heart of the sea.

It is astonishing to pass over the frothy line of a
tide-rip from the dominant, cobalt sparkle of the Mexican ocean into the yellow domain of the river. Objec-
tively it is like watching a cloud-shadow loom suddenly
over a wide, bright landscape; subjectively it resembles
the alteration of the underlying mood of the soul from
one of calm cheerfulness and hopeful anticipation to
another of vast and vague melancholy, sustaining itself

bravely only by an assumed outward gayety from the onslaught of some subliminal fear.

All the low coasts of this region of the world are dominated by the mighty vein of the planet for which there is no sufficient name. The tongue of man is not adequate to compass the idea of the feeling which the river engenders in him. His favourite names for it are like the names of ancient gods, attempts not to name it at all.

"Mississippi," he whispers, hoping the river will not hear him. "Father of Waters," said the Indian, paying it rhetorical honour, as though it were the ghost of the old man of the tribe to be appeased. And "Ol' Man Ribah, Ol' Man Ribah," sings the black man with a nice, deprecatory humour while he teases the banjo, artfully absolving himself by laughter and melody from a thought that is too great to bear.

How ritualistic is the negro's whimsy by the waters of his river of Babylon! He is not the only exile there.

Here in this low-country of moss-swathed swamps and forests, where the oldest continent bleeds to death slowly through a million bayous and half-stagnant, tidal estuaries, all men build along the banks like muskrats, hoping that the river will let them stay. Man gambles with this river as he gambles with much the same kind of thing on the slopes of sleeping volcanoes. He gambles successfully for a while—and then he loses. And his character partakes of that. He says little about it, for like other gamblers he is silent about the main chance and very gay about the little ones; melancholy and mercurial; that is your Creole.

For him the feeling of the river is always present. Like no other river it hangs like a sword above the head. The memory of it is like a ghost walled-in and murmuring. Through the generations, under the flat, horizonless sky, its secret tongue speaks menacingly. "*Mississippi, Mississippi, Mississippi*," lisp the ripples, nibbling along a thousand miles of levees. The bells of passing ships reach land faintly here. For on its lower

512

reaches men do not speak of the "banks" of this vast river but of its "coasts."

———————

Forty-two days out from Lisbon, with the weeds hanging in submarine beards from her copper, the good ship *Lothair* picked up its Cajan pilot off Breton Island and headed for Octave pass.

"We're sho' gettin' somewhar and *to* somethin'," chortled the cook's boy as he whacked open a huge watermelon the pilot had brought.

"First fruits," thought Anthony, "of a land running over with sugar and water, if rumours and the present view of things mean anything at all."

He and the three other passengers, two Scotch clerks and a Portugal wine merchant, looked at the endless expanse of swamp on all sides of them; at the muddy eddies fuming past the side, secretly disappointed at this newest part of the world, a land literally in the making, an abode as yet fit only for mud-turtles and alligators.

Glistening bones of trees lined the low, muddy beaches, shoals, and islets. Like the skeletons of defeated monsters, at a little distance they seemed to strew the legendary battlefields of time. Now and then the hand of a bleached and fallen giant drifted past the ship, writhing slowly in the current.

Here was decidedly no note of welcome. Here was indifference. There was even a hint of warning.

Through the days to come in America Anthony was often to be reminded of that. An indefinable hint in the ragged forests, an indefinite high-light like a gleam from outer space in the sunshine—and he would remember. He would become homesick for something missing; nervous about some gigantic-nothing that cast no shadow but was there. To him, at least, there was something in this continent that waited and was inimical to man.

513

In the south he found it only brooded. Yet even there, because of it, no one could ever keep still. To escape it men inveterately sought the company of one another. It did not matter whom. Anything or anybody, not to be left alone in America. The mouth of the Mississippi spoke the truth.

"Whist, Mr. Adverse," said Mr. M'Quiston, the representative of Scotch drapers who clothed the Creoles extensively, " 'tis no prattling mountain bur-rn we've blundered upon." Swinging at anchor in the mouth of the river, alone in the limitless glow of a yellow, summer twilight, even the ship seemed inclined to agree with him.

Out of deference to certain piratically-inclined gentlemen farther up the coast at Barataria, the captain had omitted a riding light. But nothing hove in sight. Only a half-submerged log nosed the ship disconsolately all night. *Bump*—all the watch sat waiting. Surely the thing must have gone by now. They would continue their yarns and then—*bump* very stealthily, and then *bump* again.

Nothing is so disturbing as to have something underneath trying to get into a ship.

Yet the next morning was bright and cheerful enough. A steady southwind swept them along bravely against the current. The low country ahead, as the "coasts" closed in, sparkled with lakes and glowed with dark, green forests of shining leaves. From the bayous and creeks ragged, long-haired habitans in dugouts came out from time to time to trade with them. After exchanging muskrat skins and snowy heron-plumes for calico and knives on the deck, they departed again into the cavernous mouths of their muddy streams.

Low, weathered houses behind veils of live-oaks and grey mosses began to look out across the water higher up. A few plantation boats were occasionally glimpsed, like moths adrift. Once a line of carts drove along a levee as though on the surface of the water and disappeared into a wall of distant canes. A Spanish warship flaunting her gorgeous colours and under bare poles drifted down, and much to their relief, drifted past.

"A guardacosta," said the captain, "bound for Havana or for Vera Cruz."

It was the only ship they passed on their hundred-mile voyage inland. Against the current they now moved sluggishly. On the afternoon of the second day they close-hauled to round a great bend in the river and came in sight of New Orleans.

Anthony climbed to the masthead. He had come half-way across the world to make this place his home, and he cast his eyes upon it with a peculiarly quickened though unconscious insight. It was the first general impression that forever coloured the infinite particulars which were to follow. To an eye used to nothing but the loneliness of waters during a long voyage, New Orleans conveyed instantly the impression of a small but rapidly growing port.

The wide, yellow road of the river, golden in the afternoon sunshine of a hot July day, swept with a magnificent curve bulging eastward and swinging west again. In the curve of the crescent the little city and its plantation suburbs stretched for a distance of about two miles from horn to horn.

It was long but it was not wide. It was only a new moon as yet.

Immediately before him, in the very centre of it, lay a cluster of three or four thousand roofs. Red-tile and slabs covered low Mediterranean-looking buildings in a bank of dusty trees. The eye ranged rapidly over this settlement—from which the blank face of a stuccoed barracks or convent stared out boldly here and there—to take in the shingled roofs of wooden houses amid gardens just behind. Then the fields and the swamps began again. There was a canal and a basin. A few straight roads and snatches of bayous led to the eastward. And beyond them, making itself visible by a mirage-like blink, lay the levels of Lake Pontchartrain.

The nucleus of the town was still enclosed in ruinous

palisades and swampy ditches. These ended in two bull-dog forts upon the levee from which floated the gold and scarlet of Spain. There was a small battery in the centre. But the city had already burst out of this military chrysalis and extended along the levees north and south.

Two guns fired from Fort San Carlos near the canal now certified to the town the arrival of a foreign ship.

A few carts kicking up the dust behind them, and slaves in bright turbans, that could be glimpsed here and there making their way somnolently along the levees, were rapidly replaced by a crowd of brightly-clad people who swarmed out of the streets of the town onto the water front. For the most part they stood waiting about a market house near the battery.

A boatload of officers, in gold braid and bright blue uniforms, put off for the ship. Somewhere under the trees in the park-like square before the cathedral a military band began to play. Over the quarter-mile of water between the ship and the levee came the "March of Fontarabia" and the smell of the town.

Ships did not anchor here. They tied up to the levee. North of the market a fleet of them stretched away, their spars at all angles. Altogether Anthony counted fifteen; about ten of them Yankees, he judged. The rest were Spanish and there was one Frenchman brightly defiant with a tricolour. But that was by no means all the commerce of the port. Anchored three or four deep farther up the river along a sandy flat below the levee was the strangest assortment of craft he had ever seen.

Arks, and keel-boats, rafts with log-huts upon them, canoes, and flat-boats formed in that direction a kind of slatternly water-city that served to extend the town. Naked children bathing, the distant barking of curs, cattle and horses grazing along the swampy banks completed its rather unkempt and miserable scene. Even a mile away it was obviously the most raucous part of the water front. It clamoured shrilly. It whooped. It relieved itself with bare backs pointed toward the

Creole town. Its savage citizens wrapped in midnight, coonskins, and delirium tremens terrorized the few sedate residents of the Faubourg Ste. Marie as they ruthlessly rolled homeward through its vegetable gardens. Such was the "Batture," or the American landing.

The old French and Spanish town was in fact already besieged on all sides by the Americans. Those who descended upon it out of the illimitable northern forests congregated upon the Batture. Those who sailed to it from Georgia and the Carolinas and Floridas anchored their schooners in the Basin Carondelet and the canal. There was always a small fleet of the latter. Every year there were more of them.

As Anthony descended he paused in the maintop to look down upon one of the curious craft from up-river which came drifting within a few yards of the ship.

It was an American edition of Noah's ark built of logs with the bark on. From its square windows looked forth eagerly the bright, hungry faces of children, houn' dogs, and calves. It glided majestically to the sweet sound of lowing. Somewhere within its bowels an egg was being laid.

Noah himself in an iron-grey beard, coonskin cap, and ragged deerskin fringes leaned against the immense, oak-like rudder over its stern and ruminated upon the wad in his cheek with the selfsame motion as the cow in the window below him. Occasionally with a superb aim and insouciance he spat into the cow's eye. A rattling of horns followed.

"Seth, you kep' that po' critter rattlin' the hull way down from La'ville," complained his wife, who was seated on the flat roof in a rocking chair, cuddling her youngest wolverine. "For *gawd's sake* shift that wad t' t'other cheek!"

Those lining the bulwarks were close enough to see the requested transfer of ammunition successfully accomplished.

Surveying the ship somewhat contemptuously from his own slab quarter-deck, the hero in deerskins looked up at the gentleman in the maintop with a smart twinkle in his eye.

"Wall, stranger, be ye lookin' over the real estate?" he asked.

"Real estate" was Greek to Anthony, who contented himself with a friendly nod.

"There'll soon be a pa'cel o' fine lots in the city. It's boun' to grow."

"I hope I shall find mine a pleasant one," replied Anthony, moved to take the man seriously by something simple and earnest in his expression.

"Eh?" said he a little confused. "Oh—sartin! Thar's lots o' corner lots left. Me, I'm low-katin' lower down." He gave the oar an impatient shove.

"Now jes' let the river take you, Seth," put in the woman, beginning to rock. He looked at her gloomily. "Easy for her," he said and spat over the new side.

As Anthony came down the ratlines, the Spanish port-officers boarded the ship. They were accompanied by a lanky man in a black suit much too tight and short for him. His bony wrists extended far below his cuffs and he wore a huge beaver hat with a black scarf about it.

The passengers' luggage had been piled on deck since early morning and an iniquitous inquisition by the self-important colonial officials began.

Never in any place in Europe had Anthony experienced anything like it. It was quite evidently the intention of the "authorities" to confiscate the major portion of his extensive outfit for themselves. Everything he had brought with him was against the law to import. Yet their most strenuous objections were instantly quieted by the exhibition of his passport signed by Godoy— which set the chief officer to bowing and scraping— and a bribe so pitiful that he was ashamed to offer it.

"Ah, if the illustrious had only said he bore letters to the governor! Ah, ah,—and—ah! And where would his nobility reside ashore?"

"Where, indeed?" Anthony had scarcely thought of

that. Yet now that he had "come home" at last, what roof was there to shelter him?

With a knowing look the customs officer in a string of Spanish civilities that made Anthony laugh presented the lugubrious gentleman in the beaver hat as one likely to solve all difficulties—"both in life and death," said he with a grin, leaving them together.

From his vest pocket, where he also kept a mossy comb, the man in black, who began to address Anthony in vile Spanish, now drew forth a large tortoise-shell card. On it was written in Spanish, French, and English:

Doctor Melancthon Conant, LL.D.
Purveyor, Victualler, Jobber, and Undertaker
at the port of New Orleans
in the Province of Louisiana.

"Speak English," said Anthony impatiently. "You're an American, aren't you?"

The man straightened up with evident relief and shoved his hat back to an impudent angle. The scarf of official mourning floated out gayly from it in the breeze.

"I calalate I am," said he. "I'm from Bosting."

Anthony looked at him doubtfully. There was something confusing to him in the man's whole make-up. He was patently pious and yet whitely-obscene at the same time.

"—and an official in a Spanish port?" he asked.

"Wall, stranger, we from our vicinity dew rize most anywhar we're put."

"Putnam?" said Anthony reminiscently.

"No, no, Conant!" cried Melancthon, again extending the tortoise shell card.

"I made myself handy here, ye see. I drawed the teeth of Don Andres Almonaster y Roxas in his own front parlour when I came here nigh seven years ago, and I drawed the wisdom teeth of the governor settin' in the Cabildo—painlessly. And he remembered me. I

519

larned Spanish and I made myself ginerally useful." A sudden gleam came into his eye. "Ye don't happen to have a gum-boil or two that needs lancin' right na-ow, do ye?"

"Not one," said Anthony almost regretfully.

"No, I can see yer ivories shine like a two-year-old hoss's. But jes' keep me in mind when they dew begin ter ache. It takes 'em a long time ter rot out. But I don't believe sufferin' helps the character. I give relief. Keep that in mind—*Melancthon Conant gives relief*."

There was no getting away from him. They were preparing to make fast to the levee now. But the man had him fairly buttonholed.

"It's a boardin'-house I want to talk to ye about. Na-ow I kin fix ye up fine." He rolled his eyes over Anthony's luggage, calculating. "A gen'leman like yourself with sound teeth, money, and warm blood ul want to live free and easy. I have a little arrangement with a free lady of colour in the Faubourg Ste. Marie. Mother Marie can cook elegant gumbo. It's lonesome. Ye can make all the noise ye want. And yet—it's right convenient. Comfortable beds and lots of company for 'em."

"I know that kind," said Anthony reminiscently.

"Ye mistake me, 'deed ye dew. Few of these gals bite, an' if they dew ye don't care. *Y'seewhatamean?*" He whisked off his hat and drew out of it, as though he were producing a rabbit, an extraordinary leather-folder which he began to unroll with a sacerdotal calm.

"Gin-u-ine portraits," he whispered, "drawed from life by a imigree artist, late of Versailles. Cost me a dollar apiece." He stood waiting for his fish to bite.

On the leather sheet now dangled before Anthony's eyes, each in its own little pocket and painted on thin ovals of ivory, were a baker's dozen of miniature masterpieces of pornography. It was impossible not to look at them. St. Anthony himself would have succumbed. The artist had been genuinely inspired. The girls, who ranged from the colour of the ivory itself to warm

520

chocolate, reclined upon the hotbeds of the imagination dimpling with hospitality. The chef-d'œuvre was reserved for the centre. It was round instead of oval, and a stepchild of the Renaissance. It represented Apollo begetting a demigod upon the body of a ravished octoroon.

"That 'air one," said Mr. Conant, "is painted on alabaster and cost me five dollars. Hold it up to the sun. Ain't it life-like? It's transparent."

"It certainly is," admitted Anthony; "but I don't think I'll be stopping at Mother Marie's."

"No?" said Melancthon, shocked into a dream of disappointment.

"No!" said Anthony. And then suddenly inspired by the devil, "But you might show these to Mr. M'Quiston, the Scotch gentleman yonder. He looks lonely."

"He does!" said Mr. Conant and hurried over to him.

Leaning against the bulwark, oblivious to the confusion of the preparations for landing going on all about him, Anthony watched the pantomime.

Mr. Conant approached Mr. M'Quiston with so pious an air that the Scotchman's face, which at first registered its usual suspicion at the approach of any stranger, suddenly shifted into the right Sabbath expression appropriate and habitual at the approach of the cloth. His hands, however, remained firmly in his trousers pockets, where he always thrust them at the too-near approach of anybody.

Mr. M'Quiston had a small purse in each pocket. He kept his eggs in two baskets.

Mr. Conant's introduction of himself was so lugubriously proper, however, that it was obvious Mr. M'Quiston felt he was being welcomed home. His face relaxed. Still he extended no hand. Mr. Conant's hat came off. Mr. M'Quiston looked a little contemptuous. And then—the leather rabbit came out of the hat.

It fell before the face of Mr. M'Quiston like a theatre curtain. There was a long pause while Scotland met Art and Lust wrestled with Avarice. Virtue triumphed.

521

Suddenly Mr. M'Quiston was heard trumpeting through his nose.

"Mon! Awa wi' it, awa wi' it! Dinna ye ken I canna e'en afoord to ogle sic a maisterpiece? Dinna ye ken ma breeks air auld sax years sine?"

Mr. Conant became the personification of sorrow again as the rabbit folded up.

Mr. M'Quiston was then left fully revealed, flushed and pop-eyed, paralysed from the waist down.

"Thank God," said he, "thank God my pockets are still like new." Mr. Conant's threatened appraisal of Mr. M'Quiston's teeth was completely ruined by the long and disturbing merriment of Mr. Adverse.

There was undoubtedly a silvery contagion in the sound of Anthony's laughter. There was nothing cynical about it. It was merely exuberance tickled beyond restraint at the vagaries of the human scene. Because the laughter seemed somehow to include himself in his own laughter, people were seldom made angry by it. Even the canny Mr. M'Quiston did not feel it was exclusively at his expense. As the power of motion was slowly reconferred upon the Scot, he was forced to grin with something like the expression of a pumpkin redly illuminated from within.

But in so flat a neighbourhood as New Orleans Anthony was himself startled to find his laughter being echoed back to him in the tones of his own voice. He turned toward the levee to find the source of the phenomenon.

And it was thus for the first time, but by no means for the last, that Anthony saw the ever-memorable Dr. Terry Mitchell holding his sides over certain spiritual implications in the fleshly scene.

He was not more than ten paces away, leaning against an old pile on the levee. He had evidently been enjoying thoroughly the events on the deck just below him while the ship was being made fast. His three-cornered, cocked hat drooped just a little over one eye that narrowed and twinkled as he took a pinch of snuff and remarked:

"So you are not going to be staying at Mother Marie's?"

With a flourish of a fine cambric handkerchief he removed at once all traces of tobacco from his nostrils and laughter from his lips. But his smile would break out again.

"I rather thought not," he added.

They both laughed again. It was curious, but a genuine fellow-feeling had already sprung up between them.

"Have you any ideas about a comfortable and decent place to stay?" asked Anthony.

"Very decided ones," replied the gentleman on the levee. "The combination you mention is rather rare in this our raw little Babylon. Unless you have friends here—"

"None in America," said Anthony.

"Neither have I," said he. "But I do happen to know of a well-kept little place. No ravishing ladies. Will that? . . . No? Well then, suppose you leave your baggage on board for a while and come along and see for yourself. I'm not a hotel runner, understand!"

"Of course not," said Anthony, and crossed over the levee. "I'm much obliged to you."

"I'm thinkin' I'll be coomin' along wi' ye mysel' the noo," said M'Quiston, who had followed him.

"Who the devil are you, sir?" snapped Mitchell, bridling. "I'm damned particular about my company."

"I'm frae the fur-rum o' McTavish, McTavish, and McTavish o' Glasga," said M'Quiston.

"Tell them all three to go to hell," blazed Mitchell.

"I'm thinkin'," began M'Quiston—but what he thought remained known to his Maker only. Three Kentuckians standing near by in coonskin caps and long knives broke out into a loud laugh in his face.

"Come on," said Mitchell grinning.

"Howdy, cap'n, howdy," said the three with great respect to Mitchell as he passed them.

"Good day to you-all," said Mitchell curtly enough, and followed by Anthony, led the way up the levee.

What appeared to be snow scattered here and there Anthony now discovered was cotton. There were a few bales of it to be seen along the levee, but they were outnumbered a hundred to one by casks of sugar and barrels of rum with which most of the ships were loading. Despite the great heat that shimmered along the water front, the scene was an animated one.

Black stevedores dressed in a mad variety of rag-fair costumes pushed, hauled, and carried for the most part on their heads, unbelievable loads of all kinds. There were only a few drays rumbling along dustily now and then. Wheeled transport of any sort still seemed scarce. French and Spanish sailors, an occasional officer or soldier in faded and ragged uniforms made up the bulk of the whites. In the shade of a long building on low white pillars, as they neared the crest of the embankment, negresses with bright turbans sat before piles of fruits and vegetables, chattering and shrieking with excitement over the arrival of a new ship. Some Indian squaws remained in one corner impassively weaving baskets and smoking, watched over by a tall brave with a single feather in his hair, who stood wrapped in a tattered blanket and imperturbability. Pickaninnies fat and gangly sprawled and raced everywhere, getting into everyone's way and out of it miraculously. Already Anthony was familiar with the begging phrases of the place, "Lagniappe, misu, lagniappe, masa, una picayune."

"Me Mericain," insisted one little nigger racing up the levee after them out of the yellow waters of the river itself. "Me savvy Goddam." He broke into a stream of hair-curling profanity, and then, dodging Mitchell's boot, pranced on ahead of them to overtake Mr. Conant, whose long, black scarf floating back from his beaver hat had gone on before without a single prospect to follow it. No lagniappe being forthcoming,

524

the boy put his hand to his nose and began to sing to Mr. Conant at a safe distance:

> "Si to te 'tit zozo
> Et moi-memo mo te fusil,
> Mo sre tchove toi-Boum!"

"Boum, boum, boum," cried the boy for every step. Several other booming urchins joined the first, and Mr. Conant, amidst general laughter, was boomed off the levee.

"He is the only white man in New Orleans they would dare to do that to," remarked Mitchell. "We both follow the medical profession, by the way. I as a surgeon; he as an undertaker. I like to introduce him as my 'distinguished colleague.' The story goes that he steals girls' corpses for Madam Marie's house and brings them to life for the night only. They go back to the tomb at cock-crow. Saves payin' 'em wages, y' see. Well, I wouldn't doubt it. Wait till you see the girls."

They now reached the top of the levee, a grassy street stretching along the stockaded walls. There was a gallows, with a number of children of the better class watched by their black nurses while at play about it. They found themselves looking across the Place d'Armes and down the Rue Ste. Anne.

It was the very heart of the little city. Hitherto Anthony had been repulsed rather than attracted by what he had seen. But the view before him was now so novel and interesting that his heart began to go out to the place instinctively.

Behind the doubtful shade of a line of dusty willow trees were the graceful arches of the Cabildo, or Hôtel de Ville, and the still towerless cathedral. These buildings stretched clear across the bottom of the square. Except that the place was unpaved and had patches of withered grass on it here and there and the charred remnants of an old picket fence, it already looked ancient and might have been mistaken at first glance for the square of almost any minor Latin town. The sides were lined with various small boutiques and restaurants and by the Halles, a large open building serving as a general market for vegetables and gayly fluttering merchandise from embroidered muslins to gaudy handkerchiefs. But if the architecture was familiar, the crowd was novel and unique. It could have been assembled only in Louisiana.

The guard mount of the garrison was over. The band had marched off to the barracks, and the crowd, which had gathered to watch it, was breaking up. Fiery Creoles carrying rapiers and dressed in the extremity of Paris fashion rubbed elbows with voyageurs, habitants, and coureurs de bois. Cajuns and breeders from the Attakapas prairies, their blue homespun cotton redolent of cattle, bawled at one another and trod on the toes of émigré nobles accompanied by yellow sirens from San Domingo speaking a honey-smooth, island French. Flaxen-haired Saxons from the "German Coast" a few miles up the river gathered about the coffin-shaped carts of Catalan and Provençal marchandes selling callas. Milk and coffee women walked about on the outskirts of the crowd like giants, balancing immense cans on their turbaned heads. At this hour they did a roaring business as did the hawkers of piratically comeby trinkets shouting "Barataria, Barataria." Dirty Houma and Natchez Indians stalked grimly about in silent contrast to the constant chatter of blacks of all types, hues, and outlines, dressed in braguet, shapeless woollen shirts or an old bag.

And surrounding all these, apart from them, seeming to be waiting for something to happen, or to be about to close in upon the noisy and happy Creole crowd, stood the Américains, the *Kaintucks* from the unknown northern forests, the Long-knives who had borrowed the sullenness if not the stoical expression of the savages with whom they had fought. They lounged in doorways or leaned against walls in small groups or strode with quick, long, nervous strides, brushing people aside. But whether they stood, sat, or walked, they all chewed tobacco and sprayed the landscape so copiously as to guarantee them the right of way in all directions as though they were the messengers of kings.

> "American rogue,
> Dressed in nankeen,
> Stealer of Bread,
> From Mr. D'Aquin."

quoted Mitchell under his breath, as a flat-boatman in homespun jeans reeled past them out of a barrel-room shouting, "I'm a bahr-eatin' cattawampus. I'm a child o' the snappin-tartle."

"Lord, *must* they come here, too?" he muttered.

"This gets in your blood," he added, waving his hands about the square. "I hate to see it turned into a hog-pen. It's a nice little country. Hope you'll like it."

"I think I shall," said Anthony.

"You mean you reckon you will," he laughed. "It's some time since I've heard English spoken.

"This is the Rue Ste. Anne. The Hotel Orleans, where I see our Scotch friend is going, is up Chartres there to your left. If you don't like my little hang-out you can go there, too. Mind you don't step off the banquette. The dust is knee-deep now. When it rains the mud comes to your hips."

They continued thus for four or five blocks, walking on the keels of old flat-boats which in some places still bridged swampy holes, until the brick and stucco houses ceased. Then they passed through a break in the old stockade into a square surrounded by gardens and unpainted cypress houses standing on piles. There was a marine basin here with a canal leading out into a tangled swamp beyond. A number of schooners lay at anchor here as though moored in the square itself, with men in great straw hats loafing on their decks.

"This is the corner of the Place Publique and the Rue

Claude. You may want to remember it if you desire to send your luggage here," said Mitchell. He swung open a wicket gate and led the way toward a neat, frame house whose ship-like balconies overflowed with flourishing potted plants.

"Ba'tiste," he roared.

A completely bald man, round and with duck-like feet, appeared at the door, flourishing a spotless cloth and wiping a long-stemmed glass.

"Ha! Miche le docteur, vat?"

"Here is another guest for you, and he's a gentleman, by God! Show him that corner room overlooking the basin. I want some human company. What's for supper?"

"Ha! hit his not so mooch, no, de stuff, has hit his dose cook, and hi hám dose cook."

Ba'tiste patted himself on the chest as he said this, and Dr. Mitchell patted him on the back.

And so it was that Anthony came to stay at that curious combination of club, hostelry, and rendezvous of gourmands known as "Ba'tiste's," and to the inner initiates of the octagon room off the kitchen as the "Bald Duck."

The long voyage, conveying the impression that Europe was infinitely remote and all its experiences left behind him forever, the novel scenes and interests into which he was suddenly plunged, but above all, a determination to make the life of the new country into which he had come *his* life—and to look to the future rather than the past for guidance—all these things had their full effect upon Anthony.

He phrased it to himself by saying that the "weather of my soul has cleared." He was released into action again without having the springs of it stagnated by such a complexity of moral, social, and practical considerations that they could scarcely flow at all. The "guilt"

528

of the past had been liquidated—he could go on. But in a new way. For there is a profound difference between proceeding on the basis of cautious experience accumulated out of the past and on hope based on one's predictions of an untrammelled future.

Freedom was not merely a political theory in a new continent, he found; that was the least part of it. One could disregard politics and government altogether, if one wished to, by simply following the track of the sun for another few degrees westward. Freedom existed in the ease of untrammelled actions. One was accountable to one's self alone. At least Anthony did not forget his accountability to himself. A good many others did, he found. His experience was like that of many other immigrants. Perhaps he differed from the majority of his fellows only by being a little more conscious of the moral nature of the change.

One immediate result of his cogitations on the subject of the new country was that his own affairs and his desire to find himself settled in Louisiana with a genuine stake and interest in the community rapidly thrust the machinations of Ouvrard and his Mexican silver not into the background, but into a purely secondary place in his regard. That is, within a few weeks after his arrival he found himself pushing forward the plans to transfer the bullion to Parish not as the end for which he had come, but merely as the means of weaving himself more deeply into the interests of the place. Yet for that very reason he worked more feverishly and circumspectly than if he had felt himself to be a mere agent acting for Ouvrard, the Barings, and the Hopes.

He found a large pile of mail awaiting him from Parish, who had kept writing to Anthony, at New Orleans instead of through Ouvrard's bank at Paris. David's letters, Anthony was amused to see, began anxiously about four months previously, became plaintive, then indignant, and were now, if not actually menacing, furious, to say the least.

Where was Anthony? What in God's name was he

doing? Did he not know that Parish had perfected his arrangements at Philadelphia, Baltimore, New York, and Charleston, and that Lestapsis was now in Vera Cruz and had drawn the first instalment of $750,000 from the Mexican treasury? Then woe on woe. Lestapsis had chartered a ship himself. It had arrived safely at Philadelphia but the insurance was 60 per cent. Out of 200,000 silver dollars only $80,000 remained.

It is plain [wrote Parish] that New Orleans is the only practicable port of entry. I beg of you in the name of old friendship, if for no other consideration, to perfect your forwarding operations with Lestapsis at Vera Cruz, and act. Otherwise, the capital advanced by the Hopes and Barings for my mercantile operations here will be exhausted. My bills are already accepted only at a mischievous discount . . .

P. S. Mrs. Parish and Mrs. Udney add their solicitations to mine.

"That is going a long way for David," thought Anthony, smiling a little to think how cool Parish had once been about the necessity of any agency at New Orleans. "So Mrs. Udney is with Florence in Philadelphia." He tossed down the letter, laughing. "Well, it looks as though I shall have to act. Ouvrard did delay me too long. No wonder David is anxious."

So he went down to the levee and without further ado chartered the schooner *Ariel*, Captain Clemm of Baltimore, to carry letters to Parish at Philadelphia, announcing his arrival and the reasons for his delay.

Within two months I hope to have the produce of Mexico under way to you [he wrote]. We had better arrange a convenient cipher, by the way. My regards and assurances to both the ladies. The

530

"postage" on this letter comes to $750 gold—
I have paid it.

Captain Clemm sailed, not without having spread a rumor that there was a madman in town who paid in gold instead of depreciated colonial livranzas. As a consequence Anthony found that anybody would do anything for him, short of committing suicide.

Standing in the shade of the old Boucheries, Anthony watched the *Ariel* drop down the river until she disappeared around the bend beyond Makarty's plantation. He wished he had thought of sending Florence some of the Indian bead-work which a squaw was just then displaying at his feet. But on the whole it was better not to irritate David.

Dismissing so casual a thought easily, he purchased some black Havana cigars at another stand, and enjoying his first genuine smoke in some months, for he had run out of the weed on the voyage, he strolled on down the levee in an enviable frame of mind to deliver his letters and the dispatches from Godoy to the governor.

He had no idea, as he crossed the little parterre at the corner of the Rue de la Levée and Toulouse Street, that he was making history. It was all most casual. The governor's "palace" was a plain one-storey building along the river front. It looked like a tavern. There was not even a military aide on duty. He wrote his name on a card and scribbled under it—"bearing dispatches for His Excellency from the Prince of the Peace"—and gave it to an old negro servant. Presently he was led through the hall to the back piazza screened with lattice-work through which some grooms could be seen rubbing down horses in the stable-yard at the end of the garden. Two gentlemen in shirt-sleeves, with their coats hung upon the backs of chairs, were seated on the porch discussing a bottle of wine.

It was hard to tell which one was the governor. In fact, neither of the gentlemen was himself at all sure about it. One was the French prefect Laussat sent by

Napoleon to receive the transfer of Louisiana from Spain according to the terms of treaty; the other was Don Manuel de Salcedo, Spanish governor-general, who had arrived from Havana in June to turn the province over to France.

The transfer had never occurred.

Since March Laussat had been waiting at New Orleans for General Victor to arrive with final instructions and the French troops necessary to garrison Louisiana. The English prevented. Neither troops nor further instructions had arrived. In March Napoleon sold Louisiana to the United States. No rumour of that event had as yet percolated to New Orleans, although it was now almost the end of July.

The interregnum, for it amounted to that, had been one of good-natured anarchy. The Spanish authority had officially continued, but the loyalty of the Creoles had always been for France, and Laussat had been cheered and fêted wherever he appeared. He and Salcedo had spent most of the time on the piazza in their shirt-sleeves, waiting for orders, drinking endless quantities of rum lemonades as the days grew hotter, and questioning Fortune.

Instead of Louisiana's being transferred to France, 2,190 livranzas had been transferred to Spain in the person of Don Manuel by the means of a dice box.

"Perdu!" said Laussat just as Anthony entered the porch—and the dice settled. "Peste," he whispered. "What can this fellow want? He looks like an American."

"In that case he will want everything," said Salcedo. "He says he bears dispatches from Madrid."

Anthony was received civilly but rather coolly, he thought. He delivered Godoy's letters to Salcedo.

While the governor withdrew a little to read them, he and Laussat sat conversing. The Frenchman was starving for news, and Anthony's Parisian gossip, less than a year old, came to him as though a breath of fresh air from the boulevards had swept through the porch lattices. He wanted Anthony to stay and talk all day. He called for a bottle of champagne.

Suddenly they saw that Salcedo was laughing. The paper with a long seal like a watchfob on it shook in his hands. He peered over the top of it and looked at the French prefect and laughed again.

Silence—a sense of something impending fell on both Laussat and Anthony.

"Do you know what has happened, Laussat?" grinned the Spaniard. "Your master has sold Louisiana to the United States."

"What!" cried the Frenchman, sweeping the dice up from the table in a gesture of agitation. The new-bought bottle of champagne tottered and rolled to the floor where its contents gurgled away unnoticed. "Impossible! What do you mean?"

"Listen to this," said Don Manuel—and read a passage of his letter from the Prince of the Peace, which even included the bathtub incident. That had rankled in Godoy's mind. He had not been able to keep it out of his dispatches, which in some respects were always childish.

Salcedo was not given to reading his confidential dispatches before strangers. The dramatic opportunity of surprising Laussat had simply been too much for his Latin temperament to withstand. He now turned to Anthony a little apprehensively.

"If you please, Señor Adverse, you will say nothing about what you have just heard in confidence here. It might be awkward to have such a rumour spread about."

"The news is already general property in Europe, Your Excellency. For that reason I have said nothing about it here. I supposed it was generally known."

"Quelle différence?" said Laussat. "I shall return to that beautiful Paris, now—and shortly."

Then they fell to questioning Anthony about European news. He spent the rest of the morning with them, and parted on excellent terms.

"I shall do what I can to speed the Mexican affair as the letters requested. But it will not be much now, I am afraid," said the Spaniard. "I shall soon be going, I suppose," he added a bit sorrowfully.

"Yes," thought Anthony, "and leaving behind you the first chance for a really good squeeze. Too bad!" He did not neglect, however, to thank Salcedo and whetted his interested hopes by suggesting that an early shipment of bullion from Vera Cruz might be arranged if one of the guardacostas could be employed to bring it over.

The governor shook his head with evident regret. "Impossible," he said. "We should then have to divide our little percentage with the navy at Havana." Then his face brightened. "I tell you what you do, señor. See the Lafittes!"

"A good idea!" cried Anthony, who had no idea in the world who the Lafittes were. "I thank you."

They bowed most affably.

Two days later a ship from Bordeaux, which had managed to give the English the slip, brought the news of the sale of the colony to the United States. The province was first to be turned over to France and then delivered to the Americans. The town seethed with excitement. The Creoles were wild with disappointment, the Americans with joy. The Kaintucks swaggered uproariously and built a great bonfire down by the Batture. While the serenos went about announcing in French and Spanish it was "a clear, dark night and all well," the glare of the leaping flames cast a portentous red glow along the levee and the Kentucky rifles cracked in triumph as Mr. Jefferson's health was drunk in raw, white whiskey, and rum.

But there was one American who did not toast Mr. Jefferson and the United States. He was Dr. Terry Mitchell.

The doctor belonged to that small but rather influential group of Americans from the eastern seaboard cities both north and south, who already some years before the purchase of Louisiana had begun to invade New Orleans. They were a curious conglomeration of far-seeing merchants, many from Philadelphia, down-easters looking for cargoes, adventurers, and gentlemen whose brilliant operations at home had conflicted with the restraints of criminal statutes or the common law.

All these, to distinguish them from their western fellow citizens, the Kaintucks, were known to the Creoles generally as "Yanquis." It was not until a great many mortgages, maturing in Boston, and the fiery protests of Virginians and South Carolinians annoyed to the point of pistols-in-the-morning taught the Creoles better, that it was realized in New Orleans that Yankees came only from the sacred, interest-drawing soil of New England.

"Dr. Terry M.," for so he loved to refer to himself, was among the first to have shot a Creole gentleman for making this geographical error. The community had not at first understood so nice a distinction. Even the unfortunate M. La Chaise, who had died in great agony with Dr. Mitchell's bullet in his liver, was perplexed to the last as to just why he had been challenged and polished-off. Only three things were evident to everybody in regard to Dr. Mitchell: first, he was a gentleman of enormous punctilio and the courage of his convictions; secondly, he was a miraculous pistol shot; thirdly, he was the best surgeon and doctor of general medicine that anybody had ever heard of—never mind what his colleagues might say.

Everything else about Dr. Mitchell was to everybody else, save a few friends and admiring cronies, obscure. In the entire city during his life there, there were only two people who ever fully understood what he laughed at. One of them was Anthony Adverse and the other Edward Livingston. It was only when he was

535

with Dr. Mitchell that Livingston could fully find the way to laugh at himself.

The three dined together, if not invariably, at least so frequently in the octagon room at the Bald Duck that *Mitchell, Livingston, & Adverse* before long began to take on some of the aspects of a firm name.

Shortly before Anthony's arrival, Livingston had left Ba'tiste's, where he had long been living, for quarters more convenient from a business standpoint uptown. The doctor had felt Livingston's absence keenly and had for that reason seized upon Anthony as a likely companion. He had not been mistaken in his impulse, he soon ascertained, and the acquaintance in the course of a short time had rapidly become an enduring one. Ba'tiste took no other lodgers. Livingston's room remained vacant, and the roly-poly little proprietor devoted himself to cooking those suppers for which he was famous.

The establishment certainly was an unusual one. The permanent residents consisted of the fanatical little cook himself, his two gentlemen boarders, and three old female slaves. These all lived in the house. At the other end of the garden, facing the square convenient to the Basin Carondelet, was an old stable that had been converted into a bar and barrel-room. It was known as "The Little Jesus" and catered exclusively to the crews of the schooners, Floridians and Georgians for the most part. These were served and kept in bounds by one William Wilson from Maryland and his powerful, wrestling Welsh assistant David Ap Poer.

Ba'tiste thus managed to serve all classes in the city with the exception of the Kaintucks. His house in the evenings was a rendezvous for Creoles who knew how to appreciate his art. They had their own salle à manger. A steadily growing clientele of the Yanquis was accommodated for the most part in the octagon room, while in the converted stable on the square Minorcans from Florida and Crackers from Georgia looked

Messrs. Wilson and Ap Poer in the eye, not always calmly.

Mitchell, Anthony soon discovered, lived upstairs in a suite of rooms with a fiddle, several cases of duelling pistols, a medical library and a chemist's outfit that gave his apartments somewhat the appearance of an alchemist's den. The doctor was greatly given to experiments. He made up his own prescriptions, and rose regularly every morning at seven o'clock for pistol practice in the garden.

The house had been built by the French military engineer Piuger and the octagon room was evidently a domestic by-product of his art. Mitchell's quips on it were endless. Anthony had the bedroom above, which partook of the same octagon shape. He became greatly attached to his high, sunny coign with its many windows looking in several directions: west by the roofs of the town; northward over plantations to the broad, yellow expanse of the river; eastward down the long canal through the swamp to the levels of Lake Pontchartrain. The basin and its shipping lay directly before him, almost at his feet.

With the doctor's fiddle crooning away down the corridor and some of his own things laid out, it was not long before he began to feel at home. To be sure, it was far, far away from—everything. And the sunsets with the high clouds like plumes blown back upon themselves towered vastly above the rude, flat lowlands. The swamp pools amid the cypresses glared with dull red eyes. It was lonely at that hour for Anthony Adverse—but then there was supper. The crowd began to drop in from the town. There were wine and cards and billiards if one wanted them. And there was always Dr. Terry M.

"I never meant to come here," said Mitchell, who had at last grown a little confidential one rainy evening,

537

sitting over some mulled wine. "But the country itself gets in your blood if you stay—along with the fever and other things. I like it. And I know I'm going to die here. I mean of old age." He smiled a little. "If the smart Americans could only be kept out, lower Louisiana under the dons or the French might grow slowly, the only way anything worth while can grow, into a fine, mellow little country. Now we are going to have floods of democrats, oratory, humbug, Protestant anarchy, and the world and man for sale at the river mouth. I hate to see it. I do! Damn Mr. Jefferson, and damn Bonaparte for selling out, I say." He held up his glass and looked through it reflectively.

"Well, don't join me unless you feel like it. But since you're soon going to be a citizen of the great republic by force of the treaty you might as well know something about it." He drained his glass and set it down.

"About forty years ago I was born in Philadelphia. I remember the place with some amusement now. My mother was a Quaker girl who was thrown out of meeting for going on a pic-nic with my father on First day. The result of their crime was a nice little house on the Wissahickon—and myself. Nevertheless, I was brought up in an atmosphere of disgrace. My father was the rake-hell of his family, because he decided to live on what he had, like a gentleman, instead of working like a navvy. And he would never have me baptized. I inherit his temperament, which he once described as a cross between Lucifer and a mule. That means he didn't believe things just because people told him. He wouldn't take orders. He liked to kick people when they tried to drive him. And he had a pride that lasted longer than any Christian conscience. Naturally great trouble for me has ensued. But I like it, and I can shoot crows with a pistol." He looked up at the ceiling.

"I remember once sneaking into a Quaker meeting with my outcast mother. We sat for two hours in a cold little room. At the end of that time an old rogue by the name of Fox had a revelation from God Almighty that the taxes in the third ward were too high. The God of Pennsylvania was speaking. He is the personification of political economy and Ben Franklin is his high priest. Morality consisted in making correct small change, never mind what you did with the rest, and doing your necessary reliefs away from home. The German farmers used to bundle.

"You don't know it?

"You go to bed with a girl to save firewood, but you have bags on to prevent accidents. It's a sort of venereal blind-man's-buff that saves fuel and virginity at the same time. I saved the fuel.

"So father sent me to Edinburgh to keep me from being married to a field of cabbages in Lancaster County, and to learn how to have my revenge on humanity by practising what is called medicine.

"I came back to Philadelphia after the late glorious Revolution and found things had gone from bad to worse. Everybody was now just as good as everybody else, even a little better. I met a young fellow by the name of Wistar who had interesting theories about medicine. They were lucid theories, and they started me thinking. My family, I found, except father, had all been patriots. That means they fought for their pockets against the king's and tried to pay for the war in paper money. It didn't work, of course, and they had to invent a government to take the place of the Parliament and the King they had driven out. They wrote down their profoundest thoughts on the subject in Philadelphia and called it macaroni. A West Indian adventurer by the name of Hamilton has reinvented collectable taxes and solvency for 'em. An uncle of mine, by the way, drew the map on which the United States was laid out during the treaty. The map is only partly accurate.

"Well, I went through a yellow fever plague at Philadelphia and then sailed for Nassau, where I heard a great many decent Tories from Virginia and the Carolinas had gone. I spent a year on a barren island called

Eleuthra, living on turtle eggs and memories of Edinburgh, and then took ship on impulse and came here. So now you have me.

"My own case is only a particular in the general mess, of course. But there were a great many people who felt just as I did about the glorious Revolution. They moved away from it; some to Canada, and some to the West Indies. I came here. And now I am going to be made a citizen of the Republic by treaty again.

"You can remember this about Americans, since you're going to be one too. There are two main kinds: those who come from east of the Alleghenies and those who are born west of them. 'North' and 'South' is what they talk about among themselves, but that difference goes only as far as the mountains. West of the mountains they are all what they call 'Kaintucks' here. The Kaintucks aren't Europeans any longer. Here is a rule for dealing with them that I ought to charge you money for: Treat every Westerner as if the world had just been created Tuesday; it is now Wednesday and you are a passive thunderbolt delighted to meet the first and only man."

"What about the Easterners?" asked Anthony.

"Three general kinds—" began the doctor, "but here comes our friend Ed Livingston. You've often heard him talk. He's one kind. Fine old New York family—caveat emptor. A little careless about municipal bookkeeping at home. Finds the climate of Louisiana permanently congenial; not nearly so hot as New York when he left it. A little worried about extradition and the text of the new treaty . . ."

"What's that?" said Livingston, who had caught the last phrase and turned scarlet.

"Sit down, sit down," cried the doctor. "I was just talking politics with Toni, the ex-blackbirder here."

It was now Anthony's turn to burn under the collar.

"Look here, Terry—" began Livingston.

"Nonsense, nonsense!" shouted the doctor. "What is the past, the Constitution, or a treaty between friends?

Ba'tiste, three bottles of burgundy, some of that white Spanish soup, bisque of crayfish, and poulet and rice à la Creole. What do you say, gentlemen? Or would you rather have it pistols-in-the-morning?"

"By God, you're a card, Terry," said Livingston as they laughed and fell to. "Now I have a little proposition I want to make to you gentlemen."

A roar followed. Livingston always forgot that he always began supper that way. But this time he succeeded in interesting them. Like so many other propositions, all that this one needed was someone else's capital to demonstrate it. . . .

"How would a hundred thousand silver dollars as a first deposit do?" asked Anthony.

Livingston reached forward searching his face. "Do you mean that?" he cried.

"I certainly do."

"Told you he was lined with it," insisted the doctor. "Ba'tiste!" He rattled the empty bottles.

"Now you fellows listen to me," said Anthony, his eyes beginning to sparkle.

Anthony had waited for some time before he had seen fit to reveal to anyone the nature of his business in New Orleans. But the opportunity offered by the rainy night and the two whom he had now come to know well enough to have confidence in had not been lost.

Livingston's "proposition" had been to start a "Merchants' and Planters' Bank." It was, of course, to be a bank of issue. When the American régime was installed, he hoped to be able to bring enough political influence to bear to have his bank designated as the depository for federal funds. Upon these an unlimited issue of wildcat money in banknotes could be issued.

"And then," said he, "there will be the Indian funds. The Natchez will eventually have to be paid off for their land. The specie will come from Washington. We can pay the Indians in banknotes and hold the coin as deposit. No one needs to tell the Indians how to cash the notes. Probably not many bills will come back from so great a distance. It will be clear, clean profit. All that we need is Toni's Mexican silver here to start the ball rolling. The knowledge that large shipments of bullion are being deposited with us is all that we should want to establish our credit. Do you really think you could arrange to leave a hundred thousand on deposit with us between shipments, Toni?"

"Provided we can count on setting up regular and fairly safe forwarding operations between here and Vera Cruz. Once we get the dollars here I have no doubt we can arrange to get them on to Philadelphia. While the stuff is in New Orleans it will have to be kept somewhere. Why not in our bank? I can't see myself burying it in the garden and sitting up over it with a pistol all night."

"You don't bury anything here," remarked the doctor, "not even the dead. You strike water six inches down."

"It isn't the water that worries me," said Livingston. "It's Lafitte and the Baratarians. How is Adverse ever going to get shiploads of dollars past those pirates? The river mouth is a regular nest of them around Barataria. For the past five years they have been bribed to let ships for New Orleans alone only by giving them complete control of the slave trade. Even at that . . ."

"Lafitte?" said Anthony. "Why, it was Lafitte that the governor spoke of!"

"I see what he meant!" exclaimed Mitchell. "Now leave it to me, Livingston. Go ahead and organize your bank uptown, I'll take Adverse to see Jean Lafitte at the blacksmith shop tomorrow. He owes me a life or two. If we don't have silver coming here by shiploads by the time you are ready to open your doors, I'll eat my hat. Now what's your plan, Toni, to get the stuff to Philadelphia?"

"I shall open up business as a general merchandising concern, dealing principally in sugar and cotton, and as a correspondent of *David Parish and Company*, in Philadelphia. I shall buy or charter a number of fast sailing craft and ship specie, unknown to anybody but ourselves, to Parish as fast as it comes in."

"Good," said Mitchell. "It looks to me as if we had both ends and the middle of this proposition in order. Now let's get on with it before the Americans take over the government and start to make laws about everything."

"Amen to that," said Anthony.

Next day he and Dr. Mitchell went to see the proprietor of a blacksmith shop on St. Philip Street between Bourbon and Dauphine. The heavy rain of the night before had made the distinction between the river and the town purely academic.

Outwardly the blacksmith shop of the Brothers Lafitte resembled—a blacksmith shop. The usual number of sorry nags were standing about on three feet with the fourth held in the leather apron of a negro smith stripped to the waist, while the hot-iron sizzled against the hoof and the nails went home. The usual number of curs stole and fought over that choice tidbit of dogdom, a hoof-paring. The usual number of children with black-beady eyes peeped in through the wide doors attracted by the glow of red-hot metal, the whale-like puffing of leather bellows, and the musical clink and ring of iron, anvil, and hammers. But that was all that was usual about the blacksmith shop of the Brothers Lafitte.

On the unusual side of the ledger it might have been entered that the negro smiths all seemed to have been chosen from a race of giants. A good many of them were scarred with both sword and whip, and one of them, the tallest, had lost an eye. The muscles of these huge fellows rippled like snakes in the mud under the black, glistening films of their sweaty hides, and they could fit iron clod-hoppers on a vicious she-mule as if Cinderella herself were bashfully extending one foot to be fitted with a glass slipper.

Add that these slaves of the lamp were bossed by a white jinnee from Georgia seven feet tall by the name of Humble, the pride of Catahoula Parish, where gouging was a fine art, and that M. Jean Lafitte was in the custom of calling upon those who owed him moneys or had trade favours to dispense, accompanied by a bodyguard of very black blacksmiths—and one need add no more.

Gentlemen who insisted upon challenging M. Jean Lafitte to duels with colchemards, the Creole short sword, or with pistols were waited upon by Mr. Humble in the rôle of M. Lafitte's second. He would greatly regret the unfortunate illness, or absence, of his principal and suggest that the matter could be settled immediately with hammers in six feet of water in the nearest swamp. Otherwise, a thousand dollars would heal M. Lafitte's asperged honour, which was sensitive about gossip. Thus horseshoeing tended to prosper.

The close family feeling between the brothers Pierre and Jean Lafitte was touching. They were not only hand in glove but hand in purse. If they had been Siamese twins it could scarcely have been more difficult to tell which one robbed you; whether it was Pierre with his gang of able ruffians at Grande Terre near the mouth of the river or Jean at the blacksmith shop in New Orleans. Those who had anything to import or export, whether merchandise or members of the family, made a point of seeing Jean in New Orleans in order to avoid seeing Pierre at Grande Terre.

Hence, the giant Humble was by no means surprised when Dr. Mitchell appeared at the smithy entrance with Anthony in tow and pointed inquiringly to a barred passage leading to the rear of the shop.

"He's thar," said Humble, "but he ain't done riz yet. How 'bout the gen'leman, doc?"

"A bobcat," said the doctor. "Take a good look at him so you don't mistake him for a muskrat when you're out skinnin' some night." He added something in a low tone to Humble.

"Yo don't say so!" exclaimed the man. "Stranger, I'm powerful glad to meet yo-all." For some days afterwards Anthony's right hand was out of business.

The yard and sheds behind the smithy were piled with an assortment of merchandise and valuables that spoke well for the enterprise of the "Privateers" at Barataria. There was the smell of spilled spices, and in one corner of the compound a couple of unshaven ruffians in red caps and greasy canvas drawers were pawing over a chest of cashmere shawls.

"It's not often they stop an Indiaman," said the doctor. "Look at that smashed teakwood screen there. But come on; they don't like you nebbin' in just after a haul."

A mulatto woman opened the door of a small, brick house at the far end of the yard, and muttering something incomprehensible in Gombo, led them into a kitchen with a dirt floor.

Seated before a table, upon which stood a large, smoking tureen of boiled shrimps, was a dapper little man dressed in an exquisite, bottle-green suit, buckled pumps, and a frilled shirt. This, with his eyes, which were very large and had curious yellow pupils that seldom shifted, gave him the air of a frog. The resemblance was still further increased by his habit of pitching pink shrimps into his mouth and gulping them as if they were so many insects. He greeted the doctor with a smile and nodded to Anthony, who did not for some time realize that here was the celebrated Jean Lafitte.

The doctor began to explain the object of their call. At first Lafitte seemed to pay no attention to him and the shrimps continued to vanish accompanied by copious streams of fragrant Java coffee. As the doctor talked on, however, the dark little man at the table shoved aside his plate, and resting his head in his hands and his elbows on the board, gazed piercingly at the two visitors before him.

At the end of half an hour, during which Mitchell had made an ardent plea for his co-operation, Lafitte began to question Anthony keenly.

Anthony replied frankly and with few reservations, for he had come to the conclusion that he would have to deal with this powerful river-baron either on the basis of a complete understanding or an open defiance. Defiance would entail obtaining and manning ships powerful enough to defy the flotilla of Pierre Lafitte at the entrance to the Mississippi. That might be impossible. It would certainly be enormously expensive, and it would surely imply an insufferable delay. It would be better to pay; pay, if one had to, through the nose. . . .

"As I understand it then," said Lafitte, "the doctor's suggestion is that on each of these shipments of bullion a moderate toll should be levied by us to permit them to pass. I should say about half would be a fair division—under the circumstances."

"That would never do," replied Anthony. "You do not quite see the realities of the situation. You must remember, monsieur the blacksmith, that you are not dealing with some helpless merchant. My principals have supplied me with unlimited resources to carry out this project, and if you do not care to participate reasonably, I shall go to Havana, outfit my own fleet, and ferry the bullion over from Vera Cruz in your teeth."

"And pay seventy-five per cent in squeeze to the Spanish authorities," grunted Lafitte.

"No, you are mistaken. I have dealt in Havana. I know the ropes there. Carlo Cibo is my agent. And besides, my principal would not permit of the squeeze."

"He must be a powerful principal," sneered Lafitte.

"He is," replied Anthony. "His name is Napoleon Bonaparte."

Lafitte wiped his lips thoughtfully. "I begin to see," he said.

"Certainly," cried Anthony. "I knew you would. You are a man of imagination. There is nothing to prevent your taking our first cargo, for instance, and keeping all of it. But that would be the end, wouldn't it? And, if you levy a terrific toll we go elsewhere—and that also will be the end without even a beginning."

"What is your proposal then, M. Adverse? Allons!"

"It is simply this: I propose to employ you and your brother to bring the bullion from Vera Cruz to New Orleans in your own ships and to pay you damn well for doing it."

"So you would trust us, eh?"

"Certainly. I am dealing with men of honour. I understood that from the first."

Lafitte could not entirely conceal his pleasure at this. "Go on," he said.

"Well, the point is that since these operations must continue for some years, you will in the end profit much more by protecting them and making delivery safe so that we can afford to load large sums every voyage instead of driblets. And there must also be no interference with the trans-shipments to Philadelphia."

"Oh, zat ees annozair sing," said Lafitte. "You pay half ven you go up and you pay half ven you come down. Vy not?"

"Come on, Adverse, we'll go to Havana," said Dr. Mitchell, rising. "They don't strangle the golden goose there as soon as it peeps. . . .

"You're one big Cajan fool, Jean Lafitte," continued the doctor, pounding on the table till the shrimps jumped out of the pan. "This is the biggest chance that will ever come your way. Think of it! The whole province will boom with this cash going through it and you will be the dog in the manger. Don't ask me to tend any gunshot wounds again. You're not worth the time I spend on you."

"Now, doc-tair, asseyez-vous," said Lafitte, gulping a little. "You are always like ze hurricane." He sat for a minute. "I tell you vot ve do. Ve go talk zees ovair wiz my brozair Pierre chez Grande Terre. Dimanche prochain."

"Good!" said Mitchell. "I thought you'd see light."

"And you tell Mr. Edward Leevings-ton go ahead wid ze bank," said Jean laughing. "Zat ees good idea, I sink. Ha! Ve all make vera mooch monay! N'est-ce pas?"

"That last remark was very encouraging," insisted the doctor as they strolled down the swampy little street together, being careful to stick to the raised banquette, although potted plants dripped on them from the little balconies overhead. "If we have many more rains like last night's there will be fever again. It never fails."

"I think Lafitte was only putting me off," replied Anthony, who regarded himself as immune to all fever since African days.

"No, no, he only wants time to communicate with his brother Pierre at Barataria first. That is why he put you off till next Sunday. You will see, Pierre will consent. It is now only a matter of terms. I will go along with you when you go to bargain at Grande Terre, if you like."

"For Lord's sake, do. How is it you stand-in so well with them?"

"There are often a good many gunshot wounds and cutlass slashes to bind up among them. I never ask questions and I keep my mouth shut. The presents I receive from these pirates permit me to live well here and to practise medicine instead of ancient magic on honest men."

"How do we get to Barataria?" persisted Anthony, who was not so interested in medicine as the doctor was.

"Wait till Sunday, and you will see," said Mitchell. "That will leave you a few days to attend to other matters. I want you to meet people here. That is always useful. Everybody, anybody. Just get around."

"Why?"

"I want to use you later on," said the doctor, "so I want you to be successful. You see, I am completely selfish about it. Now let's step in and pass the good news along to Ed Livingston."

That able promoter needed very little to encourage him. He was soon to be found hustling about the city in a large planter's hat, an alpaca coat, and long, baggy cotton trousers, enlisting his clerical help, renting a building, installing counters and a brick safe, and informing prospective depositors of the credit facilities which "our sound and enterprising financial institution will shortly be enabled to extend to those of known enterprise and integrity. The subscribed capital is already one hundred thousand dollars Mexican. Those who wish to subscribe to the capital stock of this bank of deposit and issue, in a community with illimitable prospects, are invited to do so at ten dollars a share. The offices are at the corner of Royal and Conti streets."

"Rumour, credulity, and hope form the basis of credit," said Livingston as they took dinner one day at the Orleans Hotel shortly after the interview with Jean Lafitte. Dinner was at 2.30 in the afternoon. The rest of the day until supper was devoted to digestion and liquid accelerators.

As if to confirm Livingston's remarks, who should walk up to the bar and subscribe for ten shares of stock but Mr. M'Quiston. He was doing well, he said. McTavish, McTavish, and McTavish would be "vera pleased." He himself was settling in New Orleans.

"Our friend Melancthon Conant has put down the cash for a hundred shares, and there are others in small

549

amounts," continued Livingston, who looked surprised in spite of himself. "Who would have believed it? All that I need is another thousand dollars cash to open the doors."

"I will provide that," said Anthony, who had brought $10,000 in Spanish gold pieces. "Open up tomorrow but don't make any loans till the first shipment of bullion comes in. Oh, you might discount a thousand dollars' worth of the best paper secured by merchandise just to start the ball rolling. Say, thirty days at ten per cent and three names. Keep enough coin in the tills to make change."

Dr. Mitchell roared. "With an ex-slaver, a fugitive from justice, a Scotch clerk, and an undertaking-tout as the backers of this 'great fiduciary operation,' it ought to be a pronounced success in this world."

"And why not an M.D. too?" suggested Anthony.

"Well, why not?" replied Mitchell. "It needs a touch of respectability."

That evening the "board of directors" seated about the table over turtle steak at Ba'tiste's voted the doctor one hundred shares of stock for his "valuable services in encouraging the promotion of said fiduciary institution."

Dr. Terry M. laughed. He had no idea that his collateral heirs would be made comfortable for two generations.

The next day the *Merchants' and Planters' Bank of Deposit* opened its single door. In two weeks it received $3,000 in paid up capital stock. It made loans of $2,500 and had on file applications for $180,000 more.

But the curious thing about it was that everybody believed in it. Even Anthony believed in it. An idea tossed about in conversation had actually become an interest-drawing fact. He slipped around to the Creole who owned the lot where the bank stood and bought it one morning for $450. Thus what later on was to become the famous *Citizens' Bank of New Orleans* got under way.

550

The years 1803 and 1804 witnessed rapid and far-reaching changes. In New Orleans the long somnolence of the colonial era and the dependence upon Europe passed away. Down the current of the mighty river and across the tides of the Gulf the Americans swarmed in upon Louisiana in argosies of arks and rafts, in flotillas of ships and schooners. They began to approach it overland from Kentucky and Tennessee as well.

The ceremonies of the passing of the old and of the beginning of the new order took place before Anthony's eyes.

On the last day of November 1803, he saw Salcedo on the balcony of the Cabildo deliver the keys of the city to Laussat and heard Casa Calvo, the Spanish commissioner, absolve the provincials, and incidentally himself, from all allegiance to the crown of Spain. The tricolour was raised over the Place d'Armes amidst the wild rejoicing of the Creoles, and for about three weeks Anthony found himself by legal fiction at least a citizen of the French Republic. It was during this brief interval, while the American troops were arriving and Governor Claiborne and his modest staff were preparing to take over the province, that he visited Barataria.

Very early on the appointed Sunday morning the giant blacksmith Humble knocked on the door at Ba'-tiste's and informed Anthony and Dr. Mitchell that all was ready for the journey.

"M. Jean is already at Grande Terre with his brother Pierre," said the man. "They are waiting for you."

Dr. Mitchell nudged Anthony at this as if to say, "I told you so."

They crossed the Mississippi to the right bank in a ferry worked by an old horse which forever ascended a treadmill with an expression of perpetual surprise. To the Kaintucks who lined the levee this paddle-wheel boat appeared to be a miracle of ingenuity.

They scrambled up the levee at McDonald's plantation and, striking westward through the swamp along the banks of a drainage canal, came after several hours' terrible, muddy going on horseback to a deep, narrow, and tortuous bayou. Here a long pirogue hollowed out of a single huge cypress awaited them. It was manned by ten negroes with paddles. They were chained together at the waist and watched over by an old Canary Islander, or "isleño," who had lost both ears but still had the active use of his eyes, two pistols, a cutlass, and a whip upon which he was engaged in fitting a new lash when they entered the boat.

At a grunt from this genial coxswain they set out. Now for the first time the nature of the country about New Orleans became apparent to Anthony.

The bayou, which was forty miles long, twisted and squirmed through the impenetrable swamp. Currentless, it led through a perpetual half-gloom under a tunnel of cypress and water-oaks draped, hooded, bearded, and garlanded with masses of Spanish moss. As the banks grew lower, on either side could be seen the exotic green of the southern forest, its knees and shrubs bathed in water with an occasional hummock rising out of the perpetual grey-green gloom. Turtles and cotton-mouths abounded, and innumerable herons standing on one leg in the gloomy shallows.

All was silent. Except for the rhythmical dip of the paddles and a song with endless verses in Gombo, that the paddlers took up stanza by stanza, while the swamp listened, they might have been moving through a green limbo where the creation was not yet complete.

> "Mouché Préval
> Li donné grand bal.
> Li fait nègue payé
> Pou sauté ain pé.
> Dansé Calinda, dansé."

And they would round a turn to see the inevitable

heron flapping off with its long legs tucked under it, into the shadows.

> "Li donné soupé
> Pou nègue régalé;
> So vié la musique
> Té baye la collique.
> Dansé Calinda, dansé."

And they would round another curve. . . .

About twilight they emerged suddenly upon Lake Cataouatche, just as the long lines of waterfowl came to hide in the rushes for the night. It was an infernal mere, red as a demon's eye in the sunset, surrounded by cypress swamps and a dismal hearse-draped forest resonant as darkness fell with the eery whistling of ducks' wings. As the light dwindled, the bellowing of alligators and the harsh screams of nocturnal waterfowl resounded from all sides. *"Nox, nox, nox,"* croaked the frogs. And the endless sorrows of the whippoor-wills began.

They built fires here on a bit of beach, ate supper and rested. The vastness and loneliness of the place descended upon all of them. The dim lake reflected the misty sky. It was impossible to tell where space ended and the earth began. Both whites and blacks felt it. They seemed to be lost together in a place without limits.

"What lies to the west of these swamps?" Anthony asked the Canary Islander.

"The prairies of the Opelousas," he replied.

"And beyond that?"

"Llano estocado, señor."

"And then?"

"Los Indios, perhaps. Who knows? Wide, wide!" He gestured out into the darkness. He raked the fire together as if to lighten the threatening space about him.

By the other fire, in a subdued voice breathing insufferable regret, Anthony heard one of the slaves crooning in his half-African dialect.

"Ninette, do you remember the cool brook
   Through the palm grove,
   Do you remember the green banana trees,
   And the pool there in the sunlight
   Where we lay at ease?
   Ah, what fun we had there together,
       You and I, little pet!
   But now the brook has stopped.
       It died of regret.
   The palms droop by its shore—
   Even the water could not embrace you forever—
   Do you remember the brook, Ninette,
   Do you remember anything anymore?"

Crude as were the words, the tone, the intonation, and the primal music with which they were uttered did the trick. In the brain of the white man his own complicated and magnificent music began.

Anthony lay back in his blanket in the firelight and listened to a symphony played on the invisible and muted strings of thought. It poured out over the threshold of his spirit as if the dark and bright angels of his nature had suddenly seized viols and sat within the prison house of the body blending in harmony the magic pain of the past and the golden hope for the future. It was the song of the exile turned pioneer. It began by moving him to tears and it left him buoyed up and sustained by hope.

These mental reverberations of abstract sound, a harmony that expressed completely the emotional meaning of experience, as though he and the world had been blent into one in order to hear, this music seemed to be presented to him; to be a benign gift that brought with it a catharsis for existence itself.

How long he lay listening that evening he never knew. Dr. Mitchell poked him with the butt of his pistol and "awoke" him at last. Pine torches were flaring in the darkness and they were once more on their way.

Fatigued now beyond thought of melody, the crew sang no more. The grey trees drooped like deserted tents in the late moonlight as they passed them.

"By the rivers of Babylon . . . we hanged our harps upon the willows—"

The words suddenly flashed into his memory from somewhere as he saw himself reading in his room at the Casa da Bonnyfeather as a young boy. The light burned steadily and the madonna stood in her niche. For a moment an insufferable feeling of homesickness swept over him. Would he never get home again? Home—where was it? Here?

He lit a cigar and distributed the remainder, one to every man in the boat. A sigh of satisfaction went up as the men inhaled. They looked at him gratefully.

At least the land provided an herb to dull the ache in the hearts of the exiles it sheltered.

Great is tobacco, a leaf from the foliage of paradise, a shrub rooted in contentment, manna of the west!

The men resumed the paddles again and they sped on southward into the dawn across Lake Salvador. They threaded another endless bayou, slept, crossed Lake Villiers, plunged into the Bayou St. Denis, and finally emerged from the gloomy forest into the sparkling reaches of Barataria Sound. It was on the morning of the third day that they came in sight of Grande Terre.

A fleet of six schooners and three ships lay at anchor before a settlement of about a dozen houses at the bottom of the cove. There was a battery commanding the landing, several small warehouses, and a primitive shipyard. The place wore a bright and pleasing aspect. There was a blinding white beach. Behind it rose the vivid green of the everlasting oaks and shrubbery of the coastal island where a few cattle were pastured. The chenière of Grande Terre had been inhabited from ancient times, as the large shell heaps forming mounds and banks here and there along the beach showed. The pirate town was in fact indebted to the vanished Indians for its convenient water front and raised banks. It had not yet grown into that metropolis of buccaneers and thriving mart of illicit trade to which it afterward attained. Already, however, there were long rows of slave pens hidden behind the dunes. Two of the ships in port were blackbirders, and the third, to judge by her shattered bulwarks and pock-marked hull, was a recent prize.

As they landed, Anthony could not help noting the signs of discipline and order on every hand. The town was neat and clean. The houses of brick and cypress frame, long, low and of a pleasing contour, had flowers in the windows. A whitewashed residence with green shutters at the head of the street would have done credit to a colonial official. He had no doubt it was Lafitte's. Except for the frowning battery, there was little sign of means of defence. The tortuous channels, shoals, and sandbars were, indeed, the pirates' main reliance. There were gardens and flowered dooryards behind picket fences and lines of fluttering wash—all of which domestic rather than martial appearance was explained by the number of well-dressed women and children playing about. All labour was performed by slaves, of whom the most humble seaman could have his share.

They were met by a young fellow dressed like a merchant officer, neat but weaponless, who led them to Lafitte's house. They found the two brothers together opening the letters of a ship's mail. These lay scattered about the floor of a large room furnished exquisitely but to the point of exuberance. A hundred ships' cabins had contributed to it.

"Here's your man!" said Jean to his brother, as Anthony and the doctor entered. He motioned to a woman with a baby to leave the room. "Bonjour, mon grand petit docteur."

"Pierre, this is Meester Ad-vairse. He talks Spanish."

"Welcome, señor," said Pierre Lafitte. "How was Bayonne when you last saw it? I hear you were there recently. It is my father's town."

"It still smells of fish and garlic," said Anthony, laughing.

"Ha! Tell me about it," said Pierre. "I would give a hundred dollars for a plate of fresh sardines." They sat down to talk.

Both the brothers affected green. But Pierre was over six feet tall and even in the house wore an otterskin cap and a huge cutlass with a gold-inlayed ivory handle. There were rings in his ears, and his fine white teeth and piercing black eyes flashed simultaneously into a frown or a smile. He concealed nothing. It was plain that thought, feeling, and action with Pierre Lafitte were one and the same thing.

As Anthony took his measure, he knew that the interview about to take place would be the crisis of his own commercial career—that he would have to think faster and talk more clearly and persuasively than he had ever done before.

"I am told by little Jean," said Lafitte, "that you have something important to talk about, señor."

"Gold, Señor Lafitte; Mexican silver, millions of it."

"Ah, ha," cried Lafitte, shaking the rings in his ears. "In that case, I reply like the skittish señora with the boy husband when the big matador whispered something into her shell-like ear.

" 'Let us get together, my bully one! Why not?' "

Chapter Eighteen

The Snake Changes Its Skin

I T WAS weeks later, and past the middle of December, when Anthony stood once more upon the levee at New Orleans. The "interview" at Grande Terre had drawn out into a long negotiation.

"Well, what news?" cried Livingston, who had been haunting the water front for days. "I thought Lafitte must have swallowed you and the doctor, pills and all."

"He did," said Mitchell, who liked to speak first. "He took our medicine."

"With a large amount of orange juice to make it go down," added Anthony a little ruefully. "But the upshot of the whole matter is that a shipment of bullion will be in from Vera Cruz shortly and more will follow. Jean Lafitte is bringing the first shipment himself. After that, one of his fast brigs returns for it regularly."

"Thank God, the bank's saved!" said Livingston so piously that Mitchell smiled.

"Otherwise it would have been the same as heart

558

failure with you, wouldn't it, Ed?" he remarked. "Well, you can thank Toni here. He handled the piratical brothers like a young Ulysses. Upon my word, I say hats off to him."

To Anthony this remark of the doctor came as his chief reward for two long years' work. When the first shipment of bullion arrived and was safely on its way to Parish at Philadelphia he intended to get incontinently drunk. "But there's a slip," he thought uneasily as they walked down the little street toward Ba'tiste's, chattering gayly.

It was evening and the serenos were going about the Place d'Armes lighting the dim oil lamps that swung here and there from brackets. "A fine clear night and all's well," one of them sang out from sheer habit, despite the fact that a few drops were beginning to fall and it was a dank, misty evening with a fog blowing in from the river. They laughed.

"The old watch will soon be gone, I suppose," said Mitchell. "The Americans take over on Monday, you know. Wonder what the place will be like in a few years?

"Well, these old lamps won't throw much light into the future anyway. You can't even see the present by 'em. Let's go, it's beginning to rain," cried the doctor a little impatiently.

"They're better than nothing though," insisted Livingston as he avoided the next pitfall and picked his way along gingerly. "Many an old rip's got home by 'em and—"

"A fine night and all's well," shouted the sereno they had left behind. As if to rebuke this insistent official optimism, from somewhere up the Rue de Conti came a burst of funereal singing and the glow of torches. A few melancholy shouts and the screams and wailing of a mob of women could be heard like a chorus accompanying a dirge-like chanting that grew momentarily louder.

"Some big bow-wow among the Creoles is wagging

559

his tail for the last time, I suppose," said Livingston. "Come on, let's see the obsequies."

They turned the corner on impulse, and walking down a block, took shelter in the doorway of the old Spanish tavern at the corner of Demaine Street.

"Can't be a funeral," asserted the doctor. "There's no hearse, and look at the people swarming out of the houses as they come along. Looks like a riot."

"There's the hearse," said Anthony as a high, draped object lighted by rows of torches came around the corner of the street below. It was surrounded by nuns led by the archbishop and some clergy.

The chant grew louder. Through the river mist and fine, pearly rain the procession approached slowly. The effect of the torches and the voices in the fog was indescribably solemn.

Redemisti virgam hæreditatis tuæ . . .

"Lord! I remember now," suddenly exclaimed Mitchell. "Of course! It's the Ursulines. They're leaving tonight on the last Spanish transport for Havana and taking the statue from their chapel along with them. That's what the row's about."

Leva manus tuas in superbias eorum in finem . . .

"Only some of the old girls are staying on. A good many are French émigrées and the word 'republic' has them scared stiff. They say that fine atheist Jefferson wrote them a reassuring letter that would do a Christian gentleman credit. But only a few believed him. It's carrying the Mary off that makes the crowd yowl. Listen to that, would you!"

Et gloriati sunt qui oderunt te, in medio solemnitatis tuæ.

560

"She's been here since the French came, they say—and now she's going."

Posuerunt signa sua, signa: et non cognoverunt . . .

"And a damned good riddance," added the doctor.

"That's right, doc! Jim Cyarter and all the Cyarters and their kin up-river ul say it with ye." It was a tall American speaking; along with several others dressed in fringed shirts, he had left the bar and crowded to the door of the tavern to see the procession go by.

Quasi in silva lingnorum securibus exciderunt januas ejus in idipsum: in securi et ascia dejecerunt eam.

Two acolytes swinging censers passed leading the procession.

"What are you going to give the Cyarters and their kin when she's gone, doc?" said Anthony in a low tone just by Mitchell's ear.

The doctor started a little but rallied. "What do you give a sick man when the fever leaves him?" he said.

"Pills?"

"No. Rest, reason, and fresh air."

"I was thinking of the soul."

"The soul is a priestly lie," exclaimed the doctor hardily.

"Right again, doc," cried the irrepressible Mr. Carter, who had no idea he was horning-in. "In our neck o' the woods thar's far too many trees to cut down yit to worry about yer soul." He sniffed the incense suspiciously. "I tell ye . . ."

The clergy passed. The smell of pine torches and a whirl of smoke and sparks swirled up into their faces.

Incenderunt igni sanctuarium tuum: in terra polluerunt tabernaculum nominis tui.

561

Dixerunt in corde suo cognatio eorum simul:
Quiescere faciamus omnes dies festos Dei a terra

—thundered the Creole mob taking up the chant.

Twenty-five or thirty Ursuline nuns with their heads on their breasts, many with tears running down their cheeks, were now passing directly before them. The sound of their chanting had about it that singular touch of hysterical woe, which only the voices of women can convey. Their pale faces looked out of their hoods like so many variations upon the mask of tragedy. In the centre of this black-robed group of women was a kind of ark which had been contrived for the occasion and heaped with the last late blossoms of the year. Over it was erected a miniature pavilion of cloth of gold. The sides of this little tent were of some sort of transparent gauze, sufficient to permit a number of wax tapers sheltered behind it to burn steadily with a clear, saffron light. Bathed in this quiet radiance, as though she had gathered the aura of the past about her and was departing in its golden mist, sat a remarkably gracious and life-like statue of the Virgin holding the Holy Child on her knees. In her flower-filled ark carried on the shoulders of four huge porters she seemed to be floating above the heads of the wildly seething mob amid the red glare of funeral torches in a divinely self-poised calm. For an instant even the Americans standing in the door of the Spanish tavern were reduced to silence. But not for long.

"Hell!" exclaimed Carter, suddenly wrapping a wolf-skin jacket closer about him and striding off in the direction of the Batture. His hatchet-face seemed to cleave its way through the crowd.

Disengaging himself from his two companions, Anthony slipped away to follow the procession.

It halted before the steps of the cathedral where the archbishop blessed it and scattered holy water on the crowd. A few drops fell on his cheeks. Led by a tall, fanatical monk, Father Antoine, who lived in a cell, half-hut and half-bower, in the bosk behind the cathedral, the procession now proceeded to the water front. The levee was black with the assembled inhabitants of the Vieux Carré. Like floating globes in the river mist the lights of the Spanish transport could be seen where she lay anchored in the stream farther out.

The crowd was silent now. Only the dirge-like voices of the nuns continued. The torches and the glowing ark were carried to the marge where the boats from the transport waited.

"Ah, monsieur," exclaimed an old Creole mother to Anthony while she wept under her shawl. "C'est le dernier moment que nous aurons notre belle vierge en Lousiane."

The nuns had ceased now. They were getting into the boats. The ark was lifted reverently by the Spanish soldiers and deposited in the stern-sheets of a barge. There was a sharp command and the sound of rowing.

The glowing tent of the Virgin, seemingly floating of itself a few feet above the water, disappeared gradually and dimly into the heavy mists of the midstream. As if the river were swallowing it and blotting it out, her form was seen no more. Only the giant crucifix of the monk remained elevated in silhouette in the glare of the torches.

For a while the crowd stood hypnotized. Then a cry of mingled rage, chagrin, and despair went up from it into the night.

Now that it was too late, Father Antoine and some of the more indignant gathered to protest—against what they scarcely knew—in front of the cathedral. But sheets of rain began to fall and the ardour of the crowd dissolved.

"For God's sake, Toni, what are you doing here?" Dr. Mitchell's voice came suddenly out of the darkness. "I've been looking for you everywhere. You'll get an ague staying out in this. Here put this on—" and he threw about Anthony's shoulders a dry cloak that he had brought from Ba'tiste's. "We thought you'd given us the slip and gone home."

Under the warm cloak Anthony still shivered a little, but not from cold. The effect of the scene he had just witnessed was too deep and complicated for mere phraseology. He said little to the doctor as they hurried home, knowing that Mitchell, who had not an iota of religion about him, regarded even an interest or sympathy for it in others as a weakness.

Indeed, from time to time at supper that evening both the doctor and Livingston glanced with a slightly puzzled expression at their friend.

Anthony went to sleep that night with snatches of the song he had dreamed by the banks of Lake Cataouatche, the chanson of the slave, and the dirge of the nuns in his ears. The next morning he was awakened by the thunder of cannon in the Place d'Armes. It was Monday, the 20th of December 1803.

The entire city crowded to the square before the Cabildo to see Laussat, the French prefect, deliver the province into the hands of Governor Claiborne and the government at Washington. The new American regulars and some of the Creole militia lined the square. The tricolour came to half mast as the stars and stripes rose on the same staff. For some reason the halliards slipped, and the two flags remained for a few moments tangled together, half-way up. The crowd roared, cursed, and wept. Laussat made a gesture of farewell. Then the stars and stripes rose to the thunder of cannon, the cheers of the Americans, and the strains of "Hail! Columbia, Happy Land!" A body of French volunteers laid the tricolour reverently away. Governor Claiborne made a neat speech promising justice, religious toleration, and prosperity—provided no one gave any trouble. And it was over. Louisiana was part of the United States.

"Well, how does it feel to be a citizen of the great, new republic!" said Mitchell, slapping Anthony on the back. "Come on," he laughed, "let's go to the Café des Exilés and have a drink."

Days of change, of swift and accelerating change. Time seemed to be moving in a crescendo upon an infinite scale. Life sped with a new and more profound momentum. The new pace could be measured by contrast, for the old French and Spanish City, the Vieux Carré, as it soon came to be called, positively refused to be hustled; to change its ways. It obstinately remained "foreign," a thing unto itself, cherishing the old Creole ways and hoping to the last that something, that anything, would happen to save it. That Napoleon would win, that . . . that—

Like a beautiful woman who in her girlhood had found the styles, the attitudes and manners that suited her best, and had determined to go on wearing them, Creole New Orleans continued gazing at herself in the mirror of the past until the glass cracked.

The Americans came swarming down upon and inundating the little city from the same direction and with something of the same energy as the current of the mighty river that brought them. In a short time the city council was petitioning the governor to tear down the old walls and fill up the moats. One could walk for two miles on the roofs of the flat-boats at the American landing. In the Faubourg Ste. Marie a shanty-town of bars, boarding-houses, and gambling dens awaited the flat-boats. The levee began to awaken every morning to the rumble of drays.

From the "tower" room at Ba'tiste's, where he lived for three years, Anthony saw the boom town begin to surround and besiege the old one, even to level and breach its walls. But it was as no idle spectator that he sat there. No man in the city had a more active part in its affairs than he. In many ways his past training and experience had fitted him eminently for life in Louisiana. Above all, his command of many languages now stood him in good stead, for New Orleans was a polyglot port if every there was one.

The forwarding of the bullion, once the active co-operation of the Lafittes was secured, had been reduced to the status of a commercial routine. Their powerful protection had not been secured without paying royally for it. The brig *Felicia*, under the command of a talented desperado by the name of Dominic You, made the voyage between Vera Cruz and New Orleans for the mere trifle of $10,000 a trip—and in addition there had been an initial squeeze of $100,000 to come out of the first delivery. Besides that, 10 per cent was to be deducted and paid to Jean Lafitte out of the gross total of each voyage. But even with Anthony's own commission added to these charges plus the purchase and maintenance of swift schooners to convey the bullion to Philadelphia, he found that the cost of delivering the silver to Parish was a trifle over 12 per cent of the value of the moneys furnished by Lestapsis at Vera Cruz. As the insurance between Philadelphia and Vera Cruz was 60 per cent on minted money, he felt inclined to congratulate himself.

Indeed, it was doubtful if the Lafittes would have assented to act on such terms if it had not been for the promises of large credit facilities at Livingston's bank. If Pierre was a corsair pure and simple, Jean was a business man of no mean abilities. He had his thumb in many a pie in the development of the country and understood that being able to discount notes was often a more convenient and available method of obtaining the use of capital than rushing a quarter-deck. Besides, quarter-decks were not always rushable. The British and Yankees, it seemed, were peculiarly obstinate about their marine property. On the first of April 1804, a helpless-looking West Indian trader had turned out to be H.M.S. or U.S.S. something in disguise. There was no time to find out which. Five broadsides of grape and canister had sickened curiosity, and Dr. Mitchell had been summoned to Barataria to saw off legs and arms, set bones, sear stumps with boiling oil, and probe for bullets, while strong men made whimpering noises like nestfuls of kittens. He returned looking pale, and with the entry in his notebook that wounds infected by bluebottle flies healed mysteriously well, if you let them alone.

Under the circumstances Jean Lafitte's enthusiasm for banks was not entirely mysterious. Let Pierre roar and be the devil of a fellow at Grande Terre if he wanted to. He, Jean, could walk around to Mr. Livingston's bank at the northeast corner of Royal and Conti streets and return with what he needed, on both legs, and without having been met by a blast of grapeshot. That had its advantages.

It had been a great day, of course, when the first shipment of bullion came in. You had come stamping in one morning at Ba'tiste's and summoned Anthony to the water front. The *Felicia* lay at the levee ostensibly unloading hides. Under them and along the keel were seven hundred and fifty kegs with a thousand newly minted Mexican silver dollars in each. Jean Lafitte took a hundred and ten kegs of them home to his blacksmith shop, and the rest were conveyed to the new brick vault at Livingston's bank. All this after nightfall.

But no one can keep sailors from talking. The next day the rumour was all over town. It was gold that the *Felicia* had brought. Five million of it was in Livingston's vaults. Only three million, insisted others. A gentleman from Wheeling, Virginia, had an eye gouged out by a gentleman from Chartiers Creek, Pennsylvania, over this minor difference.

Even the old Creole city turned over a little in its sleep, and the rest of the place hummed. It felt the life blood of capital coursing in its veins. The sensation was intoxicating.

"Ah reckon thar's more caboodle in that scamp Livingston's vaults than the rest o' the hul goddamned territory's wuth," announced a Georgia planter leaning against the bar at the Orleans so that the handle of a pistol stuck out between his coat-tails. No one came forward on the negative side. The slight exaggeration was felt to be too close to the mark to be arguable.

As the shipments to Philadelphia were managed with great secrecy and dispatch no one at the end of six months' time had any idea how much money was at "Livingston's." It was possible to manage the reshipment of coin without talk. The ship that sailed with it left no one behind to do any talking. Mr. Livingston was, therefore, in a delectable state. His "fiduciary institution" continued to enjoy a fabulous credit that he was not averse to exploiting.

Anthony's first adventures in the business methods of the community were with the bank and in organizing a fleet of fast schooners to keep in touch with Parish.

The latter he accomplished through the good offices of Captain Clemm, who had returned in record time from Philadelphia with a letter from David breathing relief at finding Anthony at New Orleans.

Captain Clemm was immediately sent back to Philadelphia with the $250,000 and instructions to round up five more vessels like his own with dependable skippers and crews. He was able to accomplish this gradually, and towards the end of the year found himself the commodore of a flotilla of six schooners and three lateen rigged dispatch boats that sailed like witches. The last being the idea of Mr. Adverse.

A shipyard to take care of these boats and to keep some hold on their crews while they lay in port was established on the right bank of the river opposite the city. There was a crude dry-dock, sheds, and a frame barracks for the men and log cabins for slaves. Visitors were forcibly discouraged.

Anthony had several reasons for establishing this place, which rapidly became known as "Algeciras" or "Little Algiers." From the right bank by way of the bayous he had communication with Barataria, and it became evident early in the game that the best way to bring in the silver was to land it at Grande Terre and ferry it up the bayous. The frequent presence of so many of Lafitte's men at the yard soon gave the place its uncertain reputation and the piratical name that long stuck to the locality.

There were other advantages. Several days of beating up against the river current were eliminated, and once at Algiers, the bullion could be loaded directly and dispatched without either causing rumors or having to be deposited at the bank. The latter became more and more important as time went on, for the influx of so much cash, in fact its mere presence, tended toward a disturbing inflation of credit. Anthony in Louisiana and Parish at Philadelphia both dealt with this problem as best they could. They were not altogether successful. It was a very real problem, an inevitable concommitant of Ouvrard's scheme.

Livingston, for instance, had not been content to use the 100,000 silver dollars which had been left with him on deposit out of the first shipment of bullion as basis for establishing the bank's credit. Anthony had used a rather wide discretion in thus detaining so large an account. But he felt the necessity of providing at New Orleans, in order to facilitate his own operations, a bank with the financial and trade ramifications which a bank implied. In this decision Parish had heartily concurred. But to Livingston it had been an opportunity to start the printing press.

The notes of the new bank were quite admirable pieces of design. There was an American eagle with a slightly buzzard-like expression on every bill. The gallant bird trailed a cloudy ribbon in his beak over the helpless town of New Orleans. On this appendage was curtly inscribed

"Under My Wings Every Thing Prospers"

and then—"The Merchants' and Planters' Bank of New Orleans will pay to the bearer on demand one silver dollar." It was soon a dead heat as to which was more nebulous, the motto on the cloudy banner borne by the eagle or the promise of the bank. Mr. Livingston printed two hundred thousand one dollar bills and rapidly put them into circulation by means of loans.

The unusual number of skeptics were paid off in real dollars but the new Mississippi Bubble continued to float. It was necessary, however, for Mr. Adverse to step in and stop the printing press, which he did only after an unhappy scene with Mr. Livingston. As an upshot of this several new gentlemen were asked to sit on the board. Alexander Milne, John McDonough, Bernard Marigny, Shepherd Brown, and Judah Touro served to no little effect as a balance wheel to Mr. Livingston's printing press.

Nevertheless, in three years, a half million dollars from nowhere was pumped into the city and became real enough to draw interest for the bank. With some of the profits Mr. Livingston began to buy up the land around the American landing. A great many "gentlemen" of all kinds were "much obleeged" for loans. Businesses, shops, speculators, and plantations all felt the tonic effect of the small injection of silver that had sufficed to start the heart of credit beating.

Anthony himself now began to launch out. He speculated a little in real estate, not always successfully. He began to look around for land for a suitable plantation and house. In a short while he would settle down and send for the boy. That was always in the back of his mind. It would never do, of course, to have him living at Ba'tiste's or in the city. He must first set himself up at home. He wrote his plans to Anna and to Vincent—and heard nothing. But that was not surprising. It might take a year or so to bring their replies. In the meanwhile he established himself as a general merchant by means of a floating warehouse anchored at the American landing.

He brought-up a number of flat-boats, had them caulked at the shipyard, and using them for floats, built a platform on them with stores, sheds, a house for the clerks, and a long display counter in a room rigged up as a general store. This "floatage," as it was called, was moored to the levee and had boat landings and a narrow bridge to the bank. It was a surprising affair about a quarter of an acre in area. It cost little, it paid no taxes, and it rose and fell on the bosom of the floods. Ships moored alongside, discharged and loaded.

Mr. M'Quiston was prevailed upon to become the "captain" of this floating emporium with "sax clarks" for a crew. They were all his countrymen. The business proved unexpectedly large in volume and in the end profitable to a degree. All kinds of European merchandise were exchanged for the raw produce of the country brought down the river. Among other things, a brisk trade in furs sprang up, and coureurs de bois who ascended the Red River and the Missouri to points far beyond the ken of the map makers tied their canoes and arks up at "M'Quiston's Store," along with Scotch-Irish traders from Pittsburgh, Long-knives from the "Dark and Bloody Ground," and thrifty settlers from the Western Reserve. The scenes at the counter, where the tobacco and sugar scales were kept busy all day long, where woollens from Manchester were exchanged for beaver skins from the upper Allegheny and Monongahela, held a certain fascination for Anthony. The tales of the country of the unknown West stirred a vague longing in his soul to see some day these primeval forests and to pass beyond them to the fabulous, teeming prairies of the buffalo and the horse Indians.

Consequently, he spent considerable time at the flotage. He struck up a friendship with some of the coureurs de bois who had been farthest into the unknown. He staked them generously and trusted them. And in the end he had his reward. He fitted up a bunk and room for himself, took Simba with him and lived there for weeks at a time. The Kaintucks were always offering to trade the proceeds of their voyages for Simba.

"Man, you could sic that ar' houn' dog on painters."

About the American landing Simba and his master became well known. And because they went their own way quietly, looked able to give trouble, but never worried little dogs even when they barked at them, they were liked well enough. In the city Mr. Adverse, not only on account of his possessions, although these were rumoured to be even greater than they were, was popular. Even among the Creole planters his excellent French and other qualities had gained him a peculiar standing. After all, he was not just one of the Yanquis. His occasional presence at the cathedral, although it was observed he never attended mass, was, to the Latins at least, reassuring.

With the shipyard at Algiers, the floating store at Batture, the bank, various properties, and the constant attention and adjustments incident to the shipment of the bullion, Anthony's worldly affairs engrossed a great part of his time, besides affording him hundreds of contacts and acquaintances.

The book-keeping for his own private affairs threatened to become inextricably mixed with the accounts of others. It frequently kept the light shining from the "tower-room" windows till nearly dawn. Yet he could entrust it to no one else. And that sense of order in all things that old John Bonnyfeather had instilled into him still insisted upon having its way. If others in the city did not know how their affairs stood, Mr. Adverse was always able to strike an accurate trial balance. The genial doctor, however, began to complain of his aloofness, and Anthony could see that when his correspondence with Europe should be added to his correspondence with Paris he would be overwhelmed.

He remembered old Sandy McNab living on his pension at Livorno. He made a long report to Ouvrard his excuse for dispatching a schooner to Italy by way of Spain about the end of the year 1804. Seven months later it returned with McNab, white-haired but hearty, and still wearing the identical Leghorn hat which he had bought with Anthony's shillings twenty years before. Their meeting was humorously affectionate. Sandy was installed in the room at Ba'tiste's, formerly occupied by Livingston, as the most confidential secretary that man ever had. In an atmosphere redolent of tobacco, newly-bound leather ledgers, and a tang of whisky, to say nothing of a renewed interest in life, Sandy ripened slowly like a winter apple. And there was many a heart-easing talk over old days at the Casa, while Simba beat the rug with his tail.

"It's a shame ye canna rent yon tike out for a duster," said Sandy. "There's naught in the scripture agin beasts workin' o' Sabbaths. But for a' sic minor losses, yer doin' weel, Maister Toni."

Sandy's laughter at hearing that Faith had married Don Luis was Homeric. "A fine precious pair o' toortle doves. Mark it, mon. No good ul coom o' their cooin'."

But there were some aspects of the past that Sandy never touched upon for he also had his promises to keep. And, "Wha—" said he to himself in his own quaint way, "wha would be thankfu' for haen their ain' mither proved a whoor?"

Besides, it was not the past that engrossed Anthony. The future continued to unfold itself engrossingly:

Arch Street, Philadelphia,
Pennsylvania,
June the seventh, 1806.

Anthony Adverse, Esq.,
My very Dear Sir:

Your undersigned correspondent is in a curious quandary, one which, I venture to say, is not common among the ordinary run of men of affairs. My own situation is this: I am now at a loss how to bestow the monies which you are constantly forwarding me, at once to the best advantage and in a manner consonant with my instructions from Messrs Hope & Company.

Since February 1803 I have received from you on the bills drawn by Ouvrard on the Mexican treasury, and cashed by Lestapsis, a total of 11,329,000.32$ Mex (please check). With the utmost exertion it has been possible to forward to Europe only a little over 6,800,000$, thus leaving a vast sum to be invested here in a new country where the mere presence of so much cash is instantly magnified incalculably in terms of credit and leads to a dangerous inflation.

For instance, my last purchase of Government securities has driven them up beyond all reason. Deposit in banks leads to wild loans and the emission of floods of "wildcat" notes. The withdrawal of a deposit for sudden shipment thus becomes difficult or impossible without leaving the bank insolvent. Nor will any explanations or warnings prevent this. Loans to individuals are little better.

I have loaned a large sum to a Swiss by the name of Cazanov who came recommended to me as a sound man. He has invested heavily in the lands of Northern New York State, and, to preserve my own interests, I have had to advance him further sums and to take over many thousands of undeveloped acres in that howling wilderness as security. Ouvrard warned me against this, you will recall, but I have been helpless.

I shall soon be forced, even though winter is coming on, to make the arduous journey over the Alleghenies in order to obtain from one Blennerhassett, a mad Irishman, who has built a magnificent lodge in the wilderness near the forks of the Ohio, an adequate mortgage security on his properties for sums lent him on my account by a Mr. Chevis of the Philadelphia Bank. Since my health has been precarious, Mrs. Parish has heroically decided to accompany me—and *you may be sure* that her mother will go with her.

I mention this both to give you some idea of my many difficulties and to set your mind at rest in regard to a certain fact.

You seem to have inferred from my last letter that we were expecting a domestic accretion. I know not how you could have so misread my phraseology. Alas, your felicitations are without justification in the event. I should be more willing to gratify the natural longing of a woman to hold a child in her arms did I not feel that the duties of my wife require her to grace the board of her husband's establishment rather than to languish over the cradle of his heir. But to more important matters:

Most of the money sent to Europe so far has been immense. But it becomes more and more difficult to ship anything from here, either produce or bullion, as the restrictions of the British blockade against the Emperor Napoleon are tightened from month to month. Hence, although both the Hopes and Barings are satisfied, my own difficulties increase as to how to invest safely the sums held over here, and I doubt if those at home with only a European outlook can envisage them. I have asked for assistance, and recent letters from Messers Hope advise me that Herr Vincent Nolte of Paris and Leghorn has been retained by them to collaborate in our American operations. I can assure you he will be welcome, for I am frankly unable to give adequate attention to the multitudinous demands made upon me. I am informed that you are acquainted with this gentleman. Should he arrive by way of New Orleans, pray provide him with proper entertainment and careful information in advance of his arrival in Philadelphia.

I inclose you, for forwarding to Lestapsis at Vera Cruz, further drafts on the Mexican treasury, signed, in this instance, by the King of Spain himself, for the sum of four millions of dollars. I am told that we may soon expect more! The prospect of further enormous sums to place here on doubtful security, with shipments to Europe more difficult every day, alarms me. In this dilemma I am frankly asking for your further cooperation.

Kindly invest locally as much as possible from the further shipments of bullion you receive at New Orleans. I suggest that you try to forward it to Europe in the form of cargoes of cotton, rum, sugar and such other colonial produce as may come to hand. Bill these shipments to the Barings at London, as they will then be permitted to pass the British cruisers. Let the Barings make their own arrangements for the transfer of the value of these cargoes to Holland. Our responsibility will be at an end with the arrival of the cargoes in England.

Now this is throwing more on your shoulders than you guaranteed to assume. Yet I feel justified, under the circumstances, in calling upon you, and you can name your own remuneration in reason. This is your authority for making all necessary outlays for the furtherance of the prime object we both have in view. With every assurance of continued esteem and personal regards from me and my family, who are always very particular about you, believe me always, and in any event—

Yr. humble obedient servant,

DAVID PARISH

To Mr. Anthony Adverse,
Cor. of Rue St. Claude
   and the Public Place at
New Orleans, Territory of Orleans, U.S.

This letter completely changed the tenor of Anthony's life in New Orleans. He was impelled by it to become the chief purchaser of cotton, sugar, and rum in Louisiana, and to extend himself in every direction that promised a profitable opening for shipments abroad. He took up land himself and planted a great acreage in cotton.

Parish's letter had alarmed him. The man seemed to be losing his grip. Never before had David become so personal—and so complaining. He wrote to Vincent at the first opportunity, urging him to come quickly, painting the life in the new country in glowing colours. "Bring Katrina and set up here. And, Vinc, if you love me, bring my boy, no matter what Anna may say." He wrote this and threw away the pen in excitement. To think of meeting Vincent and young Tony at the levee! "My God, life will be worth living then!" He called to Simba and rushed out to send the letter down river by a dispatch boat in order to catch a Spanish brig that had left that morning. The letter went.

On the same day Vincent Nolte was taking leave of Mr. Hope at Amsterdam in order to sail for New York. Katharina was dead. The House of the Wolf was desolate.

On the first rising ground to the west of the city, in what was then the Parish of St. Charles, Anthony built and laid out the lovely plantation of "Silver Ho" upon which he lavished the fondest dreams of his soul and a wealth of hope. The outlay was in proportion. For the first time he opened the strings of his own purse indulgently and to his heart's content. For it was here that he intended to live and die and to bring up his son. His longing to see the boy and to welcome him into his inheritance had already caused him to look upon his arrival in the near future as an indisputable fact. It was one of those "facts" which the brain dares not dispute with the heart. "Yes, at any moment young Tony and Vincent might arrive."

It was for that reason that he hastened the construction of the house beyond the precedents of the neighbourhood and built it of frame instead of brick, as he would otherwise have liked to do. But, as it was, he built well; of cedar and cypress and yellow-pine hewn out of his own swamps to the north near Lake Pontchartrain. For he had bought for his own and leased on account of "David Parish" a domain that

577

ran clear across the "neck" from the lake to the river.

The house stood on what in the low-country passed for a knoll, a kind of low ridge covered with live-oaks, ashes, great-flowering magnolias, and clumps of pine. He cleared it carefully, accentuating its park-like aspects, leaving a patch of primeval woods at a distance of about a quarter of a mile surrounding the house.

You came upon Silver Ho suddenly. You emerged from these grey woods into the green of wide, embowered lawns dotted with live-oaks, each a pavilion of tattered moss shot through with a shimmering splendour. For it is the peculiar quality of these great trees to catch the light and hold it in the masses of their mossy nets. "That is why it is called Spanish moss," thought Anthony: "No gold slips through its fingers." There was a sharp curve in a clump of these giants and then you saw the house.

From a grove of magnolias its pillared face, chequered with white and gold shadows, looked calmly at the broad reaches of the Mississippi rolling along below it a full half-mile away. Its copper roof flashing in the sun—for he had drawn upon the shipyard extensively in his building—was for some time a mark for pilots before they rounded the great curve of the river above New Orleans. At last the roof weathered with patches of green, and the house seemed to sink back into the trees surrounding it until it became part of the magnolia grave itself.

It was not in any sense an extraordinary mansion. It belonged to the time and place. Ample, well-suited to the climate and hospitable, it had wide-flung verandas, high ceilings and generous lights. Both the house itself and its surroundings breathed abundance, leisure, and a capacity and love of living which in more northern climates would have been regarded as extravagant or unmoral. Upon the interior the skilful hands of ship carpenters left that mark of neat convenience, grace, and symmetry, the secret of which perished with them and can only be imitated.

Silver Ho was peculiar, however, in one respect. It was a whim of its owner. The young architect James Gallier protested, but Anthony insisted upon having his own way. Every stairway and hall, every entrance to the interior of the house led off from the large central room whose main embellishment was a great chimney. There was, to be sure, a rear entrance to the "L." But the "L" itself led into the big hall.

This provision was perhaps not so whimsical after all. By closing one door you closed all of them; that is, you closed the house. And on Silver Ho there were to be only a half dozen white men and eight hundred slaves. Insomnia in Louisiana was not due to the climate alone. One door to a house was a positive sedative.

Simba was to sleep in the living-hall. Anthony had his desk, his library, and his papers there. In that place the master of Silver Ho was to be at home—and his son and his son's sons after him. At that date one still peered into the future with some promise of permanence. Into the chimney-place to the right of the fire-place Anthony built a niche. And into this, when the first fire should be kindled upon the hearth, he intended to put his madonna, which had been so carefully refurbished by the jewellers in Paris. Here her wandering was to have an end at last. Here about the hearth, lares and penates visible and invisible were to shed the lustre of their calm and benign presences in the fire-light. And there was to be peace.

Such dreams have been dreamed before and since. Even Vincent had agreed with Anthony that that is what banking is about.

Thus the fall and winter of 1806-1807 was intensely happy for Anthony. He was engaged constantly, early and late, upon a multiplicity of affairs that all seemed to have found a reason and a pole to revolve about at Silver Ho.

He took to horseback again, riding out to the plantation in the early mornings to urge the builders on, and riding back to town about noon for lunch with the doctor at Ba'tiste's and a swift survey of mail and accounts in Sandy's room. Then there was a meeting at the bank or a trip across the river to the shipyard when a new convey of silver came slipping up the bayous from Barataria. There was the infinite exercise of ingenuity in laying out the money in cargoes, in the sending of ships by hook or crook to England or a European port—anywhere, so long as the Hopes or the Barings finally got the goods. There were also schooners to be dispatched to Philadelphia, dispatch boats to Lestapsis at Vera Cruz, and the constant assiduous and often costly nursing of relations with the Lafittes.

Yet with Vincent and the boy in the offing, with the house nearing completion, he enjoyed and throve and grew merry upon it. He sold M'Quiston the flotage, retaining only a third interest. There was no longer time for nor the need of supervising that floating store. The town itself was now eagerly demanding more European goods than could be imported. Purchasing, instead of selling, was now Anthony's chief interest. To be a purchaser of everything is to be persona grata to everybody. He enjoyed the atmosphere he engendered everywhere in spite of the fact that he understood the cause.

He bought and imported all materials for erecting the plantation and for the partial furnishing of the house, in less than a year. There were three separate villages of huts for the slaves and houses for the general and house servants. There was also the expensive strengthening of the levee, the cutting of timber and the drainage of swamps. Not the least of the labour was a plantation road and its branches and the establishing of a ferry over the Bayou St. Jean that formed the boundary of his domain nearest the city.

As fast as he could shelter them he acquired his slaves from the Lafittes. He also resumed correspondence on the subject with Cibo in Cuba. His experience in Africa now leaped to the fore. Even Jean Lafitte had to admit that "no gen'leman in Louisiana knows as much about niggers as Mr. Adverse." Aided by Cibo, the house servants were brought from Cuba.

Carlo also began to write about paying Anthony a visit. It was a pleasant thought as he sat, now a mountain of flesh, on the veranda in the patio looked after hand and foot by Cheecha, who had received everything but her freedom.

And then, quite suddenly it seemed, for the busy months had passed frantically, Silver Ho was finished. The lowlands were green with cane and the uplands white with cotton. The chimney of the house waited for its first smoke. But no fire had yet been kindled on the hearth. Neither Vincent nor the boy had arrived. And with a curiously reminiscent and inconsistent pleasure, like that of a bachelor going the rounds of his old haunts and cronies a few days before his marriage, Anthony returned to taste of the freedom of the city while he lingered on in New Orleans.

The charm of the place lay in its enormous contrasts. He could find the raw and primitive tang of the elemental life of frontier living among the Kaintucks, coureurs de bois, and Indians at the Batture and at M'Quiston's flotage. Or he could saunter along the now thriving mercantile houses of the levee and waterfront streets, turn the corner, and by merely crossing the threshold of the Café des Exilés be in France. There would be M. le marquis de Pierfonds reading *Le Moniteur de la Louisiane* over an apéritif, the chatter of the old régime, and the ardent fluctuating hopes of the Bonapartists. He could stroll, as he so often did about twilight with the dim oil lamps beginning to burn and lanterns commencing to flit about in archways and courtyards, past the candle-lit windows of the shops of Catalans and the boutiques of Creoles along the Rue Ste. Anne, listening to the soft patois, the click of billiards behind closed shutters, to the low hum of cafés that in the summer evenings began to spread out into the half-paved streets. For every ship now brought her ballast in paving stones.

He never grew tired of the sunset on the river behind him, that seemed to be taking place in the south, and of the fires on the deckhearths of the schooners lying in the Basin Carondelet. He would look up and down the Rue Ste. Anne from one glow to the other, each crossed by a tangle of sails. And he could then go to supper with Dr. Mitchell and Ed Livingston at Ba'tiste's, but preferably with Dr. Mitchell alone.

Afterward, the punch and card room downstairs would fill up with everybody. Vain and loud General Wilkinson, and the soft Jewish voice of Judah Touro were heard there. Creole planters, Philip Marigny who had once been a page at Versailles, Etienne de Boré rich from sugar, Forstalls, Du Fossaus, Fleurieaus, and Duplessis'. Who was there that did not come or go? The silver tongue of Colonel Burr, explaining something, nobody afterward cared to remember just what, had come and gone. The garrulous Theodore Clapp argued predestination with the gentle Sylvester Larned. Members of the territorial legislature framed deals or a bill "by and with the advice and consent of Ed Livingston," as General Claiborne remarked, while Jim Caldwell and Sam Peters listened-in or discussed the new waterworks project. There was no end to what went on in the punchroom at Ba'tiste's. Nobody agreed about anything to speak of, and Dr. Mitchell in a philosophically insulting manner—carrying his liquor and the reputation of his pistol like a gentleman—disagreed with everybody, and was never challenged.

The doctor built the new hospital by the city commons largely by the sheer charm and fear of his delicately impersonal insults. One associated him with the hot atmosphere of tobacco, succulent herbs, spices and peppers of Ba'tiste's; his skill with a probe under the oaks in the morning after a duel with the skill of Ba'tiste and his long-handled saucepan over the fire. One forgave him, too. One remembered in the back of one's mind how he had delivered the baby or—if the provocation was great—one recalled how he shot champagne bottles off the heads of little niggers at fifty yards. "Now, son, watch this picayune on the wall until you hear bang." Those, after all, were great evenings. And if one tired of it—there was the open door, and *La Comédie* in St. Peter Street or the *St. Philippe* on St. Philippe, between Royal and Bourbon, only a few blocks away with *L'Ecossais en Louisiane, La Commerce de Nuit* or similar dramatic fare, and *loges grillé* if one happened to be in mourning.

Although one might possibly regret such nights as these even at Silver Ho—with nobody there, thought Anthony. "My God, would Vinc and little Tony *never* come!" Simba brought a family of thirteen into being in an old coach by a moth-eaten mistress, who had nothing to recommend her but her fecundity and soulful brown eyes. Anthony sent them all to the plantation with his blessings—and pondered over the empty house. Others were doing the same, he discovered. He accepted invitations. The year ended. No word from Vincent.

One evening as he walked down the Rue Ste. Anne near the corner of Dauphine where the lamplight streamed across the pavement in bars through some tightly closed lattices, he stopped as if he were unable to step across them. He stopped dead. In the room upstairs someone was playing "Malbrouk s'en va-t-en guerre."

He . . .

THE ODYSSEY OF MRS. UDNEY

The Parishes, with Mrs. Udney, who intended to see that something was pulled out of the mess of David's affairs for Florence, had proceeded from Philadelphia to Pittsburgh. "Proceeded," euphemistically speaking. As Europeans they had no conception of the size of North America or what the wilderness was like. Hitherto money, class distinctions, and commercial fineness,

583

in a highly organized society millenniums old, had sufficed to supply their physical needs-luxuriously and to confirm their mental prejudices. But Lancaster, a few leagues west of Philadelphia, was the west-limit of this society in the autumn of 1806. Beyond that the chemical realities of nature began.

Mrs. Udney left her bandboxes at Lebanon and David left his temper, the chaise, and most of the rest of the baggage at Lancaster. The track between there and Harrisburg was merely a passage through the forests along the banks of the Susquehanna, accomplished in a German farm wagon that pitched like a '74 off Ushant in a bad gale. Mrs. Udney and Florence wrapped themselves in buffalo robes, which they were at first inclined to regard as smelly, but ended by purchasing for gold, since their own costumes for the journey were such as to have caused the Kobolds of Penn's woods, if there had been any, to make lush noises.

At Harrisburg a son of the man for whom the town was named provided them a comfortable night's rest and a drink of white, corn whiskey that laid David out long and low. He remained two days recovering, at the end of which time another wagon with some of the baggage caught up with them, and David was enabled to go on in a pair of new boots. His old ones had been left outside his door to be polished and had been "polished off." Mrs. Udney and Florence also found themselves provided with some London millinery that permitted them to look at the Allegheny Mountains in the best form, while adorned in heron plumes. There was nothing else, however, as the man had brought the wrong trunks.

They continued on westward, into the wall of mountains, thanks to the Conemaugh River which had been rather thoughtless of nice people in the kind of desultory pass it made through the ridges. In order to strike the military road to Pittsburgh they went up the Juniata to Ray's Town. Their sufferings were intense, and David, whose feet had swollen, had to be cut out of his only boots. He was also induced to drink of a medicinal spring at Ray's Town, with harrowing results.

The intervention of a Mr. Cessna, who took them into his house at this point, according to Mrs. Udney's diary saved their lives. Cessna conferred upon David a pair of brogues, in which there was plenty of room for his feet to swell, and packed them all off in another Conestoga wagon driven by a drunken Scotch-Irishman who got them as far as Saltsburg on the Kiskiminitas River. A Mrs. Murray, who lived in a log cabin at the forks of the river, took mercy on them, sheltered them, and fed them on deer collops, hominy and sassafras tea.

David was now all for turning back. He knew already that his money was lost and he hadn't had a glass of wine for six weeks in a country which he also suspected to be running over with nothing but laxative springs. He was therefore painfully thirsty.

Mrs. Udney, however, remembered she was an Englishwoman. Going back without having collected what she felt was due her was not in her line. She made friends with Mrs. Murray, patched her clothes as best she could, and pushed on down the valley of the Kiskiminitas. Although she was now sixty-three years of age, she walked. And she forced Mr. and Mrs. David Parish to walk with her as far as the Allegheny River.

That walk was the turning point in the life of Florence.

Hitherto she had been lost. She had sat silent during the trip. She had felt like a demure schoolgirl suddenly plumped down into the midst of the largest continent on Jupiter in order to study botany. Her desire to accompany David on this western trip had not been "heroic" at all. She was bored with Philadelphia, and the tales of the settlements had filled her with curiosity. Confronted by real hardships and some genuine suffering, by large mountains that rolled away north and south like titanic walls aflame with the mad motley of the American fall, she had simply subsided into herself and ceased to listen to her husband's complaints, while her mother supplied the will power.

She was not altogether to be blamed for this. She had led a soft life. The change was overwhelming, and Mrs. Udney always had supplied the will power. Between her husband and her mother, Florence had succumbed.

But the actual physical severities of the trip since they had left Philadelphia weeks before had now awakened her. The rest at Mrs. Murray's enabled her to do some thinking. And the crisp, sensible replies of her frontier hostess to the demands of David, whose mood was one of blind self-pity, as he sat by the fire in the log cabin with his feet in a bucket of warm water and wept, had been an education. Florence made certain resolves about herself and her future attitudes to both her husband and her mother when they should return to civilization. She kept these in reserve, but she intended from now on to act upon them. Along with her mother, she now began to disregard the physical severities of the trip. Between them they got David Parish to Pittsburgh about the middle of October.

They spent a week in that little town while David completed his investigations of titles to certain land grants by the help of General Harmer and some of the Denys' who had participated with him in one of his western schemes. In the meanwhile, in a small brick house on Diamond Street, Florence and Mrs. Udney worked desperately hard making themselves new clothes while they were called upon by the Robinsons, the Nevilles, the Witherows, and the Wilsons, who regaled them with the gossip of the neighbourhood in flat nasal tones.

But if the tone was flat the gossip was magnificent. It was not only dangerous and spicy, it was international.

Colonel Aaron Burr was staying at Blennerhassett's Island. He was making love to Mrs. Blennerhassett.

Colonel Burr was organizing an expedition against Mexico. Or was it a revolution? Some said one thing, some another. Some said both. Mr. Blennerhassett was a sweet gentleman who had built a paradise in the wilderness for his lovely bride. Mr. Blennerhassett was a terrible man who had married his own niece and fled from Europe. Colonel Burr's daughter and her husband, Governor Alston of South Carolina, were at Blennerhassett's. Mrs. Alston approved of her father's love-making to Mrs. B. She did not approve. She knew nothing about it. There were meetings at night of conspirators. New Orleans was to be the capital of a new empire. Colonel Burr had been heard to say so at Colonel Wilkins' own table and Laura Detweiler was there . . .

Mrs. Udney almost squeaked with excitement as she heard all this.

"Aw-w," said Miss Lizzie Witherow, looking down her long Scotch-Irish nose, "and the warst of it is they have music and dancing on the Sabbath. I'm not sure you'll be wantin' yur datter to go there even if she is a married wooman, Mrs. Udney." But that was where Miss Witherow was wrong. When she called next day with a basket of pop-corn balls and hickory nuts for the English ladies they had both gone.

America is full of surprises and nothing in any time or place could have been more astonishing than Blennerhassett's Island in the Ohio River in the late autumn of 1806.

In the midst of the wilderness a little below Pittsburgh, and at a staggering cost, the Irishman Blennerhassett had built himself an exquisite and completely appointed English gentleman's estate. It was furnished perfectly, from a telescope in the observatory to the statues on the lawns. He brought Adam furniture over the mountains and wines up the river from New Orleans. He had a beautiful wife and beautiful children. He ate off silver and was served by slaves, his only concession to the land of freedom. The scenery was

587

wild and romantic. The hunting and fishing magnificent. And Blennerhassett was still young. Into this paradise on the Ohio walked the devil in the charming form of Colonel Aaron Burr, who had come within one vote of being President of the United States and now intended to be Emperor of Mexico—or boss of whatever he could get from Spain by the help of the money of anybody who wanted to take a chance and equip a few western volunteers.

Burr had for years been talking about his scheme to everybody from New Orleans to Pittsburgh. And he was talking about it in Blennerhassett's library when Mr. and Mrs. David Parish and Mrs. Udney arrived from Pittsburgh, coming down-river in a four-oared scow. The fact that David Parish was Blennerhassett's creditor to a considerable amount did nothing to dull the welcome. As for Colonel Burr, he regarded Parish's advent as an act of God in his favour. He admitted the first evening that all he wanted was a hundred thousand pounds.

It was impossible to be in the same house with so many able and charming conspirators and not be taken into the conspiracy. In a few days David was genuinely alarmed. If Burr succeeded, if he even delivered an attack on Mexico by way of Louisiana, the flow of silver from Vera Cruz to New Orleans would be stopped. Ouvrard's great scheme and the entire framework in the United States, which he and Anthony had so carefully built up, would have its life-blood cut off at the source. For them everything depended on maintaining the Spanish royal authority in Mexico.

He was quite successful. All that Burr needed was money. Volunteers would flock to him if he could equip them. Could or would Parish consider arranging for supplies, say, for a thousand men at New Orleans, and ship them up the Mississippi to meet Burr coming down? Blennerhassett had already pledged his fortune to the adventure, it appeared. He and Governor Alston were heavily involved. The men and boats were to start down the Ohio as emigrants going to settle west of the river. Mr. Jefferson had encouraged that. There would be no trouble. The United States was just on the brink of war with Spain anyway.

"Let the word once get home that Burr has struck the first blow and ten thousand bold spirits will flock to me," cried the magnetic little soldier. "In six months we shall have Mexico and the treasures of Montezuma in our hands."

Parish promised to think the matter over seriously— and he did so. Far from being a madman's dream, he concluded with alarm that Burr's chance of success was uncomfortably probable.

David knew one thing, however, which Colonel Burr had no idea of. He knew that General James Wilkinson, U. S. A., commander of the American forces in and about New Orleans, was in the pay of the Spanish crown. He knew the exact amount of the pension, for he had seen it entered regularly in the accounts marked "strictly confidential—destroy" forwarded him by Anthony from New Orleans. The authority for paying it was a letter from the Prince of the Peace with the endorsement of Ouvrard as the agent for the Spanish treasury.

David's first impulse was to write a letter to Anthony, warning him of the dangerous situation arising from Burr's conspiracy and advising him to apply to General Wilkinson to stop it. He actually wrote the letter. Then he thought better of it. It would be better still to go to New Orleans himself, confer with Anthony, and go direct to Wilkinson. He could arrive there as soon as a letter. Therefore, he pretended to Burr that he was willing to further his schemes and would depart immediately to New Orleans in order to do so. Burr was delighted and gave Parish a cipher letter addressed to Wilkinson who, he had every right to suppose from previous interviews, was favourable to his plans and would further them. Nothing could have suited Parish better. He had a flat-boat fitted up as rapidly and luxuriously as possible, and taking Florence and Mrs. Udney with him, bade goodbye to Burr, Blennerhassett, and the Alstons and started for New Orleans.

Parish had been greatly harassed at the possibility of all his plans' collapsing suddenly, should Burr's threat to Mexico cut off the silver shipments. He saw himself returning to Europe ruined and disgraced, for he had involved himself heavily in America along with Ouvrard's investments. In his own name he held vast tracts of land upon which payments were not yet complete. He felt he was doing all he could to circumvent Burr and to anticipate him with Wilkinson. But the slow progress down the river exasperated him. The trip over the mountains had exhausted him. His hands and feet were continually blue and swollen, and he could get no relief. At Cincinnati he dispatched a special courier to Herr Nolte, hoping that Vincent had arrived by now in Philadelphia. In this epistle was a complete exposition of his affairs. The composition exhausted him and Florence had to finish it by dictation.

"If anything happens to me," he said to Florence and Mrs. Udney, looking up during the writing, "I count on you to deliver my own letter with Burr's cipher addressed to General Wilkinson to Adverse at New Orleans." He looked out apprehensively at the banks of the Ohio slowly gliding past the boat as they slid along with the current. "Tell him I count on him to prevent possible ruin. Tell him to act without delay."

"Oh, don't be silly, David," said Florence and went on copying.

But David was not silly. He died three days later of heart disease on a chair in the cabin.

The current of the great river continued to sweep the boat steadily toward New Orleans.

. . . turned suddenly to the door and began to knock violently. The music stopped. He heard a swift scurrying rush of feet and skirts in the room upstairs—and recognized Mrs. Udney's memorable giggle. He pushed the door open and stepped in. The hall was dark, and for a moment he hesitated. Suddenly at the far end of it there was a glow at the top of the stairs.

Florence was coming down the steps carrying a single candle. She was very pale, dressed in mourning, and had a row of black pearls about her throat. In the darkness, shielding the candle with one hand, she seemed to be bathed in fire.

"Is it you, Anthony?" she said, stopping, suddenly aware of him in the shadows below.

"Yes," he whispered.

She drew breath tensely.

"Is David?" he gasped.

"Yes—or no—I don't know what you mean," she faltered.

"Don't you?" said he. "By God, I'll show you!"

The candle rolled to the bottom of the stairs.

For the first time in her life Mrs. David Parish understood what it might be like to be married.

Sitting in the front room at the little pianoforte that she had carefully borrowed for the occasion, Mrs. Udney sniffed. Something was burning downstairs.

"Mercy," she cried, looking over the banisters at the candle-end smouldering on the carpet and smoking away, "if you children aren't careful you'll set the house afire. Now come upstairs this instant. It's disgraceful."

Nevertheless, when they were once seated before her, she looked at them with a satisfaction she could not conceal.

"I shall never let go of her hand again, madame," said Anthony, suddenly trying to recover his dignity in order not to look so ridiculous.

"Lord!" said Mrs. Udney, and the tears came into her eyes.

"And before you go back to father in England next

spring you'll see us married and settled, won't you, mother?" added Florence. "I think it's only right to wait for at least six months after . . ."

"Oh, why mention his name *at all*, my dear?" replied her mother, who had not expected to sail for England until autumn at least. She brushed away the tears for a second time and looked at her daughter. Never in her life had Florence given her mother so sweet a smile.

Mrs. Udney understood that her work was over. She seized Anthony suddenly by the shoulders and shook him. "You take care of her. Take care of her, you lucky vagabond," said she crying, and kissed him.

And of course he promised.

They were married in April. Mr. Levritt, the British consul, gave the bride away. Old Sandy McNab was the best man. He never fully recovered from the pride of the occasion and the height of his stock. At least his neck grew permanently stiff. They were married by a Protestant clergyman, for Mrs. Udney insisted upon that. And they were married at the cathedral with considerable fanfare, for Anthony felt that to be not only more comfortable to himself but most advisable in the Territory of Orleans.

At any rate there was no doubt in anybody's mind that "Anthony Adverse, gentleman, and Florence Amanda Colcros Parish, née Udney," were man and wife. They went for their honeymoon to Silver Ho. Two weeks of it. Then it ended. Mrs. Udney came to see that all was going well.

Florence and Mrs. Udney had spent the early winter and spring refurnishing the house. Anthony had given them a free hand. But he was surprised at the way they revelled in it. When they had finished there was not a better appointed house nor a more shining one in the entire region. And that was saying a great deal.

There were a good many changes to make in a house that had been arranged by a bachelor for himself and his only son in order to fit it for a husband and his bride. There were changes in the "schoolroom," which became the "nursery." The unused blackboard and maps were taken down and a more or less complete crèche installed. Mrs. Udney evidently believed in eventualities and in preparing for them.

"You might let that wait, mother," said Florence.

"My dear, you know nothing about it," replied Mrs. Udney. "And I might as well prepare things as far as I can—before I go. Do you agree with me?" She was bending over an empty baby basket as she said that. There was a little wait.

"Yes, I *do*," said Florence. Then she went out to the hall and cried. But she had made up her mind. Already she found Anthony talking over everything about the house with Mrs. Udney. To relent with her mother would be fatal. Her experience with David had at least taught her that.

So Mrs. Udney sailed for England in June.

She was bright and cheerful to the last. Anthony was greatly concerned. He would miss her motherly help and affection. With a shock he realized how much he had already begun to lean upon it. And with a shock he also realized that he had missed just that much in his wife.

As for Mrs. Udney, she waved a dry handkerchief to the last and then went down into her cabin for a brief, maternal Gethsemane over an only daughter for whom she had at last pulled the cherished chestnut out of the fire. "But I know she'll never, *never* forgive me for David," she thought, "and I don't blame her. I suppose we're even." So she forgave Florence—and missed Anthony. "I would like to see that boy of his." Mr. Udney would meet her at Dover, of course, if the rheumatism let him. Lamplight found her still sitting in her cabin with her hands in her lap. There was nothing to do now. "Oh, la," said Mrs. Udney . . .

"Cards!"

At Silver Ho the magnolia shade lay with a peculiar peace on the new lawn as the master and mistress drove up to the door. Florence leaned her head against his shoulder and Anthony knew that they were married at last.

That night he took his madonna from her fine Paris wrappings and set her into the niche by the hearth.

It was the year of the great excitement over the Burr Conspiracy. General Wilkinson had not been slow to act on the information conveyed to him by the letter from Parish and by Burr's own cipher. Anthony had lost no time in placing them both in his hands with the remark that one of the best ways to spurn a Spanish pension drawn upon the Mexican treasury would be to encourage Colonel Burr.

General Wilkinson's patriotism was immediately kindled to white heat. Burr was proclaimed a traitor against the United States. The militia were called out. People were arrested right and left in New Orleans and shipped off for trial without recourse. For a while the Territory of Orleans became a pure military despotism with Wilkinson roaring and threatening anybody he didn't like. Burr was stopped at Natchez and fled east, to be captured and tried for high treason at Richmond. The Spanish troops on the Mexican border resumed a life of sunny leisure varied by pulque and cheroots—and the silver shipments continued from Vera Cruz. Two hundred dollars a week to an American general had delayed the course of manifest destiny at least thirty years.

Anthony took no part in this. He strove in every way to conceal the workings of the Ouvrard scheme which depended upon a total lack of publicity for success. His only touch with the Burr affair after Wilkinson let loose the military was to prevent the arrest of Livingston, who had lent Burr money on his Bastrop lands. For a week Livingston came to live at Silver Ho.

594

After which time, and a call upon the general by Mr. Adverse, the danger mysteriously passed.

"And I wish you would also arrange to release Dr. Mitchell, general."

"A dangerous man, sir, if there ever was one," thundered Wilkinson, "but I'll attend to the matter nevertheless. I am in debt to your own discretion about certain matters, Adverse."

"You can rely upon it, general. But it is contingent upon your own discretion in making arrests hereafter."

The general swallowed. "I hope you and Mrs. Adverse are enjoying your honeymoon at Silver Ho. A delightful place, I hear."

"Delightful," said Anthony—and it was.

Except for this sortie in the interest of harassed friends, Anthony scarcely left the plantation. He turned the management of the silver shipments more and more into the hands of McNab and the organization at Algiers. A watchful eye was all that was needed now to continue a routine. Besides, Vincent Nolte was now in Philadelphia filling the place of Parish. In a business way that was an immense relief.

Vincent had not brought young Tony with him. "I will tell you why when I see you in New Orleans next summer," he wrote. "Do not worry about the boy. He is well, and still with Anna at Düsseldorf. In the meantime I must devote myself to affairs here which the death of Parish has greatly complicated." The rest of the letter was about Anthony's marriage. Vincent said nothing about his own. He could not bear to think of it.

What would have been the result if the boy had come? Anthony often wondered.

He had told Florence about him, of course. She had taken it calmly enough. "I didn't suppose you had just been living at the convent," she said. And so he said nothing more to her about Angela, and she said nothing to him about David. There seemed to be a tacit agreement between them that the past was to be the past.

595

He burned the blackboard taken from the "school-room" and sold a boy's pony with *"unused saddle and harness, owner sacrifices for private reasons, spirited, well-bred, little horse."* And that was that.

Next April, if all went well, there was to be someone in the nursery. That fact also occasionally brought Dr. Terry M. with the best excuse in the world for a visit. The room at the end of the wing was soon known as "the doctor's chamber."

For the rest, the days slipped into one another deep with peace and contentment, bright with hope for the future, pleasantly busy with the affairs of the great plantation. But above all, complete with that double-entity, that hyphenated entirety of existence between man and wife that makes home—and that makes all other places and conditions merely more or less tolerable by comparison.

For Anthony and Florence loved each other. He did not love her as passionately as she loved him. For him passion in its highest sense could have been complete only with Angela—had been complete. And for that reason, because it was forever denied him to confer the final crown of existence upon Florence, he loved her with a transcendent pity; with a determination to have life make up that loss to her in every other way. He cherished her with a careful, thoughtful tenderness that surpassed her understanding—that frequently puzzled her.

Florence had loved Anthony as a girl at Livorno. It had been a fresh, sweet, and secret affection that *he* had felt and compared then with the mist upon banks of flowers in early spring. Upon that had fallen the frigid influence of the cold, rigid years with David and the worldly-wise guidance of Mrs. Udney. Spring had withdrawn herself and hidden through that unnatural winter. Then the sun had shone out again unexpectedly from the face of Anthony. Spring had passed. It was the summer in full leaf and flower that leaped out of the unploughed ground.

In her new husband Florence found not only what she had lost but what she had never hoped to find. In him she had at last found herself.

This was not a fragile beginning for a union for life for either of them. As time went on it burgeoned in its own way and filled their lives.

The time of the coming of the child passed, a time infinitely close and dowered with peace in which they drew nearer to the centre and core of the mystery of life. Love and tenderness were having their fulfillment. It had not been put-off and starved and asked to repeat and wear itself out. It was taking its natural course and it would soon become embodied and visible.

All that, Anthony felt and shared with his wife when he finally held the child in his arms.

Florence had given birth to her little girl with great difficulty. But she recovered rapidly afterwards and was the better and more vigorous for it. The strained expression and a touch of hardness that had begun to disfigure her expression in the days with David disappeared forever.

It was Anthony's whim, he said, to call the child "Maria." And that name seemed good to both of them. For the first time in many weeks they drove to the city in the new family coach for the christening.

By the hearth in the great living-room the ancient statue of the madonna stretched forth her hands with the babe in them into the pleasant firelight and into the darkness. The figure of the man who sometimes came to kneel before her with a heart full of gratitude and unexpected contentment she may have known. For they had wandered together from the first and in many regions. He on his part was quite sure that he had looked upon the final and most benign expression of her face. Meanwhile, unchanging, she continued to stand there in her niche.

With the birth of little Maria all things at Silver Ho seemed to its master and mistress to be caught up into the longer and more spacious rhythms that mark, for those who can feel them, both the passing and the growth of life.

Spring flashed into summer and summer burned into fall. The sun could be felt slipping down the horizon as the cooler days came. It was "Happy Christmas." Then the jasmine bloomed, the magnolias flowered, the pride of India released its incense and it was glorious June. Likewise moved the body and soul of man responding even to the minor phrases of the moon, content to feel them without knowing their cause—as who can? And in this, having her small but infinitely important part as a particular bud of the general seed from which she sprang, the child wailed, walked, talked—and sang.

Summoned from the deep out of darkness by a process apparently inadequate to the result, the child retained in herself, as do all the children of men, the ineffable secret of her cause. She was part of it. Suddenly and mysteriously there was a new personality in the house. There was another soul. Family life began.

To Anthony the science of Dr. Terry Mitchell—and science at any given date was always appallingly modern—seemed to have as little bearing upon this whole process as the doctor's hands and wooden instruments had had at the birth of the child. The hands were willing enough, but the instruments . . . they were like the good doctor's philosophy, a last and desperate mechanical resort.

In a half-bantering way Anthony and the doctor frequently renewed the argument begun that night the nuns had fled. But they never got anywhere logically. The synthesis of their friendship resided in something larger than that. It lay in their mutual humanity, in their desire to do whatever they could do to make the lot of those about them better.

Both had long given up trying to do anything for that myth called "mankind." But they did so the best they knew how, within the bounds of their ignorance, for various men, women, and children they could affect.

And their desire to help was not confined to those within the bounds of natural affection. Their sympathy —or charity, call it what you will—was greater than that. Yet it always remained personal. In a time and century devoted to the acceleration of the millennium by leavening the mass with paper in the form of political documents, money, Bibles, tracts, and newspapers, there was something to be said in their favour. At least they practised their sympathy directly in a scheme of good-doing. With Anthony it took the pattern of a large art of living; with Dr. Mitchell the form of the practice of medicine.

There was, to be sure, the new hospital on the commons in town to which Mr. Adverse gave so generously in money and Dr. Mitchell in service, but one had better concentrate, as they did, in the practice of both their arts at Silver Ho.

———————————

Fourteen thousand acres and—before Maria was four years old—over a thousand hands constituted the modest realm of their activities. There was "Sugarville," set in the broad lowlands of the plantation that marched along the levee with the yellow river rolling past them in a great bend around which disappeared into the distance the rippling fields of cane; and on the "heights" above was "Cottontown," where the plateau-levels broke out under the hot sun into a captious winter of blossoming snowdrifts of the plant which clothes man.

And before long there were corn and rice fields, and the fertile tract near the mansion given over to the raising of vegetables and fruit.

Each one of these separate industries employed its

own overseer and gang. There were gangs devoted to the animals and pastures; to lumbering in the swampy forests near the lake; gangs on the wharfs and levee, and the rice irrigation. From the upper windows of the house Anthony looked down to the ships landing at the wharfs and to the smoke of his cotton gin and press and sugar works, for the steam engine had already begun to turn even on the banks of the Mississippi.

Faced by the ever-growing difficulty of exploring and importing to Europe, Anthony strove as far as possible to organize Silver Ho as a complete and self-sufficient plantation and to depend more and more for the necessaries brought in from outside upon domestic trade.

As a consequence most of the arts essential to existence flourished on the place in the hands of expert negro craftsmen proud of their place in the community and of the separate shops and cottages which were theirs. There were few things, from carpentry to tailoring, one could not get done at Silver Ho, and done very well. And in this it did not differ so greatly from many another plantation of the time.

The centre of the infinite activities of the place was, of course, the house itself. Sugarville and Cottontown each had its white overseer's house near by, and several other white men and their families were scattered at various places over the plantation. They were mostly men from the North. The chief-overseer had a small, neat house just over the pine ridge from the mansion. He was a Quaker by the name of Josiah Fithian from the banks of the Brandywine. Anthony had obtained his services under unusual circumstances and trusted him, for he was both kindly and just. Yet despite this watchful delegation of authority, the big house was the essential centre of things.

Here before the broad mahogany desk of the master in his library was the court of last resort. Here a careful justice was administered, and here, upon occasions, the overseers met for consultation or the advice and remonstrance of the more trusted servants was listened to and acted upon. Here the great account books were kept by Anthony with endless patience, toil, and forethought. And here also was a book of moral aphorisms, a diary, and a volume of "Philosophical Reflections" frequently pored over and entered upon. On the shelves about began to accumulate the calf-bound tomes devoted to religion, learning, the sciences and fine arts, and a surprising number of books from London, Paris, and Philadelphia given over to nothing but amusement —there were even some plays. On the desk, whenever they appeared, were laid *The Louisiana Gazette* and *Le Moniteur* by a smart little "jockey" who rode into town twice a week for the news.

Everything built or planted at Silver Ho was first planned on paper at this desk and marked on a great plot of the plantation which hung curling from the wall. All who came there to bargain, to buy, sell, or steal—and their name was legion—sat in the chair before Anthony's desk, talked to him, were entertained afterward as befitted them, and departed impressed by the order and peace of the establishment.

Mrs. Adverse, the mistress, did not make a good "job" of being a wife and mother. She had never heard of such a thing as a "job" in domestic life. She bore her child in the same way that the magnolias bore blossoms; i.e., as a function of a particular type of being. She became a mother, and she acted accordingly. Neither did it occur to her that she had the "job" of running the house and a great deal of the plantation to boot. She did not divide her life into separate compartments of unpalatable labour, bored leisure sweetened by frantic amusement, and exhausted rest. She would no more have spoken of the duties inherent in her being the mistress of the plantation as a "job" than Governor Claiborne would have thought that he "held the job at being governor." He *was* the governor of the Territory of Orleans. Florence Udney Adverse was the mistress of Silver Ho.

For the same reason Mr. Audubon, who occasionally came to paint birds at Silver Ho, was never heard to remark that the mallards in the marshes made a "good job of bringing up their young." They couldn't help it. They laid eggs and the eggs hatched when they sat on them. They brooded over life just as he did. The result in both cases was something remarkably like a duck without any "jobbing" having occurred by either the bird or the artist.

The kind of bird that could make a "job" out of living was still rara avis. And as for making a living out of a "job"—a few government contractors had just begun to try it, with the usual criminal results.

Melancthon Conant was the bird about New Orleans to do your jobbing for you, whether it was pickling your deceased aunt in brine, with a smile on her face warranted to last during her shipment home for burial, or buying up a few lively gals for the new *Sure Enuf Hotel* at the American landing—"M. Conant, Proprietor"— or selling wormy beef and paper shoes to General Jackson's heroes—Melancthon was the bird for the *job*—and a very good thing he made of it. But Mrs. Adverse did not do any jobbing at all. It was a word justly in bad odour. To have told Dr. Terry M. that he was "making a good 'job' of being a doctor" would have implied either that one was insane or doubted the doctor's marksmanship. Neither God nor man was yet debased by the glorious conception of the "job." No one had yet suggested that Christ had made a good job of being a saviour. It was still a very backward time. Progress and Fair Science were just beginning to feel out each other preparatory to begetting the factory.

Nor was Mrs. Adverse worried about her position as a woman. She had no doubt of it. Nor did she, when the baby proved to be a girl, try to call it by a boy's name. She acquiesced with the universe in the difference, and in a name which admitted it. Poor woman, her status was too secure and her life too full for her even to have thought of signing herself by her father's name after she was married in order to prove that she was independent of the conventions of men.

Meanwhile, without a "job," and without having insured her domestic importance by inverting the devices of gender, she managed to employ herself a little about the house and place, acceptably, and to while away the time from about six A.M. till before or after midnight.

There were only fifteen bedrooms at Silver Ho and they were not always all occupied. Five or six was a good average. All that was required of her menus was that they should be produced on the place, ample, elastic, well-cooked and dainty. The twenty house servants prevented anything from going to waste. They and she saw to it.

Spinning most of the cloth, weaving it, and making it up into the clothes; hemming all of the imported napery, and quilting; checking various chests and closets full of linen and the hangings used at different seasons throughout the house; seeing that the wash did not appear later at remote parts of the plantation—all this tended to encroach a little on her languid southern leisure, to say nothing of making the soap and candles.

In her room there was a keyboard with a hundred and eighty-three keys on it. With the use of each, and with their combinations, she was familiar. With this "keyboard" she played upon Silver Ho as upon a splendid instrument, providing those complicated domestic harmonies which are seldom even noticed until discord ensues.

A great many articles in the house were imported directly from Europe by ships that landed at the plantation dock, others she drove to the city to purchase. She kept the accounts of such transactions as well as her household ledgers and a little book for each of the house servants. She conducted a polite correspondence of social notes and replies with the other mistresses of the neighbourhood, besides writing long letters in long-hand to her relatives and friends in Europe. She kept a diary of sensible and pious thoughts.

Most of the domestic and amatory problems of the plantation were in her hands. In one year there were twenty-seven babies born on the place. She and Dr. Mitchell had arranged a crèche and trained midwives, who needed to be looked after. Widows were to be consoled, marriages arranged, wandering lovers from other plantations restrained, stories to be exacted from black girls in trouble and the child correctly fathered. Such things were merely routine. The depredations of witches and voodoo priestesses were also to be coped with, conjurors discouraged, and the sick and ailing visited.

Every day at eleven o'clock Florence mounted her horse and made the rounds of the quarters, while a thousand tales, requests, complaints, and wheedlings were poured into her ears. She knew her people and she brought them affection, mercy, and justice in the primary relationships of life.

Dinner was at three o'clock, when she saw her husband and discussed the day's problems with him. He had been on horseback since eight o'clock, seeing that every project on the plantation was making due progress. The afternoons, especially as the hot weather came on, were spent in the house. There was a siesta after dinner and then work or play, reading or callers in the afternoon. Six hours of constant activity in the mornings, on horseback, did not require a tennis court to keep the blood moving. But there were bowling, horseshoe pitching, boating, driving to pay visits, and such hunting and fishing as the seasons supplied—and how they did supply it and the table with game.

Gentlemen and their families from up-river passing up and down to the city stopped off at Silver Ho as a matter of course. This was not considered entertaining, it was merely "hospitality." Breakfast for ten—and away they went in their barge.

Entertaining was an entirely different matter. It was considered to be rather light at Silver Ho, for the Adverses had no relatives in the neighbourhood to ride over in parties of eight or twelve to spend a couple of weeks. They concentrated on dinners, dances, and midnight suppers.

At such times Florence shone in her best London and Paris frocks and was more or less the mirror of style and fashion for the neighbourhood. Anthony indulged her in imported furbelows to the limit and for his own satisfaction. Standing on the steps and saying good night with Florence on his arm, as they bowed the Creole gentry, the lawers and bankers, the American officials, and neighbours over the threshold, marked for them both a certain apex in life.

Some of Anthony's most tender memories of the place were of these nightly parties. Little Maria was greatly excited by the music and he would slip away sometimes to the nursery to quiet her and to sit beside her, while she lay back with her eyes wide in the moonlight. Or they would go to the balcony together to look out into the gardens below, while the couples sat about under the myrtles, and the great house pulsated with the melody of fiddles, the murmur of voices, and the tread of the dance.

He remembered, too, the silver-madness of moonlight nights, the huge, white clouds sailing slowly over the place with alternate dark and shadow upon the lowlands, the sound of banjos and black voices, and the glow of bonfires. How the dogs barked! He let his people keep them. And what is day to an African compared with the warmth and softness and lustre of the southern night?

"Adverse spoils his niggers," some of the neighbours grumbled. But it was universally admitted that he was a most generous and charitable gentleman, and that he and his gracious wife and lovely little child deserved the bounty which they so evidently strove in a hundred ways to share with all about them.

Anthony had no illusions about the system of slavery. He knew its beginnings and its end better than most of those about him. But he knew no other system in the time and place in which he lived. He tried to mitigate it and to alleviate it in every way that he could, using both intelligence and sympathy. He had not forgotten Brother François. The good man had not died entirely in vain. From the little madonna by the fireplace flowed many a mercy that the spirit of Brother François would have approved.

Life was not all dancing, and moonlight, and abundance at Silver Ho. It was also grim and tragic. Among a thousand people not all were saintly characters. Most of them were men and women. But there were also the usual number of beasts—ferocious, lustful, cunning, and all the rest of the catalogue—against which due precautions had to be taken and justice meted out.

Also, there was no way of shifting burdens off onto a general community. They were dealt with by the master and mistress. Silver Ho took care of its two madmen and three-simple minded children, its several crippled by accidents, and the sick and parentless. As yet there were no aged or infirm. But there would be. Anthony could see that. It was his books that made the most profound comment on it, after all. After five years the profits of the place began to decrease progressively. This was due partly to the condition of war and foreign trade. But it was also due to the fact that the natural increase of people on the plantation began to eat up its surplus. "What," thought Anthony, "will the books show ten years from now when many are old and infirm?" He thought this over a great deal. It was his chief worry. He once phrased it morally in a little note left on a ledger: "The earth says, 'In a few decades Silver Ho will be a lie.' Something or somebody else will then have to pay for it—or it will lapse." He thought with satisfaction of certain investments in England and he also began to pull in his horns.

Vincent Nolte came to New Orleans in the winter

of 1809 and took all of Ouvrard's affairs into his own hands. It was a great relief to Anthony. He brought old McNab to Silver Ho; closed his books in the city. He also unburdened himself of the leased lands. Life generally became easier after.

Anthony was now thirty-three and considered himself to be entering upon middle-age. The dates in local cemeteries gave him warrant for that. He and Florence would have liked another child, but none came. Vincent was now much about the house. The table seated him and the doctor almost as regularly as it did Anthony, Florence, and Maria. Old Sandy preferred his meals in his room and followed the child about as faithfully as did Simba, whose muzzle was turning grey.

The memories of these halcyon days by the great river were afterwards to be like springs of water in the wilderness, like the sound of doves murmuring outside a prisoner's cell.

For all things come to an end, usually with portents. There is a certain prophetic direction and gathering of speed and momentum in even very simple human affairs. It began at Silver Ho with the death of Sandy McNab and plague among the slaves.

Dr. Mitchell had vaccinated them and everybody else who was not pock-marked. But he could do nothing against other plagues. There was a sudden outbreak of white cholera. At Cottontown, out of four hundred in the quarters two hundred and thirty-six were removed. There was no question about having to sell the people now because of lessened acreage. That had greatly worried both Anthony and Florence. They kept putting it off. And then a West Indian sloop brought something Dr. Mitchell called "cachexia" that occupied him desperately.

No one at the big house was troubled by these plagues. But in the summer two of Florence's best spinners went by yellow fever. Maria was ill of some childish complaint in the fall. Then all seemed to be well again. But those days of quarantine, enforced by

607

Dr. Mitchell to the point of violence, had brought them all closer. No visitors. Only Anthony and Florence by the fire in the evenings; the child in his lap before bedtime; a sense of dangerous wings having brushed them and gone past leaving them closer. Maria understood that, too.

At last they were released.

He sat by the fire one November evening and looked into the coals. The madonna seemed to be particularly peaceful and dreamful in the firelight again. Later on he was to ride into town for a meeting at the Chamber of Commerce.

"Oh, daddy, don't go," cried Maria. "I want you to stay tonight."

"It *is* rather blustery, my dear," said Florence. "Is it important?"

"Well, rather. Ed Livingston is creating a good deal of excitement by his claims to the land the river is making in front of his holding along the Batture. There is likely to be some pretty hot argument pro and con. He asked me to be there."

Florence made no further remonstrance. It was not often he rode into New Orleans at night.

"Bring Vincent back with you then," she said. "We haven't seen him for weeks."

"Now, child, kiss your father good night."

Maria climbed on his knees, flaxen-haired and laughing. For a moment she lay quiet against his heart, while he promised to bring her something from town and watched his favourite curl over one small ear catch the firelight.

"Good night, good night."

They went upstairs, calling back to him. Simba rose as the horse was led around.

"Stay home, sir."

The dog lay down on the porch disappointed, waiting dejectedly to watch him go.

A window upstairs opened. Florence called down to him, "I wish you'd come and fix this lock on the nursery door, Anthony. I can't get the door open. We're closed in now." She laughed at her ridiculous plight.

"We're locked in, daddy," shouted little Marie.

"Oh, it's all right. Here comes Terry now."

He heard Dr. Mitchell's voice joking with the little girl in her room. The light went out and Florence and the doctor came downstairs. He saw them pass the window in the library—Florence with her high English colouring that she had never lost, her fine, frank, level glance, and the warm lights in her brown hair; the doctor looking tired and grey but as gallant as ever, his humorous mouth just about to say something amusing . . .

He touched his horse with the spurs and rode off into the darkness, leaving Simba staring after him with his head on his paws.

It was quite windy. He wrapped his cloak about him and looped it. He reached town about nine o'clock and found the Chamber of Commerce already in full session with a good deal of shouting and impassioned eloquence taking place. Old John McDonough was booming away as he came in.

"Never covet what is not your own. That, sir, is one of the principles by which every honourable man is proud to be regulated. But how, sir, has my honourable friend Mr. Livingston applied this precept? By fencing in the land which the river has been making. It is land made by an act of God. It rightfully belongs to the city, to the free and enlightened people of this great community."

"Can't God act in *my* favour?" asked the voice of Mr. Livingston from the corner.

"Not always," shouted McDonough.

"The Almighty, you know—by definition," insisted Mr. Livingston.

A roar of laughter, catcalls, jeers and imprecations followed this sally. John McDonough sat down, wiping his brow. Anthony settled himself hurriedly into his seat. Old Cicero went about snuffing the candles, while the wind rattled the windows and the suave voice of Mr. Livingston began to explain the very complicated nature of his riparian rights.

"My friends, far be it . . .

At Silver Ho, Dr. Mitchell and Florence finished a hand of whist and turned in. Dr. Mitchell was very tired and slept the sleep of the just. The wind bellowed in the chimney. A smouldering log leaped up and cracked. It spat a fat, live coal out onto the carpet. Presently the robe of the madonna, who stood holding the child out in the darkness, began to twinkle with little flames.

The wind in the chimney at Silver Ho and the orators at the Chamber of Commerce in New Orleans roared away till after midnight. The chimney at the plantation now had more than it could do. The windows on the lower floor began to help it out. Between speeches Anthony caught a little nap . . .

He was awakened by a rough hand on his shoulder.

"Sir," said an irate gentleman, "your dog is in the street below raising hell. Won't you go down and call him off?"

"Damn him," said Anthony, taking up his riding crop. "I'll show him—" and he walked downstairs to be almost devoured by Simba, who was whining continuously and had half his hair singed off.

"Fire!"

He stumbled getting frantically to his horse. And it was then as he picked himself up that he saw—just as Signora Bovino had seen it a quarter of a century before in Livorno—a red glare in the sky.

It was northward toward Silver Ho, and it hung with an appalling glow over the river.

"Oh God!" cried Anthony, and began to kill the horse with his spurs.

With the voice of the hound preceding him like a trumpet, he rushed on through the darkness toward the pillar of fire by night. Already in his maddening thoughts it had become apocalyptic.

610

At the Bayou St. Jean, incredible as it might be, the ferryman was still asleep. He groaned aloud as he hauled the poor black man out of the shack by his heels and made a note to come back and kill him later. The ferry-boat worked slowly. Simba kept rushing about in the bushes on the opposite bank baying. The light in the sky suddenly died down to a low, pink glow. There were no sparks over the top of the ridge any longer.

Three miles more . . .

He galloped out of the last clump of oaks and came thudding over the lawn. The house—

Nothing, nothing was left but a great bed of coals that shimmered like a lake of hell when the wind blew on them and made the spot in the sky above momentarily brighter. A few wisps of flame leaped up with green tongues feeding upon the roof copper—and died away again. Out of this, three storeys high, stood the great chimney white-hot, growing black in places where the cool wind fanned it and then glowing again. It mottled its face at him. Half-way up, the nursery fire-place was growing black. The terrible heat from the place where the great mansion had stood beat up into his face. The ruined horse trembled and twitched under him. Simba sat down and gave the death-howl.

He had no doubt what had happened. He knew. Otherwise they would have come to meet him before this.

He sat on his horse, waiting to go mad . . .

"Why was there nobody here? The niggers might run away, of course."

"Florence! My baby!—what had Terry done? Why, it *couldn't* be true! It just could not be true. To be burned in the fire; with fire, fire, fire, fire, fire, fire . . ."

The mare collapsed and he sat down on her while she died under him.

He sat there beating his own head with a riding crop.

Someone came up behind and tried to stop him. He fought with several men frantically. A blind impulse

611

to rush down and tread the fire was upon him. Luciferian defiances to the Almighty ripped from his throat.

"Steady, friend, steady," said the sorrowful voice of his chief-overseer Fithian. "We would deal gently with thee." He lay still. He saw the tears running down the face of Fithian. They must have been afraid to come near him at first. He lay still and looked at the stars. The men stood looking down at him.

"Couldn't you do *anything*?" he asked Polaris.

"Thee knows," said Fithian, "that all the doors led into the great room, and it must have been there that the fire started. When we got here it was too late. We could neither get in to them nor could they get out. It is impossible to walk through flame. We tried to see if we could."

He looked at their scorched faces. Smith, the cotton-overseer, was horribly burned.

"Did you hear anything?"

There was a terrible silence.

"Tell me."

"Yes," said Smith, moving his seared face frightfully.

"Well?" He dug both heels into the earth. "What?"

"Three pistol shots."

He grasped the man's hand. "Listen, Smith, you wouldn't lie to me, would you? Not now."

"No! By God, sir, it's true. It was when I was trying to get in through the servants' way. We couldn't. The fire came out at us into the hall. We got the maids out, there. All but two, the smoke . . ."

"And it was three."

"Yes, sir, in the nursery, I think—three shots—about a second apart."

"Nothing else?"

"Nothing. Dr. Mitchell was a great man, sir, a *brave* man."

"So are you, Smith," said Anthony, rising. "And the rest of you." He looked around at the scorched group of his faithful white servants. Someone sobbed once. He thought it might be Fithian.

"God must be ashamed of himself," he wrenched out. They gaped at him in amazement. "But I'll leave Him to Terry. He's up there now." He shook his fist at the stars. "And my baby"—Smith turned away.

"O God!"

"But you *men* will listen to me. I want to tell you something. And don't ever forget it as long as I live." They closed in a little.

"This never happened. It never happened at all! Do you see?"

They stood together for a moment with the glow and heat of the fire on them and then parted.

"Thee will be spending the night at my house, friend Adverse?" cried Fithian, his voice breaking.

"Take me," he cried. "And don't tell anyone except Mr. Nolte where I am."

Half an hour later a hundred people were arriving at the plantation by both horse and boat.

The news of the tragedy was all over town next day by dawn. Those who heard the tale of the horror-stricken overseers agreed that they had done their best. Servants were pulled out of the smoke just in time. Two girls died, smothered.

"Nobody knew until they saw the light in the sky. And most of the overseers lived a mile or so away. You know how quick a pine-lined house burns. No, it was just too late. What do you think of that fellow Mitchell? Do you think he ought to have done it?"

The discussion about that was quite hot for some time.

"Why don't you ask Adverse?" said a drunken young puppy at the Orleans bar a night or two afterwards.

"Friend," said Mr. Fithian, coming clear across the floor to take him by the throat, "I heard what thee said. I will not strike thee, neither will I kick thee—but I will grind thy countenance in the dirt."

Staid gentlemen voiced their almost tearful enthusiasm over the Quaker's abilities as a grinder.

In the meanwhile Mr. Adverse was in town again—as usual.

———————————————

No, it was not impossible. It was quite true. The race survives largely by virtue of certain fictions agreed upon. It is sometimes necessary for an individual to do the same. Wise and considerate people, even though they know the "facts," will usually acquiesce in the fiction and even play up to it. That is the part of *common* decency. It is your simple-minded fool who has never had anything happen to him or someone who is too young to understand that reality can have the quality of lightning, who always insists that a perfectly candid peal of thunder must follow every lightning stroke under all circumstances.

Fire had fallen from heaven upon Anthony and crisped his wife, his child, and his friend. The same element also threatened to suffuse his brain with intolerably glowing images and memories; to send him about the streets of New Orleans giving the death-howl like Simba until friends put him away where his voice would no longer trouble the world. Yet—

His heart went on. His body functioned. The event had not stopped them. He was left, left alone in the field of his own suffering, and he took shelter under the only available tree there, his own will.

"This never happened," he had said to himself—although he knew better than anyone else that it had. He was, indeed, the only one who really knew *what* had happened. "Never," he said, and went on living the negative. He left Silver Ho without looking back, because he would have been turned into a pillar of Bedlam if he had done so. He elected to remain sane.

A few well-meaning and curious persons who stopped him on the street to offer their sympathy were met by an uncomprehending stare. They retired, some of them disgruntled and complaining of his hardness of heart.

But it was remarkable how quickly, indeed, how almost instantly, the majority of his acquaintances understood not only the rôle he was acting but the temper of the lines he was saying, and how they conspired with him also to be about town "as usual."

In particular there was Edward Livingston whose discretion and tact, whose carefully disguised but boundless sympathy constantly found time in the midst of endless business to devise "accidental" meetings with "my friend Adverse," with "Toni, my dear boy, we must have some ducks for Sunday dinner. They say the shooting at Spanish Fort is remarkably fine. I won't use live decoys. I agree with you, there's something treacherous about them. But I've had that fellow Audubon daub me a half dozen buffleheads. Man, they're so natural they make the drakes stop to make love to them. It's like shooting Romeos in front of a balcony with a wooden Juliet,"—and away they would go into the marshes for a day or two. And sometimes, sometimes he would almost forget.

There were others besides Livingston who knew. There was Ba'tiste who had received him back into his tower-room as if he had never left it; Ba'tiste who never even mentioned the doctor, who was tactfully merry as only a sad fat-man can be when the pepper gets in his eyes—and yet he must go on cooking as only a Frenchman could in order to convey his ineffable admiration and sympathy pour une pose héroïque.

And there was Vincent Nolte.

He lived in the doctor's old room at Ba'tiste's while he was setting up the working of his new mercantile firm that concealed Ouvrard's schemes for some years to come. It was Vincent alone who really knew the extent of Anthony's confusion. As they sat talking over old times together and planning the future as though Silver Ho had never been, Vincent would find that Anthony was mistaking him for Dr. Mitchell. The "never happened" formula was working perhaps a little too well. "After all," thought Vincent, "one cannot act

615

entirely as if it were just five years ago and Dr. Terry still here."

Vincent thought a good deal about that. As time went on, he began to remind Anthony of the boy and to speak of Anna, "who is like a mother to him at Düsseldorf," of his studies and his life there. "Perhaps you would care to go back some day?"

"Never," he said.

Such talk had but one practical result. Anthony put his affairs in Europe in thorough order for the boy's future. At the end of some months he was able to remake his will. He was able to read the names of Florence and Maria in the old one—and to burn it, too. And now to his relief and amazement he found that if he was careful—if he was very careful to shut out the red light in the sky—certain memories of Florence and the child came back to him with a comfort that was inexpressible.

There was one in particular that sustained him. It was one of those moments of the past, unnoted when it occurred, but cherished by the soul for its subliminal value to the individual just as the great images of poetry are cherished by the race, unreasoningly, with an insight deeper than logic—"die, critics, or we perish"— it was a moment of immortal life saved out of the ghostly ruin of mutability and physical grief.

He would be driving again with Florence and little Maria, leaning back in the comfortable little chaise with his arms around his wife and the little girl held on his knees, her face close to his own. Ridiculously enough, it was along a short stretch of Tchoupitoulas Street. Florence was talking to him. Only her voice conveyed what she was saying. The mere words were lost forever. Perhaps they had nothing to do with what she had been saying then. It was simply (as she looked up at him out of her bonnet with the violets on it) "We love each other and are made one by it. Oh, happiness beyond thought!"—and the child basking in this impalpable warmth and security clung to him. And then—Tchoupitoulas Street led off into the darkness again.

But oh, how warm it was along that salvaged stretch, how the flowers bloomed forever in the immortal light!

As the spring came on with its delicately-untraceable, its unconsciously-reminiscent odours, he must pass that way again and again.

Let the mocking birds and cardinals sing. He could bear them again; bear them even without tears.

Grief is a curious thing. It must reassure itself at last of the reality of the things for which it grieves. Had there ever been a place called Silver Ho; a man who had once been happy there? Perhaps? Almost he had convinced himself "No." Now he must go and see. He *must* see it once again. In some way he must find surcease there, or—

The weeds and bushes had grown surprisingly high about the house. Some swallows were nesting in the chimney. He walked up the fire-scarred steps that led to—nothing. And jumped off into the area of ashes behind. The swallows had made their nest in the nursery fireplace and he blessed them for it. For the first time since the fire he wept unrestrainedly, tempestuously. And after the fit was over he felt an unspeakable relief.

Someone had left some garden roses and early spring wild-flowers at the foot of the chimney. "Probably Smith's wife and little girls," he thought, "or some of the hands. They loved her." He walked over to the chimney and climbed up on the hearth where the blossoms lay. They lay there as if on a rude, fire-scarred altar of ruined stone before the statue of his little madonna.

He looked at her in doubtful amazement, where she still stood in the niche where he had last seen her—

that night. And now—there was nothing left but the figure of the woman and the child.

She stood there exactly as she had come from the hands of her maker millenniums ago. Only the fire had glazed her. It had annealed every crack and imperfection. The rivets that had marked their place had flowed away and left her whole. Only she and the child remained. The golden Byzantine diadem, the gorgeous medieval robe, the heavens of art above her and the pearly steps beneath had sublimed in the furnace through which she had passed. She stood there, rooted in the stone, still holding her son forth to the man who now lay before her on the cold hearth. . . .

The sun grew hot before he looked up at her again. What passed was not in words. He could go now. A certain patience had come upon him. He remembered another who had suffered. One who had not tried to forget and had never been forgotten.

His vision as he looked at the madonna in the niche was peculiarly acute. The fire had cracked the chimney in places. An evil mouth of darkness yawned just beneath her. He caught the glimpse of something moving in this maw. Out of it, very slowly, as if it were sick of life itself, came a filthy-looking snake. It wriggled and half-slipped down the brick-work to a level space in the sunlight, where it lay still. An occasional tremor ran through it as though it were dying.

It was this that caused him to withhold his hand. The thing was obviously in great trouble. It was a sickly-white colour like an old cocoon.

"Poor worm of nature," he thought, "you are horrible, but you are in agony, too. Perhaps I am not kind to let you live and suffer." Yet he withheld his hand and kept still.

Presently the snake began to gasp and dart out its tongue as if to taste the sunlight for the last time. Its eyes looked seared. Then the skin of its throat parted and a new head came out of the old one. Its effort had been a violent one. Like the man on the hearth only a few feet away, it now lay very still.

The man lay there for hours. The snake emerged. It stripped itself from head to tail. It lay in the sun while its new colours became more brilliant and it revived. It coiled and uncoiled itself, a glorious creature at last, the colour of flame. It flowed off into the sunlight across the ashes and left its empty husk lying behind it on the stone.

Anthony rose, stiff in every joint, for he had been fascinated for hours. He took the statue out of the niche from the stone it had been standing on and went back to town.

He spent the whole night arguing with Vincent, who was in tears—and the next morning in a few brief preparations. And then, embracing his friend for the last time, he stepped into a canoe with four voyageurs, whom he had befriended in old days at the flotage, and started up-river headed for the unknown.

As they passed Silver Ho he lay down and held the madonna close to him. With the exception of that memento and Simba there was nothing in the craft to remind him of anything in the past.

"It is finished," he said. "I go."

Chapter Nineteen

The People of the Bear

JEAN, Pierre, Pedro, and Moosh-Moosh, a light cedar pirogue, Simba, and Anthony ascended the Mississippi above the White Bluffs to St. Catherine's Landing, where about the end of May 1813 they spent a week in making final preparations for the plunge into the continent westward.

At St. Catherine's lived old William Dunbar and one Dr. George Hunter, who seven years before at the request of Mr. Jefferson had explored the country north and west toward the sources of the Red River of the South until they came to the place where hot springs break from the earth out of the mountains and hills.

"All that I can tell you about them," said Dunbar, "is that on January fourteenth, eighteen-hundred-five, while camping at the hot springs I observed an eclipse of the moon and was therefore able to ascertain their exact situation to a nicety. They lie, in a bank of vapour, which can be seen afar-off ascending from the heart of the hills where they rise, at latitude thirty-four degrees, thirty-six minutes, four seconds north and longitude ninety-two degrees, fifty minutes, forty-five seconds west from Greenwich. If you are not sure when you get there, put your foot in the water and it will boil the flesh off. There is no possibility of mistaking them."

William Dunbar was the last civilized man speaking English whom Anthony talked to. He had frequently entertained him at Silver Ho on his way up and down the river from New Orleans, and Dunbar had heard of the tragedy. The good old Scot, who was one of the notable local scientists of his time, seemed instinctively to understand Anthony's desire to plunge into the wilderness. He placed his maps and notes at his disposal and talked engagingly of the nature of the fauna and flora, of the trials and hardships, and of the wonders to be met with beyond the habitation of men. He even wished to press upon him the loan of his mathematical instruments.

"You can return them—in a year or two," he said. "I should then like to see your notebooks and journals, for I am always curious."

"My dear sir," said Anthony. "I am not going to return, and I shall keep no notebooks. As for the mathematical instruments, it no longer makes any difference to me whether I am east or west of Greenwich. You see, I can no longer find my way by mathematics. I shall follow the moon, the stars, and the sun until I come to the end of the earth."

"Peace to you," said the old man. "The lights of heaven wander but they are at least eternal. Look out upon the glories of the universe and dwell no longer upon the shadows within. That way contentment lies, I think."

Then, in order to distract his guest, he became reminiscent, speaking of his youth in the beautiful country about Elgin, of his long wanderings westward of the great river to the place where the flowered prairies begin, and of his letters to Sir William Herschel, to David Rittenhouse in Philadelphia, and to Jefferson.

"I am sure if you will only look out upon the world you will find peace as I have in merely recounting its wonders to yourself and to other men. I have found peace here at the 'Forest' just remembering what I have seen. Try it, my son."

There was something in Dunbar's face that reminded Anthony of John Bonnyfeather as the old Scot sat before the fire that last night, full of practical advice, comfort, and out-looking philosophy. He received gladly the gift of a compass which the old man pressed upon him as he left the next day.

"Even that varies," said Dunbar with a little smile. "But it is the best I can do for you. This will always be the same, though"—and he gave him a warm hand-clasp.

They went back then to Fort Adams, filled their powder horns, and swinging around the great bend to the southward, turned the bow up to the mouth of the Red River where it rolled its red marl in sanguine clouds into the yellow Mississippi.

Jean, Pierre, Pedro, and Moosh-Moosh, a light cedar canoe, Simba and Anthony.

———————————

Jean and Pierre were French and Indian half-breeds, coureurs de bois. Pedro was a Spanish Creole from the colony of Bastrop far up the Red River. Moosh-Moosh was an Osage Indian whose real name was Hill-with-Owls-on-its-Head, because he had been born in the Ozarks near a mountain devoted to screech owls. Moosh-Moosh was a nickname given him by the coureurs de bois for the reason that when sleeping he made a noise like the buzzing of many flies. Otherwise he was silent. He had keen, restless eyes and was a hunter and trapper who had been farther up the Arkansas than most geographers of the time would have thought possible. A belt made of Buffalo hides and scalps supported an arrangement of deerskin that vaguely resembled trousers. Moosh-Moosh and Simba had upon first meeting prepared for a fight to the death. They disliked each other's smell. A few days' hunting taught them mutual respect. Wounded deer no longer escaped Moosh-Moosh. Simba invariably brought them down. After many weeks the Indian one night emitted an approving grunt and laid his hand on the dog's head. Simba's hair bristled, but he merely wrinkled his lips. On the basis of this working agreement, the party was seldom without meat.

It took them a month to leave the always half-flooded lowlands behind them. Day after day, under the steady impetus of five paddles, the bow of the canoe wrinkled the red water to each side of it, darting forward and forward, always north and a little westward past the low banks lined with scrub-willows and the mouths of swampy bayous. At night they camped on the river-islands or sandbars, building fires of drift wood, driven nearly frantic by mosquitoes that forced Simba to roll in the shallows or to sit with nothing but his muzzle out of water, for he could not take shelter in the smoke as the men did.

Every two or three days they passed flat-boats being poled and dragged up-river through the shallows or coming down swiftly under five or six oars. They were loaded with goods and the bales of traders, for they were not beyond the settlements yet. Here and there on the higher reaches of the banks, or on the islands amid the bayous, were French or Spanish plantations that traded with New Orleans.

They avoided these as far as possible, stopping only now and again for yeast, tobacco, and salt. They passed the occasional flatboats easily, and began to ascend rapids from time to time. The country now began to lift itself out of the domain of the rivers into higher land where snatches of prairies began; where there were pines, sandhills, and rocks.

At Bastrop they left Pedro behind. It was from here that Burr had intended to invade Mexico by way of Texas. There was a cluster of settlements and plantations, Frenchmen, Spaniards, slaves, and a few Yanqui traders. This was the "capital" of the Baron Bastrop, who had been granted a million acres by the Crown of Spain. Here they drank wine for the last time and Moosh-Moosh filled himself to the throat with rum. Only his eyes moved as they laid him in the canoe. For a time there were only two to paddle, Anthony in the bow and Jean in the stern, for the night before leaving Pierre had blown his head off trying to light his pipe with a powder horn and flint-lock.

"It *can* be done, monsieur," said Jean, "but one must flutter the thumb rapidly and draw in even at the moment of the spark. Alas Pierre, he coughed."

Two days later Moosh-Moosh arose from the canoe, brewed himself a black broth, confided his trouble to the river, and resumed the paddle.

They ascended into a country of cascades, hills, forests, and uncountable bears. The nights grew colder, the water deeper. All traces of men except a few tree-caches along the banks disappeared. About the end of August they ascended a tremendous rapid and around a bend in the river came in sight of a prairie with some hills in the middle of it from which ascended innumerable smokes. About fifty miles to the northwest tumbled a range of blue mountains.

"These," thought Anthony, "are the hot springs, latitude thirty-four degrees north, and longitude ninety-two degrees west of Greenwich. Moosh-Moosh, do you hear that? Do you know where we are now as well as I do?"

"Ugh!" said Moosh-Moosh. "Boil-um heap fish."

They spent the fall and winter at the hot springs. There was already a bark lodge there where sufferers came out of the wilderness to ease themselves of various complaints, for the healing nature of the waters had long been known to the Indians. It was here that a whole tribe of people of the Osage had died. Hill-with-Owls-on-its-Head remembered. The bad medicine of the pale faces had smitten them with sores from head to foot and they had come here to bathe in the steaming baths that cascaded down the hillsides. Small-pox driven inward is fatal, so they had died by fives and dozens sitting in misty pools. Some of them sat there yet. The rest had been "buried" in the treetops. They came across their skeletons from time to time in the woods.

But no one disturbed them that winter. They had the scalding fountains and the country for unknown leagues about all to themselves. Only the Buffalo-people came from the north, drifting through in small herds of a few hundred at a time toward the southern salt pans. Some had arrows in their flanks, which Moosh-Moosh said had been loosed by the Sioux, far-off and westward over the great prairies. They cut off a herd of yearling bulls in a little valley, and largely by the help of Simba stampeded them over a cliff. Without horses it was useless to try to pursue these huge animals. Only a lucky shot could drop them. For the most part they rushed off wounded and bellowing to be devoured later on by wolves.

With so ample a supply of meat they felt themselves lucky and built a heavy log hut with a roof piled high with stones to protect it from the bears. With these thieves the woods abounded and they also were added to the winter larder. Jean, as the cold came on, anointed himself with their grease.

They also built for themselves a log and turf hut with an ingenious floor. Several layers of boulders covered with branches and a stratum of gravel and packed clay formed a kind of platform on a hillside upon which the house stood. Under this floor, and between the boulders, they led a stream of water from a hot spring whose multi-coloured terraces steamed and bubbled only a few hundred feet away. All winter the grateful heat of the water ascended through the floor. Even Jean was lost in admiration of this. Moosh-Moosh hibernated here rather than slept. And Simba made both the white men laugh by occasionally raising his feet and looking at them in surprise.

Jean and the Indian hunted and trapped all winter. When spring came there was a canoe-load of peltry ready for New Orleans. Jean prepared to depart.

And what had Anthony been doing? Exactly what has been related. He had learned to give himself up to being nothing but muscles to paddle with and eyes to search the river ahead; to use every faculty to slay and to keep from being slain by animals; to sharpen his five wits so keenly that the world without became the world within—and he had discovered how to master the world without and how to cope with it.

He had learned how to hunt and fish, how to make clothes for himself out of skins, the ways of a hundred animals and the uses of trees and plants. In short, how to get along in the wilderness without anything but a rifle, an axe, and a knife.

He could walk out on the little terrace before the cabin with the still-steaming water running away in its bubbling channel from beneath the floor, and hear nothing but the water and the wind, and see nothing but the view: blue mountains to the north, stretches of forest and prairie, and the ever-changing sky. He did not think about them. He saw them. And he read into them nothing but the signs of the weather and the messages of the wilderness. As though with the eyes of Simba and Moosh-Moosh he, too, looked and saw only what there was to see without remembering that he saw. He had been helped to this natural use of his faculties by the fact that nothing he looked upon reminded him of man. Every prospect about him was at once unspoiled, eternal, limitless, and new. He looked upon distant mountains; the mountains looked upon him—and he thought no more of them.

The madonna hung in a small deerskin bag tied close to the rafters. He had made it to contain her fire-scarred body. With a drawstring he tied the mouth of the bag fast.

When the spring came and the forests grew misty green, the pain of spring did not return again. He had forgotten it, he said. If he felt it vaguely, as one who is partly benumbed, he did not stop to recall what it was about. The woods were turning green. That was all. The beavers were starting to build again. It was different from fall. The earth grew warm again. In a certain way he rejoiced. He knew now that he was not going to lose his mind. He had saved it by letting the wilderness flow in upon him.

Jean left in early April. He took back a few words written on a piece of bark to Vincent and the compass to Mr. Dunbar. Anthony and the Indian remained at the hot springs, building a canoe.

When the spring floods were over they launched forth with Simba and the rifles and paddled on into the heart of the continent. Their only kit was a kettle, a small deerskin bag, and blankets. The tobacco had gone by this time. The powder lasted them till August.

By that time even Moosh-Moosh did not know where they were.

———————————————

They had been following the river for five months. About mid-summer they had passed through a succession of great gorges and rapids where the stream cut through a range of wild and forbidding hills indescribably rocky and ragged. They carried the canoe around a roaring falls. Hunting was all but impossible here, and they had nearly starved. A fawn that came to stare at their campfire one night saved their lives.

Farther up, the river widened out again into a val-

627

ley two or three miles wide, with islands, shallows, and an imperceptible current.

The valley continued endlessly between lines of steep, clay cliffs with patches of open cottonwood forests.

It was pleasant but monotonous. The red cliffs faced each other across the groves of cottonwoods and low, sandy islands for hundreds of miles. From time to time they climbed the cliffs to look around them and found themselves always in the same great prairie, an absolutely level sea of land covered with grass from horizon to horizon. The last of the distant, blue hills had been left behind somewhere in time. Anthony had lost count of the days. Only space lay before them in the shape of the endless level plain.

Game abounded. Down the trails over the cliffs from the prairie above buffalo and antelope came to drink, and herds of wild horses. The valley was full of the skulls and skeletons of animals slaughtered at the fords. Once they lay hidden on an island for a week. Horse Indians were hunting along the cliffs above, and they did not dare to build a fire. Simba remained silent, crouching under the canoe as he had been taught to do. The hunters passed on. A few days later the prairie was a sea of fire and the valley thronged with animals that in some places came over the cliff in reckless waves while the flames licked along the heights above them.

At one place they waited for three days while a herd of buffalo passed. They were going south. Moosh-Moosh looked uncomfortable and gave signs of being lost. With a stick he traced in the sand a rude map and indicated that they had somehow taken the wrong fork of the river.

He was sure of it when they came to five isolated buttes that rose out of the prairie like an archipelago from which the sea had withdrawn. He did not know these hills. They lay to the south of the river. A stream drained them and broke through the cliffs into the main valley by a gorge. They turned aside here and followed it up. A day later they were at its source, five great springs that burst out at the foot of the buttes.

These table-top mountains, for they seemed to be mountains in the middle of the plain, lay scattered about in a rough amphitheatre in the centre of which was a large black pond into which the springs drained and where the stream took its rise. This bowl between the hills was two or three miles in diameter and covered with a forest of giant pines. There were signs of an old Indian encampment but of many years past. They climbed the tallest butte and looked about them. From sunrise to sunset stretched the unbroken, flat prairie; from north to south. Across it the river zigzagged like a red gash. Southward great, dark patches like cloud-shadows marked the drifting herds of buffalo. They camped there and soon discovered why so favoured a spot was apparently ignored.

It was not approachable by a horse, the only easy access being by way of stream, and it was haunted by a grizzly bear of enormous proportions and ferocious temperament. He devoured their cache of jerked buffalo meat and scattered their camp. Without firearms they could do nothing about it. An arrow, which Moosh-Moosh launched at him from his short bow, glanced off his jaw and was almost the end of them. They would have become skeletons in treetops if Simba had not drawn him off in a hopeless pursuit. They returned to the river valley and spent the winter in a hut made of boulders and cottonwood on an island. It was terribly cold and food was scarce.

As soon as the river thawed in the spring, Moosh-Moosh prepared the canoe to depart for the settlements. He could not persuade Anthony to accompany him and he seemed concerned about it. "No rum," said he, pointing around in all directions. "No rum." Then he rubbed his stomach. Seeing that his greatest argument made no impression, he shoved off. Anthony and Simba remained by the ashes of the fire on the island.

As the Indian disappeared around the bend below, Anthony knelt down and blew up the coals. In addition to the fire and the dog, he had a useless rifle and an empty powder horn; he had a knife, an axe, flint and steel, and a certain deerskin bag tied at the mouth.

After that his life, even to himself, became legendary.

He fished and trapped. At the ford below the island Simba lay in wait and tackled the deer as they swam. From the bois d'arc Anthony cut himself a straight-grained piece and shaped a bow. It was some time before he could find anything for a bowstring. Deer hide parted. At last he took the long tendon from a stag's leg and out of these sinews formed one that hummed like a harp-string and held. The bow was not short as that of Moosh-Moosh had been. It was over two yards from tip to tip and suited the height and the strength of the man who strung it.

That man was taller than his bow and stronger. He now had muscles of iron. His golden beard, a little grey at the temples, fell half-way to his belt and was a continuation of his yellow mane. Out of this bush, above the short bare-space of tanned cheek bones, looked wide, grey-blue eyes, alert, not sunken into deep sockets, still youthful in their expression, piercing now rather than dreamful, whether they gazed over the sea of prairies or searched out the terraces along the cliffs.

He could move like a flash or sit for hours without moving a muscle, not thinking, but like the hound that lay beside him using his eyes, ears, and nose. His outward conversation was now addressed solely to that hound. But it was more extensive in its emotional range and understanding than those who are acquainted with dogs only as household pets and inferior companions might suspect.

When he communed with himself it was not upon the past nor did he always seem to be addressing some dream-companion within his own head. He could now, at times, commune in an external direction as though his whole verbal consciousness were in the mood expressed by that form of address, the use of which has almost lapsed from modern language, the attitude expressed by O.

It is only in timeless solitudes, which the traveller has discovered to be no longer solitary, that a man's lips can learn to shape themselves to the round symbol of eternity which is the crown of human talk and communion, that O complete in itself. And so at last, by becoming utterly lonely, he discovered that it was impossible to be alone. He had asked for comfort, and in some sort he received it.

The physical man busied himself in preparing physical weapons and devices to claim his daily meat from God. He made arrows and feathered them, hardening their points in the fire, for he could come by nothing as yet wherewith to tip them. He took the ramrod out of his gun, and heating it in the coals, pounded it with rocks to a sharp point and set it in a staff. He now had a spear with a bayonet-like point over a foot long. It was no mean weapon. He spent endless hours shooting with the bow and could at last, as both his marksmanship and arrow-making improved, drive true to the mark.

Thus provided, he left the river bottom towards the end of his first summer in solitude, for he had no desire to winter there alone, and returned to the valley between the five buttes, determined to drive out the bear and if possible to kill him.

It was not long before he realized that the bear was hunting him. He found his huge tracks about the camp the first morning after he camped by the pool in the pines. Only the watchfulness of Simba and a leaping fire kept him off. It was essential to find a safe resting place. With that end in view he began to examine the sides of the buttes that rose with faces of sheer cliff directly out of a steep slope of weathered rocks and shale.

Simba flushed a bobcat at the foot of the cliffs. It darted spitting up the slope, and leaping onto a ledge on the cliff, apparently disappeared into the heart of the hill. They followed with some difficulty. The ledge was only about a foot wide. It gradually tilted inward into the face of the cliff until they were passing through a knife-slice into the side of the butte itself. There was just room enough for a man to pass and for a glimmer of sky overhead. Along this cut bubbled a lively little stream through a gutter it had worn in the stone. Simba darted ahead now, and from some distance beyond came the noise of a wildcat brought to bay and voicing its opinion of intruders.

Twenty yards more, and Anthony stepped into the sunlight. The place at one time must have been an immense cave. But its roof had collapsed ages before, leaving a hole in the flat top of the butte as though a rough knot had been extracted from a level plank. The sides were about two hundred feet high, sheer and smooth, and the area at the bottom of this rocky well in the hill was several acres in extent. There was a cluster of gigantic cedars here which had grown in the perfect shelter with an unspoiled symmetry and in the course of centuries covered the ground with their needles and cones. Somewhere beneath this fragrant covering, still faintly audible, ran the stream that drained this little crater, which would otherwise have been a lake.

As he looked about him with satisfaction and amazement, Anthony found himself saying, "This is home." Just then Simba closed with the bobcat.

For a hound trained to tackle a lion, the bobcat was not formidable. Simba broke its back from behind. He then darted into a hole in the cliff and finished off a nest of savage kittens.

Anthony cleansed the place with fire and moved in.

It was a cave with a sandy floor that ran back into the cliff for nearly fifty yards. Man had been here before. Near the entrance there was an old hearth with the marks of fire on it. Later on, he found flints, a rough stone hammer, and needles of polished bone. Whoever had lived there had gone away ages before. In the ashes of the hearth he thought he recognized the half-charred nuts of a species of palm. How long ago had that fire gone out? Upon that hearth he re-kindled his own fire.

Here he was safe from all intruders except the birds. No one could find him except by climbing the sheer cliffs of the butte and peering down at him. The cleft through which the stream drained was too narrow for the bear. And he soon barricaded it effectually at its narrowest place by a gate of logs. The way along the rocky ledge left no trail. He now slept secure at nights with nothing but the hidden complaint of the stream under its bed of needles, the song of owls, and the moonlight filtering through the cedars as company, for there was not even a wind to sigh in the boughs of the sheltered trees.

He lived comfortably. He set up a rude housekeeping in the cave. He built himself a chair and a bed, a rough log table. He drove pegs into the rock to hang his deerskins upon and stocked the inner reaches of the place with an ample supply of firewood. Best of all, he could now accumulate a stock of dried and smoked meat for the winter, instead of depending upon hunting from day to day.

Some miles away over the prairie, on the opposite side of the butte, he found a salt lick where the deer and buffalo came. By a month's work he was able to evaporate several bushels of the mineral by pouring the brine into holes in a rock and dropping hot stones into it. His chief difficulty was the lack of a kettle or dish of any kind that would bear fire. The clay along the river set him thinking.

After several trials he succeeded in constructing a

potter's wheel out of a log end, a stick for a treadle, and a deer thong for a belt. His first efforts at making bowls and pots were weird. But he progressed. He built a rough kiln out of boulders and daubed clay and fired it. The results surpassed his expectations. He could, he found, not only supply himself with pots but with dishes and receptacles of all shapes and kinds. He spent hours at the wheel. He improved his furnace with a bellows and was at last able to melt sand. He made a clay mould and cast hundreds of glass arrow heads. But he was unable to contrive a blower that would work. At last he remembered the rifle barrel and was enabled to make some bottles of monstrous shapes. They were more curious than usable.

Nothing was lacking now but the skin of the bear for a hearth-rug and some grain to vary his diet. And tobacco—

Security had permitted him to declare a truce with the bear. He was not so likely to be surprised by the animal in the daytime but he was aware that when he went down into the bowl between the hills he was frequently followed. Perhaps it was only curiosity, he thought. The animal never left his haunts between the buttes to go down to the river valley or onto the plains below. He was an old bachelor with a morose temper. Gradually, although Anthony saw him only once or twice, he became acquainted with his habits. He lived in a hole in a hill across the pine woods on the far side of the bowl.

Once just as he emerged from the cliff along the ledge, he found him digging for roots on the slope below. They saw each other at the same instant. The bear rose out of the bushes. He stood over eleven feet high, pig-like eyes squinting, his arms falling before him as if he had heavy boxing gloves on. He rumbled out a defiance to his enemy on the ledge above him and made off. Once he heard him roaring and saw him pursued by a swarm of bees into the lake. One night Simba came back bleeding with deep claw marks down his shoulder. After that they both emerged from the cliff more carefully. The "truce" was distinctly over, with one of the parties lying in ambush. About the beginning of winter Anthony got a long shot at him with the bow, but it was too long. The arrow glanced off. Bruin then disappeared for some months. It was not until early March that he was seen again and under most curious circumstances.

The snowfall had been heavy that winter and the little lake under the pines was frozen solid. As he passed it one day, returning from the river valley, he heard a hoarse rumbling-chuckling going on in the direction of the pool. Simba growled and started to creep forward. Cautioning him to keep low, he crept to the edge of the trees himself and peered out, keeping his hand on the dog.

Bruin was there. He looked thin and gaunt after his winter sleep. But he was having a good time. He was sled-riding.

He would climb up a little knoll that sloped steeply to the lake, squat on his haunches, glide down with a terrific speed, and shoot out unto the smooth surface of the ice, bumbling with ecstasy. His remarks and his gestures were those of a bear who had lost all sense of gravity except when sliding, who did not care how far his tongue hung out of his grinning mouth. His little nose smoked rapidly in the frosty air as he scrambled back to the mound and repeated the performance. It went on till sunset and continued into the starlight. In the darkness Anthony finally left, forcing Simba to follow.

Later that night he returned to the pond and reconnoitred carefully. The bear had gone.

He walked over the ice, and taking his spear with the sharpened iron ramrod on the end of it, set it with its butt against a rock and the head slanting up the toboggan slide of the afternoon before. He covered it with snow, and making all as smooth as possible walked back over the ice. He remembered that at best the bear could not see very well. He went back to the cave and slept.

Simba wakened him wild with excitement. He went out and listened and then came back. That afternoon he went down and began to skin the bear.

The spear had been driven clear through him and snapped off.

Anthony was not sorry for the bear. How could he be? He was no longer even sorry for himself. And charity begins at home.

In all that vast region overlooked by the Five Buttes there was not a single being with whom he could have shared sympathy or the peace of God, if he had found it. Not one. For three years he had lived there without seeing a trace of man.

The buffalo swung back and forth with the pendulum of the seasons, following the sea of grass as it withered and bloomed. About the base of his hills broke this spray of the prairie whose tide was controlled by the sun. By this time he had learned as perfectly as might be the implacable laws of the place. From the fish in the pools of the river bottom to the eagles on the cliffs above—what animal so successful as he?

But it was not enough.

It was not enough to be the god of Simba, or to have vanquished the great bear—to walk superior to all things save himself. For he had come into the wilderness for two reasons and he had been only half successful. He had come into the wilderness to let the scars of the burning heal. By living in the present only he had enabled his mind to form its cicatrice. But he had also hoped to draw near to the All-Father in nature by becoming one of his children. And he had become a child again, able to release himself into the world about him and to play there contentedly between sleep and sleep. But of the Causer of Dreams and of the nature of Nature he had learned nothing at all. Nature had nobly sustained his body, and that was all.

It was his custom about evening to climb to the top of the butte where the cave was and to look out over the ocean of prairies from west to east. And he would also rise early in the mornings to behold the dawn. So frequently did he do this that the spectacle of dawn and sunset and of the day between them became one to him in his own mind as he sat by the fire in his cave at night.

Surely, if anywhere in the world without, the word of God might be spoken between those two flaming lips of dawn and sunset a prairie-day apart; a word clear and glorious, a thought vast and stupendous, a great yea-saying between the green infinity of earth and the blue infinitudes of sky.

But if all things from the north unto the south and from the east unto the west combined to praise Him, this was the unconscious music of the spheres and no mere opera for the heart and mind of man.

Who could write the libretto to this fundamental music or choose the words for the cosmic chorus that must accompany it in explanation? His name was Noman. Even the harp of David had not been able to compass the poem to such music, though he had caught the accents of the divine.

Anthony could find no more in it than the feeling of glory, of exaltation, of terror at the coldness of the infinite in this hymn of the prairie. But even Simba experienced the last. In winter when the light failed and the cold stars began to glitter on the sea of snow below, he would sit on the cliff's edge and howl until the quavering answer of the sadness in the hearts of his relatives the wolves and coyotes answered him. In the moonlight the canine people of the prairie went lunatic. An hour or two of their libretto was all that any man could stand.

Anthony would call Simba back with a shrill whistle,

637

and the hound would return to the fire, glad of its cheerful glow and the satisfactory and familiar limits of the cave.

It was on one of these lonely winter evenings, when the cold penetrated even to the interior of the cave, that he undertook to enlarge the area of the hearth. It was simple enough. He had merely to add a few stones. As he dug down in the sand he found that the older portion of the hearth was laid upon a bed of clay. He removed some stones from it to fit on his addition, and beneath one he found, as clear as if it had been made only yesterday, the imprint of a child's hand.

An emotion, too conflicting and too complicated to describe, overcame him, and he sat there unashamed of the tears that coursed freely down his face.

So the place really had been home once! He had given small thought to those who had dwelt there—so far in the past that they had left no ghosts, he thought. But now he could feel them about him as though it had been only yesterday. Perhaps in some such human symbol as this handprint, rather than in the word contained between the lips of dawn and sunset, was the answer to what he sought.

He removed the fire-scarred figure from its deerskin bag and set it above him in a groove of the rock where the madonna held forth the man child to him in the firelight again . . .

How well those who had tried to express the relation of God to man had done to leave the Father understood and unexpressed in the group. For was He not unknowable and inexpressible in human symbols or syllables?

Still, through all, through the fire, and the shadows, and from the beginning to the end, the divine child had been held out to him. Should he let him remain here in the wilderness, or should he take him to his own heart at last and go like Brother François to exhibit his image among men?

The cogitations of the winter were long. Before

spring came he had begun to make his preparations for departure.

Simba, who was half-blind now and old and grizzled, seemed to understand that they were leaving. But he showed no joy over it as he would have even a few years before. He crept near Anthony by the hearth, and putting his great head on his knees, wagged his tail slowly and grumbled and moaned a little as if he would say, "Have we not wandered enough, my master? Let us lie down here in peace." And the man did his best to comfort the dog. Amah's friendship had indeed followed far.

Anthony made a warm coat for himself out of the skin of the bear. He used the head for a hood and the limbs for sleeves and trousers. He was most bear-like when he laced himself into it. But he was also dry and warm. Towards the end of the winter, when his supplies ran low, he began to move about in it in the country around the Five Buttes, hunting. And it was thus arrayed that on a bleak March day, with the snow still driving hard, he came suddenly about twilight upon three old women.

They were seated near the dark lake in the pine woods around the ashes of a fire. He would have passed them in the early darkness and the heavy, feathery snow of earliest springtime, if it had not been for the nose of the hound. It was Simba who smelled them out as if they had been so many witches. Indeed, that was what they looked like.

Never in his life had he seen or imagined women so old as these. They were certainly, he thought as he drew near to them, the oldest women in the world.

They, on their part, did not move as he approached them, for they had been left there to die and to be looked after by the bear, which was the god of their tribe. They had been left as all the other old women of their people had been left before them. Their last fire had gone out, as they peered through the darkness with the final numbness of age and winter heavy upon

639

them and saw the bear approaching, as they had been told he would—they said nothing at all. That was the form in which death came to old women of the People of the Bear; to those who had lived too long. Death *was* a bear. When the bear spoke to them, when a man's head came out of the bear's head and the thing beckoned to them, they knew they were already dead and that they were being commanded to follow to the happy hunting ground of the People of the Bear. But only two of them rose and followed. The third remained where she had been sitting when she last sat down.

Thus, with two all but disembodied spirits tottering after him, the bear and his great cub Simba led the two surviving squaws home to the warmth and ease of the cave. There they drank some hot soup made of deerbones, stretched out their withered hands to the warmth of the hearth, and began to look fearfully about them to see what heaven, where the bear lived, was like. Doubtless it was for her sins in early youth that their sister had not been permitted to accompany them. Doubtless the bear had devoured her soul as she deserved. At any rate, they never saw her again. She was now nothing but a myth for ghostly gossip conducted in whispers in the morning as they built up the fire for the bear.

It was impossible to talk to these old women, Anthony found. He did not know their language, and when he attempted to address them even by signs they fell with their faces to the ground. So he brought them meat and they cooked it. They were careful to see that Simba received his due share, for it was plain from his actions that the earthly smell they had brought with them into paradise irked his god-like nose. It was also plain that their master the bear often laughed at them. His head frequently protruded from his head to do so; at which times they remembered their own sins. Who could tell what the laughter of a bear might portend even in a spiritual state?

As for the bear, he was as kind as he could be to them. But he could not help laughing at himself and at the difficulties of even beginning to follow the example of Brother François. One was supposed to begin humbly.

Meanwhile, the two old women grew fat and sleek again. They were well-fed and rested. It looked as though they might live for another hundred years. In the spring they went forth to gather roots and berries. And thereby a change came both to themselves and for their master the bear. Unfortunately, the happy hunting ground still had relations with the unhappy hunting grounds of the mundane plains below.

It was in early May of a certain year, unnamed by the People of the Bear, that the medicine-man of that tribe of wandering red men found the ghosts of his deceased grandmother digging for clamus roots on the side of a mountain. Some natural doubts as to her decease passed between them, including the story of the bear. The chief returned to his tepee to make medicine. The result was the undoubted decease of both the old women and the capture of the bear.

Only Simba escaped. He now followed Anthony afar-off, killing such of the Indian dogs as came out at night to hunt him over the prairie. He picked up the trail of his master as best he could. Old bones, wounds, and sores were his only reward and portion.

And with Anthony it was not much better. Only a man in the form of a god could have fallen as low as he had.

He was kept, just as he had been captured, in the bearskin. He was held imprisoned in the largest tepee as the Big Medicine of the tribe. Every article in the cavern had been taken along just as each had been found; everything, except the two old women, who had been left on the floor of the place with no brains left to worry them. When the tribe moved, as they did every few days, southward over the prairies, for they were following the buffalo, the contents of the tepee was loaded onto a pony and upon two poles that dragged on the ground behind him by way of a cart or traverse. This traverse the Big Medicine followed. He had become attached to the thing by means of a horsehair rope. The attachment lasted for three months. By that time they had arrived in semi-arid, alkali country about the headwater of certain rivers draining southward into the Rio Grande. No person had as yet taken the trouble to mark these rivers upon any map made in Europe. They flowed quite incognito, but they were of considerable interest to the buffalo which traversed their valleys to the rich southern ranges beyond, and hence to the horse Indians who pursued them hither.

At a certain point in the semi-arid landscape the southward tendency of the Indians became of great interest to the military authorities of New Spain. They had no objection to the wild tribes' pursuing the wild buffalo. But they had numerous objections, and strong ones, in the form of regiments of cavalry, to the Indians' continuing on into "Texas" and raiding the herds of longhorn cattle on the haciendas or the villages gathered about the missions, whose bells rang never so loudly as when the "Apaches" approached.

That portion of New Spain ruled eastward from Santa Fé was a large one. In the midsummer of 1816 the People of the Bear found themselves halted on the northern bank of the "Bitter River" in pow-wow over a message from their Mighty Father, the King of Spain. It was laconic, written in two paragraphs: the first was a dead rattlesnake stuffed with powder; the second was another rattlesnake which appeared to have died eating bullets. The caballero who brought them flung them into the lap of the chief and departed to his own camp on the other side of the river. There he became the Munchausen of his regiment by insisting that in the tents of the Indians there was a bear who had called out to him in Spanish that he was a Christian man.

This assertion having been repeated to those in authority, and received with the proper contempt due to the sublime credulity or impudence which had prompted it, the Spanish camp settled down to digesting its midday meal, while the camp of the Indians digested the message conveyed by the rattlesnakes. A good deal of dancing, *ugh-ughing*, and *woof-woofing* accompanied the latter process.

From the slit in the door of his tepee, which was tied fast as usual, Anthony could see down the street of the Indian village where the pow-wow was going on. The young braves were for continuing on after the buffalo southward; the eloquence of the chiefs of the tribe was trying to persuade them to turn back. Presently the maker of medicine began to perform a dance. It went on for hours. The squaws, two of whom generally watched him closely, gradually closed in slapping their hands together and moving their bodies to the time. Presently the medicine-man would consult the bear and make up the tribe's mind for it. The dance was merely in preparation for that. They would go north again into the wilderness. He knew. He would never hear the Spanish bugles again.

The heat in the tepee was tremendous. The man sewed in the bearskin sweated and was devoured by fleas. The dance outside went on. In the middle of the afternoon he heard Simba hunting. His voice came from across the river, strong as in the old days, full of excitement. He seemed to have struck an old familiar trail. He might have come across the spoor of a lion. A remembrance of strength and hope returned to the despairing man in the tepee. Outside the dance went on.

He rose, and taking the edge of his axe, split the bearskin down the front from throat to belly and stepped out of it. He tied the deerskin bag about his

643

neck, wriggled naked under the back of the tepee with the axe in his hand, and crawled down the slope toward the river about half a mile away.

A dry arroyo swallowed him. He continued on down it. He killed a rattlesnake with a stone. Simba was still following the trail. He might rejoin him now. One last hunt together, and they might yet be free. Ten minutes more, and he would make the river without being seen. He listened again, carefully screened by a clump of chaparral from both the Indian and the Spanish camps. The dance above was still going on. He could see the Spanish sentries below him.

Which way should he go? Into the wilderness—or back to Spain?

Suddenly the voice of the hound below him burst into the full hunting cry and began to make straight into the Spanish camp. The sentries began firing. He leaped up and started to run. As he rushed into the river, a fierce clamour broke out in the tepees behind him. The god had gone. The man in the river swam like mad toward the Spanish camp that now lay only a short distance before him. The cleansing caress of the water removed the filth of his three months of divinity and made him feel as if he were reborn. His long golden beard streamed in the wind as he climbed the river bank.

———

Simba was nearly blind. He had hidden by day and followed Anthony's trail at night. He had not dared to try to enter the Indian encampment. From time to time Anthony had heard him, and so had the Indians, howling in the wilderness. He had lived on what small game he could snap up, and learned to crouch and back off at the whir of the rattlesnake. But he was nearly done now; almost at the end of the trail; gaunt, starved, full of nothing but puzzled despair. The familiar scent of his master's footsteps was the only thing that still dragged him along over the surface of the earth. That odour was the trail of his god who could do no wrong, even if he had abandoned heaven and he heard his voice no more.

Nineteen years of odours constituted the memory of this aged and gigantic hound. As his light failed, and even sounds began to grow distant and confused, he lived by his nose alone. It had never deceived him, and he was never surprised at any of its messages. No matter how preposterous a thing might seem to be to a man, when the nose of Simba smelled it, he remembered, and he knew that it must be true.

It was, therefore, no surprise to Simba one afternoon on a prairie in the middle of America to pick up a trail he had once lost years before in Spain. Suddenly his nose came across it again. It simply resumed. It was the trail of the little man who had once lost his hat to him off a coach just outside the gates of Madrid—and that hat had also had upon it the blood of Juan. In the mind of Simba he now simply took up the chase of Sancho where he had last left off.

As Anthony climbed the river bank, that long trail was nearing its end. The hound rushed baying into the camp. At the far end of the street of tents, "El Gato," seated under the shade of a military marquee, heard him and sat up, his whiskers bristling with alarm. He remembered that voice. Even at the world's-end he could not forget it.

———————————

The honours and dignities which had fallen upon Sancho in the new world had not altered the essential nature of the little man. He was still his master's humble and obedient servant. But Don Luis was now nearly eighty-five, and he administered the province of New Spain—of which he had found himself appointed the military governor, some years before upon arriving in Mexico—largely by the help of his still vigorous wife and the ruthless little man who had once been his postilion.

It had been necessary, however, to conceal the humble origin of both Faith and Sancho even from the provincial society of the little town of Santa Fé, which was Don Luis' capital. For that purpose, and to increase his authority, Sancho had been made a colonel, and aide-de-camp to the governor, and had conferred upon him the star and ribbon of an obscure Italian order, which Napoleon had suppressed years before. The ruse had been rightly successful. Mounted upon a piebald horse with a sabre, high, polished jackboots, a cocked hat, and the order of S. Rosario about his neck, "Don Sancho Armijo" had done his master full credit.

He rode hard and far. And both the regular troops of the garrison and the levies of local lancers followed him willingly. He gave no orders which he did not expect himself to see carried out. If his men always referred to him as "The Cat," they did so respectfully. For it had long been known all over the province and on the frontiers that the Cat had claws and could use them. No one was sure just when or where Sancho might pounce. On the present occasion he had ridden northeast clear up into Kansas, burning sundry Indian villages, sacking a pueblo or two, and gathering in several Texan hunters and trappers, who had presumed to cross the vague boundaries of Louisiana into the sacred domains of Spain.

With the Texans it would go especially hard. It was the custom to send them to Mexico from Santa Fé, along with such rebels, criminals, and political disturbers as the governor might desire to be rid of. There was an annual clearance of such rubbish. Once in Mexico the viceroy had his own methods, of which no one had ever returned to complain. Since the expedition of General Pike, which some years before had come to final grief at Santa Fé, the zeal of the Spanish authorities had been especially directed against the

Americans. That two of the Texans captured on the present raid had their families with them seemed especially significant. Sancho had burned their cabins and brought them, men, women, and children, along with him, despite the hardships and their miserable plight. His encounter with the People of the Bear was a mere incident. They were not even Apaches, and his force outnumbered them fifty to one. He would give them a few hours to deliberate, he thought, as he sat under the marquee, and then send them flying. He was preparing for a siesta in a hammock slung between two tent poles, when the voice of the dog disturbed him. When it approached the camp the Cat sat up. The dog was undoubtedly hunting.

There was only one hound in the world that had a voice just like that. Fear is a marvellous conjuror. It reduces a situation to its elementals. In the mind of Sancho everything but the fact that he was being pursued melted away. The sense of his rank and authority vanished as the voice of Simba approached. When the grizzled form of the hound, with his nose to the trail, appeared at the far end of the street of tents, panic seized Sancho. There was something almost supernatural about it. The dog seemed to have come across the prairies out of the past from the other side of the Atlantic to bay Sancho's footsteps. There he was, and fast approaching. It never occurred to Sancho to stop him. The thing to do was to flee.

He snatched his feet out of his jack-boots and raced down the camp street toward the picket lines. If he could once get on horseback he might get away. But there was no time for that. As Simba struck the trail of Sancho's stocking feet he burst forth into a hellish clamour. Sancho leaped forward. So did Simba. Sancho now changed his direction suddenly and ran for a clump of trees by the river bank. The dog gained. Before his dim sight he now beheld the ghostly shadow of a cat leaping frantically to escape him, and he could hear its squalls. Simba hurtled forward and ripped the coat off his enemy's back. A sentry's rifle cracked. The cat scrambled into the cruel branches of a thorn tree. The dog sank gasping at its foot. Soldiers were now closing in from all directions.

Just then a naked man with a long, yellow beard rushed out from the covert along the river bank. The dog died with his head on his master's knees. In the branches of the thorn tree above a kind of twittering ceased. Caught on the long thorns, the body of Sancho ceased to struggle and hung limply across a limb with his eyes glazing.

Soldiers closed in around Anthony and looked down at him, where he sat with his arms about Simba.

After a while they led him prisoner into the camp and gave him some old clothing. The dog and the Cat they buried not far from each other on opposite sides of the tree of thorns.

Chapter Twenty

The Pilgrimage of Grace

DUST—not only clouds of it—but dust which flowed along the ground like liquid, that trickled into the hoofprints of the troop of horses as they trotted steadily into the southwest, that showered upon the sagebrush to either side of the trail like drops of dry water. Behind the scarves over their mouths the troopers coughed dust. The horses blew it out of their muddy noses. It clogged the corners of their eyes. Over the alkali plains dust-devils rose and twisted like waterspouts, dancing in the quivering heat. Lizards, twitching from stone to stone, left puffs of dust behind them. The long trail smoked with it for hours after the Spanish cavalry and their prisoners passed.

It was a silent land, leeched-out, bleached by the tremendous reverberations of white sunlight, with valleys like the floor of abandoned lime kilns and mountains flaunting dark ribbons of spiny lava along the sky. For Anthony, it was a country that did not remind him of any that he had ever seen before.

At night they camped by bitter, green water-holes that mirrored the stars dully, and wrinkled slowly to the horses' noses when they drank. The cool mornings were brisk and refreshing with the tea-like tang of sagebrush in the air. The distances were incredibly clear. The bugles rang, and they would start. It no longer made any difference to him where they were going.

Although he was a prisoner, he felt free and happy. Physical hardship meant nothing to him any more. The lonely years in the wilderness had both given and tempered his iron strength. He had ceased to try to make things happen. His faith in the director of events was now not only mental but physical. Whatever happened to him was "right." He lived as if he had once died in battle in a good cause, slept in eternity, and risen again to find himself still riding on.

The iron shoes of the squadrons rang on the stones of the dry arroyos, as they trotted on day after day. . . .

From the instant that he had recognized Sancho he knew that Don Luis would be at Santa Fé. Godoy had undoubtedly carried out his intention and exiled the marquis. He had sent him to be the governor of this distant province as he had said he would do. And no doubt the old man would blame him for that. Don Luis would feel that a word to Ouvrard might have prevented it. That was undoubtedly what Don Luis had been so anxious to speak to him about those last days in Madrid. But he had dodged their interview. Don Luis could never be made to understand how the statue in his patio had made that meeting impossible. No, it would probably go hard with him now—after Sancho's death! How curiously the truce between him and Don Luis had been broken! It seemed as though fate had made it difficult for either of them to keep that truce and yet still insisted upon bringing them together again.

It was this conviction of fate, plus a heightened

sense of the irrevocable direction of time and of the events towards which it drifted him—as though they already existed and were waiting for him instead of just occurring—that marked him as a different man from the one he had been before; that to a certain extent separated him from those who now surrounded him. But in that separation there was also a spiritual freedom, for he understood that something over which neither he nor his captors had any control was what finally dictated the march of life.

So the prospect of again meeting with Don Luis could no longer fill him with consternation. He regarded it as inevitable; but, therefore, with an almost complete detachment. He felt that Don Luis' judgment upon him, whatever it might be, would be uttered as though Don Luis were the mouthpiece of what controlled them both.

Yet he speculated a good deal upon their possible meeting.

That event would mark a return to the mysterious influences that had to do with the beginning of his existence; make visible the curve of his return to the mystery from which he had come. How little he had to do with that circle, half of which lay in eternity! Despite all his struggles and attempts to depart in his own direction, he had always been brought around again. He was forced, even when he thought he was flying off on his own tangent, to keep to the ordained curve of his life.

In realizing this, Anthony did not feel that he was different from other men. They too must all have their mysterious "rounds." Only in his own life, looking backward, he could dimly trace his own curve now.

Yet because he saw fate there, that did not mean he had become supine and intended to cease to struggle. It merely meant that, like a good many others who reach the age of forty, he felt the inevitability of direction in existence and the hand of a mysterious compulsion heavy upon him.

These were some of the considerations that let him ride forward quietly; that caused Major Muñoz, the officer who had succeeded Sancho in command of the expedition, to describe him as a "tractable prisoner," while they pushed on through the Great American Desert toward Santa Fé.

There was no doubt in that officer's mind about the advisability of holding Anthony prisoner. He regarded him as an altogether mysterious and suspicious character. Although he spoke Spanish, and seemed to be a good Catholic, for he carried an amulet of the Mother of God in a deerskin bag about his neck—still, he also spoke English; his dog had killed the colonel, and his account of what he was doing in Spanish territory was curious, to say the least.

Let him explain to the governor that he had been captured by Indians. Let old Don Luis look to it! He had a way of disposing of doubtful cases. And in these times—with the Yankees pouring across the frontiers into Texas and the revolutionaries out to avenge the shooting of Hidalgo by murdering the Gachupines—one could not be too careful.

Anthony found himself welcomed by the other prisoners, who had too many miseries of their own to be curious about his. The Texans, in particular, were inclined to regard as a benefactor the man whose dog had killed the Cat. The harshness of Sancho toward them had been extreme.

He rode day after day now with one of the white children held before him. He was able to lighten the burdens of the way by sharing his rations and the even more scanty dole of water with some of those who were failing. Remonstrance with the guards about their treatment of captive Indians also brought some results.

But as yet neither his fellow prisoners nor the guards knew exactly what to make of him. They looked somewhat askance upon the powerful man with the yellow beard tucked into his belt, who rode with such a serene look upon his face. What made him so happy? Perhaps, there was something a little uncanny about him? Only the child on his saddle-bow learned to trust him completely; to count on the precious sip of water as the heat and dust of the afternoon began its inevitable torture, and to come and ask for a story at night by the fires.

As for Anthony, he was glad to be back once more among the children of men.

"And there is only one way to live among them," he thought. "Brother François was right: 'Let us be kind to one another.' No man can ever harm me again, for he cannot make me harm him. I am free of everything at last: of all my possessions; of sorrows and hates; of useless curiosity about the nature of God and the Universe. All that I have left is my life and the love of the Divine Child. I sought the Almighty One among the lonely hills for my own comfort and this is the answer. 'Only among men can a man find Him!' The rest is mystery.

"Let the mountains and the oceans that I have seen bear witness to Him. Let me rejoice in, but not try to read the Word between the lips of the dawn and sunset. In me also is the Word, and through my lips and hands, O God, let it be spoken to men. Strengthen me, now that I have found the path at last. Forgive me that not by my own strength have I arrived at this, but because the world withered in fire and in ashes fell away."

Thus he said, riding on through the dust, communing with the spirit in himself, and feeling the weak body of the child before him on the saddle-bow.

And so it was that on a certain afternoon he looked down into a valley where there were a number of flat-roofed, adobe buildings gathered about a plaza. It was a small, poverty-stricken place. The prison would doubtless be none too comfortable. But he looked at it with a serene face.

"That, señor," vouchsafed one of the soldiers, pointing proudly, "is the end of our journey, the City of Santa Fé. We made a great circle when we marched so far into the desert. It has taken us a long time to get back again!"

"Yes," said Anthony, "we have come a great way about."

––––––––––––––

Don Luis had been military governor of the northern Mexican provinces and frontiers for over a decade. When he left Spain he knew he would never see it again. The Prince of the Peace had arranged his departure with a certain neatness. The appointment to a government in Mexico had been disguised as an honour, as indeed it might have been to any younger man. Don Luis' protests to the king had been unavailing. Both Godoy and the queen were finally determined to be rid of him, and they had enlisted Ouvrard on their side. Don Luis, Faith, Sancho, and a few domestics had, therefore, sailed for Mexico shortly after Anthony had left Madrid for New Orleans.

In a way, Don Luis had already had his revenge for being exiled. While he had been living in his adobe "palace" near Santa Fé, comfortably enough, Napoleon had made a clean sweep of Spain and carried off all those who had exiled Don Luis. Don Carlos IV and his queen, Godoy and his entire régime had vanished from Madrid. They were now exiles themselves.

The canny old man left forlornly at Santa Fé had long made it his study to get along with the viceregal authorities at Mexico, whoever they might be. He had made himself invaluable to them; to Don José de Iturrigaray; and in due course to Archbishop Lizana. Don Luis was now holding his government in the name of Ferdinand VII. Not that he was enthused with loyalty for his new sovereign; he had instructions from Mexico—and Don Luis' politics always agreed with

654

the viceroy's. He had now only one fixed policy. He intended to die in his comfortable adobe house in New Spain. The ruthless suppression of the rebellion of Hidalgo had taken place some years before. The shooting of that hero and his thirty companions, one a day for a month, had been managed by Don Luis for the archbishop-viceroy with neatness and dispatch. He had, to be sure, reprieved the thirty-one prisoners from June to July. But only because July has thirty-one days in it. And he had shot Hidalgo last, on the last day of the month, at Chihuahua.

No one since then had cared to raise the grito of revolution in northern Mexico.

The silver convoys had also been sent south from Chihuahua, regularly, twice a year. Don Luis made it a custom to dispatch with them such persons as might be inclined to trouble him, consigned to the tender care of the viceroy.

The regular arrival of silver and "rebels" from the North was a matter of routine at the City of Mexico. The viceroy knew exactly what to do with both.

Things were therefore peaceful enough for the time being.

"It will last my time," said Don Luis to his wife, while they sat on the porch at the Hacienda de León. He could now look at the distant snow mountains complacently enough. "After all, it *is* better than St. Helena. And I feel it in my bones, my dear, that in a short while you at least will be able to return to Spain with an estate that any widow in Madrid might envy. Taking it all in all, it is probably lucky that we were sent here. It is hard to tell what might have happened to us in the troubled times at home." The news of Napoleon's downfall had only recently arrived and had caused Don Luis to do some philosophic thinking. He laughed to think of the poverty-stricken Don Manuel Godoy still dancing attendance on the exiled queen at Rome.

To her husband's remarks Faith did not reply. For

the most part she sat in silence, waiting. It would not be long now.

Don Luis had failed greatly in the last six months. There was no doubt that his end must be near. Faith looked forward to returning to Spain and even to Paris for the years of quiet luxury that might still be hers. She felt she had earned them. She had been a faithful wife to the marquis. She looked at him now, sitting in the sun to keep warm.

The lion-like expression of his face had become accentuated. His huge hands, a surprising network of blue veins, lay relaxed upon the arms of his chair. He was a very ancient lion, wrinkled, and white-maned. Only the eyes were still bright and blazing. But even they had to close in sleep too often. On his temples the veins stood out startlingly. His neck had grown thin. His voice seldom boomed now. For the most part Don Luis piped. That annoyed him, so he too said little. Each understood the other's silence.

In his heart Don Luis wished he could die. He felt he had lived too long. He sat and thought of nothing. He appeared to sleep. It seemed to him that he was waiting for something important to happen, but he could not remember what.

Even when the news of the death of Sancho came, his expression did not alter. Perhaps, that was what he had been waiting for. He would not have to miss his old servant long. And there was a certain aptness about the passing of Sancho—as he listened to Major Muñoz recounting the incident—which still appealed to his sense of the fitness of things.

It seemed inevitable to Don Luis that Sancho should have been treed like a cat. So he had died squalling amid the thorns and branches! Hounded to death! Yes, that was what would have had to happen. For generations in Estremadura the family of Sancho had served his own. They were a peculiar race. There had been legends about them, which Don Luis did not believe. But he knew it was a fact that Sancho's people had always looked like cats. There were also pigs, asses, and mules among men. Character in plants and animals has its characteristic shapes. He thought he knew the subliminal why. Don Luis had needed a servant like Sancho to help get his work done. Soon there would be no more of either of them. Perhaps, the kind of work they were needed to do was over? Both their races had run out.

Don Luis stirred a little uneasily. He hated to think he had been used. He looked at the distant mountains as Major Muñoz departed. "What were *they* for?" he wondered. Well, he would probably soon find out now—or know nothing at all.

"It would be just like You," he said, "to send me to hell for it now You are finished with me. Just like You!"

He wished theology were more reassuring. Perhaps it would be just as well to send for a priest? Now that Sancho was gone, the end did seem near.

What an excellent joke it would be to confess himself into heaven! In the sunlight he sat and laughed a little languidly about it. And yet there were tears in his eyes before he finished. "Maria," he thought, "if she is anywhere—Maria will be there." God, how magical that springtime in Auvergne had been—a whole lifetime ago! *That* had been like paradise. That was heaven. If he had only known it then! If he had only had a child by her! It had been a boy after all. "Saints and Angels! When I meet that young Irishman in hell, I will kill him all over again!" He rose, and taking his stick, stumped into the living-room of the hacienda where Faith generally sat, waiting, and the Navajo blankets blazed with geometrical beasts and black lightnings along the walls.

It had made no particular impression upon Don Luis that the man whose dog had killed Sancho had been captured. He did not even speculate upon old trails having been resumed. That the son of Maria was so near never entered his thoughts. Tomorrow he would go down and sit in judgment on the prisoners that Muñoz had captured. Mañana! In the meantime he sat down to a bowl of atolegruel and a soft, milky tortilla.

In the afternoon he would sleep.

———————

Faith called Major Muñoz back and entertained him for an hour. She got all the news out of him that she could. Santa Fé had become inexpressibly dull to her. The death of Sancho would make a difference. She would now have to depend upon Muñoz to carry out Don Luis' policies. A great many practical details of the administration now rested upon her shoulders. It was important to keep together a junta that she could depend upon. Major Muñoz was the ranking officer of the garrison, so she strove to make his call a pleasant one and to show him that she took a personal interest in his labours.

"What about the new prisoners?" she asked.

"Just the usual lot," he replied, "a few recalcitrant Indians from the Zuñi pueblos; some Americans who settled without permission in Texas; and the man who owned the dog. I must say I can't quite make him out. He seems to be a kind of hermit from his story. But you can't depend upon that. Educated, I think. Speaks Spanish like a Castilian. But he isn't. It might amuse you to talk with him? He begged some milch goats from me for the children only this morning. I let him have them. It can do no harm. It will go hard enough with those people on the trip south. It's quite a long walk from here to Mexico."

"Poor things!" said Faith. "I'll take some shoes down to them."

"Excellent," replied the major. "From now on they will be on foot, you know. They won't be moving with cavalry." He excused himself and left.

About five o'clock the governor's wife drove down

658

to the plaza. She took along some old clothes. It had been too much trouble to find shoes. She looked through the grating at the prisoners in the patio of the city cárcel.

There were two white women with children. One had a child at the breast. The rest of the youngsters were running about. They looked gaunt but were playing eagerly, although one little girl was painfully lame. The small boys kept shop under one of the arches. Mud pies on pieces of broken crockery were for sale. Some savage-looking men strolled up and bought these childish wares from time to time. They bargained solemnly. The currency was bright pebbles and grains of corn. The purchasers were American frontiersmen clad in greasy deerskin full of rents and falling into naked holes. None of them had had their beards or hair cut for months.

Ten or twelve Indians wrapped in the remains of old blankets sat about like bronze statues in rags, saying nothing. Several squaws were making tortillas at the metates. The two white women were having a gossip. One of them, wearing the remains of a sunbonnet, had a clear, sensitive face. She was nursing the baby.

Faith was surprised to see how happy and contented these unfortunates seemed to be. An air of quiet friendliness prevaded the sunny patio of the bare adobe cárcel. Even between the whites and the Indians there was an obvious comradeship.

For a moment she stood there envying them. The bars which separated her prison from theirs were impassable. She had never really been able to share destiny with anyone. She wondered what it would be like not to be completely lonely—to have friends. Thrusting the bundle of odd items of charity that she had brought with her through the grating, she called out for someone to come and get it. A hush fell on the place and they looked at her suspiciously. She felt it and winced. Finally a man got up from behind one of the pillars and started to cross the courtyard toward her.

He was very tall, with an immense mane of yellow hair and a long golden beard. He was dressed in the scarecrow offerings of castoff military clothing. A rawhide thong suspended something about his neck. Yet she knew him instantly. It was the way he walked and his eyes.

"We thank you, señora," he started to say in Spanish.

A scream rose in her throat. She choked it and fled.

He came forward and took the bundle she had left sticking between the bars of the gate and looked out. There was no one there. In the archway beyond there was a faint play of shadows and in the distance the rumble of wheels.

"Doubtless," he thought, "it is not permitted to bring things to the prisoners. The lady did not wish to be recognized." In the courtyard his fellow prisoners crowded about him as he opened the bundle and distributed her offerings. Something as he did so made him think of the Casa da Bonnyfeather.

It was Faith's impulse to drive straight back to the hacienda and break the news to Don Luis. But on the way out over the rough road she fell to thinking. Her mind travelled backward and forward into the remote past and into the not so distant future. It was her curiosity to see what would happen that finally tipped the scales for her decision.

"Go back," she said to the young Indian driving her, "I have forgotten something."

They returned to the town and drew up before a house where a bowl hung from a red pole. She sent for the barber and made a bargain with him. The man bowed to her as she sat in her hooded cart with a seat. He was greatly pleased at being given a well-paid commission by the wife of the governor.

"My lady is *most* charitable," he said. "Only a pious mind given to good works could be so originally

660

thoughtful." He would be glad to confer so comfortable a mercy. He would see to it promptly. She could rely upon him.

Faith returned to the hacienda and said nothing about Anthony to Don Luis.

About an hour before sunset the barber appeared at the prison and offered to cut the hair of the men prisoners and to shave them, gratis. It was a work of charity, he explained. He was to say no more about it. Such had been his instructions. Let those who wished to avail themselves of his services step up.

For the first time in years Anthony slept that night with a smooth cheek against his rough pillow and a cool breeze on the back of his neck. His face, left white where the beard had been, looked like a pale mask of himself.

———————

At the Hacienda de León, under a great cotton tree, Don Luis gave judgment on such matters as came before him. The tree was said to have been planted by Coronado. It stood close-by one of the rare springs in that dry country, where the water burst out under a flat rock scrawled over with rude prehistoric carvings. Upon this rock, under the deep shade of the tree, he sat in the seat of justice with a blanket about his knees. At his feet sat a prothonotary's clerk with horn spectacles and a large book in which the decisions of the governor were written down.

The day after Faith's visit the prisoners were marched out of the city under guard and brought before him. They sat huddled together until their names were called. It was thus, with the speckled shade of the leaves of the great tree falling upon him, that Anthony looked up and beheld the old lion sitting upon the rock.

A Zuñi chief from the pueblo of Nutrias, called by the Spaniards "Bigotes" from the long moustache he wore, was the first called. He was accused by one of the padres of making missionary efforts in his region too difficult.

"A subtle heathen, Your Excellency; a sorcerer powerful in the ceremonies of his khiva; an enemy of Christ."

"Does he make trouble for the king?" inquired Don Luis.

None of the soldiers had any complaint against him.

Some of his own people then stepped forward and begged for his release, claiming that his presence would soon be essential in a dance at his village to make rain.

Don Luis smiled. "Do you not think, Fray Marcos," said he, "that in future you might confine your missionary efforts to the tribes in the river villages? I have noticed that in the arid mountains here most of the missions are in ruins. Christianity in order to flourish must be tempered with humidity. You should remember that."

Fray Marcos looked confused. He could not remember anything about "humidity" in the scriptures. Yet it sounded like a virtue. Don Luis turned to the Indian.

"Go," said he, "return to your village and make rain. The priest of the pale face will trouble you no more. But be careful that in drawing the clouds over your pueblo you do not also bring down upon it the lightning and thunder-birds of your great white father, the King of Spain."

There was a certain majesty in the old man as he uttered this—and the interpreter translated. The Zuñis retired with appreciative grunts, taking Bigotes along with them.

With the rest of the Indians the governor made short work. They were marauders or half-breed malcontents. A brief explanation by Muñoz of the reason for their arrest was followed by the sentence, "To the mines."

There was no period to the sentence. No one returned from the mines.

With the Americans Don Luis dealt at some length. He questioned each one keenly, the women as well as the men.

"Jane Chalfont . . ."

"So your husband was killed on the River of Arcansa by Indian arrows, you say?"

"Yes, sir," said the little widow with the ragged sunbonnet, holding her child close to her breast.

"Didn't you wish to return whence you came even then?"

"No, sir."

"What!"

"No, sir, me and Mrs. Johnson and her two boys just stayed on and put in the corn."

Don Luis looked at her in astonishment.

"And we was doin' good enough till your captain that the dog killed come and burned down the cabin and carried us all off into Egypt. I'm glad the dog got him. Sarved him plum right!"

"Those are 'the boys,'" said Muñoz indicating two very young ones.

"Dios," said Don Luis. "Why, they're infants! What are we going to do if these people keep on coming?"

The major shrugged his shoulders.

"Remanded to Mexico," said Don Luis. "Now then, I'll see this hermit who owned the dog. Rather unfortunate for him. A bit cracked, you think, eh?"

Muñoz had purposely reserved Anthony's case to the last. He had not shot him offhand on the plains for the death of Sancho—which he might have done, and no questions asked—because he had thoroughly despised his little commander as an upstart and owed his promotion to his death. It was not his quarrel. In addition, he could make nothing out of Anthony when he questioned him. With the ingrained propensity of the military man to avoid responsibility whenever possible, he had simply left the decision to the governor.

Bored, he now beckoned to Anthony to come forward.

Don Luis was tired. For an old man it had been a gruelling morning. He had already cross-questioned over a dozen prisoners and he felt a little nauseated and trembling. He sat for a moment with his eyes half closed, watching the play of leaf shadow on the ground. The inside of his head felt like that too.

When he looked up Anthony was standing before him.

He looked at his face. It was quite calm and serene. But it produced in Don Luis the effect of a violent electric shock. For a while he could say nothing. His own face worked, and he trembled with an access of palsy. By an effort of will that almost exhausted him he was at length able to control himself.

"Give me your book," he said to the clerk at his feet, "and your pen!"

In a script which appeared to be a nervous caricature of his own precise handwriting, he wrote something in the book and signed it. Then he looked Anthony in the eyes.

"Bastard!" said he, and mumbled something. No one could understand what. His speech was broken and thick. At last he motioned for them to take Anthony away.

Major Muñoz looked in the book. He gave a whistle of cynical surprise and shouted orders to take the prisoners back to the cárcel.

Don Luis got into his litter with great difficulty and was carried home. Faith was much disappointed. He did not say anything at all but went directly to his room. He felt faint and sent the maidservant out for some wine. It was after midday now and very warm. He sat down in a chair before his dresser and took off his wig. Beads of sweat were running off his bald crown. He could see the veins in his temples beating slowly. Suddenly a convulsion shook him. He saw his face writhing, in the mirror. Then, as if cool fingers had stroked him, one side of it became still with the eye closed. He regarded it with the other eye for an instant of eternal horror, while one half of him watched the other half die. Then he slipped to the floor.

A few minutes later Faith was summoned, by the screams of the girl who had returned with the wine, to assume immediately the grief and duties of a widow. She assumed both equally well. While she arranged with Major Muñoz for a proper military funeral for her husband, she was also able to direct the packing of as much of her own wardrobe and his personal effects as were to accompany her on her return to Spain. The arrangement for her escort and conveyance as far as Mexico was promptly completed. It was remarkable how well, and with what an eye for detail, she seemed to have thought of everything in advance. Both the mirth and the admiration of the major were moved. But he said nothing. For he considered her, despite her age, to be a woman of great determination and the remains of a strange charm.

"Dios!" said he, curling his mustachios, as her wagon and the strong detachment of cavalry that accompanied it disappeared in the dust down the road towards Albuquerque. "What a woman the old girl must have been!" It was only a few days later that he found himself in great trouble merely because of his haste with a lady in trying to reassure himself that he had *not* been born too late.

Even to the end Faith carried with her this power of disturbance. If her intercourse was henceforth purely conversational, it was nevertheless titillating even to the aged gallants who for some years afterward continued to call upon the Marquesa da Vincitata both at Madrid and in Paris—perhaps out of respect for her husband's memory. If so, they had their reward. For her piquant, though veiled reminiscences held fast her many admirers in a mutual regret for the lost pleasures of youth; regrets so skillfully fanned that they almost rekindled to flames. At least she warmed the eternal spark that remains even in ashes.

As for Anthony, time passed monotonously in the cárcel at Santa Fé, and his hair and beard grew long again. The summer waned, and the nights began to become uncomfortably cold.

———————————

It was not until late October that Major Muñoz felt it safe to start his now considerable body of prisoners on their long march from Santa Fé to the City of Mexico. His delay was due to the disturbances in the northern provinces caused by the rumours of Don Luis' death, and by the clamorous demands of the intendant at Chihuahua for a full quota of labourers for the government silver mines. So the major had waited well into the autumn, while he "arrested" more Indians and peons, and conducted a brief raid into the Moqui highlands to complete his labour quota to the number desired.

The convoy, when it did start, consisted of about sixty unfortunate mestizos and Indians bound for the mines at Chihuahua as well as the captured Americans, or "Tejaños," whose cases were to be disposed of by the Viceroy Calleja at Mexico. Before the Texan frontiersmen and their families lay a journey over the plateaus and mountains of Anahuac of some sixteen hundred English miles.

There was no logical reason for their being thus dragged into exile. All they had tried to do was to make homes in the wilderness. Unwittingly, they had crossed over certain invisible boundaries into the territory of New Spain. That constituted a political crime, at least in the eyes of their captors, and they were therefore reduced to the status of beings whose existence was an official nuisance. Their only hope lay in what sympathetic help they would be able to extend to each other and in the humanity and mercy they might arouse in the hearts of their fellow men encountered along the route.

666

Anthony had learned that he was to be sent with the Tejaños to Mexico, but he could learn nothing more. "I am sorry for you, señor," said the major, "Don Luis seemed to understand you well enough! Unfortunately, he has gone where I cannot question him as to his motives, and it is only natural that I should respect the decisions of my illustrious predecessor. I am in command here only temporarily, you know."

"No one commands permanently, señor, one's opportunity for doing good is always brief. But I am not pleading for myself primarily," Anthony replied. "You may think it strange, perhaps, but I find myself just now happy and satisfied"—"God help you," murmured the major thinking of what Don Luis had written in the book—"I thought you might care to share my happiness by providing the prisoners with shoes before we set out. There are old men, women, and children among them. I have done what I could by making moccasins out of the leather fire buckets that hung in the guard-house."

"So that is where they went!" cried Muñoz.

"Yes," laughed Anthony, "but they did not go very far. I could fit the little ones only. Your own heart must be greater than that."

"You are a clever fellow," muttered the soldier, looking at Anthony's bare feet.

"No, no," cried the prisoner, "it is more than that!"

Major Muñoz said nothing. He turned suddenly and walked away. The evening before they left there was a distribution of shoes.

Anthony held up his hand to Muñoz as they passed out of the gate next morning.

"I am glad that I didn't tell him," mused the major as he smiled back at him. "Dios, what a beard he has!" —and he thought of that prisoner no more.

The column of Tejaños and Indians toiled along the rough road to Albuquerque over the cactus-covered hills. They were under the command of a rascal by the name of José Salezar, a half-breed from Tehuacán, who was never at peace with himself or anyone else. In him the Spaniard and the Indian were forever struggling for mastery. His feelings and actions were both cruel and confused. The only abiding satisfaction he found in the world was in the collecting of things. It did not matter what, so long as they were of some value. He was a kind of human magpie. Sympathy was foreign to him, for he could not understand, nor did he care, what the feelings of others might be like.

Hence, the sufferings of the unfortunates in his charge were never mitigated by anything but the fear of future reprisals or the possible indignation of his superiors, which he could not understand. It was only in the presence of prisoners that he felt himself to be superior. He had gladly become a professional route-jailer. He delivered his charges dead or alive, for that was the way his orders read.

With the guards riding up and down the flanks and kicking dust into their faces, the prisoners proceeded in a column of fours to Albuquerque, where they spent a night in an ample jail. Half-a-day's march south of that city they were stripped of their shoes. It was Salezar's intention to sell these at El Paso and he did not want them worn out. From this point on real sufferings began.

There was now no hope of even an Indian's escaping across the waterless desert. At night the prisoners were left for the most part to shift for themselves with only a few mounted pickets thrown out.

On the high plateau northwest of El Paso the autumn cold was extreme. When the sun sank a panic began to develop among both whites and Indians lest they should freeze to death. After the miserable evening meal of half-cooked mush was over, they dissolved into groups which rushed from one dry grass clump to another in order to set them on fire. The grass flared up while they stood about it in circles; wild, ragged figures shivering in the firelight. Then the flames would suddenly die down and they would rush on to the next clump.

They trod in the ashes to keep their feet from freezing. They danced and cried out. For a mile over the flat uplands the weird scene kept repeating itself. Flames leaped into the air and died down again. The circles rushed on. Always herded in the right direction by the mounted guards, by morning they had advanced several miles along the trail and they were driven in by the mounted pickets.

It was impossible to sleep under such conditions. Those who finally lay down exhausted were afraid they would either freeze or be left behind. The terror of falling by the wayside hung over the column day and night.

On the first of these nights of bonfires and hysteria Anthony had found the Chalfont woman wandering about with her child. She had nothing to wrap about it but the thin remnants of her shawl and wisps of grass.

"My baby is going to die," she said simply. "Feel him. He is turning cold. If I only had something to wrap about him!"

He had already given his coat to one "Grumpa Carlton," an old man who appeared to be dying of a cough, and was then lying under one of the carts. He himself stood with nothing on but a pair of old military trousers and the deerskin bag about his neck.

"And see," said the woman, looking up into his face, as if he could do something. "My son is dying."

They came to him like that now. They seemed to think he must do something about it. At last she realized he was helpless.

"I should think that God would do something," said the little widow. She looked about her in the moonlight as though searching for Him.

"But no," she added violently, "no, no! Who cares?"

"Wait here," he said. "It may not be too late yet."

He went to the carts where some of the guards,

rolled snugly in their blankets, were sleeping comfortably. There were savage and brutal faces, weak, and surprised and simple faces among them, as they lay unconscious and relaxed before him. But one, that of a full-blooded Indian, bore the stamp of patience and sorrow. He took the image from the bag, and holding it up before him, quietly wakened him. The man's eyes opened. Still in a half-dreaming state, he looked at the figure in the moonlight.

"Madre de Díos," he whispered. Then he saw Anthony, and sat up startled. They looked at each other.

"Well?" grumbled the soldier.

"What is your name, my friend?"

"Pedro."

"Are you a Christian, Pedro?"

"Sí!" The man crossed himself.

"Christ is dying of cold just behind the wagons." Pedro showed no surprise. "Come with me and I'll show you."

The man wrapped his serape about him and stalked after Anthony into the darkness. Presently they came to the woman and child. She was standing just where he had left her.

"Look," said he. "It might be the Child himself."

The Indian felt the baby's icy feet and grunted. He took off his serape, wrapped the baby in it, and handed the bundle back to Jane Chalfont.

She clutched it to her, warming the child against her breast. Presently the folds of the blanked moved and a faint cry came from it.

"Ugh!" said Pedro, and clutching Anthony by the arm led him back to the carts. He groped in one, and from somewhere produced a couple of sheepskin coats. They put these on and squatted together under a cart. After a while the woman came and joined them. She went to sleep leaning against a wheel with the blanket wrapped about her and the child. Anthony and Pedro passed the Indian's pipe back and forth between them until dawn. They managed to sleep a little.

He spent every night that way for some time. In the daytime he marched bare to the waist. In spite of the coat which he had lent Grumpa Carlton, the old man finally died of pneumonia. As he lay breathing his last in an oxcart, one of the guards came up and poked his rifle in his face. The sick man saw it and cried out. The soldier snapped the lock and laughed. He did this three times. When he strolled on Carlton was dead.

Even the Texans were so exhausted by this time that they merely sat still and watched. A sergeant came and cut off the dead man's ears. They would constitute Salezar's receipt for this prisoner to his superiors, and a proof that he had not escaped. They buried Carlton that night with the ghostly Indians standing around. Some of the squaws started to keen but the guards stopped them. A silent sympathy had developed between Indian prisoners and the whites.

Finding Salezar happy on mescal one evening, Anthony had approached him and wheedled some tobacco out of him. He distributed the small bundles to both whites and Indians alike. Many brown eyes now followed him gratefully.

Things at last became a little more tolerable. At San Miguel some of the charitable inhabitants supplied them with fresh bread. The panics at evening ceased. They were now in the valley of the Rio Grande where the chaparral supplied them with firewood. The guards had been prevailed upon to give the women and children a lift in the ration carts now and then. They made so much better time this way that Salezar connived at the breach of his own orders.

Anthony cheered them along with the hope that some help would be forthcoming at El Paso, where he promised, if possible, to appeal to the authorities for relief. He was almost afraid to promise anything, for they were coming to depend upon him utterly. He was the only one who could make himself clearly understood in Spanish, and besides that, he had now gained the trust and fervent affection of every man, woman, and child in the little group of exiles who dragged themselves along toward they knew not what. His great strength, which frequently permitted him to lighten the burdens of the others, his imperturbable serenity, and his tireless efforts to cheer and alleviate their lot had permeated them all with a spirit that buoyed them up even when they were not aware of it.

One of the children was always riding on his shoulders. He became particularly attached to a little girl, Sadie Johnson, who had gone painfully lame. It was the terror of her mother that she might be made to leave her behind. The sight of her sad little face high above the heads of the others, riding on through the dust on the shoulders of the man with the yellow mane gave the woman strength and hope enough to falter after. Her husband, a tall, pale man from the banks of the Ohio, had been hurt when he was captured. He could do no more than march himself. His two young boys took themselves along manfully, but were too small to help.

Day after day on this exhausting march from Santa Fé to El Paso, Anthony heard the half-dreamful, half-benumbed humming of the child Sadie sound in his ears; a formless, endless, half-melodic murmur like the sound of the summer wind in treetops. And to this he would often reply by a little song himself. He did not remember, but it was the song Contessina had once sung to him while he played by the fountain. In the dust and panting heat of the afternoon he sometimes thought he heard the quiet murmur and refreshing whisper of those eternal waters in his ears. The child would sleep and he would plod on mechanically, one foot after the other. On the bottom of his soles was a hard, shiny callous. It was not long, indeed, before those who had been deprived of shoes by Salezar were reshod by nature with horn.

At last they arrived at the Pass of the North and camped. On the morrow they would be in El Paso.

The sunset here was unearthly. In the gorges of the savage mountains to the eastward it lingered in mellow contrast along their black cliffs. Through the dust of the tableland stretching endlessly westward, the enormously enlarged face of the sun sank dark as old blood through what appeared to be a fiery mist. Somewhere a little south of them, he could not see where, the silver vein of the Rio* Grande cut through the sombre and ragged mountains.

"El Paso del Norte!" Tomorrow he would pass through its gates.

The premonition of an utterly new and inscrutable experience before him; a flood of memories from the immense and irrevocable past overcame him as the sun sank and cold and darkness rushed upon the desert prairie as though they were one.

For a time that evening, while the mountain peaks still caught the last, high rays of vanishing day, he felt that it was impossible that he should go on. He fell face downward in despair and psychic exhaustion. He must have lain there for some minutes. It was then that a chariot came for him. It picked him up. In some fold of eternity he rode with Florence and little Maria again along that stretch of Tchoupitoulas Street, where it was always spring and the birds sang.

He never saw them again. And this was also the last time in his life that he lay in the dust and wept.

When he rose he was able to stroll back to the wagons where the fires were already leaping as though nothing had happened. And, indeed, nothing in the world had.

There was a new hope, almost a joyful atmosphere about the fires that evening. Finding himself so near the end of this section of the route, Salezar got drunk, distributed extra rations to the prisoners, and gorged his men. For the first time in many days there was plenty to eat. And tomorrow—tomorrow they would be in El Paso!

It is surprising what very small things in adverse

circumstances suffice to make people happy—a little food, warmth, and something to look forward to. Already it seemed as though the terrors of the march had never been. Van Ness and Griffith, two of the Texans, actually tried to sing a little. Mrs. Chalfont's baby was hushed. Even the Indians, although they knew they would never come back that way again, passed from mouth to mouth such pipes and weed as they had, together with the magic phrase of change and hoped-for alleviation, "El Paso del Norte."

———————

Early in the morning they struck into the valley and marched through the gorge. The last trial of their strength remained. At a little fall in the Rio Grande some four miles above El Paso they were forced to ford the river.

Several lariats were tied together. One of the guards rode across with the rope, and it was stretched taut. The river was waist-deep in most places, and chin-deep in others for all but the tallest. The Texans took the women and children on their shoulders and crossed over, slipping, floundering, and cutting their feet on sharp stones. In the cold morning air they stood shivering on the far bank, looking back at the Indians who had not crossed yet.

Salezar became impatient at the delay. He gave a shrill whistle, and the guards rode into the Indians, where they huddled on the bank. The sound of hoofs on stones, the sharp crack and dull thud of whips, the terrified cries made a hideous chorus in the quiet valley.

The Indians were driven into the stream en masse. Some of them missed the rope. They struggled with one another desperately. Three of them sank and were drowned. There would not even be any ears to show for them.

Enraged at his own stupidity, Salezar now hurried his prisoners pellmell down the road toward the town, cursing and swearing. Then he formed them in columns, and placing himself proudly at their head, prepared to lead them into El Paso. Mounted on a baggage mule with silver housings, he curled his mustachios with pride. He was arriving five days ahead of his schedule and counted on selling not only the shoes but the remaining rations. He formed up his guards in as military a manner as possible and sent his buglers forward to announce himself. The population of the town poured forth into the plaza to see the Tejaños.

To find El Paso buried in its vineyards and delicious gardens in the midst of the dusty, cactus desert was to defy all earthly comparisons to do justice to the contrast. For those prisoners who had been born in green countries it was as though they had been dragged for an eternity across the cinder fields of purgatory and had stumbled suddenly upon the first outlying vale of paradise. They crossed the first irrigation ditch, and then, as though their sins had been forgiven them, the lush verdure began.

It was not a city into which they had come. It was far more beautiful than that. It was a succession of luxuriantly cultivated villas that stretched for miles up and down the valley in a wide strip on both sides of the river, sheltered from the withering "northers" by a semicircle of frowning hills. There were broad roads lined on either side by placid little canals overarched by rows of trees and spanned by frame bridges. From the base of the mountains, the place had looked like a green, haphazard chequer-board crossed by white lines on which one might move from a square of vineyard to one of roses, or from a rectangle of orchard to a garden patch. Such, indeed, was the ancient and fruitful game in which the pawns who lived there were absorbingly engaged.

Myriads of birds sang in the thickets, and there was always to be heard, like a constant, whispered assurance of abundance, the sound of flowing water passing

675

over the wooden irrigation gates. Into this bower, which far surpassed all their expectations with its colourful adobe houses gleaming in the midst of groves and gardens, the prisoners were now marched.

The effect upon them was overpowering. The children darted out of ranks to gather flowers and even some of the men wept at the sight and touch of leaves. The day was warm, the sky a faultless blue, and the sunlight sparkled along the hedges. They had been washed in the river and their garments had now dried on them. It was like being reborn. Although some of their wounded feet still left bloody traces in the dust, they marched firmly and with a dignity and joy at still being among the living that only an escape from mortal suffering can confer. They were ridiculous and grotesque in appearance, but they were also sublime.

It was curious how the crowd that had gathered on the plaza was instantly aware of this; how it both laughed at and then pitied them, and called out in encouragement and admiration all at the same time.

The Texans were not shamefaced at their own suffering and appearance. They were beyond that. They could even join in the laughter at their own expense, a little, even when some of their faces were still wet with tears.

By the manifestation of so many complicated and even conflicting emotions at the same time, as when the various degrees of pain and pleasure are simultaneously made visible by a hundred subtle gestures and facial expressions, humanity can best recognize itself as human. For it is in his combined complexity and unity of emotion that man is pre-eminently differentiated from all other living things. Let him once see that this essentially human quality has been outraged in others, and by a touch of self-protective imagination he puts himself in their place. That is where sympathy begins. And that is why it is always most easily awakened by a display of feeling.

Perhaps, then, it was fortunate for the prisoners that

they had been so broken down by the rigours of the march from Santa Fé that they could not prevent themselves from openly showing their manifold and conflicting emotions as they were marched through the streets of El Paso. Such displays are infectious.

That is why they were described as "pestilential" in official correspondence—they begot a plague of sympathy—and why the crowd on the plaza went mad over them while it only laughed or hissed Salezar, who was obviously without many human feelings, and therefore a brute. There was no fuss at all over the Indians who were in a much worse way but were quite impassive. Sympathy was concentrated on the Texans. Even the comandante of the district, whom no one had ever thought of describing as sentimental, was touched.

Standing on the steps of his headquarters opposite the cathedral, Colonel Don Elias Gonzales, commanding at El Paso, looked down and saw approaching him above the heads of the crowd a pale, straw-haired little girl with the dark blue marks of suffering under her eyes. The face of that child smote him to the heart. She was holding a small bouquet of flowers in her hand, and her dress, a wisp of faded gingham, scarcely seemed to cover her white form. She was riding on the shoulders of a huge man stripped to the waist whose great yellow beard rippled down over his breast. His ragged trousers with a faded stripe on them flapped in tatters to his knees. As they passed the comandante the child looked up at him, and drawing back her arm in a peculiarly feminine motion of throwing, tossed him her flowers. He caught them and bowed gravely to her. Between the colonel and the man with the beard passed an understanding glance. The man and child were followed by a number of stalwart, weirdly-bewhiskered fellows in all manner of skins and rags, several with bleeding feet. Mrs. Johnson and her two boys, who were waving green branches and had something faunlike about them, came next, with Mrs. Chalfont in her still surviving sunbonnet, carrying the baby in a serape.

677

The two women were dressed in the gowns that Faith had conferred upon them, old court costumes with stomachers, bedraggled and grotesque beyond belief. At the rear limped Mr. Johnson himself, holding his wounded side and looking ghastly with a thin blue beard. Then came the Indians. Their sufferings were indecent and various. A few faithful squaws followed after their captive husbands, hustled now and again by mounted guards.

The colonel-comandante nosed his bouquet thoughtfully and looked across it at Salezar, who sat on his mule with the silver housings, a grin of assured welcome on his face. Over his saddle-bow was a string of eight ears interesting to several flies.

The colonel turned away without noticing Salezar, although he saluted several times. He went in and sat down by a window. Taking a piece of folded paper out of the bouquet, he carefully read some quite minute but very legible writing upon it. It was a diary of the route kept by one of the prisoners. After he finished he sat for a few minutes with his eyelids half-closed. Then he got up and looked out again.

The crowd had disappeared. Across the plaza the prisoners were just entering the gate of the city cárcel . . .

"Sadie, my love," said Anthony, "you threw that bouquet splendidly! How would you like to sleep in a nice soft bed tonight? I believe you will yet."

The child sighed. She no longer believed every cheering thing he told her, although she always responded.

"Anyway, it's a nice jail," she said. "There *might* be some straw."

. . . Salezar batted the flies away from his saddle-bow impatiently. He had been kept waiting for some time. His mule stamped.

"Come up here!" roared Colonel Gonzales out of the window at him. Salezar looked up in stupefaction. "You, *you damned rascal*," shouted the colonel his face purple with rage, jabbing his thumb at him, "I mean you!"

———————————

An hour later the door into the big room of the city prison opened and the colonel, a young priest, and the surgeon of the garrison stepped in. They saw a long whitewashed apartment with barred windows near the ceiling, through which the sunlight fell in slanting rays to the bare floor. At one end of it the Indians sat stoically upon the stones. The man with the yellow beard was kneeling down before a squaw seated on a bench. He was washing and binding up her wounded feet. The whites had arranged themselves as best they could in another corner. They had taken most of the benches. The two women sat together. One was nursing her baby and the other holding the little girl with the pale face. The men were already asleep or gathered about a pack of frayed cards.

"Same old three pennies in the poke," said Van Ness. "Well, Falconer, I'll raise yer on this ante. Can't ya hide yer face even with all that chaparral on it?" Suddenly they saw the three strangers at the door and the room grew quiet.

The young priest walked forward and touched Anthony on the shoulder.

"I see we both serve the same master, señor," said he. "Am I right?"

"Yes," said Anthony.

"We have come to help you. Do, leave off for a moment. The colonel wishes to speak to you. Wipe your hands on my gown. You need bandages, don't you?"

"It was you who wrote me the note, señor?" asked the colonel.

"Yes, very hurriedly this morning on a piece of paper I found in the street. It seemed to have been sent . . ."

679

"It was," said the colonel. "Now where is the little señorita who tossed me the flowers? A most touching thing, señor. I and my wife have been greatly moved. Take me to her. Now what is her name? . . . Sadee? Do I say it right?"

"How do you do, Señorita Sadee. You and your mother are to come home with me. Sí! Explain to them, señor. It is the wish of my wife. What! Two brothers, too! I am afraid—but no, why not? Come, you shall *all* go forth with me. Doctor, you will ask your good wife to look after this other woman and her baby. Look, it is sick. It has puked all over its blanket."

"They usually do," said the doctor looking a little startled.

"Come, come," cried the colonel. "Would you have me send them to the padre's house to make a scandal? Think how the tongue of his washerwoman would clack. Dios de Dios, doctor!"

The surgeon and the priest laughed.

"Now as to these,"—he pointed to the men, "—if they will give me their parole, I am sure we can find comfortable places about town for them. What do you think?"

There was no doubt whatever they thought. They gave the colonel a cheer.

In ten minutes the place was emptied of the whites and the colonel sat smiling with satisfaction and flushed with the excitement of so much kindness on one of the empty benches.

"I am sorry my house is not large enough to entertain you, too," he said to Anthony. "I am afraid you will have to go home with the padre. I will send you some clothes, and a razor. You will have no objections to that I suppose?"

"None whatever. I wish in some way to thank you!" He hesitated. "What of these Indians?"

The good colonel shrugged his shoulders. "Well, what of them?" he said. "Let the padre look after them. Here, señor, permit me to lend you my cloak. You must go home through the streets. No, no, it is nothing. It is yours." They bowed to each other and he left.

"You see," said the young priest as they walked home to his house a little later, "human kindness is not quite enough."

"That is strange," replied Anthony, "I was just thinking the same thing."

They smiled at each other.

"My name is Ramón Ortiz. As you may have guessed I am the cura of El Paso—and yours . . ."

"Here we are," he cried at last, "sometimes I think it is almost too comfortable for a follower of the blessed St. Francis. But it is just as I found it when I came here two years ago."

They passed through a vineyard and the priest swung open the unlatched door of his adobe dwelling. He drove a hen and her family out of the room. "Shoo," he cried. "Shoo!"

"Enter, brother, in His name."

From El Paso to Chihuahua wild mountain ranges march southward with the tablelands—and men march perforce along the tablelands, watching the mountains that now reach into the distance and now close in again.

It was a radically altered band of prisoners that set out upon this mighty road to Anahuac after six weeks of rest and mercy at El Paso. The Indians had long ago preceded them. Somewhere in the mountains southward they were already labouring in the mines. But they could do nothing about that. They thought of them no more, for the road that lay before them was pregnant with the mystery of their own fate. What it might finally be they considered or sometimes whispered about around the fires, but for the most part they were now content to let this fate unroll before them from day to day.

The panorama of it was magnificent.

In that hour of agony before they had come through the Pass of the North, Anthony had thought he could

681

never find joy or feel the glory in the mystical and unpronounceable Word hidden behind the veils of the outward semblances of things. But he had been wrong about that. It was renewed for him as a gift accompanying the rejuvenation and renovation of his inward being that he had also received. Never before had the Vision of Light been so radiant and yet so revealing. Never had the landscapes of the earth meant more. Now that he had forever given up questing for *what* they meant, now since he was content to feel them only as vivid words composed at once of thought and feeling in the almighty poem of the universe, his soul leapt up each morning with his body to meet the dawn.

Who has looked upon the world with the focused prisms of a clear outer and inner manhood, washed clear by sorrow and polished, not scratched and falsely angled by the grinding of suffering, might see with him. False rainbows about the edges of things were no more. The perspective was perfected, the light stronger, and the objects bathed in it were clear. He saw them whole, and therefore with a new glory upon them.

There was, it is true, a hint of something overpowering about this, an overtone of an element that was more than light. It was a mental brightness so intolerable that it might turn sunlight into a shadow—as though the light itself were the shade of the thing that cast it, he sometimes thought. So far the exaltation of the spirit might attain—and no more. But he did not recoil from these experiences exhausted. He was not overpowered. He returned with the freshness and strength of them and walked the trail in peace.

That peace was all the greater—perhaps, he only possessed it to the fullness that he did—because it was shared with him by the others who were travelling the same road.

They could scarcely be called prisoners any longer, unless from a purely political standpoint, and none of them took that. They had become, rather, a band of pilgrims travelling in friendship together toward the same mysterious fate.

They travelled in solid-wheeled oxcarts, at least Mrs. Johnson and Mrs. Chalfont and the children did, while the men rode upon mules. But that made no difference. Nor did the hardships and rigours of the route disconcert them. Hardships are, within certain degrees, merely a matter of contrast. What they were experiencing now was like a journey through the promised land compared with the intolerable inflictions between Santa Fé and El Paso.

Salezar and his crew of ladrones and picaros, who so patterned themselves after him, had disappeared. They had been returned by Colonel Gonzales to Major Muñoz at Santa Fé with the suggestion that since Don Luis was no more, it might no longer be necessary to employ wild beasts to convoy men.

The prisoners were still under guard, for the good colonel had in the end been forced to take the political view of things. He could not release them, as he would have liked to do. He was merely an authority. But he had fed them fat and rested them well. Their guards now consisted of the good-natured militia of El Paso, who were also conducting the annual caravan of travellers from that vicinity bound for the New Year's fair at Chihuahua, with apples, raisins, pears, onions, wine, and Paso Brandy. The string of carts and pack animals, muleteers, servants, and motley camp-followers—women and children—were now a thousand in number and in marching stretched out for over a mile. At night they camped in a great ring, a circle of twinkling fires.

Indeed, the checks now put upon the Texans were few. At night they were at liberty to wander among the traders as they pleased, going from fire to fire, where there was much amusement to be had. The trip was a sort of travelling carnival for the traders and their families. The excellent, fiery vino del país was broached, and much Paso passed from bottle to lip.

There was music, singing, and the clapping of hands and castanets in the dance. There were dice and cards under the carts by the light of horn lanterns, from which Van Ness and Buckthorn generally returned with pockets jingling. And there was also the characteristic sound of lamentation by those whose cart had broken an axle. Half the load of each cart consisted of axels. Lamentation was chronic. These giant wains by daylight staggered, wobbled, and groaned forward upon eccentric courses in a state of epidemic collapse. Yet what could be more comfortable at night to sleep in than one of these great wagons filled with straw, while the meteors streaked down the twinkling bowl of heaven, coyotes clamoured in the distant desert, and the fires died low?

"Listen, big man," said little Sadie one evening when he came to say good night to her, "do you know what them coyotes sounds like? Like the schoolyard back in Ohio away-way off across the river. I'd like to go back there and play." He sat silent a moment listening. She pulled him down to her. "Don't ye tell ma, will ye?"—He promised—"but I'm going home soon. I know it. Hearin' them wild voices and watchin' stars fall, told me. And I want ye to promise me suthin'. I want ye . . ."—"Yes," he whispered. . . . "I want ye to make ma leave my dolly with me. She might keep it to remember me by, and I don't want to be left all alone. I thought you'd know. It's too bad after you done toted me so far."

He walked out on the prairie a little and came back again.

It would not do to go too far. The Apaches might be about. For that reason the guards had no need to worry that their prisoners would try to escape. By day they even let the Texans range well ahead of the column, for no one had sharper eyes for hostile Injuns than they, but after darkness fell the "centinela alerta" sounded about the camp all night.

It was the night after they had camped at the Diamond Spring that Sadie had spoken to Anthony. The next two days they double-teamed it through shifting sand hills without water until they came to a spring near the trail-side called the "Fountain of the Star." It was sandy all about. There was only one stone in the neighbourhood. It was called "la puerta de piedra," and weighed at least two hundred pounds. Everyone, who could, lifted it once and threw it over his head along the road to Mexico. One Oacha, a muleteer, explained the reason to Anthony.

"It is for the glory of God, señor. There are many travellers on this road. It is their faith that sometime this stone will reach Méjico and be put in the high altar there. In my time it has moved from the Diamond Spring to the Fountain of the Star. My father told me that in heathen times it came slowly down out of the north. Perhaps, quién sabe?"

So Anthony moved it a few feet nearer to Mexico.

"A fine throw," said Oacha, "that is all that anyone can do."

A few days later they camped at a hot spring that bubbled up out of a mound in a desert of thorn bushes. Here was a great washing of clothes and of naked bodies.

He took the sick child Sadie and laid her in a warm pool. There was something the matter with her hip. The surgeon at El Paso could do nothing about it but shake his head. In the warm water she seemed to revive. He thought from then on she looked better.

"The pain *is* gone," she said.

A few days later they left the desert behind them and entered upon those grassy tablelands with streams lined by trees, and far-stretching haciendas generous as the careless sovereigns who granted them, where the longhorn cattle and the half-wild horses wander in legions over the teeming tierras templadas. Here the mountains receded dimly into the perspective, opening out like the ribs of a great fan. The distance became vaster. They were emerging upon the fertile plateaus of Anahuac.

Not far from Chihuahua, in a grassy valley which is nothing more than a depression in the plain, lies the Laguna Encillanos. Its waters are clear blue, and the prairie sweeps down to it in smooth, curving lawns that about the end of December break forth into untold myriads of nodding, purple flowers. For some reason there are no trees here. The lake lies in the prairie and looks up at heaven like an eye wide-open and fringed with blossoms. It was here that Sadie Johnson died.

They called him to her hastily. She was asking for him, they said. Death had suddenly looked out of the child's face. Her mother and the two small boys, Alec and Tom, stood by the cart frightened and weeping incontinently. Her father, too tired just then to feel anything keenly, sat near by in a kind of dreamful despair.

"Do something, for God's sake *do* something," cried the woman, seizing Anthony by the arm as he came up.

He smiled at her, and putting her hands together, went to the cart and bent over the child.

"Sadie," he whispered. She opened her eyes. They reminded him of the lake. She searched for him with her hands blindly and found his hair.

" 'Pears like night's coming soon today," she said.

"In the morning light He will come and carry you," he said.

"Sure?"

"Certain I am."

"Now I lay me . . ." she began—and then pulled him down closer to her. "I want to say it to ma."

He beckoned to her mother, who gathered her child to her.

They were all silent now, even the boys. Most of the men, having heard the news, came up quietly and stood about.

Suddenly the woman gave a scream. She dropped the little body into the straw of the cart, and running out onto the open prairie, frantically began to gather armfuls of the purple flowers.

They all began to do that. That was all they could do. They heaped the cart. The Mexicans came around chattering and big eyed.

The father did not move but sat shaking his head slowly in a kind of numb negative.

"Yer no good, Johnson," cried the woman, "yer no good at all!"

"I know it," he said, and went off to borrow a spade.

So they left Sadie with her doll sleeping together by the Laguna Encillanos.

In an inexplicable way this event drew them all closer together. From now on the men went less about the fires of the traders and stayed more about their own. The pilgrims marched southward over the plateaus more and more like one family.

It was not that they had been made melancholy or felt it essential to show their grief in an explicit way. But everybody missed the child. Anthony's shoulders ached for her. Mrs. Johnson trudged on bravely with Mrs. Chalfont beside her. The principal comfort of the older woman now was in carrying the baby. From now on it had two mothers. In a curious way the two boys had been driven closer to their father. Mrs. Johnson had for so long blamed her husband for marrying her that she had come to blame him for everything else. She looked grim when he tentatively approached the fire at supper now.

" 'Tain't pa took Sadie, ma," piped her son Tom one evening.

"Here's your mush!" snapped Mrs. Johnson. "Hush your mouth!"

That evening the boy crept under the blanket with his father and took to tagging by his side during the march. Some of the men winked at one another. They also for the first time took the shy, sensitive Johnson into their midst. His wound began to get better. To their amazed surprise he disclosed a sly, sweet sense of humour that cheered them along the way. Finding herself about to be isolated, Mrs. Johnson relented— and suddenly found her family reunited about her. She remembered how every one of the company, even the terrible Falconer, who was now sweet on Mrs. Chalfont and insisted on helping to carry the baby, had stopped to look back as they left the lake.

" 'Pears like death jes' driv us all together like a pack o' sheep huddles up when they see a wolf," she thought.

And it was true that they were all more gentle to one another because of what had happened. Falconer, Van Ness, McBride, and Johnson took to singing at night. They had suddenly discovered, after some tentative trials while marching, that they were a quartette. At Anthony's suggestion they left off the doleful ballads which at first engrossed them and took to trolling more cheerful lays. One of Burns's songs, then a worldwide favourite, they repeated again and again every night. Apparently nobody ever grew tired of it. The Mexicans themselves took to standing about the Texans' fire at night. The four voices were good ones:

"Green grow the rashes, O;
Green grow the rashes, O;
The sweetest hours that e'er I spend,
Are spent among the lasses, O."

Everyone in the cavalcade was soon singing it— "Grin-gro, Grin-go," hummed the Mexicans as the ox-carts plodded forward. And so it was that the Texans became to be known as "Gringos."

At Chihuahua, where they stayed in the prison-like Hospital of the Jesuits, they gathered one evening about the stump of one candle that flickered fitfully in the mouth of a bottle, to discuss their situation.

A journey of over a thousand miles still lay before them. Tomorrow they would go forward under a new guard, for their good-natured friends from El Paso

688

went no farther. They would be alone. And they had learned that they would have to walk. They tried to organize themselves for the long trail before them. Van Ness suggested a daily leader, "Jes to keep things straight among ourselves."

" 'Taint no use doin' that," said Falconer. "That 'ull be like the militia back home. Everybody 'ull jes take his tarn bein' sassed."

"Move we 'lect one cap'n from hya to Mexico," said McBride, a quiet Virginian.

"Adverse," sung out Buckthorn, an inveterate gambler. "He's our most hopeful odd number." There was a laugh.

"Well, what d'ya say, cap?" cried the impulsive Van Ness, springing up and prematurely pumping Anthony by the hand.

The candle suddenly burned out. There was a heavy silence. Out of it after an interval came the colourless voice of the inconsequential Johnson, "I ain't no good, I know. Even my old woman says it. But I'm willin' ter follow the only light I ever heerd tell on that cain't be blowed out. An' I tell you-all it's burnin' right here in the darkness now. Cain't you'ns see it?"

A sound of shuffling and rising bodies greeted this statement. Anthony thought they were going away. But they thronged about him in the darkness, whispering huskily and shaking his hand.

And once more he wept. But this time not alone, and not lying in the dust.

Months later, they marched incredibly ragged and footsore, but still hopeful, into the City of Mexico. It was deep twilight and the summits of the two giant volcanoes hung above the evening already settled in the valley below like islands of mystery floating on seas of sunset. They were all together yet. Even Jane Chalfont's baby, which had begun to walk, was there. It was the sunbonnet that had finally succumbed.

"Ye never can tell," sniffed Mrs. Johnson. "Some goes on through, and some don't."

"I wisht I know'd whar my young'un was agoin' to end up at," said Jane looking up at the mysterious islands in the sky.

"Maybe hit's lucky you don't," replied the older woman. "But whar we got to now?" she added.

The column of new garrison troops to whose care they had been confined only that morning, had suddenly halted.

"What's the matter?" inquired a mounted officer riding back.

"One of the prisoners is to be left here, señor capitán," replied a sergeant. "The lieutenant says there's a special order about him."

"Which one?"

"Adverse," said the young officer, hurrying up. "It's a special rescript from the old governor at Santa Fé."

The captain looked at it indifferently.

"Deposit the body of this individual at the Prison of St. Lazarus, until further orders."

He heard them calling his name. And it was then, as he looked up at the gloomy building before him and saw the dim faces within peering at him from a barred window, that for the first time Anthony understood the full measure of Don Luis' hate.

Chapter Twenty-One

The Prison of St. Lazarus

THERE is a kind of writing in the forms and lines of things by which he who reads may prophesy. It may well have been the source of the forebodings of Cassandra, for it is a sort of "palmistry" *in toto* of the implications of the future inherent in a building or a neighbourhood. Mrs. Johnson had the gift. One look at the outlines of the grim building confronting her in the now melancholy twilight, coupled with the loud calling of Anthony's name, was sufficient to cause her to scream, "They're takin' the cap'n from us, and we'll never see him no more."

The sergeant was already hammering vigorously with the butt of his rifle at a gigantic, iron-studded door. In the street the prisoners suddenly broke ranks and crowded about Anthony.

He had never realized that he had come to love them as though they were his own flesh and blood. But he knew it now. The two boys clung to him like sons.

The baby was for a moment thrust into his arms, as though it also were his, and he must bless it. The two women began that sort of talk accompanied by the kind of noise that greets the appearance of a snake in a parrot's nest. Even the conscripts knew that something terrible was happening. The men came up and wrung his hands in eloquent silence. He found it impossible to say good-bye to them. At the very last he and Van Ness were left face to face, their hands locked on each other's arms.

"Get word to the British consul somehow, Van. It's your best chance. Don't forget the plan I talked over with you. They'll all depend on you now. You're the only one that can write. Never mind about me. I'm done. But I'll see it through, with the . . ."

"Never say die, cap'n. It's not like you. You'll soon be hearin' from us."

"Here, you," shouted the young lieutenant, who had his reputation for indifference to suffering yet to establish, "leave off that English talk."

The sergeant came for him.

He snatched young Tom up and kissed him. He found himself walking numbly between two soldiers toward a small door cut in the large one, through which came a glimmer of lantern light. Behind him he heard the column getting under way. Some of them called out to him—something. They passed. . . .

Overhead the giant iron bell of the Hospital of St. Lazarus began to proclaim the abstract information that it was *one—two—three—four . . . seven—*eight o'clock, in the valley of Mexico. The locks in the door behind him shot home, and he was left alone standing in darkness. The invisible hall that lay before him was so large that gusts of air, wandering as freely as though they were not in prison, fanned his face.

"Well," said the turnkey, coming up and flashing his lantern over him critically, "what the hell's the matter with you?"

"Nothing. What makes you think there might be?"

The man gave a laugh like the grating of a rusty hinge. "We'll see about that tomorrow," said he, and gave a peculiar whistle.

A door opened behind him, allowing a bright light to stream out over the stone floor. Before him was a heavy iron grille. He could see no farther on the other side of it than its own shadows. Two more powerful and morose-looking wardens appeared at the door.

"He's a big one," said the man who had admitted him. "I thought you'd better be near while I chained him up, just in case . . ."

The others grinned.

"Ever since that quiet-lookin' little woman pulled his ear off, Pedro ain't taking *no* chances. By God, I don't blame him this time," said one of them, taking a look at the new prisoner and shrinking back a little. "Get that heavy wall chain, Roblado! It's in the old chest." The man disappeared and the clanking of irons was soon heard. On a table in the little guard-room beyond the door Anthony saw several hands of cards face downward amid the remains of a scanty meal. The sour-looking Roblado emerged with a chain attached to a steel belt. The latter they fastened around his waist and the former to the iron grille.

"If you'll not give us no trouble," said the first turnkey, "I'll give you the whole length of the chain." He grinned a little, and then looked ashamed. "Hard luck," he muttered into his beard. "It's orders, you know."

"They don't feed you gentlemen any too well here, do they?" remarked Anthony.

"That they don't, my friend. It's dogs' leavings we get—but you're the first caged bird I ever heard worryin' about what the jailers get!"

"Here's a dollar for you," said Anthony. "A priest at El Paso gave it to me for the love of Christ, and it's all I have. Now go and get yourselves a pollo and some mescal or a little wine. All that I ask is that you drink the health of the good cura of El Paso."

693

They stood looking at him dumbly for a minute. The man Roblado at last bit the dollar. "It's all right," he muttered. "I'll go!"

"And be damned sure you come back," roared Pedro after him.

"Señor," said one of the two ruffians who remained, "in the name of God, we thank you."

One of them brought him a stool and a pot of water.

He sat down and arranged the chain behind him. The door closed and he was left in the darkness again. He got nothing to eat that evening.

Long after midnight the door opened again. The three turnkeys were all drunk. With great solemnity they approached him one after the other and left three mattresses at his feet.

Dawn in the prison of St. Lazarus was not like dawn anywhere else. When he opened his eyes early next morning the white light was stealing through a succession of high, grated windows along the entire length of the vast, arched nave of a church. At one end of it was an altar that still looked as though it were occasionally used for the purpose for which it had been built. The great dome of the unfinished church, for such it was, had never been completed, and an intensely bright cylinder of light poured from the open ring in the ceiling onto the floor. Through this also poured, as though the place were sucking in faint wisps of black smoke, an army of bats. But that was not all that he saw through the empty circle.

Mirrored in the morning sky, its snow fields slowly flushing an incredible rose colour, was the volcano of the "Sleeping Woman," her mighty form recumbent upon a bed of clouds. So beautiful was this vision floating in heaven that his heart was lifted up in him out of prison, and he said:

"The day belongs to thee, O God,
And the night also,
For thou hast made the morning
With the rising sun.
The sun setteth, and the moon walketh upon the
    waters
Because of thee.
The stars signal upon thy watchtowers by night.
From everlasting unto everlasting is thy name
Made glorious forever.
The measure of the firmament is the depth of thy
    thought;
The vision of thy glory reneweth my soul.
Lo, in thy hand will I lie through the nighttime
Like a lake held by pleasant hills.
The day shall find me there,
And my voice shall be heard among the mountains.
Because of thee I will leap up and rejoice . . ."

After a while the vision of the mountain faded. It veiled itself in mists, and there was nothing to be seen through the circle which had framed it but the sky. In the prison of St. Lazarus the daily round began.

He could see where he was now. The grille was a great cage built about the region of the door. Before him stretched the long nave of the unfinished church. Along the sides of it, set in the entrances of what, if the church had been finished, would have been its side chapels, were barred gates.

Through these began to come the murmur of voices and from the one nearest squeakings and husky tones. There were evidently a great many people in the rooms and wards behind the gates. Once he heard wild laughter and chains. Some pigeons came through the circle in the ceiling, flew about inside the nave, and left again with a throbbing whir of wings. The door behind him opened and one of the turnkeys came out. He gave a grin of remembrance when he saw the new prisoner, returned, and emerged once again with the remains of the feast.

"You might as well have it," he said. "The others are still asleep. They'll think I ate it. Where did you come from?"

"Santa Fé."

The man whistled and looked at his prisoner thoughtfully. "Got any more dollars in that bag?"

Anthony took the little figure out of it and turned the bag inside out. The jailer laughed.

"Well, I guess you can keep *that*," he said. "Looks as if it's been through the fire."

"It has."

He stood pondering the figure for some time and grunted before he handed it back. "Feet sore?"

Anthony nodded.

The man began to unlock the chain. "There's a flowing water channel in the big yard," he said. "Better come along and bathe there. Wrap your chain about you or you'll sound like the damned dead walking. You'll soon get used to it. 'Taint as bad as if you'd a ball and shackles. That there steel belt is just one we use on maniacs. I thought you was crazy last night when I first seen you. You looked so bloody calm and happy. There's a woman here thinks she's St. Theresa. She's made up a song about a burning rose and the five Holy wounds. It fair cuts the heart out of you, for she has the face of an angel. But you can't trust her." He rubbed the side of his head. "She damn near chewed my ear off one morning. I was just leanin' up against the bars amusin' her a little. *Ho, ho, ho.*" The ceiling laughed back at him dismally. "Now *you* don't have any cunning tricks, do you?" He hesitated a minute over the lock.

"What do you want me to do—bark like a dog?"

"No, no, for God's sake *don't*," laughed the man. "We've got one like that already. Come on, you'll do, I guess." They both laughed. "The doctor will be here in an hour on his morning rounds."

He unlatched the grille, and they walked down the long nave together while the turnkey also unlocked several gates and drew his key jangling across the bars.

"Lepers in there. They're always so cheerful. Make the most of their time.

"That's the plague ward. Nobody there now. Last year they overflowed and half filled the church. We couldn't get them in and out fast enough."

Some nuns entered from a side door and waited until he let them in. Three pale looking sisters came out. One of them held up two fingers. The turnkey nodded. "I'll see to the stretchers," he said to her. "Small-pox. We lock 'em up at night. That's the general ward there without a gate. It's May now and pretty empty. But wait till August when the fever begins! Sometimes we get good clothes off them then. In the spring you can't count on that though. Maybe a hat or a pair of shoes now and then between us. Here's your door." He flung open a door that was not locked. "Come back when you're done. The surgeon will want to see you. I've got St. Theresa and the dog to water and feed and there's a lot of others. Want to see 'em?"

Anthony declined the pleasure and all but fled through the door. He stepped through it into the open air and sunlight, and for a moment felt free again. But only for a moment. As he looked about him he began to understand the plan of the place into which he had come.

He was standing before the unfinished front of a great formless church, one of many left unfinished by the Jesuits when they had been driven out. From its sides protruded the various wards of the hospital which had been built onto it; long, low buildings, white-washed, and with round barred windows. There were six wards on one side and none on the other. The huge, grey building with its numerous "offspring" reminded him for all the world of a sow suckling its farrow. In the architecture there was something that seemed to decree that the six "youngsters" be given curly tails.

But the front of the church was overpowering and sinister. There were deep, shadowed niches with half-executed carvings; giant saints with square, block faces, featureless, or with the rudiments of mouths and noses; their hands nothing but grey stone knobs, stub-fingered or crossed over their rough breasts, still encased in gloves of stone. Their eyes glared out of rocky sockets left rough as when the chisels had ceased. They were a grisly and depressing company covered with scales of bird lime. He turned from them in horror.

A wall forty feet high surrounded him on all sides. It formed an ample square about the Hospital of St. Lazarus, several acres in area. It joined onto the walls of the church in the rear. There were some spare, neglected shrubs planted in this waste plot that was still covered with the rough blocks and débris of the builders. Through it flowed a water course in a channel of stone. In this he bathed, stripping himself of all except the steel belt and chain. He sat on a great block to dry in the sun. It was thus that Dr. Lopez, the head physician, found him.

"What's the matter?" said he. "You look like a gladiator."

"Nothing," repeated Anthony.

A thorough examination standing on the block—"Now I know how the slaves felt at Gallegos," he thought—confirmed the prisoner. The doctor sat on another block and talked with him for half an hour.

"So the enmity of the old governor at Santa Fé is the only reason you can think of, eh?"

"My dog killed his man, as I said. And Don Luis was a Spaniard of the old school, you know."

"In the time of the old viceroy, Iturrigaray, we had some 'cases' like yours sent to us," said the doctor. "They were sent here to rot. But they didn't. They . . . not that I would encourage you too much," he hastened to add. "Understand me. I do *not* intend to interest myself in your case *outside* of this hospital. I have my small salary here, four children, and a wife with a temper. I do not intend to mix myself up in any political quarrels. I might find myself released. Do I convey my meaning, señor? I am adamant."

"I respect your reasons," Anthony replied.

"Good!" said the little physician. "Inside, I will see what I can do. Let us return. I can see no reason just yet for the maniac's belt. We shall begin by dispensing with that." They entered the church together.

A number of figures walking and limping were busy about the place with mops and brooms. They reminded him forcibly of the statues on the front of the building. He looked at them and quailed.

"You must get over that," said the doctor. "No one knows how you get leprosy. I try to give these poor people something to do. Now try to bear up, my friend. Let me urge you to do so. In that event—" He waved his hands vaguely, and laughed. "But," he insisted, "consider—Your case is really no different here than any other place. Death dogs everybody—and eventually, you know. Here the process is visible. That is all."

He called to the turnkey and gave orders. "Let him sleep in the vestibule. Give him a new pallet and he can lay it on the stone bench there. That will at least be outside," he mused. "Take off the chain and don't use it unless"—he looked at Anthony significantly—"he offers to make trouble for you. In that case chain him to the wall.

"Do you hear, señor? I trust we understand each other. I am adamant. Perhaps you can occupy yourself by helping a little here and there. You will run no more danger than I do."

The little doctor laughed, gave him a cigar, and strolled off on his rounds.

"Come on," said Roblado. "Give me a lift on these stretchers. You're strong, are you! All right, let's see if you are."

To the prisoners of the hospital time glided almost imperceptibly. It was marked for them in nature only by the slow erosion of certain of the bodies of the inmates and by the sterile blooming and withering of some of the sickly shrubs in the surrounding close. In the open vestibule, where he slept, Anthony saw the shadow of the extended hand of the stone St. Lazarus swing from one joint in the masonry to another, and then creep back again. Into that stone hand the days of his life were slowly being dropped, one golden coin after another, like a trickle of precious alms. Altogether some four hundred of them had now been given away, gratis.

According to all respectable romances, he told himself, he should by this time have filed his way through the bars, overpowered the turnkeys in their drunken stupor, or have managed to scale the wall. At the very least he should have communicated with powerful friends on the outside and arranged to bribe the authorities. There were also several less orthodox methods of jail delivery which he contemplated that at first did seem feasible, but in the end came to nothing. If he had simply been incarcerated as a political offender in an ordinary prison he might possibly have managed to emerge—but the Hospital of St. Lazarus!—that was a different affair altogether.

He did manage through the good offices of one of the priests, who came to bring the host of the dying, to get a letter to the English consul. The gentleman came to see him and talked to him through the grille. He sent him some wine, books, and cigars. He also turned his case over to the American consul, which was exactly what Anthony feared he would do. The efforts of the representative of the United States on his behalf were strenuous enough to call the attention of the new viceroy to his existence. General Calleja then departed to fight the rising tide of revolution which was eventually to sweep Spain clear of Mexico. That, however, did not keep the municipal authorities from preventing the inmates of the plague hospital, and the maniacs who were also sent there, from getting out again. On two occasions he smuggled out letters addressed to friends in New Orleans, but nothing came of them. It looked as though the slow swinging back and forth of the shadowy hand of St. Lazarus was the only thing that would finally bring him release.

Yet despite this, Don Luis had not triumphed. He had meant to leave the son of Maria a legacy of immortal hatred and despair, but once again he had failed. He had merely provided an opportunity for Anthony to understand and to participate in hate's eternal opposite. For it was in the prison of St. Lazarus that he was finally born again into freedom and new hope. He lost the fear of death. Here, where the bodies of men perished and withered horribly, he saw the spirit of love in them working. And he participated in that work. He became a part of it.

When the plague fell upon the city, the second summer after his arrival, he at last gave up trying to penetrate the walls that surrounded him, and looking for hope and freedom to come from the outside. That way lay nothing but hope deferred and prolonged despair. Apparently, no earthly postman could reach his friends with messages. And then suddenly he found that all he had been looking for lay within.

Towards the end of the dog days they began to bring the first fever sufferers to St. Lazarus—and to take them away. The tide grew. It threatened to inundate the establishment. The great nave of the church filled up. There were no more beds. They laid them in rows in cotton blankets on the floor. There were no more blankets. They laid them in rows. A thousand times, in every direction that he looked, the scene in the cabin of the *Ariostatica* was being repeated. There was no scale against which the sights he now saw were describable. None except that of the nature and destiny of man.

A band of devoted nuns and priests, a brotherhood

and sisterhood of lay nurses in hoods so that their merit might not be known, appeared, and attempted to administer what bodily and spiritual comfort they could. He saw them sicken, too, lie down, and be carried out. Others took their places. He laboured with them night and day as did the very turnkeys themselves. He lay down and slept, felled by exhaustion. He got up again and went on, his services accepted without question. He understood now that Dr. Lopez, although his science prevented no one from dying, was a sublime little man.

"Well," said that little physician one night toward the end of the hopeless struggle when the nave lay comparatively deserted again, "I see you aren't afraid of a mere leper any more!"

"No," he answered, "I find them marvellously cheerful. I often go into their room now to share that with them. I have friends there."

"So have I," said the doctor. "And I know what you're thinking. No, I wouldn't say that you'll get it. I haven't. Quién sabe? Come out and take a swim with me. That water course through the old priests' garden here is a godsend these sultry nights. It runs into the big canal on the other side of the wall."

"Yes, through a heavy stone grating so narrow a duck couldn't get through after her little ones the other day."

"I dare say you have investigated," smiled the doctor. "Have you heard anything from your friends?"

"Nothing. But somehow I don't seem to care now. After the last few weeks I think, 'What is the difference?' "

"There is a certain perversity about fate," cried the little man, preparing to plunge into the water. His head reappeared above the surface to continue his remarks—"It is just when you are feeling like that, that somebody is likely to appear and insist upon your resuming life again. You see, I, at the present time, for various domestic reasons, *I* am somewhat inclined to envy you. Believe me, señor, when I return home from this hospital it is from the sublime to the ridiculous. My mother is piously sentimental and wishes me to contribute to her sodality devoted to paying for masses for souls. Can you imagine it? 'Everyone should practise some charity,' she says, and rattles the box with money in it in my face. Two of my children died of the plague. I couldn't keep them in their bodies. And now—their grandmother rattles that box with pesos in it in my face."

"Where are all these people that we have just buried?" cried Anthony. "They are still, and we are alive swimming in the water here. Look, I can move. What does it mean? Without my hands I could not make even a ripple. What do you think? Tell me!"

"Life is like this," said the doctor. He cupped his hands and plunged them in the channel, bringing them up again like a brimming cup. "I now remove the hands. Look into the stream and tell me where the water has gone.

"Do not try to think about the soul after death, señor. It is like talking about a lake without any surrounding land. Now I, as a man of science, have certain theories about the body. It is possible that some day we shall prevent this fever, which you and I have so far escaped. But," he cried, throwing a stone in the water vehemently, "there is only one thing certain about man; that animal has an incorrigible habit of dying, no matter what you do for him. I have just been trying to do the best I can!"

They began to swim about once more and to splash each other like a couple of boys. It was an expression of their triumph at still being alive and also served to cover their embarrassment at admitting an interest in mysteries. They splashed a good deal. They had a good time.

"By the way," said Lopez at the door of the church. "I signed the Yankee consul's request for your release. It didn't do any good. It was like medicine. You're still here in spite of it. But I did say what kind of a life I saw you living here. I . . . I . . ." He stopped overcome by embarrassment. He had never intended to admit it. It was his favourite expression that he was adamant.

"Nonsense," cried Anthony. "Why, I'm only doing the best I can!"

In a place like San Lazaro, where so many came to stay, and were carried away hastily, those who were able to remain for any considerable period inevitably developed not only a proprietary air about the establishment but an intense neighbourliness and free-masonry among themselves. Death was the only stranger, although he visited them often. Yet to the casual observer the cheerfulness and the gayety, a certain intensified nonchalance and *carpe diem* among the incurables seemed incredible and grotesque if not cruelly indifferent. Grotesque, perhaps—in reality it was not hard-hearted. It was merely a manifestation of a kind of wisdom practised only by those who feel strongly that their days are certainly numbered, and who understand that it is a waste of precious time to try to assume for others the burdens which are individual by nature. Thus, when a person finally came to die, he was left severely alone except in so far as he needed or demanded necessary attentions. And it was the same with those in pain, they were not harassed by the constant reiterations of communal sympathy. They received only what could actually be given them.

Casual visitors, of whom there were a few, were shocked and pained by this surface of indifference at San Lazaro. They expected at least to find an atmosphere of dolour, and were bravely prepared to encounter a universal whine. A considerable number of professional cheer and charity mongers departed, therefore, without that which they had come to obtain from

704

the lepers, their own edification. And then there were others driven by a certain morbid curiosity to enter the place in the name of charity, but who could not conceal that what they did was a kind of imaginative alleviation of themselves. "Suppose I were a leper, how brave, how noble I should think those were who came to be kind to me. How horrible they are. How sorry I would-be-am." And they would leave with a certain hastiness, a few running steps and a skip through the door, which they could not conceal. They also went away disappointed; without the admiration they had hoped to get.

Dr. Lopez, indeed, had little use for such sympathy, and these casual visitors were always accompanied by an attendant as they made their rounds. The place took little notice of them beyond snatching their tangible gifts and quarrelling over them. In the presence of strangers the inmates felt they were in a zoo, and they acted like it. "Naturally!" said the doctor in disgust, "but Doña Anna Salledro, and her like, are influential persons, so what can I do about it?"

"Let her come. Maybe she will learn something at last," said Anthony.

The doctor shook his head.

"Not so long as she's healthy herself. Among people who try to practise luxury and charity at the same time the only ones who ever learn to care about other people, outside of their own families, are those who are attacked by a mortal disease themselves. Besides, this is not an educational institution, it's a respectable lazar house."

Every three months they were visited by a priest in charge of young lads in training at a near-by seminary. In order to learn humility the boys were each made to kneel and serve one of the lepers from a nest of dishes they brought for the occasion.

There was no escaping this visitation. All the inmates, except those suffering from a virulent disease, were subjected to it. There were more boys to learn humility than there were vile persons to kneel before. So even the turnkeys were requisitioned.

Somewhat awed by the flustered youngster who knelt before him in the vestibule, with the stony saints looking down upon him while he arranged the dishes on the floor with a shy awkwardness, Anthony strove to ease the natural embarrassment of the situation by engaging the boy in talk.

But he did not succeed very well, he thought. He asked him some questions. The replies were truthful, he felt, but brief. He discovered, however, that the youth was bored, homesick, and not anxious to be a priest.

"I am the third son, and my father has only a small hacienda. It would not do to divide the pastures. So you see, señor, the only field I inherit is the church. The grazing is pretty scant there. We bring you the best meal of the year—to teach us humility!" Suddenly the youth put his hand over his mouth and looked up in terror at the man he was serving. He had not meant to say that. Tears came into his eyes and he closed them. He did not open them for some time. He did not dare to. He was being fed from the dishes he had come to serve.

"Not all of it, *not* the pineapple frijole, señor."

"Sí, all of it, Tertio," insisted the big man with the beard, "to the last spoonful. Thou must learn how to share thy gifts with others. It is the essence of humility."

Tertio packed the empty dishes, blushing deeply, and departed after presenting his gift. "It is a horse that I carved myself," said he. "But look! He does lift his feet as though he spurned the dust."

"I am charmed with it," cried Anthony. "Anybody can see that it is a noble animal. It can go."

The boy gravely bade him farewell. Anthony remembered another boy in a long priest's garment and sat thinking.

He dropped the fine little horse that Tertio had carved into the deerskin bag.

Three months later he found himself sought out and served again. This time, still in the quiet of the vestibule, they shared the meal together and the boy began to question him. Thus at three-month intervals their acquaintance ripened. In all Anthony saw Tertio seven times.

The boy had grown greatly in that time. The man could feel himself reliving his own youth. Inexplicably he felt it being renewed within him. And with it returned something of his old ardour for life; his desire to fare forth again. If there had been a tree in the prison close, he would once more have climbed it. He told Tertio that story—but there were only stunted bushes in the prison yard.

He now began, all but unconsciously at first, to keep an eye about him for possible means of escape. He was even riper for it than he thought. He began to imagine that he might—if he could—go back to Europe—to Düsseldorf. By this time his son would be well into manhood. Perhaps, Angela might . . . and then a terrible sense of the futility and the degradation of returning to them, like a ghost come back to claim their property, would rush upon him. No, dead men had no right to rise.

"Lazarus, come forth."

How *that* would interfere with things! What was there, what was there that he could expect by returning to the past? To return would be to return to all of it, too. It would only be in the end to resume the shirt of Nessus that he had been able to wear—and cast off—only by the Grace of God. He might yet be chained up in the steel belt in the corner along with "St. Theresa," poor soul, if he started to don the past again.

But there was the future to look to, he could not deny that. It seemed as though he would live a long time yet. People died around him and he was left untouched. Even in the pesthouse of Mexico. Sometimes he had hoped—what?

"Never!"

Why, outside it was spring again! From some garden near by, the scent of orange blossoms drifted to him across the wall. He went and lay in the sun and breathed in the odour. The world outside must be mad with bloom. Somehow—he must take his time and consider well—it would never do to be recaptured—but somehow he must see it again. He opened the bag that night and the little horse fell out.

"Anyone can see that it is a noble animal. It can *go*." He heard himself saying that to young Tertio almost two years ago now. "Go!"

At last his own suggestion rang in his heart like a command.

The festival of San Lazaro takes place on the eleventh of March. For some days before that event the inmates of the hospital spent their time and ingenuity in preparing for the only visitation of charity which they were genuinely enthusiastic about. It was their own festival they prepared for. Others came to share their joy with them. It was the custom on the eleventh of March for all classes in the City of Mexico to go and visit the leprosos.

On that morning the vision of the great mountain through the empty dome had lifted up the heart of at least one of the prisoners with a renewed sense of hope —and an impulse toward freedom. Perhaps, it was only the unwonted sense of joy about him in the prison that seemed to sweep him on with it. But that morning he knelt before the great altar in the nave, where the festival of the saint of the abandoned and the lepers began, and received the wafer for the first and last time in his life.

The entire company of the prison from Dr. Lopez to

the Indian cooks, everyone who could still walk, sat down together and ate with the priests who had celebrated mass, from a board furnished sumptuously by public benevolence and served by masked and hooded gentlemen.

The leprosos had decorated their room with festoons and flags; with bright, pathetic devices cut from all kinds of coloured papers. These were strung abolt the walls and streamed from the lamps and brackets. Even the bars of the windows were gayly trimmed. The word *caridad*—charity—predominated. Its neatly-cut, paper letters were pasted upon various wreathed baskets and boxes placed where they would most readily strike the eye of visitors. The floor had been stained a bright yellow tint. Strips of red, white, and green muslin were arranged like an arabesque on the ceiling. The cots of the lepers themselves were wreathed with flowers.

They now changed the clothing upon their beds and began to dress themselves in the finery of the world they had left behind them but whose joyful garments they still cherished. No one could gaze upon them now without astonishment. It seemed as though the dead in various stages of dissolution had suddenly emerged equipped in glaring holiday finery; dressed as fearful, flaunting cavaliers and giddy, drawing-room belles. All that was needed was a few skeletons for bailarinas—and the dance would begin. One expected at any moment to hear the infernal castanets and the demoniacal guitars. And there *was* music, the sound of some stringed instrument touched in the shadowy corners of the room by a hand without enough fingers.

Anthony had seen this festival before, but he now looked upon it with a different understanding. It was not a dance of death, grotesque and obscene. Even in these decaying bodies the eternal joy of life, the triumph of the living spirit of man over the matter that contains it was being manifested. He saw past the bizarre clothes covering the grotesque bodies into the tongues of flame that sat upon the flower-wreathed bedsteads, laughing, leaping in the face of death. And within him his own spirit burned with them again mightily.

The big gates at the end of the room had been carefully closed and two small side doors especially prepared for the occasion. They were guarded by attendants, who knew the inmates, so that none could leave without scrutiny, but they were thrown open so that anyone might enter. About nine o'clock the crowds from the city began to assemble outside.

Entering by one of the side doors, the visitors would slowly make the circuit of the rooms, talk to the various inmates, leaving with them such presents as they had brought, and then depart by the door on the opposite side. Yet in spite of the attempts of the attendants to keep the line moving, by noon the throng in the huge chamber was immense and engaged in a kind of carnival in which the laughter and encouraging gayety of the visitors was punctuated by the husky and squeaky voices of the lepers, the rattle of dice boxes, the blurred twanging of instruments, the popping of corks, and the clicking of castanets. For in various places misshapen couples were dancing fandangos beyond description, encouraged by the good-natured shouts of the bystanders.

The beds of the disabled, and the tables of others behind which those who still had discernible faces sat with expectant grins, were piled high with gifts: loaves of bread, cakes, packets of cigars, cigarritos and puros; oranges, pineapples, and mangoes. The constant ring of coins, clacos and medios, silver dollars and gold pieces dropped into the jars provided for the purpose, accompanied the scene with a metallic clink. On the beds and tables of the youngest sufferers piled up offerings of flowers and toys.

"Amigo," said a tall Spaniard whose days were obviously few, "will you receive for me at my table a while? I must lie down for a little. Gracias, may God reward you!" He sank back on his cot, while

Anthony took his place on a chair behind the table.

He began to call out with the others begging for charity. His clear voice rang through the room.

"Let not the humble be turned away with confusion;
The poor and needy shall praise thy name."

A peon advanced impulsively and gave him his sombrero. A beggar contributed a silver coin. The voice continued. They understood he was begging for the man on the cot. The Spaniard thanked them magnificently. The gifts increased. In his grey face the sufferer's eyes gleamed with satisfaction.

The room was now aswirl with excitement and colour. The crowd ran the gamut of classes from a city where the diversity of population is as complex as any that exists. There were caballeros with silver spurs, and beggars; priests with shovel hats, and soldiers; girls dressed in the poblana,—short and gaudy petticoats, fancifully worked chemises, gay satin shoes, and no stockings,—girls with hardly any dress at all. There were monks, gamblers, and ragamuffins; ladies attired in mantillas, jewels, and satins; friars and peons, and the families of the lepers gathered about their cots. A party of high-born and fashionable women arrived with a meal which they served themselves.

The second hour of the afternoon marked the height of this orgy of charity. The table before Anthony was now heaped high. He made a last appeal and was about to go,

"Forget not to the end the souls of thy poor."

A lady disengaged herself from the richly dressed group which surrounded her and approached his table. One of a hundred others who had dropped a coin in the jar that day, he did not look up. He saw her hand dropping a gold piece in the jar. It fell onto the floor.

"Is it possible?" he heard her exclaim.

"Not lost," he cried. "I'll find it for you!"

He got up and found himself face to face with Dolores.

He reached out impulsively and took her hands. She let them lie in his while in each other's faces they sought to read something of the story of the past. Then a look of horror came and she snatched them away.

"Señora, I am clean," he said.

They stood for a while in eternity. The room vanished. Then she took his hands again.

"No matter," she exclaimed, "I shall never let go of them now."

And so it was that on the festival of all-beggars he received the best gift of all.

Chapter Twenty-Two

The Stone In
the Heart of the Tree

BEFORE the death of her husband Dolores already
found herself in charge of his far-flung haciendas,
his mines, and various mansions. Don Guillermo
had for several years been hopelessly feeble. They had
no children, but he had long kept a large, hungry
pack of his collateral relatives, who looked forward
with undisguised enthusiasm to gathering him to his
fathers. Some of them, who had more courage than
cash, had even proposed among themselves to hasten
his demise, should a seasonable opportunity present
itself. The skill and diplomacy of the old hidalgo's wife
had prevented them, and permitted nature, who is so
indifferent to collateral heirs, to take her own tedious
time.

And very tedious it was, especially for Dolores. While
the old gentleman, to whom she had been joined in
matrimony by an allegedly Christian ceremony, sat in

the patio of his great house at Guanajuato and played with moonstones and white rabbits, for he had a senile passion for both, she had watched her mirror reflect nothing but the slow effect upon her of the sterile embraces of time.

It was only natural, under the circumstances, that she should at least permit herself some dreams of what might have been, and a more than usual preoccupation with romantic incidents of the past; incidents that under different circumstances she would undoubtedly have forgotten or remembered with an indulgent smile. As it was, her meeting with Anthony at Havana, the golden night in the courtyard, and the few seconds in the arms of her lover there rose like an Olympus from the drab plain of her experience. Her encounter with Anthony at Madrid had only served in the end to intensify her few memories of him by providing a little more reality upon which to feed them.

And yet Dolores was not romantic. Had anyone suggested that she was to the disappointed relatives of her late husband, he would have been laughed at and told, between curses, that she was known to the family as the "Lady Miser." There was also a number of young, and some middle-aged caballeros scattered over the country who would have confirmed the family. They had one and all admired either her person, her property, or both, and found her unapproachable. She was capable of only one passion, they said; a passion for property. As for the women, while they admired and secretly envied certain qualities in Dolores, which they were afraid to imitate, they were also inclined to agree with the men.

And this remarkable unanimity of opinion in regard to Dolores had, as usual, something to build upon.

She had been married off to Don Guillermo de Almanara shortly after her return from Havana to Spain. The alliance—it was nothing more—had served to cement legally two of the greatest feudatories in Mexico, where the possessions of both her own family and

714

her husband's were immense. More territory, revenue, and people were involved than in many a marriage of minor European sovereigns. But Don Guillermo was sixty-four and Dolores nineteen when he brought her home to Mexico. She found herself confronted with the choice of existing in futile luxury till he died; of idly playing with fire; of enjoying the genuine power, influence, and prestige which the active administration of vast estates and interests might bring her.

Dolores was of a pure Gothic type. She was at once ardent, obstinate, and determined. She had great beauty and a clear, firm mind. She had all the fierce pride of her ancestors, who had harried the Moors from Valladolid to Valencia. She was not inclined to become the mistress of philandering cavaliers even if she had fallen in love with them. She considered her situation carefully, and made her choice. She devoted herself to the administration of her mines and haciendas.

Those who threatened her interests or trespassed upon her property she fought like a tiger with cubs. Indeed, the care of "her people," as she called her peons and dependents, and the improvement of her property became for her the equivalent of a family. She lavished upon this work the tireless energy of a woman who was not barren but childless.

The gradual lapse of her husband into senility provided her with both the excuse and opportunity to carry out her plans. In a short while it was not Dolores but Don Guillermo who spent his life in secluded luxury. She encouraged him in it. She finally sequestered him at Guanajuato, after first having seen to it that his will was in proper order and safe keeping. She provided him with endless moonstones, a platonic harem of white rabbits, and carefully selected attendants. He died in peace, and was buried with that complete manifestation of sorrow which only blue blood and riches can confer.

The reading of his will, however, was followed by

a somewhat less conventional and restrained gnashing of teeth. The entire estate, with the wise exception of a fixed income to any viceroy as long as he held office, was left to his wife. Thus Dolores had finally secured what her marriage had been meant to accomplish; the bringing together of certain estates. Because she had paid for this result with the greatest of sacrifices, she defended it passionately.

She gave her husband's relatives pensions in exact proportion to the trouble they were able to make. She encouraged them to live abroad and educate their children there. She held forth the promise of legacies. But she was also obdurate. Once having settled the amount of a stipend, she would not for any reason whatever increase it. She had therefore become known as the "Lady Miser."

Despite the fact that she still desired to complete herself and to have children, she could not easily be persuaded to remarry. She could not overcome her repugnance merely to accepting the necessary man. And besides that, her marriage to anyone in her own circles would have involved immense legal and political difficulties.

Mexico was in the throes of revolution. The Spaniards had been driven out. Iturbide was just about to become emperor. It had taken all the skill and finesse that Dolores possessed to preserve her property in an era of confiscation and dissolution. She had played both sides admirably and she had been lucky. The dictator was indebted to her for his cavalry remounts and other timely contributions. Temporarily she was safe.

But it had been a time of terrible anxiety, and she was tired of it. Even more than a husband, she wanted security.

Yet a marriage with any of the able or influential Mexicans who sought her would have involved her hopelessly in the interests of the particular faction to which any one of them belonged. Upon several occasions she had decided that this would never do, and

716

she had had to say so with all the diplomacy that could possibly be attached to a firm "no." Each of her suitors had easily been persuaded that a man who was as charming as she admitted him to be could only be repulsed by a heart hardened by avarice. Thus opinion tended to confirm itself. Dolores was generally regarded as an able, powerful, and worldly woman. She was received everywhere with fear, favour, and respect—but with nothing more.

And, of course, that was not enough for Dolores. She wanted life. Despite the death of her husband, and her position, it seemed as though she were going to be robbed of it. Desire and prudence threatened to come to a static balance in her and to leave her holding the scales between them without her daring to let go. The worst of it was, she knew it. She was almost forty. It would soon be too late to act, in any event.

Some weeks before her visit to St. Lazarus an amiable but much disappointed man had in the stress of a final interview with her so far forgotten his gallantry as to point this out. She replied stingingly. Don Elyano rode off in a tingling fury.

Perhaps, if he had returned, she would have accepted him. For in his angry reproaches she had recognized the insults of truth. And it must be remembered that this interview was conducted in Castilian; in that magnificent and punctilious idiom that is so capable of expressing the mother wit of fishwives.

For once the poise of Dolores had been shaken. She had almost lost her balance and been precipitated into hasty action.

She had gone about for some time afterward feeling that she would live to regret what was probably her last chance in a decision for life. She was still doing so when she had recognized the voice of the man who had once been her lover calling for charity in the House of Lepers. "Is it possible?"—her first words to him—had therefore expressed both the supreme doubt and the utmost hopes of her being. She had given him her hands from an impulse she could not restrain.

To both of them this providential encounter provided a way for an escape into life and action. Neither of them hesitated, but they were none the less cautious. It was some time before Anthony was liberated. Now that release was so near, for the first time he began to worry greatly about his contact with contagion. It was possible, even likely, he felt, that he might now be taken off. But fate was even more capricious than he expected. It was Lopez, the little physician, who died.

"When you get out of here, my friend, if you ever do, remember my children," he begged.

In the meanwhile Dolores made her arrangements. She began to take a great interest in prisons in general. A number of other women were also interested. For a while it became the fashion to visit the oppressed. As a result of this, nearly fifty persons incarcerated by tyrannical measures during the Spanish regime found themselves blinking in the light of day again. Among them was a man with a long golden beard from the prison of St. Lazarus. Seeing an excellent chance in this wholesome deliverance to curry favour with the liberals, Iturbide had these fortunate ones marched to the plaza and released after a patriotic harangue and the presentation of a small purse.

The unfortunate prisoner, whose patriarchal appearance had rather tended to fix attention upon him, then disappeared. He aroused a barber late that night to shave him and dress his hair. The next day there was no more reason to associate the quiet, well-dressed and dignified gentleman, who spoke a very careful Castilian, but was thought to be an Englishman, with the late inmate of San Lazaro than there was to connect this utter stranger with the name of Doña Dolores. Yet they met frequently.

Anthony lingered for about a week in the City of Mexico, making arrangements for travelling; satisfying himself that certain American prisoners had really been

718

sent to New Orleans two years before, as the records showed, and that the family of Dr. Lopez had a pension settled upon them from a mysterious but charitable source. At the end of that time he set out for the North, well mounted and provided with a small escort.

He traversed rapidly the same route over which he had toiled southward only a few years before. He was received with great respect by the major-domo in charge of a great hacienda two days north of Chihuahua. The hacienda, which belonged to Doña Dolores de Almanara, stretched indefinitely northward beyond the Rio Grande. It was bounded in that direction by a river which lost itself in the desert, a mountain with a village on it, and the somewhat more definite though hostile ideas of the horse Indians as to where their hunting grounds began. Surveying in that direction was too closely connected with the loss of hair to be accurate.

Dolores followed Anthony after a short interval. She closed her great town house in Mexico and made her will, which was so phrased as both to encourage and to restrain her husband's relatives. It was considered a feminine vanity on her part that she still insisted upon certain clauses relating to the heirs of her body. She announced that she was retiring permanently to the country, owing to the disturbed state of the capital, and bade farewell to her friends without permitting them to make much ado about nothing. Her last care was to see that a young renegade by the name of Tertio was sent abroad to study.

A few weeks later Anthony and Dolores were married by the padre in charge of the church at Ysleta, a small village at a ford on the Rio Grande between El Paso and Socorro. Their wedding feast was served by the Indians of the place. And if Anthony remembered another "wedding breakfast," he did not show it. There was a calmness and an assured serenity about him which was reflected in the face of the noble woman who had become his wife.

719

They expected little; they hoped for much. They rode northward into the desert together, accompanied by a few of Dolores' people, some animals, and a half-dozen solid-wheeled carts. Their objective was a certain detached mountain with a village on it. Dolores had once visited it years before and remembered it as an abode of peace.

It was the season when the yucca was in bloom. Through these candelabra of the gods, hung with delicate white bells as though for a wilderness festival of lilies, they advanced slowly, driving their flocks before them; some longhorns, extra horses, burros, and sheep. The beds of dry arroyos, still firm and damp from the recent spring rains and freshets, were their winding roads. Here and there pools still lay in rocky holes under the banks. For a few weeks the desert had become an exotic park, planted, it seemed, upon an almighty plan by inhuman landscapers for the delectation of stony-faced deities. The dust was laid; the sagebrush a deep cypress green; the cacti glorious with complex and brilliant, fleshy blossoms inflamed with the lust of life, and haunted by myriads of bees. Gophers twittered at them from the entrances of their burrows. The shadows of birds passed like the shades of memory across the glaring sands. At dawn and twilight their eery, piping chorus seemed to be the song of ghosts lost in this peopleless land.

They rested in the heat and glamour of noon under the shade of the carts, and pushed on again until the flowers of the desert above them bloomed with light. Their marriage bed was a great oxcart filled with straw. On this they lay, whispering of the life that lay before them. Once more Anthony heard the wild coyote-voices as though the loneliness of the cosmos were giving tongue, and watched the falling stars, and turned, not this time to comfort the dying, but to take triumphant refuge in the arms of life. Upon the face of Dolores gradually spread the deeper shade of the desert and a reflection of the peaceful glory through which they advanced. Through the day the man and woman rode side by side, reading the promise of the future in each other's faces.

Westward, a range of bronze-coloured mountains tumbled into the blinding north. They rose onto the higher and more arid plateaus, where an occasional buffalo or cow skull marked the trail of the horse Indians and cautioned them to build small dry fires in sheltered places and to keep watch by night. Presently, almost directly under the pole star, a lonely peak began to show itself above the horizon.

They raised it slowly. At first it was only a glowing mound above the far level of the plateau. It rose gradually into heaven as they advanced. Its highest ramparts were covered by a cloud that gathered at night and dissolved in the morning into streaks of rain. These could be seen, even at a great distance, slanting down upon the forests and meadows that clothed the mountain's forehead. It was like a giant with green hair. The desert lapped it around and rose half-way up its side in a furnace of cacti and red lava rocks. The small river, that trickled like a vein of perpetual perspiration down its face, plunged through a gorge and lost itself in the desert. El Tronador, this mountain was called, because of the thunder-storms that gathered about it in the springtime.

Four days after first sighting it they entered the flowered meadow which marked the death struggles of the little river with the desert at its feet. The sheep and cattle rushed forward bawling to crop the sweet herbage. They camped that night hearing the bells of flocks far up the mountain. In the morning they began to ascend the narrow gorge toward the grass and timberlands above them.

It was a day's journey to the village of La Luz near the top. Half-way up they were met by the priest and headmen from the town, who gave them welcome, but learned with amazement that the master and mistress of the lands they cultivated had come to make their home among them. Looking at the flocks and goods they had brought, their restrained suspicion turned to unrestrained joy. It was after sunset when they arrived in a great bowl of meadows just below the rain line, where the pine forests began. On one side of the meadow, against a dark background of forest, the lights twinkled as they approached it through a haze of almond orchards in violet and starlike bloom.

And neither Anthony nor Dolores had any doubt that they had at last come home. He lifted her over the threshold of the first house they entered.

The years at La Luz did not deny them what they had hoped. Experience had taught them not to expect too much. They were prepared for sorrows and pain as an inevitable share of their destiny. Surcease, health, and happiness are rare jewels on the string of time. They counted such beads as wonderful, and thankfully added them to the treasury of memory, mindful of the time to come when the recounting of them might be their sole comfort. Happiness came to them not as something ordinary to be ruthlessly used; not as a mere norm always to be transcended by passion, if they were really to feel alive, but like a new gift brought secretly at night by some mysterious and generous spendthrift, who they knew they might find almost any morning had failed to remember them. They did not speculate about it nor spoil it by impossible precautions and useless apprehensions. Like a plant, whose end is sure, they let it grow, blossom, and seed in its own way upon the hill where it stood.

But they were doubly blessed in this: the best of the fruits of time that they gathered together did not come to them as if they were snatched from niggardly hands as wages sharply due them for their honest toil and sweat. They did not live to make ends meet. They still toiled. At La Luz, as elsewhere, the whole daily round of life went on. No one can escape it without having some part of him begin to die—but their rewards came to them now like the two unexpected children whom Dolores bore to Anthony; they came as the result of living as part of a scheme the ends of which, since they cannot be sighted, can never be made to meet.

"At La Luz," mused Anthony one evening toward the end of their third year there, "I think I detect a little overtone from paradise. Or perhaps it is something in the sunlight, a golden reflection from that age which poets can never remember enough about to coin them out of their dark garrets. I am glad that I did not try to live by dreams alone; glad I tried as best I could to pour molten dreams into the mould of life. This is a good mould here at La Luz to let the hot metal of thought cool in. All the shapes of things I see about me are suitable; made beautiful by the sweet necessity of daily human use. Such images are the stuff out of which good dreams take shape—to be recast.

"It is always like that: the dream into the mould; from the mould the dream again. I am glad that I have come to some balance in this flux by living; that I am whole now; that I am neither a mere dreamer nor just a mammal. I am glad that I am a man compounded out of both; that I live; that is, that I can act in between. I have not achieved this just by taking thought and then acting.

"Three things have made me out of a mammal that dreamed into something that resembles a man: Mystery burning in the furnace of experience; Dolores, whom it is pure mercy and good fortune to have found; and a life here at La Luz that changes no faster than a man can change with it. God grant that I be not torn away from this place to wander again, for I am weak, and the grace to prevail might not again be with me. It is for this grace I pray. Life is two things. It is never anything in itself. It is always *like* something else. Only when I compare it with him who is both the dreamer and the thing dreamed can I see that it must be perfect. That is my vision of light . . ."

La Luz changed; that is, the houses and the mountain upon which they stood weathered with the processes of the centuries. The men and women in it renewed themselves and were always there in varying forms. They lived and breathed with the rhythm of the seasons; they experienced slowly, but calmly and to the full, the whole round of life; childhood, youth, and old age. Around them the forests and meadows also renewed themselves with the processes of the years. Between the years and centuries the people of the village remained poised. Their economy for continuing to exist was as perfect as could be invented. It suited the earth; it was not invented by thought alone. If the people changed it was with the mountain.

Anthony and Dolores had become a part of this village and its life. Gallegos and Silver Ho had taught him his lessons. He did not try to change the place, to improve it, and to tear from the earth a surplus and superabundance, which exhausts the soil upon which man stands. From too great abundance, he had discovered, came the chief curses to the bodies and spirits of men. So the master and mistress of the place restrained themselves and let La Luz alone. It was beautiful and self-sufficient. "And that is all we need to know about it," he said to Dolores, "that is the sign manual of the approval of God."

They built their house after the manner of those in the village. It lay a little higher on some land they and their people had cleared amid the trees. It was built of stone and adobe. It contained all they needed and only a little more. Here Inez and Flora, their two daughters, were born and flourished through childhood. Only three times in ten years were they disturbed.

724

Once by some Spanish gypsies who wandered from Paraguay to Mexico. They were smiths and mended the great copper kettle of the village that had come down with the first Indian inhabitants from the north. They closed the hole in it that fire had made.

"That is well," said Fray Pedro, the village padre. "I shall bless it, and then whole lambs can be boiled again."

Once they were disturbed by a pilgrimage of Penitentes whipping themselves, walking upon glass and hot stones. They departed for a place called the "Mountain of the Cross" that lay westward over the desert. "Some of them," said Fray Pedro, "may crucify each other. I have heard of it." They took some half-maddened converts from the village with them and left others behind. Fray Pedro did not bless this work. "These are the old devils of the land breaking out again," he said one evening when he had come to call at the house amid the trees. "It is very difficult to drive them away. They even assume the form of Jesus. Do you know what they will do? Just before a penitente dies those about him break his arms and legs. It ensures them paradise, they think, for they say that those who are treated thus have suffered more than Christ who was not so broken when he descended from the cross. Is that not a cunning temptation for simple minds? An enemy has done this!" He sat for some time looking sad and perplexed. "I wish," he said at last, "I had a beautiful image of the Mother of God to hold up mercy before them in the chapel."

Anthony rose and taking the little madonna from the deerskin bag, where he had long kept it, he gave it to Fray Pedro.

"Take it," said he, "I have kept her with me long. I can never lose her now."

And so with due festival the little madonna went home to the village church. She stood in a niche above the altar and the villagers dressed her again.

"How can you part with her?" said Dolores, who knew much of her story.

"I do not part with her," he cried. "Her image still remains in this house." They clung together in the darkness.

Fray Pedro was not entirely satisfied, however. The villagers had insisted on placing their new madonna on a certain stone. "It is a holy one," they said, and would say no more.

"So I have let them do it," he cried, "just as after the Easter services I let them hold a corn dance before the church. What do you think?" he asked Anthony.

"It is well to try to control as best you can, Fray Pedro, but I think it is useless to try to prevent and prohibit. All these things you mention are contained in life. They may eventually lead up to the image on the the altar, and beyond."

"And *beyond*, señor?" said the padre.

"Yes," he replied. "One cannot prevent that either."

The padre departed still troubled at heart. He could not always understand the señor.

"But, after all, it was he who gave the image," he thought, and was comforted.

When Inez, the older child, was five years old the Indians attempted to creep up on the village from the plains below. They met them in the gorge and drove them back again. In this, the great event of their lives. the men of the village become brothers in battle.

"These are not my People of the Bear," thought Anthony. "They are wolves," he said to the man next to him, as the smoke cleared away. "Listen to them howl."

"Si, señor, they go back again. They will trouble us at La Luz no more. Once every generation they try to come up here. They forget. For us now, it will be nothing but peace till we die."

And so it was—the peace of pasture, field, and forest; the peace of the village; the peace of the house—

while in the chapel the madonna held forth the image of mercy to all who could see it. . . .

And then one day he took a sharp axe in his hand and went out to cut down a tree.

It was one of those calm, cool days at the close of summer that presage the fall. Dolores had taken Inez and Flora to the village to be present at a little playmate's name-day feast. He raised the axe to them in a happy gesture of farewell as they disappeared over the crest of the hill from his view. Dolores saw the blinding flash of the metal in the sun. There was no one left about the house. The people of the hacienda were all busy that day on the far side of the mountain, building sheep folds in the new east pasture.

The path he took ran west. The great tree stood in the middle of a field. The sun would soon be going down behind it. There was just about time to cut it down before evening. Tomorrow they could cart it away. Its dense shade spoiled the best field he had. He did not like to cut it down, for it reminded him vaguely of the tree in the convent courtyard. But what must be must be. He took a few deep breaths. How sweet the air on the mountain was! Wine with the sunlight dancing through it. He swung the axe up and began.

The tree was very old. In past ages it had taken up a stone, as it grew, into the heart of it. And now it was waiting there—the stone in the heart of the tree.

The hard chips flew; the gash made by the metal widened. Suddenly the axe twisted in his hand as though it had been turned against him. The steel rang. The sharp edge bit into the flesh of the man. He staggered backward, clutching himself. From the great artery near his groin, a wide arc of blood spurted into the sunlight with every heart-throb.

For a moment he was only amazed. Then came terror. Then no more of that forever. He struggled desperately to stanch his wound. It was difficult to get at it. He succeeded in stopping the flow of blood a little with his scarf and belt. It would do, he thought. He must drag himself to the top of the hill and call for help. Dolores would hear him when she returned. He could lie still there until she came for him. Already the bright pasture was turning a little grey. "Night *is* coming," he thought. "How strange!"

His blind determination remained. He dragged himself up the field, his life running away through the grass. He came to the place where he could go no farther. He knew that. "O God, Dolores! Be with her!" he cried.

It seemed long ago. He began to pray to his madonna. He was going to sleep. His eyes opened slowly and wide. Looking down over the slope of the field, he saw the great tree still standing there with the sun sinking behind it. His eyes gazed steadily. He no longer winked. He was in the courtyard again. The light began to stir with strange forms.

The Bronze Boy and the Missing Twin fell in a furious rain of greyness from heaven and strove with each other and the ground. They dashed up flames out of the fountain. From the midst of the fire sprang the great tree. It hung between heaven and the ground. Its branches shaded the whole earth. Through them swarmed the forms of everything he had ever seen. In the midst of lightnings, which perpetually passed through its leaves, he saw himself climbing, and then, he saw himself no more. At the top of the tree the madonna bloomed. She held the child out into the light. Behind her head the sun burned intolerably, shooting forth golden and spiked rays into his eyes. The head faded. From behind a mere shadow of it the light still came. All else grew dark now. Suddenly the rays of light themselves dissolved and began to sweep into his eyes like grey seeds of darkness. He shuddered. All was black now. The . . .

EPILOGUE

THE great mountain continued to look upon the plain. In the springtime the thunder-storms still gathered about it as before. The stream ran into the desert, and the forests grew. But the village of La Luz in the pleasant bowl of meadows near its top was silent. Its dying almond orchards still blossomed feebly but their starry wonder brought no pleasure to men.

Long ago Dolores had taken her two children and gone to El Paso. Some of the villagers had left with her. With how she struggled to retain a part of their inheritance for her daughters; whom they married— this story has nothing to do. It must suffice that all the blood of the man who was their father had not been spilt in the field by the tree which he could not cut down. The tree still grew. He slept in the chapel under the floor below the altar. The madonna still stood above the altar but she was now alone.

The Indians had once crept up the mountain. They did not come by the gorge that time. The roofs of the houses and the chapel had fallen in. Only the wild goats remained to look down from the little hills. Trees grew in the patios of the dwellings where no one dwelt— and the mountain looked down upon the plain.

Like the hill of Gergovia in far-off Auvergne, it too overlooked an ancient human road and seemed to watch it. No one knew how old the trail was. It had been used before man wrote or travelled upon wheels. There had been a good many travellers following it lately. They did not travel as individuals or even as families. They came in great droves and flocks in wagon trains. Their white, rolling tents smoked across the dusty desert and made for the Pass of the North. Most of them went by the mountain, content to water their oxen from the stream at the foot. They looked up and coveted the pastures above them, but the mountain was high. Then they went on in a great hurry. Somewhere else there seemed to be a promised land.

At last a party of newcomers climbed the mountain again. They drove their sick cattle up the gorge to the pastures. They found the old people's road to good grazing. They were from Missouri. "Show us," they said to those who said it couldn't be done, for there were a few people from other states amongst them. They camped in a circle of wagons in the great meadow open to heaven and let their cattle and horses roll in the grass. They thoroughly explored the ruined town. Something might have been left. You can never tell. But there was nothing valuable. All that they found was the little madonna.

It was some of the children who found the madonna. They came peering into the little chapel, half afraid of the shadows. Who could tell what might be there? They soon found themselves at home, however.

"This is the church and this is the steeple,
Open the doors and see all the people,"

they sang, dancing about on the bare stone floor.

Under the stone something crumpled. In the skull of the sleeper was neither music nor dreams nor the vision of light. He was not troubled by anything at all. What was left of him was completely material. He had got down to business at last. He grinned. The rhythm of childish feet had only jarred him. After a while they ceased.

It was not much fun playing church. There wasn't as much to it as the old rhyme said. There were no doors and no steeple; the roof had fallen in. There was only the people. So they started to play house, which was much better. It was then that Mary—she wished she had a real Bible name like Esther-Susannah—found the doll. It was splendid playing house after that. The doll had a baby in her arms.

"This is the house and this is the people,"

they sang. They stopped a minute but no one could make up the rest.

"And here we are,"

sang out a little boy. They all laughed for some reason. There ought to have been more, they felt—and there wasn't. They screamed.

All went beautifully then until the boys wanted to play store. The altar made such a good counter. Mary Jorham walked off with her doll. She loved it. She stood at the door of the ruined chapel looking at it in the light.

"Oh, you darling," she said. "I'm agoin' to take ya along with me."

Then she covered it quickly with her apron. Abner Jorham, one of the drivers of the wagons, approached. He happened to be her father.

731

"What you got there, sis?" he said, extending his open hand. "Give it ta me."

She knew better than to refuse him. She put the image in his hand.

"Why, swan to man, if hit hain't a heathen idol!"

"Hit's not," she said, suddenly growing pale with anger. "Hit's my dolly, par."

"Whar did ye get her?"

"In thar," she said.

"Thought so," said he. "I won't have ye playin' with no sich trash. Now run along to yer mar. She's been callin' yer."

"I'll tell her," she called after him. "I'll tell her ye took it away from me." She burst into tears.

Her father waved his hand a little uneasily and sauntered off. He was quite a fellow with "the boys" from Pike County. They began to arrange a shooting match. "I got the very thing fer a mark. Look here! The kids found it rootin' round in the ruins."

They disposed themselves for the match.

" 'Bout three hundred yads eh?" said Mr. Jorham.

"Make it three hundred and fifty," said a man from Tennessee. "You can stand the mark on the rock there." They waited till he returned, ramming their charges home. Mrs. Jordan came stalking up.

"Whar's that doll you took from Mary, Abner?" she demanded.

" 'Tain't no doll," he said.

" 'Tis," countered his wife. "I don't believe ya know what yer talkin' about."

"Wall, tha she's settin', if ya wants ter find out," he said, grinning and pointing toward the rock at which five rifles were already pointing.

"Right to left, and a full ten counts between so there can't be no argument," said the Tennessean. He was on the left and the others cursed his arrogance.

But it took the man from Tennessee to do it. The rifle on the left cracked and the figure on the rock sprang into a thousand pieces.

732

"Thar's nothing like bar's grease for rifle patches," said the winner.

"Ya might have let her have it," still insisted Mrs. Jorham. "She's lonely, and God knows . . ."

"Aw, forget it," cried her husband. "Can't ya see it's too late. I'll buy her a doll at the store when we git to El Paso."

By the wagon Mary dried her eyes and looked about her. There seemed nothing to do. "I wisht we'd get to a home," she thought. "Par, he's alers fer movin'." She fished out her Bible that the Reverend Jacob Todhunter had given her back East and tried to read in it. "Shucks," said she, "hit's only a book arter all." Then she looked about her a little scared. She wanted that dolly. She needed something to talk to that was hers.

She walked over to the edge of the meadow. There was a gap there in the forest and she could look down upon the blinding plains below her. In all that moonlike landscape there was not even the shadow of a thing to which she could confide the enormous fear and loneliness of her heart.

"Do, God! Give us *something*," she cried.

THE END